Praise for *Every Knee Shall Bow*

"Bristling with tension and undergirded by impeccable historical research, this tale of courage, defiance, and humble submission to God continues the captivating saga of two unlikely allies in the age of imperial Christianity."

Inspirational Historical Fiction Index

"Fast-paced, with plenty of adventure and intrigue. . . . the story will fascinate fans of drama and history."

Compass Book Ratings

"If you've read the first book in this series, then you will enjoy the continued adventures of Rex and Flavia. . . . Litfin dives deep into research to set up accurate portrayals of the time period as well as supporting historical characters. If you like this type of history (as I do), then you will enjoy sitting down and spending some time with this book."

Write-Read-Life

"All good fiction brings the reader into another world so that they might think differently about their own."

Marks of a Disciple

Praise for *The Conqueror*

"Bryan Litfin brings a historian's background to the story he tells about Constantine the conqueror, giving you a feel for the time and actions of a historic figure. This is still fiction, but it tells a good story well. Enjoy."

Darrell Bock, *Executive Director for Cultural Engagement, Howard G. Hendricks Center for Christian Leadership and Cultural Engagement; senior research professor of New Testament studies*

"With an eye for detail and an engaging fictional story, Dr. Bryan Litfin makes history come alive. If you've ever wondered what life was like for early believers, you will love *The Conqueror*."

Chris Fabry, author and radio host

"*The Conqueror* is a wonderful mix of excellence in storytelling and keen insight into the setting's historical context. This is what you get when a historian crosses over the authorial divide into the world of fiction. Read this book! Read all of Bryan's books! They are enjoyable from beginning to end. This is certainly on my list of Christmas presents for the readers in my family."

Benjamin K. Forrest, author and professor

"A deftly crafted and fully absorbing novel by an author who is an especially skilled storyteller."

Midwest Book Review

"I thoroughly enjoy a well-researched novel concerning ancient Rome, and Litfin did not disappoint. *The Conqueror* is filled with rich Roman history and lush tidbits of the early church in Rome. If you're a fan of this time period and history, it will definitely need to find a way to your bookshelf."

Write-Read-Life

"Entertaining and overall well-done. Litfin gives readers an enjoyable and thought-provoking story with relevant theological themes."

Evangelical Church Library

Books by Bryan Litfin

FICTION

CONSTANTINE'S EMPIRE

Book 1: The Conqueror
Book 2: Every Knee Shall Bow
Book 3: Caesar's Lord

NONFICTION

Getting to Know the Church Fathers
Early Christian Martyr Stories

CONSTANTINE'S EMPIRE

BOOK 3

CAESAR'S LORD

BRYAN LITFIN

Revell

a division of Baker Publishing Group
Grand Rapids, Michigan

© 2022 by Bryan M. Litfin

Published by Revell
a division of Baker Publishing Group
PO Box 6287, Grand Rapids, MI 49516-6287
www.revellbooks.com

Printed in the United States of America

Library of Congress Cataloging-in-Publication Data
Names: Litfin, Bryan M., 1970– author.
Title: Caesar's lord / Bryan Litfin.
Description: Grand Rapids, MI : Revell, a division of Baker Publishing Group, [2022] | Series: Constantine's empire ; book 3
Identifiers: LCCN 2021062752 | ISBN 9780800738198 (paperback) | ISBN 9780800742461 (casebound) | ISBN 9781493438792 (ebook)
Subjects: LCSH: Church history—Primitive and early church, ca. 30–600—Fiction. | Rome—History—Constantine I, the Great, 306–337—Fiction. | LCGFT: Historical fiction. | Christian fiction. | Novels.
Classification: LCC PS3612.I865 C34 2022 | DDC 813/.6—dc23/eng/20220218
LC record available at https://lccn.loc.gov/2021062752

This is a work of historical reconstruction; the appearances of certain historical figures are therefore inevitable. All other characters, however, are products of the author's imagination, and any resemblance to actual persons, living or dead, is coincidental.

Baker Publishing Group publications use paper produced from sustainable forestry practices and post-consumer waste whenever possible.

22 23 24 25 26 27 28   7 6 5 4 3 2 1

To Carolyn,
my beloved wife
and faithful companion
in all of life's ups and downs

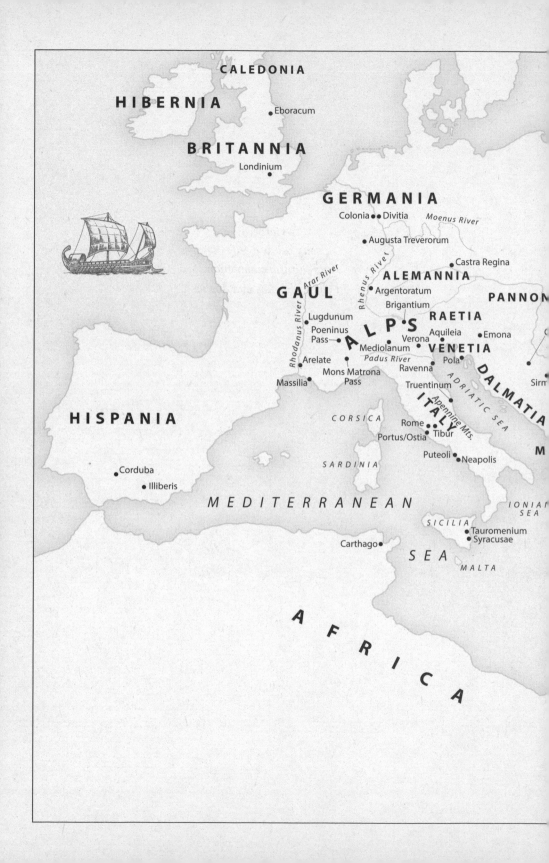

CALEDONIA

HIBERNIA

Eboracum

BRITANNIA

Londinium

GERMANIA

Colonia • • Divitia   *Moenus River*

• Augusta Treverorum

• Castra Regina

ALEMANNIA

GAUL   Rhenus River

• Argentoratum

Brigantium

PANNON

Arar River

Lugdunum

RAETIA

Poeninus
Pass

ALPS

Verona   Aquileia   • Emona

Rhodanus River

Mediolanum

VENETIA

Arelate   *Padus River*   Pola

Ravenna

DALMATIA

Mons Matrona
Pass

Truentium

ADRIATIC SEA

Sirm

Massilia

ITALY

Apennine Mts.

HISPANIA

CORSICA

Rome

Portus/Ostia   Tibur

M

Puteoli   • Neapolis

Corduba

SARDINIA

• Illiberis

MEDITERRANEAN

*IONIAN
SEA*

SICILIA

Tauromenium

Syracusae

SEA

Carthago•

MALTA

AFRICA

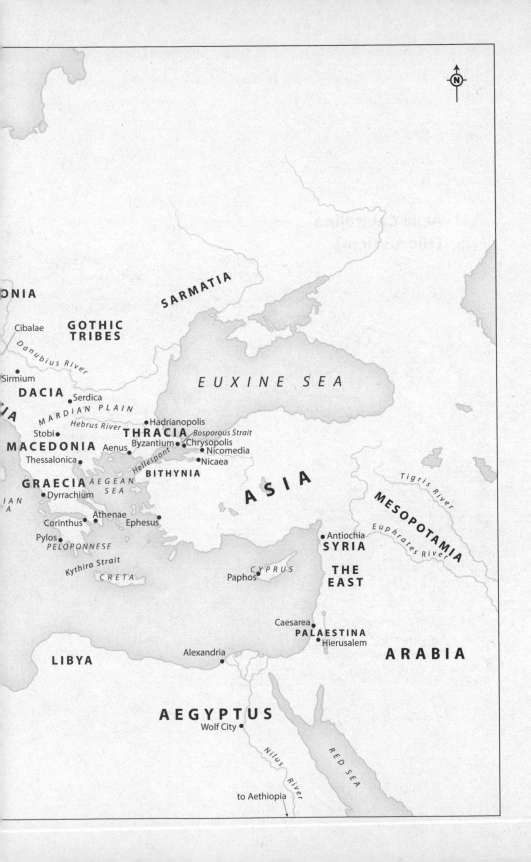

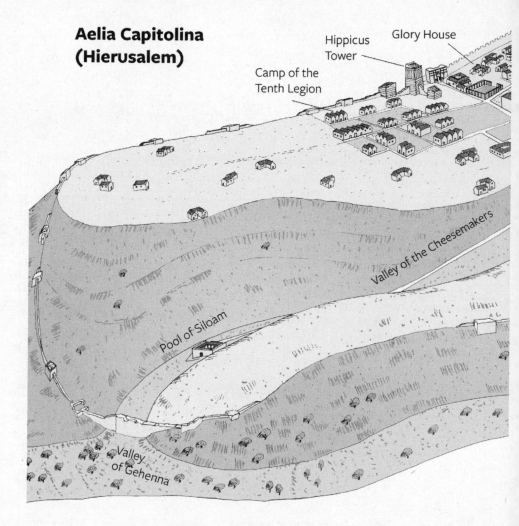

Aelia Capitolina (Hierusalem)

Glory House

Hippicus Tower

Camp of the Tenth Legion

Valley of the Cheesemakers

Pool of Siloam

Valley of Gehenna

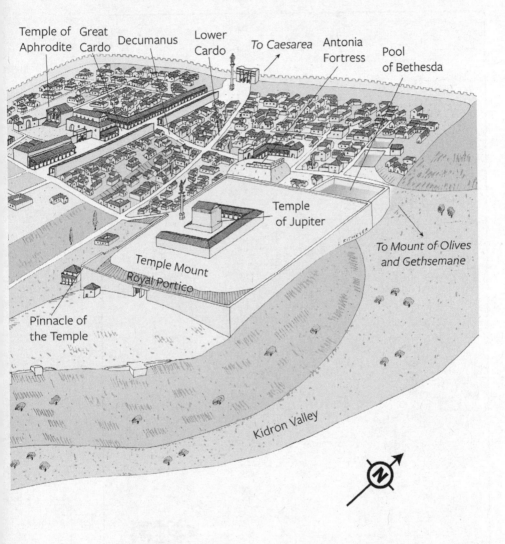

Temple of Aphrodite

Great Cardo

Decumanus

Lower Cardo

To Caesarea

Antonia Fortress

Pool of Bethesda

Temple of Jupiter

Temple Mount

Royal Portico

Pinnacle of the Temple

To Mount of Olives and Gethsemane

Kidron Valley

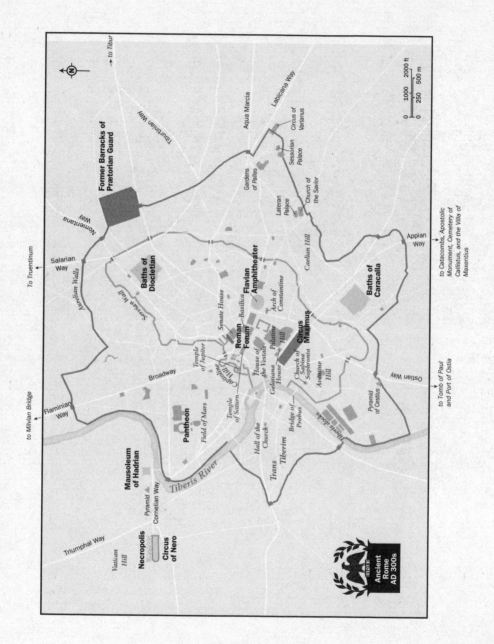

Ancient Rome AD 300s

N

to Tibur

Tiburtinan Way

To Truentinum

Salarian Way

Aurelian Walls

Nomentana Way

Former Barracks of Praetorian Guard

Servian Wall

Aqua Marcia

Labicana Way

Circus of Varianus

Sessorian Palace

Gardens of Pallas

Church of the Savior

Lateran Palace

Baths of Diocletian

Caelian Hill

Appian Way

to Catacombs, Apostolic Monument, Cemetery of Callistus, and the Villa of Maxentius

Baths of Caracalla

Senate House

Basilica

Flavian Amphitheater

Arch of Constantine

Roman Forum

Palatine Hill

Circus Maximus

to Milvian Bridge

Flaminian Way

Broadway

Temple of Jupiter

Capitoline Hill

Temple of Saturn

House of the Vestals

Gelotiana House

Church of Sabina Sophronia

Aventine Hill

Ostian Way

to Tomb of Paul and Port of Ostia

Pantheon

Field of Mars

Temple of Mars

Hall of the Church

Bridge of Probus

Tiber docks

Pyramid of Cestius

Mausoleum of Hadrian

Pyramid

Cornelian Way

Trans Tiberim

Tiberis River

Vatican Hill

Necropolis

Circus of Nero

Triumphal Way

0   1000   2000 ft
0   250   500 m

Contents

Historical Note

THE EARLY FOURTH CENTURY (the AD 300s) was one of the most pivotal times in church history. Everything changed dramatically for the Christian church in a span of about twenty years. I have set the *Constantine's Empire* trilogy in this era for precisely this reason. It is the fascinating moment when Emperor Constantine was coming into power, and at the same time, gradually realizing what the Christian faith was all about.

Historians debate the exact timing of his personal conversion. In fact, some scholars debate whether it was a genuine conversion at all or just a clever political ploy. In this novel, I treat Constantine's conversion as both real and something he grew into as he left his pagan worldview behind. Over time, he became more fully committed to Christianity, backing up his beliefs with government support and generous funding for the church.

The sequence of Constantine's personal conversion began with the famous "solar vision" in which he saw a brilliant, crisscrossed figure in the sun. He interpreted it as a Christian omen that told him to conquer by the powerful sign of the cross. In contrast, his brother-in-law Maxentius was a tyrant and occultist who oppressed the people of Rome. Confident in the power of the cross, Constantine set out for Rome to meet Maxentius in war. The run-up to this confrontation and its climax at the Battle of the Milvian Bridge form the historical background of book 1, *The Conqueror*.

Book 2, *Every Knee Shall Bow*, tells the story of Constantine's civil wars with another brother-in-law, this one named Licinius. Their struggle took place within a political framework that distributed power among four emperors, an arrangement the ancients called a "college." (Modern historians call it the Tetrarchy.) Two great battles were fought and the outcomes of both were inconclusive. After a fragile truce was reached, a few years of relative calm allowed Constantine to initiate his plan of supporting Christianity. It was during this time that the foundations were laid for the great Roman churches of Saint John Lateran and Saint Peter's Basilica.

But the peace within the Tetrarchy was not to last. By AD 323, the two brothers-in-law were back at war again. In *Caesar's Lord*, you will read the story of Constantine's final confrontation with Licinius by land and sea, as well as the important events in church history that happened afterward. I won't offer any plot spoilers here, but I will tell you that the key cities were Alexandria, Nicaea, Rome, and Jerusalem.

As always in a work of historical fiction, some characters in this novel are real figures from history while others are made up. Though Rex and Flavia are not real people, the basic historical storyline that they follow is true. I have not violated any known historical facts in order to tell a better tale. The characters whom we know actually existed are:

Emperor Constantine

Emperor Licinius

Helena, Constantine's mother

Fausta, Constantine's wife

Constantia, Licinius's wife and Constantine's half sister

Caesar Crispus, Constantine's son by Minervina, not Fausta

Constantine II, Constantius, and Constans, the sons of Constantine by Fausta

Licinius Junior, son of Licinius and Constantia

Sophronia (but the name Sabina, which I have attached to her, is imaginary)

Pope Sylvester of Rome

Bishop Ossius of Corduba

Bishop Alexander of Alexandria

Arius, a heretical priest of Alexandria

Athanasius, a deacon of Alexandria

Bishop Eusebius of Caesarea, the church historian

Bishop Eusebius of Nicomedia, an Arian

Bishop Macarius of Hierusalem

Cyril of Hierusalem, a young acolyte who later became the city's
bishop

Lactantius, a Christian rhetorician and theologian; the tutor of Caesar
Crispus

Vincentius, a Roman priest

Abantus, a naval officer

Alica, a Gothic ally of Licinius

Rausimodus, a Sarmatian warlord

Perhaps in this third and final novel, I should say something about the historicity of Lady Sabina Sophronia, the heroine's mother. She is listed above as a real person. However, all we know about her is the record of her noble suicide. Bishop Eusebius, in his *Church History* and *Life of Constantine*, mentions an unnamed Roman woman who was the wife of the city prefect. She committed suicide to avoid being abducted and ravished by Maxentius. The Latin version of Eusebius's Greek work, translated by the ancient scholar Rufinus, reported the woman's name as Sophronia. She would go on to have a long literary history, appearing as an archetype in works such as *Foxe's Book of Martyrs* (1610), *The Second Maiden's Tragedy* (1611), and *The Honour of Ladies* (1622). Sophronia (or a character like her) no doubt appeared in many other pious tales through the ages—including the one you are now reading!

The fictional element I have added to Sophronia is twofold. First, I have imagined that while her death by suicide was widely believed by her contemporaries, in fact, she secretly survived. Second, I have imagined that she can be equated with a woman named Sabina, who is associated with a church on the Aventine Hill. Atop that hill today, there stands one of the loveliest buildings in all of Rome: the Basilica of Santa Sabina. This church was constructed in the early 400s and still retains much of its original appearance. We know nothing of the "Saint Sabina" for whom the church is named, since the legends about her aren't historically valid. In fact, this person probably didn't even really exist but was just a creation of popular Christian folklore.

Therefore I have imagined in my novels that Sophronia (who is actually attested in history) and Sabina (whose real identity is unknown) are the same person, and that she lived with her husband in a mansion on the Aventine Hill where many senators had their homes. Archaeologists haven't excavated beneath the church of Santa Sabina, but if they did, they would probably find the remains of a Roman house. This would be the house that I portray as the childhood home of Flavia, where she lived with her godly mother and rascally father until she set out on her adventures with Rex. Then it was turned into a house church. Later, after the time frame of these novels, Flavia's house was demolished and the current Basilica of Santa Sabina was built on the site—or so I imagine. In truth, however, no one knows whose house originally occupied the site where the beautiful church stands today.

Another important historical question in this novel is, What Bible version did the characters use? At that time, the Bible didn't yet exist as a single book. It was a collection of separate texts. Though the exact boundaries of the canon were still being determined, there was widespread agreement among Christians about the core, such as the Mosaic law, the psalms, the four Gospels, and the Pauline epistles.

The Greek Old Testament of the ancient church was the Septuagint, or the Translation of the Seventy. In this version, the numbering of the psalms was usually behind our modern numbering by one. This was because the Septuagint combined psalms 9 and 10 into a single psalm (and there were some other discrepancies elsewhere). Prior to the fifth century, virtually no ancient Christians read or translated the Hebrew text like modern Bibles do today.

The New Testament of the early church was identical to our Greek New Testament, at least at the macro level, though the specific wording varied among manuscripts. Some rough Latin translations of the Greek also circulated in the western Roman Empire. At the time in which this novel is set, the church father Jerome had not yet published his famous Vulgate. Also, our modern divisions into chapters and verses had not yet been invented.

Here are a few other historical notes that may be of interest:

- The Romans had an advanced travel system as part of their post office whose purpose was to send official government messages. People with high-level access could use this system and travel quickly by exchanging horses at intermittent stations (like the Pony Express in US history). Inns were stationed about a day's ride apart. In this novel, "a mile" refers to a Roman mile, which was about 90 percent the length of our modern mile.

- There is no actual record of an Arian assault on the Church of Theonas or a Manichaean attempt to invade and occupy the Lateran Basilica. However, something similar did happen a little later in Milan, during the time of Bishop Ambrose. This was an age of highly inflamed religious passions on all sides.

- The Romans calculated their dates by counting the days (inclusively) prior to three key points in each month: the Kalends, or the first day of the next month; the Nones, either the fifth or the seventh day; and the Ides, the thirteenth or fifteenth day. By the time period of this novel, the Romans had a twelve-month calendar with the same names (in Latin) as the months we use today: Januarius, Februarius, Martius, etc.

In terms of an overall timeline for the trilogy, the events of the Constantine's Empire novels take place from AD 309 to 328. These are perhaps the two most crucial decades in all of church history. Why? Because the tide-turning battles, triumph over persecution, rise of beautiful church architecture, councils and creeds, initial steps toward finalizing Scripture's canon, and the formation of a Christian society instead of a pagan one all fundamentally changed the nature of Christianity forever.

These momentous events make for great storytelling. In my three novels, I have tried to blend real history with thrilling plotlines to narrate a grand, epic saga. It is my heartfelt prayer that you will enjoy reading this adventure as much as I have enjoyed writing it.

Dr. Bryan Litfin

The Dynasty of Constantine

KEY:
+ marriage
▾ children
= siblings
(*not all siblings and relatives are depicted*)

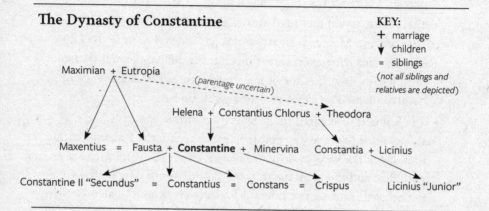

Maximian + Eutropia

(parentage uncertain)

Helena + Constantius Chlorus + Theodora

Maxentius = Fausta + **Constantine** + Minervina   Constantia + Licinius

Constantine II "Secundus" = Constantius = Constans = Crispus   Licinius "Junior"

Gazetteer of Ancient and Modern Place Names

Note: the modern names of *Rome* and *Italy* are used in this book because of frequent appearance.

Aegyptus. Egypt

Aelia Capitolina. Imperial name of Jerusalem; some Christians called it "Hierusalem"

Aenus. Enez, Turkey

Aethiopia. Ethiopia

Africa. Corresponds to Libya, Tunisia, Algeria, and Morocco

Aila. Eilat, Israel

Alexandria. Alexandria, Egypt

Alps. Mountain range across northern Italy and central Europe

Ancyra. Ankara, the capital city of Turkey

Antiochia. Antioch, Turkey

Aquileia. Aquileia, Italy

Arelate. Arles, France

Ascalon. Ashkelon, Israel

Athenae. Athens, Greece

Bosporous Strait. Strait of Istanbul, Turkey

Britannia. Corresponds to England, Wales, and parts of Scotland

Byzantium. Istanbul, Turkey

Caesarea. Ancient ruins are now part of Caesarea National Park, Israel

Capernaum. Ancient ruins are now part of the archaeological site of Capernaum, Israel

Carthago. Ancient Carthage, near Tunis, Tunisia

Catacombs, the. Catacombs of San Sebastiano, Rome

Chalcedon. Kadıköy, Turkey

Chrysopolis. Üsküdar, Turkey

Classis. Military port of ancient Ravenna, now the archaeological site of Classe, Italy

Constantinople. Istanbul, Turkey

Corduba. Córdoba, Spain

Creta. Crete

Dacia. Corresponds to parts of Bulgaria and Serbia

Danubius River. Danube River

East, the. Diocese of Oriens, at the eastern end of the Mediterranean Sea, corresponding to parts of Israel, Jordan, Lebanon, Syria, and Turkey

Eboracum. York, England

Euxine Sea. Black Sea

Gaul. Corresponds to France, Belgium, Netherlands, and portions of a few other countries

Gaza. Gaza City, Palestinian National Authority

Germania. Corresponds to areas north of the Rhine and upper Danube, including Germany, Poland, Czechia, Austria, and other central European countries

Graecia. Greece

Hadrianopolis. Edirne, Turkey

Hadrian's Wall. Defensive wall near today's border between England and Scotland

Hall of the Church. Basilica of San Crisogono, Rome

Hebrus River. Maritsa River, Bulgaria, Greece, and Turkey

Hellespont. Dardanelles Strait, Turkey

Hibernia. Ireland

Hierusalem. Christian name for Jerusalem, Israel

Hispania. Spain

Iericho. Jericho, Palestinian National Authority

Iordanes River. Jordan River, Israel and Jordan

Kallipolis. Gelibolu, Turkey

Kythira Strait. Waterway off the southern coast of Greece, known for hazardous passage

Libya. Libya, North Africa

Mediolanum. Milan, Italy

Mons Aetna. Mount Etna, Sicily, Italy

Mons Olympus. Mount Olympus, Greece

Neapolis. Naples, Italy

Nicomedia. İzmit, Turkey

Nilus River. Nile River, Egypt

Ostia. Ostia Antica, an archaeological site today, but the original port of Rome

Palaestina. Corresponds to parts of Israel, Jordan, Lebanon, and Syria

Paphos. Paphos, Cyprus

Peloponnese. Large peninsula comprising all of southern Greece

Pola. Pula, Croatia

Portus. Secondary port of Rome, which eclipsed Ostia; today it is at the tip of the runway at Rome's Leonardo da Vinci International Airport

Propontis. Sea of Marmara, Turkey

Ravenna. Ravenna, Italy

Rhenus River. Rhine River

Sarmatia. Corresponds to southern Ukraine

Serdica. Sofia, Bulgaria

Seres. China

Sicilia. Sicily, Italy

Sirmium. Sremska Mitrovica, Serbia

Tarsus. Tarsus, Turkey

Thessalonica. Thessaloniki, Greece

Thracia. Corresponds to parts of Bulgaria, Greece, and Turkey

Tiberis River. Tiber River, Italy

Trans Tiberim. Trastevere neighborhood, Rome

Verona. Verona, Italy

Glossary

agora. The central marketplace of a Greek town, equivalent to the Latin *forum.*

argenteus. A silver coin of significant value, though not as much as a solidus.

augustus. A traditional title for the emperors, used within the Imperial College to designate one of the two highest leaders.

ballista. Torsion-powered weapon for projecting darts and missiles with great force.

bireme. A rowed warship (usually also having a sail) with two banks of oars on each side.

caesar. A traditional title for the emperors, used within the Imperial College to designate one of the two junior rulers.

calda. A warm drink made of wine, water, and spices.

caldarium. A hot room in a Roman bath.

canicula. A Latin term for a female dog.

capsa. A tube-shaped container for carrying books or scrolls.

cardo. Primary north-to-south street laid out in a Roman legionary camp or city.

catechumen. A person who has believed in Christ and entered into preparation for baptism.

chi-rho. The first two Greek letters in the name of Christ, superimposed to form ☧, a Christogram often used by Constantine.

chiton. A simple, loose-fitting dress worn especially by Greek women, held in place by pins.

codex. A book of papyrus or parchment pages bound inside covers, readily adopted by Christians to replace the scroll.

college. A legal association of like-minded people, whether a civic club like a guild or the Imperial College ("Tetrarchy") of four emperors.

corbita. Roman merchant ship, propelled by sails, not oars.

cubicularia. An attendant who oversees an aristocrat's bedchamber and personal quarters in a palace.

decumanus. Primary east-to-west street laid out in a Roman legionary camp or city.

denarius. (pl., *denarii*) In late imperial times, it was no longer an actual coin, but a monetary unit of low value; e.g., an unskilled laborer would make twenty-five *denarii* per day.

domus. A Roman city house, as opposed to a country villa.

donative. Periodic distribution of large monetary gifts to soldiers to increase their annual pay and keep them loyal.

Falernian wine. The wine perceived as the very best by the Romans, grown in the Falernian region between Rome and Naples.

fossor. Gravediggers employed by the church to oversee Christian cemeteries.

Gnosticism. Ancient heresy that took many forms; centered on the idea that knowledge (*gnosis*) of heavenly truth, not the historical work of Jesus on the cross, leads to salvation.

hippodrome. Eastern term for what the Latin-speaking world called a *circus*: an oblong racetrack for chariots with a central spine, surrounded by seats.

jugerum. (pl., *jugera*) Unit of land measure, about two-thirds of an acre.

Kalends. First day of a Roman month, from which the previous month's days are counted backward (inclusively) to the middle day of that month (known as the Ides).

labarum. The battle standard of Constantine, marked with a chi-rho (the origin of its name is uncertain).

liburnian. A lightweight warship prized for its speed and agility.

mile. A Roman mile, equal to a thousand paces, or about 4,860 modern feet (nine tenths of a modern mile).

monoreme. A rowed warship (usually also having a sail) with a single bank of oars on each side.

nummus. (pl., *nummi*) The general name for a coin, including bronze coins of little value, like a penny.

odeon. A small semicircular theater for musical, poetic, or dramatic performances.

optio. A Roman army officer with various duties, serving under a centurion.

ornatrix. A domestic slave specializing in hair and makeup for the lady of the house.

ostracon. (pl., *ostraca*) A piece of broken pottery reused as writing surface by ink or incision.

peristyle. The rear garden in a Roman house, surrounded by pillars supporting a shady arcade.

posca. A cheap drink of soldiers and lower classes, made from diluted vinegar and herbal flavorings.

solidus. A late imperial gold coin of significant value.

spatha. A long sword that had come into common use by soldiers of the late imperial era, replacing the shorter gladius.

speculator. A Roman special forces agent, like a spy (from *speculari*, to observe, explore, see).

stadium. (pl., *stadia*) A Roman unit of distance, imprecise, but perhaps about two hundred yards. The word also meant a foot-racing venue of that length.

thermopolium. Hot-food restaurant counter found on many urban streets.

tonsor. A barber.

trireme. A rowed warship (usually also having a sail) with three banks of oars on each side.

vellum. The finest parchment, made from calfskin.

vexillarius. Standard-bearer of a Roman troop, who carried the war banner (*vexillum*).

Prologue

SEPTEMBER 323

Despite the bloody sword in my hand, the captured Sarmatian kneeling before me had a defiant look in his eye. His name, so I had learned, was Rausimodus. He was the chieftain of his people and their warlord in battle. I found his swarthy face arrogant, especially for someone kneeling in bondage before an emperor of Rome. For a long moment, I considered thrusting my blade into his throat so his smirk would offend me no more.

There was a day when I would have done just that. But then I learned to execute my prisoners in a more useful way. It became my custom to throw the vanquished barbarians into the arena, where their deaths would do me some good. How the crowds would cheer as those once-mighty chiefs were ripped apart by the beasts! No one could dispute the invincible dominion of Rome.

Now, of course, I have rejected my former violent habits. I have become a Christian. Granting mercy has become my new way of life—mercy to even a captured enemy with a rebellious gleam in his eye. Truth be told, this virtue doesn't come easy to me. I am Constantine, a ruler who must be feared. *But mercy is God's will*, I reminded myself as I sheathed my sword and turned away from the haughty Sarmatian.

"Lock him up," I commanded my camp prefect, "and give Rausimodus a fair trial. If he has fought nobly, send him back to his people with his thumbs cut off so he can never again hold a weapon. But if he is guilty of treachery . . ."

The prefect smiled wickedly as he tried to finish my command. "Crucify him."

"No!" I shouted. "The Savior's death is unworthy for any man. It is cruel, and I forbid it. If capital punishment is required, give Rausimodus a merciful death. Execute him by the sword, and swiftly. But first let him defend himself before a magistrate, which is only right in the eyes of God."

"Yes, Your Highness," the prefect replied as the guards dragged the prisoner away.

I shivered and drew my cloak around me as I gazed across the wide and placid Danubius River. It was a cold day on the river's windswept plain. That we were upon the northern bank of the Danubius, not the southern, was significant. Here, my army was outside the Roman Empire, in territory belonging to the barbarians. They had started crossing the river and raiding the empire last spring, taking captives and much loot. A prolonged campaign that stretched into September had been required to subdue them. But now they were defeated, and Rausimodus would trouble my subjects no more. Our victory would bring long-lasting peace with the Sarmatians. Unfortunately, the way it had happened would probably lead to war with someone else: my prideful brother-in-law, Licinius.

Across the Danubius, I could see a detachment of Licinius's army eyeing us warily, though not with a threatening deployment. Now wasn't the time to pick a fight. Both sides knew this. Yet a civil war seemed inevitable.

Even as I watched the troops, a rowboat was launched from the southern bank, whose earth belonged to the Roman diocese of Thracia. Over there, the troops stood on imperial soil, while the stuff beneath my feet belonged to the wild barbarians. We were free to wage war on this side; no laws or agreements restricted us. However, my army had been forced to cross through Thracia in pursuit of the Sarmatians. I suspected Licinius was going to make a fuss about that. Technically, it was a violation of our treaty. Many wars had been sparked by lesser offenses than this.

I beckoned to my camp prefect. "Now is the time for that scroll," I told him. He scurried off to fetch it while I waited for the rowboat to land.

When it skidded into the mud, the leader who disembarked was a blond-haired German wearing upscale Roman clothing. His soldiers, too, were Germanic mercenaries. Yet despite his foreign ethnicity, I knew he was coming to me with Licinius's full authority. All Roman commanders were using mercenaries these days. The only thing that differed was the tribe they were from. Interacting with barbarian lieutenants was normal in this age of scarce imperial troops.

Interestingly, the man who approached me walked with a limp. Though he had a powerful build and was probably still dangerous, this fellow wasn't fighting in battles anymore.

"I am Geta," he announced when his party came and stood before me. "I am a son of the great and noble Augustus of the East, Gaius Valerius Licinius."

"A son, yet not a caesar," I observed. "You are the spawn of a wench, then."

Geta stiffened at this. Though his eyes narrowed and an angry flush reddened his cheeks, he dared not respond with a threat. Bodyguards stood behind me; an army was encamped around me.

"I am a prince of the emperor by a humble woman," he said through gritted teeth.

"And what do you seek from me, Princeling Geta?"

The man gathered his composure before he spoke. "My lord Licinius is offended. You have violated the treaty you made at Serdica six years ago. At that time, you clearly awarded Licinius jurisdiction over Thracia. You agreed not to occupy his lands without permission."

"I am not in his lands. Nor are any of my men."

"True," Geta admitted, "but you marched troops through his territory."

"Not against him," I said mildly. "Only to defeat our common enemy. The Sarmatians are a mobile and elusive people, as Licinius would know if he ever bothered to defend his subjects from foreign raiders."

"The duties of Licinius are not the issue at hand, Augustus Constantine."

Though Geta's tone was calm, his words and his face were bold. I could see he wasn't frightened of me, for he knew I wouldn't give his master cause for war by doing something more egregious than I had already done.

I smiled benignly. "Tell me, Princeling Geta. What is troubling the great man's heart? I have done nothing except eliminate a threat that was harming our people."

Geta held up an object in his fingers. "This is why I have come! Licinius is angered by this!"

The object in the emissary's hand was a little silver coin, newly struck by one of my own mints. How Licinius had obtained it so quickly, I didn't know. A spy at the Sirmium mint had probably rushed it to him. I motioned to my camp prefect, who took the coin from Geta and brought it to me. I gazed upon it in my palm. My own image was there, my brow wreathed in laurels. I flipped over the coin and gazed at the reverse image: a victory goddess with a palm branch and a trophy in her hands. A prisoner was bound at her feet. Around her were written the words *Sarmatia Conquered.*

I glanced up from the coin. Rather than apologize for it, I announced to Geta, "Indeed, the Sarmatian threat to our empire has been vanquished. Now I am taking a new title: Sarmaticus Maximus, for I am the one who accomplished this needful thing."

Geta recoiled at this announcement. Even my own guardsmen were shocked. It was a title that should have belonged to Licinius. The fact that I had taken it instead was a slap in the face, a reminder to everyone that Constantine was taking care of what Licinius was too timid to accomplish.

But I wasn't finished with my shocking announcements. In times like this, when peace hung in the balance and war loomed like a vulture on a branch, it didn't pay to be timid. The initiator who made the first move and threw his opponent off-balance was likely to come out ahead. And so I reached toward my camp prefect and received the scroll I had sent him to fetch.

"You have given me a token," I said to Geta. "Now I have something for you to take back to your so-called father." Though the insult angered the German again, I didn't relent. "It has come to my attention that Licinius has also violated our former pact. We had agreed that the Christians in our lands would be at peace. Yet I have learned that Licinius has been forcing bishops to sacrifice to the gods. Surely Licinius has aroused the wrath of the Highest God! That is why I have issued this law"—I pitched the scroll to Geta, who caught it awkwardly as it bounced off his chest—"which mandates a harsh beating or a heavy fine for any official who requires a Christian to sacrifice to the filthy demons whom you call gods."

Geta unrolled the scroll and scanned it. His expression of dawning comprehension told me that although he was a barbarian, he could read Greek. After taking it all in, he looked up. Then, with what some would call courage but others might call impudence, he began to limp toward me.

Instantly my bodyguards rushed to my side, their spears lowered. Yet Geta kept coming. Though he was unarmed, he seemed determined to approach. After stopping a few paces from me, he met my eyes. His jaw was square, his chin dimpled, his blond hair woven into a braid that draped down his back. He seemed to be in his early thirties, yet he had the trim and muscular build of a younger man.

"I will take your law with me," Geta said, "but I must warn you, Licinius does not favor those Christian vermin you adore so much."

"Vermin?" How dare he offer such an insult. This man knows I am a Christian too!

My hand fell to the pommel of the sword on my hip. Everything in me wanted to draw it . . . swing it around . . . sever this fool's head and hang it from a branch by its blond braid. My body knew exactly what to do after so many years of combat. It would be easy. Every fiber of my being cried out to do it.

But I refrained.

Why did I hold back? Out of Christian mercy, like before? Perhaps. Yet I also knew I wasn't prepared for war right now. My legion—a force plenty big enough to defeat the Sarmatians yet not capable of resisting Licinius's army should it close around us because of a diplomatic affront—was out here on the frontier. To slay this imperial legate, this illegitimate son of the eastern augustus, would be to slay myself as well. Licinius would have just cause to attack. I would be captured and killed.

And so I released the hilt of my sword.

Even so, I didn't back down from arrogant Geta. I stepped toward him and was gratified to see him give way to my advance. I glared at him with all the disdain I could muster. He was a tall man, but so was I, and our eyes were even. "You will take that decree to my brother-in-law," I told him fiercely, "and he will enforce it, or there will be hell to pay." My statement pleased me, for it had a double meaning. God would punish Licinius's persecution of Christians with blades in this world and fire in the next.

To his credit, Geta didn't answer with a meek reply. Instead, he said, "When I return to Hadrianopolis with this law, my lord shall spit upon it."

I could no longer hold myself back. My hand whipped out my sword in a move so quick that my bodyguards had no time to react. The tip of my blade was under Geta's chin, pressing a dimple in his throat, though not drawing blood.

"Know this, spawn of Licinius," I growled as I stared into Geta's blue eyes. "I am the only lord who matters here. Now get out of my sight, lest I send you back to your father limping in both of your legs!"

Geta grimaced and took a step back, then returned to his boat. Only after the craft had eased into the water did I shove my sword back in its scabbard and turn away from my illegitimate nephew who had dared to challenge my reign.

"Will it be war?" the prefect asked as we left the riverbank.

"*Iacta alea est.*"

The prefect glanced sideways at me. "I only know Greek, my lord."

"Those were the words of Julius Caesar when he started a civil war. 'The die is cast.' And so it is once again."

ACT 1

EXCLUSIVITY

1

Even after seven years of marriage, Flavia's heart still leapt when Rex came home. He was a tall man with a purposeful walk, so the sound of his footfall was distinctive in the hallway outside. And he had a way of always bursting into their apartment with a commotion that Flavia found endearing. That was who Rex was: a big, rowdy bundle of zest and energy. Flavia delighted to welcome him into every part of her life.

"I've got lake perch!" he exclaimed as he barged through the door, holding out the purchase he had made at the thermopolium, where hot food was served. The flaky white fish was wrapped in palm leaves to keep it warm. Olive oil dripped from it onto the recently mopped floor, a minor mess that Rex hadn't noticed in his enthusiasm for the evening meal. Flavia placed the fish on a wooden platter and made a mental note to clean the spill later.

She kissed Rex on the lips—not passionately, for it was not yet time to stir those flames—but sweetly and with genuine affection. As she turned to take the fish to the kitchen area of the apartment, she felt a playful pinch on her bottom. Glancing over her shoulder, she saw Rex's bearded face grinning back at her. He was thirty years old now, and truth be told, even better looking than when she met him at eighteen. Back then, he was just a boy. Now he was a good and godly man—a fine husband and provider. She winked at him, acknowledging his playful flirtation. "Let's eat on the balcony," she suggested. "Go out, and I'll bring the dinner in a moment."

"Good idea," Rex agreed. "It's another beautiful day in Aegyptus."

Flavia divided the fish onto two ceramic dishes and sprinkled the fillets with fennel and sea salt. Next to them, she arranged some pieces of flatbread slathered with hummus. A handful of dates would add sweetness to the meal, while a few olives would counter it with salt. And of course, Flavia opened a jar of beer and inserted two straws. It was one of Rex's favorite aspects of living in Aegyptus: the people here made beer like back in his homeland of Germania. Nobody wanted to drink the infectious water of the Nilus. The Aegyptian beer was made with emmer wheat, yielding a hearty and nutritious brew. Since a sludge floated on top, the straws helped the drinkers reach the fluid below, creating a sociable, communal experience. Though Flavia had been raised as an Italian wine drinker, she had come to enjoy sharing a jar of beer with Rex at the end of a long day.

He was reclining on a divan with a cushion under his arm when Flavia came out with the food. She lay down on the other divan and set her tray on a little table between them. Off to the west, far down the Aegyptian coastline, the red sun was setting into a veil of ragged clouds. Much closer in, Alexandria's city gate was visible in that direction. The Moon Gate, it was called, because the Sun Gate faced the dawn on the opposite side of the city.

Rex had a wax tablet beside him, brought home from the Catechetical School where he had recently taken an appointment as a teacher. The Alexandrian church had ordained him a deacon not long ago, and now one of his primary duties was the doctrinal instruction of youths. Yet Bishop Alexander couldn't help but notice Rex's impressive physique, so the other part of his diaconal service was to lead a detachment of *parabalani*, the brawny stretcher carriers who scooped up invalids from the streets and brought them for care at the Christian hospital.

"I took some notes from a guest lecturer today," Rex said, waving his tablet. "Listen to this." He cast his eyes to the Latin writing he had scratched into the wax. It was a quotation from the church father Tertullian, whose hometown of Carthago was somewhere down the coast where the sun was now setting. Rex read aloud, "It is proper for the faithful not to take any food or go to the bath without first saying a prayer. For refreshing and sustaining the spirit should take precedence over sustaining the flesh, since heavenly things always take priority over the earthly." And with that wise admonition from a century ago, Rex said a prayer over the meal.

The married couple ate in companionable silence for a while, enjoying the pleasant evening. Flavia found herself lost in her thoughts as she gazed across the cityscape of her adopted Aegyptian home. The apartment's balcony had a good view, for the building rose a little higher than most. It sat on the slope of one of Alexandria's few hills, the hillock atop which the Serapeum was perched. At this prestigious center of pagan learning, the church rented rooms for its Catechetical School, which meant Rex's trip to work was just a short walk uphill.

As Flavia was sopping up fishy olive oil with a piece of bread, Rex caught her attention. He pointed across the low buildings to the city's waterfront in the distance. The lighthouse on the island had just been lit, its glow beckoning ships into Alexandria's wide and spacious harbor. "That is one of the greatest wonders of the world," Rex marveled. "Who could imagine that men could ever build such a lofty thing?"

"It's an amazing construction. But the real lighthouse of Alexandria is over there."

Rex glanced to where Flavia was pointing. His eyes came to rest on the building that stood on the main avenue next to the Moon Gate: the Church of Theonas, which was Bishop Alexander's episcopal seat. "Christ is the Light of the world," Rex agreed. "His beacon is never extinguished but always invites the world to salvation." Flavia nodded at her husband's eloquent words.

At last, the sun ducked beneath the horizon, leaving a pink glow in its wake. Venus was visible now, burning white and fierce above the sun, and a few other stars soon followed. Though Alexandria was a warm city, it was March, so the nights could still be cool. Rex's divan was a wide one with a soft mat. "Sit with me?" he invited. Flavia willingly obliged. The pair snuggled under a woolen blanket and listened to the city's sounds shift from the daytime bustle to the more placid rhythms of night.

A public park was near the apartment, and two boys playing there caught Flavia's attention. They were curly haired Aethiopians from far up the Nilus River, the land where the hot sun caused people's skin to turn black. The boys were playing a game with their father, laughing hysterically as they pitched a ball back and forth. Apparently, the boys' goal was to get past their father while holding the ball without being tagged. Flavia found herself riveted by the competition, and soon Rex got into it too. "Go, little man!" he cheered as one of the boys finally succeeded in his noble quest.

When the mother of the family arrived at the park, the two boys ran toward her. Their combined force was so vigorous that they almost bowled her over, but her husband was there to steady her. She smiled at her man, her white teeth flashing in the evening dusk. He patted her stomach gently, and Flavia discerned that it bore the roundness of pregnancy. A little sigh escaped her lips.

Rex pulled Flavia closer under the blanket, taking her hand in his.

"I wish . . ." she started to say, then let her words trail away.

"Me too," Rex replied.

"But we still have a beautiful life."

"We do. And perhaps soon, the Lord will make it even more beautiful."

"I hope so," Flavia said sadly, though without despair.

Rex nuzzled Flavia's ear. "Do you want to hear a theological truth I learned today at the Catechetical School?" A playful tone was in his voice.

"Tell me, o wise one."

"The man was a scholar from Caesarea. He said Mary's virginal conception was a onetime event. It will never happen like that again."

"Is that so?"

"Mm-hmm," Rex replied. "It's an absolute truth. Only once like that—ever."

"Then I suppose that leaves the normal method for everyone else."

Rex laughed as he tossed the blanket aside and stood up. "It's getting chilly out here," he declared. "How about if we go inside? Maybe you can help me understand what you mean by 'the normal method.'"

"There are many definitions, Rex. I have so much to teach you."

"And I'm quite willing to learn." He winked at Flavia, then added, "O wise one."

Rex went to the door of the apartment and opened it. As he paused there, he was silhouetted against the lamplight from within. With his broad shoulders and narrow waist, his manly shape was appealing. He glanced back, inviting Flavia to follow him with a sly tip of his head. She felt her heart begin to race.

I really do have a beautiful life, she said to the Lord, then followed her husband inside.

―――

When the imperial coach came to a stop, Emperor Licinius immediately felt his stomach begin to rumble. He was ready for a hot lunch. And he was even more ready to be rid of the philosophical blabbering he'd been enduring all morning on the long ride to Hadrianopolis.

Everyone said the philosopher Diogenes was the best teacher around. Licinius had decided to take them at their word despite the man's unimpressive appearance. The little fellow was unusually scrawny, and now his great age had shriveled him even more. How that shrunken body could sustain so great a flood of words, Licinius didn't know. It was a wonder the wheezy old man was still alive, much less capable of teaching philosophy.

Yet teach he did, this chattering geezer. His mouth ran constantly, spewing profound thoughts that Licinius only half understood. Yet Licinius didn't consider himself dull-minded. It was just hard to think about philosophy when he had an empire to run.

Licinius had spent the previous winter shoring up his defenses at Byzantium and Nicomedia. Troop deployments had to be managed, provisions laid in, walls rebuilt, and Gothic mercenaries recruited. That was just for the land army. Any confrontation with Constantine was going to require sea battles as well. The navy needed more triremes right away, as many as could be amassed. Maybe some could be found at—

"Are you listening to me?" Diogenes demanded, interrupting Licinius's war planning. The philosopher's voice had the bold tone that old men often took. Their lives were near the end already. What more could anyone do to them?

"I'm listening," Licinius said, "though only with one ear."

Diogenes made a displeased *tsk!* at this. "Both ears are required for philosophy, Emperor Licinius. Can an archer shoot with one arm? Can a racer run on one leg? Can a surgeon operate with one hand? Total effort is needed for those tasks! How much more, then, are all your mental faculties required for the greatest of human pursuits?"

41

"I'm not sure philosophy is the greatest human pursuit," Licinius muttered.

"Well, sire, you're the one who hired me. You must have wanted this."

It was an impudent thing to say, yet true nonetheless. As Licinius had been making his rounds through his eastern domains, he had become painfully aware in those elegant circles—steeped as they were in six hundred years of glorious Greek culture—that his own peasant background was embarrassing. Licinius knew war-making very well, but in truth, not much else. Running an empire properly was going to require some higher learning. Diogenes was the handy solution.

"It's been a long morning and I'm tired," Licinius admitted. "We've reached the sacred grove now. Let us resume our studies after lunch and a nap."

"Let us keep your studies going," the old man countered. Licinius ignored the remark and exited the coach.

The sacred grove that had been chosen for the lunch stop was a picturesque dell with mossy cliffs and big, old oaks. A beautiful stream watered it, making the grass thick and lush. Long ago, some ancient gardener had been hired to turn the place into a religious shrine. Now many idols stood at the base of each tree, making the grove into a *pantheon*, a sanctuary for all the gods.

But Licinius had lunch, not worship, on his mind. After a fire was quickly kindled, the chef of the imperial caravan began to cook sausages for the emperor and his entourage of advisers and lackeys. Yet Diogenes was unwilling to let his philosophical teaching take a lunch break. He called his pupil over to the grotto's lovely stream. Since Licinius was thirsty anyway, he obliged.

Diogenes had girded up his tunic and was standing knee deep in the stream when Licinius arrived. "I am about to teach you the most important principle in all of philosophy," he announced. "This is the central debate from which all other philosophies emerge—the problem of the One and the Many."

"I shall get a drink while you're at it," Licinius replied as he waded into the stream and began to cup water to his mouth.

With a grand flourish, Diogenes dropped a twig into the current. "Behold the great truth!" he exclaimed. The two men watched the stick float away.

Licinius wasn't impressed. "So that's the great truth?"

"Indeed, it is, sire. What you have just witnessed is the meaning of the universe."

"Is that so? Well, I'll be sure to think about your cosmic twig while I eat my sausage."

Licinius had waded back to the grassy bank and started toward the fire when he heard the philosopher yell to wait, so he turned around.

"Come back!" Diogenes said, beckoning with his hand. "There is one more thing you must learn. Stand here in the water."

Rolling his eyes, Licinius reentered the stream. The sausages wouldn't be ready yet anyway.

Diogenes drew a handful of water and let it dribble between his fingers. "Is this the same stream you entered before?"

"Of course. I walked into it, got a drink, and walked out. Now I am in it again."

"But look around you. Is any of this water the same? Or is every drop that surrounded you before now gone? Isn't it all far downstream, along with the twig that still floats upon its surface?"

"I . . . I guess the water here is different," Licinius admitted.

"Then is this stream a permanent thing?"

"Yes. It flows between these two banks, here and there, and nowhere else."

"What flows here?"

"Water, obviously."

"Yet not a single drop that now touches your shins is the same water that touched you before. That water is long gone on its way to the ocean. It had a twig upon it that is no longer here. Your assertion that this stream has permanent existence is just an illusion. In fact, the stream is entirely different now. And the whole cosmos is like that. Everything is constantly changing. There is no *being*, only *becoming*."

"Some things do stay the same."

"No! Not when you analyze them minutely like I just did. You must awaken to the fact that everything is in a state of flux. Though we try to impose coherence on what we see, it is just a trick of the mind. We strive to give uniformity to what is actually a chaotic and disordered mess."

Licinius considered the philosopher's claim, trying to grapple with the possibility that it might be true. "Are these your ideas, or someone else's?"

"They are the beliefs of the ancient philosopher Heraclitus, whose motto was 'Everything flows.' Heraclitus said you can never enter the same stream twice, because he realized what I am telling you now. There is no single existence binding everything together. That was the view of Parmenides—and Plato and Plotinus after him—but they were wrong. Look around! This grove will not last forever. Nor has it always been here. In our world, there is only the conflict of opposites crashing into each other. Winter vies with summer, the wolf vies with the deer, and even the things that are supposedly the same are in conflict. Each drop of this stream fights for its desired place. Yet as soon as it is achieved, another drop pushes it away. Licinius, listen to me! Reality is like that cookfire behind you. It is constantly changing at every moment. The only thing you can do is accept this truth, then enjoy the chaos while it cooks your sausage."

Licinius scratched the back of his head, wrestling with Diogenes's claims. A spark of insight had been kindled in him, though he couldn't yet define it. Licinius had the feeling he was on the cusp of a mental breakthrough—one that would have implications for his policies as emperor. "So nothing is permanent," he mused as he stared at the current rippling past his legs.

"Exactly. Only change."

"There is nothing stable and lasting behind it all?"

"Not in the human experience. Constant change—the struggle of opposites—is the only truth. There is no great One, only the Many in perpetual conflict. That is all mankind has ever had, and all we will ever know—chaos and complexity, lacking ultimate meaning. So then, my son, enjoy whatever you can until you collapse back into the absurdity from which you came."

"That's not much to look forward to—a constant cycle of absurdity."

"Have you ever seen the lush grass upon a grave? It feeds the goose, who feeds the man, who feeds the soil, until it all starts over again. It means nothing. There is no intention. That's just the way it is."

"Somehow . . . I'm not sure how, but somehow, I think this relates to . . ."

Licinius's words trailed away as he tried to sort out the implications of the philosopher's assertions.

"It relates to everything!" Diogenes said with urgency. "This is the great truth behind all philosophy, all art, all politics, and all religion."

"Yes!" Licinius exclaimed, his eyes widening. "Religion! That's it!" Now he waded deeper into the stream to where Diogenes stood, ignoring the soaking of his royal tunic. He grasped the old man by his frail shoulders and stared into his eyes. "This is the question behind the clash of religions that's happening in our empire! Unity or diversity? The constant battles of the gods or the will of one God? I stand for Heraclitus, and Constantine stands for Parmenides. These two great ideas are striving once again for supremacy!"

"Yes, sire. This debate is exactly what separates our many gods from the Christians' one God. But they are wrong. A God who gives meaning to the world doesn't exist. Reality is like your campfire over there. One man uses it to cook sausages, another to heat his home, a third to burn the Christians for treason. Since there is no ultimate purpose for fire, you can do with it what you please. Universal truth is just an illusion for the weak."

"I do not intend to be weak."

"May the gods forbid it! As a supreme ruler, you must instead be wise. And today, although you resisted it at first, you have finally seen the light and become a wise man."

"I shall rule with wisdom," Licinius agreed as he shook the philosopher's hand. "Kind sir, I am in your debt forever."

Turning away from the old man, Licinius hurried back to the imperial caravan. "Candles!" he shouted to his lackeys. "Bring me candles right away!" Quickly, a fistful of beeswax tapers was located and brought to the agitated emperor. He bent to the cookfire—unmindful of the sausages now—and lit one of the wicks.

"Follow me, everyone!" he shouted to his entourage of bureaucrats and bodyguards. Dutifully, they crowded around him, waiting to hear what their lord would say.

Licinius walked to one of the idols in the sacred grove. It depicted stern Artemis, the many-breasted mother of all humanity. Kneeling before the goddess, Licinius wormed his candle into the soft, moist earth. Using the ancient words of pagan prayer, he intoned, "Holy Artemis, behold, I give, that you might give."

Lighting another candle from the first, Licinius went to the next idol. Again he repeated his prayer: "Almighty Jupiter, behold, I give, that you might give." All the officials surrounding the emperor murmured their agreement. Together they made their way around the entire pantheon until candles were twinkling like stars before every idol in the grotto.

Now Licinius walked to the center of the shrine and stood in the midst of his entourage. Words welled up within him, making him feel more eloquent than normal. He assumed the stance of a rhetorician giving an important address before the Senate. His Curator of Correspondence, a man named Zeno, took out a tablet and stylus to record the speech in shorthand.

"Friends and comrades!" Licinius cried. "These are our empire's gods. We honor them with worship derived from our most ancient ancestors. But he who leads the army that opposes us has denied the religion of his forefathers. He has adopted blasphemous ideas instead, honoring a weird, unheard-of deity."

"A strange, Jewish god!" came a shout from the crowd.

"Do not fear, though," Licinius went on. "The moment has arrived to prove which of us is mistaken. The war shall decide between our gods and the one whom our enemy professes. And the outcome will surely declare the victory to be ours, displaying to all mankind that our gods are the true saviors and helpers of the world. But if Constantine's God, who comes from who knows where, should prove superior to our deities—who are many and have the advantage of numbers—then go ahead! Let everyone attach themselves to that God's superior power, and give him the honor of victory."

"Never shall that happen!" cried another fierce voice.

A third speaker, a soldier in chain mail, raised his spear. "The ancient gods shall reign!"

Licinius lifted his palms to quiet the agitated onlookers. "Do not let your hearts be troubled, and be not dismayed," he said to his entourage with the confidence that only a deified emperor could possess. He reached out to the soldier who had brandished his spear, borrowing the weapon to make his point. After planting its butt in the ground as if to stake out territory,

Licinius gripped its wooden shaft and continued his exhortation. "We need not fear the upcoming war, my brethren! And if our gods triumph, as they certainly will, then we will press the war against the Christians. We will crush those fools, those wretches, those despisers of our ancient gods!"

At these triumphant words, a huge cheer rose among the emperor's advisers. Caught up in the moment, Licinius urged on their fervor. "Curse the arrogant Christians who insist that Jesus alone is Lord!"

"We Romans were right to crucify him," snarled the chain-mailed soldier, shaking his fist.

Licinius put his finger onto the sharp point of the spear. A quick movement of his hand pricked his fingertip. Using the red blood that welled up as holy ink, he dabbed two letters onto the spear's shaft, one above the other: P.P.

Returning his attention to the crowd, Licinius showed them what he had done. "Pontius Pilate defeated Jesus once already," he declared to his followers. "Now the man who stands before you shall finish the job."

<hr />

The trudge up the hill to the Serapeum brought a little sweat to Rex's brow, not because the walk was far or the incline too steep, but because of how muggy it was today. The sky was hazy and gray, and the air felt uncomfortably thick. He hoped the odeon where he was headed might catch a little breeze.

"I never like coming up here," Flavia said to Rex as they walked side by side. "The Serapeum is impressive, with its colonnades and statues and all that. But spiritually, it's dark."

"I know what you mean," Rex replied with an understanding nod. "I feel it too. Yet what better place for Christians to rent rooms than where we can dialogue with the best pagan philosophers?" Flavia seemed to contemplate this point as the pair silently continued their climb to the magnificent temple complex of Serapis.

The little odeon was a semicircle that would seat about a hundred people on its stone risers. It was near the archives where the surviving books from Alexandria's famous Library and Museum—destroyed by a civil war a few decades ago—were now kept for safekeeping. A theological debate had been scheduled for today. Several eager students from the Catechetical School were already sitting on the front row of the odeon when Rex arrived, and he greeted them all by name. They welcomed him warmly, along with Flavia too, for she had previously attended lectures, so the young fellows knew her.

"This Arius is full of caca," one of the students declared after the couple had taken seats. "He's a heretic, pure and simple!"

"I heard he is righteous in character, though," countered another young man. He was a thoughtful student from Carthago who usually remained quiet and listened because he wasn't yet fluent in Greek.

"I guess we're about to find out," Rex said. "There he is."

Father Arius entered the odeon with an entourage of students who seemed chattier and more boisterous than they should have been in this dignified setting. Father Arius was a tall man whose confident demeanor made him likable and charismatic. His hair, the color of gray concrete, was tied in a ponytail at the nape of his neck. He also had a gray beard that he oiled into a point.

Bishop Alexander entered with Arius. As the city's highest church leader, he served as the honorary president of the Catechetical School. Its original purpose was to instruct new believers in the basic doctrines and morals of God prior to baptism. But now, thanks to the legacy of the scholar Origen, deeper theological investigations also took place here. Whenever guest lecturers were invited to address the students, the bishop tried to be present to offer a gracious welcome. The same was true today, even though Arius, a local priest, had opposed Alexander for the past six years. The theology he advocated was viewed as heresy by some and gospel truth by others. Bishop Alexander firmly opposed the Arians, whom he considered a threat to Christianity. Yet because Alexander wanted to see truth prevail by theological investigation instead of force, he hadn't forbidden today's lecture. Rex wasn't sure how the local church was going to resolve this complex matter.

A platform occupied the focal point of the odeon's half circle. The acoustics of this arrangement allowed the speaker's words to be heard by all. Alexander offered a brief and somewhat strained introduction, then Arius was given the stage. After a few pleasantries and words of greeting, he launched into his speech. Rex leaned back on the riser behind him and settled in to listen.

Arius's central claim was that Jesus Christ was a creature whom God had made for important purposes. Because the Savior wasn't eternal, his divinity was on a lower level than the Father's. "Didn't Jesus himself tell us this?" Arius asked with a rhetorical flourish of his hand. "From his own holy lips, he said, 'The Father is greater than I.' And the *Book of Proverbs* says about him, 'The Lord made me the beginning of his ways.' Christ's inferiority to God is scriptural truth!"

As Arius was speaking, he descended from the platform and approached an Aegyptian man on his left. The fellow was seated next to his wife, much like Rex and Flavia were seated next to each other—except this woman had a newborn infant swaddled on her lap. Arius asked the couple to stand. "What is your baby's name?" he asked the father. When the reply was, "Shenoute," Arius cried, "Aha! You have a little boy!" And the parents nodded.

"We are now in the month the Romans call March," Arius went on. He took the baby into his hands and held him up for all to see, but he spoke directly to the father. "Do you know when your little son was begotten?"

At this point, Shenoute began to wail, not recognizing the hands that held him. The mother looked disturbed, and the audience grew unsettled. The Latin-speaking student from Carthago leaned over to Rex and whispered, "I don't know that word, *begotten*."

"It refers to the conception of a son," Rex told him. "Like when 'Abraham begat Isaac.'" The succinct answer seemed to satisfy the inquisitive Carthaginian.

Arius decided to hand the baby back to his mother, which immediately soothed the child. Now that the little one was quieted, Arius repeated his question: "When was Shenoute begotten?"

"Nine months ago," replied the father. "I remember the beautiful moon and the warm breezes on that night."

Arius brazenly placed his hand on the mother's belly. "And what was inside your wife's womb before this?"

"Nothing, sir. Shenoute is my firstborn son. Before he was begotten, he was not."

"Exactly!" cried Arius, whirling to face the crowd and raising his finger to the sky. His triumphant word echoed around the odeon like a victory shout. "Before a son is begotten, he does not exist! His existence begins at conception. So then, if Christ is the only-begotten Son of the Father as the scriptures declare, there must have been a prior time when he was not."

This provocative statement agitated many of the gathered priests and theology students. Rex could feel the tension building among his friends. While Arius's doctrine did have a kind of logic behind it, the implications were troubling. Did Jesus deserve less worship than the heavenly Father? Was there really a time when he did not exist? Was the Son of God part of the creation instead of eternal deity?

Yet Rex could see the other side too. If Christ was equally divine with the Father like Bishop Alexander taught, did that mean there were actually two Gods? And how did the Holy Spirit fit into this? Were there three Gods? Or just one, like the Jews believed? The debate was a thorny theological dilemma.

Energetic discussions broke out in the odeon as the listeners formed small groups. Arius allowed them to continue because he seemed satisfied with the way things were going. Flavia leaned close to Rex and whispered, "Arius sounds convincing because of his logic. But his conclusion is blasphemous. The Lord Jesus isn't a creature. He is God come down in the flesh."

"But what kind of God is he? Maybe a lesser version?"

"He's the exact same, Rex, just like the bishop says."

Before Rex could reply, the students and nuns who had entered with Arius began to chant a song. The tune wasn't from one of the church's holy hymns. It was a lively drinking song popular in the taverns.

"There came a time to make the world, so Jesus was begot!" chanted the Arians. "But long before God made his Son, there was when he was not!" Then that refrain was repeated by the singers: "There was when he was no-o-ot! There was when he was no-o-ot!"

"Blasphemy!" cried Bishop Alexander, standing off to one side. Yet it was no use. The catchy song had taken over the odeon. No one was listening to the bishop.

A short, brown man suddenly burst from the crowd and strode purposefully toward Arius. He was youthful, perhaps in his midtwenties. Everyone turned their attention to the new arrival, for it seemed as if fisticuffs might be imminent. Rex began to rise from his seat. He had seen rocks thrown at Arius before, drawing blood, and he didn't want another riot to break out. Such behavior wasn't worthy of Christians.

"Let him speak," Flavia said, putting her hand on Rex's arm to restrain him. "Athanasius isn't violent. Let's wait and see what happens."

"Alright. But if I see anything threatening, I'm going to stop it." Rex settled back on the riser, keeping a wary eye on the feisty Aegyptian deacon who had come forward.

Athanasius beckoned for the married couple with the baby to join him next to Arius. When they were on the speaker's platform, Athanasius fixed his eyes on little Shenoute. Everyone in the odeon fell silent, waiting for the deacon to speak. Yet all he did was stare at the infant. Soon, everyone else was looking at Shenoute too.

"Hail, Glorious Lord!" Athanasius suddenly shouted. And with that, he fell to his knees and began to worship the baby.

The sacrilege shocked the audience. Everyone began to boo and jeer, both the Arians and catholics alike. Yet Athanasius didn't relent. He bowed his face to the ground again and again, crying, "Mighty God! Blessed Lord!"

Bishop Alexander could contain himself no longer. "Rise up, my son, and stop this nonsense."

At the sharp episcopal command, the little deacon got to his feet. Gesturing to Shenoute, he asked the crowd, "What's wrong? You think this boy deserves no worship?"

"Of course not, you blasphemer!" shouted someone from the audience.

"Aha!" cried Athanasius, pointing to the man who had shouted. "So you agree that some things belong to God and not to humans! Not everything that is true of God is true of man. The properties of each are distinct."

A murmur of approval rippled through the crowd, so Athanasius pressed ahead with his point. "This baby was conceived by his parents through the act of marital love. It happened last summer, as his father has informed us. And before that, Shenoute did not exist. But what is true of human children isn't necessarily true of God's own Son. The Almighty lives outside of time. He doesn't conceive through physical generation. We cannot assume a precise analogy in every way."

Athanasius descended from the platform and walked up the steps of the odeon until he stood over a lad of about twelve. "Young man," the deacon said, "what is your name?"

"Clement, sir."

"And do you live with your father?"

"Of course. He is a good Christian man."

"And what chores does your father ask of you?"

"It is my job to feed the cows. And milk them, and bring it home in jugs."

"So your father issues commands and you obey. Is that correct?"

"Yes, sir. At least, I try to."

"And why do you obey?"

"Because it is right, and because my father is good to us."

"Do you love him, Clement?"

"Yes, sir. I wish to please him."

Athanasius turned back to the crowd. "My friends, many things define sonship. The essence of being a son isn't his beginning or lack thereof. To the contrary! The essence of being a son is to be *beloved*. That is what it means for Christ to be the Son of God. Out of deep and eternal love, the Father sent forth his Son for salvation. And what did our Lord say when he met the Samaritan woman at the well? 'My food is to do the will of him who sent me.' He delights to obey! The sonship of Jesus consists of loving obedience to his Father who commands him, just like Clement has demonstrated so well."

Now Arius stepped forward, waving his palms in a dismissive manner. "Unfortunately, the scriptures refute you, deacon! They say that Jesus was begotten. Begetting happens at a point in time. Before that, the Son did not exist. Therefore his divinity must be of a lesser sort. The creator is greater than the created."

"The Son is eternally begotten of the Father," Athanasius replied. "He has always existed. His deity is entirely the same. His sonship consists of obedient love, not an origin in time."

"Error!" came a cry from the crowd.

"Truth!" shouted someone else.

And then the heavens added a word of their own: a mighty thunderclap rumbled in the distance. The muggy day had grown turbulent, and a storm was brewing up fast. Far away, lightning flashed on the horizon. A few big drops spattered the ground, and the crowd fell still. On the platform, the tall, ponytailed Arius and the short, brown-skinned Athanasius glared at each other in silence.

Bishop Alexander's pastoral words broke the tense moment. "These deliberations are sufficient for today," he said gently. "Let us now return to our homes. Yet be alert, my children! I think we can all perceive that a great tempest is surely on the way."

—◦◦◦—

Springtime in Rome was always a glorious season. To Pope Sylvester, the highlight of spring was the holy week of Pascha. It started with Palm Sun Day, the day of Christ's triumphal entry into Hierusalem, and culminated with the celebration of his victorious resurrection. Yet in between those highs, of course, was the low of the crucifixion. Today was Great Friday, the dark and dreadful day when the King of Glory was slain like a common criminal. *How fitting*, Sylvester thought, *that the Manichaeans are choosing to open their new building on this sorrowful day*. The advance of heresy was always a gloomy occasion.

"This is their front door," said Father Vincentius, an intelligent and earnest priest from Hibernia who now lived in Rome. "Though the façade of their place is unassuming, I have been inside. It is roomy enough for many to join their misguided conventicles."

"It's directly across the street from our church!" Sylvester exclaimed as he looked over his shoulder at the entrance to Santa Sabina. That building had once been a house church owned by Lady Sabina Sophronia, a pious and wealthy aristocrat. When it came into the church's possession, it was converted to full-time liturgical use. Christian worship on the Aventine Hill had been centered here for the past thirty years. Now the Manichaeans were trying to pluck some sheep out of God's flock—not like wolves who sneak around at night, but brazenly, by the light of day!

"It is truly an affront," Vincentius agreed. "Yet there's nothing to prevent them from doing it. Constantine's policy is to provide religious tolerance for everyone. Unfortunately, that gives these false cults the ability to set up shop wherever they want."

"Very well, then. We will resist them not by persecution but by proclamation. Let the truth of the Lord go forth and defeat their error."

"Speaking of error, look who's coming now," Vincentius muttered as he glanced over Sylvester's shoulder. "It's sneaky Felix himself."

Felix—formerly Father Felix, for he pastored Santa Sabina before lapsing into heresy—was a handsome man of around forty. His jet-black hair and trim physique made him seem younger than he really was. Not a few of his followers were women. Clearly, it wasn't just his doctrines that gave him such wide appeal.

The man bowed politely as he greeted Vincentius and Sylvester. "I see you have come to examine the House of Mani," he said, gesturing at his front door. "You are welcome any time to leave the darkness of your hovel across the street and come sit in the presence of the Divine Light."

Sylvester sighed and shook his head. "So you think you have found the true way, Felix?"

"I know I have. The path of enlightenment runs through Manichaeism, not your catholic faith, with all its physical, material concerns."

"You're just teaching Gnosticism under a new name. It's the same seductive promises as before—the pride of enlightenment, easy morality for the congregation, and a heavenly hope that never has to count the cost of discipleship."

"I have discovered many hidden secrets," Felix said cryptically.

"That is because you ask unclean spirits to lead you along," Vincentius accused. "It's just what Saint Paul predicted. In later times, people will abandon the true faith and follow deceptive spirits and the doctrines of demons."

Felix scoffed at this. "Our spirits are heavenly beings, angels of divine light."

"Satan himself masquerades as an angel of light," the pope declared. "Come now, Father Vincentius, let us leave this unwholesome threshold and cross over to the holy place of Christ. We must not have fellowship with darkness, as both Paul and John have instructed us."

The two men left Felix on the sidewalk and entered Santa Sabina. Though it was once a residential building, its interior had been remodeled for its new use. Now there was a beautiful central hall with columns on either side. Crystal-paned windows gave light from high above, and an attractive mosaic decorated the floor. Though Vincentius was its pastor now, Sylvester had come to join him for the evening's Great Friday service. It wasn't often that the bishop of Rome came all the way up to the Aventine Hill for a visit. The congregation had been looking forward to it for weeks. The liturgy would begin in about an hour, and Sylvester expected the service to be packed.

When the time arrived, however, his hopes were dashed. Only a smattering of worshipers stood in the aisles when he led the entrance procession down the center of the nave. The bishop and priest stood side by side at the altar and celebrated the Eucharistic service with all the dignity it deserved. Numerous oil lamps gave the hall a reverential glow, while the God-honoring aroma of incense permeated the air. The lector read the gospel account of the crucifixion, Sylvester gave a homily on it, then all the worshipers partook of the bread and wine with befitting reverence. There was only one problem: hardly anyone was in attendance.

After the service, Sylvester hailed a middle-aged woman whom he knew. "Lucretia, come speak with me." She was the wife of a poor shopkeeper who often received the church's charity. When the woman drew near, Sylvester asked, "Where is your husband tonight?"

At this inquiry, Lucretia's face became distraught. "Holy Father, I am embarrassed to tell you, Justin refused to attend."

"He refused? Justin has always been a faithful Christian! Why did he stay home?"

Lucretia stared at her feet, reluctant to answer. Finally, she said with shame in her voice, "He . . . he is across the street."

"With the *Manichaeans*?" The revelation was shocking to Sylvester. "Why, Lucretia?"

Though she didn't lift her eyes from the floor, her pent-up frustration came bursting out. "It is that feast they offer! They set up an idol of Mani on a throne, and he forgives all their sins of the past year. Then he presides over a lavish banquet. Justin says he's never tasted such sweet pastries. And there's so much meat, Holy Father! For the poor like us, it is almost irresistible."

"They are just bribing your husband with food. Instead of using the tithes for charity, they throw lavish parties."

"I know. But it works! Justin says he can indulge all he wants because his real self is just a spark inside his body. The deeds of his outward body are meaningless. And their salvation is so easy! Their leaders just declare forgiveness. To them, Jesus didn't have to go to the cross. His body wasn't even real, just an illusion so he could talk to us."

"That is the heresy of Docetism, which the Gnostics started and the Manichaeans are continuing."

"Whatever you call it, Justin loves this religion. Felix tells him, 'Stick with me. The hard life is for those losers across the street.'"

Though Sylvester kept his peace, inside he seethed at the blasphemous words spewing from the false prophet's mouth. Such devious doctrines were leading astray good men like Justin. "May God repay Felix for what he has done. Wide is the road that heads into error. Although the way of Christ is narrow and difficult, it leads to eternal life."

"I believe it," Lucretia whispered as tears welled up. "That is why I am here—all alone."

Sylvester gently cupped Lucretia's chin. Tentatively, she lifted her eyes and looked at her pastor. He gazed back at her, infusing her with courage. "I will pray earnestly that Justin returns."

With a sudden cry, Lucretia fell to her knees and began to weep. She clutched the fabric of Sylvester's robe, repeating the words, "Thank you, bishop . . . thank you."

Sylvester stroked the woman's hair until she had calmed enough to stand again. After wiping her eyes, she kissed the bishop's hand, thanked him once more, and hurried away.

When all the worshipers had finally left the building, Sylvester stepped outside with Father Vincentius. The cool night air felt refreshing as the two spiritual brothers examined the ups and downs of the holy day. Sylvester was about to go back inside and retire to a guest bedroom when he heard a loud belch nearby. He turned to see a man staggering toward them. As he approached, Sylvester realized it was Justin.

"Cheers, you old scoundrel!" Justin cried, too drunk to realize how socially improper his greeting was.

"Hello, dear friend. It grieves me to see you like this."

Justin swatted his hand, which almost made him lose his balance. "Bah! I'm happier now than I ever have been. I get to fill my belly in this life and come back better in the next!"

"There is more to life than full bellies, Justin. There is the upward call of

God. I urge you, my brother: return to the Christian church. Join Lucretia again, like before. Return to Jesus Christ, the true Light of the world."

"Jesus Christ?" Justin scoffed as he swayed on his feet. His inebriation gave him a boldness he never would have had otherwise. "That Jewish prophet from long ago? Was he really crucified? Who can even say that he lived? Maybe he was just a vision of God!"

"He was a true man, with a body like yours and mine. He was crucified by a Roman governor in real history."

"But Felix told me . . ." Justin paused and scrunched his face, clearly trying hard to recall what Felix told him.

"I know what that heretic teaches. Jesus had no real body. He only seemed to be a man so he could convey wisdom. But that is wrong, Justin. The Lord suffered upon a cross for your sins, the righteous for the unrighteous, to bring you to God. He was put to death in the body but made alive in the Spirit."

Whether Justin understood these words, Sylvester did not know. The drunken man's only response was to bend over, vomit on the pavement, then straighten up and try to wipe his mouth. He stood there with meaty flecks in his beard, unsure of where he was.

Turning to the front entrance of Santa Sabina, the bishop called over the husky doorkeeper who guarded it. "Escort this man to the house of Lucretia," he ordered. "It wouldn't be safe for him to wander the streets in this stupor." The doorkeeper nodded his assent. "And give this to his wife," Sylvester added, pressing a coin into the servant's hand. "It will buy them food for a month."

Once the doorkeeper had departed with Justin, the pope blew out a long breath. He shook his head to clear his mind, then glanced at Father Vincentius. "Only prayer will help that man now."

"Look at what Felix is doing—breaking up families, ruining lives. I wish the city prefect would arrest him. He shouldn't be allowed to do these things!"

"And then what, Vincentius? Should we reverse the persecutions that have just ended for us? No, my son, that is not the way. We must live into our times, and be faithful each day, and proclaim the truth with power and humility."

57

"You are right, Holy Father," Vincentius replied with an affirming nod. "I just want our empire to know the truth of the Lord!"

"Jesus Christ is surely coming to the Roman Empire. The only question is, whose Christ will it be? The old gods and the new heresies are going to fight tooth and claw against the Savior."

Vincentius made the sign of the cross by touching his forehead, his chest, and both shoulders. "Maranatha," he whispered under his breath. "Come quickly, Lord Jesus."

APRIL 324

It wasn't often that the bishop of Aegyptus summoned one of his congregants to a personal meeting, especially not at the second hour of the day. But Rex had received such an invitation from Alexander, so he thought he had better get up early and look his best before heading over to the Church of Theonas.

Holding a bronze mirror near his bedroom window, Rex inspected his face by the early morning twilight. Though he no longer wore his hair down below his shoulders like in Germania, it was still longer than the Aegyptian style, which was short for men unless a wig was used. Rex had no intention of adopting that local fashion so popular among the Alexandrian aristocrats. His blond hair was notably Germanic, and his beard made him even more distinctive in the clean-shaven Aegyptian culture. He smoothed back his locks with a comb and a little oil, just to make sure he didn't look like he had come straight from his bed when he met the bishop. After setting the mirror on the washstand, he quietly exited the apartment and left Flavia asleep in the stillness.

Rarely did Rex walk through the streets of Alexandria without marveling at the city's unique features. Its shape was oblong, being much wider than it was deep. This was because of the strategic location chosen by its founder, Alexander the Great. The famous conqueror's namesake city possessed a long stretch of coastline in a spot tucked behind Lighthouse Island, which created a sheltered harbor. Yet urban expansion inland was limited by a freshwater lake not far from the coast. That lake was linked to the Nilus by canals; and the Nilus was, of course, the backbone of Aegyptus. The ancient pharaohs had even dug canals to connect the river with the Red Sea, providing access to the exotic seaports of the Orient.

All this meant that Alexandria was located at the juncture where the trade artery of the Nilus River met the maritime commerce of the Mediterranean Sea. In the city's many shops, you could buy silk that had just arrived from Persia or woolen cloth that had just come down from Britannia. Pungent Indian spices might sit beside Spanish lead or tin. But this morning, Rex didn't want anything imported from the farthest reaches of the west or east. He wanted only a little breakfast to quiet his rumbling stomach before he met with the bishop.

Most of the shopping in Alexandria took place on the market street called Canopus Avenue. This grand boulevard bisected the city, running its entire width from the Moon Gate in the west to the Sun Gate in the east. Rex reached the street and glanced down its colonnaded length toward the rising sun. Far in the distance, bright light was visible in the sky, though the sun itself had not yet risen high enough to be seen above the city walls.

"Hey, handsome, I got what you need over here," called a she-wolf hoping to snag one last customer for the night. Prostitution was rampant in Alexandria.

"I'm happily married, miss," Rex replied with a friendly smile, then headed toward the Moon Gate with a different bodily urge in mind.

Although most shops along the colonnade were closed at this early hour, Rex finally found a bakery whose door was cracked. Delicious aromas wafted from within. A few bronze nummi bought him warm bread and a thick breakfast beer.

He had just finished the loaf and discarded the cheap cup when he reached the Moon Gate. The episcopal church of Alexandria stood adjacent to it. Named for the martyred bishop Theonas, who founded the church in his home, the building was now—like so many going up across the empire—a newly built basilica that Bishop Alexander had dedicated to his godly and courageous predecessor. The church's main entrance faced directly onto Canopus Avenue, making it the first building travelers encountered when entering through the Moon Gate. The location was good for Christianity's increasingly public presence in the empire's cities.

A deacon welcomed Rex and ushered him to an interior courtyard. Since Rex had been summoned by episcopal command, his visit clearly was expected.

It wasn't long before the bishop emerged from his private chambers to welcome his guest. Though Alexander normally wore a wig like the aristocrats from whose ranks he came, this morning he was without it. Rex thought the bishop looked almost unrecognizable with his head shaved smooth. Yet it was a sign of his humility that he wasn't too proud to be seen in this way.

"Peace to you in Christ," the bishop said, kissing Rex on the cheek. Not all churches still practiced the holy kiss, but Alexander believed it was important because it was commanded five times in the scriptures.

"I honor you, Reverend Bishop," Rex replied with a dip of his chin. The two men took seats on benches beneath a potted palm.

For a few moments, Alexander appeared to gather his thoughts. Finally, he said, "We are facing grave times in our empire, Brandulf Vitus Rex. Grave times indeed."

"I can always tell the times are bad when someone uses my full name," Rex replied with a gentle smile. The wry remark elicited a chuckle from Alexander, who seemed to appreciate the momentary alleviation of the strain so clearly etched on his face. Yet the relief quickly faded, and the bishop's heaviness returned.

"The future hangs in the balance," he declared. "I don't just mean politically, though a civil war will probably start this summer. But I mean theologically—or you might say, spiritually. The Christian church faces a fork in the road. The choices made now will lead to very different outcomes."

Rex nodded. "If Licinius wins, the persecutions will start again. The churches will close, and Christian blood will flow."

"Ah, Rex, have you ever seen it?"

"Bloodshed? I was a soldier, you recall."

"I mean the blood of the martyrs. Truly, it is the seed of the church. Truly, it is a heroic moment of steadfast courage. Yet I tell you now, martyrdom is nothing to glamorize with pious stories! When you see that redness in the sand, when you hear the screams of hideous pain, when you see your wife . . . your son . . . the youngsters you converted and baptized . . ."

The bishop's words drifted off as he gazed into space. Rex knew it was because horrific images were rushing into his mind. To be pastoring in Aegyptus today was to have seen things that no eye should ever have to witness. Rex waited quietly for the bishop to collect his thoughts.

At last, Alexander shook himself from his terrible reverie. He looked straight at Rex and said, "You must go to Rome, my son. Right away. First ship tomorrow."

Now it was Rex's turn to be taken aback. He stared at the tiled floor of the courtyard as jumbled thoughts rushed through his mind. *Go to Rome?* It was the last thing he had expected to hear. For almost seven years now, Aegyptus had been his home. He and Flavia had arrived here as newlyweds, so Alexandria was all they had known as a married couple. In all that time, they had not once been back to Italy.

"Holy Father, you know I will obey you," Rex finally said when too much silence had elapsed. "But it was Pope Sylvester of Rome who sent me here to Alexandria. He told me to support you in any way I could. This I have done—as a deacon, a teacher of youth, and a carrier of the stretchers."

"And also a kind of bodyguard, Rex. Your former military training has made you valuable to me on many occasions. Your skills are unique among the Christians here. That is why I have selected you for this mission. The stakes are high, and treacherous enemies are involved. To thwart them will take a resourceful and experienced man."

Rex waited only a moment longer with his eyes cast down. Then he let out a deep breath, looked up, and nodded in a way that signaled his firm resolve. When a commanding officer issued an order, a good soldier didn't waver or delay. He strapped on his sword and did his job. Rex had always taken orders like that from his military superiors. How much more should he do so from his bishop?

"I will go gladly to Rome," he said, looking Alexander in the eye, "and I will carry out your commands in every detail. What is my mission?"

Alexander turned around and beckoned through the doorway to the deacon. The man brought a stiff leather tube on a strap. Alexander received the capsa and held it in both hands. "This scroll case contains a letter I have written to my brother in the Lord, the esteemed Pope Sylvester of Rome. It is a request for unity, a locking of arms against our common foes. It is time for the Alexandrians and the Romans to put rivalries aside and cooperate. We are the bishops of the empire's two greatest cities. Only by fraternal unity can we defeat the many forces that stand against our Lord. Sitting still while the threat grows simply isn't an option."

"Emperor Licinius must go down," Rex agreed. "He has reverted to paganism with vengeance on his mind. He will spread that ancient poison across the empire, rolling back all the church's gains."

"The pagan gods are but one of our enemies, Brandulf Vitus Rex. You were present when Arius gave his presentation. You saw how many people follow him. But I ask you: Can his Christ save us—this creature whom God supposedly made to be our example? 'Imitate the life of this great moral teacher and you will be saved.' No, Rex! Christ must be fully divine to bring us back to the Father God."

"Indeed, eternal souls hang in the balance."

"We face two great enemies: the polytheists who deny the uniqueness of Christ and the Arians who deny his divinity. I cannot face these threats alone. I need the fellowship of Rome, the strengthening support of my brother Sylvester." The bishop tied down the lid of the capsa with thongs and handed it to Rex. "You must convey my invitation to him. There may be those who seek to stop you! I send you alone on this mission, though not without the support of the Paraclete who always attends the ways of the believer."

With these final words, the bishop stood up, so Rex followed his lead. Bowing, Rex vowed to carry out the mission. After a quick prayer with the laying on of hands, Alexander dismissed him, then the deacon led him out to the street. Rex thanked the man, slung the capsa over his shoulder, and began to walk home.

The morning sun was still low in the east when Rex reached his apartment on the flank of the Serapeum's hill. He entered cautiously, lest he wake Flavia, but she was already up and about. When he told his wife about the mission to Rome, her reaction was what he had feared. A look of sadness came to her face, and she clasped her forehead with deep disappointment.

"I will return quickly," Rex said with as much tenderness as he could convey. "As soon as the mission is over."

"I know you will. And I support you, Rex. You're the right man for this job. It's just that I know what else this trip will mean."

"What?"

"Well, obviously . . ."

"Tell me, Flavia. You can say it. What is it?"

Flavia's lip quivered and moisture came to her eyes, which she quickly wiped away. Though her hair was tousled from recent sleep, it wasn't enough of a veil to hide her deep emotions. "It will mean more months when we cannot conceive," she said. "More waiting, Rex. How long must I wait to become a mother? An eighth year? A ninth?"

Rex remained silent, realizing that now wasn't the time for soothing gestures or empty promises. Flavia just wanted to be heard. "Yes, it is hard," was all he said.

"It's *so* hard!" She pounded her fist on the washstand in their bedroom, then dipped a rag into the cool water and wiped her face. Silently, she stood with her hands gripping the stand, staring at her reflection in the basin. Then she turned to face Rex again with a look of resolve on her face.

"I choose to support your calling, my husband," she said, reaching for him. "All else belongs in the hands of the Lord."

Rex came and embraced her. For a long time, he held her close. Slowly, Flavia's stiff body relaxed as some of her tension drained away. She separated and looked up at him with imploring eyes. "One last try?" she asked.

"May God bless us," Rex replied.

⟞ ⟝

Harbors, Flavia had decided, were double-minded places. Sometimes they offered you the world. Magnificent ships awaited to whisk you away on grand adventures. But other times, a harbor could steal the thing you loved most. And today was one of those days.

The booming grain trade between the Nilus delta—resupplied every year with fertile soil from the river's flood—and ever-hungry Rome meant that ships often traveled back and forth. Except in the winter months, anyone with the means to pay could purchase passage on a grain freighter. Because Flavia had inherited a fortune from her rich uncle, she and Rex were financially secure. Although they could have afforded extravagant luxuries or a beautiful Alexandrian villa, they chose to live frugally like Christians should. Yet when it came to important things like travel, the funds were available for whatever was needed.

"I'm going to miss you, my beloved," Rex said as he stood at the foot of the gangplank. The huge ship was moored alongside the pier and had already been loaded with the remnants of last season's wheat from the nearby granaries. The sailors were busy throwing off the ropes and preparing to set sail.

"Ah, Rex, I can't believe you're boarding a ship and leaving me behind. I have bad memories of this."

"I know. I came back to you, though."

"Yes, but as a pirate!"

"Hey!" Rex protested with a grin. "Not a pirate! I was a naval tax collector." The couple laughed as they shared a memory.

Reaching into the satchel that dangled from her shoulder, Flavia withdrew a small glass vial covered in silver filigree. "Do you know what this is?"

"Medicine?"

"No, smell it." Flavia removed the stopper and held it under Rex's nose. As he sniffed, his eyes lit up with recognition. "Your perfume!"

"Yes. If you ever start to forget me, have a whiff of this." Flavia smiled sweetly as she put the stopper back in the little bottle and offered it to her husband.

"I could never forget you," Rex said, though he gladly took the bottle and stowed it in his pack.

A horn blew from the ship's stern, signaling to everyone that it was about to shove off. The tugboats were ready to move the great behemoth into position for the sail to catch some wind. In the distance, the lighthouse of Alexandria stood on its island like a slender queen with a blazing crown. It was the second tallest man-made structure in the world, behind only the Aegyptian pyramids. At forty stories high, it dwarfed even the Flavian Amphitheater or the Colossus of Rodos. Though Flavia had always found the white spire beautiful, today she felt jealous of it. The lighthouse was like a voluptuous seductress stealing away her man.

Rex hoisted to his shoulders the rucksack that contained the scroll case from the bishop. He was used to traveling with a heavy pack, for in his youth, the army had trained him as a special forces operative called a speculator. Still adept in his training and bold by personality, Rex knew how to navigate whatever situations came his way. Flavia relied on her husband's natural competence every day. Now she was feeling the sting of how much she was going to miss him.

"I love you," she said, standing on her tiptoes to kiss his whiskered cheek.

"Forever and for always," he replied, then turned and ascended the gangplank.

The crewmen in the tugboats leaned into their oars. Soon the grain ship was positioned in open space so that its sail could be unfurled. The linen fabric snapped crisply and bowed into an arc as it caught a breeze. Slowly, the ship headed past the white pinnacle whose column of smoke ascended into the sky. Then, with a westward turn, Rex was gone.

Flavia didn't wait around at the fickle and greedy harbor. The walk back to her apartment took her first to Canopus Avenue. Arriving at the wide thoroughfare, she peered down its length in both directions. At one end was the Church of Theonas, while the other end exited through the Sun Gate into the rough countryside known as the Boukolia district. That was Arius's power base. The scruffy shepherds out there admired him, and the shrine of Saint Mark was his church. Some people said the apostle's relics were interred there, but the more learned Christians denied that legend because the earliest Alexandrian records did not attest an apostolic visit from Mark.

Since Flavia needed to buy a few groceries today, she had brought some money in her satchel. She strolled along the colonnade until she had acquired flatbread, oil, and lentils. Now she stopped at the stall of a wrinkled, white-haired fishwife whose smelly wares lay before her on a cart.

"How fresh are your mussels?" Flavia asked.

"Hee-hee!" the old hag cried in a high-pitched cackle. "Put your nose a little closer to 'em, and you'll find they ain't fresh at all."

"Then why are you selling them?"

"I'm not! I just set 'em out to draw the nose. Then when someone walks up, I sell what's in my shop behind."

"And what is that?"

"Live oysters," the hag said, "which a young broody hen like you could prob'ly use."

Flavia was surprised that the conversation had taken this direction. Yet the fishmonger's words struck a nerve. "I've heard mothers say that oysters can help conception," she acknowledged.

"O'course they can! I guarantee you, little lady, they'll have you on the birthin' stool by the start of the new year. Follow me."

The hag led Flavia into her shop. Surprisingly, the fishy smell wasn't as bad there. The elderly proprietor had draped flower garlands on her walls. A censer on a tripod sent up a tendril of aromatic smoke that drifted out of a high window.

"My little baby makers are down here," the crone said as she removed the lid of a ceramic vat that had been set into the floor. The inside of the vat was cool and damp, with no bad smell coming up. "These can surely help you. Steam 'em and eat 'em with garlic oil. But just so you know, I have even better wares for your purposes—if you got the means to pay."

"What's better than oysters?" Flavia asked, intrigued by the claim.

"It'll cost you an argenteus."

"An argenteus! That could buy me a hundred oysters!"

"Do you want the baby or not?" the hag grumped.

"I do. I'll buy whatever it is. Show me."

The old woman beckoned Flavia to follow her through the shop's back door. Across a narrow alley was an imposing wall made of heavy limestone blocks. The wall had a little door in it. Pushing it open, the hag led the way into the dark interior. The smell of frankincense immediately greeted Flavia's nose. Yellow lamplight flickered ahead. With her heart beating fast, Flavia emerged from the tunnel and looked up to discover where she was.

The Temple of Isis!

The idol sat enthroned in silent, golden splendor: Isis, the mother goddess of Aegyptus, with the infant Horus upon her lap. A staff was in her hand, a sun disk crowned her head, and an ankh cross adorned her breast. Instead of staring straight ahead with blank eyes, Isis's head was inclined toward the earth. Her expression was benevolent and compassionate. "I am here to help you," she seemed to say. "Just ask me for what you need."

A brazier sat on the floor in front of the idol. Red-hot coals glowed in its basin. Beside it was a pair of scissors and a little wooden coffer with a slot in the top.

"For forty years, I was a priestess of Isis," the hag announced. "Now I am retired. Even so, I still bring before our Holy Mother any seeker who has a need."

"No," Flavia whispered, backing away. "I am a Christian."

"Christians have needs too. Has your God smiled upon your womb? Or is he making you wait?"

"I'm . . . still waiting."

"Give him some help, then," the hag urged. "He's probably busy with other things. The Mother will pay more attention to you while the Father is occupied with bigger affairs."

"No! I can't."

The hag shrugged. "Sure you can. It's easy. Watch." She walked over and picked up the scissors and the coffer. "Put your argenteus in here," she said, holding out the little coin box.

Flavia fished the coin out of her satchel. *It's a necessary price to escape this place*, she told herself as she dropped it in. The coin made a tinkling sound against the others below.

"And now," the hag went on, "the goddess requires a more corporeal gift. To put something into your body, she must take something from your body as well." Before Flavia could protest, the hag snipped away a lock of her hair and held it between pinched fingers. Walking over to the brazier, she dropped it onto the coals. A thin line of smoke went up to Isis—and then it was gone.

The hag now began to say an incantation, not in Greek or Latin, but in the Coptic language that had been in use since the time of the pharaohs. The words were inscribed upon a copper sheet with pictorial glyphs. Though Flavia didn't understand the words, she knew exactly what this was: a fertility spell, an ancient magical invocation to make the seed of a man take root in a woman's womb.

When the spell was over, the hag came and stood in front of Flavia. She placed both hands on Flavia's belly. "May you soon conceive a child by the power of the Holy Mother."

And with those pagan words, Flavia could endure no more.

She burst from the main door of the temple and rushed down the steps onto Canopus Avenue. The midday sun was bright, so she squinted from the glare after being trapped in the temple's gloom for so long. Her heart was beating wildly, and she seemed to be breathing harder than she should have been from the short run. "Oh God, oh God," she panted in ragged gasps, "oh God, what have I done?"

Just then, a man's voice hailed her. "Candida!"

It was her baptismal name. "White" was its meaning—the color of cleanness, of spiritual purity. Only one person in Alexandria addressed her that way. Flavia turned, dreading to confront the figure she knew would be standing there.

Bishop Alexander stared back at her with a stunned expression. "Candida," he said, his eyes wide and his eyebrows arched, "did you just . . . ?"

No words would come from Flavia's mouth. No excuses for this dreadful sin could be made. The shame was overwhelming. There was nothing to do but run. Turning her back on her bishop, Flavia fled from his presence and left him agape and astonished in front of the hideous house of Isis.

2

It didn't matter if a traveler had been away from Rome for seven days or, like Rex, seven years; returning to the Eternal City always stirred the soul and amazed the eyes. The city's architecture was too stunning, its size too vast, and its legacy too grand for the human mind to comprehend. It was impossible not to pause outside Rome's gates and marvel at what was inside. There was no place like it on earth.

Rex approached Rome at its Ostian Gate, where the road from the port met the Aurelian Walls that defined the urban boundary. Some ancient senator with aspirations of Aegyptian grandeur had built his tomb here in the form of a pyramid. Rex had seen it many times, for it wasn't far from Flavia's old house. Yet now he could only chuckle at the pitiful little edifice that had once seemed rather impressive. "You should see the real thing, mister," he said to whomever had decided to bury himself like an Italian pseudo-pharaoh. With a shake of his head and a little chuckle, Rex renewed his grip on his staff and passed through the city walls.

The Ostian Gate—which the locals had started calling Saint Paul's Gate because a chapel was being built over the apostle's tomb on the road outside the walls—was in the southern part of the city, not far from Rex's final destination. Yet before he could arrive at the Lateran Palace and seek an audience with the pope, he desperately needed something else first: a bath. Rex had left Alexandria on the second day of April, and now it was twenty-six days later—a good time for the difficult westward trip, yet not one that afforded any leisure for visiting bathhouses along the way. A cleanup and haircut were definitely in order before he could deliver Bishop Alexander's letter to the pope.

Fortunately, the majestic Bathhouse of Caracalla was on the way to the Lateran Palace. Though these public baths were now a hundred years old, they were no less impressive today than when first built. Rex approached the massive complex with a mixture of gratitude and awe: gratitude because he could finally wash away his grime, awe because the architecture was so stunning. Not only were the baths overwhelming in their vast size, but they also dazzled the beholder by the sheer quantity of their columns, statues, fountains, courtyards, mosaics, gilded ornaments, and multicolored marble inlays that met the eye wherever you looked. The Bathhouse of Caracalla was one of the most astonishing places in the whole empire.

Although entrance was free to all citizens, Rex gladly paid the fee for a slave to guard his belongings with the promise of a nice tip when everything was safely retrieved again. After stripping in the changing room, he oiled himself and scraped his skin clean, then went three times through the rounds of hot, warm, and cold water that the baths offered. A long soak in the caldarium's hot pool—situated beneath a dome that gave the Pantheon a run for its money—was especially relaxing. After a final swim in the outdoor pool under the bright Italian sun, Rex re-dressed, collected his things, and stepped into the broad, sunny courtyard that surrounded the baths. He had one more place to visit before he left: the Latin library just across the courtyard.

Although the bathhouse offered a Greek library too, Rex had frequent access to Alexandria's archives at the Serapeum, so he was less interested in eastern literature right now. He wanted to see which of the Christian Latin writers might be available here in Rome. As he perused the walls, with their cubbyholes full of scrolls and codices, he noted the presence of Minucius Felix, Novatian, Cyprian, Victorinus, and best of all, Tertullian. Rex pulled Tertullian's *Against Praxeas* from its storage nook and opened the codex. Taking it to a nearby couch, he flipped the pages and familiarized himself with the argument. Although this text was written more than a century ago, it dealt with many of the issues the Alexandrian church was now facing with regard to Arius—the very issues addressed in the letter that Rex had carried across the sea. Finally, he closed the book, returned it to its nook, and left the bathhouse with theological debates about the "persons" and "substance" of God swirling in his mind.

The Lateran Palace was only a short walk from the baths. Upon his arrival, a doorkeeper relayed a message inside and Rex was soon admitted. The first person to greet him was his old friend and former catechist, the Hibernian priest Vincentius.

"Vitus!" the priest cried, using Rex's baptismal name as he welcomed him with an embrace. "It has been far too long since I've seen you! How fares the church in Aegyptus?"

"It thrives under its bishop yet is riven by the faction of Arius. I have brought an urgent letter from Alexander about this matter."

Vincentius nodded gravely, for he was an orthodox theologian always on guard against heresy. "I will arrange a meeting with Pope Sylvester first thing tomorrow."

After a sociable afternoon and a good evening meal, Rex was shown to a guest room whose door opened off the palace's rear garden. The tiny room was furnished with only a cot, a rough-hewn table, and a stool. Yet despite the spartan accommodations, Rex could see that this was the best of the guest rooms. One of its walls adjoined an outdoor fireplace that faced into the garden for whoever might wish to sit around the flames at night. Since the bricks of the fireplace and its chimney formed the guest room's right wall, the radiant heat from the firebox made the space cozy and snug. Rex pushed his cot up against the warm bricks, climbed under his covers, and slept through the night like a man dead to the world.

The next morning, Sylvester welcomed Rex and Vincentius into his personal study, an honor he accorded to few people. The conversation began not with pleasantries but with sincere pastoral concern as Sylvester inquired about the state of Rex's soul. After a time of personal reflections and even some admonishment, the subject turned to the reason for Rex's audience with the pope. Rex untied the lid of the capsa and withdrew the scroll. For the next half hour, Vincentius read the lengthy letter aloud while the other two men listened.

Once Vincentius had finished, the three men reflected quietly for a time, sipping hot wine while they considered what they had heard. Finally, Sylvester said, "It appears we have a third enemy on the horizon." Vincentius immediately agreed, but Rex had to ask who the first two enemies were.

"Here in Rome," the bishop explained, "we have long been pressed by the pagans. Their worship of multiple gods, indeed their entire view of the world, is opposed to the Christian view of one God. More lately, we have been pressed by heretics—specifically the Manichaeans. That sect is on the rise in Rome, led by the former priest whom you will surely remember, Felix of the Aventine Hill."

"Felix! I thought he must have disappeared after his treachery over the bones of Saint Peter."

"Unfortunately, the man is still making trouble among us, though I have no idea what happened to his associate, the fellow with the snake tattoo."

Rex frowned as he contemplated what Sylvester had just told him. Two great enemies were arrayed against Christ—the pagans and Manichaeans—and now the letter from Alexander was introducing a third—the Arians. No doubt this was a heavy burden upon the pope. Yet in hard times, it was better to identify one's enemies than live in oblivion.

Sylvester's face, however, did not signal despair. With liveliness in his eyes, he said to Rex, "Vincentius tells me you've been reading Tertullian on these matters. Good for you! That African was one of the church's greatest minds. His wit was acerbic, and his tongue was sharp. Yet back in his day, no one got it right more often than Tertullian."

"I believe Tertullian offers a solution to the debate between Alexander and Arius," Rex said. "He uses the word *Trinity* to speak of three 'persons': the Father, Son, and Holy Spirit. Yet God is one because their 'substance' is united."

A smile played at the corners of Sylvester's lips. "Look at what happens when we send a barbarian off to Alexandria," he said with a laugh. "He comes back to us as a theological scholar!"

The joke made Rex toss back his head and laugh too, for he knew what the bishop meant. It was more than just a wisecrack about the famous intellectualism of Alexandria. Pope Sylvester understood that theology transforms a person because it addresses the most beautiful subject in all of human inquiry: God himself.

Sylvester rose from his desk and went to a cabinet behind him. Returning to his guests, he seated himself again with something clenched in his fist. Looking at Rex with a steady gaze, he said, "Brandulf Vitus Rex, I still recall the day I baptized you. It was not at the Pasch, as is normal for us, but at the dedication of our new baptistery. How beautiful was the dawn that morning! But even more lovely was the grace of Christ upon a man of idols and bloodshed. Such a man were you, Vitus of Germania. 'But you were washed, you were sanctified, you were justified in the name of the Lord Jesus Christ and by the Spirit of our God.'"

"I remember that day too. It is vivid in my mind."

"As it should be! For if I recall correctly, there was another lovely vision that day."

"Yes. My bride."

Sylvester nodded, then opened his fist and held out his palm. A gold signet ring was there, inset with a red carnelian engraved with a dove and a key. "Vitus," the pope said, "I am deputizing you as a papal legate whose doctrine is sound and whose orthodoxy is unimpeached. On occasions when I authorize it, you may represent me on official church business across the empire."

"It is a high honor," Vincentius added. He showed Rex that he, too, had a ring with the same emblem.

Rex bowed his head, feeling overwhelmed by the new responsibility yet grateful for the affirmation. "Your Holiness, I promise to stay true to the path of Christ in everything I say and do." He received the ring and slipped it on the third finger of his right hand.

"Excellent! Then our meeting today is complete. And may I suggest that while you are here, you should take a look at the new Church of the Savior outside. It looks very different than it did on the day of your baptism and wedding."

"I shall do it," Rex agreed.

The three men stood up. After Rex had thanked the bishop and taken his leave from him and Vincentius, he made his way out of the palace and across a courtyard to the basilica Sylvester had mentioned.

The Lateran Church of the Savior was impressive and inviting even though it was still under construction. Scaffolding surrounded some parts of it, but the outer shell was more or less complete. Rex went inside and walked down the hall's length toward the apse. Though a floor of beautiful marble was being installed, not all the tiles were yet in place, leaving bare spots here and there. Somewhere beneath that floor were the foundations of the buildings that had stood here before: the barracks of the cavalry fort that Rex had joined . . . how long ago was it now? *Twelve years*, he realized after he did the math. *More than twelve years ago, I came here to spy on Maxentius. I had a cot in the barracks that were here. Over there, I rode the Cantabrian Circle to impress the recruiters enough to let me into the horse guard. And then, a few years later . . .*

Rex arrived at the altar, a simple block of marble that probably would be replaced by a finer version once the basilica was complete. The last time Rex was here, the barracks had been demolished because they had belonged to Constantine's enemy. However, the place was still a grassy field under an open sky, with no part of the basilica yet started except the foundations of the exterior walls. The altar back then was just a pile of jumbled stones to mark the spot where a real altar would one day stand. Yet it was here that Rex had married Flavia, crowning her not with a golden tiara or a circlet of silver but with laurels of victory plucked from a nearby bush. *That is perfect*, Rex decided, *because Flavia and I triumphed over so many obstacles to be standing together that day.*

Near the altar was one of the bare patches in the floor that had not yet received its marble overlay. Rex went to it and knelt down. Scratching his fingers through the substrate, he reached the soil underneath. After making a little hole with his finger, Rex opened his rucksack and rummaged in it until he found the vial that Flavia had given him at the harbor of Alexandria on the day he left. Removing its stopper, he let a droplet of her perfume—its floral aroma so much a part of who she was to him—trickle into the hole. He smoothed the place over with dirt. Now Flavia's presence would be there forever, resting quietly beneath the floor of the Lateran Church in Rome.

"Never could I forget you, Lady Junia Flavia Candida," Rex said as he stood up and gazed at the sacred spot, "nor the eternal vows that we made in this holy place."

✧

Caesar Crispus could feel the cool winds rolling down from snowcapped Mons Olympus as he sailed past its great bulk on his left. He stood in the prow of a warship headed into Thessalonica's harbor at the head of a massive fleet. Everyone was calling the new construction "Dug Harbor," because for the past three years, Constantine's workers had been dredging silt from the ocean floor to deepen the moorings. A long breakwater had been built of local stone, serving as a protective arm to scoop arriving ships into its safe embrace. Constantine's new harbor was expansive, with plenty of room for a naval fleet. Crispus resolved to congratulate his father on the fine achievement. They both knew it would be needed soon in the confrontation with Licinius.

The emperor was standing on the pier when the flagship drew near, and Crispus was delighted to see a little boy at his side. It was his half brother, also named Constantine, but called Secundus by everyone to avoid confusion. Crispus thought the lad had grown up quite a bit since he had seen him last. Secundus was about seven now, with the bug eyes and homely features of his mother, Fausta. But despite his awkward appearance, he was a sweet boy, and Crispus was glad to share the rank of caesar with him in the Imperial College.

"Well done, my son!" Constantine cried as Crispus stepped onto the pier from the gangplank. "What a magnificent fleet you have brought! Your galleys look like a flock of noble swans drifting into the harbor."

"Except these swans will soon turn into fierce hawks in search of their prey, Your Majesty!" Though Crispus didn't normally use such formal titles with his father, he did so now to signal his respect before all the dignitaries gathered on the pier.

Constantine smiled and nodded, for he knew the "prey" of which Crispus spoke. All winter, the two of them had been war planning against Licinius. Soon that troublemaker would be removed from the Imperial College, along with his son Licinius Junior. That would leave Constantine alone in the rank of augustus, while Crispus and Secundus would occupy the two junior positions as caesars. Imperial rule would once again be in the hands of a single dynasty, just like in the glory days of Rome.

"Your new harbor is splendid," Crispus said after receiving a warm embrace from his father. "What a magnificent achievement!"

"Come along," Constantine replied with a wave of his hand. "It is not the harbor that counts, but what's in it. I want you to see the ships I have. I'll be interested in your evaluation of them in comparison to the ones you've brought up from Athenae."

"The Thessalonian shipwrights are nearly as famous as the Athenian ones. I'm sure they make excellent watercraft here." Crispus turned toward the boy at Constantine's side. "Shall we take Secundus with us? It's never too early to start learning the details of naval warfare."

"Yes, please!" the boy cried with eager eyes and an urgent clap of his hands. Clearly, he viewed his half brother with a heavy dose of hero worship.

"Indeed, bring the lad! We shall go together like a family should." Constantine turned and led the way as the threesome headed toward the shipyard adjacent to the harbor.

One of the Thessalonian galleys had been drawn onto land for repairs, a stout liburnian with weathered but still-functional planking. Crispus approached it with his father and brother. "How many total vessels do you have?" he asked.

"Eighty in the harbor, plus the hundred 'swans' you just led up from Graecia."

"A good fleet, but we should try to find a few more and get to two hundred before we sail out."

Constantine winced. "Licinius is reported to have three hundred."

"But he doesn't have General Crispus at the helm!" Secundus cried.

Crispus turned and shook his head with a gentle grin. "It isn't me, nor Constantine, and certainly not Licinius who decides the outcome of a war. The battle belongs to the Lord. Two hundred ships will do just fine."

Secundus seemed encouraged by the pious reminder. He nodded and made a cross over himself like the grown-ups around him so often did.

Crispus beckoned his little brother to follow him close to the galley. He showed the boy its graceful lines and let him stroke its wood. "Now look here," Crispus said. "I want to show you how this works." He bent down and picked up a shipwright's adze. Using brisk, accurate strokes, Crispus planed away thin strips of wood from a plank between his feet. With each fall of the adze's metal head, aromatic cedar shavings curled up like cheese sliced by a knife. Soon he had created an angled surface at the end of the plank so that its tip was now a slender wedge.

Emperor Constantine approached his two sons. "That's a nice scarf joint," he said approvingly as he looked over Crispus's shoulder. "See that, Secundus? It will fit right here." Constantine showed the boy the other plank on the ship's hull, the one to which this one would be joined end to end. "Crispus has made a perfect fit! The hull of this galley is in great shape. Let's go check her out from the inside."

The three visitors ascended a ladder to the main deck. After looking around a bit, they went below. The rowing deck was stuffy and smelled of stale sweat. Secundus slid his bottom along a rower's bench and peered through one of the oar holes that lined the sides of the ship. Since the oars were stowed while the ship was being repaired, Secundus could see to the outside. After staring through the hole for a bit, he glanced above his head. "I've seen galleys with the rowers stacked in three levels. I hope one of those monsters rams Uncle Licinius broadside!"

Crispus glanced over at Constantine. The two men exchanged looks, for this had been a matter of debate between them last winter. Constantine had wanted to amass a fleet of the three-tiered battleships called triremes, which for so long had formed the backbone of the Roman navy. Everyone knew Licinius was acquiring many triremes of his own. But Crispus had favored the one-tiered ships called liburnians, which were lighter, faster, and had more flexible hulls. Cutting-edge naval tactics these days called for maneuverability and speed, not sheer bulk. To Constantine, the liburnians seemed like rabbits trying to take on a wild bison. Crispus had replied that the proper picture would be wolves against a bison—a swift and mobile attack that would work just fine under the right circumstances. Eventually, Constantine had acquiesced to his son's plan, though not without some misgivings.

"Our uncle's flagship will surely be sunk," Crispus declared, avoiding the delicate subject Secundus had unknowingly brought up.

"And when it is," Constantine added, "I'll have his flag cut into handkerchiefs for all my officers. You can have one too, my boy!"

The threesome left the stuffy rowing deck and went topside. The cool wind coming down from the mountains across the Thessalonian gulf felt good on Crispus's face.

Secundus, still excited by the aura of grand adventure, ran to the ship's prow. He peered down at the bronze ram for a moment, then raised his eyes and stared at an imaginary enemy slicing through the waves at full speed. "I shall defeat you!" he cried, shaking his fists. "Our ships are faster! Our joints are stronger! Our tactics are better! Our men are braver! No one can defeat the armies of Constantine!"

The lusty battle cry elicited a hearty chuckle from the emperor. "Ho, look at my boy! What a warrior he'll be someday."

"He is a brave lad," Crispus agreed, joining his father at his side.

"I hope you're right about these liburnians," Constantine said. "Everything is riding on the outcome of this war—for me, for you, and for that little one right there."

Crispus gazed across the choppy bay at the peak of Mons Olympus. "Licinius is such a fool. He thinks Jupiter sits up there—or Zeus, as they call him around here. Dionysus sips his wine, Apollo plays his harp, Hera nags her husband, Aphrodite seduces whomever she can. What nonsense! I heard that last summer, a local huntsman got all the way to the top. He said he found nothing up there but rocks and goat dung."

"It is truly nonsense. But it's powerful nonsense. Desperate people look to those gods for help."

For a long time, the two men were silent. Then Crispus said quietly, "I have lifted mine eyes to the hills. From where shall my help come?"

"My help comes from the Lord," Constantine whispered in reply, "from he who made heaven and earth."

Crispus slipped his arm around Constantine's shoulder. "You are right, my father," he said as they watched the Olympian winds ruffle the Aegean Sea. "You are right indeed."

MAY 324

Flavia ducked between two stalls in the fish market on Lake Mareotis, hoping the man she had spotted across the market hadn't seen her. He was one of the last people she wanted to interact with right now. He wasn't a dangerous man. In fact, he was her friend. But Flavia didn't want to talk to him: Athanasius, the right-hand man to Bishop Alexander.

"Hey, lady, wanna buy some perch?" asked the fishmonger whose stall Flavia had approached.

Keeping her back toward the area where she had seen Athanasius, Flavia quickly bought some fish and a few wafers of flatbread. Still feeling flustered, she hurried out of the market and strolled aimlessly down the wharf that ran along the waterfront. She came to a lonely dock that thrust into the wide, blue expanse of Lake Mareotis. Only when she was seated out on its end with her legs dangling over the water did she realize her mistake: she had bought raw fish when she had meant to buy cooked. Now all she had for lunch was the dry bread and a gourd of water.

Flavia had just taken a bite of the crusty wafer when she heard a voice behind her ask, "May I join you?" She turned—and of course it was Athanasius.

He sat down beside her before she could respond. From a basket, he brought out something wrapped in waxy palm leaves. Opening them, he revealed two steaming white fillets with char marks from the grill. He also had a bowl of cheese spread seasoned with pepper and herbs for dipping. And to top it off: an earthenware flagon of wine.

"I know I'm just a little fellow," Athanasius joked in reference to his short stature, "but I have the appetite of three Goths."

Flavia gave her friend a smile. "I guess that's too bad for me. Your lunch looks delicious, and I have none."

"I suppose I could give you some," Athanasius replied, playing along. They both knew he had come here on purpose to share the meal. He handed Flavia one of the fillets. For a while, the two of them ate in silence, dipping their bread in the bowl of soft cheese and drinking wine straight from the flagon like a couple of rustic peasants.

When they were finished, Athanasius let out a loud belch. Flavia didn't mind. Her friend wasn't used to womanly company, so he was rather earthy in his habits. He swept his hand across the wide expanse of Lake Mareotis, then pointed to the canals that exited it. "The Nilus is the lifeblood of Aegyptus," he declared. "Only its water makes life possible in this desert."

"I haven't been very far inland. My world is across the sea, not in Upper Aegyptus."

"Ah, my dear Flavia, our land is truly beautiful! You and Rex should go sometime and experience the Nilus, the desert, and the ancient cultures. Alexandria is too filled with other peoples to be fully Aegyptian. It is an edge city for us, a boundary with other nations."

"I know. We are on the westernmost branch of the Nilus. Our gaze is always toward Rome."

"But the rest of Aegyptus is available to you! It is all there to the south. And beyond that is an even wider world." The deacon pointed to the southeast. "The Red Sea is over that way. From there you can reach Arabia, Persia, India, or even Seres, which is a faraway land of much silk."

"Or you can reach the Promised Land, as the Israelites discovered."

Athanasius chuckled. "Indeed, you can! But unless you can call down some manna, I suggest you catch a ship in the harbor and arrive a few days later in Caesarea."

"Someday I shall go to Hierusalem," Flavia announced. Though her statement came out unexpectedly, it didn't feel like a whim—more like a vow.

"I hope you do, my dear Flavia."

She turned and looked at her friend. Although he was a churchman, he refused to call her Candida because he said it felt too formal. He wanted her to know he was more than just a pastoral figure. Athanasius was a dark-skinned man of Coptic origin with jet-black hair and a delicate chin that fit his small stature. He was still young, maybe around twenty-five. Yet he was no weakling. This man could breathe fire and make the earth quake when the Spirit of God was upon him.

"You are kind to me," she told him.

"It is what friends do. They seek to meet needs."

"Do you think . . . I have needs?"

"You needed fish," Athanasius said simply, "so I brought some."

"Is that the only reason you came?"

"If you want it to be."

"What if I want to talk?"

"Then you can do that too, if you wish."

Flavia sighed and fiddled with the empty palm leaf in her lap. *I do want to talk . . . but where to begin?*

Athanasius provided the way. "Bishop Alexander told me about seeing you in the street."

Now that the subject was broached, tears came to Flavia's eyes, but with them came the necessary words that had been pent up inside. Each one was like a jagged shard of glass in her throat, needing to come out yet hurting as it did. "I did what no Christian should ever do," she confessed, wincing and hanging her head. "I worshiped a demon. I hailed an unclean spirit as my lord and savior instead of Christ. I gave to that filthy goddess what rightly belongs to God."

"I stand with you," Athanasius said, "as a sinner too."

"But not like this! I did what the martyrs gave their lives to avoid!" The shame of Flavia's deed was overwhelming. During the persecutions, many Christians had endured torture, mutilation, enslavement, rape, or the killing of their families. They had refused to worship the gods even under such dire threats. Yet Flavia had freely chosen to call upon Isis, giving worship to a divinity other than God himself—all because of her desire for a baby.

"I violated my baptismal oath," Flavia said bitterly. "That is what we call it in Rome, Athanasius—an oath! Our word is *sacramentum*. Standing in the water, we renounce Satan and swear to follow Christ forever. Now I have broken my vow. Surely I am no longer saved."

"Flavia, dear one, remember these words of holy scripture: 'He has saved us not by the works of righteousness we have done, but according to his mercy, through the washing of regeneration and the renewing of the Holy Spirit.'"

Although Flavia wanted to believe that God's mercy could be so great, the gravity of her sin overwhelmed her. Worshiping a goddess, paying lip service to Satan himself, was as displeasing to the Lord as anything she could imagine.

Athanasius reached into the basket in which he had brought the food. "Look here," he said. "I have a gift for you."

The deacon brought forth a small codex and held it in his smooth, dark hands. He showed her the title: *On the Incarnation*. Flavia had heard of it, for it was a popular theological work that Athanasius had written a few years ago. Many people in Alexandria were still talking about it.

"What you need now," Athanasius said gently, "is a reminder of why Christ came to this earth. He knew that we always reach for what is unreal, until we ourselves fall into oblivion. But God loved his creatures too much to let this dilemma prevail! And so he sent us a Savior, Christ Jesus our Lord." The deacon handed Flavia the book, then folded his hands in his lap. "Take comfort, my friend. The incarnation is the answer."

With these words, Athanasius stood up. "I think you need some time alone with God. Sit here under his bright sunshine and feel the wind that moves these boats along. You might find that the Holy Wind fills your sails too. My prayers will be with you, dear friend."

After the deacon had left Flavia on the end of the rickety dock, she did what he had instructed. Closing her eyes, she focused on the sun's warmth on her cheeks and the breeze in her hair. Her fingers played with the leather-bound covers of the book in her lap. At last, she looked down and opened it. The pages were fine vellum, the scribal hand bold and clear. Her eyes immediately fell upon a passage whose words arrested her attention:

This is above all why Christ came to live with us. His purpose was this: after he had proved his divinity from his works, he went on to offer a sacrifice on behalf of all, handing over his body to death in our place.

"A sacrifice on behalf of all," Flavia whispered as her finger traced the life-giving words. "His death in our place." She wanted to believe it was true. Yet the guilt of her transgression would not let go. She wrestled with her thoughts for a long time as she sat on the old, rugged dock. Finally, she gave in. "I accept it, Lord," she said aloud. "I choose to believe in your grace."

Flavia tied the leather thong around the book's sturdy covers and gathered her things. But as she began to rise from the dock, her foot caught on her hem and set her off-balance. In the same moment, a hard gust of wind buffeted her. As she reached out to steady herself, the book slipped from her grasp. Before Flavia could catch it, the little volume tumbled over the edge of the dock and disappeared into the waters of Lake Mareotis.

No! My lovely gift! Though Flavia considered jumping in and searching, she knew that the water was too deep, the lake bed too muddy. And even if she could find the book, the ink would be dissolved beyond recognition. Deep sadness seized Flavia as she realized the precious gift was gone.

Was it a sign? Was God chastising her? Was he banishing her soul to the abyss like the holy book she had dared to touch?

Flavia put her hand to her belly, covering it as if to protect what might be there. Since the day Rex had left the city, she hadn't experienced the monthly sign that tells a woman there has been no conception. For all she knew, a child might be growing in her womb right now. "Please, Lord," she said to the heavens, "don't turn your back on me!"

For a long moment, Flavia waited for an answer, desperate for God to speak. But there was no word from heaven, not even a cooling breeze. The only response was a dreadful silence and the searing heat of the empty Aegyptian sky.

Emperor Licinius knocked a candied cherry from his son's hand just as the boy put it to his mouth. "Enough of that! You're such a pig!" he shouted. "There isn't a warhorse in the empire that could carry a load like you! Quit eating all the time!"

At these words, Licinius Junior began to bawl like a newborn baby. Though at age nine he was old enough to know better, he ran to his mother and hid behind her skirts. He cowered there, whimpering and rubbing his hand where Licinius's slap had left a mark.

"Why must you discipline the boy so harshly?" Constantia demanded with hard eyes.

"So Junior doesn't turn out as fat as you," Licinius shot back. He hoped that the brusque reply would make his wife go away, but she seemed determined to lurk around their private apartments, as if a woman should be part of his war planning.

Turning his back on her, Licinius went to a window and gazed out at the Thracian city of Hadrianopolis. It was locked up tight, fully provisioned with food and armaments. Situated on the Hebrus River, Hadrianopolis was well protected by that natural barrier on one side and stout walls on the other three. Every tower was manned by defenders, yet that was only the beginning. Licinius's entire army was stationed along the near bank of the river for a distance of fifty miles. It was a powerful force of one hundred thousand men, with fifty thousand more troops back at Byzantium if he needed to retreat there. All in all, Licinius was well prepared for battle with his brother-in-law. *So why do I feel so nervous?*

Little Junior—not so little, actually—finally quit his blubbering and began to pick at a scab on his arm. Constantia left him at his picking and approached Licinius. "Do not fret, my love," she cooed in a voice that tried to be soothing but was just annoying.

"How can I not fret? Do you see that river there?" When Constantia peered out the window and nodded, Licinius said, "Your brother's army is sailing to the place where the Hebrus meets the sea. They'll march upriver and be here in a matter of days. Your brother has already beaten me twice. Who's to say it won't happen again?"

"He's only my half brother," Constantia said in an attempt to show loyalty.

"He's about to be your dead brother."

Licinius strode across the room and picked up a spear that rested against the wall. It was just a standard-issue cavalry lance with a sturdy ashen shaft and a tapered steel head. But one thing about it was special: it was the spear he had marked with the letters "P.P." in his own blood. That unexpected moment at the roadside pantheon had seemed to infuse the weapon with special power.

"I'm considering having this made into a war banner," he announced, speaking ostensibly to Constantia but really just thinking out loud. "It is sacred to me."

"Good idea! I remember when you fought Daia. You had a Christian banner, and your men said a prayer to the Supreme God. Do the same now, my love."

"*Pfft!* That was just a ploy to impress the bishops. It wasn't the Christian God we prayed to. It was the Invincible Sun."

"Perhaps you meant it to be Sol. But another ear heard your prayer: the Sun of Righteousness, Jesus Christ."

Rage flared in Licinius's heart, and he whirled to face his wife. "Never mention that name to me again!" he snarled. He cocked his arm and hurled the spear in Constantia's direction—not straight at her, yet close enough to inspire fear. The spearhead impaled itself in a chest of drawers nearby. Constantia shrank back with her eyes wide and her hand on her bosom. Though her mouth hung open, she appeared unable to speak.

Still enraged, Licinius uttered a string of curses against Jesus that were as vicious and foul as he could think up. A divine power seemed to overtake him, enabling him to express the harshest profanities, the crudest accusations, the vilest mockeries he had ever produced. Satisfied by the extremity of his blasphemy, Licinius went over to the spear and yanked it from the furniture. "I hope I have made myself clear," he said as he set the spear against the wall. Constantia offered only a meek nod.

Licinius ordered the handmaiden who stood in the corner of the room to fetch his Curator of Correspondence. A short while later, the fellow appeared. Zeno was a rodent of a man with a pointed nose and the quick, shifty eyes of a rat. But also like a rat, he was inventive and always on the move. He was a very good scribe.

"Greetings, my lord," Zeno said as he dropped to one knee and bowed. He clutched a wax tablet and stylus to his chest as he genuflected. Such obsequious behavior would have been considered strange in the early days of the empire, and it was unthinkable in the old republic. Yet Diocletian had introduced it a few years back when he demanded to be called "lord" instead of "first citizen." Most emperors since then had continued to require such servile gestures as part of their reign. In fact, the only one who didn't was Constantine.

"You may rise, Zeno," Licinius said in a dignified voice. When the man was on his feet, Licinius announced, "I have decided that my troops need spiritual focus for the day of battle. Therefore it is my divine will to make Christianity illegal again."

"No!" Constantia shrieked, finally recovering her voice. "You cannot!"

"It is a wise course," Zeno countered, "for those people are impious, and they attract the wrath of the gods upon our armies. To support the Christians is to guarantee a loss in battle."

"You ended the persecutions at our wedding," Constantia protested with a face contorted by horror. She even had the audacity to come and clutch her husband's expensive Dalmatic tunic. "Ever since your edict at Mediolanum, the age of martyrdom has been over. You cannot restart it!"

Licinius yanked his sleeve from Constantia's grip. "I can do whatever I want! I am the lord and savior of this empire—not that pitiful carpenter of the filthy Jews."

"What are your commands, sire?" Zeno asked as he put the stylus to the wax. "Tell me, and I shall prepare a rough draft for you by the end of the day."

"Send a new edict to all the governors under my authority. Tell them to go after the clergy—those who shepherd the flock. Make up charges against them if necessary. Hire false witnesses. Just get the clergy in custody and execute them in public so everyone will know the high price of being a Christian."

"It shall be done right away."

"And, Zeno, one more thing . . ."

"Yes, my lord?"

"Make it gory. I mean, *gory*. I want people fainting and vomiting at the sight."

"As you wish," Zeno said with a weaselly smirk.

Constantia came and faced Licinius with determination in her eyes. Gone now was her syrupy piety and typical female hysteria. A note of warning was in her voice when she asked, "Are you certain Jupiter is behind you in this?"

The question caught Licinius off guard. "Of course I'm certain. I am his favorite son."

"But the gods are whimsical! How can you be so sure you are in Jupiter's good graces? I suggest you wait to persecute the Christians until after the battle. Then you will know Jupiter favors you. You can do whatever you please once you have won."

Although she was only a woman, Constantia's counsel actually had some merit. Licinius was mulling it over when Zeno said, "May I suggest an alternative?"

"Tell me, my son."

"If you wait until the battle is over, you will lose the value of restarting the persecution—the encouragement of your troops. Therefore I suggest a better way to determine whether you have Jupiter's favor."

"And that is?"

"Take the auspices. If the omens are favorable, send out the edict. If not, you can wait until your political position is more secure."

"Bah!" Constantia exclaimed with a dismissive wave. "Watching the flight of birds to tell the future? It's nonsense."

Licinius glared at her. "You're the one full of nonsense, woman! Augury is ancient wisdom." And with that, it was decided.

Two days later, on an overcast day with the threat of rain, Licinius, Zeno, and a gaggle of priests and military advisers met on a hillock outside Hadrianopolis. A large contingent of troops had been summoned to stand beneath the rocky outcrop at the summit—close enough to see the proceedings, though not allowed to ascend to the crags. The Chief Augur was at Licinius's side, along with some other soothsayers. Two of them carried a pole on their shoulders from which a bulky object dangled. It was draped by a purple cloth with gold tassels.

"Behold!" cried the Chief Augur, looking heavenward and raising both hands. "The sky is the domain of the spirits! All creatures that rise into its heights are kissed by the powers of the air, beloved by the rulers and principalities in the heavenly places. And so the birds of the earth can become vessels of celestial revelation."

After more flowery words like these, followed by several incantations to make the spirits propitious, the purple cloth was removed to reveal an iron birdcage. Inside was a white-tailed eagle with strong, clear eyes and a noble bearing.

"Arise, creature of the air!" said the Chief Augur as he removed the top of the cage.

Now there was nothing above the eagle's head as it gripped its perch in its curved talons. Spreading its immense wings, the eagle lifted off and quickly found an updraft. It spiraled upward, flying higher and higher until it could barely be seen. At such a great height, the soaring creature surely must have achieved union with the gods.

And then, just as the eagle reached its zenith, a tremendous thunderbolt exploded in the heavens. Its flash was blinding and its concussion seemed to shatter the sky's gray dome. For a long time afterward, the thunderous echo rumbled on. All the soothsayers—and even the gathered troops—cowered in fear of the heavenly portent.

"It is a mighty sign!" the Chief Augur declared when everyone had collected their wits. "An omen beyond all that could be expected! Jupiter's lightning has indwelled that lofty bird. As it returns to us, it brings godly power down to earth—a divine presence in our midst."

"Does Jupiter favor me?" Licinius asked, clutching the augur's robe.

"Like his own beloved son."

"Yes!" Licinius exclaimed, pumping his fist. "I knew it!"

Now the eagle came circling back to its masters. As it drew near, the troops on the hillock began to cheer. The noble bird made one last swoop through the sky, then settled onto its perch again.

The Chief Augur reached into a pouch at his waist and sprinkled something into a handheld censer. "Jupiter, Highest and Best, we welcome you to earth," he said as the resinous aroma of frankincense and myrrh wafted from the golden censer.

Licinius approached the eagle on its perch. With the help of its handlers and a thick leather glove, he induced it to stand upon his arm. Now he approached the edge of the outcrop and looked at the troops assembled beneath the crags. "Do not fear the day of battle, my men!" he cried with the mighty bird raised to the sky. "As you have seen today, we fight by the power of the true god! We shall prevail over all pretenders!"

"Hurrah!" the men cried, rattling their swords against their shields. From their exuberant faces and courageous demeanor, Licinius could see that he would surely be victorious on the field of war.

Strangely, however, the eagle made no response to the great commotion. Unlike before, when its bearing was regal and alert, it now stared into the distance and seemed unaware of its surroundings. When Licinius spoke sharply and the bird did not turn its head, he realized it had been deafened by the thunderclap. Its tongue lolled in its gaping yellow beak, and it shifted nervously on his arm. Licinius returned the dazed bird to its perch. Quickly, the soothsayers caged and covered the animal before the troops could notice that anything was wrong.

As the eagle was being taken away, a single feather drifted from the cage. Licinius stooped and picked it up. Its edges had been singed by the lightning, and the smell of it was acrid. Licinius beckoned for Zeno to approach.

"I am at your service," the scribe said with a dip of his chin.

"Do you have the edict prepared?"

"Of course, my lord." Zeno displayed a writing board to which a vellum document was attached. An inkwell was in the corner of the board. Zeno offered Licinius a reed pen. "After you sign it, the edict shall be copied and disseminated throughout your realm."

Licinius, however, spurned the reed pen and demanded that a nib be cut into the eagle's quill. When it was ready, he dipped it into the ink, wrote out his name, and nodded to his scribe when he was finished.

"Your signature is infused with the power of Jupiter," Zeno said.

"The Highest and Best," Licinius replied. "Now send out that edict and let the martyrdoms begin."

<hr />

JUNE 324

It felt good to Rex to be back on a ship after several weeks in hot and crowded Rome. He had been forced to wait longer than expected to catch a return ship to Alexandria since most of the grain fleet was now arriving in the capital instead of departing. Yet he had put those weeks to good use by meeting several times with Pope Sylvester about the Arian heresy, learning more about the responsibilities of a papal legate, and even receiving some in-depth theological instruction from Vincentius. All in all, it had been a productive trip. But Rex was ready to get back to Flavia.

His ship was a tubby Graecian corbita with a sternpost carved into the shape of a goose's head. She carried a red square sail on her Lebanese cedar mast, assisted by a substantial foresail on an inclined spar that projected over the bow. The captain was a grizzled and bowlegged fellow who called his ship the *Vixen*. For being such a round-bellied cargo vessel loaded with amphoras of wine, Rex had found the *Vixen* to be surprisingly agile in the sea.

The captain was up on the stern deck one morning when Rex approached him. "Looks like fair sailing today," Rex said after a glance at the sky.

"Aye! But we've a tricky stretch ahead. The Kythira Strait. Even Homer speaks of it blowin' Odysseus to ruin."

Rex knew the area well: a notoriously hazardous strait off of Graecia's Peloponnesian Peninsula. "It's safer if you sail close to Cape Malea," he told the captain with the confidence born of experience. "Most ships are tempted to swing wide, but that keeps you in danger for longer. You should take advantage of this weather and shoot past the cape before a storm blows up. It's risky, but usually worth it."

The captain gave Rex a strange look. "What does a German know about such things?"

"I was a seaman once," Rex said casually. It was all he was willing to admit. The captain didn't need to know that Rex had once commanded a pirate ship in the Kythira Strait. Changing the subject, he said, "Once we make it through, I think we can be moored in the lee of Creta before moonrise tonight."

Again the captain was impressed with Rex's nautical knowledge. "Aye, that's my aim, German. Pray that Poseidon favors us."

Instead of answering, Rex crossed himself to signal he was a Christian, then winked and smiled at the old captain and left him to his navigation.

Throughout the morning, God smiled upon the *Vixen* despite the captain's misplaced loyalties. The weather was sunny, the winds light and steady off the stern. The captain took Rex's advice about steering close to the cape, and by noon they were through the strait and out in the open Aegean again. They had just begun a southward turn toward Creta when a lookout cried from the stern, "Sail abaft! Coming on hard and overtaking!"

Instantly, the entire crew was on alert. Neither warships nor cargo vessels behaved that way. Only one kind of craft did. Very quickly, it became obvious to the corbita's eight-man crew that they were in a chase with a pirate ship.

The captain assumed his place on the stern deck and began to issue sailing commands that would increase speed. When the pirate ship kept closing the distance, he ordered even more drastic measures. "Fifty amphoras overboard!" he shouted to a man down in the hold. Then an hour later, "Fifty more!"

Yet even with the lightened load, the pirate ship still gained on the *Vixen*. By late afternoon, it was clear that the enemy ship would catch up to the corbita before it could reach the safety of Creta. The pirates were in a much sleeker vessel, one that had oars as well as a sail and a bronze ram upon its prow.

But the merchant captain wouldn't give up. He decided to make a final run for Creta and hoped to encounter a naval warship that would scare the attackers away. "Empty the hold!" he ordered. "Everything must go!"

The crew immediately started heaving the remaining amphoras overboard. Yet when one man began to throw out some extra rigging and tools, Rex stopped him. "Let me have those," he said, plucking a shipwright's sledgehammer and saw from the sailor's hands. Though the man's expression was quizzical, he acquiesced. But Rex knew exactly what he was doing. It was his only chance to save the ship from capture and the crew from probable murder.

The captain was visibly agitated when Rex approached him on the stern deck. As an experienced seaman, the captain knew all too well what would happen once the pirates closed the final distance. When Rex explained his plan, the captain looked at him like he was crazy. "It'll never work!" he said.

"It will," Rex countered. "I've had it done to me, to great effect." Again the captain looked surprised by Rex's mysterious seafaring past. Rex kept insisting. "It's the only way. It's either this or capture." Finally, the captain relented and authorized the plan.

With a hard pull on the steering oar, the *Vixen* now made a foolish maneuver: it turned broadside so that its starboard hull was directly exposed to ramming by the oncoming ship. It was like tying up a rabbit in front of a hungry wolf. The vicious predator, moved by a primal instinct, couldn't help but pounce.

As the pirates bore down, Rex put the crosscut saw to the starboard side of the tall cedar mast. Aided by a brawny seaman on the other handle, he carved out a notch at knee height above the deck. Other sailors manned the ropes, keeping the mast upright now that it was subject to dangerous new stresses.

The pirate ship kept coming. Its fierce crew roamed the prow, snarling threats and brandishing their swords. A few arrows came arcing across the turbulent sea, but not many, for there was no need to waste the shafts when the prey would be so easy to capture.

Rex and his helper now set the saw blade against the portside of the mast, directly behind the notch. "Saw as hard as you ever have!" Rex ordered, and the two men began slicing a line into the wood. When a crevice opened up, Rex shoved a wedge-shaped piece of iron into the gap and hammered it partway in. Now the mast groaned and creaked as the wind buffeted it. The sailors on the ropes could barely keep it upright as it swayed back and forth like a wheat stalk in a whirlwind.

"Brace yourselves!" the rudderman shouted. "The enemy's coming in fast! Impact in ten! Nine! Eight!"

Rex set his foot against the base of the mast and drew back his sledge-hammer.

"Seven! Six! Five!"

"Isis, protect us!" the captain shouted, clutching the gooseneck that was her symbol.

"Four! Three! Two!"

"Only one," Rex declared, and smashed home the iron wedge.

The clang of metal against metal rang out on the deck, followed immediately by an ear-splitting *crack!* as the mast broke from its stepping. It toppled along the line of the notch that had been cut from its other side. Just as the pirate ship was about to ram the *Vixen*, the cedar trunk came swooping down from the sky like the avenging arm of Gabriel. The falling mast demolished the enemy's prow, hurling chunks of wood and broken bodies into the churning waves. The enemy ship's forward motion, deflected by the colossal impact and the ruin of its hull, was diverted from its former course. Its momentum carried it harmlessly through the wake of its intended target.

A triumphant cheer arose from the crew of the *Vixen*. They all rushed to the stern to stare at the destroyed ship that only moments ago was the destroyer. Nobody aboard the enemy vessel was thinking about pirating anymore. Not only was its prow a wreck, but its own mast was also ensnared in a tangle of wood, sailcloth, and rigging. Shouts of confusion and groans of anguish arose from the deck in a great clamor. The pirates who had survived the impact were trying to remain aboard the dangerously listing ship. Others wailed as the agony of broken bones took hold. As for the men floating facedown in the water—they had no concern now except the judgment seat of Christ.

The *Vixen*, of course, was also immobilized without her mainmast. Yet her hull was intact. Despite some damage to the side rail, the ship was seaworthy. The crew quickly trimmed the foresail on the forward spar. Though it wasn't intended to provide primary impetus, the canvas caught enough wind to create some separation from the pirates. Soon the enemy was far behind, and the crew was visibly relieved.

"Well, boys, looks like this voyage is a bust," the bowlegged captain said when he had assembled the sailors on the deck. "We got a dismasted ship and no cargo to sell. But at least we got our lives!"

"And drinking water," the rudderman added, patting a keg beside him that hadn't been tossed. "Enough to get us into some harbor."

"Where to, then?" Rex asked.

The captain considered it for a moment. "Athenae is the nearest port with shipwrights. And I can get a new cargo there. Maybe it can cover our losses."

And I can find a new ship to Alexandria, Rex decided, but he kept the thought to himself.

The sun was low in the sky when the limping *Vixen* drew near to an uninhabited island. A tiny cove provided shelter for the night, and a stream that trickled into the sea allowed the keg to be refilled. A few wafers of seabiscuit were doled out to each man, along with a shared bottle of vinegar. After sour porridge for dinner, the sailors wrapped themselves in blankets and fell asleep on the *Vixen*'s deck while she swung at anchor in a gentle breeze.

But Rex couldn't sleep. Rising with his blanket around his shoulders, he went and stood on the stern deck and stared out at the open sea. The direction was north—away from Flavia but toward Athenae, where he must go to return to her. Long ago, Flavia gave a speech in that great city, pleading for her mother's release from enslavement to a rich silver merchant. The oration was successful, and the businessman freed Sophronia rather than bear the reproach of his friends. Rex remembered being incredibly proud of Flavia's preparation, skill, and courage that day.

"May God keep you, my beloved," he whispered to the wind. Then he added, "May he grant what we desire." Smiling at that hopeful possibility, Rex settled onto the deck, tightened the blanket around him, and fell into a deep sleep beneath the Aegean stars.

Constantine knew that the man and wife who were about to arrive in his presence would make him even angrier than he already was. Not angry at them—they were courageous heroes. They would make him angry at his vicious brother-in-law, Emperor Licinius.

"I think I shall have Licinius crucified once we capture him," he told Crispus, who waited beside him in the reception hall at the imperial palace of Thessalonica.

Crispus glanced over at Constantine. Both men were seated on thrones, the father in the higher one as an augustus, the son slightly lower as a caesar. "You abolished that barbaric practice not long ago," Crispus observed mildly. There was no rebuke in his voice, only an observation of fact.

"I was thinking of reviving it one last time because it is fitting."

Crispus seemed to ruminate on the matter for a while. Finally, he said, "Your laws are known to be wise and charitable toward mankind. You have forbidden slaves to be branded on the face with hot irons. You have made Sun Day a day of rest for all. You have allowed bishops to liberate slaves so that many have joyously gained their freedom. And you have forbidden crucifixion. So, I wonder, if you go back on this one law, will your people fear that you will go back on others? Will you look fickle and unsteady?"

"Good point, Crispus." The emperor stroked his smooth chin as he considered his son's wise advice. "I shall offer mercy to Licinius," he finally decided. "Imprisonment and exile."

"Such mercy will be celebrated by everyone, more so than the cruelty of a cross."

With the matter settled, Constantine lapsed into silence again. A short while later, the doors opened at the opposite end of the hall and the African professor Lucius Caecilius Firmianus Lactantius strode into the room with his two guests.

"Hail, Your Majesty," Lactantius said to Constantine when he arrived before the imperial thrones. The salutation was respectful, though without any groveling. "And hail to you, Caesar Crispus." Lactantius smiled broadly, then added, "I hope you have been keeping up with your scripture reading, young man!"

Constantine chuckled, for Lactantius had been the boy's tutor for many

94

years—not just in the classics like Virgil and Livy, but also in the sacred words of God. Constantine attributed much of Crispus's piety and spiritual maturity to Lactantius's influence. He was an excellent teacher of literature and a wise shepherd of souls.

"Of course, my master," Crispus replied, still respectful toward his teacher despite the vast difference in their power. "Just this morning, I was reading the story of Daniel."

"A fitting text," Lactantius declared, "for the circumstances that face us today are similar. A wicked Nebuchadnezzar is raging once again, and I have brought before you a faithful Daniel and Susanna."

With these words, Lactantius stepped aside and made way for the two visitors, a man and his wife just arrived from Amasea in Pontus. Clearly, they had come straight from hard travel. Both were dirty and wore ragged cloaks around their shoulders. Their hair was disheveled, their faces grubby, their cheeks gaunt. And their eyes had the furtive wariness of people who had recently experienced terror and trauma.

"You are safe here," Constantine assured the bedraggled visitors, "for you are among Christians." When this warm welcome got a grateful nod, Constantine asked the husband, "Sir, what do you do for a living?"

"I was a furniture maker in Pontus. I owned my own shop. My product was high quality, and my customers were of the upper class."

"Lactantius tells me you were a leader of the church in Amasea?"

"Yes, Majesty. As a literate man, I was appointed a reader of the scriptures in the liturgy of our Lord."

"Tell me your story," Constantine said.

It took the man a while to organize his thoughts. His wife, an attractive middle-aged woman with high spirit, prompted him. "Start with the arrest."

The husband nodded and drew a deep breath. "They came for me by night—Licinius's men. They were the local police under the governor's command, but everyone knew they were doing the augustus's bidding. I was jailed overnight. The next morning, the tortures began. This was not just the normal harshness that is always directed at criminals, but weird and unheard-of torments, a gory spectacle made public for all to see. The whole town was forced to watch." At this terrible memory, the man stopped speaking and the wife stepped a little closer to him. The two of them stood side by side, huddled deep in their cloaks like frightened rabbits in their burrow.

Constantine gave the couple some time to collect themselves, then said, "Go on, friend. What happened next?"

"It is not something I shall ever forget. It will haunt me forever. Families of the clergy were assembled on a riverbank. They were made to watch as their husband or father was dissected with knives and shears. The cutting began on the tips of his limbs and worked inward. The flesh was collected in baskets. Once the limbs were gone, the pieces, along with the still-living torso, were thrown into the river as fish food. And then it began on the next man of the church."

The shocking story, involving a cruelty so extreme it was obviously the work of Satan himself, made Constantine want to rise from his throne, board the nearest warship, and head straight to Hadrianopolis. Of course, he couldn't do that—not yet, anyway. But in a matter of weeks, the fleet would sail out. "I shall have vengeance soon," Constantine declared.

"Vengeance belongs to God," Crispus countered. "Seek justice instead."

Constantine turned his attention back to the husband. "You were a lector of the church, a man destined for punishment. Yet you stand here today. How did you escape these horrific torments?"

"I did not."

Now a dreadful silence descended on the throne room. From beneath his cloak, the man brought out his right hand with no fingers or thumb. Blackened, crusty scabs occupied the places where his five digits once met the palm.

"You are a confessor of the faith," Crispus said with awe in his voice. "I honor you, sir."

Constantine's eyes were fixed on the man's maimed hand. *God curse Licinius! I will surely have him crucified!* "How did it happen?" he asked through gritted teeth.

"I was tied to a pole with my arms outstretched. They began the process on me, knuckle by knuckle."

"He did not scream," the wife added, "but bore it with eyes upraised to heaven."

"The pain was terrible. Yet by God's grace, a thunderstorm arose, and they stopped their devilish work. Night came on. Then my beloved wife"—he glanced at her with deep affection—"came to the soldiers with strong wine. Of course they harassed her, but she resisted them and got them drunk. While they were in a stupor, she cut my bonds. We escaped Amasea with nothing but these ragged clothes and a bag of coins. We came straight here to tell you of this. Our brother in Christ arranged an audience with you."

Lactantius, who had been standing off to the side, now came and stood before the two thrones again. "There is more bad news. The word from the east is that Licinius plans to extend the persecution. From now on, it won't just be against the clergy but all Christians in his domains."

Constantine could stay in his seat no longer. Leaping up, he cried, "We must stop him immediately!"

"Indeed, we must," Crispus agreed. "It will be a just war, a Christian undertaking."

The strong words made Lactantius purse his lips and nod in a thoughtful way. "The matter is complex. The Christian church has been divided on this topic. Our Lord gave us the ethic of turning the other cheek, of loving our enemies. Yet we see many righteous wars in the scriptures. We can think of Joshua, who was our Savior's namesake. He was ordered to conquer Canaan. King David, whose hands were trained for war, is another example. Clearly, in ancient times God commanded battles and empowered warriors. But what is the appropriate use of warfare today?"

Taking his seat on the throne again, Constantine asked, "How do you answer that question, Lactantius?"

"I have come to believe that earthly judges are considered just when they punish wrongdoing, for this reflects God's character. It would be cowardly for judges to do nothing about men who maim and destroy. My principle is, 'He who punishes evildoers guards the safety of good men.' The apostle Paul says precisely this at the end of *Romans*. This, Your Highness, is my view."

Unexpectedly, Constantine found himself irritated by Lactantius's reply. "What am I supposed to do?" he demanded. "Capture all the soldiers of Licinius and bring them before judges? The courts would be clogged for decades, and no other business could be conducted. That's ridiculous!"

"I do not think," Crispus said soothingly, "that our brother Lactantius is suggesting such a thing. If I am not mistaken, he is saying that warfare can serve the same purpose as law courts. When Saint Paul mentions the government's power of the 'sword,' it is by no means clear if the weapon belongs to the executioner or the legionary."

"Perhaps both," Lactantius admitted. "It is not only the violent who injure people but also the passive men who spare the injurious from reprisals. Just rulers must be willing to use force to punish aggression."

At these words, the furniture maker from Amasea stepped forward and knelt before Constantine. He held out his maimed hand—a raw, misshapen stump that looked even worse up close. "I do not ask for revenge, nor for cruelty, nor for any actions outside the law," he said. "I ask only that justice be done for this crime. Let it be prevented from ever happening to someone else."

Constantine raised his eyes from his petitioner and sat up straight in his throne. "Listen well, all you gathered here! Today I declare war upon Licinius. His evil deeds threaten the peace and security of all mankind. But God has given me the armies to defeat him. And so I swear to move out by land and sea, to meet him in a just war, and to bring retribution upon him so the whole empire may flourish once again and not be ravaged by a tyrant."

"I thank you, Your Majesty," the kneeling man said. He tucked his wounded hand back inside his cape.

Constantine gazed upon him with respect. "Rise, faithful servant, and you may go. And thank you for this important report."

The man and his wife had started to exit the throne room when Crispus stopped them with a sharp command. After they turned around, Crispus said, "Go directly to my personal physician. Tell him I sent you. He will clean those wounds and put balm on them. Then when you are fully recovered, I offer you a job as a master instructor in the furniture guild at Nicomedia. You must pass on your lore to the rising generation of woodworkers. And as you teach them, speak of the even greater work that has been done in your soul by the carpenter of Nazareth to whom you have testified so bravely."

"Bless you, Caesar Crispus!" the man exclaimed with his mouth agape.

His wife, too, seemed overjoyed by the announcement. "It is gracious beyond all expectation!"

"It is but a small way to honor a confessor of the faith," Crispus replied.

Constantine glanced over at his son, who was extraordinarily wise for his young age of twenty-six. He was well-built and handsome, with the high cheekbones and reddish hair of his mother, Minervina. *I miss her*, Constantine thought. *I never should have set her aside.* Yet no sooner did this twinge of regret come to him than he was comforted by a future hope. *At least I can look forward to seeing what God will do in the life of my beloved son!*

3

It took a ridiculously long time for the *Vixen* to reach Athenae's harbor on just its foresail, but with careful rope work and close attention to the wind, the wounded and empty ship finally arrived. The harbor's surrounding town was known as Piraeus, a bustling port only five miles from Athenae itself. The *Vixen*'s captain was anxious to get repairs started and acquire a new cargo. Rex, however, was ready to be free of the ship and find another way to Aegyptus.

He walked down the gangplank with his rucksack on his shoulders and a renewed sense of optimism. Things were busy in Piraeus today, and a lively energy permeated the air. Everyone knew that an armada was being assembled by Caesar Crispus. The final few warships of the New Aegean Fleet were about to sail out. But Rex had no intention of hitching a ride aboard any of them. They were headed for the northern Aegean coast, the opposite direction from where Rex wanted to go. A freighter full of Greek exports to Aegyptus was his goal instead.

Down along the pier, three young men were seated on stools around a barrel that served as a table. They were playing knucklebones and exchanging bronze nummi after each throw. Among the trio, one man stood out because of his impressive muscles. His tanned arms protruded from his tunic, revealing bulges that usually meant one thing: he was a rower in the imperial navy. The oars created a kind of physique that was hard to attain any other way.

"Greetings, gents," Rex said with an affable air. "Any luck with the bones?"

"Today's my lucky day," the strong oarsman crowed. "My stack is growing with every round!"

Rex waited until the oarsman—whose name was Herakles, according to the curses his adversaries were hurling his way—had won a few more rounds. When the man sat back after yet another victory, Rex said, "Well played, my friend!" He paused, then asked, "I'm seeking passage to Alexandria. Can anyone recommend a good captain of a fast ship?"

Now Herakles turned and smirked at Rex. "I know such a man."

"And his name?"

Herakles gestured at his winnings. "I don't give out rewards for free, stranger. If you want something from me, you've got to play the game."

"I can pay," Rex said, reaching into his belt pouch for a nummus.

But Herakles waved it off. "I didn't say 'pay.' I said 'play.'"

Now Rex brought out a silver coin worth twice as much as Herakles's whole stack. "How about if we raise the stakes? One throw each. You win, the silver is yours. I win, and that pile of nummi is mine. Either way, we part as friends who played the game, and you tell me where to find the ship that's heading to Aegyptus the soonest."

"It's too good to pass up!" another one of the players said. "His silver against your bronze. Take the wager!"

"Deal," Herakles said, then scooped up the bones.

Herakles shook the sheep bones in his fist for an extra long time. His brow was deeply furrowed, as if he were trying to impart luck directly from his brain into his throw. Finally, he made the cast. When the bones stopped tumbling, Herakles raised his fist and cried, "Thirty-six! Beat that, stranger!"

Rex just smiled congenially and remained silent. His motive was not to win but to get information. He collected the knucklebones, shook them for a moment, then threw them on the barrelhead. They rolled to the rare score of forty.

"You lose!" the other two players exclaimed to Herakles, gleeful that their former opponent had just gone down.

Herakles's face scrunched into a scowl. He was a swarthy, bristle-browed man with the typical Greek hot temper. Standing up from his stool, he demanded, "Play again!"

"First, tell me the name of the ship," Rex countered, "like you agreed."

"I ain't tellin' you nothin' until you play me again!"

But Rex wasn't willing to keep putting down more silver. "Just name the captain, friend, and I'll be off."

Herakles grew even more belligerent. "Again!" he insisted, stamping his foot on the dock.

"Keep the bronzes," Rex said with a wave of his hand, and began to walk away.

"That's not how Herakles plays the game!" he roared.

"Do you actually know any ships heading for Aegyptus?" Rex shot back. "Or am I just wasting my time?"

"By the gods, I do! My cousin owns a ship. He's heading there tomorrow with a load of Greek pottery!"

Intrigued, Rex moved back toward Herakles. "We played the game, like you said. You have to tell me where to find him."

"I can do better than that, Goth. I can take you to him and introduce you. One word from me and you'll depart on his freighter tomorrow with a hammock and vittles included. But without me, you can beg all you want and he won't take you. And there won't be another ship departing for Alexandria for more than a week, until Crispus gets these warships out of here."

"I'm Alemannic, not Gothic. Now take me to your cousin, unless you have no honor."

"Let me win my money back," Herakles countered, "unless you have no honor."

Though Rex didn't think honor demanded that he keep playing the game until the loser finally won, he decided to go along. "Alright. Another throw?"

"I ain't got any more money to bet. You took it all."

"Then how?"

Herakles sized Rex up and down. "You look like you might've turned an oar back in the day."

"Aye," Rex said. "Former navy man. What do you have in mind?"

"We row two skiffs across the harbor. First man to touch the opposite pier is the winner. If it's me, I get my bronzes back plus your silver. You win, you keep it all and I have to recommend you to my cousin like you're my own kin."

Rex nodded to his adversary. "You're on. Show me the boats."

Herakles led the way to two rowboats that served as tenders to the larger ships anchored away from the pier. They were identical, so the match would be decided by skill and stamina, not a superior watercraft. Herakles untied his boat and Rex did the same.

When both competitors were situated in the thwarts, one of Herakles's friends ran ahead to the opposite side of the harbor while the other man stayed behind to start the race. He raised his hand. "Ready?" he cried. "Then . . . begin!" As soon as his hand swept down, Rex gave the oars a heave and started rowing with all his strength.

Although it took a few revolutions of the sculls for the boat to gain momentum, the sturdy little craft was soon slicing across the harbor like a sleek delfinus. Rex knew from experience not to try and achieve speed through jerky or frantic motions. Instead, he concentrated on smooth, steady strokes with good form, seeking maximum catch on each drive and feathering the blades on each recovery. The boat responded by shooting swiftly toward its destination.

Halfway across the harbor, the burn set in. Rex's thighs, shoulders, and stomach muscles went from a low flame to a steady blaze to a white-hot inferno that demanded immediate relief. But there was no way he was going to slow down. Herakles was directly alongside him, his face contorted by his own intense effort. Rex could see from his motions that he was a skilled rower. The man was strong and fit, probably five years younger than Rex's thirty. *He's got nothing on me*, Rex reminded himself, and kept rowing.

As the race reached its finale, Rex glanced over his shoulder to check his line. He was surprised to see that a crowd had gathered at his destination. Raucous cheers drifted across the water as he drew near. The unexpected race through the middle of the harbor had captured the attention of everyone along the docks.

Herakles's boat pulled a little ahead of Rex's. "I got you, Goth!"

"Alemann!" Rex shouted back as he summoned his last bit of strength.

The cheering was intense as the two racers approached the pier like twin arrows shot from the same bow. Rex heard some people urging on Herakles, while others were shouting for "the German." But he took no comfort in having fans; his body was in too much pain for that. His lungs heaved. His thighs burned. His hands were raw and bloodied. Nausea roiled his gut, and sweat streamed down his face. *Only three more strokes! Then turn and slap the post!*

"Look out!" someone cried.

Crunch!

Rex's boat slammed into a half-submerged log that no one had bothered to warn him about until it was too late. The rowboat immediately capsized, hurling Rex overboard. He surfaced to see that Herakles had also hit the obstruction. Both men were sputtering in the drink as they tried to gather their wits.

Yet no sooner did they make eye contact than each man realized the race wasn't over. Instantly, they lunged into action, swimming hard for the same post. Rex decided to go underwater. He swept his exhausted arms through the murky depths and propelled himself with powerful scissor kicks. The thrashing nearby told him Herakles was doing the same.

Just as Rex's breath was about to run out, he surfaced again. The post was right in front of him. He dove toward it with his arm extended, his hand outstretched.

"I win!" the two men cried as they slapped the post at the same moment.

A great hurrah exploded from the crowd above. Everyone on the pier seemed delighted by the race's fitting conclusion. Rex glanced over at Herakles, whose shaggy hair was plastered to his cheeks. Water dribbled down his nose. Both men were breathing hard.

"Good rowing," Rex said.

"You too, Alemann. Well done."

From up above, an authoritative voice addressed the two competitors. "Excellent work, gentlemen! A fine example of seamanship and competitive spirit! Now climb up that ladder and come here. I wish to speak with you both—but especially you, Rex."

Rex? Who knows me by name in Piraeus?

He glanced up to see who had addressed him. A man was peering over the edge of the dock, but Rex couldn't discern his identity because the sun was in his eyes. He raised his hand to shade his face so the person would come into view. Only then did Rex recognize the speaker. It was Flavius Julius Crispus—son of Constantine, Caesar of the West, and commander of the New Aegean Fleet.

"I'm coming, Your Majesty," Rex said, then grasped the ladder and began to haul himself up with the vague suspicion that his life was about to take an unexpected turn.

<hr />

Although humans had been living at Athenae for almost two thousand years, and the Greeks had made the city famous for its philosophy, it was the Roman Empire that had given the city its current agora. The town square was adorned with buildings that had been celebrated around the world until an invasion by the warlike Heruli destroyed it sixty years ago. Judging by the damage those fellow Germani had inflicted, they were experts at wrecking stuff. *Stupid barbarians*, Rex thought. *Always destroying instead of building. At least they'll never take Rome.* He smiled at the absurdity of that idea, then glanced at the sun's low angle as he continued to wait for his afternoon appointment to show up.

After the race at the harbor, Caesar Crispus had commended the two competitors and given them each a gold solidus. But to Rex he had also said, "I remember you as my father's bodyguard. Meet me in the Athenian agora at the eleventh hour, and we shall tour the ancient city together." Although Rex had had little interest in touring Athenae, he had told himself, *Who am I to disobey a member of the Imperial College?* So here he was.

The afternoon heat had finally begun to let up a little when Caesar Crispus arrived with his entourage of politicians, military officials, and bodyguards. He greeted Rex cordially, though not with personal friendship, which wouldn't have been appropriate in light of their different stations in life.

"Shall we go up now?" Crispus asked after a few pleasantries were exchanged. Rex nodded, though he was still confused as to why the emperor wanted him to join the tour of the Acropolis. Yet it wasn't his place to question such things, so he dutifully agreed, and the whole party began to trudge up the slope.

They reached the saddle of Mars Hill and turned left toward the Acropolis. After ascending a ramp, they climbed through an impressive gateway. As they arrived at the top, Crispus paused to admire the world-renowned temple of Athena. She was a celibate goddess, so her shrine was known as the Parthenon, from the Greek word for a virgin. Crispus could only shake his head in awe as he stared at the temple's perfect dimensions. "It is truly a marvel of architectural—"

A crossbowman burst from behind a clump of shrubs. His weapon was leveled at the emperor. "Assassin!" someone screamed.

Rex didn't stop to think. His training as an imperial guardsman took over, making his body act before his mind could issue a conscious command. He enveloped Crispus and took him to the ground. In the same motion, he turned his back to the assassin. Rex's rucksack was stuffed with his belongings. It might stop or at least slow down the bolt.

Whap!

The impact against Rex's pack felt like someone had struck it with a club. Holding perfectly still, he shielded the emperor from further attack while the bodyguards subdued the assassin. And he waited for the pain to start.

Silence.

No one moved.

And there's no pain . . .

"Well done, Rex," Crispus said. "You may stand up and release me."

Now completely confused, Rex did as he was told. Glancing around, he found all the military officials and bodyguards smiling. Even the man with the crossbow had a big grin on his face. Rex's eyes fell to the bolt on the ground. Its end was tipped with padded leather like the bolts used in mock combat drills. *The attack was a ruse!*

"What's going on here, Your Majesty?"

"A test," Crispus replied, "and you passed it beyond all expectation. I had to know whether you still possessed your instincts and skills—and where your true loyalties lie."

"But . . . why?"

"So I can commission you back into the army. I need you, Rex. Your emperor summons you to war."

Stunned, Rex could offer no reply. The announcement was so unexpected that his mind had to grapple with it for several moments before the meaning of Crispus's words could register. At last, Rex realized he needed to speak. "M-my ship leaves tomorrow," he managed to say. "Herakles arranged it."

Crispus said nothing. His face was unreadable.

"How do you even remember me?" Rex finally asked. The question had been bothering him all afternoon. Though he had served as Constantine's bodyguard long ago, and in those days the young prince was often nearby, Rex had never actually exchanged words with Crispus before today.

But the answer was simple. Crispus shrugged and said, "How could I not remember you? As a boy, I secretly admired you—a handsome Germanic warrior with huge muscles. I have followed your military career over the years. And of course, there was the incident at Verona. It was due to my urging that my father finally forgave you. Let it be known that any questions about your courage are banished forever. We have just seen that you were willing to take a crossbow dart for your lord."

Now it was Rex's turn to remain silent. The "incident at Verona" was a source of shame for him—a time when he left Constantine's side in the heat of battle so he could pursue an enemy who carried a grudge against Flavia. Chasing and killing that man was a legitimate action in war. Yet Constantine had taken offense at Rex leaving the field, so he condemned him to be a menial rower in the imperial navy. Apparently Crispus had been instrumental in turning things around.

"Thank you," Rex said as he struggled to make sense of all that was coming at him.

"Here is the situation," Crispus explained. "The New Aegean Fleet is fully assembled. Our warships number two hundred, supported by a flotilla of transports. We depart in two days for Thessalonica, and from there I shall lead the navy against Licinius. Meanwhile the infantry will march overland to Hadrianopolis under my father's command. That is where you come in. We need field scouts—explorers and speculators. But the captain of our scout force has contracted a deadly cancer. Though the junior officers are skilled operatives, none of them is a natural leader. Warfare, I have learned, requires more than tactics and techniques. Victory demands a captain who can win the hearts of his troops by his courage and quick wits. You, Rex, are such a man."

"But, Your Majesty . . . I am in service of the church now."

"Who is your bishop?"

"Alexander of Alexandria. And in time of necessity, I represent Sylvester of Rome as well."

"Do those men wish to see Christ's name exalted in our empire?"

"Of course, sir."

"And do they wish to see the pagan temples fall into disuse because the gods are shown to be false?"

"That is indeed their goal."

"Then fight with me, Rex! Fight with me and my father, Constantine. We want the same thing. Only Licinius stands in our way, demanding that the gods be worshiped and staining the earth with the blood of those who refuse. I have seen the carnage with my own eyes."

Rex was silent for a long time. The officials of the imperial entourage stared at him while the young emperor waited expectantly. Though Rex wanted to say yes to the summons, there was so much to consider. *Lord, what is my duty here? How should I respond? Show me!*

"I know what that is," Crispus said.

Uncertain about what Crispus meant, Rex did not reply.

Now the emperor indicated that one of his bodyguards should hand him a sword. The man immediately obeyed. Slowly, Crispus withdrew the sword from its sheath. Metal slid against metal, a sound every soldier knew well. The exposed blade gleamed in the bright Greek sun. It wasn't ornamental. This weapon was made for death.

"I know what that is," Crispus repeated, and began to advance toward Rex.

Rex straightened his shoulders and lifted his chin. He met Crispus's eyes as the emperor approached—not in a rebellious way, nor fearfully, but with the confident dignity that a soldier should possess.

As Crispus walked forward, he extended his arm and brought his sword close to Rex's throat. Its tip rested lightly on his collarbone. No one dared to move, for no one knew what was coming next.

"I know what that is," Crispus said for the third time. And then, with a flick of his blade, he withdrew a necklace from beneath Rex's tunic and cut the leather thong as soon as it was free. The gilded pendant started to fall, but Rex instinctively caught it before it could reach the ground.

Slowly, he opened his fist. The pendant lying in his palm was engraved with a cross. It was the Christian amulet given to him by Constantine long ago, at the outset of Rex's first mission. Everyone exhaled at the sight of the mighty emblem.

"In this sign . . ." Crispus said, then turned his weapon around and offered the hilt to Rex.

". . . you shall conquer," Rex replied as he received the sword from the Caesar of the West.

———

JULY 324

Flavia was in a good mood, delighted that her mother, Sophronia, had joined her for a shopping excursion on a pleasant evening with cool breezes coming off the sea. It was a get-together they tried to observe at least once a week. Their custom had started as soon as Sophronia moved from Sicilia to Alexandria about a year after Rex and Flavia arrived in the city. Sophronia was a nun, so she didn't often leave her convent attached to the Church of Theonas. But a brisk walk down Canopus Avenue browsing the shops and buying the week's necessities was a good way for mother and daughter to spend some time together and catch up on each other's lives.

"Look at this," Flavia said as the two women paused outside an herbalist's shop. "It's lavender essence. And the bottle is so pretty. Let's get it."

Sophronia chuckled at the idea. "I'm forty-eight and a nun, Flavia. What do I need with perfume?"

"It's not just perfume. It's good for infections, the health of the skin, and calming the spirit. Besides—a woman is never too old to feel lovely."

"I have no one to feel lovely for," Sophronia said as she stared absently into the distance.

Flavia glanced at her mother. By anyone's estimation, Sabina Sophronia was a beautiful woman. Her hair and eyes were dark—more so than Flavia's chestnut hair and hazel eyes. Yet despite this difference, everyone said the two favored each other, and people of both sexes tended to compliment their beauty. Though Flavia was thirty and Sophronia was forty-eight, each woman was attractive for her age. Flavia didn't want her mother to think

109

she couldn't be considered pretty. "I'll buy it for you," she insisted. "You can use it as you wish."

For a moment longer, Sophronia's mind remained in some far-off place, then she returned her attention to the present. "I'll use it for health reasons," she said, and Flavia made the purchase.

"Now all we need is lamp oil, and we're done," Sophronia said. "I believe Osiris's shop had a good price last week. We might be able to work him down again."

"I, uh . . . I prefer that little shop on the corner with Aspendia Street. Better oil there."

"It's exactly the same stuff! That place is twice as far and in the wrong direction. Why go there when Osiris's store is a few steps away? Come on, let's see what kind of deals he's offering."

Sophronia moved in that direction, so Flavia reluctantly followed. She didn't want to tell her mother the real reason she wished to avoid the shop: because getting there required passing in front of the Isis temple. It was a wicked place, a place of demons, a place where she had grievously sinned. Sophronia, of course, didn't know about that. Flavia had only confided in Athanasius. And the bishop knew it too. Beyond that, no one else did.

Since it was dusk now, the torches outside the temple had been lit by the time Flavia reached the building, giving its façade a weird and eerie glow. With her eyes cast down, she passed on the other side of the street. No sooner was the temple behind her than she caught a refreshing breeze and her discomfort dissipated.

"Osiris is going to want to bargain hard," Sophronia said, "but if we—"

"Aahh!" Flavia screamed as a wrenching pain stabbed her in the belly. She clutched the excruciating place with one hand and grabbed her mother's forearm with the other.

"Flavia! What is it?"

"It hurts!" She grimaced as the pain dug in hard, crescendoed, then waned and finally let go. Beads of sweat were on Flavia's brow.

"Step into the latrine, quick!"

Flavia stumbled into the dark and smelly place behind her mother. Fortunately, no men were using it now. Though the interiors of such places were always dim, at night they were especially gloomy. A single oil lamp in a wall niche provided the only illumination. Sophronia picked it up and helped her daughter lift her hem.

"Blood," she said in an ominous tone. "Let's get you home right away."

The walk back to the apartment near the Serapeum was interrupted by two more agonizing spasms, both spaced closer to each other than they were to the first. As soon as the women arrived, Flavia climbed the stairs to her second-floor residence and tumbled into her bed as another cramp took hold. Unlike the others, this one felt . . . substantial. Flavia knew exactly what was happening. "Boil water," she told her mother as tears came to her eyes. "There are linen rags in the cupboard."

Sophronia stayed with Flavia for the next sad and painful hour. At the end of it, everything had changed. Flavia would not—at least for now—be a mother.

"I am sorry, my love," Sophronia said quietly as she stroked her daughter's hand. Flavia's only response was to utter a helpless whimper.

The moon rose in the sky, casting a white glow through the bedroom window. Flavia felt herself awaken from a kind of stupor as she noticed it. "It's late," she said to her mother. "You need to get back to the convent. You cannot stay out unexpectedly."

Sophronia nodded. "I shall come again at first light."

"Knock on Philip's door downstairs and ask him to escort you. He is a stretcher carrier for the church. No one will bother you while you're with him—not with a frame like his."

"I will," Sophronia said. "Philip is a dove in an ox's body. But out on the streets, no one will know that."

After kissing Flavia's forehead, Sophronia exited the apartment and closed the door behind her. Immediately, the place fell into a deathly stillness. For a while, Flavia simply lay on her bed, exhausted by her ordeal. At last, she decided to read from the scriptures. Since the apartment had grown dark, she carried the lamp into the study where the books were kept in a cabinet.

Flavia had just retrieved the book of Paul's epistles when she noticed that the landlord had delivered a letter and laid it on the desk. After breaking its seal, she found it was from Rex. Excited, Flavia began to scan it by the light of the oil lamp in her other hand. At first, Rex's affectionate words thrilled her. But when she came to the part about "a commission from Caesar Crispus" and "a campaign through the fall" and "honorable duty," her heart sank. Although she supported Rex's main reason for rejoining the army—to save her fellow believers from future persecution—Flavia couldn't help but feel the personal sting. She had been hoping to see her husband again soon. Now he would be delayed for several months, in danger the whole time and unable to communicate. It felt like another blow from on high.

Lord, is your hand against me?

Such a woeful thought was an indulgence in self-pity. She knew God was loving and kind. He was never against his children. Yet after the terrible experience of the miscarriage, followed by the letter delaying Rex's return, Flavia felt overwhelmed with sadness. God might not be against her . . . but could he be rebuking her for her sin at the Isis temple? Was this a divine chastisement because she hadn't sufficiently repented?

Flavia laid the letter on the desk and returned to her bedroom with the Pauline scriptures. Cool ocean breezes blew in through the apartment's windows. After stirring the charcoal brazier, she set the lamp on her bedside table and settled onto her bed to read.

The Holy Spirit led Flavia to a passage in Paul's *First Epistle to the Corinthians*. Flavia was meditating upon the apostle's guidance about marriage when a strong gust of wind extinguished her lamp.

Stiffly, she climbed out of bed and took the lamp to the brazier. Soon a cheerful flame once again danced in the lamp's mouth. Its warm glow illuminated the room and soothed Flavia's soul on this hard and gloomy night.

But as she was returning the lamp to its stand, an aftershock from the miscarriage seized her abdomen. As her hand instinctively went to her belly, she fumbled with the lamp and dropped it. The flame went out and the oil spilled across the floor, plunging the room into darkness again.

Flavia endured the pain until the cramp finally passed, then turned her attention to the lamp. "Noooo," she said as she knelt and found it broken. She was about to go get another lamp when she remembered that the apartment was out of oil. Because of the distressing circumstances of the night, she hadn't bought a new supply.

Mournfully, she got back in bed and drew the coverlet up to her neck. The room seemed oppressively dark. *I'm like one of the Five Foolish Virgins who had no oil*, Flavia thought. *What did Jesus say to those women who did not prepare? "Truly I say to you, I do not know you."*

"Lord, do you know me anymore?" Flavia cried to the ceiling. But there was no reply.

For a long time, her mind drifted. Outside, clouds rolled over the moon, darkening the house and Flavia's spirits even more. Her thoughts went to the passage she had been reading from *First Corinthians*. According to the apostle, abstinence from sexual relations was useful when spouses needed to devote themselves to prayer. Flavia resolved to implement the ascetic practice for several months after Rex's return. *Maybe then God will return his favor to me!*

Another breeze blew into the room, fanning the coals in the brazier. Briefly, a red glow illumined the walls. Then it faded and returned the room to darkness. "Was that you, Lord?" Flavia whispered. She hoped it was. Yet as she closed her eyes for sleep, the disquiet in her soul suggested it might have been something else.

<hr />

Two weeks of marching had brought Constantine's field army within sight of Hadrianopolis's high, white walls. The route from Thessalonica had taken the troops along the Egnatian Way to the Hebrus River near Aenus, where they turned upstream and followed a branch of the main highway to their destination. Rex had been surprised, though not alarmed, to arrive on the last day of June and find Licinius's army deployed on the eastern side of the river for about twenty-five miles above and below Hadrianopolis. Constantine's army remained on the western riverbank until a plan of attack could be formed. *And that's where the scouts come in*, Rex had reminded himself. *Time to get to work.*

The squad of elite speculators numbered twelve men. Upon meeting these special forces operatives, Rex had immediately understood Caesar Crispus's concern. While these speculators were skilled in their craft, they were all young, ranging from their late teens to early twenties. And because the empire had been at rest since the peace treaty at Serdica seven years ago, none of these warriors had seen army-on-army combat. Though they had skirmished with barbarians like Rome had been doing for centuries, they had never actually scouted an enemy supply line, spied on a city like Hadrianopolis, or devised an attack against a fortified position. The barbarians didn't require such tactics—but the imperial army did. Caesar Crispus had realized that to take on Licinius, leadership experience in actual army reconnaissance was going to be required. And so he had commissioned Rex back into the army.

"Here's what I want," he told his assembled men. "Half of you go upstream and half go down. Bring me word of two things: the narrowest place to cross and the shallowest." He threw two coils of rope on the ground in front of the troops. "Measure both crossings by sending your best swimmers across at night. Hold one end of the rope on this side and have the man cut it at the far bank. By tomorrow, I want these ropes to be exactly as long as the distances between the riverbanks at both crossings."

The next day, the speculators gave Rex the two ropes. They had found the narrowest crossing to be a swift, deep, and dangerous place at the base of a wooded hill. The shallowest crossing, however, was a much wider place in the river—and as an obvious place for an attack, it was more robustly defended by the Licinians on the far side.

Now Rex went to the headquarters tent and sought permission to speak with the emperor. Constantine called Rex inside along with his old general, Arcadius, whom Rex knew from previous battles. In contrast to the tall and slim Constantine, General Arcadius was short but powerfully built. It was he who spoke. "What's your plan, soldier?"

Using a belt and some other objects on the emperor's desk to represent the Hebrus River and the two crossings, Rex outlined his idea. Arcadius and Constantine listened closely. When Rex was finished, Arcadius said, "The Batavi, eh? You think they'll do the trick?"

Rex nodded. "I'm Germanic too, sir. I know how deadly we can be in war. And those men have some special skills beyond just valor and ferocity."

"Let's do it," Constantine said. "Arcadius, make the arrangements. And may God be with us."

A construction project was begun at the wide, shallow crossing. After trees were felled, the army carpenters hewed them into logs and started lashing them together. "It has to work like this," Rex said to the head carpenter. He put his right fist to his left shoulder, then swung his arm straight out, keeping it parallel to the ground. "Like a hinge, swinging downstream."

"I get it," said the carpenter, who passed on the orders to his men.

Soon a floating bridge had been built, intact and ready to use but held back from the riverbank because it would be in range of the enemy archers once it was deployed. Using the speculators' length of rope as a guide, the bridge had been made exactly the width of the river crossing. Sharp stakes were fastened to what would become its far end. The men nicknamed their creation "the Wolf" because the stakes hung down like pointy fangs, certain to catch into the mud flat on the opposite shore.

At sunrise the next morning, while the enemy was still sleepy, a squad of husky men picked up the Wolf and hustled it toward the riverbank. A hail of arrows began to arc across the river, but Constantine's bowmen returned the shots and forced the enemy archers to take cover. A few of the men carrying the bridge fell beneath the onslaught, but others stood ready to swoop in and take their place.

As quickly as possible, the carriers laid the bridge in the water along the length of the shoreline. One end of the bridge was lashed into place with ropes that had a little play in them. These ropes were fastened to boulders on the riverbank. But the other end of the bridge—the end with the "fangs"— was tethered by only a single line that could easily be released when the right time came. With a push from a pole, the current would swing the bridge out and the fangs would catch in the mud on the far side. The connection would be solid, allowing the troops to cross swiftly and engage the enemy. Yet today was not that day.

Night fell, and campfires twinkled to life one by one among the trees on both sides of the river. All the men were restless, knowing an attack was imminent. Rex gathered his twelve speculators at the horse corral. "Mount up," he told them. "We ride tonight to our staging area. The attack begins at dawn."

The twelve riders followed Rex down a deer path that snaked north through the forest. Soon the ground began to rise. As they neared the top of a knoll, they heard a gruff voice hail them. "Password?"

"Beer and sausage," Rex said. For a moment, there was only silence. Then there was a chuckle, followed by words spoken in guttural German. "You may pass, brothers," said the sentry, and the twelve speculators rode into the fireless camp of the Batavi.

The Germanic mercenaries were fully armed and armored. Their ponies were enclosed in a dense copse of thorny bushes that would keep the creatures nearby yet block any sounds they might make. Over eighty Batavian cavalrymen were encamped here with their captains, all of them expert horsemen and devastating warriors. And just down the back of the hill, away from the river, was a camp of five thousand archers whose quivers bristled like porcupines. Not one of the men wore armor. Everything was ready for Rex's plan.

Hours passed as the troops chatted in whispers or dozed wherever they could. Though a few men chewed on pieces of hardtack or jerky, nobody had hot food, for campfires were strictly forbidden.

In the darkest and quietest hour that always precedes the dawn, Rex gave the signal for the troops to mount up. The twelve speculators were all trained in a skill that the Batavi were famous for inventing: riding a horse into a river, slipping out of the saddle as soon as the hoofs left the bottom, and jumping back into the saddle as soon as the mount found purchase on the other side.

Only the strongest horses could swim with an armored man clinging to them like dead weight. Yet the right horses could do it if the crossing wasn't too wide. And Rex's speculators had located the ford where the river was at its narrowest. Their rope had proven it was twenty-five paces wide—the upper limit for such a turbulent crossing, yet doable. A whole army couldn't ford here, but elite forces could—and these were the best of the best. Licinius's men had no idea what was coming.

Careful to make no sound, Rex's riders picked their way downhill through the trees until they were lined up just inside the foliage at the river's edge. For what seemed like a long time, they waited in total silence. Suddenly, far downstream, a trumpet sounded. Constantine's men were pushing the Wolf's fanged end into the current. The contraption would swing out on its flexible ropes until the spikes lodged firmly into the other side. Rex waited a moment longer until he heard what sounded like battle cries. Then, without saying a word, he prompted his horse out of the shrubbery and into the Hebrus's swift flow.

The hundred riders surged into the water like a fierce Aegyptian crocodile entering its natural element. The speculators and the Batavi immediately dismounted, always on the upstream side of the horse lest they lose their grip and be swept away. Rex's pony was a sturdy dapple gray from the Sarmatian plains. It clearly knew its work, churning ahead with its powerful legs fighting the river's flow. Halfway across, only the heads of the horses and their riders were above the surface. The water was icy cold, and the current was pushing the animal in a diagonal line as it crossed. Yet Rex had planned for that, identifying a fallen oak downstream as the rendezvous point for his men.

Rex could feel the change in movement as the dapple gray's hoofs made contact with the riverbed again. He slid into the saddle and rose up from the river as his mount charged into enemy territory. Now it was time for a battle cry. "For Constantine!" he shouted with his spear raised to the dawn. "For Constantine!" all the men echoed, and the Battle of Hadrianopolis began.

The cavalrymen broke out of the trees that lined the river and immediately encountered resistance on an open field. Yet the Licinians had been taken by surprise and were badly out of position. Some of them didn't even have their helmets or shields, for they had been startled from sleep and leapt into the saddle without adequate preparation. The muddled troops were no match for either the expert warcraft of the speculators or the skillful horsemanship of the Batavi. A horn sounded a retreat, and the enemy fell back. Rex urged his men to follow the fleeing riders and press them toward the Wolf.

But partway toward that wide, flat crossing, the retreating Licinians ran into a contingent of their own comrades who had determined that the attack at the bridge was a ruse. Since no one from Constantine's side had actually crossed after the trumpets blew, the guards had guessed that the real attack was happening upstream. Leaving their post, they had rushed to defend against the assault.

Rex signaled for his horsemen to stop. The Licinians whom he had just sent running were mingled with the defenders arriving from the bridge, creating a chaotic mess on the field ahead. Rex told his horn blower to call for a barrage of arrows. The man trumpeted out the notes, and the shafts immediately descended from the five thousand Constantinian bowmen who had swarmed behind the Batavian cavalry, swimming unarmored as they crossed to the empty riverbank. Now the defenseless Licinian troops were mown down like wheat stalks under a scythe that cut them from above.

"All pull back!" shouted some brave soul who had assumed leadership of the disorganized enemy. As the men retreated, Rex pressed ahead and took the relinquished ground. Corpses were strewn across the battlefield with feathered shafts protruding from them. The speculators and the Batavian cavalry galloped over the slippery carnage and kept pushing the enemy toward the Wolf.

But upon their arrival there, the Licinians found a deadly foe awaiting them. After the defenders abandoned the Wolf to engage Rex's attack, General Arcadius launched a force of heavy infantry onto the makeshift bridge. They had surged across the solid timbers and were now on the eastern shore, mad as hornets and ready to fight. Caught between Rex's riders and the newly arrived footmen, the Licinians were continuously rained upon by the archers' perfectly placed shots. They were in a killing zone. No escape was possible. The men fell by the thousands, and the rout was on.

Now the work of the scouts was done. The legionaries from the bridge had capable commanders who didn't need Rex to help them finish their job. After disengaging his force of elite warriors from the fray, Rex gathered the young men in a sheltered place. He couldn't help but breathe a sigh of relief as he realized that his risky plan had worked to perfection.

"Well done, sir," said a wiry, teenaged speculator with a cocky grin. "Nice riding for an old-timer."

Rex scoffed at the remark. "I eat kids like you for breakfast," he said, then used the flat of his spearhead to bang the man on the helmet.

"What now?" asked another young speculator.

"We say a prayer," Rex replied, "because God just gave Constantine the victory at the Battle of Hadrianopolis."

—❧—

For the rest of the day, the Constantinian troops swarmed across the river and obliterated Licinius's army. Around sunset, Rex learned that the enemy's field camp had been captured. Only when night fell did the slaughter finally stop.

When the victory trumpet sounded, the whole army let out a great cheer. Rex joined the chorus and raised his sword to the sky. But the looting that usually followed a victory did not occur, as Constantine had put his men under strict orders not to enter Hadrianopolis lest they be unable to resist the temptation to plunder it. All the gates were to remain locked with the citizenry inside and unharmed. "One does not blame the horse that is bitten by a horsefly," the emperor said, "nor the swimmer who picks up a leech. This city did not ask to be infested by parasites, so it shall not bear the punishment of harboring Licinius."

That night, after a dinner of potato soup and boiled leeks, Rex curled up by a campfire and fell into the sleep of the exhausted. At dawn the next morning, he was summoned to the imperial tent, which had been moved to the eastern side of the Hebrus, not far from the city walls. Apparently even Constantine was refraining from going inside the city—perhaps to show solidarity with his men, or perhaps because he didn't want to risk changing his mind about his clemency.

The tent had been set up in a flat, grassy area beneath a canopy of slender beech trees. All the dukes, tribunes, and other officers who had led the various legions had been summoned for the morning report. They encircled the front of the tent and waited for the emperor to emerge. Since Rex was only a junior officer commanding the field scouts, he took up a place behind the higher-ranked men.

Soon Constantine exited the tent with General Arcadius at his side. Constantine walked stiffly, for he had been wounded in the thigh in yesterday's hostilities. A small lockbox was in the emperor's hand, which he opened and displayed. Bright gold gleamed inside, making all the men marvel. "This is just a tiny bit of the treasure we have captured," Constantine announced. "In all, it is a magnificent sum, and I proclaim a donative of two thousand denarii per man. As for the Batavi who led the first charge"—Constantine searched the crowd until he caught Rex's eye—"I proclaim four thousand! How did those boys learn to swim horses like that?"

"Because the barbarians can't build bridges," Arcadius said gruffly, though not incorrectly. "How else can they cross rivers?"

Rex ignored the remark. "The Batavi honor your generosity, Your Majesty," he answered with a polite tip of his head. "I shall inform them straightaway."

Now General Arcadius proceeded to give some facts that had been learned overnight. The estimated number of Licinian dead was thirty-four thousand. Several thousand more had surrendered and expressed a desire to switch over to Constantine's side. Fourteen high-ranking officers in the enemy army had also been captured. When one surly duke shouted for their immediate execution, Arcadius shook his head. "Our merciful leader has decreed that they shall not be killed, but be stripped of their rank and posted at the edge of Britannia, north of Eboracum, at Hadrian's Wall."

I know it well, Rex thought, for he had grown up in that region while his father served Constantine there. *It will be a cold and rainy place to live out their final years. But at least they will still have their lives!*

"What of Licinius?" the grumpy duke asked. "Surely he will be executed?"

Arcadius grimaced and shook his head again. "Emperor Licinius escaped. He has retreated upon the Military Highway with a substantial force of his surviving troops."

At this, the men groaned and muttered. They all knew what this meant. Licinius was headed for Byzantium, a powerful city everyone considered impregnable. It was surrounded on three sides by the sea, and its fourth side had a stout wall built by Emperor Septimius Severus, during whose reign the empire had reached its maximum dimensions. Nobody could besiege Byzantium without also surrounding it by a naval blockade. Even then, it would take a long time to capture such a mighty citadel. Licinius was proving to be a wily and formidable enemy.

"Be at peace," Constantine admonished his restless men. "God goes before us to fight our battles. We shall prevail. It is only a matter of time."

The officers had quieted a bit and stopped their grumbling when a messenger arrived and knelt before the emperor. With his head bowed, he offered a wax tablet in a wooden case to Constantine, who took it and began to read. His face showed surprise, followed by grave concern. He handed the tablet to Arcadius. Upon reading the message, his face also grew alarmed.

"Well? What is it?" demanded a highly decorated tribune.

Arcadius grimaced and folded his hands behind his back. "We put one of the captured officers to torture, and he revealed some dire news. Licinius's admiral, Abantus by name, has taken up a position in the Hellespont. His ships are hidden in coves at the place where ingress into the strait is the most difficult."

A trap, Rex realized, and he wasn't alone in this realization. The other men perceived it too. Rex knew Admiral Abantus from a journey he once took with him. Back when Rex was a newlywed, he chartered passage on Abantus's warship. Rex had found him to be a likable captain, shrewd in the ways of the sea. His crew had even called him "Amandus" because he was "beloved" to them. Why the man was serving Licinius, Rex couldn't fathom. In any case, Abantus's shrewdness was about to become a serious threat to Constantine's navy. The narrow strait of the Hellespont was hard enough to enter without enemy opposition. Its outflow current was strong, making forward progress incredibly slow, sometimes even pinning ships in place as they tried to advance. A surprise attack from the flank at that moment would be deadly.

"My son's fleet is anchored in the Hebrus estuary at Aenus," Constantine said. "When word reaches him of Licinius's retreat, he will swiftly advance on Byzantium—and right into the teeth of Abantus."

"Crispus must be warned," Arcadius said. "Today."

"Rex!"

Emperor Constantine's sharp tone immediately grabbed Rex's attention. He stepped forward and saluted. "Yes, Your Majesty?"

"How old are you?"

"Thirty, sir. Thirty-one in about a month."

"Is there any man here who is younger?" Constantine looked around, but no one spoke up. They were all senior officers. He looked back at Rex. "It'll be a hard ride, but you can do it. Ninety miles in a day, then probably some infiltration at Aenus because there will still be some Licinians lurking around. Somehow you've got to slip past them and get aboard Crispus's flagship. Then show him this." Constantine opened the tablet, pressed his signet ring into the wax beneath the writing, and closed it again. After securing the clasp, he handed it to Rex. "Tell the hostler I said to give you the best horse he's got. You're going to need it. Farewell, Rex, and may God go with you."

After bowing to his lord, Rex left the circle of men and hurried to the corral on the western side of the Hebrus. The hostler found him a strong and well-rested mount that could go the distance: a long-legged Arabian used exclusively by the army couriers. Within half an hour, Rex was on the road toward Aenus, heading south on a warm July day. He alternatively walked and cantered his horse at a pace that was brisk but wouldn't be exhausting. The mare was going to need to conserve her strength.

Fortunately, the highway was straight and level, with few people on it since travelers tended to stay home when unpredictable soldiers were around. Rex rode throughout the day, stopping only a few times to rest and water his mount. A pouch of salted pork, eaten in the saddle and washed down with posca, served as his only meal.

The sun was setting on the distant ocean horizon when Rex arrived at Aenus. Though he hadn't encountered any Licinians on the branch highway he'd been using, he hadn't forgotten Constantine's warning that some enemy scouts might still be in the area. He hoped most of them had retreated down the Egnatian Way toward Byzantium by now. Yet in war, it paid to be cautious. One never knew what was around the bend.

Upon reaching the city's harbor, Rex found the imperial tax office to be flying Licinius's flag, not Constantine's. This region had been Licinian territory for a long time, so the political shift wasn't going to happen overnight no matter what had happened at Hadrianopolis. Rex gave his horse to a local hostler and paid him to rub down the tired mare and feed her good oats. She had done her job well. Now it was time to move from land to sea.

Since the harbor authorities of Aenus would be of no help, Rex wandered the pier in search of a different solution. A fleet of Constantinian galleys was anchored out in Aenus's sheltered bay. Most were at rest, with their sails furled and their oars stowed. But a few were starting to move out—and one of these was Crispus's flagship, the *Faithful*. It was surely headed for the Hellespont, for Crispus would want to lead the way to the next place of battle. Then the rest of the fleet could follow tomorrow. Little did they know they were headed into an ambush.

I've got to get out there tonight, Rex realized, *or there will be no catching up.*

Off to the side of Aenus's harbor was an enclosure where the port authority boats were moored. The fastest-looking craft was a little sailboat with one of the new lateen sails. Its crew consisted of two oafs making crude banter and foolishly cooking their dinner over a charcoal brazier on board.

Glancing around, Rex spotted a supply chest sitting on the dock nearby. He discovered nothing of value inside except the one item he had hoped to find: the distinctive cap that all the Licinian sailors wore. Its insignia was the eagle and thunderbolt of Jupiter. Rex donned it and approached the two buffoons in the sailboat.

"Get up," he commanded with feigned authority. He brandished the wax tablet. "I've just come from the battlefront, and I've got a message from Licinius himself. I have to get out to Crispus right away."

One of the sailors looked scared and started to comply, but the other man's fat face drooped into a scowl. "Prove it!" he spat.

Rex stepped on board—careful not to overturn the hot brazier—and opened the tablet. "See here?" He pointed to the letters scratched into the wax, which reported the trap that Abantus had laid. "Clearly, you can see how Emperor Licinius seeks fair terms and a parley for peace with his beloved nephew. And there is his personal seal, pressed into the wax by his own signet."

"I see it!" Fat Face said with indignation in his voice. "Do ya think I'm some kinda fool? I can read letters as good as you."

"Of course you can. So hoist the sail, and let's get out to the *Faithful* before she catches a night breeze and is gone."

Rex used thick rags to pick up the brazier and dump the charcoal overboard while the two scruffy crewmen got the dinghy out of the harbor. The lateen sail made her unusually swift, raising a nice ruffle at her prow as she sliced toward the emperor's flagship. Though the sun had already gone down, a round moon illuminated the bay with a bright glow.

"They might shoot the ballista at us," Fat Face said as the sailboat drew near. "They know we're Licinians. They'll wonder what we're up to."

Rex tied one of the rags onto a short javelin. "I'll signal for a truce. Now, pull us close, and don't do anything stupid." *For once in your life.*

"Halt where you are!" came a sharp command from the high deck of the *Faithful*.

"Important message from Constantine!" Rex called back as he waved his flag. "We come as allies!" He glanced over his shoulder at the two crewmen and added, "That should fool them. They'll think I'm from their own leader." The sailors guffawed at the clever ruse.

"Draw alongside, stranger. One wrong move and we open a hole in you the size of an egg!"

Rex had no intention of doing anything to invite a ballista bolt from the main deck. After discarding his Licinian cap, he remained calm and unthreatening as a rope ladder was dropped. He ascended it, then clambered aboard the *Faithful* and was immediately surrounded by marines with their swords drawn.

"As you can see, I am unarmed. I come only with this." Rex held out the tablet toward the centurion who faced him.

"What is it?"

"I wasn't lying when I said it's a message from Constantine. I have come straight here from the battlefront at Hadrianopolis. This morning we learned there's an ambush waiting for you in the Hellespont."

A look of concern immediately came to the centurion's face. "An ambush?"

"Yes. Admiral Abantus awaits in hidden coves to attack you when the going is hardest. It's all in this message." Rex opened the tablet. "And here is the seal of Constantine, which Crispus will surely recognize as authentic."

The centurion took the tablet from Rex. As he scanned it, his eyes widened in alarm. Turning to his optio, he said, "Go tell the pilot to drop anchor and furl the sail. We aren't going anywhere until we get this figured out."

From over his shoulder, Rex heard a clear and authoritative voice say, "Well done!"

He turned. It was Caesar Crispus, dressed in the kind of military splendor that befitted a fleet commander. A gold circlet was upon his brow and a purple cape was around his shoulders. He carried an admiral's baton.

Rex put his fist to his heart and dipped his head. "I am just obeying the commands of my lord," he said.

"As am I," Crispus replied.

⚬⚬⚬

The Hellespont looked to Caesar Crispus more like a wide river than the sea lane it actually was. *It's got a current like a river too*, he thought, having battled it all morning and finally broken through to more placid waters. The waterway, pinched by land on either side, formed a long connection between the Euxine Sea and the Aegean. The constant exchange of water between those two seas made navigating up the Hellespont especially difficult. Admiral Abantus's ambush would have been disastrous had the speculator Rex not brought news of it just in time.

But armed with the knowledge of the waiting ships, Crispus had spent the previous day drawing out the ambush and neutralizing it. He had sent some liburnians up the Hellespont on high alert and ready for an immediate retreat, which they performed as soon as the enemy came out of hiding. Having lost the element of surprise, Abantus's slower, heavier ships couldn't catch Crispus's more nimble ones as they scooted away. The enemy's triremes were left bobbing in the middle of the strait, impotent and frustrated. The initial confrontation was chalked up as a draw, and the game board was reset for a second match. This time, it would be admiral against admiral in a fair fight, and may the best man win.

"I see them, sir!" called down an eagle-eyed youth who had shimmied up the mast of the *Faithful*.

"What formation are they in?"

"It's a blockade strategy, sir. All the way across the waterway. I'd estimate two hundred ships in all."

Just as I suspected. Crispus chuckled at his opponent's predictability. *A wall of triremes from shore to shore.* And behind it was the grand prize: the city of Byzantium, where Licinius was safely ensconced. Though one side of the city faced Constantine's land army, the three other sides faced the sea, which would provide easy resupply with food, water, and more troops. Licinius had nothing to fear in a setup like that. Everything hinged on who had control of the waters around Byzantium.

Crispus went to the stern of his ship, where his pilot manned the steerboard. The *Faithful* was, like most of Crispus's fleet, a long, slender liburnian with a single row of fifteen oars on each side of the hull. Though he had some heavier ships in reserve, his strategy today called for using these so-called "thirty-polers" to their maximum efficiency.

The ancient wisdom among navy men was that monoreme warships couldn't take on triremes. A single level of oars was deemed inferior to three decks when it came to top-end speed and sheer bulk for ramming. But the rising generation of naval theorists had realized that neither speed nor size was the essential thing in battle. *Agility* mattered most. Crispus believed it too—not just in theory, but enough to stake his fleet, and perhaps his life, on the validity of the new wisdom.

"It's time," he told the pilot whose hand was on the steering oar. "My officers have been ordered to follow my lead today, so you must do exactly as I say."

"Aye, sir," the weather-beaten pilot said, "and may the Lord be with us."

Crispus set his eyes on the dark line of enemy ships that blocked his way. "Right up the middle we go, straight toward the *Dominant* like David charging at Goliath. No fear. Just faith. You may commence action."

The signals were relayed down to the beat keeper, and the oars began to turn. The pilot set a course through the center of the strait in the deepest part of the Hellespont. Eighty ships had been detached from Crispus's fleet—all light, fast monoremes taking on warships that weighed twice as much. Yet they were swift and eager for the fight. The galleys formed a triangular arrowhead aimed at the center of the enemy blockade, with the *Faithful* at the tip of the point.

"Paddleships ahead!" cried the lookout from the mast.

The announcement surprised everyone, including Crispus. The paddleship was a recent invention not previously used in war. Some generals even refused to believe they existed, claiming they were just a rumor, though numerous spies insisted they had seen them. These massive ships had capstans below deck that were turned by yokes of oxen. A set of gears transferred the rotation of the capstans to paddlewheels on either side of the hull. Once the wheels got turning, they could propel a battleship at speeds human rowers could never achieve. The weight of the ship, with all its interior machinery, gave it colossal force when it finally rammed an opponent.

Assuming they can catch the opponent, Crispus reminded himself. He resolved not to let that happen and instead decided to take out a paddleship today.

The blockade of enemy galleys looked impenetrable as the Constantinian attackers sped toward them. Crispus knew his men's fighting spirit was high, for these were bold and experienced sailors. At the same time, the attack had an audacious or even foolish air that couldn't help but raise the tension. What could puny liburnians do against the naval power Licinius possessed?

"Cease rowing," Crispus told his pilot.

"But sir," the man said nervously, "they'll be able to—"

"Just do it!"

"Right away, sir," replied the chastened pilot. With a single command, the *Faithful* immediately slowed.

Now the attacking fleet of Constantinian ships drifted toward the center of the Licinian blockade on their own momentum. The crimson banner of Jupiter rippled on the staff of Abantus's flagship. Flanking the *Dominant* were two paddleships whose prows were painted with angry yellow eyes. Affixed to the stem at the waterline were fierce bronze spikes for ramming. The behemoths seemed like fierce mastiffs guarding their master on either side.

"Come about," Crispus ordered. "Prepare to turn and run."

The pilot's face betrayed a shocked, even angry, expression as he received the command. "We don't have time to get away! They'll surround us!"

"Steady," Crispus said, his eyes fixed on the enemy line. "Wait for my orders."

Having broken off their swift attack, the cluster of eighty Constantinian ships sat idly in the water before the line of two hundred triremes. The tempting bait was more than the battle-hungry enemy could resist. Lured by what looked like vulnerable prey, Abantus's flagship surged ahead on the strength of its three tiers of oars. The paddleships advanced along with them. And down the line on either side, the triremes began to close on their victim like a crocodile's jaws snapping onto a juicy tidbit.

"They believe our courage has failed," said Crispus, "and they suppose victory is at hand."

"Sir, we've got to move!" The pilot's voice was urgent. "We'll be slaughtered! Shall I give the order to attack?"

"Hold still."

Now the *Dominant* was so close that Crispus could see the warriors' eager faces upon its prow. Both lines of the crocodile's jaws had closed fast, and the cluster of Constantinian ships was about to get hit hard by a flanking maneuver from either side. Even so, Crispus held his ships in place.

"God help us," the pilot said.

"He will," Crispus replied, then launched his ships into action.

Following the lead of the *Faithful*, the eighty liburnians engaged their oars and began to row at top speed. The agile ships—each one having been told beforehand what to do—aimed for the open sea through the gaps between the triremes that were bearing down on them. Like water trickling through the holes in a sieve, the galleys of Crispus found openings wherever they could and darted past the enemy craft. Sometimes the triremes tried to close the gaps to prevent escape, but the liburnians were quick enough to adjust their course into the new gap created on the other side. A few of the ponderous warships even crashed into each other or enmeshed their oars as they sought to corral the escaping liburnians. Although futile volleys of arrows were launched as the swifter ships slid past, none of the liburnians took a ramming from Abantus's fearsome navy.

After clearing the knot of enemy ships, Crispus found himself under a bright, blue sky in wide-open space. "This is our time!" he cried. "Come about hard and press the attack!" The pilot—now with a big grin on his face—immediately complied. And all the other liburnians did the same.

As the *Faithful* completed a graceful turn, Crispus was gratified to discover that the Licinian ships were still a jumbled mess in the middle of the Hellespont. After their prey had slipped by untouched, their own momentum had carried them toward their comrades who were closing from the other side. Shouts of confusion and angry orders arose from the frothing mass of tangled battleships. No one had any room to turn or maneuver. As soon as any of the rowers put their oars into the sea, the pinewood shafts struck the oars of the adjacent ships trying to do the same. Their prows were all pointed toward each other, and their sterns were exposed to rear attack.

"Hit them hard, boys!" Crispus called to his oarsmen below deck. "Full speed ahead."

"Straight up the sternpost, sir?" The pilot's former anxiety had now turned to glee. His long hair was blowing in the wind, and sea spray glistened in his beard. The longtime navy man recognized a victory when he saw it. And he was about to get a good one.

"Knock a hole in their arse!" Crispus replied with a grin, then braced for impact.

One by one, the liburnians smashed the enemy triremes in their rear quarters. That area of the hull was a galley's weak point, for the high, curving sternpost did not allow fighters to congregate there for defense. Normally, a warship would never let its stern be exposed like that. But today the triremes were too entangled with one another to take evasive action. All they could do was clench and wait.

Crispus had ordered each of his ships to take out two enemies if they could. In solidarity with his men, he first rammed a trireme straight on its sternpost where it met the waterline. The timbers crunched under the force of impact, and sea water rushed into the breached hull, making the craft list dangerously. The steering oar on the starboard side was broken as well. Crispus's experienced rowers immediately reversed their strokes, backing out the *Faithful* so it wouldn't be dragged down with the sinking ship.

But Crispus wasn't finished. Scanning the chaotic scene around him, he finally spotted one of the paddleships. Although it wasn't very maneuverable, it had used its bulk to plow its way into open waters again. "Hit that paddlewheel broadside," he ordered. "All ballistae and archers to the fore, now!"

The troops obeyed and immediately began to fire on their opponent. The enemy ship, of course, had missiles of its own to launch. A barrage of arrows whistled toward the *Faithful* as it made its deadly approach. One of the ballista bolts impaled the mainmast with a loud *thunk!* Though some of Crispus's archers fell before the onslaught, the ship kept surging ahead.

When the impact finally came, it shook Crispus so hard that he stumbled to his knees. Once again, the *Faithful* immediately backed out. Only then could Crispus see that the paddlewheel had been reduced to splinters. As he left the crippled ship behind, he caught the sound of terrified oxen bellowing from inside the hold.

"Victory!" cried all the soldiers and rowers as they surveyed the damage their attack had caused. And they were right. Broken and immobilized triremes were strewn everywhere. Some had even capsized or begun to sink. The ones that had escaped damage had retreated. The day had gone to Constantine in every way.

With the Licinian blockade shattered, Crispus's entire fleet could now proceed up the Hellespont. A smoke signal was raised to summon the rest of the ships. "Head for Kallipolis," Crispus instructed his pilot. "We'll shelter there overnight and finish this thing tomorrow."

Feeling exuberant after the great victory, the devout helmsman held the rudder in one hand and raised his other palm to the sky. "Praise God!" he exclaimed. "David has defeated Goliath!"

But Crispus shook his head. "Not yet, my friend. Byzantium still awaits."

4

JULY 324

Rex could only laugh as he wiped sweat from his face with his new handkerchief. The cloth was red, and there was a little piece of gold embroidery on it, a fragment of a lightning bolt that symbolized Jupiter's power. It was cut from the flag of the *Dominant*, which had been breached in Crispus's attack, then was smashed on jagged rocks the next day when an afternoon thunderstorm caught the remaining Licinian ships too close to the shore and ran them aground. In all, three hundred and fifty Licinian ships were destroyed in the two days of combat, and the enemy navy was no more. After capturing Admiral Abantus, Crispus cut his war banner into little squares to award to those who had contributed to the win. Rex was glad to have a token of the victory. Yet he was even more pleased that the Battle of the Hellespont had, like the Battle of Hadrianopolis before it, gone to Emperor Constantine.

"Using it as a sweat rag, eh?"

Rex turned from his quiet spot in the prow of the *Faithful* to see Crispus approaching him. "It's a hot day, Your Majesty. The rag is just what I need."

"I like to use mine like this." Crispus loudly blew his nose into his square of red cloth. "Oops. Sorry, Jupiter."

Rex chuckled at the emperor's impudent action. *I like this man,* he thought, though he kept the sentiment to himself lest it sound like flattery.

Crispus gestured toward the distant horizon as his flagship moved farther up the Hellespont. "We should be in sight of Byzantium's walls by sundown. Have you ever seen it, Rex?"

"Never have. Heard a lot about it, though."

"It's an incredible city! The Greeks founded it, you know. Around the same time as Rome. And they picked a great spot. It sits on the Bosporus Strait, which is like the Hellespont but even narrower. Nobody can get from the Euxine Sea into the Mediterranean without sailing right past Byzantium."

"A strategic location."

"Yes, and not just by sea. Two continents meet there as well. Byzantium is on the European side. But Asia is only half a mile across the Bosporus. So the city commands maritime traffic between two seas and land traffic between two continents. My father is very impressed by that. He remarks on it often."

Although Rex had learned some of those details during his brief stint as a pirate, he didn't want Crispus to know about that. So he just nodded appreciatively and said, "It sounds like quite a place! I can't wait to see it for myself."

"You'll see its exterior in a few hours. As for its interior"—Crispus gave Rex a confident wink—"that will depend on how long my uncle's courage can hold out." The emperor slapped Rex on the back and moved on to other business, leaving him alone again in the *Faithful*'s prow.

The afternoon winds were favorable, and Crispus's prediction proved true. Around sundown, the city appeared on the horizon off the port bow. The sun's rays gave an orange sheen to the magnificent walls that rose from the water's edge on three sides. And although Rex couldn't see it, he knew that Constantine's land army was camped outside Byzantium's fourth wall, chipping away at the city's defenses while they waited for a naval blockade to put a stranglehold on the people inside. Now that the New Aegean Fleet had control of the waterways, it wouldn't be long before Crispus's ships surrounded Byzantium and invested it. Then the hungry times would begin.

Night fell, dark and still, with just a thin sliver of moon. The anchor was dropped and set in the deep water of the Bosporus. With their day's work done, the *Faithful*'s crew began to mill around the main deck. The total crew numbered sixty men: thirty rowers on the oars, twenty marines to fight the battles, five sailors who were skilled with ropes, and five officers with various duties. Normally the crew went ashore at night and slept on the beach. But with a blockade in place, the men were forced to sleep aboard the galley. Caesar Crispus, however, had been taken away to some other location.

Since a warship had no space for rations, the *Faithful* was victualed by tenders that came from the supply transports. Rex was served a mushy stew of anchovies, chickpeas, and ship's biscuit, washed down by sour wine. With his belly full and his eyelids heavy, he found an empty space on the deck, pulled his cloak around himself, and settled in for sleep. It wasn't long before he was out.

Late that night, a sound awakened him. *What is it?*

He listened, but there was only silence. A sleeping man snuffled, smacked his lips, and rolled over. Silence again.

High above, clouds had obscured the moon. The only light was a single lantern hanging from the sternpost. Rex concentrated on every sound, trying to discern what had awakened him. Occasionally he would hear waves lap against the hull, a fish jump, the ship timbers creak, or the rigging rattle as the wind stirred it. All of that was normal.

And then he heard it again: the distinct sound of a yard moving against a mast as a sailor adjusted it to the wind. Someone was out on the sea, violating the blockade.

Nearby, the centurion's second-in-command was asleep on the deck. Rex stirred the optio until he was awake. "There's a boat on the water," Rex whispered.

The optio rubbed his eyes and sat up. "You sure?"

"Yes. Come have a look."

The two men stood at the ship's rail and peered into the gloom. For a long time, they saw nothing. Then the clouds parted and the sea brightened a bit. "There it is," Rex said.

"It's tiny. A fishing boat under sail."

"What's it doing out here at night?"

The optio shrugged. "He probably wants to fish at sunup and sneak back tonight. His catch will sell for ten times the normal price inside an invested city."

"That's risky. If he gets caught, he's dead."

"Some people are risk-takers. Go back to sleep, Rex. That guy is no threat to us."

"I think we should check it out."

"My men just fought a two-day battle. They need to rest for whatever's coming next. I'm not sending anybody out there in the middle of the night just so they can confiscate a couple of mackerel."

"Then I'll go," Rex declared. "He shouldn't be out there. I'm sending him back to the city with a stern warning."

"Suit yourself." The optio unbuckled his sword and offered it to Rex. "You'd better take this, just in case."

Rex nodded to the optio and went to the ship's ladder. Down in the water was the dinghy that the cook had brought from the resupply freighter. After climbing down, Rex lit the boat's lantern and cast off.

With an oar in each hand, he rowed the dinghy on a trajectory he thought would intercept the illegal fisherman. Though at first he saw nothing, the third time he glanced over his shoulder, he caught sight of his quarry in the dim moonlight. After adjusting his line and speeding up, Rex soon drew alongside the trespasser.

"Imperial navy!" he barked. "Halt and prepare to be boarded!" Rex threw a line around the sailboat's steering oar so it couldn't get away. But before clambering aboard the captured vessel, he rummaged in the dinghy's supply locker and quickly found what he wanted: a pot of the red paint that trimmed virtually all navy ships.

The fisherman in the captured boat was a wiry old fellow with the look of the sea about him. "Please spare me!" he implored with his fingers interlocked. "My family is starving."

"I doubt it, old man. You just got invested today. You're not out of food yet in Byzantium."

The man immediately hung his head and nodded. "You're right. I was just trying to make some extra silver. Figured it wouldn't hurt anybody if I took a few fish."

"That isn't for you to decide. You're under an imperial blockade." Rex opened his paint jar and heaved its contents onto the fishing boat's sail. The red paint made a huge, messy splotch on the white fabric. "Get back to Byzantium right now," Rex ordered. "If this boat is spotted again at sea, we're sinking it, and I hope you can swim."

"Yes, sir," the old fisherman said. "I'll turn around right now, sir."

"See that you do." Rex turned away from the Byzantine scofflaw and loosed the rope from the rudder. He was about to climb back into his dinghy when a water keg sneezed, and everything changed in an instant.

Rex had his sword out of its scabbard before he had even reached the keg. He snatched off the barrel's lid and raised his arm to thrust the blade into whatever might emerge from its dark recesses. Nothing did—and then the fisherman threw a net over Rex.

"Kill him!" screamed the old man. "Quick!"

Rex stumbled backward, ensnared by the net's tangles. As he struggled to free himself, the man hiding in the barrel finally popped out. *Licinius!* Though the emperor was dressed in common clothes, Rex recognized his face from countless coins and statues. Licinius was a thick-necked man with close-cropped hair and stubble on his chin. A vicious gleam was in his eye, and a dagger was in his hand.

"You'll never take me!" he snarled, then dove at Rex with his blade outstretched.

Trapped in the net and cornered in the boat's stern, Rex was helpless. His own weapon was unable to parry. To try and fight Licinius would be to die. There was nothing to do but leap away from his assailant and dive overboard.

The water was frigid when Rex tumbled in. Darkness enveloped him, for the abyss was inky black. Without the use of his arms or legs, he immediately began to plunge into the underworld. He thrashed in the net, striving to throw it off, yet it only tangled him more. Rex was horrified at the thought of coming to rest on the muddy bottom far below the surface.

Though terror began to take hold of him as he sank deeper, Rex forced himself to remain calm. Deliberately, he used his sword to cut one strand after another. For a long, scary moment, the net refused to relinquish its grip. Then to Rex's great relief, he felt the flaxen strands give way under his fierce tugging. He shook off the deadly mesh and was free.

Kicking hard, Rex surged upward through the gloom. Just as his breath was about to give out, he broke the surface with a desperate gasp. He exulted in the blessed intake of sweet, fresh air. For a while he could only float in the water with his mouth agape, panting as he recovered from his ordeal.

When he had finally regained his equilibrium, he glanced around until he spotted the dinghy. It had drifted away when the fishing boat sailed off. He swam over to it, hauled himself over the gunwale, and took a seat in the thwarts. Letting out a frustrated sigh, he wiped water from his eyes.

Off to his left was Europe. Byzantium stood there in the moonlight—proud, ancient, and unafraid. To his right was the coast of Asia. Rex could see the lights of Chrysopolis, a modest-sized town that marked the beginning of a new continent.

"That was a close one," Rex muttered as he grasped the oars and started heading back to his ship. *Much too close!* The emperor's dagger had almost impaled him. The sea had almost swallowed him. Yet here he was: alive, uninjured, and ready to fight another day. And that was what he would have to do now that Licinius had slipped through the imperial blockade. The tenacious emperor would assemble a new army in Asia and make another stand.

"We'll chase you all the way to Persia if we have to," Rex said toward the east. "But I wish you'd quit running and get this over with. I've got a wife waiting for me at home."

—◦◦◦—

AUGUST 324

The doctor named Hillel who lived outside the Sun Gate was said to be the best in Alexandria for treating women's issues. Renowned for his gentle demeanor and mastery of herbs, he was part of Alexandria's ancient and venerable Jewish community, which was noted for its exceptional doctors. Flavia had heard his name numerous times from her female friends but had never actually visited him. Yet her ongoing problems with her womb had finally made her decide to go.

The Sun Gate stood open on this August afternoon when Flavia reached it. The gate was in the northeastern city wall, all the way across town from her apartment in Alexandria's southwestern corner. It had been a long, hot walk. Yet the trip would be worth it if Hillel could help with her frequent bleeding and cramps.

Flavia exited the city and entered the suburb known as Boukolia, whose name was derived from the Greek word for animal herds. Although much had changed in Alexandria over the centuries—whether under the Pharaohs, the Greeks, Queen Cleopatra, or the Romans—this suburban district had always remained a rural area for pasturing goats, sheep, and cattle. To serve the herdsmen of the area, a suburban village had grown up between the pastures and the city walls. The doctor's home was within sight of the Sun Gate.

It turned out that Hillel was everything he had been advertised to be. His bedside manner was gentle and caring, and his knowledge of herbal medicine was encyclopedic. Though he was a great advocate of the healing power of prayer, he also believed that God had provided the plants of the world for human flourishing. He prescribed Flavia a potion made from the vitex tree, which everyone called the "chastity tree" for its dampening effect upon sexual desire. Its berries and leaves were said to be useful for gynecological problems. The prescribed medicine also contained ginger root and shepherd's purse. Hillel assured Flavia that soon she would be feeling much better.

After paying the doctor and heading back to the main road with her prescription, Flavia decided to eat a quick meal before the long walk home. Her search for a thermopolium took her into the side streets of the village that had cropped up outside the city wall. The gates of large cities often created subcommunities like Boukolia at the interface of the urban and rural environments. And of course, those people needed to eat just like anyone else.

It didn't take Flavia long to determine that since this was a shepherding village, meat was available everywhere. The mouth-watering aroma of roasted mutton met her nostrils as she approached a respectable-looking establishment. She stepped up to the counter and bought a saucy lamb kebab over a bed of greens and barley. The wine was a good vintage too. Flavia felt thoroughly refreshed by the delicious food.

As she was finishing up her meal, the thermopolium's proprietor glanced at a sun dial, then beckoned for Flavia to eat her last bite so he could take back the dish and cup. He wanted to close down his restaurant. "Church is about to start," he said.

"You're a Christian?"

"Aye, very devoted to the Lord," the man answered. He was a brown-skinned Copt with a cheap wig that wobbled as he nodded. "And you?"

"A believer also."

"Then you should come to church with me, sister. Come hear our priest. He's an excellent preacher."

"Who is it?"

"Brother Arius, an orthodox theologian of our faith. His church is the Martyrium of Saint Mark."

Arius!

In her concern about her medical issues, Flavia had forgotten that the Boukolia district was Arius's territory. The chapel out here was old—so old that it claimed to house the relics of John Mark, the companion of Paul, scribe of Peter, and writer of the second gospel. The view that Mark had planted the Alexandrian church was widely believed by the local people. However, it had little historical backing. The previous Christian scholars of Alexandria made no mention of Mark's evangelistic work. Bishop Alexander accepted that Mark could have made a visit to the Aegyptian city. Yet he believed that the relics beneath the Martyrium's altar were false—just like the doctrine held by the Martyrium's priest.

Even so, Flavia decided she might as well take the opportunity to accompany the restaurant owner to church and listen to Arius in his own setting. She had only ever seen Arius giving academic lectures at the Serapeum. What would he be like with his flock?

The service today wasn't a Holy Eucharist but just a feast day for a minor Aegyptian saint whom Flavia had never heard of. The liturgy included a litany of scripture readings, several lengthy prayers, and of course, a sermon that celebrated the departed saint. But Arius wasn't one to linger on the details of a pious life when he could instead be addressing his favorite subject: the Son's inferiority to the Father because of his creaturely status. It wasn't long before the homily on the saint's life had veered into this familiar Arian territory.

Father Arius was, Flavia had to admit, a dignified and articulate man. He had a powerful presence as he spoke from his acacia-wood chair at the front of the church. His words were erudite and persuasive. Even though he was approaching seventy years old, his voice was still strong and his demeanor dignified as he preached. His primary text was from the *Proverbs of Solomon*: "The Lord established me at the beginning of his ways, for his works." While Flavia didn't agree with Arius's theological conclusions, after listening to his sermon for a while, she began to understand how he got there—mistaken though he was.

"The proverb that lies open on my lap uses an important word," Arius declared. "The lector read it to you a few moments ago: *established*. This precious word in our Greek scriptures, which the seventy Jewish fathers of our city translated from the Hebrew so long ago, has several other meanings that must be recognized. The term *established* can also mean 'created,' or 'brought into being.' Surely that is what King Solomon had in mind when he wrote the proverb by divine inspiration! The Heavenly Father created his Son at the beginning of all things so he could make the cosmos through him. Listen to that, brethren! Is it merely some strange idea from an ancient Israelite king?"

Now a timid hush descended on the church as Arius waited for a response. No one wanted to break the silence that permeated the Martyrium of Saint Mark. Yet Arius seemed to want an answer. He held out his hands, inviting a reply. "Come now," he said warmly. "Is it strange and mysterious to say that the Son was created at the beginning of God's work for the sake of creating everything else? Or is that something you might have heard in a more familiar place?"

Flavia could stay silent no longer. "You are thinking of *Colossians*," she offered, "at the beginning of the epistle."

"Yes, my sister!" Arius's face brightened as his gaze alighted on Flavia, and he smiled at her through his pointy, waxed beard. "And how does that passage go?"

Flavia summarized the text as best she could recall it. "Saint Paul refers to our Lord as 'the firstborn of all creation.' Then he says, 'By him all things were created, in heaven and on earth, visible and invisible.'"

"You see?" cried Arius, raising his finger in triumph and looking around the hall. "The Son is the first of all created things. After he was made by God at the very beginning of time, he created the rest of the universe. It appears that King Solomon and the Apostle were in total agreement—which is only fitting, since the scriptures are a single book from the Lord's hand."

"But that doctrine is wrong," Flavia countered. "John's gospel says, 'In the beginning was the Word. He was with God and he was God. He was there in the beginning.'"

"That is what I just said, dear sister. You have proven my point. Christ was there at the beginning, when God made him. Then God made the world through his Son. It is a beautiful plan! And it is the scripture's own teaching."

Now Flavia felt flustered. She knew there were biblical passages that taught the eternality of Christ, but at the moment, her mind couldn't produce them. She lapsed into silence, feeling embarrassed that she had publicly corrected a priest at a church where she was just a visitor.

When the service was over, Flavia quietly slipped out. She thanked the restaurant owner for inviting her, then hurried back to the main road. Once she entered the city again through the Sun Gate, she was back on Canopus Avenue. The walk to the opposite side of Alexandria was a long one, yet it gave Flavia time to rehearse what she should have said to Arius. She thought of several replies she wished had come to her mind. But of course, it was too late now.

At last, she reached the Church of Theonas. Its interior was cool and dim as she entered, a welcome relief after the glare of the Aegyptian sun. Confused and disturbed by the events of her day, Flavia felt the need to seek God's face before heading home. She picked up a small lamp and carried it over to a wall where the women of the church often prayed. Beautiful paintings lined the wall, pictures of the great heroes who had already "run the race with endurance." Flavia went to a niche where King Solomon was depicted. She set down her lamp and knelt to ask the Lord's discernment in matters of doctrine. When she was finished, she stood up and made the sign of the cross over herself.

The image of King Solomon, so grave and dignified, seemed to stare at Flavia with piercing eyes. She felt burdened by the difficult task of exegeting the scriptures. It was hard to separate truth from falsehood, retaining the gold while discarding the dross. "What did you mean by *established*, you wisest of kings?" she asked the artful icon.

"Certainly not a creature," said a voice from behind.

Flavia turned to see who had spoken. As she had suspected, it was Athanasius. The little deacon stood there with a benign smile on his face.

He chuckled and said, "It sounds like an Arian has been whispering in your ear."

"Not an Arian, but Arius himself! I know his doctrine is false, but then he quotes scriptures like 'The Lord established me at the beginning of his ways' and 'Jesus is the firstborn of all creation.' It's so confusing!"

"Only because they make it so, my dear Flavia. Those texts do not mean our Lord is a creature, for nowhere do the scriptures ever say such a blasphemous thing. Rather, this language speaks of Christ's oneness with the created world. It is the language of his deep union with the human race, his brotherhood with us, his divine descent in which he takes true flesh to himself. Those scriptures describe not the Word's creatureliness but his incarnation."

Athanasius's forthright words seemed to clear a mist from Flavia's mind. "Thank you, my friend," she said. "You have comforted me. Once again, I am in your debt."

"I know a way you could repay that debt," Athanasius said.

Flavia glanced over at him. The deacon's eyebrow was arched, and an impish smile was on his lips. Flavia sensed that something big was on his mind. "How, my brother?"

"The church of Alexandria has a great need. A holy mission must be sent to a place far from here. It will be an expensive journey. But you have the means to pay for it."

"To where?"

"I cannot yet tell you. But what I know is this. With your wealth, you could cover the costs of this important church business."

The decision wasn't hard for Flavia to make. God had given her a substantial inheritance not to pay for a lavish lifestyle but for purposes such as this. If the Holy Spirit decided to speak through Athanasius, her job was simply to obey. "Behold, I am the handmaiden of the Lord," Flavia said to her friend and mentor, quoting the words of the blessed virgin. "I am willing to pay for the mission if the bishop has such a need."

"I believe he will," Athanasius said, "and I think our quiet days in Alexandria are coming to an end."

"We need fifty thousand more just like you," Emperor Licinius said to the long-haired Goth with a physique like a marble sculpture and a face like a god. His name was Alica. He was probably just a man. Yet Licinius couldn't help but suspect that someone so muscular and handsome might actually be an incarnation of Thor himself.

"There's only one of me," Alica replied through the manly beard that jutted from his square jaw. "But I can bring you fifty thousand Gothic warriors who won't disappoint."

"How soon?"

"Depends on the price."

"I'm thinking fifty million, plus two jugera of farmland per man."

Alica arched his eyebrows at the exorbitant sum. "You're good for that?" His Latin accent was throaty and guttural like all the Germani, yet somehow it sounded agreeable upon this man's lips. Licinius thought even Cicero wouldn't have minded it.

"I'm good for it," Licinius replied. "I'll get you the money if I have to sack my own cities to do it. This is my last stand against Constantine. Either I do it now or I'm dead. So this is my oath: your men will receive fifty million denarii in silver coins plus all the farmland around Sinope, or my life is yours to take."

"I'll need to have blood for an oath like that."

Licinius drew a jeweled dagger from his belt. For a moment, he hesitated. But when he saw Alica watching him with a skeptical eye, he mustered his resolve and drew the blade across his palm. He grunted at the fiery pain, then immediately wished he hadn't uttered the sound. It probably made him seem unmanly.

"Fool!" Alica said—an audacious thing for a barbarian to call a Roman emperor. "Never damage the hand that wages war." With that, Alica took the knife and made a tiny nick on the back of his head. He pressed his finger to it, then brought a smear of redness to Licinius's wounded palm. "We have a deal," Alica declared, as blood met blood. "You shall have fifty thousand Goths at your service before a week goes by. Payment shall be due once I have crushed Constantine under my heel like a wriggling worm."

"If anyone can do it, you can, Th—I mean, Alica."

The tall barbarian didn't acknowledge Licinius's slip of the tongue. He merely nodded in a polite though not submissive way. Then he turned and left the imperial tent with the briskness of a man who had a job to do. *Fifty thousand Goths*, Licinius mused. *Added to my legionaries, that makes an army of a hundred and thirty. More than enough to beat Constantine—especially since a Goth is worth two Romans!*

Now that Alica was gone, Licinius went to his field trunk and found a silk handkerchief to wrap around his hand. After drinking a willow-bark potion for the pain, he rinsed the bitter stuff from his mouth with a swallow of wine, then went outside to survey his camp.

The rolling, grassy area between Chrysopolis and Chalcedon had been Licinius's home for the past month, ever since he had escaped Byzantium by night. He had elevated one of his generals to the rank of caesar—a move that had infuriated Constantine—and sent him down to Lampsacus to hold the coastline against an invasion. Fortunately, Crispus's navy was tied up making the blockade around Byzantium, so they couldn't muster a sufficient landing force to establish a beachhead in Asia. Meanwhile, Constantine's army was besieging Byzantium from its landward side to root out its garrison, but to no avail. The long stalemate had allowed Licinius to regroup, establish a new camp, and send emissaries across the Euxine Sea to the Goths. Their chieftain, Alica, had been only too happy to answer the call for mercenaries. Now that Licinius had a field army once more, he felt he had a realistic chance of finally winning against Constantine. But there was one more thing he needed to do.

Between the new military camp and the edge of the Bosporus, the ground formed a shallow bowl that sloped down to the water. A wooden platform had been constructed at the bowl's rim, creating a perfect place for a commander to address his troops. Licinius went there alone and stood next to a war banner that had seen action at Hadrianopolis. Its edges were frayed, and it was stained by splotches of mud—or maybe it was blood? The spearhead above the banner had grown rusty and its edge was nicked. The butt end of the shaft had been wedged into a stand with the front of the flag facing toward Byzantium, which was visible directly across the Bosporus.

"Curse you, Constantine," Licinius muttered as he stared at the city.

He imagined his enemy on the other side of it, arrogantly attempting to capture what didn't belong to him. "For a brother-in-law, you sure are a piece of caca."

Licinius yanked the old war banner out of the stand and brandished it toward Byzantium. He felt a deep sense of outrage well up inside him. "You can have that hellhole!" he shouted at the city. "Stupid Europe is a wasteland, anyway! I am Licinius Asianus, Lord of the East! This continent is mine, and by Jupiter, you aren't taking it from me!"

Unfortunately, Jupiter hadn't been listening well lately. In the last two battles, the god had remained atop his thundercloud without intervening. *Is that because his image isn't represented on the army's war banners?* The one in Licinius's hand was just a regular flag of the legions that depicted a rampaging wild boar. He took the tattered standard back to his tent and propped it against the goatskin wall. Then he picked up a different spear: the one he had obtained at the roadside pantheon. It was marked with the initials of Pontius Pilate in blood.

"Go get the vexillarius," Licinius snapped at his manservant. The obsequious fellow instantly nodded and darted outside.

A short while later, the standard-bearer entered the tent and bowed. "You called for me, Your Majesty?"

Licinius handed him the Pilate spear. "I have a great plan. Listen carefully to what I say." He outlined to the man exactly what he wanted, omitting no details. "How long will it take?" he asked when he was finished.

"No more than a week, sir."

"Get it done by the time the Goths arrive." Licinius waved the man away and turned his mind to other things.

Five days later, the vexillarius reported that the new standard was ready. Good weavers in Chalcedon had been commissioned to make the flag out of fine-spun wool. Embroiderers had added its primary emblem: the symbol of Jupiter, a wingspread eagle with thunderbolts in its talons. However, for this special banner, instead of lightning, the bird held something else in the claws of its left foot: a fish, the ancient symbol of the Christians. In this way, the banner would proclaim Jupiter's triumph over Jesus.

Licinius admired the banner in his tent when the vexillarius brought it to him. It had a strong wooden shaft whose "P.P." marking had been enhanced with red paint. The blade at the top was made of the finest steel, honed to a keen edge. This was a working spear, not a military toy.

To the shaft's length a crossbar was attached from which the flag hung. The fabric was crimson, the universal color of war. Dangling from the flag of Jupiter were eleven medallions that depicted the other Olympian gods. A multicolored band running horizontally through the fabric symbolized the uncountable number of lesser deities. And the feather from the eagle that had soared among the clouds also adorned the flag, fastened by a chain of gold to the pole where it met the crossbar.

Below all this, set into the wooden shaft, was a gold disc upon which had been struck an image of Licinius and his son, Licinius Junior. Very soon, the two of them would rule the empire together. The whole banner was a magnificent accomplishment, a true work of art. It was worthy to lead the troops into battle.

But is it infused with divine power? Only time will tell.

Early the next morning, the troops, their officers, and all the auxiliary slaves were summoned to the grassy bowl outside the camp. The sun was still low in the east, so its rays sparkled on the water of the Bosporus and made Byzantium stand out in sharp detail. Licinius took up his position on the wooden platform at the rim of the bowl. He had brought the war banner with him, which was wrapped in nondescript cloth and remained hidden at his feet.

Now a group of priests stepped up to make a ritual sacrifice. A castrated bull was brought forward on a lead rope. Its hide was pure white. The smashing blow of a sledgehammer to its skull brought the mighty animal to its knees. Then a priest gripped the stunned beast by its nostrils and yanked back its head. A slice across the throat was the last thing the white ox knew before the god received its lifeblood. The priests made a burnt offering upon a rock outcrop, and high above in the clouds, Jupiter accepted the holy oblation.

Like every good general, Licinius recognized that the moment had come when a rousing oration was required from the commander in chief. Though he was by no means an accomplished rhetorician, he knew exactly what would play well with his men: a speech that recalled Rome's greatness, extolled Rome's gods, and celebrated Rome's crucifixion of Jesus Christ.

And Licinius gave it to them. He spent the better part of an hour re-counting the great battles of Roman history, intertwining his narration with the fabulous myths of the gods. But it was the speech's conclusion that really got the troops riled up. Licinius heaped scorn on the carpenter of Nazareth—that filthy Jew, that charlatan who led people astray. Jesus claimed to be a king but died naked and impaled by the true lord of lords: the caesar of Rome.

Lifting his fist to the sky, Licinius shouted at his men, "What did the crowds say to Pontius Pilate?"

"Crucify him!" came the raucous reply.

"And what will we do to Constantine?"

"Crucify him!"

Now Licinius raised his voice to its maximum volume. His words came out in what sounded like an eagle's screech. "And what will Jupiter do to the Christian God?"

"CRUCIFY HIM!"

With the troops now excited to a fever pitch, Licinius decided it was time for his big reveal. He stooped and unwrapped the war banner, though he still kept it out of sight on the platform.

"You have heard it said that the Christians revere the cross," he yelled to his frenzied men. "Our enemy has put that accursed sign on his flag, the so-called labarum. It is an evil thing, and I charge you, in battle, do not look at it lest it bewitch your eyes! Avoid its devilry at all costs! Keep your gaze far away, for its power is from hell. And yet, my brethren, do not let your hearts be troubled. You believe in Jupiter; believe also in me! Today I give you an even more powerful gift. Behold the true cross, the true wood that saves, the true sign of divine triumph!"

With that, Licinius scooped up the new war banner and raised it before the watching soldiers. The roar of their cheer was like a giant wave, rolling from Byzantium across the Bosporus and right up onto the coast of Asia. Licinius could feel its supernatural energy hit him like a physical force. *Aha! Divine power has finally arrived! The men are filled with it!*

"Hail, Jupiter!" cried a centurion near the front.

"Caesar is lord!" added another man. Although that phrase was outdated, the acclamation was too ancient and customary not to use on a day like this.

The centurion who had spoken first threw himself facedown before the platform on which Licinius stood. "Save us, lord!" he exclaimed.

"Save us, lord!" echoed several other soldiers, who likewise prostrated themselves before the emperor. Suddenly, as if the wave of divine energy had bounced from Licinius and was now rolling back through the crowd, everyone fell down in the grass—except one person.

Licinius stared at the lone woman, a Dacian prisoner of war who served as a camp prostitute. She looked beautiful as the wind stirred her long, dark hair. Her back was erect and her chin was lifted high. Clearly, she knew what she was doing by remaining upright. Now her impudence was going to cost her.

"Fall down before your savior!" Licinius ordered. His voice was hoarse from his long oration, but he managed to make himself heard.

The woman said nothing. And she made no move.

Enraged, Licinius descended from his platform and stormed over to the woman. "What is your name?"

"I am Zia."

"Rebellious Zia! Why do you not bow like all the rest?"

The woman had a defiant gleam in her eye—a regal demeanor unworthy of someone as lowly as a sex slave. She looked straight at Licinius and said, "I was a ruler among my people until I was abducted by your soldiers! Now my days are a nightmare and my nights will never end. Yet here also, I have found the Lord Jesus Christ. To him alone do I bow—not to you, proud emperor, nor to Jupiter, nor even to my ancestral gods! To Christ alone."

For a long moment, Licinius glared at Zia as rage coursed through his body. It infiltrated every limb, every joint, every corner of his dark and twisted soul. He quivered as he beheld this dirty canicula who dared to defy him while all his troops lay prostrate on the ground. Finally, a semblance of words came bubbling from his lips. "You . . . worship . . . me!"

"I worship Jesus," said the Dacian queen.

"Then go to him!" Licinius screamed, and ran Zia through with the Pilate spear. The blade pierced her stomach easily and sank all the way to the crossbar. Licinius held the shaft in both hands as Zia stared at him with wide eyes, until, with great dignity, she closed them and released her soul.

The emperor yanked out the spear and turned away as Zia's limp body collapsed to the ground.

"Look up at me!" he shouted.

All the prostrate men lifted their faces from the dirt and beheld their glorious lord. Licinius touched the flat spearhead with his thumb and wiped off a dollop of Zia's blood. He held it up to the gods.

"Now this banner is ready for war," he declared.

And from the ancient soil of Asia, the legions of Rome began to cheer.

—◦◦◦—

SEPTEMBER 324

The *Faithful* was making good time up the Bosporus Strait on one of the beautiful blue-sky days that so often came in early September. The flagship was leading not only the liburnians of the New Aegean Fleet but also a motley assortment of supply transports, repurposed fishing vessels, and haphazardly constructed rafts. The whole thing made a crazy armada the likes of which Rex had never seen. Yet despite its absurd appearance, he knew this was an invasion force of immense power.

"Look out there," Caesar Crispus said to Rex and the two bodyguards who always accompanied him. The foursome was standing at the side rail of the warship with a sea breeze on their faces. "It's the Sacred Promontory. It marks the entrance into the Euxine Sea."

Following the emperor's extended finger, Rex could see how the green coastlines on either side of the Bosporus disappeared about a mile ahead. There, at the place where the promontory jutted out, the narrow strait opened into a vast sea whose distant shores were inhabited by barbarians outside the Roman Empire.

Rex pointed ahead and to his left. "There's a gray haze on the European side."

The observation brought a smile to Crispus's face. "Yes! Cookfires! Looks like my father's army has already started to arrive."

A week ago, the decision had been made to abandon the siege of Byzantium. The war machines were making no progress against the impregnable citadel, and Licinius wasn't even inside anyway. Instead, Constantine had decided to cross the Bosporus, invade Asia, and take out his rebellious brother-in-law once and for all. Then Byzantium would probably surrender, and no one would be left to rule the empire except Constantine and his sons.

However, to transport a hundred thousand troops and their supplies across the channel would require an uncontested crossing. That was why the location selected for the landing was far away from Licinian territory: twenty-five miles up the Bosporus at its mouth where it opened into the Euxine Sea. The Asian coastline was dotted with a few villages here but was otherwise uninhabited. To get the troops across, every available boat had been rounded up and log rafts had been built that could be towed behind the warships. By the time Licinius learned of the invasion and started to mobilize, the army would already be across. Then the final battle could commence.

Over the next two days, the crossing was successfully made. The soldiers, horses, and materiel were loaded into boats—often overloaded, Rex thought—and ferried across the strait. Early on the second day, his twelve speculators arrived on the European side, so Rex took his leave from Crispus and reassumed command of his men. They crowded onto a raft and were towed over to Asia, where they reclaimed their horses and gear. Since they were skilled horsemen, the speculators had been tasked to function as a nimble and high-impact strike force wherever quick action was needed on the battlefield.

Once the whole army was safely across in Asia, Constantine and Crispus—the augustus and his caesar—led a triumphant cavalcade toward Chalcedon, where Licinius was based. But because the forward scouts began to make enemy contact around Chrysopolis, the army stopped on its outskirts instead. A field camp was constructed at the edge of a broad field surrounded by rolling hills. The Licinians moved up and camped on the other side of the open space. Now the game board was set. The pieces could only sit and wait for the match to begin.

After the tents had been erected and the ditches dug around the camp, Rex climbed a knoll and surveyed the contours of the battlefield. It was mostly level, though a few gullies and ravines split the land here and there. The view from the knoll was idyllic and pastoral, but Rex knew that wouldn't last much longer. Soon the wide, green meadow would be churned into a bog of brown mud and red blood.

The augustus and his son had ordered a prayer tent to be set up outside the camp. It functioned as a place of retreat and spiritual preparation. Crispus's former tutor Lactantius served as its chaplain. As the day of battle approached, a prayer service was appointed there on Sun Day at dawn, the hour of the Lord's resurrection. Since Rex was a deputized legate of Bishop Sylvester, he was invited to attend the ceremony as a representative of the Roman church. It was held under an open sky in front of the tent.

Surrounded by the officers and centurions, Lactantius delivered a rousing sermon from the story of David and Goliath in the first of the four *Books of Kings*. Using the gruff voice of the Philistine giant, Lactantius cried, "Am I a dog, that you come at me with sticks? I curse you by all my gods! Come now, you runt, so I can give your flesh to the birds of the air and your bones to the beasts of the field."

Then, switching over to David's more noble voice, Lactantius summoned all his rhetorical power and proclaimed the courageous reply of God's anointed: "Thou comest at me with a sword, and a spear, and a shield. But I come in the name of the Lord God of Hosts! And the Lord shall deliver thee into my hand. Then shall the whole world know that the Lord delivers not by sword or spear but by his own power and might. For the battle is the Lord's, and he shall deliver thee into our hands!" The cheering that this proclamation aroused was so loud, Rex thought it could probably be heard all the way to Licinius's tent.

At last, the day of battle arrived. It dawned bright and clear, with a crisp coolness in the air that hinted of the autumn to come. The hundred thousand Constantinian soldiers had arrayed themselves at the edge of the battlefield to face the hundred and thirty thousand enemy troops. In the center of the line were Constantine and Crispus, along with their standard-bearer, who wore a lion skin over his shoulders and carried the mighty Christian labarum. It was marked with the Greek letters chi and rho, the first two letters in the name of Christ, superimposed on one another: ☧. The army of Constantine would conquer by the sign of the cross.

Rex, however, was stationed off to the side with his speculators. Each man was fully armed. They wore high-quality chain mail and had iron helmets with green plumes for easy identification. Since their strategy was to be mobile, their horses had been selected for quickness and agility in battle.

"Let's get this job done," Rex said to his men. "Fight hard today and you'll be back to your women before the first snow, with gold in your purse and honor on your brow."

"And home cooking in our bellies!" added a freckle-faced youth from Gaul, a province where they knew a thing or two about fine food.

"That's right," Rex replied as he fastened the helmet's thong at his chin. "Now, tighten up your straps, boys. And may God go with us."

The sun was above the trees by the time the first sorties took place. The armies were like two pugilists testing each other with a few early jabs. But soon the battle was engaged in earnest. It was a traditional pitched battle with a preliminary exchange of missiles followed by successive clashes of infantry whose wings were protected by cavalry.

The most elite of Constantine's legions were stationed near the labarum. Its banner was made of brilliant purple cloth, and its top was crowned by a jeweled wreath that surrounded a chi-rho made of gold. Rex could see that wherever the labarum went, the Licinian legions fell back. Clearly, they perceived it to have dreadful power, so they wanted to fight in other places until the battle had turned their way. This afforded the Constantinian troops a significant advantage. They could initiate contact wherever they wanted and expect a retreat.

Yet as the labarum surged forward and was about to break the enemy lines, another combatant entered the fray: a detachment of Gothic mercenaries led by their muscular chieftain, Alica. His gods were of another tradition, so the Germani held no fear for the peace-loving God of the Christians. Alica fought his way toward the Christian war banner under the power and impetus of Thor. And Thor wasn't afraid of Christ.

Meanwhile, Rex's speculators had skirmished their way along the fringe of the battlefield to a location where a flanking strike would be effective. Their strategy had inadvertently brought them close to the place where Alica was striving to intercept the labarum. The battle grew fierce as two powerful forces converged at that spot. The ground was broken and uneven, making maneuvering difficult for the combatants. Death claimed many men from both armies.

Slowly, however, Constantine's legions began to prevail. Fighting with confidence and determination, they succeeded in pushing back the Gothic warriors. The battle was turning their way. Victory felt close. And then tragedy struck: a javelin came hurtling from the sky like a thunderbolt from Asgard. It impaled Constantine's standard-bearer through the chest. He collapsed to the ground and sent the labarum tumbling into a craggy ravine at the base of a gnarly oak.

"Now is our time!" Rex cried, putting his heels to his horse's flanks. "Follow me!" The labarum was the rallying point and inspiration for the whole Constantinian army. Holding it high was essential for securing a victory. Now it was down in a ditch. Rescuing the flag in the heat of battle was just the kind of mission for which the speculators existed.

As the twelve men galloped toward the ravine, they immediately encountered resistance. Sling bullets made of lead flew past them with high-pitched whistles or made loud bangs when they struck helmets and shields. The slingers' attack slowed down a few riders, but Rex pressed on and led them deeper into the fray.

A horde of Goths, locked in hard combat with the best of Constantine's legions, blocked the way to the ravine. Rex's men hit the rear of the Gothic contingent but didn't stop to engage them. Yet the Goths were fierce fighters, so any clash with them came at a cost. Blood was spilled as the speculators barreled into the melee. Finally, they managed to break through the tumult and reach the edge of the ditch. Rex headed for the gnarled tree where he had seen the labarum go down. He intended to recover it or die in the attempt.

But another band of Gothic riders had set their eyes on the craggy ravine as well. They, too, understood the symbolic significance of the Christian flag. These men had broken free of the main combat and were charging toward the tree. Instead of turning aside, Rex decided to meet them head-on. He urged his mount to go faster. His twelve warriors accelerated into the confrontation as if borne along by angels' wings.

The collision of the two sides was an enormous smashup. Bodies flew from saddles. Rex saw a severed Gothic head spin past him like a comet. He took an arm-numbing blow on his shield, then ran his spear through the throat of a mustached warrior with battle lust in his eyes. No sooner had he taken down that opponent when something clobbered him on the back of his helmet. Bright lights flashed before Rex's eyes. His body went limp. All sound disappeared. He fell sideways. A wall of green rushed up to meet him.

Rex hit the ground hard. Though the impact was bone jarring, it also knocked him back to reality. His instincts and training kicked in, causing him to roll across the turf to absorb the blow. Finally, he came to rest. Rising onto his hands and knees, Rex squinted and shook his head, trying to overcome the pain and disorientation. *Get up!* demanded a voice in his head. *Do it now or die!*

He scrambled to his feet and drew his sword. Glancing around, he saw no immediate opponent. The gnarled oak was a few paces away. Rex ran to it. After sliding down the jagged side of the ravine, he scanned the ground for the labarum. At first, it was nowhere to be seen. Then he spotted it—not lying on the ground but clenched in Alica's triumphant fist.

The Gothic warrior was a specimen of manhood like few Rex had ever seen. He must have been a foot taller than Rex, with shoulders so wide he could have set a yoke on them and put the oxen to shame. His arm muscles bulged inside his sleeves as if he had stowed melons there. Alica's helmet had fallen off, causing his long blond hair to blow in the wind like filaments of gold. The braid of his beard dangled from his chin with the kind of girth that made other men shrivel and shrink. Alica seemed like a pagan god walking the earth. Even so, Rex gripped his sword and began to advance. It was time for the old gods to die.

"That banner belongs to me," Rex said, "and I'm coming to take it."

Alica spat a gob of saliva on the flag. "I curse you and your god," he replied in deep, throaty German. Then he dropped the labarum, drew his sword, and charged at Rex with utter disdain.

The force of the warrior's onslaught was impressive, but Rex was experienced in war and had fought strong foes before. He didn't yield any ground but took the blows upon his shield and countered with thrusts of his own, forcing Alica to defend himself and not simply attack. Wooden splinters flew from the two men's shields as they hacked and slashed at each other. In between their assaults, they stepped back and circled each other with wary eyes, catching their breath, alert for any opportunity to make a killing strike.

Alica growled like a feral beast, his pale gray eyes fixed on Rex. "You cannot defeat me," he snarled. Yet even as he spoke, he circled toward the edge of a furrow in the earth that he hadn't seen.

Rex positioned himself so that his charge would make Alica step backward into the uneven ground. "You are defeated already," he declared, then threw himself at his opponent.

The Gothic chieftain held his stance as Rex came charging in. The two warriors found themselves locked in a contest of strength as they shoved each other with their shields. Neither man could bring his sword into action at such close quarters. Each combatant struggled to force the other one back. Then, in a surprise move, Rex brought up his knee and smashed Alica in the groin.

"Argh!" the Goth cried as the pain made him withdraw. His foot landed awkwardly in the rut behind him, and he tumbled onto his back. His sword skittered from his hand. And in that helpless instant, Rex stabbed Alica through the heart.

For what seemed like a long time, Rex returned the man's fierce yet impotent stare. At last, Alica's eyeballs rolled back and his eyelids fluttered. The light faded from his countenance. A final, raspy gurgle escaped his throat. Then death claimed him.

"And so it ends," Rex said. Still panting from the fierce exertion, he turned away from Alica's corpse and went to retrieve the Christian labarum.

Peeking out of the ravine, Rex found that the battle had shifted to a more distant place. His own men were farther away now, still engaged with the Gothic riders. Closer in, a squadron of Licinian cavalry had paused near the ravine to regroup. If a soldier in Constantinian armor were to emerge from the ditch with the labarum, the Licinians would descend on him like a swarm of demons. Unfortunately, some of Alica's men were now moving up the ravine in search of their commander. At any moment, Rex would be spotted by one enemy or another.

The Constantinian battle line was two stadia away across an empty field. It would be hard for a rider to outrun his pursuers over such a great distance. Mounted archers would be shooting at him the whole time. Yet hiding in a hole like a scared rabbit would only lead to discovery and death. There were no good options. The Goths were drawing near. Rex's best choice was to grab a horse and make a run for it.

Alica had hitched his mount to the gnarled oak when he went after the flag. The animal was no compact pony from the Sarmatian grasslands but a huge stallion with draught-horse bloodlines. The mighty beast was built for an all-out charge—which was a good thing because that was what Rex was about to try. After making the sign of the cross over himself, he clambered from the ditch and untied the stallion. Rex was in the saddle, labarum in hand, before any of the Licinians noticed him. But that obscurity didn't last long. A single shout arose, followed by a roar, and the chase was on.

The stallion wanted to run, so Rex had no problem motivating his mount to rise to a gallop. Its pace was smooth and its stride was long as it ate up the ground. Yet a glance over Rex's shoulder told him how much trouble he was in. Around a thousand men were surging after him like a wolf pack in pursuit of a wounded fawn. The labarum meant everything in this battle. Rex was its lone defender. Every man in the ravenous horde wanted to be the one to claim it.

Arrows began to whistle past Rex on either side as his pursuers loosed their deadly missiles. It was only a matter of time until one of the points struck the stallion's rump—or worse, Rex's spine. He had to get out of their range.

Squeezing his thighs, Rex directed the stallion toward a low, grassy slope. Though it wasn't on a direct course toward the Constantinian army, Rex thought that passing over its top would protect him from the arrows long enough to reach the safety of his own battle line. At least, he hoped it would.

Clang! An arrow grazed Rex's helmet with enough force to knock his head forward. Had the point hit him square on, it would have pierced his iron headpiece. He urged the stallion to press harder. If its courage and willpower failed, both man and beast would perish on the field of war.

Rex reached the base of the knoll and began to rise up its slope. Behind him, he could hear his pursuers' curses and shouts. Arrows flew past on the left and right. Rex felt his shoulders tense as he anticipated one of the shafts piercing him through.

But the top of the rise was close now. "Just a little more!" he shouted to the brave horse. "You can do it!"

The stallion dug deep and found even more speed. At last, Rex reached the summit. And as he crested the knoll, he beheld a sight he would never forget.

Galloping up the back side of the hill was a vast legion of Constantinian cavalry. There had to be five thousand riders surging up the slope, unseen by the Licinians who were chasing Rex. This mighty host was about to reach the crest and go spilling over its rim like lava flowing down the flanks of Mons Aetna. Death and destruction would follow in their wake.

Atop the knoll's summit, Rex reined up his horse and spun it around to face the enemy. The noble stallion reared on two legs and pawed the air with its hoofs. From within its broad chest it uttered a defiant whinny. "For Christ and Constantine!" Rex shouted as he raised the labarum to the noonday sun. And at the sound of those words, the five thousand riders surged past Rex and descended upon the terrified Licinians like the avenging whirlwind of God.

—◈—

OCTOBER 324

Constantine had decided he was tired of staring at city walls from the outside. After remaining outside of Hadrianopolis and Byzantium, then bypassing Chrysopolis after the victory on the battlefield, Constantine was looking forward to resuming a civilized, urban life again. In particular, he wanted a real bath. The city of Nicomedia was about to provide it.

"We won't have to capture it," Crispus suggested to his father as the two men examined Nicomedia's walls from their encampment before its western gate. "All we have to do is sit here and wait. That city will vomit out Licinius like a piece of rotten meat."

Crispus's prophecy was fulfilled even sooner than Constantine had expected. Later that afternoon, the gates opened and two people exited with their attendants. Guards immediately swarmed them and escorted them into the imperial camp.

The captain of the royal bodyguard approached Constantine. "Your Majesty," he announced, "an audience is requested by your half sister, Lady Julia Constantia, and the venerable Bishop Eusebius, along with their handmaids and deacons."

"I grant it," Constantine said, and the guests were brought to him.

It had been many years since the emperor had seen his half sister. Laying eyes on her now, he marveled at how much she looked like their father. Constantius had been a heavyset man. Similarly, Lady Constantia was a curvaceous, full-figured woman. Both of them had striking features and smooth, pale skin. Anyone would consider Constantia beautiful—except Licinius, who always mocked her as "fat." *Another crime to add to his list.*

The greetings were polite as the guests bowed before Constantine and Crispus, both of whom were seated on ornate camp chairs beneath a shady awning. Obviously, the visitors had come to beg for mercy. The battle at Chrysopolis had been a total rout, with twenty-five thousand enemy soldiers slain after the surprise charge over the knoll broke their spirit. In the end, Licinius's troops abandoned him, so he fled to Nicomedia. The Gothic mercenaries disappeared once they realized no loot was forthcoming. Now Licinius was holed up inside Nicomedia with a tiny garrison, surrounded by Constantine's vast army. His defeat was certain. Victory was near.

"My husband is ready to acknowledge your sole reign over the empire," Constantia declared after she greeted her brother with many compliments. "He is humbled and repentant for his odious misdeeds."

"Mercy is the way of the Lord," Eusebius added. He was a tall, skinny fellow with a beak-like nose and stringy white hair that draped to his shoulders. Constantine sensed in him the smooth aura of a political conniver. The two of them were distantly related, a connection the crafty bishop would no doubt exploit.

"Your words are true," Constantine acknowledged to Eusebius, "but the *Epistle to the Romans* also grants the power of capital punishment to the governing authorities. It is how God executes judgment on wrongdoers. As a man of the scriptures, you surely know this."

Before Eusebius could reply, Constantia turned and beckoned to her handmaids. They stepped aside and sent forth a short, thick-bodied person wearing a robe with a low-hanging hood. When the hood was pulled back, the person was revealed to be Licinius Junior. "Have mercy on your little nephew!" Constantia cried. "He needs a father!"

Constantine grimaced at what felt like an emotional ploy from his sister. Nevertheless, he agreed with the basic premise that Jesus Christ asked his followers to demonstrate extravagant mercy. "Take heart," he said in a kindly voice. "If Licinius the Elder will lie prostrate before me and swear loyalty, his life and that of his son will be spared. You shall live sequestered lives at Thessalonica, adequately cared for, though restricted to your dwelling. This I swear before God."

The sound that escaped Constantia's lips was a spontaneous squeal of relief. "Oh! Bless you, kind brother!"

"Go in peace," the emperor said.

As the emissaries from the city prepared to return, Crispus stopped Eusebius with a sharp command. "Wait, bishop!" Eusebius reluctantly turned back toward the stern-faced caesar. "Why did you support Licinius in this great war?"

"Your Majesty, he was the emperor of my territory. What else was I to do?"

"Licinius was a persecutor of your flock! A shedder of Christian blood! A man of obscene morals! What do you mean, 'What else was I to do?' You should have resisted this pagan persecutor like bishops have been doing for centuries! The blood of the martyrs cries out against you. When the hired hand sees the wolf coming, he abandons the sheep and the wolf pounces. But the good shepherd lays down his life for the sheep."

"I was hoping . . . that is, I asked God to let me keep my friendship with Licinius so I could—"

"So you could what? Face no danger? Shed no blood yourself? Keep your riches?"

"It was a strategy, Your Highness! When the persecution passed, I would be able to—"

"Be quiet!" Crispus ordered with his palm outstretched. "The prophet Jeremiah proclaims this word against you: 'Woe to the shepherds who destroy and scatter the sheep of my pasture!' Because of your dereliction of duty, Eusebius, you shall not preside at the thanksgiving service one week hence."

A red flush rose to the clergyman's face, suggesting both anger and shame. "Then who will lead it?"

"Bishop Ossius of Corduba, a man of true piety and wisdom, will celebrate the Eucharist. Now be gone from us, sir, before you are stripped of your clerical office altogether."

As the humiliated bishop turned to go, Constantine observed, "That was a stern rebuke, my son."

"Yet it was warranted, I believe. The blood of the martyrs is nothing to treat lightly."

Constantine nodded at this but said nothing. Privately, though, he marveled at his son's knack for discerning the spiritual ramifications of things that he himself often missed. *What a fine Christian augustus this young man is going to be! I will be honored to turn things over to him on my deathbed.*

A busy week passed during which Constantine entered Nicomedia and took up residence in the lavish palace of Diocletian. It was Emperor Diocletian who, forty years ago, had organized the fourfold system for governing the empire. But now that Imperial College was gone. Once again, Rome's vast domains had only one emperor ruling over them. And Constantine intended to let everyone know that the single emperor of the single empire had a single God. Christian monotheism, not pagan polytheism, was the future of Rome.

On the day of the thanksgiving service, Constantine and Crispus greeted Bishop Ossius in the reception hall at the palace. He was a distinguished Spaniard with silver locks and a debonair quality about him. Yet he was no superficial dandy. Everyone acknowledged the man's profound intellect and mature Christian piety. Crispus's former tutor, Lactantius, accompanied the Spanish bishop.

"Step out here to the balcony," Constantine invited his guests. "You must see the view."

As the four men went outside, they were met with a glorious vista of Nicomedia and the sea called the Propontis. But even more glorious was the view of the Christian basilica that had recently been rebuilt atop a nearby hill. Lactantius, in particular, seemed moved by the sight. "It's beautiful!" he exclaimed. "How well I remember when the great persecution started. What a terrible day that was, my brethren! The church that stood there was torn down by the Praetorian Guard with sledgehammers and axes. Everything was ransacked. The scriptures were burned. And then the blood of the martyrs began to flow across the empire."[1]

---

1. Lactantius recorded this story in his book *On the Deaths of the Persecutors*, ch. 12. A translation of his Latin text appears in my book *Early Christian Martyr Stories: An Evangelical Introduction with New Translations* (Grand Rapids: Baker Academic, 2014), 142.

Constantine shook his head and smiled broadly, gesturing with both of his palms lifted to heaven. "No more! From now on, everything shall be just the opposite. The church is standing strong, martyrdom has ended, and the Christians who were banished to the mines or stripped of their properties are being restored. It is a day for celebration!"

"Glory to God in the highest," Ossius said. The foursome nodded reverently, then went back inside and prepared to head over to the church.

When they arrived, the basilica was decorated with elegant tapestries and golden lampstands. Constantine did not assume the central seat in the apse, for that chair was reserved for a man of the clergy. Instead, he and Crispus remained standing like the rest of the congregation. They took up places near the rail where the congregants came to receive the bread and wine from the hands of the deacons, or even from Ossius himself.

The Spanish bishop gave a brief yet eloquent sermon on the theme of thanksgiving. The Greek verb *eucharisteo*, he said, was uttered at the Last Supper when Jesus "gave thanks" as he broke the bread and distributed the cup. The Holy Eucharist was named for, and pointed toward, this supreme reason for Christian thanksgiving.

After the scripture readings and homily were finished, the service moved into the Eucharistic liturgy itself. In solemn procession, the faithful came forward to receive the bread and wine. Constantine watched the service unfold without moving. Since he had not yet been baptized, he could not partake. Yet as he considered the beautiful surroundings, he decided it might be nice—at some distant point in the future—to be baptized in this magnificent church at Nicomedia. He wasn't sure, though, who could perform the ceremony now that the local bishop had been shamed. It was a question for another day.

A man who looked vaguely familiar came forward to meet Ossius and receive the communion bread. His wife was beside him, holding his hand. Constantine scrutinized the fellow for a moment, trying to place him. And then he remembered: the furniture maker from Thessalonica! The last time Constantine had seen this man, he was bedraggled from hard travel and his tortured hand was sorely infected. Now he was here at Nicomedia, working for the furniture guild and passing on his lore. He was clean, healed, and happy again.

"This is the body of Christ for you," Ossius intoned, offering the fragment.

"Thanks be to God," replied the furniture maker as he took the bread into his fingerless palm and passed it to his mouth. "The pagans who assaulted us are defeated. The empire is ruled by a Christian. I never thought I would see such a day as this!"

ACT 2

DEITY

5

The four oxen chosen for the holy duties today were completely white, symbolizing their purity and perfection. But Constantine didn't intend to shed their blood like was done in so many pagan rituals, or even like the Jews when their temple still stood in Hierusalem. Instead, the four oxen, yoked in pairs, were about to do their normal work: plow a straight line through the earth.

The whole imperial family stood before the main gate on Byzantium's landward side. Unlike when Constantine was here last—encamped on a knoll while attacking the massive walls in a siege—the gate now stood open to its rightful ruler. The road that emerged from the gate was the beginning of the great highway called the Egnatian Way. Constantine gazed down its length toward the west, marveling that it ran all the way to the coast of the Adriatic Sea. From there, it was but a short sail to the boot heel of Italy, then up the Appian Way to Rome. In a very real sense, the rising city of Byzantium was linked to the old capital by the paving stones beneath the emperor's feet.

Shaking away his musings about symbolic geography, Constantine returned his attention to the matter at hand. The ancient ceremony planned for the day was called a "delineation," the marking of sacred lines where new city walls would rise. It was time to expand the size of Byzantium. The crowd of onlookers, well-wishers, and imperial functionaries all wanted to know how far out from the old walls Constantine would draw the new line.

"Shall we be going?" Empress Helena asked. It was a chilly day, and she was shivering in her fur-lined shawl. "The carriage awaits. And truth be told, I'm freezing."

"You should ride in the coach with Fausta and the boys, Mother. Crispus and I shall ride in the saddle like generals."

The imperial procession set out with the royal carriage leading the way. Behind them was Constantine on an Arabian stallion whose tack was tasseled and gilded. He rode side by side with his son, who was on a Spanish mare in similar array. Then came the various palace bureaucrats, bodyguards, and civic leaders of Byzantium. Behind them walked the two pair of oxen with their handlers. A crowd of curious commoners brought up the rear.

When they reached the first milestone on the Egnatian Way, everyone expected the procession to stop. This was already much farther out than anyone had guessed the line would be drawn. The peninsula on whose tip Byzantium had been founded grew wider as a traveler moved inland. So with each passing footstep toward the west, the city grew bigger, not only along its east-west axis but also north to south as the peninsula widened. A massive new territory was being incorporated into ancient Byzantium— and that was just what Constantine wanted. He signaled for the journey to continue past the first milestone.

At a mile and a half, Crispus turned to his father as they rode through the suburban countryside. "This is quite a new city you're making here," he observed. "The newcomers will have plenty of room to build their houses. How far out do you plan to go?"

Constantine smiled and indicated the carriage ahead of him. "That's your fussy grandmother riding up there. She'll want to stretch her legs at some point. I'll just keep going until she who goes before me decides to stop—and we shall call that God's will!"

The emperor's prediction proved true at just past the two-mile mark. The coach halted and Helena alighted from it, followed by Fausta and her two eldest sons. Everyone called eight-year-old Constantine II "Secundus" to differentiate him from his father. The other boy had the similar-sounding name of Constantius. Fortunately, another family namesake wasn't present today to add to the confusion: Constantine's fourth son, Constans, was still just a toddler.

"How much farther must we go?" Helena asked as she smoothed her rumpled gown. "The road is rather bumpy out here."

Constantine glanced around at the beautiful countryside, then looked back at the thin line of the city walls two miles behind him. "This is the spot!" he proclaimed as he leapt down from the saddle with a spear in his hand. "Here the new walls of Byzantium shall rise!"

Bending to the earth, Constantine used his spear to carve a long line in the soil. Its northern end pointed to the coastline that met the estuary called the Golden Horn. The southern end of the line pointed toward the waters of the Propontis. To the east, the existing city faced the Bosporous Strait and the continent of Asia. And to the west, the Egnatian Way continued on to Rome.

After drawing a short intersecting line, Constantine planted his spear at the center of the cross. "My new Christian capital shall be a crossroads," he declared to those who had crowded around him. "By land, Europe is joined here to Asia. By sea, the Mediterranean is joined to the Euxine. And while the landscape you see all around is rural, it won't be for long! I am decreeing that a new senate shall be formed in this city. Any aristocrat from Italy who wishes to move here will be granted free land. Soon, people will be flocking here from afar. Byzantium will become the jewel of the world, a city with a glorious future!"

After these rousing words were met with approval from the onlookers, the two teams of oxen were brought to the cross in the earth. They were hitched to plows, facing opposite directions. Then at Constantine's command, one team began to cut a furrow to the north while the other proceeded south.

"Do not stop until you reach water," he ordered the plowmen as the oxen moved away. Then he added, "Let the masons start building the wall tomorrow."

"I'm freezing," Helena complained. "It's so cold today."

Constantine gave his mother his own cape in addition to hers. "Let's get you home," he said kindly, then the procession turned around and headed back into the city that was about to quadruple in size.

Two days later, the weather was much warmer when chariot races were scheduled for Byzantium's impressive hippodrome. Originally built by Septimius Severus to placate the citizens after he besieged their city during a rebellion, the giant racetrack was able to seat almost as many spectators as the Circus Maximus in Rome. Unfortunately, it was now 120 years old and showing signs of decay. As Constantine surveyed the massive edifice, he decided it could use an overhaul. If properly refurbished, the place could be truly magnificent.

Constantine turned to his wife as they sat in the imperial box and watched the chariots circle the spine in the track. "What do you think?" he asked. "Should I make this place my first priority?"

"It must be second after the walls," Fausta replied. "A city needs stout walls, or the next warlord to come along will ruin all the work you've done."

Crispus leaned over and joined the conversation. "Put the walls second and the hippodrome third. Make the Church of Holy Peace your first priority. Then everything else will fall into place."

Although Fausta rolled her eyes at this pious advice, Constantine thought it had merit. "So many competing priorities! But yes, God must come first."

When all the chariot races were finished, the Greens had won the day over the Blues, Whites, and Reds. The drivers were awarded trophies and rewards, while up in the stands, the spectators exchanged the money they had won or lost in their betting. But the day's festivities weren't over yet. Constantine had three great surprises in store for the people who had assembled.

A trumpet fanfare rang out, signaling to the crowd that all talking should cease. In the hush that followed, Constantine stepped to the front of the imperial box and began to speak in a loud voice. The acoustics of the hippodrome were such that his voice carried for a long distance, allowing thousands of people to hear him. And he knew that whatever he said would be passed along to those in the farthest seats, like sparks borne along by the wind.

After a warm greeting that expressed his paternal affection for the populace, Constantine began to make the announcements he had planned for the day. "For many centuries, everyone in Rome has received a daily ration of grain so that no man has to work for his daily bread. The people here deserve the same. Therefore I proclaim to you that from now on, the citizens of Byzantium shall receive a grain dole just like the Romans!"

The cheer that erupted at this amazing announcement went on for a very long time. Constantine took the opportunity to have Crispus and Secundus come and stand on either side of him. When the trumpets had finally quieted the crowd again, he proceeded to the second of his three announcements. "Behold!" he cried. "Your two caesars stand to the right and left of your augustus. But did not the great Diocletian devise a college of four? It must be so again! Today I elevate Constantius to the rank of caesar as well. And to commemorate this moment, every person in this hippodrome will receive a silver coin bearing his image!"

Once again, the cheering was almost unstoppable. Little Constantius, only seven years old and wide-eyed with wonder, came and stood in front of his father and two brothers at the railing of the imperial box. The exuberant spectators waved at him, and he waved back with boyish enthusiasm. Constantine beamed at the joyful proceedings, rejoicing in the knowledge that the people would forever associate his third son with a silver coin that had brought something nice into their homes.

The trumpets blared repeatedly, until a hush returned to the expectant crowd. Now Constantine was ready for his third and final announcement. "A thousand years ago, the great sailor Byzas came to this region from faraway Graecia, looking for a place to settle. He could see that this spot could command two seas and two continents. Since that day, the city of Byzantium has borne his name. But my people, listen to me! Today it is time to set aside the old and embrace the new. It is time for the west to give way to the east. And so, as your father of the fatherland, I proclaim that henceforth this city shall be the empire's new capital. From now on, it shall be called New Rome!"

For a long moment, a stunned silence hung over the crowd. Constantine assumed it was the calm before a storm of thunderous applause—but the applause never came. Instead, the silence turned into a general confusion among the crowd, with only some scattered and half-hearted clapping. Friends turned to one another to ascertain whether they had heard the words correctly. Everyone seemed bewildered. Clearly, the idea of replacing the old capital with a new one didn't have the appeal Constantine thought it would.

"Behold New Rome!" he repeated with his arms raised. But still, the crowd did not respond.

From somewhere in the stands, a voice shouted two words in Greek: "*Konstantinou Polis!*" Someone else repeated the two words right away. Soon, the whole area around the imperial box was shouting the same thing and stamping their feet. Like a wave rippling across the sea, the chant spread to the farthest reaches of the hippodrome. The building shook as everyone roared in unison, "City of Constantine! City of Constantine! City of Constantine!"

The surprised emperor let the chant continue for a long time. Eventually, the acclamation melted into general cheering. When the crowd's energy had finally run its course, Constantine was able to speak. He raised both hands and quieted the last of the boisterous spectators. The crowd fell silent, waiting to hear Constantine's response.

After holding still until the tension was about to reach its breaking point, Constantine issued his verdict. "Our new capital must be viewed as New Rome," he insisted, "for I intend to make it even more spectacular than its predecessor in the west. However, the name you have supplied today is good as well, for it comes from the affection of your heart. Therefore I proclaim, O people of former Byzantium, that I accept the name you have chosen!"

The announcement was greeted by a massive wave of adulation. The ovation from the hundred thousand spectators was deafening. Constantine could only step back, cover his ears, and try to take it in. There was nothing else to do; the people had spoken. Although he had intended for them to be New Romans, the people themselves had decided to be the citizens of Constantinople.

—◈—

As the ruler of a unified Roman Empire with a new capital, Constantine had decided to tour his newly acquired eastern domains—a decision that worked out perfectly for Rex. The emperor's final destination was going to be Alexandria, so Rex was invited to tag along with the entourage at imperial expense. His old friend Ossius, the emperor's trusted adviser, had made the request. Yet Constantine had needed no special persuasion. He was happy to reward Rex's faithful service in war. Now Rex expected to be in Flavia's arms before the end of November.

A ten-day journey by sea had brought all the travelers to Antiochia, a city Rex had long wanted to visit. He had read much about this ancient metropolis in his studies for the diaconate, especially in the *Acts of the Apostles*. It was here that the followers of the Way were first called "Christians" almost three hundred years ago. It was also from this city that Saint Paul had been sent on his evangelistic missions. Now, Rex approached the city gates under a political situation those earliest believers could never have imagined: the ruler of the Roman Empire was himself a Christian. The imperial entourage would even be visiting a church dedicated to Saint Peter. Antiochia's apostolic heritage was rivaled only by Hierusalem's. Rex looked forward to seeing what such a great Christian city might have in store for him.

Constantine was received into Antiochia with the same boisterous welcome he had received in every city during his tour of the East. The people of these newly conquered lands seemed united in one thing: they were glad to see Licinius go. Or at least, that's what all the citizens along the route were saying to the emperor who now ruled them. But Rex thought they weren't faking it. The warm reception felt real. And why not? Licinius had been a tyrant. Anyone would prefer a benevolent emperor like Constantine.

Bishop Ossius rode up next to Rex on horseback as they reached Antiochia's western bridge and gate. It led to a large island in the Orontes River where the imperial palace was located. "Rex, did you ever think we'd see such a day?" the gallant Spaniard asked with a smile. "What a change! We've been through some deep waters to get to a place like this."

"The first time I met you, you were literally in deep water," Rex remarked. "And it was on fire too."

"I remember it! You poured bitumen into the sea and set it ablaze. Ha! Those pirates were so frightened! They jumped overboard like rats on a sinking ship."

The two men exchanged memories about the day when Rex rescued the bishop from slave traders. After reminiscing about several other events, Ossius asked, "So how is Flavia? And . . . her dear mother?"

"They are both well, or at least, they were when I left them. But that was more than seven months ago. I can only hope the Lord has protected them while I've been gone."

"I'm sure he has, my son. He is the merciful keeper of his children. You must miss them."

"I do. Very much."

"Me too," Ossius said. Then he quickly added, "That is to say, I miss those days when we were traveling on the pope's mission. It was quite an adventure."

"Indeed, it was," Rex agreed, suppressing a smile. He said no more, and the two men parted as Ossius prompted his horse to a slightly faster pace.

The emperor's reception at Antiochia was even more enthusiastic than it had been in the other cities along the route. It seemed like every citizen had turned out to see their new ruler. They waved flags, many of them emblazoned with the chi-rho. This ancient Christian symbol had come to be firmly identified with Constantine's reign.

A three-day stay in Antiochia was planned for the imperial entourage. The travelers were glad for a rest after the wearying sea journey. Technically, Rex was still serving as the captain of the scout force for Caesar Crispus. Yet because the war was over and the speculators had been assigned to other duties, Rex had unlimited free time to enjoy the city. He took advantage of it—exploring churches, getting to know the local Christian population, and listening to the old-timers recount their ancient memories. He even met a direct descendant of Ignatius, the famous martyred bishop of Antiochia.

On the morning of the third day, however, Rex was summoned to the palace's throne room for an official event. An ecclesiastical embassy had arrived from Alexandria with urgent news for Constantine. The visitors were going to be welcomed with a dignified imperial reception, for Constantine now wanted all Christian bishops to be treated with the same honor as government officials.

In the little bedroom Rex had been assigned, he washed his face, combed his hair, and oiled his beard. He put on his best outfit—a long, maroon tunic with decorative emblems on the hem, worn over buff-colored trousers. After lacing up his newly shined boots and belting on an ornate sword, he stepped out of his bedroom and into the hallway. And when he did, he saw something that made his heart lurch, his eyes widen, and his jaw drop.

A woman was there, waiting for him.

Flavia!

He ran to her, and she to him, and they fell into an exuberant embrace, rejoicing at the end of their long separation.

"Oh, Rex!" Flavia exclaimed. "I've missed you so much!"

"And I've missed you, my beloved!" Rex kissed his wife on the lips—a joyous kiss of reunion more than a passionate one. The dignified halls of the imperial palace weren't the right place for amorous behavior. Yet Rex wasn't about to greet Flavia after a seven-month separation without a kiss.

"How come you're here?" he asked when they finally parted. He held both her hands and gazed into the beautiful face he had pictured every day since he left.

"A mission from Bishop Alexander. He sent Deacon Athanasius with an urgent letter for the emperor. It has to do with the schemes of Arius, back in Aegyptus. We were going to bypass Antiochia until we heard that Constantine was here, so we detoured."

"I guess you must have funded the trip. Is that why they let you come along?"

"Yes, but it was more than just gratitude for the donation. Athanasius is an insightful man—I would even say prophetic. He believes the time has come for me to reenter church affairs after a season of quiet. So he insisted that I join the men. But I had no idea I would run into you! When Bishop Ossius told me you were here, I rushed to the guards' quarters to find you."

"Did Ossius inquire about your mother?"

"He did," Flavia answered, then exchanged a grin with Rex.

Long ago, Ossius and Sophronia seemed affectionate with each other. Since their spiritual vocation of celibacy prevented anything romantic from developing between them, they settled for chaste friendship. Though life had parted their paths for a time, apparently their warm feelings hadn't faded. But that was a discussion for another day.

Rex offered his arm to his wife. "We'd better get going. We don't want to miss the reception."

Flavia took Rex's arm with a delighted smile. "Lead the way, handsome. I'm going wherever you are."

The couple arrived just as the event was starting. Constantine was seated in the apse of the throne room with a royal relative on either side: Caesar Crispus on his right and Lady Constantia on his left. The emperor's sister had been restored to a place of prominence now that her husband and son were banished to Thessalonica. Constantine had always had a soft spot for Constantia. To his credit, a spirit of mercy was triumphing over his normal tendency toward bitter revenge for any perceived betrayal.

After going through the initial pomp and circumstance that such imperial events required, the participants got down to the heart of the matter. They spoke with the flowery, formal speech always used at these occasions. Deacon Athanasius, representing the bishop of Alexandria, had come with bad news: the Arian faction had done what even Christ's crucifiers had not dared to do: rend the seamless garment of the Lord in half. The Arians had torn asunder the catholic church, which God intended to be whole. They had split away from their bishop and formed their own faction.

"Your Highness, you have read Alexander's letter," the fiery deacon said. "All the charges contained in it are true—the plotting, the greed, the conniving, the blasphemies. But worst among them is this: They say, 'There was a time when the Son of God did not exist' and 'Christ was just like us, able to do evil.' So they make Christ into a normal man—not truly divine, just a prophet who did righteous deeds. But I ask you, O pious Constantine: Was the Christ who gave you victory against Licinius just a regular man with good morals? Or is he the Lord of the cosmos who decrees all things?"

Rex could tell from the emperor's contemplative expression that the argument held weight with him. Constantine had a strong attraction to a cosmic Christ who ruled the universe from above. He believed that Christ had chosen him to rule the Roman Empire below, bringing peace and justice to lands where tyranny and persecution once reigned.

Before Constantine could reply, his sister leaned over and whispered something in his ear. Constantine listened to her words and nodded thoughtfully. Then he turned his attention back to Athanasius.

"I rebuke Father Arius," he announced, "for splitting the church at the very moment when, after forty years, the empire has been reunited under one ruler." Athanasius seemed gratified by this statement. But then Constantine startled the room with what he said next. "I also rebuke Bishop Alexander for raising inscrutable questions of theology before the sheep whom he should tend in simplicity. This sort of bickering does no service to the people of God! The debate is pointless and ought never have been raised among the common folk. It seems that both these brothers have erred in significant ways."

Though Athanasius was caught off guard by the unexpected criticism of his mentor, he did not back down. Pointing his finger at Lady Constantia, he said, "Your sister is an aqueduct of befouled water, Your Majesty! She pipes in the contamination of Eusebius of Nicomedia—and through him, the sewage of Arius!"

The bold statement, so shocking in its audacity, made the room fall silent. Though Constantia's eyes were wide, she held her tongue because her own situation was politically delicate. As for Constantine, he only grimaced and stared at the floor for a moment, then waved his hand and beckoned for Ossius to step forward.

"What is it, Your Highness?" the bishop asked when he was before the emperor.

"Brother Ossius, your reputation for wisdom comes from as far away as my empire stretches, from the land where the sun sets upon the end of the world. Therefore I task you with a job that demands a wise man. Accompany the good deacon back to his home at Alexandria. Make peace between Alexander and Arius, so that my heart will no longer be stricken by this strife and disunity."

"I will do my best, Your Majesty. Does this mean you shall not be continuing to Aegyptus yourself?"

"I shall not. By ridding the empire of Licinius's tyranny, I had hoped to bring unity and harmony to all mankind. But now that I see how Africa is rent by divisions, I can no longer continue my happy journey there. This quarreling over meaningless doctrine distresses me! It is back to Nicomedia for me. Yet I shall send you to Alexandria with a letter urging that these disputants forgive one another and restore my peaceful days and tranquil life. Take it hastily, Brother Ossius, so that this trivial squabbling can cease."

The bishop closed his eyes and dipped his chin to acknowledge his acceptance of the mission. "As you wish."

Though many in the tense throne room breathed a sigh of relief at these conciliatory words, Rex found himself unsettled. He looked over at Flavia. From her glance, he could see that she was troubled too. "Trivial squabbling?" he whispered to his wife. "I think it's more important than the emperor wants to believe."

Flavia nodded. "These doctrines determine who Jesus is. It is no trivial thing to call him a creature and a mere man."

"If Christ isn't divine, he can't forgive the sins of the world."

"It isn't the sins of the world I'm worried about," Flavia replied, "but the sins which are my own."

<hr>

DECEMBER 324

The sea journey to Alexandria took only nine days, and that included two days stuck in the port of Paphos on Cyprus while a thunderstorm raged. Flavia was so glad to be with Rex, she didn't mind the delay. She was also glad that their skipper had more sense than Saint Paul's captain in the *Book of Acts*, who foolishly set out in bad weather and shipwrecked his vessel. Though the skipper of Flavia's ship was a cautious little fellow who feared late-season sailing, he was opportunistic enough to transport high-paying passengers on an imperial mission. So long as he could sit tight whenever a storm blew up, it was a risk he was willing to take.

The route beyond Paphos required open-sea sailing, which meant all the passengers had to sleep aboard. Nighttime privacy was nonexistent, since everyone just wrapped up in woolen blankets on deck wherever they could find space. Yet even on land, the inns were crowded and the lodging was communal. The presence of Athanasius and Ossius made things even more awkward. Although Flavia would have preferred to have her own quarters, the public accommodations at least relieved her of one concern. She hadn't yet gotten up her courage to tell Rex about her vow of celibacy for a season of prayer. The ship's lack of privacy would defer that conversation until another day.

On the ninth day of the journey, a column of dark smoke from Alexandria's lighthouse was sighted off the bow. The ship made a beeline for it, and soon Flavia found herself disembarking in the harbor of her adopted city that now felt like home.

Rex inhaled deeply through his nose, seeming to savor the familiar scents. "I forgot what date palms smell like," he said with a satisfied smile. "And I can even smell the desert on the wind. It's good to be in Aegyptus again."

Bishop Alexander had come to the dock to welcome the Christian travelers. He went first to greet Athanasius and his esteemed guest, Bishop Ossius, who had never been to Aegyptus before. Flavia was much more excited to see her mother than her bishop. She ran to Sophronia, embracing her joyously even though they had been separated for only a few weeks. Sophronia also gave Rex a warm greeting. After commending him for his military service, she admitted that she was relieved to have her son-in-law back to care for her daughter again.

"Greetings to you, my lady," said a polite voice from behind the reunited trio. Everyone turned to see Ossius standing there with a kind of dashing nonchalance. The sea breeze had tousled his silver hair, leaving a lone strand dangling over his forehead. It would have made most men look disheveled, but somehow it made Ossius seem roguish and jaunty.

"Bishop Ossius, how wonderful to see you!" Sophronia answered smoothly. She leaned toward her friend and turned her cheek away. The bishop did the same and they made a kissing sound. The greeting was no different from the way two Christians of the opposite sex normally exchanged the kiss of peace at church. Even so, Flavia knew that for her mother, it was something more.

After a little chitchat and catching up, Ossius took his leave, but not before inviting everyone to a colloquium at the Catechetical School in two days. Alexander and Arius would present their views in a spirit of charity. It was hoped that common ground between them would be recognized by all. Sophronia promised to be there, which made Ossius smile and nod. "Let us pray for the Lord's peace," he said, then went on his way.

On the day of the colloquium, Flavia ascended the hill of the Serapeum behind her apartment building. Sophronia was with her, but Rex had gone ahead to save seats. The designated room was a lecture hall whose windows offered a beautiful view of the city. The seats were travertine benches on which Rex had set some cushions. A low platform made of red marble was at one end of the hall. Upon it stood an elevated pulpit with steps, ready for the disputants to take turns speaking. Ossius would serve as the neutral moderator. A good-sized crowd had already packed the room, so the late arrivals took seats on the floor.

The first order of business was to hear the letter sent by Emperor Constantine. A lector ascended to the pulpit and read it aloud. The emperor took the same approach in writing as he had taken in the reception hall at Antiochia. He expressed dismay at the theological rift that had emerged within the catholic faith just as it was supposed to give unity to his new empire. Then he chastised both Alexander and Arius for fomenting discord over metaphysical speculations that have no real importance. Constantine instructed the two men to be reconciled immediately. "Restore to me my calm days and carefree nights," the emperor implored, "so that from now on, the pleasure of clear light and the happiness of a peaceful life might be preserved for me."

Ossius then added his own exhortation: "Gentlemen, your emperor has spoken. Your theological squabbling must cease. We all believe that 'in the beginning was the Word' and 'the Word became flesh and dwelt among us.' Now it is time to agree upon what that means. Bishop Alexander, you may give your preamble."

With the august seriousness that befitted a bishop, Alexander rose from his chair and started for the pulpit. But then he stopped. Surprising everyone, he knelt on the red marble stage. After producing a piece of chalk from the folds of his robe, he drew a long vertical line. On one side he wrote *eternal*, and on the other, *creature*. Only then did he ascend the wooden pulpit. Several books of the scriptures lay nearby in case either of the disputants wished to quote from them.

Alexander cleared his throat. "Eternal God? Or God's creature? That, my beloved flock, is what must be decided today. There is no middle ground. Our Lord Jesus Christ is one of these, or he is the other. He cannot be both. And I cannot—I will not!—seek a reconciliation of views at the expense of doctrinal truth." After an emphatic pause, the bishop descended and took his seat again.

Now Arius hurried up the steps of the pulpit. "You forget, Master Churchman! In Aegyptus, priests have the right to decide their own doctrines. No one can tell me what to believe. If I want to call Christ a creature, I will—for that is exactly what he is."

"Watch yourself, brother," Ossius cautioned from his chair. "All pastors must submit their views before the rest of the church, before the archbishop of the flock, before the sacred scriptures, and ultimately, before God himself."

Arius wasn't at all chastened by the rebuke. He kept insisting that Alexander had no right to impose his views on everyone else. With polished eloquence, Arius made his case for priestly independence from episcopal oversight. At last, when his preamble was done, he began to speak in earnest about the doctrine of Christ.

"Too often, this debate has been made philosophical," he declared. "But what matters most for you and me, as people with sins upon our souls, is *salvation*. And let me tell you how it is achieved. Hear now the good news! Jesus Christ was a man capable of sins. Therefore he had to work hard to do right and earn God's favor. This Jesus—such a godly man was he!—kept striving toward God's high standard throughout his whole life, all the way to death on a cross. In the end, he was found to be a perfect creature who had done everything right. God honored him by taking him as a son. So, too, we have to imitate God's highest and best creature with similar obedience. If we do this, we, too, can earn God's favor—like our Brother Jesus who set before us such a fine example. Then we will also be sons of God, and we shall be welcomed into his blessed kingdom. That, my friends, is true Christianity."

Although the speech went on to say more than this, Flavia found that her emotions had become stirred and she lost focus. Strangely, she felt heat rise to her cheeks, so she fanned the neckline of her dress to cool herself. Eventually she was able to return her attention to the last part of Arius's oration. He summarized the things he had said at the outset, then concluded with a rousing exhortation to ascend to heaven through great moral effort.

Now it was Alexander's turn to take the pulpit. Although he wasn't nearly as eloquent as his skillful opponent, a holy fire burned in his eyes when he spoke. "This man claims to offer 'true Christianity' to you, but he is a liar like his serpentine father! Salvation doesn't consist of achieving virtue—an idea no different from what the Greek philosophers have long offered. Salvation is a gift of grace! It comes from God's initiative when he saw us falling into the sin of Adam. The Son of God, divine from all eternity, took on flesh and became a man. He lived a perfect life, offered himself upon the cross, and paid the debt of sin. Then God raised him to new life. Friends, listen to me! Salvation doesn't come from a creature whom we imitate. It comes from the eternal Word who defeated Satan, trampled death, and conquered sin on our behalf. You must believe in this gospel, and it alone, for salvation."

Alexander fell silent for a long moment. In the hushed silence of the room, he descended from the pulpit and went over to his chalk writing. There he scuffed out the word *ktisma* with his toe, taking his stand on *aionios* instead. "My beloved flock, hear the word of your pastor! Only this"—Alexander tapped his foot on the word *eternal*—"is true Christianity."

When Alexander said this, the restless feeling in Flavia's soul came rushing upon her again. Now she perceived the reason for her distress more clearly. Arius and Alexander were both talking about salvation. But Arius was offering steps the sinner could take to gain God's favor. In contrast, Bishop Alexander's advice was to rely solely on Christ. *But what if there are limits to how much God can forgive? Then there's nothing I can do to fix it!*

A panicky feeling tightened within Flavia's chest. There wasn't enough air to breathe. The crowd seemed to press too close. Leaping to her feet, Flavia bolted from the lecture hall.

Rex followed her immediately. He found her leaning against a column and trying to calm her breathing. "What's the matter?" he asked with concern on his face. "Are you alright?"

"I'm . . . I'm fine. It was just, you know, a fainting spell. It happens sometimes to me. I'm not sure why."

"Has it passed?"

"Yes, my love. I just needed some fresh air. It's gone now. We can start walking home."

"Are you sure? You still look shaken."

Flavia nodded and took her husband's arm. "Everything is fine," she said reassuringly. "Don't worry about me, Rex. Let's go home. There's nothing wrong at all."

—◦◦◦◦—

Though it rarely got cold in Alexandria, the winter mornings could be pleasantly crisp. Rex stood at the railing of his apartment's balcony with a cloak around his shoulders and a steaming cup of calda in his hands. He sipped it slowly as he watched the city rise, stretch, and begin its day.

When his cup was empty, he went back inside. He had hoped Flavia might come out and join him as she often did. Yet she remained in the bedroom, asleep under her covers. It was midmorning when she finally arose and Rex was able to speak with her.

"How are you feeling?" he ventured.

"Fine."

"In my experience," Rex said gently, "that answer usually means the opposite."

Flavia turned her attention from the potted ivy she was pruning and glanced over her shoulder at Rex. She offered a faint smile. "Maybe sometimes it does. But this time, I meant it. I'm fine."

"Are you feeling better after yesterday? I've rarely seen you so distressed like that."

Instead of answering, Flavia rose from the table and filled a vase from the faucet where running water entered the apartment. It was a luxury that those who lived near the Serapeum enjoyed, for water was piped to that high place from underground cisterns fed by a Nilus canal. Many nearby apartments had a supply from the Serapeum, and Flavia had always been grateful she could water her plants with its flow. Yet now, as she returned to her project, the wet vase slipped from her hands and shattered on the floor. Staring down at the broken shards, she began to cry.

Rex came and stood in front of Flavia, encircling her waist with his arms. She leaned into him, but her crying did not cease. "Don't worry, I'll clean it up, and I'll get you a new vase too." He paused, knowing these things weren't the real problem. Finally, he asked, "Are you sure you don't want to talk?"

Flavia didn't answer, but just let her tears flow freely. Eventually, her crying became a soft whimper, and then she was silent for a long time. Rex waited, holding her close while not offering any words. He knew from experience that his wife wanted only his presence at a time like this. When she was ready, she would share what was on her heart.

At last, she seemed ready to speak. And when she did, her words were shocking. Without raising her eyes to look at him, she simply said, "I worshiped the demons."

Though Rex managed not to flinch, he was taken by surprise. Idolatry was a terrible sin for a Christian, a transgression on the same level as murder or adultery. Many martyrs had shed their blood to avoid it. Those who hadn't been able to resist the compelled idolatry of the persecutions were asked by the church to go through a process of repentance and restoration after the persecutions had passed. For a Christian woman—especially someone as godly as Flavia—to enter a temple and hail a demon as lord was . . . well, it was indeed a grievous sin.

Yet Rex didn't say any of those things aloud, for Flavia already knew them. Instead, he said, "I don't judge you, my beloved. No one but our Savior resisted all temptations. It belongs to humans to fail. And it belongs to the God of grace to restore us when we do. There is hope for you."

"I believe that," Flavia said forlornly. "But then I read the scripture where Jesus said, 'Those whom I love, I rebuke and discipline.' Rex . . . I think God has disciplined me in a difficult way."

"How so?"

"*Ah!* It is so hard to tell you!" Tears returned to Flavia's eyes, but she pressed on with her confession. "We had a baby, Rex. From just before you left for Rome. Then after I worshiped Isis, I lost it. Do you think it was God's judgment?"

"I don't think God is like that," Rex whispered in Flavia's ear as he held her close. "He uses hard things to teach us. But he doesn't strike us out of anger and spite. We lost a child once before, and it drew us nearer to God. We can try again. God hasn't abandoned us."

Now Flavia separated from Rex's embrace and looked intently at him, searching his face. Her cheeks were wet, her eyes red and puffy. "You don't think I'm under his wrath?"

"God didn't destine us for wrath but to obtain salvation through our Lord Jesus Christ."

"Is that in the scriptures? I can't recall."

"Yes. The end of *First Thessalonians*."

Flavia's face brightened at Rex's mention of that biblical epistle. "Remember when we saw it? The original letter from Paul, right there in Thessalonica. Just before those bad men burnt it."

"I do remember it. Very clearly."

"Bishop Basil lost a hand trying to protect it," Flavia mused as sadness returned to her countenance. "Yet I couldn't even trust the Lord for a simple pregnancy. I had to appeal to a goddess like an unbeliever."

"But within the church, there is forgiveness."

"I know. I've begun a process of restoration with Athanasius. He is a spiritual adviser to me." Flavia let out a deep sigh, then glanced at Rex with tentative eyes. "Something important has been laid on my heart. You might not like it. But I think . . . I think it is from the Lord."

"Tell me."

Now Flavia grew apprehensive about what she wanted to say. Rex took her hand in both of his, stroking it gently, and that seemed to help her. She gathered her courage and told him about her desire for abstinence during a season of prayer, as mentioned in *First Corinthians*. The news was surprising to Rex, yet he tried to understand his wife's perspective. "Is it like a penance?" he asked.

"No! It's so we can be devoted to prayer about holiness . . . and about the possibility of children."

Rex wasn't sure what to say next. The news had caught him off guard. He wanted to be supportive. Yet the decision would come with a cost. To test the way forward, he asked Flavia a practical question: "How long are you thinking?"

"I don't know," she answered. "Long enough to have a spiritual effect. That's all I can say at this point. Rex, do you understand my heart? Do you agree with me on this?"

Stepping close to Flavia, he gazed down at her beautiful face. Her reddened eyes had cleared and had a look of hope in them again. With his thumb, he wiped away the last of the moisture from her cheeks. He smiled warmly to show his support. "I agree with you," he said, then kissed her lightly on the forehead.

She fell into his arms, embracing him tightly. "Oh, Rex," she sighed. "I love you so much."

"I love you too," he answered, "and love never fails."

<hr />

Arius opened the door and welcomed his eight guests into his private study, a well-appointed room attached to the Martyrium of Saint Mark. The visitors were all large men from surrounding Boukolia, and they had the rough appearance so common to herders. Some of them tended sheep, others looked after goats or pigs or cattle. The smell of their bucolic occupation was thick upon them. Yet they were beloved children of God—and also, Arius reminded himself, very useful for God's purposes.

"We are honored to be invited here," said a long-limbed shepherd clutching his cap in his hand.

"The honor is mine," Arius replied smoothly, "for we are brethren united against a common enemy. Look here!" He snatched a pamphlet off his desk and showed it to the men. It was exactly the kind of papyrus handbill that advertisers made for political elections or gladiator games—except this one was making a theological statement, not a commercial one. Since Arius knew his guests couldn't read, he relied on the picture to make the pamphlet's point clear. It showed Arius with his pointy beard preaching to a congregation, but with the body of a snake. Meanwhile, Bishop Alexander, recognizable by his wig, looked on with disapproval. And a divine hand held a sword over Arius's serpentine image.

"It's a disgrace!" said the leader of the herdsmen. "It mocks you, Father Arius!"

"I agree. Even though it comes from the commoners and not the bishop, it still shows the kind of leader he is. Now we must respond with countermeasures of our own."

"We stand ready to help," the shepherd said, and his seven associates earnestly nodded their agreement.

"Good. I know I can trust you men. And let me be clear about what is at stake. Souls will go to hell because people aren't motivated to pursue the good works that earn salvation."

"We cannot let that happen!" cried the shepherd.

"We must not," added a husky fellow wearing the high boots of a pig herder.

"You shall not," Arius declared, "and here is how you can prevent it."

After Arius had outlined his plan to his assistants, he dismissed them before any worshipers arrived for the liturgy. Now that Sun Day was an imperial holiday due to Constantine's decree, church services were no longer held at dawn because people had leisure throughout the day. But soon the congregants began to show up. When the Martyrium of Saint Mark was full, Arius proceeded down the middle of the hall with his deacons, acolytes, and lectors. He took a seat behind the altar in his acacia-wood chair. Once the greetings, prayers, and scripture readings were finished, he began to preach. His text was the passage at the beginning of John's gospel where Jesus clears the temple of money changers.

The people were thoroughly engaged with the sermon, and Arius could feel their energy. After about an hour of stirring oratory, he sensed it was time to issue a call to action. "Do you notice, my brethren, which holy psalm came to the disciples' minds? It is the sixty-eighth, where it says, 'Zeal for thine house hath consumed me.' So I ask you, does such holy zeal consume you as well?"

At this prearranged signal, the tall shepherd cried out, "It does! What must we do?"

Without missing a beat, Arius replied, "Do what Christ did, my brother! You must cleanse the house of the Lord with purging fire and overturn the tables of his false worshipers. Is this the will of God's people?"

"It is!" shouted the eight herders who had met earlier with Arius. Immediately their enthusiasm caught on, for the foundations of zealotry had been well laid by the rousing sermon. Soon everyone in the church was proclaiming their agreement.

Now Arius arose from his chair and withdrew something from beneath it. He kept the item hidden as he approached the altar. Everyone fell silent and stared at him, since it was strange for a priest to stand up during his sermon. They waited to see what he would produce from behind his back.

"Let the faithful expel the trespassers from God's temple!" Arius cried, then dropped a herder's whip onto the altar that stood above the relics of Saint Mark.

For a long moment, no one spoke, nor even moved. Then the leader of the herders dashed to the altar and snatched up the whip. "Zeal for God's house consumes me!" he exclaimed to the congregation with a loud crack of the lash. And then, like a volcano erupting, an agitated crowd of Arian fanatics surged out the church's door and spilled into the street.

~⚬~

One of Rex's occasional duties in the diaconate was to serve as a lector during the service of the Holy Eucharist. It wasn't a duty he enjoyed, because

Greek was his third language, after German and Latin, so he didn't feel especially fluent. His conversational Greek was fine, but reading the words of scripture in front of the church took him out of his comfort zone. Even so, he performed the duty whenever he was asked because God preferred humility over expertise.

Rex was reading the psalm for the day when he heard a distant commotion outside. Since all cities had disturbances from time to time, he wasn't particularly concerned. Yet he also knew that no one in the Church of Theonas had the ability to fend off an angry mob if things took a bad turn. Rex was the only person among the hundred or so assembled today who had that sort of training.

He broke off from his reading—ironically, it was "he trains my hands for battle"—and hurried to the church's only entrance. A gang of inflamed herdsmen was marching down Canopus Avenue. Rex heard enough theological jargon in their howling to realize that his church was the object of their wrath. One of the men spotted him and shouted a curse. Then they all broke into a run.

Rex dashed to the altar and seized a bronze candlestick that stood beside it. Returning to the door, he found four husky men with clubs about to rush inside. Though Rex's combat training kicked in, he refrained from the use of deadly force. A few head shots with the heavy candlestick could have easily killed the four unskilled ruffians. Instead, using the bronze rod like a quarterstaff, he broke a few ribs and left the attackers writhing on the church's porch. But the rest of the mob was close behind. Rex slammed the door and barred it with the candlestick instead of its normal wooden slat.

Turning back to the congregation, he saw a frightened look in their eyes. Only Flavia looked unafraid. She came forward with Athanasius, who was in charge of the service today because the bishop was visiting the monks of the desert. Although Athanasius was a bold and courageous churchman, he was also a short fellow with a slender frame. "What should we do now?" he asked.

Before Rex could answer, a fireball came sailing through a high window in the clerestory. Since the Alexandrians didn't use windowpanes because there was rarely any cold or rain, the burning object was able to sail right through. The people shrieked and dodged out of its way as it landed on the floor in a shower of sparks. It was a pitch-soaked bundle of rags that had been tied into a wad and set aflame. Clearly, the mob outside intended to burn down the church.

Someone pounded on the front door. "Open it!" the rough voice demanded. "Or we'll burn you inside if we have to!"

"We should go out," Athanasius said. "It's better to take our chances in the public streets than die in a—"

The little deacon broke off his words as a second fireball hurtled down from the windows, followed immediately by a third. Black smoke billowed among the rafters, while dark tendrils trickled from under the front door. It would only be a short time before the air in the church was unbreathable. Already, many of the congregants were coughing, and the elderly were leaning on others for support.

"Rex, if we go out that door, blood will be shed," Flavia said. "Some of our people will surely be killed."

"But we'll all die if we stay in here," Athanasius countered. "We have to open the door."

Now everyone looked to Rex to make a decision. Instantly his mind grasped the situation and he assessed each possibility. *Other exits? None. Windows? Too high. Smother the fires? Too many. Out the door? People will die. What's left?*

Down!

Rex knew that the Church of Theonas was built over the former site of a Mithraeum. The followers of Mithras were often mistaken for Christians because they also worshiped a savior deity who descended into the underworld and returned. Mithraeums, where those worshipers ate a sacred meal, were built to look like caves. Rex turned to Athanasius and asked him exactly where the Mithraic shrine was located beneath the church's floor plan. "Not far from the street," was his reply.

Near the front door of the church was a flagstone whose mortar had grown crumbly. Rex returned to the altar and grabbed the second candlestick on the other side. After yanking the candle off the pricket, he inserted the sharp spike into the groove around the stone. Using the rod as a pry bar, he lifted the stone until some other Christian men could pull it out.

Rex scooped away some dirt to reveal the top of a brick vault in the hole. "Stand back," he said to the people standing nearby—then smashed the butt end of the candlestick against the brick.

After four hard strikes, the vaulted ceiling broke away. Rex knocked off some remaining pieces of brickwork with a couple more jabs until the opening was big enough for him to fit through. He knelt and peered into the hole. In the gloom below, he saw the marble face of Mithras staring back at him with wild, ecstatic eyes.

Dropping into the opening, Rex used the statue of Mithras slaying a bull as a stepping-stone to reach the ground. The Mithraeum was dank and musty, not having been open to fresh air for more than a hundred years. It had benches along both sides. Unfortunately, its staircase that once exited onto the street was now completely blocked.

Frustrated at being thwarted, Rex glanced around for another way out. The smoke was thick in the church above, and many of the Christians were coughing and hacking. The danger to them was growing with each passing moment. And then Rex's eyes fell on the solution he was looking for. He spotted a hand pump on the wall.

Unbeknownst to the citizens of Alexandria, the ground beneath their feet was honeycombed by a vast, subterranean city that only the watermen ever saw. The whole urban landscape was superimposed upon a series of interconnected cisterns that filled up every year when the Nilus River flooded. Rex knew that if there was a pump in the Mithraeum for sacred washings, it had to be drawing from a cistern on the other side.

"Flavia!" he shouted through the hole he had made. "Hand me the candlestick, then start bringing everyone down!"

She grabbed the bronze pole and passed it to Rex. While she clambered down into the Mithraeum and began to help the others descend, Rex knelt beside the pump and passed his hand back and forth across the wall. Soon he found what he was looking for. A tiny hole was admitting a flow of air, which meant there had to be a cavity on the other side that was connected to the surface.

Bracing his feet securely, Rex held the candlestick in two hands and smashed its sturdy base against the weak point where the hole was. This time, multiple strikes weren't required. The fragile old wall broke under the powerful impact. Rex kicked away more stones from the hole, then squatted and looked inside. The cistern's water level wasn't far below. Though the water was murky, Rex was gratified to see a little light glinting on its surface. That meant there was an exit nearby.

After sticking his feet through the opening he had just made, Rex jumped in. His feet touched bottom with the water up to his chest. Splashing across the cistern to its far wall, he peered into the conduit that brought in the water. Not far down the line, a shaft of sunlight shone into it from above. Rex pulled himself out of the water and wriggled into the conduit. The pipe was big enough for him to crawl ahead. When he was under the access hole for the watermen, he stood up, pushed the iron grate out of the way, and peeked out at street level. The place was a deserted alley around the corner from the Church of Theonas.

After crawling back to the cistern, Rex found that Flavia had already entered the water and waded across to meet him. He helped her clamber into the conduit. Behind her, the escaping Christians followed her lead. One by one, they entered the conduit and crawled down its length to the access shaft. Rex and Flavia climbed out and began to help the people get up. Once everyone had emerged from underground, Rex sent them to their homes through a lane that went in the opposite direction from the riot at the church.

Only Athanasius remained behind with Rex and Flavia. All three were sopping wet and cold, yet that was a small price to pay for escaping the wrath of the Arian radicals.

"Bishop Alexander will be furious when he hears about this attack!" the little deacon exclaimed.

"Constantine will be even angrier," Rex said. "Burning down the other side's church wasn't what he had in mind when he told the two factions to make peace."

Flavia sighed and shook her head. "We've reached a new low. I don't see how a resolution can be found. The Alexandrian church is split in two. We need help from outside."

"That's right, Flavia," Athanasius agreed. "We need wisdom from the rest of Christ's body. We must try something that has never before been done in the history of our faith."

Rex was intrigued by the deacon's words, and he could see Flavia was too. "What is it?" he asked.

Athanasius gazed at the heavens for a moment, then returned his eyes to his friends. "In the providence of God," he declared, "the time has come for a worldwide council of the whole Christian church."

6

DECEMBER 324

Though the wintry Sun Day was bright and beautiful, Flavia couldn't get her heart settled on worship. She felt frustrated that she couldn't be in her own church today. The rampage at the basilica the previous Sun Day had destroyed the beautiful door and left smoke marks everywhere. The carpenters who inspected the roof found many charred spots where sparks had lodged in the rafters. Flavia thanked God that his divine hand extinguished those flames before they could bring down the building. Though it was a close call, the Church of Theonas would survive. Yet its repairs meant Flavia had to worship in a different neighborhood today, a former house church in the city center.

After the service, Flavia spent some time with Athanasius in confession and spiritual devotions. Her season of marital abstinence still continued, not only out of choice but because Rex had once again departed the city. Bishop Ossius had left Alexandria immediately to take news of the Arian assault to Constantine. The imperial mission to achieve peace had failed, and now the goal was to summon a worldwide council with the emperor's permission and funding. Rex was asked to accompany the bishop because the riot had proved that tensions were running high. Violence and bloodshed were no longer out of the question.

Flavia understood why Rex was asked to go along. Yet she had been surprised—and pleased, actually—to learn that her mother had also been

191

invited to assist Ossius. Sophronia's relationship with the Spanish bishop, while entirely chaste, was nevertheless one of genuine affection. Their co-operation resulted in mutual blessing. Flavia was glad those two could gain from each other the warm companionship both of them needed.

"Your mind seems to be wandering today, my friend," Athanasius said with humor, yet also with a hint of reproof. He was sitting with Flavia in the rear courtyard of the urban domus that now served as a full-time church.

"I'm sorry! I think the riot has thrown me off-balance. I keep thinking about it, then I lose my focus and my mind drifts to other things."

"It was a scary experience."

"It's not even the scariness that bothers me. I've been through much worse. It's just the outrage of it all. For so-called Christians to attack another church—and during the Eucharist! Who would do such a thing?"

"Now we know, don't we?"

Flavia glanced over at Athanasius, a man five years younger than she yet already endowed with the spiritual power of an ancient saint. Athanasius had been saying that he sensed Flavia's life was turning, that it was time for her to become active again in larger affairs. Now an idea occurred to her that fit his description. It was the sort of audacious deed that had marked Flavia's life before she settled in Alexandria. "Would you be interested in some sleuthing?" she asked her friend.

The young deacon's face was noncommittal. "What do you have in mind?"

"The city magistrates are dragging their feet in prosecuting the rioters. They say they have no reason to believe the mob got its start at Arius's church. If we could find some evidence there—torches or pitch or something like that—we could make sure those criminals are brought to justice."

"Did you notice the patch that some of those men had sewn on their tunics?"

"Yes! The eye inside the triangle. What is it?"

"I believe the Arians consider it a symbol for their view of God. But it's really just the Eye of Horus, a god whom many conflate with Jesus. If we found garments with this insignia at the Martyrium of Saint Mark, it would prove that the arsonists were sent from there."

Flavia shuddered as she recalled seeing the infant Horus in the lap of Isis at the temple. Instead of dwelling on that painful memory, she said, "Shall we go out to Boukolia and see what we can find?"

"Lead the way, Flavia," Athanasius replied. So she did.

The two sleuths headed down Canopus Avenue and exited through the Sun Gate. They arrived at the Martyrium—*so-called* Martyrium, Flavia reminded herself, because the relics of Mark weren't actually there—after the service when everyone had already gone home. The church was still open, so they went inside, hoping they'd be seen as worshipers seeking a quiet place for prayer.

The building was simple, and it didn't take long to determine they would find nothing of interest there. The empty hall was demarcated into three parallel sections by two rows of columns. At the far end was the altar and a preacher's chair like every other church. A door led to a private room for Arius, but it was locked. A quick scan outside revealed that the room's windows were shuttered tight.

Athanasius looked at Flavia and shrugged. "Should we head back?"

"Not yet." Though she wasn't a trained speculator like Rex, Flavia had picked up a lot of his spycraft in their adventures over the years. "Some of those rioters were herdsmen, right?"

"Yes. The men of Boukolia keep animals here because of all the grass. They're a rough lot. Robbers, many of them. Even some murderers."

"Did you notice the ones who fought Rex on the porch? They had the eye insignia sewn on their tunics. And they weren't herders. They had a different occupation."

Athanasius looked perplexed. "Really? How do you know?"

"Their tools!" Flavia said triumphantly. "There were carrying tools to damage our church. When Rex hit them with the candlestick, they dropped them on the porch."

"I didn't notice."

"I did. Hammers and chisels. Those men were stonecutters."

Now Athanasius's eyes widened as the significance dawned on him. "Fossors!" he exclaimed, then pointed over his shoulder. "From the necropolis!"

The Martyrium of Saint Mark was located near many Christian and Jewish graves. The area between the chapel and the coastline was filled with ancient tombs. Many of them were aboveground, forming little houses for shrouded corpses or their cremated ashes in urns. The outskirts of Alexandria even had some underground catacombs, though not many, since the local bedrock was harder to cut than the soft tuff around Rome. Though Flavia didn't think the day's spying would require a subterranean visit, the contents of the gravediggers' headquarters might be interesting—if they could find a way to get inside.

Flavia and Athanasius approached the city of the dead with the hoods of their cloaks pulled over their heads. A few people were visiting the tombs of their family members, but for the most part the place was deserted. A little wandering brought the two sleuths to the hall where the fossors gathered for the meetings of their college. A man was inside, snoozing on a stool with his feet propped up.

"Ah! We can't get in," Athanasius said. "We were so close! But they have a guard."

Flavia glanced sideways at her friend, her eyebrows arched. "Are you kidding me? We're going right in. Here's our plan."

After Flavia explained her strategy, Athanasius hurried over to a donkey hitched to a two-wheeled cart. The young deacon unlooped its reins from a post. Once seated in the cart, he snapped the reins hard enough to elicit a bray from the startled beast. As it started to gallop toward the distant seashore with Athanasius jostling behind, the sleepy gravedigger emerged from his office. "Someone stop that man!" he shouted, then took off running after the supposed thief.

Now Flavia had the fossors' headquarters to herself. Since tradesmen's guilds typically offered meals for their members, the place had a small dining room. Though it was empty, when Flavia peeked into the kitchen, she spotted a storeroom on the far wall.

The storeroom shelves were filled with various foodstuffs but no torches or pitch-soaked rags. Nor were there any weapons. Yet a basket on a top shelf looked intriguing. Flavia took it down. Inside she found needles, thread, and a wooden box. She opened it. *The Eye of Horus!* Flavia reached into the box and plucked out a patch like the ones sewn on the garments of the men who attacked the church. Here was the evidence she needed to tie the crime of arson to the gravediggers of Arius. She was about to go when a man grabbed her by the shoulders.

"Caught ya, thief!" he cried.

Flavia's captor was a big brute with pimple-covered cheeks. She protested and tried to wriggle away, but the man was too strong. "You're comin' with me," he snarled as he dragged her out to the main room.

Another man was there, a more intelligent fellow who identified himself as the chief fossor for the cemetery. While the pimply thug held Flavia in place, the man in charge began to ask her a series of questions. "Why did you come here with Deacon Athanasius?"

"Prob'ly sinnin' in the bushes!" exclaimed the brute.

Flavia ignored the crude remark and tried to fib about a dead relative needing burial. But the chief fossor wasn't buying it. "I know you're married to that tall German who works for Alexander," he accused. "You're working against the true faith! Tell me where Bishop Ossius went or things are going to go real bad for you."

"I don't know anything about Ossius. He's here in the city somewhere."

"She's lyin', boss! Put the fire to her arm. Then she'll sing!"

"We can leave no marks," the chief fossor said, "but I think this lady could use a good baptism."

With a wicked cackle, the pimply brute forced Flavia to her knees. A mop bucket filled to its brim with filthy water was scooted under her face. Before Flavia could snatch a breath, her face was forced into the slop. She struggled, but the fingers on the back of her neck were like an eagle's talons. Even when her air started to run out, her tormentor didn't let her up. Flavia's lungs were in agony, and the urge to breathe was more than she could stand. *God help me! These men are going to drown me!*

At last, the man released his fierce grip and Flavia threw back her head. She gasped and choked as she tried to suck in the air she so badly needed. Her lungs heaved. Water trickled down her throat and made her sputter. Globs of black slime dribbled from her lips. Panting, she remained on her hands and knees with her head hanging down until she finally caught her breath. Exhausted, she could only whimper at the terrible ordeal.

"Do it again," the chief fossor ordered, and the talons once again tightened on Flavia's neck.

"Nicomedia," she said.

"What was that, little lady?"

"Bishop Ossius went to Nicomedia yesterday." Flavia spat out another wad of grime, then raised her head and stared into the chief fossor's beady eyes. "That's right! He's on his way there now. The emperor's most trusted adviser is about to tell him everything that happened here. Your attack on our church will be reported to Constantine's ears within a fortnight! Then your violence will be brought into the open. Constantine will side with us!"

The chief fossor gave Flavia a disdainful look. "I doubt it. Not if he hears the story from our side first." Gesturing toward his pimply henchman, he said, "Throw that dirty heretic out the door, then go find Father Arius. Tell him I have some important news. We have some travel plans to arrange."

———

JANUARY 325

Rex walked down the gangplank of the Phoenician freighter carrying three heavy packs—his own, along with Ossius's and Sophronia's. The two of them were discussing departure plans with the ship's captain while Rex got their luggage onto Caesarea's dock. The stopover on the way to Nicomedia would last a few days, so everything had to be unloaded. Though neither Ossius nor Sophronia were frail, Rex still preferred to do the heavy lifting for his esteemed friends. *And it never hurts to keep your mother-in-law happy*, he reminded himself with a chuckle.

The trip up from Alexandria had taken ten days instead of the usual five because each time a winter squall arose, the captain hunkered down in a port, including three wasted days in Ascalon. But Ossius wasn't too concerned about it. Since there wasn't a deadline to bring Constantine the news about the Arian attack on the church—and Ossius wasn't looking forward to reporting his failure to make peace between the factions—the bishop thought it best to visit some Christian leaders along the way and solidify their support. Rex, however, just wanted to get home to Flavia as soon as he could. Yet it wasn't his call to make.

Now he was in Caesarea, commonly called Seaside Caesarea to differentiate it from others with that name. From what he had already seen, Rex could tell it was a remarkable place. Its ancient patron, Herod the Great, had made it into a glorious city by building long moles into the sea to form the harbor where the freighter was now docked. This created a safe port that allowed ships to come from afar to this otherwise smooth stretch of coastline. It was an impressive construction, though Rex thought the lighthouse on the breakwater's tip looked rather small compared to the one back in Alexandria.

By far the most imposing sight at Caesarea was what Rex was looking at now. Though the terrain was flat, King Herod built a high platform surmounted by a temple for the worship of his patron: the founder of the empire, Caesar Augustus. The temple gleamed as if lit from within, though Rex reminded himself God's sun actually illumined it. Only darkness could be found in emperor worship, a pagan requirement that had claimed the blood of many a Christian martyr.

A familiar voice from behind made Rex turn around. "Many thanks, my brother, for being not only our guardian but our camel!" Ossius said with a smile as he descended the gangplank, followed by Sophronia.

"And thank you from me as well," Sophronia added, "though I have to admit, I have never seen a three-humped camel before!"

Rex was about to make a joking reply about the heavy luggage when a man interrupted them, hailing the threesome with an enthusiastic welcome. He was a short, chubby fellow with a scalp that was bald except for shaggy tufts behind his ears. His tunic was decorated with chi-rho emblems set in roundels on the hem.

"Bishop Eusebius, it is a pleasure to see you again," Ossius said with a gracious dip of his chin. Introductions were made to Sophronia and Rex, then the portly bishop led his guests through Caesarea's streets to a quiet neighborhood in the north. It was a lovely area near the coast, yet not as opulent as the imperial city center or the monumental south, where Herod's old palace was built.

The main church of Caesarea didn't yet use the new architectural model of a basilica. The building to which Eusebius led his guests was instead an urban domus whose second story had a wide balcony that gave a view of the sea. Eusebius turned to Ossius with a twinkle in his eyes. "This house has always been in Christian hands, ever since the days of the apostles. Can you guess whose it is?"

"The centurion Cornelius?" Ossius ventured.

"A good guess, but no. It belonged to Philip the deacon—he who baptized the Ethiopian eunuch and had four daughters who prophesied. The canonical *Acts* tells us that Philip gave hospitality to the apostle Paul on his way to Hierusalem. Great Christian events happened here!"

"Then this is the perfect house of worship for a church historian like yourself."

"Historian and librarian," Eusebius said with uncontainable enthusiasm. "Follow me and I'll show you."

The energetic little bishop ushered his guests into what was once a peristyle garden with two stories. Above and below, bedrooms opened onto a covered walkway around the garden, but these rooms were no longer used for sleeping. Instead, the walls of each were lined with book cupboards. Rex immediately recognized where he was, for he had heard of this famous place. It was the Christian library of Caesarea, whose biblical and theological holdings surpassed even those of the Catechetical School at Alexandria.

Sophronia pointed to a massive codex that lay open on its own table. The book was so big that it was surely never moved about, only consulted where it lay. "What is that great volume?"

Though Eusebius seemed to grin constantly, somehow his smile grew even wider. "Come and see!" he cried as he waddled over. His guests followed him.

Every page of the book was divided into six columns. The first was Hebrew, the second contained Greek letters that made no sense to Rex, and the final four were versions of the Greek Old Testament. "This is the work of Christianity's most brilliant scholar," Eusebius explained. "It is the *Hexapla* of Origen, who is from your city but sojourned in ours as well. When he died from a persecution, his scholarship was taken up by my mentor, Pamphilus, who was also martyred for our Lord. Now I am the great book's keeper."

"What is the second column?" Sophronia asked. "The letters spell no words."

"That is a transliteration of the Hebrew text into Greek characters. Origen was one of the few Christians who knew both languages. He had many learned discussions with the local rabbis." Eusebius paused, as if redirecting his thoughts back to the present, then said, "But enough with the church history! No good host should reveal his house's treasures until his guests are first refreshed from their journey. Follow me to the bedrooms—for we do have some that contain beds instead of books."

The bedrooms were comfortable and well-appointed, which was fortunate since the traveling party ended up spending two rainy days in Caesarea while the captain of the freighter waited for better weather. Rex enjoyed learning more about the history of Christianity from Eusebius, who was the greatest expert on that subject. Yet when the discussions turned theological, it was obvious the rotund bishop had strong Arian sympathies. Rex often noticed Ossius frowning at Eusebius's remarks. Alexander had convinced the Spanish bishop about the dangers of Arianism. He didn't like what he was hearing from Eusebius.

On the third morning, a clear sky greeted the travelers at dawn. Word came that the Phoenician freighter would depart within an hour. Eusebius announced he would be joining the trip because, as he put it, "I, too, have a stake in this report being made to my friend, the Emperor Constantine." Since Ossius was in no position to forbid it, he welcomed Eusebius to the expedition.

Unexpectedly, the travelers were joined by yet another bishop just as the ship was about to depart. He was Macarius, bishop of Hierusalem. Though that city's official name had been Aelia Capitolina ever since Emperor Hadrian took it from the Jews and dedicated it to his own family and to Jupiter, its current bishop didn't like to acknowledge this pagan political reality. So Macarius called the city Hierusalem like the scriptures did, and many other Christians followed his lead.

As the ship made its way up to Antiochia, Rex found that he enjoyed Macarius's company. The man was young to be a bishop, maybe about forty years old. His hair was jet black and hung down to his shoulders in a rugged, masculine way. Unlike most churchmen, he also had an impressive physique, with muscular arms and a trim waist. "I didn't come up through the ranks of the church," Macarius explained. "I was a woodworker like our Lord—still am, actually."

But despite his rustic occupation, Macarius was by no means unlettered. His mind was sharp and his theological interests were wide ranging. Rex wasn't surprised to learn that, like Bishop Ossius, Macarius also held suspicions about Eusebius's affinity for Arianism. This made things a little tricky because Caesarea's bishop held ecclesiastical authority over Hierusalem in the hinterland. Macarius always tried to be respectful toward Eusebius, even though he found the senior bishop's theology to be errant.

The simmering tension between Eusebius on the one hand and Ossius and Macarius on the other broke into the open when the travelers reached Antiochia. About sixty regional churchmen had gathered to elect a new bishop since the previous one had recently died. The newly installed bishop also supported what everyone had started calling the "Alexandrian" view: that the Father and Son were coeternal and equally divine.

But Eusebius took a firm stand on the saying from John's gospel that "the Father is greater" than the Son. "I mean no disrespect to Jesus," he insisted. "Yet the scriptures say he was inferior to God. And the Spirit ranks third within the Triad. A hierarchy—one, two, three—makes perfect sense."

Macarius of Hierusalem couldn't remain quiet at this. "Your name means 'piety,' brother, but your view is impious! What irony that the two foremost Christians with your name, the Eusebii of Caesarea and Nicomedia, both hold to the falsehood of Arius."

"The emperor has already chastised the other Eusebius," Ossius remarked, "and I fear he will chastise you as well."

Now Eusebius's round face grew flushed, like when he had lifted himself up a staircase. "I am Constantine's personal friend! By my own hand, I am writing his biography—he who represents on earth the will of our Lord in heaven. Constantine will not rebuke me!"

"Do not put your hopes in the emperor's friendship," Ossius implored. "Instead, win the friendship of your brethren by holding to sound doctrine."

But Eusebius remained unmoved. Crossing his arms over his ample body, he declared, "The emperor will soon be seeing things after the manner of Arius."

All the other bishops shook their heads at the bold assertion. "How can you be so sure?" Macarius asked.

"Because Arius has sent a letter ahead of you to the imperial court."

The startling statement made everyone in the room fall silent. Even Rex, who was only observing the discussion from the perimeter, could sense the dismay of the stunned bishops. Ossius finally broke the silence. "Explain yourself, Bishop Eusebius."

"After you left Alexandria, Father Arius caught wind of your return to the emperor with a negative report. Immediately he wrote a letter explaining his side of things and dispatched it with a swift courier. The man reached Caesarea while we were still there. In fact, he was aboard that ship we saw leaving an hour before us. He reached Seleucia the same day we did, but he did not follow us inland to Antiochia. Instead, he continued his sea voyage. By now he is well along the coast of Asia. He carries a truthful letter about the events in Alexandria—a letter that God is speeding toward its noble recipient in Nicomedia."

Now the bishops began to talk furiously among themselves while Eusebius sat in their midst with a smug expression. After a long, heated exchange, a plan was agreed upon. The report Ossius was bringing to Constantine would have to be sent ahead by its own speedy courier—but not by sea. Although the overland trip was seven hundred miles, the bishops believed that with the use of the imperial relay system and the help of Almighty God, it could be delivered faster than with a ship. The timing would be close. Yet the bishops agreed it was vital for their letter to arrive ahead of Arius's. The first person to tell a story always shaped how other versions would be perceived.

Despite the bishops' theoretical agreement about the plan, one of them, a man named Zenobios, thought the feat would be impossible. "Do you know what the interior of Asia is like in winter?" he asked his fellow churchmen. "It's full of high mountains, cold winds, and barren plains with no shelter. And what about the Cilician Gates? That gorge is infested with robbers!"

"Even so, the deed must be done," insisted Macarius of Hierusalem. "The matter is urgent. Someone strong enough to do it must be found."

For a long moment, the bishops were quiet as each one wrestled with his thoughts and tried to find a solution. And then, once again, Bishop Ossius broke the silence.

"I know just the man," he said.

—◈—

The warrior Geta crouched beneath Thessalonica's massive city wall, examining its height in the pale moonlight. Although the sea walls seemed to rise straight from the water, in fact, a tiny bit of gravelly land was at their base. All was quiet, for the spot Geta had chosen was an out-of-the-way place where boats did not pass since there was no dock for a mile in either direction. Here, the only living things were fish, birds, and barnacles on the seawall. Now they were joined by a speculator from Germania who knew how such walls could be scaled.

On the third attempt, Geta's grappling hook found purchase in the battlements above. The rope attached to the hook was knotted, a humiliating yet necessary adaptation. A speculator ought to be able to ascend a simple rope. But many years ago, Geta sustained a broken shin that left him lame for life. He could only ascend the rope with the help of the knots as footholds.

Once he had reached the top of the wall, Geta paused to catch his breath. No guards patrolled the parapet, for Thessalonica was at peace and security was lax. The gates were wide open by day, so whoever sought entry to the city could simply walk in. No one had a reason to scale the walls—no one, that is, except the lone speculator on an extraction mission.

In the quiet moment while Geta was calming his breath, he gazed upon the stunning urban landscape bleached by the pale light of a crescent moon. The sea bordered one side of the city, and across its ruffled waters gleamed the snowy summit of Mons Olympus. Within the city walls, not far away, was the palace complex built by Emperor Galerius. There was a lavish imperial residence, and next to it was a building of equal importance: a hippodrome for chariot races.

Below Geta's lofty perch was a tiny yard. Two of its sides consisted of the city wall and the back end of the hippodrome. The other two sides were high walled as well, forming a secure enclosure with a single, stout gate. Inside the yard was a grassy area and a two-room building that abutted the city wall. Its front room had windows, so perhaps it was somewhat pleasant. The rear room, however, was windowless and no doubt dreary. Yet this was the home—or indeed, the prison—of the man Geta had come to see: Valerius Licinius, the true emperor of Rome, and Geta's beloved father.

After all these years, it has come to this. The son who was given life by his father is about to give life in return!

After checking his grappling hook to make sure it was securely set, Geta hauled up the knotted rope from where it dangled down the outside of the wall. Then he dropped it inside the yard, allowing its end to coil upon the roof of the two-room building. With utmost silence, Geta climbed down. Kneeling on the roof, he carefully moved a single tile ever so slightly. He winced at the scraping sound it made, for he knew guards were always stationed in the front room. Yet nothing stirred, so Geta moved the tile a little more until a small hole was revealed. He lay down on the roof with his mouth near the opening.

"*Psst!*" he whispered into the rear room.

No answer. Geta waited. Finally, a hushed voice said, "Who are you?"

"A lifelong ally," Geta replied in the barest of whispers. "One who seeks to free you."

There was another long silence, then the question was repeated: "Who are you?"

Powerful emotions rose up within Geta. He hadn't spoken with his father for many years. Since he was an illegitimate son, he'd never had a political destiny. Yet Licinius had loved Geta's mother—if *love* was the right word for a courtesan—so he had helped Geta enter the army, and had even commissioned him as a spy. Would Licinius remember those things? It was time to find out. "I am Geta," he declared.

Down below, Licinius paused, then asked, "The son of the beautiful Saxon?"

He remembers! "Yes, Your Majesty, the son of Inga."

"Inga was beloved to me. We sent you to the speculator academy, yes?"

"You did, the academy in the Alps, where I excelled as a cadet. Then upon my graduation, you commissioned me as a spy in Rome during the time of Maxentius."

"What happened to you after that?"

"I left combat duty because of an injury. Yet I have stayed committed to you through all these years. Once, I even sought to assassinate Constantine. My allegiance lies only with you."

"And why have you come here tonight, loyal son?"

"To free you and once again see you rise to the noble height you deserve."

"A worthy cause. Unfortunately, I am trapped like a bird in Constantine's cage. He has defeated me again and again."

"Not forever, my lord! I am in touch with the Gothic mercenaries who roam the Macedonian hinterlands. I speak their language, so they trust me. These men have regrouped and are willing to serve you again in exchange for plunder and land. All they demand is your physical presence in their midst. They will not serve an idea or a promise. But if they see you free, they will rally to you, and you can defeat Constantine at last!"

"That is my heart's deepest desire," Licinius admitted. "But how should I be freed? My birdcage is surrounded by wildcats at all times."

"Yes, they surround it. But they are not on top of it."

"You propose that I escape through the roof? Impossible. To open a tiny hole is one thing. But to break open an exit sufficient for a man? The noise would have the guards rushing in at the removal of the first tile. Then Constantine would have a legal pretext to execute me. Your escape plan would be my death sentence, son of Inga."

"Not if the guards didn't hear it. I am sure they are alert. But no one can hear the sound of a tile when thousands upon thousands of men are yelling nearby. And that very thing will be happening here, one week hence."

Licinius let out a chuckle, though he kept its sound low, like the words of this secret conversation. "Your speculator training has taught you well. This is a bold plan you propose. Yet perhaps it could work, under the cover of so great a noise."

"Are you willing to try it?"

Licinius inserted a curled finger through the hole. Geta took it into his own hooked finger. "I will see you in one week, Geta, my son," said the true emperor of Rome.

The day of the chariot races was also a feast day for Hercules, which Geta believed was a propitious omen. Ever since childhood, he had worshiped Hercules as the Roman version of his mother's devotion to Thor. Surely the muscular god would reward such lifelong reverence by giving success to the escape plan.

Geta rowed swiftly to his secret place at the base of the wall because he didn't have the cover of darkness to hide him. When he left his meeting with Licinius a week earlier, he risked leaving his knotted rope tied to an iron spike that he had driven into a crack, knowing it would save him the time of throwing and hooking the grapnel. His boat arrived at the bottom of the rope, which was almost invisible as it dangled against Thessalonica's rugged, timeworn wall. Ascending the rope as quickly as he could with his deformed leg, Geta reached the top of the wall and crouched on the rampart behind the battlements. Once he had ascertained that the courtyard below was empty, he pulled up his rope hand by hand, then lowered it onto his father's prison. A moment later, he was upon the roof.

Although the tumult of the hundred thousand spectators in the hippodrome made a constant sound, its cadence had intermittent lulls and crescendos. Between the races, there was just a steady rumble. But when the starting trumpet sounded and the chariots exploded from the gates, the noise was deafening until someone finally won. The duration of a single chariot race would be long enough to make a hole for the escape.

In the interval until the next race began, Geta lay flat on the roof to keep the lowest possible profile in case someone had a sight line to his location. It wasn't long before the tension started to build as the chariots took their positions in the starting gates. As soon as the trumpet blared, the cheer from the spectators went up like a volcano belching its guts into the sky—and under the cover of that thunderous commotion, Geta started removing the tiles.

As he removed each one, they made a loud, scraping sound. When Geta accidentally dropped a tile into the hole and it shattered, he was sure the guards would become bursting in from the front room. Yet the noise from the adjacent hippodrome had its intended effect. No one entered Licinius's cell. Soon the hole was the size of a large tree trunk, so Geta pitched the end of his knotted rope into the opening. "Climb up!" he said, beckoning to his father.

Licinius emerged onto the roof, blinking in the bright sun. Geta reached out and steadied him, then led him to the city wall where it abutted the accursed house of confinement. The knotted rope ran up and over the battlements to the iron spike Geta had installed. He gave the rope a hard yank to make sure it was still secure. It didn't yield at all, so Geta sent Licinius to the ramparts first, then clambered up behind him.

"The sea!" Licinius exclaimed when he was atop the wall. "I haven't seen it in so long! How beautifully it shines before my eyes."

Geta had already hauled up the knotted rope. Now he threw it outside the walls again. "I have a rowboat below us. In a moment, we shall be upon that beautiful sea, making good our—"

"There they are! Seize them!"

Geta turned and saw a contingent of soldiers about a hundred paces down the rampart. The men had bows, so to leap over the wall now would only result in a rain of arrows that couldn't miss while he and his father were defenseless on the rope. Yet Hercules had provided a solution! Between Geta and the soldiers was a watchtower with a door in it. Such doors were designed to deny sections of the ramparts to invaders who had managed to gain the walls. Now, the door would be used to block the city's garrison instead.

"Climb down!" he shouted to his father as he broke into a run. "I'll be right behind you!"

Geta was much closer to the door than the soldiers were, so he believed he could get there first. The door was stout, and it had iron latches on both sides since no one knew where an attacker might reach the walls. Shutting it would keep the soldiers at bay and prevent the archers from shooting at him while he escaped. But as Geta ran, the awkward gait created by his deformed leg slowed him down. As he neared the door, he saw it was going to be close. The soldiers had the advantage of greater speed.

Ignoring the pain in his leg, Geta sprinted for the tower. He reached it first and seized the wooden door. With a thrill of triumph, he swung it shut—and it banged against the spear shaft that someone had just thrust into the opening from the other side.

Unable to latch the door, Geta found he was no match for the combined strength of the soldiers. They came barreling through, hurling him back. Spears were everywhere, and Geta had only a dagger. Though he tried to run, he had gone only a few steps when an arrow bounced near his feet and ricocheted off the ramparts ahead. "Halt!" shouted a commanding voice, "or the next one's in your spine!"

There was nothing else to do. Geta stopped, turned around, and found himself face-to-face with Caesar Crispus. The false caesar held up an iron hook with four tines. "Did you forget something, sir?"

My grapnel! When Geta set the spike for the climbing rope, he forgot to take it along. No speculator should ever do such a foolish thing. Leaving evidence at the scene of a mission was the stupidest mistake an operative could make. Even a first-year cadet would know better. This was a colossal failure that only confirmed what Geta already suspected: he had lost every skill that once made him great. He was no longer a speculator. Now, whatever was left of his pathetic military career was ruined.

"We've been waiting for you," Crispus explained, then gestured to the battlements. "Take a look."

Geta peered over the wall. Down at the water, three navy patrol boats surrounded his father. A soldier held him by the collar, while another man stood next to him with a drawn sword. Licinius's face showed total defeat.

"Kneel down and put your hands behind your back," Crispus ordered.

Geta obeyed. As the manacles were fastened to his wrists, he muttered, "I'm your cousin, you know." Though he hoped it might get him some mercy, he hated himself for uttering such pitiful words.

"No, you're my prisoner," Crispus replied as he hauled Geta to his feet. "And if you try anything foolish, you'll be vulture food instead."

⚉

After writing a full dossier for Emperor Constantine, Bishop Ossius had secured permission for Rex to use the imperial transport system. A rider who was willing to push himself could cover sixty miles a day, exchanging tired mounts for fresh ones at the imperial way stations along the road. Since the terrain around Antiochia was mostly flat, Rex was able to make good time on the initial leg of his race to Nicomedia. He rode hard for two days, traveling without the weight of armor or a bedroll to maximize the endurance of his horses. They were specially bred and trained to have a smooth gait that ate up the miles yet was comfortable in the saddle.

At dawn on the third day, Rex left the flat area along the coastline and turned north toward the Anatolian Plateau. Before reaching the high plains, he knew he would have to pass through the notorious Cilician Gates. Soon the road began to rise into this treacherous gorge that climbed to a high pass. Rex arrived at a way station around midday, but he only changed horses without stopping for a rest. Then he began to ascend along a narrow track with rock walls towering on either side.

The horse labored all afternoon. Though Rex rested the mare a few times and fed her oats from a bag, still, the noble creature was being pushed to her limit. Yet Alexander the Great had successfully traversed this pass, and so had countless settlers, pilgrims, and armies before him. More recently, the apostle Paul had gone through here on his second missionary journey. Rex was determined to do the same. A little sleet began to fall as he approached the pass, so he tightened his cloak's fur-lined hood and donned woolen mittens. The pass was swathed in clouds when he finally reached it. There was nothing to do but keep going.

The downhill side of the pass was easier on the mare's lungs but harder on her legs. She plodded along with her head hanging low. Around dusk, the narrow defile opened up a bit. Now Rex could see the Anatolian Plateau several miles ahead. In the gathering darkness, he spotted something that encouraged his heart. Far out on the plain, the proprietor of a way station had set out a lantern to serve as a beacon for exhausted travelers like Rex.

And then it happened. Two horsemen materialized in the gloom ahead, standing still and blocking the road. Rex glanced over his shoulder and saw two more riders behind him. When they started closing in, he knew they had to be bandits.

Instantly, Rex sized up the situation and devised a plan. His horse was too tired to outrun the attackers even if he could somehow barrel past the men ahead. A wide, icy stream ran along the left side of the highway at the base of a sheer cliff. On the right, a craggy slope rose up from the road. Rex knew he couldn't overcome four mounted men in such a tight place. Rather than fight a losing battle, he dismounted, grabbed his lone saddlebag with the all-important dossier in it, and scrambled up the boulder-strewn slope. Though one robber stayed with the horses, the other three leapt to the ground and began their pursuit.

The slope grew steeper, and Rex was forced to climb hand over hand. He slipped when a stone rolled beneath his foot, causing his shin to bang hard against a rock, but he grunted and kept climbing. Because Rex was in better physical condition than his pursuers, he soon widened his lead. Yet as he scrambled over a ledge, he realized he had come to a dead end—a concave nook whose rear wall was unclimbable. There was no way up, and his enemies were right behind him. Rex would have to make his stand here.

Peering over the ledge, Rex saw that the three attackers had spread out as they wound their way through the crags by different routes. One man was directly below. Rex knelt and put his back against a jagged boulder.

By pressing hard with his legs, he was able to loosen the stone. He turned back around and shoved the boulder off the ledge. There was a scrabbling sound as the chunk of granite tumbled through the scree . . . then a thud and a sharp scream . . . then silence. *One man down.* Yet the other two robbers weren't deterred by their comrade's demise. Rex drew his sword from his belt sheath and prepared to defend his tiny castle. If he failed, he would probably be killed, or at least sold into slavery.

The first man onto the ledge bore a stout wooden shield in addition to his sword. He was a swarthy fellow with a thunderbolt and the number XII tattooed on his arm. "The Thundering Twelfth, eh?" Rex said as he circled the former legionary.

"Come meet the lightning," the man growled, and the fight was on.

Though Rex was the superior swordsman by far, the ledge's tight confines and the man's shield served to even the conflict. Rex had to use his weapon to parry, while his opponent could push with one arm and attack with the other. At one point, the two men clinched, and the robber managed to nick Rex's scalp. Rex stepped back and wiped bloody sweat from his eyes. "You're dead!" the ex-soldier screamed as he moved in for the kill.

But he was overconfident. As he came in, he raised his shield too high. Instead of keeping it against his torso where it could be controlled, he momentarily extended it in front of his face. Rex saw the mistake and struck like lightning, shoving the heel of his palm against the shield's top rim. It smashed against the bridge of the man's nose, sending a cascade of blood down his face. Stunned, the ex-legionary lowered his defenses, and Rex took the opening. He plunged his sword into the man's throat.

The robber staggered backward, his eyelids fluttering. As he started to sink to his knees, his grip on his sword went limp. At the same moment, Rex noticed movement out of the corner of his eye. Just as the dying robber was about to drop his sword, Rex smacked the weapon with his own blade and sent it spiraling into the air. Catching it by the hilt in his free hand, he whirled and sent the sword hurtling toward the second assailant, who had just clambered onto the ledge.

That man had his crossbow pointed at Rex. The sword struck him just as he depressed the trigger. Rex heard the bolt whizz past his head and smack into the cliff behind him. As for the crossbowman—he stood still for a long moment, staring with wide eyes at the hilt protruding from his chest. Then, without even uttering a scream, he took a step back onto nothingness and disappeared over the ledge.

Exhausted from the combat, Rex leaned on the rock wall and panted to catch his breath. The robber with the shield and the crossbowman were both dead, and whoever had been struck by the boulder was in no more position to fight than his two comrades. But Rex wasn't safe yet. If the fourth fellow who was guarding the horses decided to move off with the mare, Rex would have to spend the night in the mountains without any protection against the cold. He had to keep moving or he could still meet his death in this frigid and lonely place.

After retrieving his saddlebag, Rex descended to the place where the crossbowman's body lay. Four darts were in his belt quiver, and his bow was nearby. Rex took the arms with him as he returned to the road. The guardian of the horses was still there, glancing around nervously now that the sun had gone down and his partners hadn't returned. Using a stealthy line of approach, Rex drew close to the man, then rose from the crags with a sharp command. "Drop your sword!" he shouted with the cocked crossbow in his hands.

The man hesitated, but Rex didn't. He approached closer until even a child couldn't miss. Now the robber knew he was beat. His sword clattered onto the rocks, and he showed Rex his empty palms. "D-d-don't kill me," he begged. "Those men forced me to serve them!"

Though Rex thought it was probably a lie, he didn't want to kill a defenseless man if he could help it. Instead, he said, "Strip!"

"Wh-what?"

"You heard me! Strip naked . . . now!"

The terrified robber complied, dropping his trousers and tunic alongside his sword until his bare skin was whitewashed by the moonlight. He hugged his body, trying futilely to stay warm.

"Now get in the stream," Rex ordered.

"That'll kill me!"

"So will this dart! Do it in five! Four! Three!"

The man chose the lesser of two evils, breaking the ice and splashing into the water with a high-pitched squeal. Rex made him swim all the way out until only his head was visible. Then, while keeping one eye on his captive, Rex made a train with the reins and tails of the four horses and put his own mare in the fifth position. Before mounting the lead horse, Rex unlashed a bedroll from its back, along with a satchel that contained some vittles and a fire striker. He pitched the items on the ground, then swung into the saddle.

"You can come out now," Rex said to the frozen robber. The poor fellow hurried out of the stream and staggered to his gear, shivering like a frightened rabbit.

"Th-th-thank you," the man said through chattering teeth as he threw a woolen blanket around his shoulders.

"Your three friends are dead," Rex informed the erstwhile bandit. "I'd suggest you take this opportunity to start a new life." Then, with the man nodding vigorously at this word of advice, Rex started his horse toward the way station at the exit of the Cilician Gates.

—◦∾◦—

Constantine awoke in the dim light of a winter morning at Nicomedia, but he didn't get out of bed. It was one of the nice aspects of no longer being on military campaign: not having to rise at dawn from an army cot to supervise the war planning. Life in the imperial palace could be as slow-paced and relaxed as he wanted it to be. *Now that I rule the whole empire, will I ever have to go out on campaign again?* Constantine laughed at the ridiculous idea of a sedentary life for an emperor. Although Licinius was residing peacefully in Thessalonica and the civil wars were over, plenty of other opponents remained outside the empire. Shapur, king of the Persians, would have to be dealt with at some point. And there would always be barbarian tribes to fight on every border.

Constantine's mind drifted to his recent visit to Byzantium—or New Rome, as he had renamed it. The delineation of the walls and the presentation of his son as the third caesar had gone extremely well. Yet he had been surprised that the people wanted their city to be called Constantinople—the "city of Constantine." It was an honor that pleased him, for it meant he had their affection, unlike so many other emperors in recent memory. Constantine was determined to build on that affection and create a peaceful, harmonious empire in which Christianity was the foremost religion.

But the church split at Alexandria was a troublesome development. Such squabbling about trivial points of doctrine had to cease. If some people wanted to view Jesus as a divinized creature and others wanted him to be equal to God . . . what harm was there in such disagreement? As Constantine finally sat up in his bed and swung his feet to the floor, he prayed that a middle-of-the-road compromise would triumph over theological precision.

Two days later, however, a messenger arrived at Nicomedia with new information that challenged Constantine's morning ruminations. The visitor was the speculator-turned-deacon named Brandulf Rex—a man who always seemed to be at the center of important matters. Rex had come on an urgent mission from Ossius at Antiochia, completing the difficult overland trip in just twelve days despite an attack by highwaymen. He had brought a dossier of letters and treatises from the good bishop. After Constantine examined the packet, he summoned Rex to appear before him in a little hall with a throne in the apse.

"Brandulf Rex, I don't know your secret, but you seem not to age," Constantine remarked before his questions began. "You look as fit now as the day you entered my bodyguard. Do you remember your ride across the battlefield on the Rhenus with shields draped all over you?"

"I do, Your Highness. It was either cover myself in shields or take a Frankish arrow in my arse. But I had to get across that field. Just like now, I had important news for you then too."

Constantine chuckled at Rex's rugged, self-confident demeanor. He had always found Rex to be a likable fellow. His arms still bulged with muscles, and his long hair and beard were masculine without being too barbaric. "You've been distinguishing yourself on the battlefield ever since that day, Brandulf Rex. The Milvian Bridge. Cibalae. The Mardian Plain. Hadrianopolis. Chrysopolis." Constantine paused as a wry smile came to his lips. "And yes," he added with his brows arched, "at Verona as well."

"Thank you, Your Majesty," Rex said with a dip of his chin.

Constantine could tell his guest was especially pleased he had included that last remark. The emperor cleared his throat and redirected his thoughts, for it was time to discuss the matter that had brought Rex to Nicomedia. "The dossier you delivered was quite illuminating. Did Father Arius's followers really attack the episcopal basilica?"

"Yes, with fire and hammers. I had to lead the people to safety by smashing through the floor and escaping through the cisterns."

"What an evil crime! Such a thing should never happen among Christians."

Before Constantine could say more, a palace steward approached the throne and whispered in his ear. The theologian Lactantius, who had been summoned earlier, had just arrived and was waiting at the far end of the hall. Constantine beckoned for Lactantius to come and stand next to Rex. "It seems you were right about Arianism after all," the emperor said to the eminent scholar and rhetorician. "The issues under debate are more consequential than I first imagined."

Lactantius nodded gravely. "Christianity stands at a junction, Your Majesty. How the catholic church addresses the Arian question will determine what it will become for the rest of its existence."

"I perceive that fork in the road more clearly now," Constantine admitted. "I thought I could just have the two sides sweep the matter under the rug. But there are fundamental doctrines at stake here—along with much pride, bickering, and hard feelings."

"Unfortunately, it's all wrapped together," Lactantius agreed. "But we mustn't let the sinful part obscure the core issues about who Christ really is."

Constantine switched his gaze to Rex. "Tell me what happened down at Antiochia. Did they really excommunicate Eusebius? I like that little scholar, even if he is a bit of a toady."

"I think Eusebius's heart is in the right place. It's true, he does want your approval, and he's willing to flatter you to get it. He also wants the approval of other bishops. Yet he's got a stubborn streak, so when they tried to correct him, he wouldn't budge. He's digging in his heels on Arianism. That's what got him excommunicated. However, they're giving him a chance to repent at the big council they want to convene."

Constantine glanced down at the documents in his lap. "They're calling it a 'magnificent council of the clergy.' It sounds like they want everyone in the east to attend."

"Yes, sir. Ossius said he wants every bishop who can get to Ancyra this summer to go."

"Why Ancyra, of all places? It's remote and unpleasant."

"I just passed through there a few days ago, and I couldn't agree more."

Now Lactantius intervened. "If I may explain, Your Majesty, I think the reason is both geographic and strategic. All the eastern bishops can travel there by land, whether down through Nicomedia or up from Syria, Palaestina, and Aegyptus. As for strategy—I believe the bishop there is fiercely anti-Arian."

Constantine frowned. "It wouldn't be a fair council, then, would it? We're not having it in Ancyra."

"Very well. How about your capital of New Rome?" Lactantius suggested.

"No, that would make it look like I'm meddling in church affairs. The council needs to be close to my oversight, yet not in an obvious place of imperial power."

"I have an idea," Rex said. "I just came through a town I found to be pleasant. It was the first way station on my trip where the horse trough didn't freeze overnight. I think it would be nice in the summer. And there's an imperial palace on a lake."

Constantine was intrigued. "And this place is?"

"Nicaea. About a two days' carriage ride from here."

"The city of victory! That is a good idea, Brandulf Rex. It will be the perfect place for a 'victorious' council that puts an end to all this strife. I only hope some of the eastern bishops will explain to their western brethren the hidden meaning of the town's Greek name."

Rex and Lactantius exchanged glances. Constantine remained silent and let his guests linger in their surprise, until Lactantius finally said, "Do you mean . . . there will be Latin speakers at this council? Men who do not know Greek?"

"Of course. Because there are many Latin-speaking Christians in our far western lands."

"So you intend to summon all the bishops of the whole catholic church to this council? Even from the west? A worldwide gathering?"

"That is exactly what I intend, Lactantius. And I shall pay for it out of the imperial treasury. We shall send invitations to Britannia and Gaul and Hispania, to Africa and Aegyptus and Syria, and to every church along the Euphrates and the Danubius and the Rhenus. The whole world will run to Nicaea, the city of victory, like sprinters from the starting line!"

"There is one bishop whose agreement is especially important," Rex remarked. "Without him, this council won't seem truly catholic, even if it involves other bishops from the four corners of the earth."

"And who is that?" Constantine asked.

"My former pastor, the man who baptized me, Pope Sylvester of Rome."

"Aha! This is true indeed. If the bishop from the city of Peter and Paul doesn't approve the outcome of the council, it won't have the proper weight of authority."

Turning toward his steward, Constantine clapped his hands. When the man hurried over, the emperor said, "Bring me the stable master, for I have a special command and I wish him to hear it directly from me."

Since the palace at Nicomedia wasn't immense, it didn't take long for the steward to return with the stable master—a tall, thin fellow with a beaked nose. Constantine overlooked the fact that he had manure on his boots in the imperial throne room.

"Listen to me closely," the emperor said, "for this matter is important. I am sending an envoy to Rome, someone who is loved with great affection by the Christian church there. Because it is winter, the trip must be mostly by land, so I want my best carriage refurbished to the highest standards. Upholster it everywhere with cushions and silks. Seal out the cold, but leave windows that can be opened whenever the weather is nice. I want only the finest mules to draw it, and you shall exchange them for the best ones that the stations can offer along the way. In other words, make it the most comfortable trip possible for my special envoy."

"It shall be done just as you ask," the stable master said, bowing at the waist.

"This must be quite a special man you're sending," Lactantius observed.

Constantine chuckled. "Although you are a brilliant theologian, Lactantius, you are mistaken on this one. I am sending no man, but a lady of impeccable character and unmatched social graces. As for who she is—well, I shall give her the honor of finding out about this mission from me. You may learn her identity afterward. And now, gentlemen, may God bless your work as you begin preparing for the momentous Council of Nicaea."

7

"I've been looking forward to this bath for a month," Empress Helena said as she disrobed in the changing room with her ladies-in-waiting. "The rigors of the road take a toll on the body in every way."

"We haven't seen a real bathhouse since we left Nicomedia," agreed a handmaiden who served as the queen's cubicularia, the chamberlain of the royal bedroom. "At last, we are civilized again!"

The ladies made their way to the tepid room to adjust themselves to the warmth after the short walk from the Sessorian Palace. Today was a chilly day in Rome, and most experts advised against sudden swings in temperature. It was better for the body, the doctors agreed, to grow accustomed to the heat gradually. Helena took a seat on a marble bench and slipped her feet out of the wooden clogs she had used to cross the heated floor. The pleasant feeling of radiant warmth immediately made her sleepy. She leaned against the wall and closed her eyes.

But some of the other girls were chatty, so they prattled among themselves about the things they had seen and experienced on the road from Nicomedia. The trip had been about as enjoyable as Helena could have hoped for, especially since Constantine had made the carriage so comfortable. The only difficult part had been crossing the Adriatic Sea from Macedonia to Italy. It had taken a full day to get the fine carriage stowed securely on a ship, which turned out to be time well spent when a winter squall made the waters choppy. But the embassy had made it safely across, and the rest of the trip up the Appian Way was uneventful. The queen, her ladies-in-waiting, and her bodyguard had arrived in Rome this morning. The bathhouse next to the Sessorian Palace was the first place Helena had decided to go. If she was going to meet with the pope, she intended to do it with a clean body and a refreshed spirit.

After a while, the women felt ready for the caldarium. As they entered the hot room, a servant gave them each a sachet to wear around their neck. The little pouch, made with a porous fabric, was filled with nuggets of myrrh and peppermint leaves. After settling into the steaming water—almost too hot to stand, Helena thought—the women periodically squeezed the packets to release the natural oils. The pool's hot water caused pleasant menthol vapors with soothing aromas and healing powers to rise up to the ladies' faces.

It wasn't long before Helena felt stifled by the heat, so she ladled cool water over her head from a silver pail. Though it helped, something still seemed off. The Sessorian baths were old, even decrepit in certain places. Often if the chimneys in a bathhouse weren't well maintained, too much heat would build up in the pools. Helena was about to do something about it when a servant entered the caldarium with an item that made her forget about the heat for the moment. Rather than directly approach the queen, the servant gave the item to the cubicularia, who brought it across the pool to her mistress. "It's a lovely resemblance!" the girl exclaimed as she handed it to Helena.

The item was a gold coin that depicted Helena's head adorned with a pearl diadem. Around the bust were the words *HELENA AUGUSTA*. The brand-new solidus, fresh from the Roman mint, was designed to reflect a new political reality. A few weeks ago, Constantine, the sole augustus of the Imperial College, did something that had been done only once before in the forty years of the college's existence: he raised a woman to the rank of augusta, a position equal to his own. Helena's previous rank was Most Noble Woman, a symbolic title of honor. Now she was a coruler of the empire with her son. The only annoying thing about Constantine's momentous decision was that he had granted the title to his wife, Fausta, as well.

"Let's see the reverse," the cubicularia suggested.

Helena turned over the coin in her palm. The words *SECURITY OF*

THE REPUBLIC were emblazoned around its edge. Inside the inscription was an image of Lady Security in a relaxed and carefree pose, holding the olive branch of peace. "I don't know if I can bring peace and security to my people," Helena murmured, "but with God's help, I will try."

"You will do great things for this empire," the cubicularia said in a tone marked by genuine confidence rather than flattery. "You will leave a lasting mark upon this earth, my lady."

The sudden reminder of Helena's great responsibilities weighed heavily upon her and made her want some time to herself. She rose from the water and tucked the coin in the sachet at her neck. Leaving her handmaidens to their lighthearted chatter, she went to the bath's cold room. A dip in the chilly waters of the plunge pool immediately cooled her off, leaving her skin tingly and flushed. Now it was time for the sauna, a place Helena had often found conducive to spiritual thoughts; for with the purging of the body came the purging of the soul as well.

The sweat started immediately, but that was what Helena wanted. A good sweat was a pleasant thing as long as it didn't last too long. She sat quietly in the sauna, enjoying the heat and trying to clear her mind of resentment toward Fausta. That woman was always undercutting Crispus's career or maligning him despite his high moral character. Fausta wanted to advance her biological sons instead of Crispus, who was the child of Constantine's former concubine. Though the three boys were all caesars in the Imperial College, everyone could see it was Crispus who was destined to rule after his father. That popular sentiment infuriated Fausta, filling her with a kind of insane jealousy. Helena often felt she was the only person standing between Crispus and serious violence from his stepmother.

The pleasant intensity of the sauna's dry heat soon became too much for Helena. Once again, the Sessorian baths seemed to be functioning poorly, making what should have been a leisurely sweat feel more like torment. Helena rose from the bench and crossed to the door, her clogs making clip-clop sounds on the marble floor.

But upon reaching the door, Helena found it stuck. The old wood had warped from the bath's constant moisture, the hinges had rusted, and the paving stones outside had shifted to make an obstruction beneath the door. For a moment, Helena began to panic when she realized she wasn't able to get out. The thought of being trapped in this overheated room frightened her. Calming herself, she took a step back and lowered her shoulder. Then, like a commoner fighting his way through a crowd at the amphitheater, she gave a shove to the door. It opened, though not by much. Another hard strike with her shoulder was sufficient for Helena to squeeze through. The cool, sweet air that flooded her lungs was a great relief.

"Attendant!" she called, but there was no answer. *Since when does a bath-house not have an attendant nearby for the augusta of the empire?*

Thoroughly irritated now, Helena went to the changing room and donned a silk wrap, then made her way downstairs to the subterranean level. Though she had never been down there, she knew exactly what three things she would find: firewood, a furnace, and people to tend the flames. Every bath-house had a team of slaves constantly working beneath the beautiful facility above. Since it took a long time to heat the whole building, the fire had to be kept going continuously or the process would have to start all over. Bathing in Rome required a lot of manpower and logs.

An orange glow around the corner told Helena where the furnace was to be found. From this one source, hot air would circulate beneath the floors and through the walls, as well as heat the tanks for soaking. Helena rounded the corner and found the fireman to be a pale, misshapen fellow in a loincloth who was hurling logs into the furnace instead of maintaining a low, steady fire. Clearly, the furnace was overheated. The fireman couldn't even stand close to the blazing inferno. Yet he kept pitching more fuel into the furnace's gaping maw.

Helena loudly cleared her throat, but the man didn't respond. At last, she said, "Look at me!"

The slave turned, and when he did, he became the most pitiful spectacle Helena had ever witnessed. He fell to his knees with his deformed leg stick-ing out to one side. His eyes bugged with fear. Clasping his hands in front of himself, he wailed, "Please, lady, no whip me!"

"I'm not going to whip you," Helena said. "I just want to know why you're trying to steam me like a lobster."

"I no steam you! They bring me from mines. I no make fires there!"

The mines. That explains the man's terror. The imperial mines were a hell-hole that would break any man's spirit. Certainly they had broken this man's body, and it hadn't healed well. Nor had his mind healed from the trauma and mistreatment. Yet somehow he had been brought here from that living death. Now he had been put to work underground again, even though he knew nothing about tending a furnace. It was a ridiculous decision that was bound to fail. *Fausta would no doubt scourge this man, along with the supervisor who had assigned him here.*

But Helena had no such intentions. She approached the crippled slave, who lowered his eyes and whimpered as she drew near. For a moment, the augusta said nothing. Then, softly, she put her hand on his shoulder. "Rise up."

The terrified slave didn't have the courage to obey, so Helena drew him up by the elbow until he was standing. Because of his deformed leg and bent torso, he was even shorter than she was. His skin was pale from his many years in darkness. The gulf between this man's lot in life and her own was as wide as could be.

"No whip me," the man moaned.

"I do not intend to whip you, sir. I intend to free you."

The expression on the man's face showed he did not understand what Helena had just said. So in plain words, she informed him that he was now a freedman, then explained what that meant. Slowly, the man's countenance changed as the light of humanity was rekindled within him. Helena could see hope return to his vacant eyes.

"What is your name?" she asked.

"Juvenal, lady. I am Juvenal."

"And what did you do, Juvenal, before you were sent to the mines?"

"Tonsor."

"Then that is what you shall do again. There is always a need in our palace for shaving and hair cutting. You will not have to walk about and can stay in one place to do your job. And you shall receive wages for your work."

"Lady, see!" cried Juvenal. "My face is happy!"

And indeed, it was—his grin seemed to spread from ear to ear. Helena smiled at Juvenal in return. "There is one more thing you need," she told him. "A thing to help you get started. Hold out your hand."

Though Juvenal was still tentative from his long history of abuse, he managed to extend his hand without flinching. Into his palm, Helena placed the gold coin from the sachet around her neck. Its reverse face was showing. She stared at the coin as it glittered in Juvenal's hand by the light of the fiery furnace.

"For the security of the republic," Helena said, repeating the slogan on the coin. "One person at a time."

———— ⁓⁓⁓ ————

Pope Sylvester left the Lateran Palace on a bright winter morning while frost was still on the north-facing roofs. He wore a warm cloak over his tunic, and his socks were made of wool beneath good leather shoes. His journey took him over the low height of the Caelian Hill, then down into the urban lowland—long ago, a swampy meadow—where the Circus Maximus now stood. From there he began to ascend the flank of Rome's most elegant hill, the Aventine, home of senators and aristocrats who desired mansions away from the hustle and bustle of the city center.

As Sylvester neared the hill's crest, he noticed a man not far ahead whom he recognized: the disgraced priest Felix, now a leader of the heretical sect of the Manichaeans. Felix was walking in the same direction as Sylvester, so the pope found himself following the man at a distance.

Felix arrived at a large mansion whose owner Sylvester didn't know. Outside the front door, two litters were waiting, each borne by eight slaves. The powerful city leaders who emerged from behind the litters' curtains caught Sylvester by surprise. One was the chief of the Urban Cohorts, the only military force left in Rome after Constantine dissolved the Praetorians and the imperial cavalry. The other man was the urban prefect, Acilius Severus, the highest-ranking civic official in the city. Sylvester watched as the politicians greeted Felix with the Persian-style bow of the Manichaeans—such men despised the kiss of the Christians—then entered the mansion together.

Passing by the mansion without bothering to give it a glance, Sylvester continued until he reached his destination on the Aventine's summit—the church of Santa Sabina, whose priest was the orthodox and upright Vincentius. Sylvester leaned on his staff while he caught his wind from the uphill hike, for his breathing was labored these days. Though he could have taken a litter, he preferred to walk, in the humbler fashion of a Christian. Jesus and the apostles walked everywhere, so the bishop of Rome thought he ought to do the same. When his respiration was regular again, he rapped on the door with his staff.

The doorman ushered him into an atrium with a pool and a fountain at the center. Father Vincentius emerged from the study with a warm smile. He was young for a priest, perhaps in his midthirties, with a fiery personality that matched the red hair of his Celtic heritage. "Welcome, Holy Father!" he exclaimed, then the two men retired to a dining room to break their fast with some food and drinks.

"The church seems to be thriving under your care, judging from the amount of new construction I see," Sylvester said when the two men were settled on divans around a low table.

"Yes, we've put on a new roof, and we converted the baths into a baptistery. And the people are always telling me how much they love the mosaic floor. At some point, the congregation will outgrow this building and we'll need a basilica. But not anytime soon. Too many people have left us for the Manichaeans."

"May you have a need for expansion sooner than you expect—for it would mean the growth of the people of God."

"Being cramped on a Sun Day would surely be better than having an empty hall," Vincentius agreed. "For now, though, we're fine in this old house. And that reminds me, some of my people told me they discovered the former owner's grave in the countryside. They wish to venerate the place. I believe you knew Sabina Sophronia, yes?"

Vincentius's question presented Sylvester with a dilemma. He had certainly known Lady Sabina Sophronia, and also her daughter, Lady Junia Flavia. They had lived in this house before he became the bishop of Rome. But a terrible series of events transpired not far from where Sylvester and Vincentius now reclined. The enraged tyrant Maxentius sent pimps to capture the holy matron for lascivious purposes, with her brutal murder sure to follow. Rather than suffer that shameful death, Sophronia was believed to have committed noble suicide by a dagger to the breast. Then her house, which was already a meeting place for Christians, passed into the ownership of the catholic church. The believers who met here today respected Sabina Sophronia's courageous act as a form of martyrdom.

But that story was only partially true. While Sophronia did indeed stab herself with a dagger, the speculator Rex found her before she perished and saved her life. He gave her a potion that put her into a deep sleep. Then he broke off the blade of the dagger and placed the hilt in her bloody wound. When the wicked pimps found her like that, they took her for dead and left the house. Sophronia survived the ordeal; and after she healed for several months in a remote place, she went into retirement as a nun. Now she was living in quiet and happy anonymity in Alexandria. Sylvester knew this because Vitus Rex reported on Sophronia's well-being when he came with the letter about the Arians. Yet these things couldn't become widely known in Rome, or Sophronia's privacy would be violated.

Sylvester opted for a simple reply to the complex matter Vincentius had raised. "Let us not give credence to Christian legends," he advised. "There is no tradition of Sabina Sophronia's resting place. So these discoverers haven't found anything authentic." And with that, the matter was dropped.

The conversation turned, as it often did among church officials these days, to the problem of the Manichaeans. They were expanding rapidly, and not just among the common folk. Many powerful men from the aristocracy were also joining the sect. "It is hard to believe that even the city prefect has embraced the doctrines of Mani," Vincentius said after Sylvester recounted what he had seen on the way over.

"Now the political power in the city and the police force will be sympathetic to them. That isn't something to be feared. Yet it is a thing to be watched by us, as wisdom demands."

Vincentius nodded as he set down his glass of pear juice. "I suppose that must be why Constantine made his mother an augusta and sent her here. He doesn't want to live in Rome himself, but he wants his views represented in the heart of his empire."

"You are half correct." Sylvester smiled at his protégé across the breakfast table. "But, unknown to you, there is another reason for Helena's presence in the city. And it is the reason I have come to visit you today." When Vincentius indicated he was listening, Sylvester went on to explain. "You remember the urgent letter from Aegyptus? The one brought by Vitus?"

"Certainly. Bishop Alexander was seeking our cooperation against the doctrines of Arius."

"That heresy isn't widespread here. But the Arians are for the eastern-ers what the Manichaeans are for us. They have a false view of Christ yet are close enough to the truth to deceive many. Some of their terminology overlaps with ours. Their teachers try to say that the differences are minor."

"But they aren't!" Vincentius exclaimed with fire in his eyes. "A Christ who is the creature of God isn't the Christ of the true faith."

"Indeed, he is not. At first, Emperor Constantine didn't see those issues for what they were. Even Ossius believed a middle ground could be found. But now they've decided to do something about it. They are summoning a council of bishops from the whole church. From Hispania to the Euphrates, from the Rhenus to the Nilus. Two delegates shall represent Rome at Nicaea this summer. And Vincentius—I want you to attend the council."

The announcement seemed to catch the young priest by surprise. "I will certainly go, Holy Father. But why me? The Roman church is full of priests, many of them more senior than I."

"Yet none who are more theologically astute. Vincentius, I have watched you since you were a catechist. Your doctrine is orthodox on every point. And where theological matters are still open for determination, I have ob-served that your instincts are always inclined in the right direction. You stand for the glory and majesty of God, the full equality of the Son, and the life-giving power of the Spirit. On these things, you do not budge, no matter how much pressure is put upon you."

"Because that is the witness of apostolic scripture," Vincentius said sim-ply. "We must not deviate from the things that God's word has declared to humankind."

Sylvester smiled to himself. *This is exactly why Vincentius must attend*, said the voice in his heart—a divine whisper that confirmed his prayerful decision.

"When will we depart?" Vincentius asked. "I believe a sea journey to Nicaea would take at least three weeks. Maybe closer to four, if we travel slowly and take your comfort into account."

Before Sylvester could answer, a deacon entered the dining room to clear the table now that the meal was finished. The two diners adjourned to a sitting room whose charcoal brazier was putting out pleasant warmth and the soothing aroma of incense.

When the men were seated, Sylvester gave Vincentius the news that would probably disappoint him. "I cannot go to Nicaea. I have developed a malady of the lungs—labored breathing, accompanied by the coughing of blood. My physicians insist that a months-long trip is not possible for me."

A concerned expression came to Vincentius's face, but Sylvester assured him the doctors had the illness under control. Once the young priest was comforted, Sylvester could see the weight of his new responsibility settle like a heavy rucksack on his shoulders. "Do not fear, Vincentius. I am sending you with a man of great influence. The second delegate I have chosen is Leo, the chaplain of Empress Helena Augusta. He, too, wears the ring of a papal legate."

"Yes, I know the man."

Sylvester arched his eyebrows. "From your tone, my son, you do not seem enthused by that choice. Does it not please you?"

"The decision is yours, Holy Father. I am but your servant."

"Your humility is praiseworthy, Vincentius. Yet you may speak freely. Why not Leo?"

The Celtic priest seemed to consider his words before speaking. At last, he said, "Leo is a pious man, of that I am certain. Everyone says he is moral and upright. Yet he comes from a privileged background. He is a patrician, and his family has been Christian for three generations. Rarely has a hardship come into his life. Rarely has he been tested by fiery trials, even during the persecutions. And by no means has he seen sin up close. He is almost perfectly clean."

"That is a bad thing?"

"I have found," Vincentius said cautiously, "that the holiest Christians are the ones who once were terrible sinners. Only they can truly comprehend the depths of God's grace."

Sylvester thought on this point for a while, believing it insightful and worthy of contemplation. The scriptures affirmed what Vincentius had just said. Surely the apostle Paul was a man like that—a sinner saved by grace— which explained his deep love for God and burning zeal for the good news. "Who would you send instead?"

"Vitus."

"*Vitus!* A man of former bloodshed?" Such a startling idea had never entered the bishop's thinking.

But Vincentius seemed convinced of it. "Yes, Holy Father, he is precisely the man I would send. I taught Vitus his baptismal catechesis. I know him well—his mind as well as his heart. You yourself made him a legate on your behalf. He wears the same ring I do. Vitus is already empowered to represent you."

"True enough, but I hadn't imagined he would do so at an ecumenical council on a pivotal point of doctrine." Sylvester tapped his chin in a contemplative way. "Now that you suggest it, though, I can see how it could be valuable. Do you suspect there will be foul play at the council?"

"Unfortunately, such intrigue isn't out of the question. But that isn't why I am recommending Vitus."

"Why, then?"

"Because the man who can see the clearest is he who has been laid the lowest. And Brandulf Vitus Rex has been down to that most humbling place. There is no greater qualification for a theologian than lowliness of spirit."

The pope glanced up at Vincentius. "Very well, my son. Vitus shall join you on my behalf. And may the true doctrine of God be discovered at Nicaea."

≈◊◊◊≈

The city of Nicomedia, though it was one of the capitals of the Imperial College, wasn't all that impressive to Rex. Perhaps it was because he had grown used to Rome and Alexandria, the two biggest cities in the empire. Yet even places like Antiochia and Thessalonica seemed to have more going for them than this sad excuse for a capital. Rex could understand why Constantine was in the process of moving his capital to Byzantium. When that splendid city—so perfectly located between east and west—was ready to assume its place as New Rome, it was going to be glorious for the next thousand years. But until then, the emperor was stuck with Nicomedia. And for the time being, Rex was stuck here too.

He wandered along the waterfront, a little bored after several days with nothing to do. Once he had delivered Ossius's theological dossier to Constantine, his work was done. Rex had reached Nicomedia just one day before the sea courier from Arius had arrived. Though the emperor did receive that man, the packet of Arian documents didn't impress him. When the courier explained that he had been delayed by a tempest, Constantine had asked him, "Was that normal winter weather or the intervening hand of God?" According to Lactantius, the emperor was frowning when he said it. "We will consider all sides of this matter," Lactantius had said graciously, and the courier was sent away. Now things were at a stalemate. The great council at Nicaea was going to determine the future of Christian belief about the Triad of God.

A fleet of fishing boats was docked at Nicomedia's harbor on the Propontis. Rex paused his stroll and watched the sailors scurry around with their work. He knew he'd be boarding a vessel like one of these later this spring, since a short hop along the coast was the quickest way to get inland to Nicaea. Rex was certain he'd have to go to the council, because Bishop Ossius had come to rely on him for the practical services he could provide. Rex had found himself naturally assuming the role of a Christian utility man and jack-of-all-trades. If nothing else, he assumed he would need to be at Nicaea so he could escort Sophronia back to Alexandria after the big event was over.

A sadness came to Rex at the thought of his mother-in-law, for it reminded him of Flavia. Turning away from the sailors in their boats, he walked farther along the waterfront to the imperial post office. There he gave the clerk a packet of letters, well protected inside oiled leather and sealed with strings and wax to prevent tampering. The clerk had been told to expect this correspondence from local church officials, so he already knew it was being sent to the bishop of Alexandria.

As Rex handed over the packet, a sigh escaped his lips at the thought of his own letter inside with the others. Now it was dispatched—gone from his hand and ready for transit across the ocean. The day would soon come when Flavia would receive it and read it with sorrow. No amount of loving words could take away her pain at learning Rex would have to remain away until the summer.

The trip to Nicomedia, Rex's second extended journey in recent months, felt a lot like a military campaign. In the army, he had seen this kind of sadness many times. Soldiers wrote to their sweethearts with deep affection, all the while knowing they couldn't be reunited anytime soon. Rex considered his current mission a kind of deployment on behalf of the catholic church.

He consoled himself with the reminder that unlike his earlier commission by Caesar Crispus, at least this time his life wouldn't be in danger. The army of Christ fought with words, not swords—and just like in warfare, some causes were so important that they transcended a man's desire for hearth and home. Sacrifices had to be made in warfare; how much more in the service of God?

A tavern called Poseidon's Trident was three doors down from the post office. Since Rex was feeling a little melancholy, he decided a cup of hot wine on this chilly winter day would revive his spirits. Poseidon's Trident was the sort of place where people from all walks of life congregated. Beautiful mansions lined Nicomedia's waterfront, so when their owners came in for a drink, they sat alongside fishermen and dock workers. A common brick-layer from the imperial palace might sit at the same table as the master of construction who employed him. Naval officers and high-level bureaucrats drank next to the scoundrels and riffraff that a seaport always attracted—and no one seemed to mind. Good wine often had a unifying effect like that.

It is good stuff, Rex had to admit when the serving wench brought him a steaming cup of calda. The dark amber wine had been mixed with honey for sweetness and ground peppercorns to give it spice. Rex let his mind drift as he sat alone in a corner, watching the customers laugh, drink, and gamble. He was halfway through his second cup when a woman walked through the door whom every man in the tavern couldn't help but notice.

She was a tall, voluptuous blonde from one of the Germanic tribes, with thick, flaxen hair and a face so beautiful it would make Aphrodite jealous. Her cheeks and lips were painted with flattering colors, not garishly, but the work of a skilled ornatrix. Beyond her stunning good looks, the woman had an elegant and high-class demeanor. The way she glided into the room with aloof self-assurance signaled that she was accustomed to an elite life.

The woman was accompanied by a large man with arrogance in his stride. His dalmatic was made of expensive silk, and his shoes were studded with gems. He had jet-black hair that Rex thought was probably dyed. Only one flaw marred his middle-aged good looks: he had the cauliflower ears of a boxer or wrestler. The best competitors could make a fortune by racking up victories, and clearly, this man had done so. He lay down on a private couch in a nook at the rear of the room with his beautiful escort reclining across from him. "Falernian!" he demanded, and the waitress jumped to serve him the tavern's best wine.

Rex returned his attention to his cup, but soon the arrogant wrestler was forcing his way back into everyone's awareness. He had grown angry with his companion—Persephone, he called her—and his voice became harsh. For her part, Persephone remained dignified even though she was taking a fierce tongue-lashing. The man was calling her crude names and mocking her appearance, despite her having no physical inadequacies that any man could ever discern.

"You sorry whore!" he berated her. "I never should have taken you from the gutter!"

"I was born to noble blood in Germania," Persephone answered calmly.

"Bah! You're a slave captured in war, and you'll never be better than that!" Persephone didn't reply, which seemed to frustrate the man all the more. He thrust his finger toward the door. "Get out of my sight!"

"I am free now, and not yours to command."

"You'll do what I say!" the wrestler shouted. Rising from his couch, he snatched his cup of wine from the table and threw it in Persephone's face. She scrambled to her feet, shocked and sputtering. A red blotch stained her elegant gown of white wool.

"You scoundrel!" she cried, humiliated in front of everyone. "Do you think you're more of a man now?"

The accusing words brought a bestial grimace to the wrestler's face. His gaze was fixed on Persephone, and he growled at her like a wild animal. "You're going to pay for that," he vowed through clenched teeth, "in blood."

The wrestler seized Persephone's arm with his left hand and balled his right into a fist. She tried to pull away but was unable to break free. The wrestler cocked his fist behind his head with a sadistic grin on his face. Then he leaned into his punch, putting the full force of his weight behind a blow that would surely break Persephone's jaw.

But it never landed. Rex caught the man's wrist in an iron grip before the blow could strike the helpless woman. "You don't want to do that," Rex said.

Infuriated, the wrestler turned to see who had taken hold of him. For a brief moment, the threesome was locked in a standoff, each held in the grip of another. Then the wrestler realized that to attack Rex, he would have to release his captive. When he turned her loose, Rex let go of the man's wrist. As the two adversaries squared up, the rage in the wrestler's eyes told Rex that a fight was unavoidable. It was only a matter of how it would end.

"Do you know who I am?" the wrestler snarled.

"I never even knew who you were, old-timer."

The insult was more than the prideful wrestler could endure. Gnashing his teeth, he launched himself at Rex. It was the kind of fierce attack that had probably overwhelmed many a wrestler, not to mention whatever rabble the man had taken to bullying at the local bar. What he didn't know was that this time, he had chosen to attack an elite special forces operative whose training was not for sport but for war.

The wrestler was in good shape for someone of middle age, and his strength was still considerable. Perhaps he could have made a decent fight of it if he hadn't been so overconfident. After feinting a left jab, he swung a right haymaker that would have knocked another opponent senseless. But Rex saw it coming before the guy's fist even started moving. Instead of ducking or dodging, Rex leaned into the punch and smashed his left elbow against the attacker's biceps, a painful and jarring blow. He also threw his right forearm into his attacker's throat. In the same instant, Rex stepped between the man's feet and used the pivot to throw the man to the ground. To make sure the fight was over, Rex stomped on the wrestler's gut, knocking the wind from him. He lay on the tiled floor, gasping and moaning.

Unfortunately, not all the men in Poseidon's Trident appreciated Rex's gallant intervention. He was a stranger here, while the wrestler apparently had friends in the room. Several other bulky men rose from their tables and began to approach. They all had the same cocky demeanor of former athletes who were used to pushing people around. "You think you're some kind of fighter, eh, German?" one of the men sneered as the other three spread out and surrounded Rex. The speaker had a close-cropped haircut and a big gap where a tooth was missing.

Through an open doorway behind the aggressive athletes, four armored soldiers entered the tavern. Having been drawn by the commotion, they had their weapons out. Rex immediately recognized their arrival as his best exit strategy. Raising his two palms toward the whole room, he said loudly, "I've got no fight with anyone here. My lady and I are just on our way out."

"She ain't your lady!" Gap Tooth cried.

"I am his lady," Persephone said, catching the eyes of the soldiers as she stepped close to Rex and took his hand. "We're leaving now, and we don't want any trouble. There's a silver piece on the table that will cover a round of drinks for everyone."

The unexpected generosity brought a cheer from the room and a surge toward the urn of spiced wine at the bar. In the sudden hubbub, Rex and Persephone slipped out the door and left Poseidon's Trident behind. After rounding a corner, Persephone released Rex's hand. "I'm in your debt," she said.

"I don't think it's over yet," Rex replied as he peeked around the corner. The four athletes had emerged from the tavern and were spreading into the streets to take up their pursuit away from the soldiers' watchful eyes. One of them hailed two nearby friends, who dropped what they were doing and joined the chase. "Guys like this form a tight gang," Rex explained. "A defeat of one is like a defeat of them all. Until they think they've gotten the best of me, they won't stop trying to regain their honor."

"They'll try to get the best of me too—but in a different way. I know how depraved those men can be."

Rex turned toward Persephone and looked her in the eye. "Don't be afraid, alright? I know what to do here. I'll stay with you until you're safe."

The reassuring words brought obvious gratitude to the beautiful woman's face. "What's your name?" she asked, surprising Rex by switching over to throaty Alemannic German.

He introduced himself in the same language, then beckoned for Persephone to follow him into an alley. "Are you married to that wrestler?"

"No! He bought me from army slave traders after my village lost a battle. I lived with him and kept him happy until he signed the papers for my emancipation. Now I'm free. But I have nowhere to go. The money was all his."

"We'll find you a place to stay. I think you can shelter with—"

"There they are!" shouted a voice, followed by the sound of running feet. Rex grabbed Persephone's hand. "Stay close. I'll get you out of this."

They took a zigzag route through Nicomedia's narrow alleys behind the waterfront shops, yet the angry athletes kept up their pursuit. Twice Rex had to dodge into a side street because he saw one of the searchers ahead.

Finally, he spotted what he needed: a direct route out of the maze. "Stand here," he told Persephone.

She obeyed, stepping onto a wooden pallet attached by ropes at its four corners to a single hook overhead. The hook dangled from the boom of a crane being used to repair an aqueduct, though no one was at work on it now. Rex climbed into the crane's treadwheel and began to walk. Persephone uttered a little squeak and grabbed one of the ropes as Rex hauled her up. She was so light that the big machine, designed to lift heavy blocks of stone, easily raised her.

No sooner had Persephone stepped from the pallet onto the top of the aqueduct than one of Rex's pursuers spotted him in the treadwheel. "Over here!" the man shouted to his comrades, and they began to close in. Rex scrambled out of the wheel's interior and began to ascend the boom. Its tip was quite a bit higher than the aqueduct, and a gap intervened between the machine and the water conduit where Persephone stood waiting.

"Throw off that pallet!" Rex shouted to her as three pursuers reached the crane and began to climb up after him.

By the time Rex reached the tip of the boom, Persephone had managed to release the loops that supported the pallet, which landed on the pavement below with a loud crash. Now there was only an iron hook dangling at the end of the boom's line. Rex gauged the distance to the aqueduct's surface where Persephone stared back at him, wide-eyed at the thought that he might be about to jump. It would be almost impossible to leap so far and remain on the narrow width of the aqueduct. Rex's momentum would surely cause him to tumble off its edge. Instead, he beckoned to Persephone for the hook. She pitched it to him, and he caught it. Then, just as one of his pursuers made a lunge for his heels, Rex leapt from the crane's boom.

Swinging at the end of the cable like a pendulum, Rex let his momentum carry him past the aqueduct. After reaching the end of his arc, he spun himself midair and focused on catching the side of the aqueduct with his feet to arrest his motion. He managed to do it, though not without smacking his ankles against the immovable stone edifice. Wincing at the sharp pain, Rex set both feet firmly on top of the aqueduct, then raised his eyes toward his pursuers.

The three of them were squatting on the boom like apes in a tree, with

Gap Tooth at the tip. "Looking for this?" Rex asked him, holding up the hook.

Gap Tooth had no response except to snarl in impotent frustration. Rex turned away from the crane and hurled the hook into the branches of a nearby oak. It snagged there with its cable far from the aqueduct, tangled and unable to be drawn back to the boom.

The three pursuers started hurling curses across the unbridgeable gap, but Rex ignored them. Instead, he turned to Persephone and gestured to the wide, smooth top of the aqueduct that stretched away in both directions like a sidewalk in the sky. "Shall we go for a stroll?" he asked her politely.

"Ja, mein Freund," the beautiful woman replied, then took Rex's arm and let him lead her away.

⚊⚊⚋⚊⚊

The city guards had just opened Alexandria's Moon Gate for the day when Flavia arrived at the Church of Theonas. Instead of entering the church, whose services wouldn't begin for another half hour, she walked to the gate and peeked out. "We'll keep an eye on ya," a friendly guard said. "Ain't no one around this early, anyways." And with that encouragement, Flavia left the city for a few moments of quiet reflection.

Unlike the eastern gate, the Moon Gate didn't have a suburban village outside of it, only a small necropolis and some garden plots. The coastline was nearby, so Flavia walked over to the sandy beach where the waves lapped against the shore. To her right was the western harbor of Alexandria, the Harbor of Good Return. It was separated from the Great Harbor by a long causeway that ran out to Lighthouse Island. A canal emptied into the sea here, admitting barge traffic from Lake Mareotis and the entire length of the Nilus. Even though so much commerce converged on this one spot, the city hadn't quite awakened yet on this Sun Day, so Flavia found her seaside location to be lonely and quiet, at least for the moment.

"Rex, what have you got planned for the day?" she wondered aloud, as if her words could be carried across the sea to his listening ears. Though being separated from her husband again was difficult, Flavia was glad that at least he faced no dangers like when he was commissioned into the army by Caesar Crispus. Nevertheless, she missed Rex sorely. The additional absence of her mother made things even more challenging. Yet Flavia had resolved to trust the Lord in this time of separation. Like many military wives, she understood that enduring time apart was just part of life.

The morning sun glittered on the water, and a light wind raised whitecaps out at sea. Though it was late February now, it rarely got cold in Alexandria, so Flavia needed only a light cloak to ward off the chill. She pulled it tight around her shoulders, then extended her hands with her palms upraised in a gesture of prayer. There on the beach, she prayed for Rex's service to the church, his safety, and his speedy return. *At least it isn't like Sicilia*, she reminded herself after her prayers were finished. During those years as a nun, she used to stare at the sea and wonder if she'd ever see Rex again. That uncertainty felt far worse than just being separated from her husband for a few months. *Thank you, Lord*, she added to her prayer, *for giving this man to me!*

Returning through the gate into the city, Flavia entered the Church of Theonas and found a place to stand among the other women in the left aisle. Soon, the clergy proceeded down the center of the nave, then the liturgy of the Word began. After the scripture readings and singing, Bishop Alexander gave a sermon on a passage from *Isaiah*. When he was finished, the liturgy of the Eucharist offered the body and blood of Christ to the people through the symbolic figures of bread and wine. Just before the dismissal, the bishop took a few moments to make some announcements—and one of them caught Flavia by surprise. She moved forward among the women so she could hear a little better.

"Our most excellent and pious emperor has sent us a letter," Alexander informed the congregation, "and its contents deserve to be heard by all." The bishop then proceeded to read Constantine's letter in which he announced the convening of a great council at Nicaea to determine the proper understanding of the Divine Triad. Delegates from far and wide were being summoned to that city in May, with the privilege to use the imperial postal system for their travels. Bishop Ossius would preside over the council's proceedings. Constantine's letter to Alexander concluded with the words, "Therefore I urge you to assemble promptly at Nicaea with four attendants of your choosing to assist you in all things. Be diligent to come speedily so that you may be present as a spectator and participant in our various deliberations about holy doctrine. God keep you, my beloved brother."

The church service ended with a pastoral blessing and the people began to leave, but Flavia lingered in the hall, waiting for a chance to speak privately with the bishop. After he had finished conversing with the last congregant, Flavia approached him. He smiled warmly at her and said, "Beloved Candida, let us step outside where God's sun shall warm us." The two of them adjourned to a sunny courtyard adjacent to the church.

After exchanging a few pleasantries with her pastor, Flavia got right to the point. "I wish to attend the council at Nicaea."

Alexander arched his eyebrows in surprise. "To what purpose, dear one?"

"My reasons are several," Flavia explained. "For one, I have come to see the doctrines of Arius as dangerous, and I wish to be part of their defeat within the church. I also know my husband and mother will surely be at the council—for wherever Ossius goes, they must follow. So I would like to see them sooner rather than later, if possible."

"Are those your only reasons?"

"There is another," Flavia admitted, though she found herself feeling uncertain about voicing it. Gathering her courage, she said, "It is a spiritual reason, coming from a prophetic word spoken to me by Athanasius. He says my life of retirement is ending, and I have a role to play in church affairs again—though what it is, I do not know."

Alexander turned away from Flavia for a moment, appearing uncertain about his reply. At last, he reached into a pouch at his waist and brought out five clay tokens, each marked with the post office's insignia. "Do you see these, Candida? Only five of us from Alexandria may attend this council. Consider the duties that are needed. Athanasius must go with me to help address theological matters. There must also be a scribe to take down notes and records. The fourth person must be a brawny man such as Philip, for the overland journey will take two months and the road isn't safe without a bodyguard. And then, of course, my personal manservant must attend to my daily needs. So as you can see, the five are already accounted for."

"I do not ask for the use of a token, nor for anyone to pay my way. I am able to cover all my expenses, if you will only let me join you. Please, Holy Father, I ask it of you."

Now Alexander grew uncomfortable. He rubbed his forehead, then absently brushed a braid of his wig away from his face. "There is a further problem, Candida," he said. "You are a woman. You cannot come with us men. Such a thing is not done in the church—not for a council like this."

The bishop's statement was startling to Flavia, to the point of being offensive. Instead of backing down, she said, "Such a thing *is* done in the church! Many years ago, I attended the council of Arelate at my bishop's invitation. Even now, my own mother is offering a woman's gifts to Ossius in the holiness of their friendship. There's no reason I couldn't accompany you to Nicaea."

Though Bishop Alexander seemed surprised by the strength of Flavia's protest, he didn't relent. With a new firmness etched upon his face, he again told her no, then quoted a scripture from *First Corinthians*. "'Woman was created for man,'" he intoned. "'For this reason, a woman ought to have authority over her head.' So says the apostle Paul. It is the natural order of God's design."

Since Flavia knew how that passage concluded, she didn't hesitate to speak the rest of the words aloud. "'Nevertheless,'" she added, "'in the Lord, a woman is not independent of man, nor is a man independent of woman. But everything comes from God.'" And with that scriptural affirmation still hanging in the air, Flavia bowed to her bishop, bid him good day, and left him alone with his thoughts in the church courtyard.

Over the next several weeks, the exchange with Bishop Alexander continued to bother Flavia. The more she thought about it—and the more she listened to the whisperings of her heart—the more convinced she became that Alexander was wrong to deny her the right to attend the council. If God was calling her there, no man should stand in her way, not even a bishop. The insights of God's daughters would be just as needed at Nicaea as those of his sons.

A plan came together in Flavia's mind. After several days of careful thought, she resolved to pursue it. She would join the trip as a private passenger, paying her own way in the carriage and asking for nothing in return. If the Christian travelers welcomed her, that would be fine. But if not, she would make her way to Nicaea alone. She would follow God's will in this matter, not man's. Flavia packed a traveling bag made of durable cloth, one she could handle by herself, and waited for the day of departure to arrive.

As always in the spring, the large ships of Alexandria were preparing to be loaded with grain for the annual delivery to Rome. Few, if any, were sailing to Nicomedia, the port from which an inland trip to Nicaea could be made. For this reason, and also because the bishop wished to visit some churches along the way, the Christian travelers intended to go by road, which meant they needed to leave plenty of time for a lengthy journey. Their departure in March would put their arrival at Nicaea in May. No doubt they would be joined by many other bishops along the road to create a holy caravan on its way to the city of victory.

Flavia found herself restless and unable to sleep the night before the departure. Finally, she rose from her bed about an hour before dawn. Although she could have waited for the company of Philip, who lived in her building and was serving as the trip's bodyguard, she decided to head over to the Sun Gate by herself. The Christian expedition would depart through the eastern gate onto the Canopus Way. After leaving the lush Nilus delta at Pelusium, the travelers would take the ancient highway up the coast of Palaestina to Antiochia. From there they would swing into Asia, traversing the treacherous pass called the Cilician Gates and the windswept plateau beyond it, before finally arriving at Nicaea.

A private litter bore Flavia from her apartment to the Sun Gate since she didn't want to lug her bag across the entire width of Alexandria. Alighting from the litter, she paid the leader of the porters, then walked toward the hostler's station just inside the gate. The smell of hay and manure was thick in the air. A man stopped her at the entrance to the stable enclosure. "Your token?" he demanded.

"I am traveling with the churchmen, but I must purchase my own token and pay my own way."

"Wait here," the hostler said, then stepped inside the office.

The eastern sky had grown lighter now, though the sun still wasn't above the horizon. Flavia tightened her cloak around herself against the predawn chill. As she waited, an uneasy feeling began to creep into her mind. Technically, she wasn't part of the official embassy to Nicaea, so for her to use the imperial travel system required a kind of bribe. Though Flavia hadn't lied to the hostler, she was not a legitimate member of the delegation. It didn't feel right to start such a holy expedition by skirting the truth.

She glanced to the city wall above the gate. A handsome guard stood there, watching the landscape lest any shady characters approach the city by night. Now the dawn was near, and his duties were almost finished. And then, with the sudden clarity that often comes to prophetic women, a scripture struck Flavia's heart and melted her resolve to take this ill-considered journey. God spoke to her through the 129th psalm, whose words were so powerful and distinct, it seemed as if a heavenly voice had uttered them aloud: "I wait for the Lord, yes, my soul does wait, and in his word do I hope. My soul waits for the Lord, more than watchmen for the morning."

I must wait, Flavia realized. *I must wait for God to lead me into whatever he wishes to do through me for his church. Not my timing, but his.*

Immediately, Flavia left the hostler's station with her bag upon her shoulder. The porters were lingering near the gate with their litter, hoping for another customer. Flavia beckoned to them, and they were only too happy to receive a double fare by taking her right back to where she had started. They dropped her off at her apartment building on the flanks of the Serapeum hill. The streets of Alexandria were still quiet, and only a few pedestrians were about. Everything was as it should be. It felt good and right to be home.

Flavia was about to trudge upstairs, at peace with her change of plans, when a voice hailed her from behind. She set down her bag and turned around. *Bishop Alexander!*

He approached slowly. As he drew near, Flavia thought he had a look of contrition upon his face. Reaching out, he took her hand in both of his. "Over these last weeks, the Lord hasn't released my heart for the way I brushed you aside," he told her solemnly. "Your words stayed with me, no matter how much I tried to ignore them. And your interpretation of scripture was more correct than mine. Will you forgive me, Candida?"

"Yes, Holy Father, of course! Every Christian needs the Lord's grace."

Now a smile returned to the bishop. "I am relieved!" he said with restored energy. "And it brings me to another matter." Alexander held out his hand. A token of the imperial post lay in his palm. "I believe you'll be needing this," he said with a twinkle in his eyes, "for I have decided that my documents at Nicaea must appear in the beautiful handwriting of a holy daughter of God."

—◦◦◦—

Though the surface of the aqueduct was smooth and flat, it wasn't extremely wide. Rex found that he and Persephone could walk two abreast, but there wasn't much room on either side. Since Persephone seemed nervous about falling off, she nestled close to Rex and clung to his arm, which seemed reasonable given the drop-off. Her perfume smelled of roses and myrrh—a pleasing aroma, Rex decided.

The aqueduct passed through a run-down neighborhood of Nicomedia, whose inhabitants were too downtrodden to care about a couple of pedestrians strolling overhead. As Rex and Persephone walked along, they chatted in the Alemannic dialect of German about inconsequential things like the weather and imperial politics. But soon the conversation turned to more personal topics.

"You're from the homeland, I take it?" Rex asked.

"Ja! From a village along the Moenus. Not far from where it joins the Rhenus."

"Me too!" Rex exclaimed. "I lived my first years there. Such great memories of those forests and streams. Then we moved to Britannia, with the legions at Eboracum."

"An army family, eh? Your father must have served with King Chrocus."

Rex fell silent for a moment, unsure of how much personal information he wanted to share with this stranger. Yet she seemed like a good person, a woman in need and not one to be feared, so he decided to be honest. "Actually, my father is King Chrocus," he admitted, then waited for a response.

It was a long time coming, but when it finally came, Persephone's single word nearly knocked Rex off the aqueduct. "Brandulf?"

Rex's head swung around. With his mouth agape, he stared at Persephone's perfectly shaped face. "You *know* me?"

"I am Gisela."

Gisela! She was a little tyke a few years younger than Rex from the next village upstream in Alemannia. Rex remembered her as an elfish playmate with whom he used to romp in the woods—the only girl who could keep up with him and didn't mind getting dirty in the process. She had hair so fair it was almost white, always plaited into two braids that fell upon her shoulders. And she could throw axes better than him, a fact he had never forgotten.

"My old friend!" he exclaimed, still speaking in German. Leaning in, he embraced Gisela, then released her quickly lest she get the wrong idea. He smiled at her and shook his head. "I can't believe it's you, after all these years! We used to have so much fun, running around in the wilderness like little barbarians."

"The old country seems like a different world to me now," she replied sadly, her gaze falling to her feet. "Much has happened since then."

"Let's continue to walk," Rex suggested, "and we'll tell our stories, as much as we wish."

The pair resumed their arm-in-arm walking down the length of the aqueduct. They decided to continue with their current names rather than revert to their childhood ones since Germanic names would signal their outsider status. Gisela had received the Greek name Persephone when she was captured as a teenager and trafficked into the empire. The warriors of her village had staged a raid against a Roman outpost, and in retaliation, the Romans burned the village and enslaved its residents. Her father, the village chief, was executed. Persephone's beauty had led her into the world of high-class courtesans. Lately, she had been running in Nicomedia's elite social circles. But now her future was uncertain.

"How about you?" Persephone asked. "I would have guessed an army career, but that sharp tunic makes you look more like a successful business-man than a soldier."

"I started out in the military. Did a stint in the special forces, attached to the Second Italian Legion. Rowed in the navy too. I picked up the name Rex in cadet school when they found out my father was a king. It was more about mockery than respect, but anyway, the name stuck. Now I'm out of the army. I live in Alexandria with my wife. I'm a catechist for the catholic church, and I also carry the sick on stretchers for medical care."

"Oh, Rex," Persephone said with genuine admiration, "it's so noble what you Christians do. I wish I could believe in your God."

"Why can't you?"

"Well . . . until now, I haven't been allowed to believe what I want. My masters have dictated my religion. Now that I'm free, I guess I could explore other things."

"Come to church with me," Rex invited. "You'll find Jesus to be the opposite of every other lord you've ever known. He gives to you instead of taking away."

"Much has been taken from me by my lords," Persephone admitted, and Rex understood not to press any further.

The conversation moved on to other topics. Now that it was early afternoon, the walkers found themselves overdressed beneath the direct glare of the sun and removed their cloaks. They came to an access hatch in the aqueduct covered by a stone slab with an iron ring embedded in it.

"Can we drink from it?" Persephone asked. "I'm so thirsty."

Rex shrugged. "I don't see why not. The water here is the same that comes out of the faucet."

Kneeling beside the hatch, he grasped the ring and lifted the heavy slab. Cool air whooshed up from the opening as he set the slab aside. The sound of gurgling water met his ears. Leaning down, he was able to scoop it with his cupped hand and take a drink.

"Is it good?" Persephone asked, kneeling across the hole from Rex.

"It's great. Try it."

Smiling mischievously like the little imp Rex remembered from long ago, Persephone reached into the hatch and scooped water of her own. "It's so pure and sweet!" she said with delight in her eyes. Again and again, she brought up more water, leaning far down and cupping it in both hands. It dribbled down her chin, but she didn't seem to care. She leaned into the hole again, and Rex noticed a trickle of water run down her slender throat and—

"It sure is sunny today," he remarked, glancing at the cloudless sky. "I'm glad we found this drink."

"Me too," Persephone replied as she guzzled water from her hands like she used to do from the bubbling brooks of Germania.

When their thirst was slaked, Rex replaced the hatch cover and the pair resumed walking. Their destination was Nicomedia's main bathhouse, the Baths of Antoninus, named in honor of the emperor who restored the grand building after an earthquake.

Arriving at the baths, Rex found that the aqueduct terminated at a holding tank open to the sky. Water poured out of the conduit and into the tank as if a countryside waterfall had been transported to the middle of the city. Pipes sprouted from the sides of the tank, serving the bathhouse or nearby mansions. But on the far side of the pool, Rex spotted the structure he was hoping for: a staircase that allowed maintenance workers to reach the rim of the tank. Its top step was just above the water's surface, and it descended to the ground outside the tank.

He glanced at Persephone. "Up for a swim?" he asked, gesturing at the pool.

"When have I ever said no to that?"

Before Rex could reply, Persephone dove into the water in a graceful arc. Astonished, and with no little admiration for her plucky spirit, Rex dove in after her.

The pair swam to the stairs, hauled themselves out of the water, and descended to the ground. They were soaking wet in an unknown part of the city, but they didn't care. It felt good to be on level ground again. Persephone's white dress, with its wine stain still upon it, clung to her lithe body in a way that made Rex avert his eyes. She shook her hair, spraying droplets everywhere, then smoothed her blonde locks back from her head. Her sandals were in her hand, making her seem like some kind of barefooted water nymph. Rex wrung as much water as he could from his tunic, but he didn't remove his boots. They were of a military style, open between the lacings and made to shed water.

"Where to?" Persephone asked.

"I'll get you to a safe place before I take my leave," Rex told his friend. "I think we can find shelter for you among the Christians. Let's head to the basilica. I know people there who can help you start a new life."

Persephone, however, had a different idea. "I might take you up on that later, but I think we should get dry first. I have a friend at a mansion near here. A courtesan like me." She paused, then corrected herself. "Like I used to be."

The mansion was only a block away, situated in a row of other fine homes near the city's grand baths. The master of the house was away on business, and as it turned out, Persephone's friend was absent too. Yet the household servants obviously knew Persephone and were accustomed to her coming and going. Instead of regarding her as a fellow slave, they deferred to her elite status within the master's social circle.

A valet showed Rex to a small bedroom off the house's atrium. He shed his wet clothes and was given a plain garment to wear while his tunic and trousers were dried by the fire in the kitchen. "Keep my boots away from the heat or the leather will dry out," he told the valet, who nodded obediently as he took away the clothes.

Barefoot and wearing what amounted to a night shirt, Rex returned to the atrium. Persephone was already there, reclining on a divan in a silk wrap tied at the waist with a sash. Her long legs were folded beneath her, and a cup of wine was in her hand. She tipped her head to indicate the decanter on a nearby table. "Have some," she invited.

Rex poured a cup for himself and tasted the wine—a sweet red with not much water mixed in. "A good vintage," he acknowledged, then took a seat on a couch opposite Persephone.

For the next several hours, the two friends chatted in Alemannic German, recalling many fond memories and sharing stories as the time slipped by. The language of Rex's youth came naturally to him, even after so many years of speaking Greek and Latin. It felt good to utter words that started from the throat and had real punch when they came out. The wine put Rex in a relaxed mood, and he found Persephone to be an excellent conversationalist.

Around dusk, the servants came in and lit the lamps in the atrium. The warm glow reflected off Persephone's smooth skin and seemed to make her hair glitter like gold. She smiled at him shyly yet also coquettishly . . . an unbelievably attractive woman.

But Rex was no fool. He knew himself, he knew how the world worked, and he knew it was time to go. He was relieved when the valet entered the atrium and announced that his clothing was dry. The man held Rex's folded tunic and trousers in his arms, with the boots on top in a woolen bag.

Rex took his garments from the valet and stepped behind a fine tapestry into the adjacent bedroom. The little room was lit by a single lamp, its dancing flame causing shadows to flicker in the corners. He took off the borrowed shirt and pulled on his trousers, a Germanic form of attire that the Romans had adopted too. When Rex sat down on the edge of the bed to put on his boots, he caught the scent of aloe and cinnamon arising from the linen covers. He had just stood up and was about to tug his maroon tunic over his head when he heard a single word whispered from behind.

243

"Brandulf."

He turned. Persephone was there, her hourglass figure backlit by the glow from the atrium. She let the tapestry fall into the doorway behind her, bringing her into clear view. Rex's heart began to pound in his chest, and his entire being was aroused by the intoxication of the moment.

Persephone reached to the knot of the sash that held her wrap together. "I have always wanted you," she told him as she began to untie it. "Taste and see."

"I will," Rex replied.

8

MAY 325

The road from Nicomedia to Nicaea traversed a rolling landscape dotted with farms, vineyards, and orchards of pears, apples, pistachios, and olives. Although the road trip could be reduced by sailing a short distance from Nicomedia and taking the most direct inland route, Constantine didn't mind making the entire journey by carriage, even if it would take a bit longer to arrive. The scenery was beautiful, the region lush and verdant. In fact, one of the most highly regarded experts on agriculture, Diophanes by name, was born in Nicaea. His writings on agricultural methods were still read today, four hundred years after his lifetime. *The city of Nicaea produces food for the body*, Constantine mused as he stared out the carriage window, *but will it also provide nourishment for the soul?* Only time would tell.

Although the emperor was enjoying his leisurely ride, the weight of anxiety was never far from him. The stakes were high, for much was riding on the outcome of this council. Constantine had summoned bishops from the whole empire—from the Euphrates River to the western ocean at the end of the world. At last count, over three hundred bishops had signaled their intent to attend. Many had already arrived in Nicaea, and others were on their way, mostly from the east, though a few from the Latin-speaking west as well. Such a great investment of time, effort, and resources couldn't be allowed to go to waste. The doctrine of the Triad—or the Trinity as they called it in Latin—would have to be determined at this council, one way or the other. Constantine intended to make sure everyone got on board with whatever was decided.

On the second day of the two-day journey, the emperor invited Lactantius to join him in his personal carriage. The Christian professor of rhetoric had served him well over the years as a valued adviser for religious affairs. Years ago, Lactantius rose through the ranks at Nicomedia as a public orator. During the age of persecution, he returned to his native Africa, then he did a stint in Gaul as the tutor to Caesar Crispus. No one had been more influential than Lactantius in forming that lad into the mature believer he now was. Constantine would always feel indebted to this godly professor for shaping his beloved son into such an upstanding young man. Now, Lactantius's wisdom was needed once again.

"There is a weighty matter I wish to discuss with you," Constantine announced as the carriage rolled along. "It is theological, yet it doesn't relate to the topics of the council."

"I have the scriptures here in my satchel," Lactantius replied, patting the leather case on the seat beside him. "So then, Your Highness, let us discuss the things of God and seek truth together."

Constantine grimaced, not in displeasure at the professor's words, but at the thought of the matter he had to bring up. Yet there was no way around it, so he plunged in. "Recently I learned that my brother-in-law attempted to escape and stir up a rebellion. Despite the mercy I granted him after our wars, Licinius plotted against me at Thessalonica. He contacted an army of Goths and tried to break out of the city. He was given a fair trial before a magistrate, and the evidence was damning. The verdict was high treason. As you know, that is a capital crime."

"Ah, I see. You wish to discuss the power of the sword. It is given by God to the ruling authorities. So says the apostle Paul in the *Book of Romans*."

"I am familiar with the passage, for I have reflected often upon it. God establishes all governing authority. Those who obey have no need to fear. Only those who disobey do, for they are defying what God has instituted. This brings them under rightful judgment. Human authorities are God's servants. Their sword executes God's wrath against wrongdoing. This is what the blessed Paul writes. It couldn't be clearer."

"And yet you feel conflicted in the case of Licinius?"

"I do—not because he is my relative, nor because I doubt the things I have just recited from *Romans*."

"Then why?"

"Because of things written in other scriptures. The sayings of Jesus about turning the other cheek. The mercy taught in the Christian church. How does that fit with governments bearing the sword in capital punishment, or indeed, in war? There are few men I trust more than you, Lactantius. As your emperor who is tasked to carry out these things, I seek your guidance."

To his credit, Lactantius didn't answer right away. Such deep questions shouldn't be answered with quick responses or glib replies. After a time of thoughtful consideration—or maybe prayer—Lactantius said, "Do you remember the confessor from Pontus whom I brought before you with his wife?"

"The fellow with no fingers? How could I forget such cruelty? The sight of his maimed hand is etched upon my mind."

"Mine too, for it was a heinous deed inflicted by a tyrant. And this brings us to the question of the government's sword. Many theologians believe that wars can be called just when they stem the tide of aggressive evil. Perhaps no Christian should participate in them. That is an ancient teaching of the church, and some believers still hold to it, though no longer everyone. Yet whether or not Christians can participate directly in killing, the wars must still be fought to protect the innocent. My own views on this have changed."

"And what do you now teach, my brother?"

"He who punishes evil guards the safety of the good. Who is guilty of violence? Not the authority who institutes just punishments. Nor the soldier who fights against marauders. Rather, he is guilty who injures an innocent person—but also guilty, Your Highness, is the judge who spares the aggressor so he may injure more. The farmer who lets a weasel run loose in his henhouse when he could have stopped it is just as responsible for the bloodshed as the weasel itself."

The image was vivid, and Constantine reflected on it as he stared out the carriage's window. Once, as a boy, he entered a henhouse to collect eggs. A weasel had invaded during the night, and its carnage was wanton, pointless, and complete. It seemed as if the whole henhouse had been painted red inside. Some creatures were just vicious killers by nature. If no one stopped them, they kept spilling the blood of the helpless.

"It is difficult enough being a Roman emperor," Constantine said at last. "But I am finding that being a Christian emperor is the hardest thing of all."

"We are praying for you to find wisdom, Your Highness. The church's leaders don't expect you to be perfect. We understand you are trying to balance many difficult things. But we can certainly see the difference between you and those who were hostile to the things of God."

Constantine nodded, feeling grateful for Lactantius's answer. He glanced out the window, then pointed into the distance. "Look! There is Nicaea on the horizon."

"Many new things are on the horizon," Lactantius said. The two friends lapsed into congenial silence as they approached the city.

Once the imperial carriage reached Nicaea's encircling walls, Constantine saw that an encampment had sprung up in the countryside. Since Nicaea was a small city, there wasn't sufficient room in the imperial palace, nor among the householders who could take in boarders, to lodge three hundred bishops and all their attendants. Constantine had arranged for leather tents to be sent ahead for the council's delegates.

Fortunately, the springtime weather was pleasant and the tents weren't uncomfortable. After taking a brief tour, Constantine was gratified to find that an upbeat, festive atmosphere permeated the camp. The bishops believed their cause was important, and they were excited about finding a solution. The visitors had plenty to eat, thanks to the produce of the regional farms and the abundant fish from Nicaea's lake. An aqueduct supplied pure, running water from the nearby mountains. Everything was set for the momentous event that was about to commence.

After a week of preparations, Constantine decided it was time for the council to be called into session. All the bishops and a few of the most senior priests gathered in the throne room of the lakeside palace. Seats had been provided for the churchmen, not only because some were frail on account of age, but also because many bore injuries from the persecutions that had only recently ended. Constantine had commanded that a special seat be placed up front for Bishop Paphnutius of Thebes—a faithful confessor who had been condemned to the imperial mines after refusing to deny his faith. Paphnutius had been intentionally crippled when his hamstring was severed and his eye gouged from its socket. The bishop surely would have perished in the mines had Constantine not defeated his enemies and rescinded the laws that persecuted the Christians. Now Paphnutius was at Nicaea to offer the special kind of wisdom only the confessors could supply.

No trumpet fanfare signaled Constantine's entrance into the hall because its brash sound would have been unseemly at such an august event. Nor did an armed military escort accompany the emperor. Yet his purple robe, adorned with gold trim and gemstones, was his very best. It was the same as he would have worn at a formal state occasion, for a meeting of God's leaders demanded no less respect than human dignitaries would have been accorded.

Constantine proceeded down the center aisle toward a gilded throne while the bishops filled the hall on either side. But when he reached the dais where his throne was situated, he paused. "I am merely a fellow Christian," he declared to his guests. "This is a convocation of the prelates of God's church. It is no imperial gathering but a spiritual one. Therefore I seek your permission to take a seat in your midst."

At these humble words, a murmur rippled through the room. "Sit with your brethren!" someone shouted from the crowd. "We invite you!" cried someone else. An acclamation went up that Constantine was welcome at the council. Only after the bishops had taken their seats did the emperor finally sit down.

Bishop Ossius, the formal convener of the council, now rose from his place and offered some opening words and a prayer of invocation, followed by a hymn. When he had returned to his chair, an expectant hush fell upon the hall. Constantine cleared his throat, then began to speak in Latin while an interpreter at his side translated his words into Greek.

The central theme of Constantine's speech was Christian unity. After giving public thanks to God for his recent victories over Licinius, he declared, "My brethren, now that all the impious tyrants have been removed from this earth by the power of God our Savior, I pray that the evil spirit who delights in divisions might be defeated as well. In my view, the existence of strife within God's church is far more dangerous than any human war or conflict. That is why these theological differences of yours grieve me more than political discord could ever do."

Constantine paused to let these heavy words sink in. The bishops nodded sagely and stroked their beards as they contemplated the evils of disunity within the body of Christ. Then, to take things in a more positive direction, the emperor continued, "Nevertheless, I rejoice as I sit here beholding this sacred assembly! I brim with optimism at what might be achieved over the coming weeks. My prayers will be fulfilled when I see you all united in one judgment, sharing the bond of peace among yourselves. Such unity is fitting for those whose labors are consecrated to the service of God. And I believe this lofty goal shall be achieved!"

These words elicited cheers from the gathered bishops. While they were celebrating, a servant brought in a charcoal brazier and set it at the emperor's feet. When Constantine had the room's attention again, he displayed a thick pile of documents. They were the many petitions that had been submitted since his arrival, with this or that churchman engaged in petty arguments about topics they wanted the emperor to adjudicate. After explaining what the documents were, Constantine announced, "Far be it from me to decide such disputes on behalf of the church! Instead, I call upon you to imitate the divine peace of God and be reconciled to one another in brotherly love. Withdraw your accusations, and let the harmony of Christ prevail among you."

With every eye on him, Constantine rose. He dropped the petitions into the brazier, and a fire immediately sprang up. While the churchmen gawked at this dramatic turn of events, Constantine raised both hands toward heaven. The flames danced at his feet, and the smoke of the burning petitions sent flecks of parchment swirling around him.

"Delay not, dear friends!" he cried. "Delay not, you ministers of God and servants of our common Savior! From this moment on, set aside the divisions that have existed among you. Embrace instead the principles of peace! For in so doing, you will not only please the Supreme God, you will also grant a boon to me, your fellow servant in the Lord."

At this prearranged moment, a door opened to Constantine's right. He exited quickly, leaving the smoke from the frivolous petitions rising into the rafters and wafting out the windows. Constantine could hear the tumult of the marveling bishops as he left the hall. *Thank you, Lord*, he prayed once the door had closed behind him. He knew the council's historic opener had made an impression that its witnesses would never forget.

For a long time, the emperor stood quietly at a window. He slowed his breathing and calmed his spirit as he gazed upon the lake of Nicaea. Sunlight sparkled on the blue expanse. The scene was tranquil, and Constantine allowed the gentle breeze to caress his face, bringing the scent of jasmine to his nostrils. It was a soothing feeling, and he delighted in it—until a servant's voice interrupted the quiet moment.

"I am sorry to disturb you, Your Majesty," said the Curator of Correspondence, a man named Horace. He extended a wax tablet and stylus toward Constantine. "The courier is leaving within an hour, and if this doesn't gain your signature now, it will be delayed by several weeks."

Constantine received the tablet, then frowned as soon as he saw what it was. Instead of postponing the inevitable, he scrawled his name in the appropriate place and pressed his signet ring into the wax. After bowing respectfully, Horace took the document away. It was the death warrant for Licinius's execution.

"It's hard being a Christian emperor," Constantine muttered with a shake of his head. "May the Lord have mercy upon my soul."

⚬⚬⚬

Rex handed his military-style knapsack to a tattooed sailor, who set it amidships without lashing it down since the weather today was going to be fair. The man reached out again, and Rex passed him the more lady-like traveling bag of Sabina Sophronia. When this, too, was stowed, Rex stepped into the boat, then turned to his mother-in-law behind him on the dock. "Ready?" he asked, extending his hand to help her into the unsteady craft.

"More than ready," she replied, taking his hand as she stepped from the dock. "There's nothing like lying abed for a week to make you want to see the sun and feel the wind on your face again."

Sophronia looked pale and gaunt, so Rex agreed with her comment that the fresh air and sunshine would probably do her good. She had been in Nicomedia for about a month now and, unfortunately, had caught an illness around the time that Bishop Ossius was departing for the council. Unable to travel to Nicaea, Sophronia had remained behind at the imperial palace, attended by the emperor's personal physician. Now she was ready to travel again. Ossius had asked Rex to bring her down to Nicaea as soon as possible, escorting her along the route and staying with her upon arrival. Rex thought that if they hurried, they might even arrive before the council's opening session.

Once the two travelers were seated in the fishing boat, a crewman pushed it away from the pier and another man hoisted the sail. It caught the breeze and snapped taut. Soon the craft was out of Nicomedia's harbor and into the open waters of the Propontis.

Since the goal was to reach Nicaea in one day, the two travelers hadn't taken the time to eat breakfast this morning. When Rex's stomach growled loudly, Sophronia knelt beside her leather bag and brought out a loaf of bread, some soft cheese, and a little clay jar. "Never let it be said that I didn't feed my son-in-law when he was hungry," she said with a smile. After tearing off a piece of bread, she slathered it with cheese and some fruit spread, then handed it over. Rex was gratified to see her take some of the food as well. Even though she was feeling better, she needed to keep up her strength.

"I hear they've set up tents outside Nicaea," Sophronia said as she munched on the bread. "The emperor sent them for those who can't stay in the palace. Ossius said he'd have one waiting for me, and you can stay in it too."

Rex licked a bit of jam from his thumb, then glanced at his mother-in-law. "You won't stay in the palace near Ossius?"

"We did consider it," Sophronia admitted. "In the end, though, we decided it'd be best not to. For appearances, you know? With so many bishops around, I wouldn't want to do anything to taint his reputation."

Rex had rarely discussed with Sophronia her relationship with Ossius, for it was her own business and there was no need to pry. In one sense, it was a perfectly normal relationship, since many priests practiced celibacy while inviting a woman to live under his roof to care for household duties. Yet such women—called "beloveds" by those who adhered to the practice— were often the subject of public scandal. Sometimes their illicit behavior at night was just a rumor, though all too often, it was real. Either way, the suspicion was always there, among not only Christians but also the mocking pagans. Many bishops wanted to use the occasion of Nicaea to make a church law against this disreputable practice.

Ironically, Bishop Ossius was one of the foremost critics of priests bringing women to live with them in their homes. Back in Hispania, he had presided over a council that condemned this common Christian practice. Ossius was strict about never spending the night alone in a house with Sophronia. In public, he didn't touch her physically, nor display any romantic affection. And yet this attractive couple was . . . *what*? Though Rex wasn't sure how to put it into words, it was clear a bond existed between the dashing Spanish bishop and the beautiful woman whose husband divorced her long ago. Rex decided to ask Sophronia about the relationship, though not to press the matter if she didn't want to discuss it.

"You know," he said cautiously, "I've always admired the friendship you have with Ossius. It's holy and admirable."

"Thank you, Rex. We have worked hard to maintain its holiness, though we aren't beyond temptation at times."

Sophronia's word *temptation* stirred up an unpleasant memory that Rex had tried to put behind him: his encounter with Persephone a few weeks earlier. That strange day had ended with her invitation to "taste and see." But Persephone had inadvertently used words from the church's liturgy, and they sprang to Rex's mind when he heard them. "I will," he had replied. "I will taste and see that the Lord is good." Then he left the mansion before she could disrobe and tempt him further—or before he could continue down the dangerous path he had lingered on for too long. Later, she tried to contact him at the palace, but Rex sent a godly widow to check on her instead. He hadn't seen Persephone since that night of risky temptation.

Shaking away the memory, Rex returned his attention to Sophronia. "I think that in another life, you and Ossius would have married each other. But God had a different plan for you."

The comment didn't seem to make Sophronia sad. "He would have made a fine husband," she said matter-of-factly. "I don't know a godlier man than he. Yet think also of this, Rex. Think of how much would have been lost to the church if Ossius had settled down in Corduba to raise a family. His divine calling lay elsewhere, that much is clear to me. Ossius was chosen by God for the purpose of helping Constantine find his way into the Christian faith. And I am honored to assist his ministry however I can—as a woman and a friend."

"Do you love him?"

Sophronia turned her head away and gazed across the blue expanse of the Propontis. For a long time she seemed lost in thought. Seagulls hovered overhead, trailing the boat's wake. Finally, Sophronia returned her gaze to Rex and said, "Of course I love him. But what is love? We have only one word for it in our tongue, maybe two if you count 'affection.' But the Greeks have several, and all of them apply to my relationship with Ossius. *Agape . . . philia . . . storge . . .* yes, even *eros*, though you probably don't want to know about that."

Rex chuckled and nodded. "I definitely do not. Yet I love you, Sophronia, and I know you're human. All of this makes you who you are. So I accept it—and like I said, I admire it too."

The sweet words brought a look of tenderness to Sophronia's face. She came and sat beside Rex on the crate he was using as a bench. Slipping her arm around his shoulder, she held him close. "You're a godly man too," she said. "I am glad you found your way back to Flavia. I couldn't have asked for a better husband for my daughter."

Rex looked sideways at the face that so often reminded him of Flavia's. "You raised her well. Thank you for accepting me into your family." For a while, the two of them fell silent beneath the warm and pleasant sun. Then, with a playful smile, Rex said, "You know what?"

"What?"

"I'm still hungry."

Sophronia threw back her head and uttered a melodious laugh. "Not if I can help it!" she cried, rising to her feet and returning to her traveling bag. She began to rummage in it. "No man will go hungry in my presence—least of all you, Rex."

"Amen," Rex replied as he received another slice of jellied bread.

It was midmorning when the boat reached a fishing village along the Bithynian coastline. Rex and Sophronia disembarked, then immediately found a hostler with a carriage drawn by two mules. Everyone in the region had been alerted to the great council, and the sudden influx of imperial funds had benefited the local residents. All the farmers, shopkeepers, fishermen, and teamsters were enjoying the unexpected prosperity. Rex and Sophronia were on the road within half an hour of leaving their vessel.

Around dusk, they arrived at the outskirts of Nicaea. Though the tents had been erected in haphazard fashion, a spirit of chaos didn't prevail at the place. Everyone seemed to be abiding by a reasonable code of rules. A pious old man named Nicholas, bishop of the city of Myra, had been named the "mayor" of the tent village. He was a skinny fellow with a long, white beard and a propensity for laughter. His reputation for generosity, especially toward needy children, had endeared him to everyone. The atmosphere at the camp was merry and upbeat.

Nicholas welcomed Rex and Sophronia warmly. When he caught her name, a look of recognition came to his face. "Sabina Sophronia?" he asked in a hushed tone.

"Yes, that's me," she replied, glancing around lest anyone should hear her full name. There were Italian bishops here who might know her, and representatives from Rome had probably accompanied Sylvester to the council. Everyone from Italy, except the pope himself, believed she was deceased. Sophronia needed to stay unrecognized at the council to maintain the life she now lived.

"Ossius tells me you wish to remain anonymous," Nicholas said. "Whatever the good Spaniard desires is fine by me. I will not speak your name again. Come along, follow me. Let me show you to your accommodations."

The goatskin tent indicated by Nicholas was roomy enough to billet eight soldiers. Upon entering it, Rex saw that Ossius had gone out of his way to make the place comfortable. Instead of bare earth, a woolen carpet covered the floor. Sophronia had a cot laden with cushions and sheepskins. A washstand with an ewer and pitcher was in one corner, and a small trunk was in another. An oil lamp hung from the apex of the tent to provide light like a real bedroom. Beneath a vent in the roof stood a brazier to take the edge off the chilly spring nights. Clearly, Ossius had considered everything Sophronia might need. And there was still plenty of room for Rex to lay a bedroll on the floor.

"I'll let you get comfortable," Rex said, then left the tent to give his mother-in-law some privacy.

Later that evening, he was chatting around a campfire with some Africans who had served as bodyguards for their bishops when a rider reined up nearby. "Aha! There you are!" the new arrival exclaimed as he dismounted.

Rex immediately recognized the Celtic lilt in his voice. It was his former teacher, Vincentius of Rome.

"Hail, brother!" Rex replied, advancing to greet his friend. The two men exchanged the kiss of peace, then Rex invited Vincentius to sit by the fire.

Vincentius, however, shook his head. "I've got some big news for you."

"What? Has Sylvester made you a bishop already? You're not even thirty! But some Italian town would probably bend the rules and take you."

Again the Celtic priest shook his head. "It's not about me. It's about you."

Rex was surprised by his friend's words. He hadn't been in Rome since last summer, almost a year ago. Since Rex had few connections there anymore, he couldn't imagine what message Vincentius had brought from that city. "Alright, tell me," he said with a shrug.

"An illness prevented Pope Sylvester from coming to Nicaea—"

"Is he in danger?"

"The doctors say he'll be fine. But he couldn't travel, so he won't be here. And, Rex, listen to this. He named you and me as his two legates to the council!"

The staggering news made Rex's jaw drop. "You mean like his official representatives? Attending the sessions? Voting, and all that?"

"Precisely! Look here." Vincentius extended his hand to show Rex his ring, whose red carnelian was marked with the papal insignia of a dove and a key. Rex raised his own hand next to his friend's. The ring upon his third finger matched the one worn by Vincentius.

"I'm just a deacon," Rex protested. "A teacher of youths and a stretcher bearer. I don't deserve this honor!"

"Who does? The high and mighty in the church? Those untouched by sin? Or those who have experienced the depths of God's grace? I think you understand grace better than anyone here."

"I do," Rex admitted with a wince and a nod. "Few Christians started out lower than me. I worshiped unclean spirits and was quick to shed blood— until God found me in the muck and saved me."

"That's why you're right for this moment, my brother! The Trinity isn't about logical arguments. It's about salvation. And no one understands God better than dirty sinners who have been made clean by his goodness." Vincentius put his hand on Rex's shoulder and looked him squarely in the eye. "So will you join me at the opening session tomorrow?"

Instead of protesting any further, Rex decided the strange circumstances must be from God. All he could do was be carried along by what the Lord had decreed. "Very well," Rex replied as he met his friend's gaze. "I will take my stand at Nicaea for the holy Trinity."

◦◦◦

For two months, Flavia had been enduring the rigors of the road. Though long-distance travel could often be physically taxing, she didn't hate it. The jostling of the carriage, the long stretches of boredom, and the lack of privacy were counterbalanced by the excitement of discovering what was around the next bend. And the fact that Rex was probably waiting at the end of the journey made every hardship worthwhile. Flavia decided she would gladly step into the traces and pull the carriage herself just to see her husband again. *We probably wouldn't get very far each day*, she thought, laughing at the absurd idea. *Better to ride inside and leave the pulling to the mules.*

Yet now that the long, arduous trip from Aegyptus to Nicaea was finally coming to an end, Flavia found herself strangely sad. While she was definitely ready to arrive, she had also bonded with her traveling companions in the shared conviviality of the road. After Bishop Alexander invited her to serve as the delegation's scribe, his original reluctance to include her was replaced by enthusiastic acceptance. He often sought her counsel about important matters or consulted her notes about the events she was recording. "The church has always welcomed godly women in its midst," he told her one night around the campfire. "I fell back into the pagan way of thinking that women are inferior." Flavia once again assured Alexander that she had forgiven him, and he finally dropped the subject.

By the time the delegation rolled into Nicaea, the original party of five had swollen into a huge caravan of ecclesiastical travelers. Bishops from other cities had decided to accompany the Aegyptians, and the farther they went down the road, the more delegations joined the parade. Flavia guessed that around two hundred people had just arrived at Nicaea, adding their numbers to those already here. The encampment outside the walls just kept growing.

Fortunately, Flavia wasn't designated to sleep in the tents. There was a house of devoted sisters inside the city, and Flavia was one of the few attendees who could lodge with them. For about a week, she lived quietly with these new friends, whom she found to be prayerful and congenial companions. No one knew exactly when Rex and Sophronia might arrive. And then, one bright morning, everything changed when Flavia answered the door and her husband burst into her life again.

"Rex!" she exclaimed as she saw his handsome, smiling face. He came to her swiftly, scooping her into his arms. Instead of speaking, Flavia let her passionate kiss convey what words never could. Rex's embrace felt so strong, so comforting and familiar, so utterly *good* that she felt she might burst. Her tumultuous emotions were a combination of joy, relief, exhilaration, and desire. Yet beneath them all was a deep and abiding love for this boisterous, courageous, rock-solid man.

Separating from the embrace, Rex stared at Flavia's face. "You look so good to me," he said softly, holding her cheeks in his hands. He kissed her again, then added, "I forgot how beautiful you are, even though I pictured you in my mind every day."

"And I thought of you, Rex. Every morning. Every meal. Every time I put out the lights. It went on for so long! I'm glad you didn't forget me after all these months."

"Forget you? Never! Look at this." Rex reached into his belt pouch and brought out the little perfume bottle she had given him long ago at the harbor of Alexandria. After unstopping it, he turned it upside down—and nothing came out. "I often dabbed a little of this on my beard at night so I could remember your smell. I kept doing it until I ran out."

"That's sweet," Flavia said.

She came close to him again, and he bent down his head so his bearded cheek was next to hers. Rex inhaled deeply, then sighed with satisfaction. "I missed you, my darling," he whispered with obvious desire.

"Me too, Rex. So, so much." She took a step back so she could see his face. "Two separations are enough. No more trips!"

"Agreed—unless we go together. From now on, we walk side by side wherever we go."

"Yes, starting now. Where are you staying? I'll bring my things."

"Out in the tents, with your mother. We arrived yesterday."

"How did you know I was here?"

"I ran into Philip this morning. He told me you came with the Aegyptians. Let's hurry and get your bag so I can take you to the camp. I have to get back to the palace for the council's first session of debate."

"What for? Are you guarding the emperor?"

Rex chuckled and shook his head. Holding out his hand, he showed her the carnelian ring. "You're not going to believe this. I'll explain everything while we walk."

After Flavia had retrieved her bag, she and Rex left the convent and headed out through Nicaea's northern gate. Rex's news that he was one of the pope's representatives at the council was surprising to Flavia, though not shocking. She knew the esteem everyone had for him, even if he couldn't quite see it himself.

As Rex carried out his duties over the next few weeks, Flavia saw that respect on full display. On many occasions, while she quietly took notes in the background of the council's deliberations, she smiled to herself when something Rex said was met with nods of appreciation from churchmen much older than him. It gratified her to see her husband held in such high regard. *There was a time when I wondered if this day would ever come*, she reminded herself. *Thanks be to God!*

As the last days of May gave way to the warmer month of June, Flavia slipped into a daily pattern of note-taking, cooking, and relaxing with her mother while Rex was occupied with council affairs. A second tent adjacent to Sophronia's had been set up for the married couple so everyone could have some privacy. Though the new tent didn't have any furniture in it, the floor was carpeted like Sophronia's, and the sheepskins were thick and comfortable. Flavia considered that a good thing now that her vow of abstinence had reached its end. "Come back together again," the apostle Paul had instructed the Corinthians. Flavia found this biblical injunction incredibly easy to observe.

After exploring her surroundings a bit, she discovered a place where she could get away from the hubbub of the council and catch a few moments of peace. It was a hidden spot in the woods where someone long ago—maybe even centuries ago—had placed a stone bench next to a trickling stream. The place felt secluded, because to reach it, the walker had to follow a narrow trail through dense foliage. Only after navigating through what looked like impenetrable underbrush did the trail reach the beautiful clearing where the bench was located. To top it off, an apricot tree stood above the bench. Flavia was delighted to have discovered such a quiet, restful place. She went there almost daily to sit on the bench, munch on a sweet apricot, listen to the bubbling stream, and lift up holy hands in prayer.

One warm afternoon, Flavia knelt beside the brook and took her fill of the cold, clear water. She stood up and wiped her lips with the back of her hand, then turned her eyes to the apricot tree. Most of the fruit had either fallen by now or she had plucked them from the low-lying branches. Though shaking some higher limbs would have dislodged more, Flavia was reluctant to do that because many fruits would fall, spoiling them for future eating. To preserve her harvest, only picking would do.

Flavia examined the lowest limbs and decided she could stand on the bench and easily climb up. Fortunately, she had left her mantle back at the tent, so she was wearing only a loose chiton that fastened at her shoulders and left her arms free. Her legs, however, were too encumbered for climbing. Since there was no one else around, Flavia gathered the folds of her dress around her hips and knotted the fabric, leaving her long legs exposed in a decidedly unladylike fashion. And then, like a frisky squirrel, she clambered into the apricot tree's leafy canopy.

The closest fruit to the main trunk was near the top, so Flavia climbed all the way up. She had just plucked a perfect apricot when she caught the sound of voices approaching below. Embarrassed to be discovered in a tree like a naughty schoolgirl, she held still, hoping the visitors would quickly leave.

Three men approached the base of the tree. When they finally came into view, Flavia was surprised to discover they were three of the most important figures at the Nicene council. Two were the famous Eusebii: the tall, thin bishop of Nicomedia and the short, pudgy bishop of Caesarea. And the third man was Arius himself!

Now that the men had reached the secret clearing, they launched into a heated debate about council strategy. "The other side has the numbers to win," Eusebius of Nicomedia complained. "More bishops are supporting them every day. Alexander is convincing them all. And that little deacon of his is like a bee-eater, flitting everywhere and chirping in everyone's ear."

"Athanasius is full of energy," Arius agreed.

"We need a new strategy," the Nicomedian bishop said. "You saw what happened when I put my creed out there—they ripped it up! Everyone refuses to believe the Savior is a creature of God. I don't know why that's so shocking, but it is. Now I'm disgraced even more than I already was."

The shorter Eusebius wiped his bald head with a kerchief. "I can't go back to Caesarea having changed my views. My people will know I gave in, and they'll scorn me for it."

"Here's our solution," Arius said. "We have to write up a creed with vague language and get the council to accept it. Then we can still hold our views under the cover of imprecise words. The trick is to use the language of scripture without actually defining it. That way, we can point back to those terms and be considered orthodox."

The shorter Eusebius nodded craftily. "What terms?"

"Common ones, like 'Lord Jesus Christ.' The 'Word of God.' 'Light from Light.' 'Life from Life.' 'Only-begotten Son.' As long as we don't define the terms, everyone wins."

"We should add a phrase from *Colossians* as well," the taller Eusebius said. "'Firstborn of all creation.' They can take it however they want. But we'll know it means he was the first creature made by God."

For a while longer, the trio plotted about how they could convince the council to accept their vague creed. It was decided that Eusebius of Caesarea would bring it forth as a long-standing creed from the apostles. The church of his city went back to the earliest days in the *Book of Acts*. If everyone agreed to accept the Caesarean creed as original and accurate, the Arians could continue to hold their views and point to the biblical words as their authority. Christ would be a noneternal creature of God, and no one could say otherwise.

Once the plan was in place, the threesome left the secret clearing. Flavia waited on her perch in the dense foliage until she was certain the men were gone. It galled her to think that these shepherds of the church were plotting to teach heresy by obscuring the meaning of holy scripture. The nasty politics, the deception and misdirection, and worst of all, the blasphemy against Jesus—all of it gave her a sick feeling in her stomach.

Once everything was quiet again, Flavia descended to the ground with the apricot still in her hand. She examined it thoughtfully, then took a bite out of it. "A woman and a fruit started this whole mess," she said after she had swallowed the mouthful. "But Lord, I promise you—this woman with a fruit is going to fix what she can!"

⚬✧⚬

June 325

Though many of the great theological debates at Nicaea were taking place in the city's public theater, Rex had discovered that the council's real business happened inside the emperor's lakeside palace. He had enjoyed listening to those fiery public debates, when one rhetorician after another gave a speech about the issues on the council's agenda. The deacon Athanasius had become something of a star among the debaters, not because of his verbal eloquence but because of his theological brilliance and uncontainable energy. Even so, despite all the sparks flying in public, the outcome was going to be decided during the closed-door sessions with Constantine in attendance. And one of those gatherings was scheduled for today.

Earlier this morning, Vincentius had awakened Rex with the news that another formal session was being convened at the sixth hour. "Everyone thinks we might vote today," Vincentius had said—an announcement that Rex was sorry to hear. Things seemed to be headed in the direction of a bland compromise, just like Flavia had overheard. Rex didn't want to see that happen.

"You can't let the Caesarean creed get accepted," Flavia said after Vincentius had left the tent. She was sitting on the carpet in front of a mirror that she had set on a trunk, brushing out her hair after sleep. "You've got to find a way to block it."

"I'll keep at it," Rex promised, though he wasn't sure what more he could do.

Flavia's discovery that the three bishops were conniving to put forth a vague creed, hiding their heretical views behind scripture's undefined words, had energized Rex. Unfortunately, his efforts to bring attention to this strategy hadn't caught on with many other council members. Bishop Ossius knew the emperor desired compromise and harmony, so he didn't want to hinder a process that seemed to be coming to an acceptable conclusion. Even Bishop Alexander was succumbing to the immense pressure to find a middle ground. "The words of the Caesarean creed do exclude the Arian view," he insisted.

But Rex was convinced that they didn't. If the words were twisted just so, the creed left open the possibility of Christ being a creature. Only Vincentius and Athanasius had joined Rex and Flavia in resisting the creed. Yet Athanasius was at Nicaea as an assistant to Alexander, so he couldn't vote. The opposition of Rex and Vincentius wouldn't be enough to sway the entire council, even though they represented Rome. Unless something big happened, the council seemed likely to adopt the ambiguous Caesarean creed.

Bishop Ossius convened the day's formal session, not in the palace's audience hall but in its rotunda. This circular room with an overhead dome had become a popular place for the bishops to address one another. Unlike the audience hall, where everyone had to face forward, this room allowed the delegates to be seated in the round. Though the debates in the public theaters had often been fiery, here they were more circumspect because each speaker had to look his opponents in the eye.

Chubby little Eusebius had the floor now, and he was making the most of his opportunity. "My hometown of Caesarea is a city of harmony," he declared to the gathered delegates. "Recall the momentous events of scripture that took place not far from my church. With my own eyes, I have seen the house of the centurion Cornelius. There he met with Saint Peter, and unity was achieved between Jew and Gentile. A sheet descended from heaven with all kinds of creatures upon it. 'God shows no partiality, but everyone who fears him is acceptable,' said the blessed Peter. And so, my brethren, let us demonstrate that same truth today! Let us agree upon a creed and prove to the world that love overcomes all."

"Harmony is a worthy goal for all believers," Constantine said, and everyone murmured their approval of the emperor's words.

Vincentius, however, leaned over from his seat next to Rex and whispered, "It is indeed a worthy goal—but at what cost?"

"The deity of Christ, apparently."

"May it never be," Vincentius muttered.

Constantine gestured toward Eusebius's parchments. "Read us the words about Christ in your creed."

After the bishop had gathered his documents on a reading lectern, he quoted the christological affirmations that he was proposing. "'We believe in one Lord Jesus Christ, the Word of God, God from God, Light from Light, Life from Life, only-begotten Son, the firstborn of every creature, begotten from the Father before all ages.' And then it goes on to speak of Christ's work of creation, his earthly life, his suffering, and his resurrection."

Constantine stood up from his golden chair. "These are my beliefs as well," he announced. "My brothers, I urge you: let us accept these words in a spirit of unity! Everyone can agree with such holy sentiments. What is there to deny?"

Rex could sense that an ovation was about to erupt in the rotunda. The group's collective will to find an agreeable solution would take hold and become unstoppable. Without hesitating, he rose to his feet and shouted, "Nothing . . . and everything!"

Constantine fastened his eyes on Rex. The cold stare of the emperor's eyes felt like being stabbed with twin daggers. "How many times, soldier, are you going to oppose your commander's will?"

"As many as I must, Your Majesty. Though not as often as I carry it out with duty and honor. Both are a form of service to you."

Surprisingly, Constantine didn't rebut that bold statement. "There is truth in your words," he admitted after he thought it over for a moment. "You may speak freely at this council, Brandulf Rex. You have earned that right."

"Thank you, Your Majesty." Rex could feel his heart pounding now, for he knew the future of the Christian faith would hinge on what he was about to say. *Lord, give me the right words*, he prayed, then began his oration. "My fellow believers in Christ—"

"Silence!"

Rex was thrown off by the unexpected interruption. Turning, he saw that the speaker was the other Eusebius, the lanky bishop of Nicomedia. The man's stringy white hair brushed his shoulders as he wagged his head, denying Rex the right to speak. He thrust out his finger in an accusing way. "This man is an adulterer!" he declared to the council.

Immediately, a ripple of disapproval coursed through the room. Rex felt heat rise to his neck and cheeks. Before he could reply, Eusebius added, "I know for a fact that this man sinned with a courtesan of Nicomedia. He lusted for the harlot Persephone and took her by force. This has been proven beyond all doubt. Such a foul sinner should not dare to lecture us about our pure and spotless Lord!"

"Is this true?" Ossius demanded.

"No, of course not!" Rex cried—but it was too late. The room had turned against him. Perhaps he could explain the facts and, in time, clear his name. But not here. Not now. The moment for declaring trinitarian truth was lost. Every eye was staring at Rex with suspicion and disdain. Like a battlefield when things turn bad, his only hope now was a strategic retreat.

Straightening his shoulders and standing erect, Rex met his accuser's fierce gaze. "You spew lies," he told the Nicomedian bishop. "But I refuse to dignify them in this holy council by rebutting them. I will take my leave until I can clear my name in the proper way."

"Good riddance, you dirty sinner," Eusebius spat with venom in his voice.

Though Rex wanted to throw back an insult, he held his tongue. *Be silent like Christ was*, he reminded himself, then exited the rotunda without saying another word.

Flavia was standing outside her tent at the grill fire, removing a rack of lamb from the flames, when she spotted Rex coming toward her at a fast clip. *Uh-oh*, she thought. *Probably not good news*. The only reason Rex would come back from the session so early would be if a vote had been taken—and that would mean the Caesarean creed had been ratified. But when Rex arrived at the tent, Flavia could tell from his expression that something else was wrong.

"Bad news?" she asked.

"Yes, but not about the vote. Eusebius of Nicomedia slandered me in front of the whole council. He made up a terrible lie. I had to leave in shame."

"Oh, Rex!" Flavia came close to her husband and took his hand. "I'm so sorry! What did he say?"

"You remember how I told you about Persephone?"

"The woman who came on to you? Your childhood friend?"

"Yes. Eusebius must have learned that I helped her. He told everyone I took her by force. He said he had 'proof' that I was an adulterer."

The terrible words hit Flavia like a punch to the stomach. To think that the council delegates would believe such a thing about Rex made her want to run back to the meeting hall and defend her husband. She put her hand on Rex's cheek, then lifted his chin and locked eyes with him. "I believe what you told me," she said. "I know this slander isn't true."

"It's not! I swear it!"

"You don't have to swear, my beloved. Your character is your oath. I will stand by you and help you clear your name."

Something happened then that Flavia had rarely seen. Tears welled up in Rex's eyes and dribbled into his beard. "Thank you," he said softly, wiping his eyes.

She embraced him, encircling his wide chest with her arms and laying her head on his shoulder. "I love you, Rex."

"I love you too," he replied, and the quiver in his voice told Flavia how hard this was for him. Though Rex was strong, he wasn't invincible. She knew that lies, when given credence, had just as much power to hurt as physical weapons—maybe even more.

Vincentius arrived at the tent a moment later, breathless from hurrying. Like a true friend, he offered words of affirmation in addition to Flavia's encouragement. The Celtic priest said he believed Rex's name could be cleared quickly, for many delegates were wary of Eusebius's trickery. The council session was adjourned after Rex left because no one knew exactly what to believe.

Though the two men went inside the tent to consider their next steps, Flavia didn't join them. She decided instead to visit her secret clearing for a time of prayer. The little glade was deserted when she arrived. Rather than sit down on the bench, she knelt in front of it and began to pour out her heart to God.

As she was praying, an idea crystallized in her mind that she couldn't dismiss. It was an audacious plan, yet not so audacious as to be impossible. "I'll go as far as you open the doors," she told the Lord. "And if you close a door at any point, I'll know it's not from you."

Instead of heading back to the tent, Flavia entered Nicaea and made her way to the imperial palace on the lake. Like most palaces, it had a forecourt open to the public, but the emperor's personal area was protected by bodyguards. Flavia approached one of the men, a husky fellow with Scythian features.

"You're late," the guard said gruffly.

"I am?"

"Don't play dumb with me. The steward expects his girls to be on time." Before Flavia could answer, the guard took her by the arm and gave her a little push into the restricted area. "You know where he is. Third door around the corner. Hurry up. Then check back with me when you're done with him."

Lord, I wasn't expecting that one! Flavia thought as she rounded the corner and ignored the room where the lusty steward was going to have to keep waiting.

A few bureaucrats passed Flavia in the halls without paying her much mind. She carried herself purposefully, and her attire was sufficiently dignified for such a place. Though she didn't know where the imperial residence was, she was determined to find it. She was going to tell the truth about Rex to Emperor Constantine.

"Well, look who it is!" said a female voice from behind.

Turning around, Flavia was shocked to discover that the speaker was Empress Fausta. Immediately, Flavia bowed at the waist. "I greet thee humbly, O great Augusta," she said.

But Fausta wasn't inclined to be formal. "You may rise. There is no need for such flowery words between us."

"As you wish, my lady."

"It is a surprise to see you in these halls. Yet I imagine I know why you're here."

"You know me?"

"Yes, through your husband, whom I've known for many years. Ever since he hung my father from the crossbeams of my own bedroom. That's not an easy thing to forget." When Flavia had no reply to this terrible statement, Fausta added, "Do not fear—it needed to be done. A hanging was too good for him, in fact." After shaking away the memory, Fausta said, "Have you come to defend Rex's innocence?"

"Yes! How did you know?"

"I heard what happened at the council. What else would bring you here? It's exactly what a proper Christian wife would do. And by all accounts, that is what you are."

"Rex is innocent, my lady. I wish to say it personally to the emperor."

"I know he is. Rex is one of those few truly good men. And there's nothing Eusebius wouldn't say or do to get his way. If he weren't Constantine's relative, I doubt he'd still be the bishop of Nicomedia. He certainly doesn't have the holiness for such a job. But he's got all the craftiness a politician could ever want."

Flavia decided not to get sidetracked with other matters, but to press toward her main objective. "So, then . . . may I speak to the emperor? As one wife to another, I ask you—may I defend the honor of my man?"

Fausta chuckled. "The higher Rex goes in life, the more futile such a task will become. Too many people will want to bring him down. Trust me. It's impossible to defend against all the accusations."

"But this one has consequences. The outcome of the council depends on it. Vital theology hangs in the balance."

"Theology?" Fausta's lip curled up. "It is a subject irrelevant to women."

"No," Flavia said gently. "Theology is the joy of women—for in it, they discover they are welcomed by God. That is a truth men have hidden from them for eons."

The augusta regarded Flavia with a cocked eyebrow and an appraising eye. Finally, she said, "You interest me, Junia Flavia."

"May I speak, then, with the augustus?"

"Yes, but only on one condition."

"And what is it, my lady?"

"That you talk about more than just your husband."

"But he is the reason I have come," Flavia said. "What else should I discuss?"

"I think Constantine needs to learn some theology from you."

—◦◦◦—

Constantine lay on his couch in the semidarkness of a shuttered room. It was his summer bedroom at the palace, one that faced north so it would be cooler during the heat of the day. Having awakened from a nap, he was lingering in the space between waking and rising. Never would he have done such a thing when he was a young man crisscrossing the empire on his rise to power. *But I am in my fifties now*, he reminded himself. *I have earned a little rest in the afternoon if I wish.*

He had just risen from the couch and poured himself a glass of water flavored with citron fruit when the steward entered. "Lady Fausta to see you," he announced. "Accompanied by a visitor."

"Send them to the patio," Constantine replied.

He carried the water jug and some extra glasses to the little courtyard adjacent to his bedroom. A leafy citron tree loomed over four wicker chairs around a low table. Constantine had just set down the serving tray when Fausta entered with her guest, a beautiful woman of about thirty years old with dark hair and a slim figure. She was dressed in a stylish yet modest fashion. Although Constantine thought she seemed familiar, he couldn't quite place her.

"I bring you Lady Junia Flavia," Fausta said, apparently discerning her husband's lack of recognition. "She is the wife of Brandulf Rex."

Of course! I knew I had seen her before. Constantine dipped his chin politely. "I welcome you, Flavia. Your husband is a mighty warrior, and your mother is a noble lady. She provides needed companionship to Ossius, and for that I am grateful. A lonely man is not at his best. And I need Ossius at his best. Won't you have a seat?"

When the women had settled into the wicker chairs, Constantine sat down opposite them. After pouring two more glasses of the tart citrus water, he served the women, then asked the visitor, "What can I do for you?" Although Constantine suspected he already knew the answer, he thought it best to let the lady speak for herself.

Flavia got straight to her point. "My husband is innocent of the accusations made against him today. He did not take Persephone to bed—neither by force nor by will. There was no adultery."

"I know. I have already investigated the matter. Then I rebuked Eusebius for spreading rumors."

Flavia seemed at once surprised and gratified by this announcement. "How . . . how do you know this?"

"Every emperor knows what happens in his palace. It is his steward's job to be aware. Today I learned that the woman, Persephone, tried to gain entrance to the Nicomedian palace where Rex was staying, claiming to be his lover. He refused to see her. She grew angry and made accusations. It is these which the bishop must have heard. But it is well-attested that Rex refused the woman's advances. As for what might have happened beforehand—this I do not know."

"Nothing happened," Flavia insisted. "I would know if Rex were lying."

"I believe you. Rest assured, we will clear your husband's name."

The look of gratitude that came to Flavia's face pleased Constantine, for he recognized it as a response to the gracious way he intended to reign. Gone were the days of tyranny, cruelty, and double-dealing. A Christian emperor should rule with truth and mercy.

Sensing that the meeting had come to a swift and fruitful conclusion, Constantine was about to bid his guest farewell when Fausta opened the door to a new subject. "It may surprise you to learn that this woman is more than just a housewife," the empress said. "She is a theologian of the church as well."

Constantine glanced at Fausta with surprise. "Since when does theology interest you?"

"I am no pagan!" Fausta answered defensively. "I teach our sons the things of God. About the Heavenly Father, and the magic of Jesus, and all of that. Women can be theologians too! I am very interested in such topics, and so are our three boys."

Constantine chuckled, understanding his wife more clearly now. "So Crispus isn't the only pious one in the family, eh?"

"Certainly not! I am much more theological than he. And I'm passing on my deep faith to your sons. They will be fine Christian rulers, not very long from now."

"Indeed, they will. All four of them." Constantine turned his attention back to Flavia. "So you are a theologian?"

"Every Christian is, Your Majesty."

"Well said! Then what do you think should be achieved by this great council?"

"Clarity. That is what is needed most here—clarity. I know for a fact that

Arius and his party wish to hide their ideas behind vague words. Athanasius has seen them whispering and snickering at the council. They believe they can accept terms like *only-begotten* and still hold their doctrines."

"That term comes straight from John's gospel. 'For God so loved the world that he gave his only-begotten Son.' What could be wrong with it?"

"I will tell you," Flavia said. "It declares Christ to be God's only Son. But it doesn't say exactly when the Son began. Has he always existed for all eternity? Or is he like human sons, who do not exist before they are begotten by their fathers? John's term said nothing about eternality, so the Arians can hide behind its imprecision. They can claim the Son didn't exist before he was begotten. He was the first creature to be made at the beginning of the world's ages. But that would make him inferior to God."

"You are very learned in these matters."

"I am no more than a student of the scriptures, Your Majesty."

"Be that as it may, most of the men here disagree with you. The creed of Caesarea appears to be acceptable to the bishops. They're almost ready to sign it. Peace can be obtained, and everyone can go home happy."

"But is that really the kind of peace you want? You wouldn't accept such a peace in your earthly empire. Why would Christ on high accept it? You do him a disservice by endorsing so false a peace."

"Is that so?" Constantine sat back in his chair, letting the little patio fall silent. There was no breeze, and the air was thick with the smell of citrus. Empress Fausta shifted in her seat, no doubt aware how dangerous it was to speak so boldly to an emperor.

Nevertheless, Flavia seemed undeterred. "There is no middle ground," she said. "You must choose a path and follow it where it leads. Define your terms. Then live with them."

"And how would you bring clarity to this matter, Flavia? I ask you genuinely, for I perceive you to be wise."

"There is a word the Arians cannot abide. I have been serving Bishop Alexander as his scribe, and I have noted this many times. Whenever it comes up in discussion, the Arians grow anxious, for it is the one term that excludes their views completely."

"And what is it?"

"*Consubstantial*. If the Son shares the same substance as the Father, they must be coeternal. And that means the Son cannot be a creature who once did not exist."

"In Greek, what is this word?"

"*Homoousios*. If it were part of the creed, everyone would know the Arian view is excluded as heresy. Then you would have the true peace that accompanies clarity, rather than the false peace of saying nothing at all."

For a long time, Constantine was silent as he reflected on Flavia's words. This extraordinary woman had somehow worked her way into his palace, then confronted not only his doctrine but his very leadership of the empire. Few women would have dared such a thing. But Christian women weren't like others. They had the holy fire of God inside them.

"You know what I think?" Constantine said at last.

"What, Your Majesty?"

"I think you are more than a theologian."

"I am?"

"Yes, Lady Junia Flavia. I think today you have become a prophetess of God."

<hr />

July 325

Rex received the reed pen from Bishop Ossius and stepped up to the table on which the Nicene creed had been laid. The table was situated directly beneath the dome of the palace rotunda. Encircling it were the three hundred delegates who had gathered for the signing ceremony. Emperor Constantine watched the proceedings with an approving eye, though he had no intention of signing the creed. This was a day for the church's leaders to express their theological harmony without any interference from politicians.

The document on the table consisted of seven pages: the creed itself, written out in beautiful Greek calligraphy, followed by six blank pages for the signatories. Ossius, as the convener of the council, had signed first. Next, Pope Sylvester's two legates were given the privilege of signing. Then all the other bishops would sign as well.

After Rex had affixed his name to the document, writing "Vitus of Rome" beneath the name of Ossius, he glanced at the creed. Though some of its language overlapped with the earlier Caesarean one, substantial modifications had been made so that this creed was entirely different. At the insistence of Emperor Constantine—influenced by Flavia's prompting behind the scenes—the words *consubstantial with the Father* had been included. Rex felt gratified to see the words written in bold script on the page. There was also a clarification of the term *only-begotten*, stating that the Son was "from the substance of the Father." Everyone understood what these phrases meant: since the Son shared in the substance of the eternal Father, there was never a time when he didn't exist. At the end of the creed, there was even a firm denial of some Arian slogans. The catholic church had once and for all rejected a creaturely Christ.

"Having second thoughts?" Vincentius quipped from over Rex's shoulder.

Rex turned around and handed his friend the pen. "Just taking it all in," he replied with a smile.

He made room for Vincentius to step up to the table, then left the rotunda and went to the palace's nearly empty throne room, taking a seat next to Flavia. A grand speech from the emperor was scheduled after the signing ceremony, but with so many signatories waiting to write their names, that event was at least an hour away.

"Were the Eusebii in the rotunda?" Flavia asked. "I imagine neither of them would wish to show his face."

"Believe it or not, they were both there. Somehow they had convinced themselves to put their names on this creed. Only three people refused to sign: two Libyans and, of course, Arius himself."

"My mother heard from Ossius that there was a confrontation when they exiled Arius. Like someone was going to hit him on the way out the door."

"Well, the bishop of Antiochia did take a step toward him with his fist clenched. But guess who intervened?"

"You?"

"I was thinking about it. But no, it was Nicholas of Myra. 'Step back,' he said. 'Christians do not behave that way.'"

"Nicholas! He's such a jolly man. I can't imagine him being firm like that."

"He was very firm. And the other bishop backed down."

Flavia nodded. "As he should have."

She and Rex continued to converse quietly while the creed's signatories gradually arrived in the reception hall. It took more than an hour for the room to fill, but at last, they were all assembled. The emperor entered in grand procession and took a seat on his throne. His speech, which he called an "oration to the saints," demonstrated a depth of theological insight that Rex found surprising. Unlike earlier in his reign, Constantine now rejected every kind of idolatrous worship, even the sun god, whom he used to equate with Christ. Clearly, the emperor had grown in his understanding of the gospel. His faith seemed genuine to Rex, though of course, only God knew the heart.

After his speech was finished, the emperor surprised everyone with an announcement about his future plans. "It was nineteen years ago that the troops at Eboracum acclaimed me as emperor," he declared in his strong, clear voice. "To commemorate my upcoming Twentieth Year, I shall embark on a grand tour of the empire. In each place I stop, I shall spread the word of God and proclaim my hope for peace and harmony. Then, one year from now, I shall culminate the tour in Rome. There I shall join the holy bishop of that city in thanking God for my victories and in beseeching the Almighty for his continued blessings on our Christian empire!"

The momentous announcement was met with cheering from the assembled bishops. Rex leaned over to Flavia and said, "It's a good idea. I think it will bring some needed healing after all the splits and divisions we've endured."

"Harmony isn't easy to achieve, but today it feels possible," she agreed.

When the speech was over and the bishops were dismissed for the evening, Rex and Flavia didn't head back to the encampment outside the walls. Since they would be leaving Nicaea tomorrow, they decided to find a hot-food counter for their last meal. After receiving a jug of wine and a dish heaped with roasted pheasant over vegetables, the pair found a bench on the lakeshore in front of the imperial palace. Across the water, the sun was setting behind the hills, giving the sky a rosy hue that faded to dark blue. Rex could see the thin line of the highway that led to the coast—the road he and Flavia would be traveling tomorrow.

"I'm ready to get home," he said wistfully.

Before Flavia could reply, a Germanic soldier in chain mail approached the bench and said, "Stand up. The augustus and his wife wish to speak with you."

Quickly setting aside their food, Rex and Flavia rose from their seats.

The bodyguard was right: Constantine was walking up to meet them—and Fausta was at his side.

"Tonight is a night to celebrate, for we have achieved a great victory at the City of Victory!" the emperor said when he had drawn near.

"It shall be remembered through the ages," Rex said.

"Such a victory is worthy of a grand tour so my subjects can share in what God has done. Don't you agree?"

Rex nodded. "My wife and I both said so. We pray that the Lord will bless this endeavor."

"Actually, there is something you could do to help those prayers be answered." Instead of waiting for Rex to inquire what it was, Constantine followed up his words and said, "We want you to come with us."

"Both of you," Fausta added. "We want you to spend the next year with us on the tour."

Rex glanced at Flavia. Judging from her expression, she seemed just as shocked as he was. Turning back to the emperor, Rex asked, "What do you want from us, Your Majesty? The empire is at rest and the legions are available. You have no need of a bodyguard."

"That's right. Your services are no longer required for military purposes."

"Then what?"

"For counsel, Rex. For insight into church affairs. And beyond this, I believe the company of your wife will bless Lady Fausta, who has much to learn about the practice of the Christian faith."

"We shall cover all your expenses," the empress said, "and at the end of the year, we will pay you handsomely."

Flavia looked toward Fausta and respectfully dipped her chin. "We are honored to be asked, my lady. But why do you choose us for such a task?"

Now it was Constantine and Fausta's turn to exchange glances. They smiled at each other, then Fausta replied, "Because the two of you will tell us what we need to hear, not what you think we want to hear!"

"So what do you say?" Constantine pressed.

Stepping away from the royal couple for a moment, Rex asked Flavia, "Is the apartment in Alexandria in good hands?"

"Locked up tight, with the rent prepaid for six months. A second payment can be arranged with the landlord."

"Then . . . do you want to do this?"

A bright smile came to Flavia's face, and she nodded vigorously. "Let's have another adventure, Rex!"

Turning back to the emperor, Rex bowed in grand fashion. "So be it!" he said with a flourish toward the west. "Let us go to Eternal Rome."

"Nay, let us go to the city of God," Constantine replied.

9

Pope Sylvester often felt that being the bishop of Rome required him to find the right balance between pastoral opposites. When to speak up and when to listen? When to thunder and when to whisper? When to pray and when to act? When to conceal and when to reveal? When to chastise and when to forgive? When to fast and when to feast? "To all things there is a time," said the *Book of Ecclesiastes*, "and a season for every matter under heaven." The pastor's duty was to determine which time was at hand.

But today, at least, Sylvester knew what the day was about: reconciliation. This evening, after the heat of the Roman sun had abated, five repentant sinners would be reconciled to the church after their period of penitence. It would be a time for forgiveness, celebration, and feasting. These five lost sheep had been recovered from the brambles of heresy by the loving hand of the Good Shepherd.

Sylvester had arrived yesterday at the Hall of the Church, one of Rome's original congregations that went back to the time of the apostles. He had been accompanied to the Trans Tiberim neighborhood by Archdeacon Quintus, his longtime assistant and a man of great erudition. Quintus was a dignified older man who had served the previous four popes as their chamberlain and secretary. Though normally placid, lately, something seemed to be bothering him. Quintus was restless in a way that wasn't normal for him. "A malaise is upon me," he had said.

"Perhaps it is from this roasting summer heat?" Sylvester had suggested.

"Perhaps," had been Quintus's only reply.

Sylvester walked to the central fountain in the atrium of the guesthouse where he was staying. Previously, the fountain had depicted a naked water nymph with flowers in her hair, but that sculpture was replaced when the catholic church acquired the house. Now a doe with a gracefully arched neck spewed water into a sparkling pool at her feet. Sylvester cupped his hands in the stream and drank his fill of the cool water, then wiped his mouth on his sleeve. A bishop didn't need to be fussy about such things, at least not in private. A simple life was best for the leaders of God's church. And besides, the silver goblets left by the house's previous owner had been moved to the church next door for the Holy Eucharist.

The front door to the house opened, letting in a blast of heat from the sun-soaked street, only to close again quickly. Then Quintus emerged from the vestibule with a little sweat on his forehead. "We have a long-awaited visitor," he announced, indicating a man behind him. "I have just escorted him here from the Tiberis docks. Look who it is!"

When Quintus stepped aside, the atrium's skylight revealed a lanky visitor whose shaggy red hair made him immediately recognizable. "Brother Vincentius!" exclaimed the pope. "Welcome home!"

The two men embraced and exchanged the kiss of peace while Quintus moistened a cloth in the fountain. After Vincentius had received the cloth and wiped away the sweat and grime of travel, the trio took seats in the coolest part of the atrium where the direct sunlight never reached. "Tell me everything," Sylvester said. "But first, tell me the final outcome! Then start at the beginning and give details."

"The Arian view was rejected at the council," Vincentius announced.

"Praise God! Our Savior is no mere creature. Now the church has recognized it forever."

Vincentius reached inside his satchel and brought out some parchments. "I have here a copy of the creed. Less than a month ago, the council ended its sessions and the emperor departed. I came straight here with this document for your eyes."

"The calligraphy is beautiful," Sylvester observed as he received the parchments.

"It was copied by Junia Flavia, the wife of Vitus."

Sylvester was too absorbed in his reading to reply. He pored over each word of the creed, which had been translated into Latin. After examining the list of signatories, he read the creed again. Attached to its end was a repudiation of certain heretical slogans. "The rejection of the Arians is clear," Sylvester said. "The catholic church condemns those who say 'There was a time when he was not' or who call the Son of God a 'creation.'"

"It was a great victory," Vincentius said. "The emperor finally saw the importance of truth instead of bland compromise. The eastern heresy was defeated. Now if only we could say the same about the Manichaeans infecting our city."

"Your voice is a little raspy, brother," Quintus observed, rising from his seat. "Allow me to get you a drink." The archdeacon excused himself and left the other two men to their discussions of the Nicene council.

Once Vincentius's report was complete, it was clear that the new creed had articulated orthodox doctrine in ways that would be hard to refute. Though the Arian party would surely attempt countermeasures and theological debate would continue, Sylvester felt confident that the eternal deity of Christ had been firmly established.

By the time Quintus returned with three wooden cups on a tray, the conversation had moved on to other matters. The men conversed a little longer, then Sylvester urged Vincentius to go refresh himself after his long journey. Since the house had a small bath facility, Vincentius could clean up, then catch an afternoon nap before attending the reconciliation service in the church next door.

The glare of the sun was no longer in the blue dome of heaven when Sylvester left the guesthouse and entered the Hall of the Church. It was a relatively plain building, rectangular in shape and decorated only with a simple fresco of Abraham offering his son Isaac on an altar. Next to the altar was the ram that served as a substitute that day. The faithful had already assembled when Sylvester arrived, the women on the left and the men on the right. The bishop proceeded to the far end of the hall and turned around to stand in front of the altar.

"My beloved children, I greet you in the Lord," Sylvester began. "We are gathered today for a most holy purpose: the reconciliation of penitent sinners, whom we welcome with open arms, as does our God, whose mercies are everlasting."

"Amen," the people said in unison. And the most emphatic of all were the five penitents standing at the front of the church.

After some opening remarks from the scriptures, the bishop asked his five lost sheep—now found again—to come stand beside him. Each of them offered a simple word of public confession. "I joined the sect of the Manichaeans," they admitted. "I denied my Savior, whose ways are blasphemed in that cult."

"And is your repentance genuine?" Sylvester probed.

"Yes, Holy Father," each of them affirmed.

"And have you made an outward sign of your inward repentance through a season of prayer, fasting, and almsgiving?"

"Yes, Holy Father," the penitents repeated.

"Then hear this word of scripture: 'In our Lord Jesus Christ, we have redemption through his blood, the forgiveness of our trespasses, according to the riches of his grace that he lavished upon us.'"

"Amen!" exclaimed the five penitents, signing themselves with the cross.

Now it was time for the laying on of hands. Sylvester approached each of the penitents—two women and three men—and placed his palm upon their heads. Then he touched their ears and their mouths, signifying that what goes in and what comes out of them was cleansed by God. All five of the restored Christians had tears in their eyes when they received the bishop's healing touch after having so grievously sinned.

Sylvester then raised his hands over the congregation. "My people, come forward and embrace your brethren! In Christ, their sins are forgiven, like yours and mine as well. I pronounce these brethren clean!"

The congregants surged forward at these welcoming words. They surrounded their beloved fellow Christians with warmth and acceptance. Tears were flowing freely now—tears of exultation at the sweet release from bondage. Sylvester noticed one woman in particular whose eyes glistened and whose face was marked by radiant joy. She was the godly woman Lucretia, whom Sylvester had seen at the Great Friday service upon the Aventine Hill. Lucretia was being held close in the embrace of her forgiven husband, Justin. When Sylvester had last seen that man, he was vomiting

on the pavement in a drunken stupor. Now here he was, restored to his wife
. . . to the church . . . to God himself. No longer would Justin gorge himself
on the delicacies and wine with which the local Manichaeans bribed the
people. From now on, Justin would feast beside Lucretia upon the body
and blood of Christ.

After the reconciliation service was over, Sylvester didn't get a chance to
sit down until the last congregant was greeted and the Hall of the Church
fell silent. It was a good church—not as beautiful as the newer ones, yet
tastefully decorated and spacious enough for meeting since the building
had once been a granary. Sylvester sat on a little wooden bench to quiet his
spirit and reflect on God's powerful work in this place. Centuries ago, the
apostle Paul was kept under house arrest not far from here. A Christian congregation of converted pagans and Jews sprung up in Trans Tiberim. Even
today, this was a vibrant and historic meeting place of Rome's Christians.

"Do you have a moment to talk?" asked a speaker whom Sylvester could
not see. He turned his head to find that Quintus had entered by a side door.

"Indeed! Come and sit beside me, brother."

When Quintus had taken a seat, Sylvester discerned that he was troubled.
Sylvester was about to inquire about his friend's distress when the archdeacon spoke up. "I am leaving the catholic church," he declared.

For a long moment—very long, in fact—neither man spoke. Finally, Sylvester said, "How come?"

"It is complicated. But the simple answer is, I am joining the Manichaeans. I will be leading a congregation that meets in the old Pantheon."

Sylvester found himself in one of those pastoral moments when many
opposing reactions were possible. What response was needed here? Sharp
rebuke? Skillful rebuttal? Prudent silence? Earnest pleading? Though all
of these had their place, Sylvester chose none of them. Instead, moved by
what could only be the Holy Spirit, he said, "I reject those doctrines. They
imperil your soul. But, my brother, I will never reject you."

The words seemed to bring immense relief to the archdeacon. "That
wasn't what I expected you to say."

"You have served God's church for many years. You are my friend. I
cannot reject you. Yet I fear to see your soul lost to perdition. Is your mind
made up in this matter?"

"Yes, firmly so. It is the next step in my intellectual journey. I can no longer remain in the simplicity of the catholic faith. The Manichaeans appeal to my mind in a way that the church does not."

"They only seem to be intellectual, Quintus. It is an illusion that will evaporate under closer scrutiny. And our own faith has a rich tradition of thinkers. Men like Justin the Martyr, Irenaeus, Tertullian, Origen. Brilliant minds, all of them."

"You omit ones like Valentinus and Basilides."

"Those men were not orthodox. They denied the true humanity of our Lord. He only 'seemed' to be human, they said."

"I have read their secret books. They contain a deep wisdom not found in your congregations."

"It is pseudo-wisdom. Not the real thing. Not truth."

"What is truth, Sylvester?"

The two men glanced at each other, communicating with their eyes instead of using words. Both of them knew the scriptures well enough to recognize who had first uttered those words: Pontius Pilate, the executioner of the Lord.

Another long silence lingered between the two men. At last, Sylvester rose to his feet. "The Christian faith is freely entered into, so it can be freely left as well. Whether God will let you leave is another matter altogether."

Quintus stood up too. "I must find out. There is no other path for me but this one."

"If this is the path you must take, so be it."

Sylvester left Quintus's side and walked to the altar in the Hall of the Church. However, he didn't remain facing it. Instead, he turned and beckoned to the somber yet resolute archdeacon who was still beside the bench. "Come close, my friend," Sylvester said.

When Quintus had drawn near, Sylvester threw wide his arms. Quintus accepted the gesture and let his longtime bishop clasp him tight. For a while, the two men were locked in a sad and silent embrace. Finally, they separated.

"I thank you for that," Quintus said with tears in his eyes. "Will I ever see you again?"

"I pray it shall be so," Sylvester replied, "right here, at the altar of God's church, when the Good Shepherd recovers you to himself."

—◦◦◦—

JANUARY 326

Flavia's autumn in Nicomedia had seemed more like a holiday than real life. It had not, however, been a time with nothing to do. Though Constantine didn't depart for the west immediately after the Nicene council was over, his entourage did make a few circuits through Asia and Thracia as preliminaries to his grand victory tour. Rex and Flavia participated in those trips, not only providing counsel to the emperor but serving as goodwill ambassadors to church leaders in every city. The job was invigorating, encouraging, and exhausting all at the same time. Flavia felt honored to be meeting so many bishops, along with their wives or other prominent Christian women. Yet the emperor's trips always circled back to Nicomedia. It wasn't until late January that Constantine finally departed from his palace with his eyes set on Rome.

The entourage went first to New Rome—or the "City of Constantine" as the locals preferred to call it. Flavia could sense the city's high energy because the emperor was making it his new, eastern capital. The heightened prestige and influx of imperial funds had set everyone abuzz.

"They seem like bees making a new hive," Flavia told her mother on the day they left New Rome after a three-week stay.

Sophronia, who was sitting in the carriage across from Flavia, nodded her agreement. "This is God's beehive," she replied, then quoted a proverb. "'Gracious words are honeycombs, and their sweetness is healing to the soul.' Let us pray that New Rome will be such a city."

From his seat beside Sophronia, Bishop Ossius offered another biblical proverb that served as a warning: "'It is not good to eat much honey, nor glorious to seek one's own glory.' I hope this city remembers that as well." The somber words made the travelers fall silent as they contemplated two possible futures for Constantine's grand capital.

The calendar had just turned to March when the entourage reached Thessalonica. Constantine was planning a lengthy stay here, for this city had deep Christian roots going back to the missionary journeys of Saint Paul. Rex and Flavia were assigned a modest room in the imperial palace, with Sophronia in an adjacent room. Ossius, of course, stayed in an entirely different wing of the palace.

After a formal dinner on the night of their arrival, hosted jointly by Constantine and the city's current bishop, Flavia joined Rex for a nighttime stroll. Both of them were in a reflective mood, for their memories of this place were a mixture of good and bad. The former bishop, Basil, had welcomed them warmly the first time they had come here. He had even shown them Saint Paul's original letters to the Thessalonians, written by the apostle himself. Yet evil men had destroyed those letters and cut off Basil's hand, leading to his eventual death. Rex had also been imprisoned in a waterfront jail. Flavia couldn't help but feel that Thessalonica was a city of contradictions.

Though she and Rex had only planned to wander the streets tonight with no destination in mind, somehow—perhaps by subtle intent—they came to a large mansion that both of them knew. It was the house of Cato and Marcia, where Flavia was once cruelly enslaved as a handmaiden to the mistress. Lady Marcia eventually emancipated Flavia, and even seemed willing to profess Christ at that time. But Flavia lost touch with her mistress after she left Thessalonica.

"Should we stop in?" she asked Rex.

"Let's speak with the doorkeeper and see what kind of man he is."

Flavia followed her husband as he approached the husky guard at the house's entrance. The overhead door lamp cast a flickering glow on his swarthy face. "Hail, friend," Rex said. "I greet you in the name of the Lord."

"Christ's peace be upon you, brother."

"Aha! You're a Christian, then?"

"For many years. I was baptized by Bishop Basil."

"He was a fine man! Is this a Christian house?"

"Aye, for that is the only kind of servant the mistress wants in her home."

"She is a believer too?"

"Lady Marcia is a woman of our faith. Her husband has yet to believe. We pray for this often. All the servants pray together every night before extinguishing the lamps. Master Cato seems to be softening to the things of God."

"Are they home?" Rex asked. "We used to know them."

"The master is away because he's being transferred to a distant port to the east. They shall move there this summer. The mistress has gone to the countryside in the meantime."

Now Flavia approached the friendly Christian doorkeeper. "You must give the mistress an important message from me. It is a word of encouragement from someone who helped her along the path toward Christ."

"What is your message, sister? I won't forget."

"Tell Lady Marcia that Flavia, her former ornatrix, gives her a warm greeting. Tell her that I wear this"—she put her hand to her throat, touching a gold pendant bejeweled with a ruby—"with the honor of a fellow sister in the Lord. Tell her I think of her with love."

"I will be sure to pass on these things," the doorkeeper said.

After a few more pleasantries, Rex and Flavia turned to go. Flavia was only a few steps away when she turned back around. "Is Marcia a cruel mistress or a tender one?" she asked.

"She's tender," the guard said, "though it doesn't always come easy for her."

Thank you, Father. You are a worker of mighty deeds! Flavia crossed herself in a spirit of holy awe, then bid the guard goodnight.

Several weeks passed in Thessalonica, full of banquets and ecclesial celebrations. But by early April, Flavia could tell the emperor was growing restless again.

"Do we have to leave so soon?" Empress Fausta complained one Sun Day morning after church.

"We have stayed too long already," Constantine countered. "The road beckons."

"I hate the road," Fausta muttered.

Constantine gestured toward Flavia. "You shall ride with my wife. Encourage her in the Lord as you go along. Speak of theological things."

"Yes, Your Highness," Flavia answered with a bow of her head.

Fausta simply shrugged. "Better than crusty old bishops, I guess."

The road from Thessalonica headed north through the mountains toward the regional capital of Sirmium. Now the travel became noticeably rougher, and the carriage jostled on its iron-rimmed wheels. Though Flavia tried to chat with Fausta as they rode along, she could tell the empress was getting more irritable by the hour.

Instead of bothering the queen further, Flavia made lighthearted conversation with the three princes: Constantine Secundus, Constantius, and bright-eyed little Constans. They were sweet boys, and Fausta doted on them. Yet even maternal love couldn't overcome her frustrations with the rigors of travel.

When the entourage reached the outskirts of Heraclea, located deep in the Macedonian mountains, Fausta reached her boiling point. Her complaints in Constantine's ear could be heard by the whole camp through the fabric walls of the imperial tent. Though her harping infuriated Constantine—never a good idea, Flavia thought—she kept pressing him with gripe after gripe. Finally, she made the ultimate demand.

"I want to go home!" she shouted.

"You can't leave the tour!" Constantine shot back. "A queen is needed at my side!"

"No more of this accursed road," Fausta insisted. "I can go back to Nicomedia and await your return."

"Impossible!"

Though Flavia wouldn't normally have intervened in the emperor's affairs, her months of closeness to the royal couple had given her more confidence in such matters. She approached the tent, and the bodyguard recognized her and waved her close. Peeking his head inside the door flap, he said, "Your counselor to see you, m'lady."

"Send her in!" answered a voice—and surprisingly, it was Constantine's.

Flavia slipped past the tent flap and found the husband and wife facing each other in a fierce staredown. Rather than continue to let the anger simmer, Flavia said, "I have a possible solution."

"Spit it out," Constantine replied irritably. "Maybe you can talk some sense into this bothersome woman."

"I suggest a solution that balances both of your desires. We have arrived at a fork in the road. The highway to Sirmium is rough as it continues north. And the journey to Rome is far beyond that. But the Egnatian Way goes straight to Dyrrachium and reaches the coast on the fourth day."

Constantine shook his head. "That isn't on our route. I have to visit Sirmium. And Mediolanum too. They're important cities." Rolling his eyes, he added, "This is your great solution, Flavia?"

"Hear me out, Your Majesty. From Dyrrachium, one can sail to Rome. Surely there will be ships departing now that the seas are open. You could send the empress ahead, and she would be waiting for you in the capital. Isn't that where you need her presence most? Perhaps she isn't needed in all these lesser towns."

"I'm for that!" Fausta exclaimed. "Just four more days of bumping along. Then a pleasant sail. Then luxury again."

Unlike before, Constantine now seemed interested. "That sea voyage would take only ten days," he mused. "Two weeks, and you could be in Rome. And you could bring some instructions for Sylvester."

"Send me to Rome," Fausta urged. "There is no better solution."

"So be it," Constantine replied.

Two days later, Fausta and her three boys were on the Egnatian Way. A detachment of soldiers was sent with them, and Rex was put in charge of those guards. Flavia's job was to keep the empress in a pious state of mind as she rolled along. Some cooks, teamsters, and maidservants rounded out the entourage. Everyone else would stay with Constantine—including Sophronia and Ossius.

Now that Fausta was separated from her husband and all the accompanying demands of being a royal wife, her mood improved and she even became lighthearted. She chatted more freely, not only with Flavia but with the servants as well. Her bodyguard, Pantera, an Aethiops with skin the color of ebony, had a quick wit that seemed to amuse the queen. "You are clever like the raven!" she exclaimed.

"And fierce like the panther," he answered with a wink.

When the travelers reached the port of Dyrrachium, the teamsters and most of the cooks were paid off and dismissed since they were no longer needed. Even some of the bodyguards were sent away because the rest of the trip would be by ship with a naval escort, so piracy wasn't a threat like highway robbery could be. Yet when Rex was deciding which guards would be retained and which let go, Fausta intervened. "Keep the funny Aethiops," she commanded, "the man they call Pantera."

"I don't recommend it," Rex told her. "He isn't trustworthy."

"He has served me well, guardsman. Do as I say."

Rex shrugged. "As you wish." Flavia was glad he didn't protest further, for the empress's mind seemed made up. And the fact that she had called Rex "guardsman" indicated she was in no mood to be contradicted.

The sea voyage Constantine had predicted would take ten days ended up taking only nine. The travelers took passage on a Dalmatian freighter with a light and easy cargo of honey, high-end wines, and fine Greek pottery. By day five, the ship had cleared the dangerous strait between Italy and Sicilia. On day seven, the skillful captain reached Neapolis and called for a day of rest for his crew. Rex was also given a day off from his bodyguard duties while Pantera was made to work instead. Flavia was glad for the extra time with Rex. They spent the day at the seaside village of Puteoli, where a small chapel commemorated the long-ago visit of Saint Paul.

Early on the ninth day of sea travel, the Dalmatian freighter arrived at Portus, the harbor of Rome. Flavia stood at the ship's prow beside Rex, holding his hand. "Remember the last time we were here?" she asked him.

"Of course." Rex squeezed her hand affectionately. "We were newly married and headed to Alexandria."

"Everything was still out in front of us then. Our life was a big, unknown adventure."

Rex glanced at Flavia as the ship eased into its berth at Portus. "It still is, beloved. And I'm glad we can discover it together."

"Side by side," Flavia agreed.

Once the ship was docked alongside the quay and the gangplank had been lowered, Rex helped unload the queen's baggage while Flavia kept an eye on the three boys. Messengers had been sent ahead to alert the local authorities of Fausta's arrival, so a luxurious river barge was waiting at the canal that connected Portus to the Tiberis River. Oxen stood on the adjacent towpath, ready to begin their work. The royal entourage boarded the barge and was towed upstream beneath a shady awning.

By the time the travelers reached Rome's river docks, the awning was no longer needed since the sun had gone down behind the city's endless tenements. Fancy litters, carried by eight porters each, awaited the empress and her sons on the wharf. Flavia was allowed to ride in one of the litters, while Rex and the rest of the guards and servants marched before and behind. Strangely, Pantera was assigned to guard Fausta's litter instead of Rex.

Although the route through Rome's streets went past the empress's former palace, the entourage didn't stop there. The House of Fausta had been donated by Constantine to Pope Sylvester, who lived in it now and administered the Roman catholic church from its halls. Fausta didn't even give the place a glance as the litter passed by.

Instead, the entourage continued to the Sessorian Palace, which had become the primary imperial residence in the city. Since senators and civil servants ran the Roman bureaucracy from the old palace on the Palatine Hill, the Sessorian was considered a more relaxed and homier place to stay than the bustling hilltop where the great caesars once lived.

No sooner had the porters set down their litters in front of the Sessorian Palace than Empress Helena emerged from its main door in full regalia. "Welcome, travelers," she said with more decorum in her voice than genuine affection.

"We greet thee," Fausta answered her mother-in-law with just as little warmth.

Helena gestured toward the front door. "Come now, enter my palace and be refreshed."

"You mean, my palace," Fausta corrected, "for I am the augusta of Rome."

"We are both augustae, if you recall."

Fausta ignored the remark. "I am weary," she announced as she brushed past Helena. "I shall go straight for the baths. Come along, ladies."

As the queen's maidservants followed her into the palace, Rex stepped close to Flavia. "We're going to have to be careful," he whispered in her ear. "There's a war of succession happening here, and violence isn't out of the question."

"May God forbid it," Flavia replied.

MAY 326

The imperial navy trireme wasn't alongside the quay, nor had a single hawser been secured, when Crispus clambered onto the ship's rail and leaped across the watery gap onto the pier of Ravenna's naval port, a fortified harbor known as Classis. Three bodyguards immediately followed him, for their job was to escort the caesar at all times and protect him from bodily harm.

"You shouldn't have jumped so far!" one of the guards said after he had regained his footing on the pier.

"Nonsense," Crispus scoffed with a wave of his hand. "I've leaped farther than that onto an enemy ship with an open blade in my hand."

"I've seen it," another guard acknowledged. "He killed a marine before his feet even hit the deck."

Crispus was about to respond with a self-effacing remark when a loud thud behind the four men made them turn around. A gangplank had been laid against the ship so the sailors could disembark. "I'll use that from now on," Crispus promised. Though his bodyguards nodded gratefully, Crispus knew these cocky speculators actually preferred that he live dangerously. Or at least, they liked it when he did, even if it made their job a little harder.

The naval harbor at Classis was situated on a shallow lagoon that lay a short distance from Ravenna itself. Ignoring the stink of the nearby marshes—so unappealing compared to the fresh sea breezes—Crispus set out for the headquarters building. Though his father was still back at Sirmium while his victory tour crept along, Crispus had decided to forge ahead in a surprise visit to check on his former crewmen. Most of the New Aegean Fleet was redeployed here after Licinius's navy was crushed. It was only right for a caesar to stop in for a visit and authorize a donative for excellent service. Many of the sailors whose sleek liburnians were docked at Classis had distinguished themselves in the tricky maneuvering and intense fighting of the Hellespont. They deserved to be rewarded.

No sooner had Crispus started walking toward the headquarters than a voice rang out. "Look! It's the caesar!" someone yelled. Immediately, a crowd began to gather along the pier.

"So much for my surprise visit," Crispus muttered to his bodyguards. "I had hoped to go unrecognized, at least until I reached the commander."

"Your face is on every coin," one of the guards reminded him. "The people love you."

"Hey, handsome!" called a middle-aged prostitute with red-painted cheeks. "I've still got what it takes if you've got the time! No charge!"

Crispus smiled gallantly at the woman. "No charge? Such beauty is worth a premium!" He tossed the prostitute an argenteus as he passed her by. "Take the day off and enjoy yourself, madam. Today is a day of rest." The delighted woman caught the valuable coin midair and tucked it in her bosom with a grin.

The three bodyguards formed a triangle around Crispus and drew their swords. Though they had no intention of using their weapons against the cheerful well-wishers, the sharp iron points were still useful for establishing space as they led the caesar through the crowd that had gathered along the entire width of the pier. Crispus was just leaving the waterfront and turning onto the wide avenue toward the headquarters building when a commotion broke out at the edge of the dock. "Help!" shouted a desperate female voice. "My baby was knocked in!"

"Get a rope!" someone else cried. "Throw her a line!"

Crispus immediately ran toward the distraught mother. Why everyone was dithering on the pier, he couldn't fathom. He hurled his cape from his neck as he neared the dock's edge, sending his gold brooch flying. The thrashing little girl went underwater just as he caught sight of her. Crispus didn't even stop his run, but dove straight in.

The mucky water was dark, and the moorage here was deep. Crispus kicked his way to the bottom and began feeling around in the gloom. Nothing came to hand, not even seaweed. He reached this way and that, stirring up a billowing cloud of mud. His lungs ached. *Help me, Lord!* he prayed as his breath began to run out. Dismay seized him at the thought of the little girl's death.

And then he found her.

Crispus burst from the water's surface like Leviathan spewing Jonah back into the land of the living. The girl was limp, but when her tiny body sensed air again, her throat spasmed and water came out. She coughed violently for a moment, heaved in a huge breath, then opened her eyes and looked up at the sky. Everyone on the dock exploded into a mighty cheer.

"Throw down the line!" someone shouted above the din—and again Crispus wondered why it hadn't been done already. Most people were shocked into inaction by unexpected events. But as Crispus knew from experience, when trauma struck, that was precisely the time to act.

After the loop on the mooring line was securely fastened around the girl's torso and under her armpits, she was lifted to safety. The rope was lowered again, but instead of allowing himself to be hauled up like a tuna, Crispus ascended hand over hand.

"Look at him go!" said a swarthy marine on the dock.

"I'd like to have him next to me at a castle siege," added another.

When Crispus clambered back onto the dock, the crowd gave him an ovation like he had just won the pentathlon at the Olympic games. He grinned back at the people as he wiped muck from his eyes and wrung water from his dalmatic. One of the bodyguards put Crispus's dry cloak around his shoulders, and another handed him the gold pin that fastened it.

The little girl who had fallen in the water was a fair-haired creature with a ragged tunic that spoke of poverty. She was cradled in her mother's arms with her face burrowed in her mother's neck. Crispus approached the child.

"Was that a scary swim?" he asked gently. The girl nodded without turning to look at him.

"Would you like something shiny and pretty?"

That question was too much to resist. Ever so slightly, the girl turned her head, peeking at Crispus out of one big, blue eye. He held up the brooch, which was made of solid gold and gleamed in the sun.

"Would you like it?" he asked.

"Your Majesty!" the mother cried in awe. "That is a year's wage!"

Crispus pressed the brooch into the girl's pudgy hand. "Sell it and use it on your daughter's behalf," he told the mother. "Give her a chance at a good life."

"God bless you!" the mother exclaimed. And once again, a huge hurrah burst from the crowd at this happy turn of events.

The next four days at Classis were spent examining the seaworthiness of the fleet and the readiness of the men. Crispus found both to be in admirable shape, and he commended the fleet admiral for his excellent leadership. After announcing that a donative of gold coins would be delivered from the mint at Aquileia, Crispus finally crossed the lagoon and entered the city of Ravenna itself.

Now a less martial and more administrative week passed in the imperial complex as Crispus adjudicated disputes and addressed various financial matters. Then a letter arrived by courier from Constantine. "Do not return to my victory tour, beloved son," it said. "Proceed onward to Rome. I have enclosed instructions, and more will soon follow. I need a man whom I trust to make preparations. And there is none I trust more than you." Crispus dictated a respectful rescript saying that he would gladly accept his father's assignment. Two days later, on the Nones of June, he left Ravenna on the Flaminian Way and started down the Italian peninsula.

Only a small entourage accompanied Crispus—a valet, a secretary, a chaplain, and the three bodyguards—so he made good time. The ancient highway cut straight through the Apennines. On the third day of travel, the party navigated a high pass that included a tunnel carved out of the rock. The good weather held, and on the eighth day, they crossed the Milvian Bridge and entered the city of Rome.

Unlike the surprise visit at Ravenna, this one required some pageantry. Crispus's secretary had gone ahead to arrange the proceedings. A small bath facility near the Flaminian Gate had been emptied of its customers so Crispus could refresh himself and change into imperial regalia that befitted a caesar. Once he was clean, he stepped into a four-horse chariot—the traditional conveyance of victorious emperors—and expertly maneuvered it onto the main avenue called Broadway. A military convoy of legionaries in dress uniforms with silver-gilt helmets escorted the chariot on either side. Cheering crowds lined the avenue all the way to the Capitoline Hill, crowned by the dazzling Temple of Jupiter.

Although Crispus knew that many of the onlookers expected him to mount that pagan hill and sacrifice to the demon, he passed it by. Instead, he entered the Forum—but again, he surprised the crowd by not stopping at the ancient Senate House from which Rome had been ruled for almost a thousand years. Ignoring the people's shouted questions and speculations, he continued through the Forum. After riding past the basilica that contained an enormous statue of his father, he arrived at the Flavian Amphitheater. But those who suggested he would stop there to proclaim a holiday with animal games and gladiators were also mistaken. Crispus guided his chariot around the arena and through the gate in the old Servian Wall, a crumbling barrier surpassed long ago when Rome grew beyond it. The crowd, now intensely curious about Crispus's destination, surged along the street on either side of the chariot.

Fortunately for the expectant onlookers, they didn't have long to wait. Crispus arrived at the Lateran Palace to a prearranged trumpet fanfare. His grandmother emerged from its front doors in all the imperial finery that befitted an augusta. Yet it was Pope Sylvester whom Crispus greeted first as he stepped down from the chariot. He bowed to the bishop of Rome and was embraced with a kiss.

"Greetings, my son," Sylvester said.

"Peace to you, Holy Father," Crispus replied, then turned and greeted Helena as well.

For a moment, the crowd was quieted to a murmur while they contemplated this reversal of protocol. Then someone's voice broke into the stillness, shouting, "Crispus the Pious!" Immediately, everyone began to repeat the refrain: "Crispus the Pious! Crispus the Pious!" The cheers of goodwill were still ringing in his ears as he followed Helena and Sylvester into the Lateran Church of the Savior.

The great building was now almost complete. Though a little scaffolding remained inside for the workers to put on some final decorations, the marble floor was in place and a beautiful altar had been installed in the apse. The basilica was a large hall with five aisles marked out by splendid Corinthian columns that stood in rows like trees in an orchard. High windows in the clerestory lit the interior, while chandeliers and lampstands were available for evening services. The resinous smell of incense filled Crispus's nostrils as he proceeded toward the altar and stood before it with his palms raised in prayer. Behind him, the doors had been left open so the crowd could peer inside. It was important for a caesar to show the people by his example what was important—and what wasn't.

When his prayers were finished, Crispus lowered his hands and opened his eyes. He found Helena gazing at him with a ruler's approval of wise actions combined with a grandmother's natural delight. But Pope Sylvester was more sober when he spoke. "We are glad you are among us," he said, "for the times indeed are challenging."

Crispus frowned a little. "How so? The empire is at peace under my father's reign."

"Physical peace, yes. But not spiritual peace. Heresy grows strong in the city."

"We shall stand against it," Crispus vowed, "not with persecutions, which are unworthy of God, but with 'the true Light which, coming into the world, enlightens every man.'"

The pope nodded. "You have memorized the scriptures, I see. Then let me quote for you another one. 'To whom much has been given, much will be required.'"

Crispus didn't immediately reply but only stared at the floor where a shaft of sunlight illumined the swirls in the marble. At last, he looked up. "Thank you for that reminder, Holy Father," he said. "But in truth, it is never far from my mind."

⁓⁓⁓

JUNE 326

The mansion atop the Aventine Hill was a place of deeply ingrained memories for Rex. Not as many as Flavia, of course, for this was her childhood home. Yet Rex had experienced life-changing events here that he would never forget. Inside that mansion, he was sorely betrayed by his best friend from cadet school, Geta, a powerful warrior. The betrayal resulted in a fierce duel in which Rex was forced to shatter his friend's shin to survive. Rex almost killed Geta that day. Only Flavia's intervention stopped Rex from murdering his helpless brother-in-arms. Yet that restraint allowed his foe to escape. Geta then defamed Rex and got him condemned to exile.

What if I had killed Geta that day? Rex wondered while gazing at the front of the mansion—now the Church of Sabina Sophronia. *Would I be where I am now? And more importantly . . . would I be* who *I am?* As he contemplated these questions, he felt Flavia slip her hand into his.

"Rex?" she said.

"Yes?"

"You are still the bravest man I have ever known."

Turning toward his wife, Rex drew her close. "I love you, Junia Flavia," he whispered into her ear.

"I love you too, my darling."

After savoring the embrace for a moment, Rex parted from Flavia and smiled. "Are you ready to become a heretic?"

"Let's get it over with," she replied, then the two of them turned away from the church and approached the Manichaean house of worship across the street.

Rex, of course, had no intention of leading his wife into heresy. But with Caesar Crispus in town, there was new hope among the Roman Christians that imperial support would sway public opinion against the growing cult of the Manichaeans. It was widely known that the royal family—with Constantine on his way and Helena and Crispus already arrived—espoused the doctrines of the Nicene Creed. Many Christians expected the new theological statement to gain favor among the populace at the expense of Manichaean precepts.

Pope Sylvester had even learned that the Manichaeans were feeling nervous about that possibility. "Go attend their meetings," he had told Rex and Flavia. "Find out what they're saying to their people about the creed. Then let me know what they teach."

Rex and Flavia had agreed that the House of Mani on the Aventine Hill was the natural place for them to do their theological investigations. Its leader, Felix, had once been the pastor of Flavia's childhood congregation but had crossed over to Manichaeism in his later years. The man was learned and articulate. He would certainly speak forcefully against the Nicene Creed.

However, as Rex and Flavia were about to enter the house with the other worshipers who were arriving, Felix stopped them at the door. "The path of light suffers no shadow to fall upon it," he said in the cryptic way that he often spoke.

But Flavia was having none of this nonsense. Before Rex could reply, she said, "This whole house is a den of darkness, Felix. No light is found in there."

"Then why should you wish to enter?" he shot back.

Rex looked back at the handsome sectarian who barred entrance to his building. "The followers of Mani have always admitted visitors," he pointed out. "The ranks of your Hearers seem to grow by the day. We assumed we could enter, just as the crowds have always been let in to seek their conversion."

"Not anymore! The Elect have decreed an end to such practices in these difficult times."

"What have you got to hide?" Flavia challenged.

"No more than you hide in your so-called 'Eucharist,' child! Or have you forgotten how I used to dismiss the unbaptized from that part of the service when I followed the errors of your church?"

Rex and Flavia glanced at each other. Although no words were exchanged, they both recognized they were in the presence of a skilled debater. Felix wouldn't be tricked or cajoled into admitting them to his secret rites. Unless it was by some kind of forcible entry, Rex and Flavia weren't going to gain access to the House of Mani. And neither of them had come here today to cause that kind of commotion.

"Let's just leave, Rex," Flavia said.

Felix raised his hand, holding his palm outward in a kind of farewell gesture. "May Jesus the Radiant lead you to discover the light within you," he intoned in his mystical voice.

"Jesus the Radiant is risen from the tomb," Rex said to Flavia as they walked away, though he didn't speak loudly enough for Felix to hear. Sometimes it was better not to engage a fool with words that he would mock if he heard them.

Though Rex felt frustrated at having been stymied so quickly, Flavia didn't seem discouraged. She took his arm as they walked down the slope of the Aventine, discussing alternate plans as they went along. When they came to a street intersection, Rex felt Flavia give him a tug. "The Sessorian is this way," she said. "Aren't we headed back to our room?"

But Rex drew her in a different direction. "Let's head for the Field of Mars. I have an idea."

"You always do," Flavia replied with a grin, then fell into step at Rex's side.

The couple walked along the Tiberis's eastern bank toward the north. When they passed the circular temple of Hercules the Victor, Flavia drew Rex a little closer to her side, almost like she was protecting him. "I've left that god behind," he reminded her. "I am baptized into Christ, a new creation."

"I know. But the old gods never die. They just take new forms so they can appeal to us in new ways." Rex nodded thoughtfully at Flavia's words but said no more about the matter.

Finally, they arrived at Rex's intended destination: the Pantheon, Rome's famous temple to "all the gods." Its shape was a cylinder, with a porch in front and a dome on top whose crown had a circular skylight called the "eye." In past centuries, the Pantheon served the needs of the city's immigrant population as a kind of catchall shrine for their many deities. But as

Rex gazed at the impressive building, he could see it had deteriorated over time. Since no single priesthood claimed it, no one bore the expenses of its upkeep. Recently, however, the Manichaeans had begun meeting there. They had secured permission to make some repairs to the ancient temple's façade.

Rex and Flavia took seats on wooden stools outside of a hot-food bar on the plaza in which the Pantheon stood. Both of them studied the building while they ate garlic toast with melted cheese. After a while, Flavia said, "I know what you're thinking."

Amused, Rex turned to look at her. "You think so?"

"Uh-huh. You think we can attend the Manichaean rites here instead of at the Aventine. Archdeacon Quintus has gone over to that cult. He would be full of strategic information. But the problem is, he knows me. He knows you too because you're the papal legate who attended the council. And you're hard to forget, Rex. So Quintus isn't going to let us into his mysteries any more than Felix did."

Rex laughed as he swallowed his bite, then wiped his lips with the back of his hand. "You're right that I want to hear what Quintus is saying. What you haven't guessed is how I'm going to do it."

"Tell me."

Rex turned and gestured toward the Pantheon. "Looks like they're doing some repairs to the top of the porch."

"I see it. Scaffolding. Pulleys. Ladders. Stonemasons and roof tilers are at work."

Now Rex returned his gaze to Flavia. "If they won't let me in through the door, maybe I can sneak in another way?"

"How? That building has no windows. There is no way in except the door."

"There's one other way."

Flavia's mouth fell open, and a shocked expression came to her face. "Rex! You're not thinking of going in through the eye?"

"Why not? That scaffolding would get me to the porch. Then I can reach the dome and go right to the top. All I need to do is lower a rope through the eye to the floor. I can do it by night and hide inside, then listen to what they're saying the next day."

"Don't you think they'll notice a rope dangling from the skylight?"

"That's where you come in. We'll anchor the rope near the ground outside. I'll signal you from inside when I'm safe on the floor. You draw back the rope, take it away. Then all I have to do is hide and wait."

"It could work, I guess," Flavia admitted.

"Of course it will. A week from now, they'll meet again. And I'm going to be hidden in the Pantheon, listening in."

"I'm with you," Flavia said. "Let's do it."

During the intervening week, Rex went out to Ostia and bought the best sailing rope he could find. He didn't want his line to break while he was dangling high above the Pantheon's marble floor. The rope was made of strong flax fibers. Rex spliced several pieces together to get the full length he would need.

The night before the Manichaean ceremony, he and Flavia stayed in the nearby home of a Christian but left their guest room in the darkest, quietest part of the night. The plaza was completely deserted. They crept to the Pantheon's base, where Rex tied the rope around one of the porch's massive columns. He used a slipknot that was tight along the tension of the rope yet could be easily undone by pulling the tail. "Do *not* pull that until you hear my voice on the floor inside," he warned, and Flavia nodded. Rex took the other end of the rope and fastened it around his waist. Now it was time to ascend.

Though the stonemasons' scaffolding was rickety, it was adequate to support Rex's weight. He climbed the access ladder while Flavia played out the line behind him and kept it from getting snagged. Soon Rex reached the porch's roof. After ascending even higher along a decorative pediment, he pulled himself onto the flat roof of the temple itself. In front of him the dome curved up in a smooth arc, its bronze veneer gleaming in the moonlight.

Rex walked easily up the surface of the dome but stopped short of the eye. Now that he was close—but still well back from its gaping maw—he unfastened the rope from his waist and pitched its end down the hole. Then, grasping the line in two hands, he inched to the eye and peered over the edge. All was dark inside the Pantheon except for a circle of moonlight on the floor, very far below.

Seating himself on the bronze sheathing at the rim of the eye, Rex put an s-curve of the rope between his boots and prepared to descend with a military technique. He scooted a little closer to the edge with his feet hanging into the abyss. *Just like my days back in cadet—*

Crack!

A piece of concrete beneath the bronze—already carrying immense strain at the apex of the dome—broke away under Rex's added weight. He plunged into the hole, flailing wildly as he fell. Though the rope had been in his hands, he lost his grip on it when he tumbled in. But as the line brushed against him, Rex's instinct kicked in and he grabbed hold of it. Hot fire burned in his palm as he slid down the rope's length. He grabbed the line with his other hand too, then snagged it with his feet and arrested his downward plunge. When he came to a stop, everything was dark and still—except for the wild pounding in Rex's chest.

For a long time, he rested on the rope with his weight supported on his feet. Gradually, his eyes adjusted to the dim light. The Pantheon's vault was spherical, its coffered ceiling extending downward in a perfect curve. Multicolored marble decorated every surface. When Rex finally got oriented to his position in the temple, he could hardly believe where he was poised. Releasing the rope, he dropped lightly to the floor just a short distance below him. "That was too close," he muttered.

With the risky descent completed—even if not as planned—there wasn't much left to do. Rex hurriedly discarded the chunks of broken concrete, then walked to the temple's huge bronze doors and rapped lightly on them. He heard Flavia's muffled voice on the other side.

"Are you safe?" she asked.

"I'm on the floor. You can pull up the rope." A moment later, its snaky length began to slither up through the eye. Before long, the dangling rope was gone from sight.

Idols stood in niches spaced around the Pantheon's cylindrical interior. In one of them was muscular Hercules with his club resting on his shoulder and the Nemean lion at his feet. Rex clambered into the niche and slipped behind the blocky pedestal on which the false god stood.

"I used to think you helped me," he said to the idol, "but now I know better." When the mute idol said nothing in return, Rex chuckled to himself, then settled down to wait for the dawn of the one, true God.

⚊✎⚊

Although Fausta didn't really enjoy the gladiator matches, the Roman citizenry loved them, which meant she needed to put in an appearance. In preparation for her husband's arrival in Rome, a week of games had been declared to get the people in a celebratory mood. Yet Constantine's instructions had been specific: no gladiator matches were to be held while he was in the city. He didn't approve of their violent spirit, and in fact, he had recently ordered that convicted criminals mustn't be sentenced to mortal combat in the arena. Yet if hunters wanted to fight wild beasts and professional gladiators wanted to fight each other—rarely to the death anymore—Constantine wasn't willing to banish this incredibly popular pastime. When it came to the restless mob, even emperors had their limits. Therefore some games had to be held, and the imperial family had to be seen there.

The morning had been spent in animal hunts, matching men with spears and nets against wild beasts. Now it was time for the afternoon gladiator contests. Fausta arrived at the Flavian Amphitheater just as the first match was about to begin. Since it was June and the sun was hot, the linen awnings had been extended to provide shade for the people. Even so, Fausta found the imperial box to be uncomfortably warm when she arrived.

"I'm tirsty," said little Constans, who was at her side. "I wants a trink."

Fausta motioned for a servant to fetch water. But before the attendant could even leave the box, Crispus arrived with a silver two-handled tray. A crystal pitcher was upon it, along with five jeweled cups. "It's going to be a hot one today," Crispus said cheerfully. "I brought iced water for us all."

"Tanks, Uncle Crispus!" Constans said, reaching out his hands. The princes often referred to Crispus as their uncle because of their age difference, though he was actually their half brother.

"Very thoughtful of you," added Constantine Secundus with the proper decorum that befitted a future emperor.

Crispus set down the tray and poured water into the cups, serving Helena first and then Fausta before the boys. Last of all, he poured himself a drink. "God's grace to us all!" he said, raising his cup as if making a toast at a banquet.

"God's grace," Helena replied brightly.

What a show-off he is, Fausta thought as she sipped the refreshing citrus water.

The roar of the crowd signaled that the first two gladiators had come out to the arena floor. One was a husky Pursuer, a fighter with a large shield, some body armor, and a helmet protected by a face mask. He was armed with a short sword. The other was a quick and agile Net-Man, barefoot and wearing only a loincloth. He lacked bodily protection except on his left arm. His weapons were an entangling net and a trident, with a dagger as backup. At the referee's command, the gladiators drew close and the fight was on.

Fausta watched suspiciously as Crispus came over to two of the princes and put an arm around each of their shoulders. "These games are bloody, and we look forward to the day when they are no more," he told them. "Until then, let us draw lessons about bravery and cowardice as much as possible."

Though Constans was too young to care much about the combat, Secundus's eyes were riveted to the battle on the sand. "The Pursuer seems likely to win," he observed. "His armor cannot be penetrated by that trident. And the Net-Man missed with his net."

"You never know," Crispus said. "Things can reverse quickly."

A moment later, Crispus's assertion was proved true. The Net-Man used his trident to snag the fallen net, which he immediately flicked onto his opponent. Though the action snarled the trident's fork in the webbing and made it useless for further attack, the Pursuer himself was also terribly entangled in the mesh. Unable to wield his sword or adequately move his shield, he was defenseless. The Net-Man drew his dagger from his belt and stabbed his opponent in the thigh. Instead of continuing to fight, the Pursuer cried out, dropped his sword, and fell to his knees.

Now came the moment that the crowd loved. The fallen gladiator would either be spared or meet his doom. Raucous cries demanded that the cowardly Pursuer be killed. The bloodthirsty crowd made stabbing gestures with their hostile thumbs. Fausta's eyes—like everyone else's in the amphitheater—went to the editor standing nearby. He was the show master who staged the games. His job was to tell the Net-Man whether to finish the job or spare his vanquished foe.

But the editor knew that the royal family was in attendance today. He glanced to the imperial box for guidance. Since gladiator executions were a rarity these days, Fausta was unprepared to make such a decision. And without Constantine in attendance, it was unclear which of the two augustae should make the final call. Fausta was contemplating what to do when Crispus stepped into the sunlight at the front of the box. Now the crowd fell silent in this poised moment. Everyone awaited the caesar's word.

Crispus extended his arm with his thumb enclosed in his fist—the sign of a sheathed sword, the order for a reprieve. "Show mercy!" he shouted into the stillness. "And may God show mercy to us all!"

"The Gate of Life!" cried the editor, gesturing to the eastern gate through which defeated gladiators were allowed to leave alive. And then the Net-Man did something remarkable. After making the sign of the cross over himself, he reached out a hand and helped the Pursuer to his feet. As the two bloodied warriors stood side by side, an image of noble comradeship in war, the crowd exploded into roars of approval.

This man will rule the world, Fausta realized with cold clarity. *Unless I put a stop to it.*

⁓⧉⧉⧉⁓

The incident at the gladiator games consumed Fausta's mind for the rest of the day. Instead of staying for another match, she took the princes—annoyingly reluctant to leave their hero's side—back to the Sessorian Palace. After sending them off with a pedagogue, she retired to her room, dismissing all her handmaidens so she could have some time to herself.

Yet being alone in her chambers gave Fausta no relief from her bitterness. The rooms she had been assigned were in the opposite wing from her mother-in-law. Fausta's windows looked out not upon pleasant gardens or bubbling fountains but on a derelict circus built by a corrupted emperor from long ago. After it fell into disuse, the new Aurelian walls had cut right through it, ensuring the racetrack's permanent place as a relic of times gone by. *When Constantine comes, we'll leave this stupid palace and take up residence where all emperors should dwell—the Palatine Hill, like the caesars of old!* Fausta averted her gaze from the crumbling circus and slammed the shutters to block the ugly view.

As Fausta walked over to the divan in the private salon outside her bedroom, her eyes fell upon a silk kerchief draped over a chair. She took it with her to the divan, then inhaled deeply of its smell while she reclined. It smelled like *him*—the man who was lithe, and sly, and fierce like the great cat for which he was named.

Pantera.

And he was coming tonight.

Fausta's heart began to race at the prospect of imminent delights. No one knew about her trysts with Pantera, and that made them all the more exciting. She let her mind drift, imagining how the night would go. Lust had ahold of her now.

It was dusk when Fausta rose from the divan and went to the wine cart in her sitting room. She unstopped the decanter and poured two glasses of Falernian—not an imitation, but a real vintage from the famous wine-growing region in Campania—then replaced the crystal stopper. Since the chambermaids had been dismissed, no one had lit the lamps, and Fausta realized she didn't actually know how. She would have to ask one of the girls to return and do the job. But first, Fausta decided to get an unpleasant task out of the way.

Next to the wine was a tray of medicines and tinctures. None of Fausta's daily tonics was pleasant, but the vial she hated most was the blue one, which contained the distilled essence of wild carrot seeds. Fausta knew how to take the medicine, for she consumed it whenever she was away from Constantine. The best method was to mix one spoonful of the bitter oil with a glass of something sweet and swallow it down. Yet nothing could take away the nasty bitterness. Perhaps the dilution helped a little. But the medicinal drink was horrible to consume even when mixed with a sweetener.

As Fausta reached for the blue vial in the dim light, she accidentally knocked it from the cart. The delicate glass shattered against the marble floor, wasting all the contraceptive elixir. More could be obtained, of course. Yet not for another day or two.

No matter, she assured herself. *I'm just as glad not to have to take that disgusting stuff.*

A tiny statue of the mother goddess stood on the wine cart next to the medicines. Though the bronze figurine would have to be put away before Constantine showed up, for now, it could stay where it was. Fausta picked up the well-worn idol and caressed it with her thumb. "Mother Venus, I beseech thee to protect me," she said in a low whisper, having adopted the habit of secrecy about pagan practices in her home. "Shield me, O Mother, from all harm and consequences."

After setting the idol back in its place, Fausta groped her way to the door. The salon was in deep shadows now, and so was the rear bedroom. She was about to open the door and summon a chambermaid to light the lamps when a knock sounded on the other side.

"Who is it?" she asked.

Instead of a verbal reply, the only sound was a deep, feral growl. When Fausta opened the door, Pantera stood there with an oil lamp in his hand. His eyes were green. His chest was bare. His black hair was oiled upon his head.

Pantera glanced around the room. "It is dark," he said.

"I am dark," Fausta replied as she took her lover's hand and drew him in.

10

"Mother, don't forget your veil," Flavia said to Sophronia as the two women stepped outside the guest room at the Lateran Palace.

"I was about to put it down," Sophronia replied as she lowered the gauzy fabric over her face. The guest room—formerly a servant's quarters but now reserved for Christians receiving hospitality from the pope—was set off by itself in a quiet wing of the papal palace, so no one was likely to see Sophronia there. Even so, whenever she went out on the streets, she always covered her face. "I'll wear my veil," Sophronia said, "but in truth, the people of Rome have forgotten about me. That's my protection now, more than a piece of linen."

"It would take only one person to recognize you. Then a lot of unpleasant rumors would start."

Sophronia took Flavia's hand and squeezed it. "You're a good daughter. Thank you for looking out for me."

"Because I love you, Mother." After lowering her own veil, Flavia smiled brightly, then said, "Alright, let's go! I know how much you value these walks. You're almost like a prisoner in this palace."

"I prefer to think of myself as a nun in quiet retreat, but sometimes it feels like a little of both," Sophronia admitted as the two women left the private wing and made their way to the palace's unobtrusive side door.

Flavia had been overjoyed when Sophronia arrived in Rome with Bishop

Ossius about two weeks ago. Constantine had sent Ossius ahead to make arrangements with Sylvester for the grand entrance into the capital city. "The emperor is delayed in Mediolanum on military matters," Ossius had explained to the pope. "The Alpine passes have to be fortified, because the day could come when barbarians invade Italy through them. But when that's taken care of, Constantine will come straight here." Although Flavia found the notion of barbarians invading Rome far-fetched, she was glad it meant her mother had arrived in the capital earlier than expected.

Now the two women left the palace and started toward the city walls to take a leisurely stroll. The battlements were lightly patrolled these days, so Flavia and Sophronia had found that the city walls were a pleasant place to walk, offering a smooth surface and a pretty view of the suburban countryside to the south.

After a pleasant leg-stretcher, the women returned to the stairs by which they had come up to the battlements and descended to ground level near the papal palace. As they passed the adjacent Lateran Church of the Savior, they paused to admire its beauty. "When I left Rome many years ago, this was just an empty field," Sophronia remarked. "A ruined army camp. Now it is a beautiful basilica of God."

"My memories run deep as well." Flavia walked over to a laurel bush next to a fountain no longer in use. She broke off a leafy twig and brought it back to her mother. "This bush was much smaller back then. Rex wove some branches into my bridal crown. With that on my head, Bishop Sylvester wed us under an open sky before the Lord—right where the altar now stands inside the church."

For a long while, the two women shared a contemplative silence. Flavia's thoughts went to the strange and winding path that had brought her to this moment. No doubt, Sophronia had similar memories of her own. Yet despite all the twists and turns of life, here they were, a mother and daughter reunited in the city where they were both born and raised. No longer were they aristocrats. Luxuries and politics had no meaning anymore. Now they were Christians, and the affairs of the church drove the wheels of their lives instead of the Forum or the Senate.

"Shall we peek into the baptistery?" Sophronia asked when her thoughts returned to the present.

"Why not?" Flavia agreed, and led the way.

The door of the octagonal building was open when the women reached it. Stepping inside the baptistery, Flavia found it to be as beautifully decorated as on the day of her baptism. Eight porphyry columns stood in each of the corners. The water in the central pool was absolutely still, its surface as smooth as a mirror. A single column arose from the water. On top of it was a golden censer sending up the aromatic smoke of balsam incense. A lamb made of solid gold and seven silver stags adorned the font's rim. They were connected to the plumbing so that they could spout water into the pool—though the water wasn't jetting out at the moment. A statue of John the Baptist stood next to one of Jesus, with the inscription "Behold the Lamb of God, who takes away the sins of the world!"

"How lovely this place is!" Sophronia exclaimed, as awed by the sublime architecture as Flavia was. "I remember the day you were baptized. You came up out of that font as naked as the day you were born."

"Because on that day, I was reborn," Flavia answered. "I was wrapped in the swaddling clothes of the Lord and fed honeyed milk like a baby."

Sophronia gazed at the ceiling as other memories came to her. "You took the church's milk better than mine," she finally said with a smile and a shake of her head. "What a wiggly little infant you were! Always interested in everything but the breast. You would stare up at me with those big, hazel eyes. How I loved you, Flavia. You'll never know how much."

Sophronia's tender words, meant to convey the warmest maternal affection, had an unintended meaning whose sting Flavia couldn't help but feel. "Maybe I'll understand someday," she said softly.

Sophronia turned quickly toward her daughter. "I'm sorry, my love . . . I didn't mean . . ."

"I know, Mother. I know."

Yet the words had been uttered, no matter what had been meant, and Flavia's attention was now turned toward her barrenness. She thought of it often, though the busyness of her recent life had helped occupy her mind with other things. Even so, the sadness of not being a mother was ever-present. It lingered beneath the surface, always ready to emerge if given the chance by a stray word or a visual reminder.

"Would you like some time alone with the Lord?" Sophronia asked.

"This is a place of new life. Perhaps some contemplation here would be a balm to your spirit."

"Yes," Flavia said, and her mother understood to exit quietly without another word.

A peaceful hush fell upon the baptistery now that Flavia was alone. Today was a cloudy day, so no sunbeams came streaming through the high windows, only the diffused light that gave the place a soft and silent feel. Flavia approached the baptismal font tentatively, like an Israelite contemplating the sea and wondering if escape from Pharaoh would truly come. Though the water didn't part as Flavia knelt at its edge, it rippled a little as a breeze from the door wafted across its surface. She cupped the water in her two hands, letting it dribble between her fingers and fall back into the font.

"Arise, be baptized and wash away your sins, calling on his name," she whispered. The words were spoken to Saint Paul after his blindness on the Damascus road. Now Flavia made them her own—for she, too, knew what it meant to be blinded, to be met by Christ, and to be healed of willful transgression.

Rubbing her fingers together, Flavia contemplated their wetness from the baptismal waters. Her mind went back to the day of her baptism, an experience so profound that she could never forget it. When the first light had reddened the eastern windows, the female candidates had disrobed behind a curtain that shielded them from male eyes. Nothing from the old world was left upon their bodies—no garment, no jewel, no ring, not even a ribbon in their hair. A deaconess had assisted the women into the font, one by one, while Sylvester spoke the baptismal formula from behind the fabric screen. Flavia had descended from the west . . . affirmed the apostles' creed . . . renounced the pomps of Satan . . . been immersed into the Trinity . . . and arose in the east in union with the Sun of Righteousness. *My salvation didn't begin that day*, Flavia mused as she knelt beside the font. *Christ had touched my soul long before. But here in the water . . . he touched my body too.*

That was the amazing thing about Christianity—its tangibility, indeed, its *fleshiness*. "The Word became flesh and dwelt among us," the beloved disciple had declared. His friend Jesus was a real and true man. No other religion could make such a claim.

Flavia was reminded of the day she and Rex toppled an idol of Aphrodite. The marble statue shattered into jagged pieces against the floor, sending stone dust billowing out of the temple. What did that prove? That the gods and goddesses were known to humans through lifeless stone. But not Jesus. He came into the world as flesh—not even as a man at first, but merely a helpless babe. And because of the divine will to become enfleshed, Jesus was still known to his people in tangible ways. He was experienced through water that washes and gives birth . . . through the bread that breaks and the wine that bleeds . . . through the fist against the breast in sorrow for sin . . . through oil that comforts the brow.

And what does that mean for me? Flavia wondered. *Am I forgiven of my idol worship?* It was a question that haunted her darker moments, though intellectually, she knew the answer was yes. She had known it even as she rushed from the demon's foul temple. Out of those depths, she had cried to the Lord: "Hear my voice! Attend to my pleas for mercy! If you should mark iniquities, who can stand?"

"I hear you, my beloved," Jesus had responded. "Be not afraid, for with me there is plenteous redemption." And Flavia knew it was true.

Yet knowing that truth mentally and knowing it bodily were two different things. Bending forward, Flavia reached into the water again. After wetting her hands, she touched her face, recalling the feeling of arising from the font like a newborn daughter of Christ. "I name you Candida," the bishop had said. "For though you were stained with sin, now you are white as snow."

Behind Flavia, the door made a creaking sound that broke the silence and ended the holy moment. She turned to see the pope's new archdeacon enter the baptistery. Flavia didn't know his name, only who he was. The godly old man had replaced Archdeacon Quintus after he went over to the Manichaeans. Now this new archdeacon was assisting the pope in practical affairs. A workman accompanied him—a plumber, judging from the lengths of pipe he carried.

"I am sorry to disturb your meditations, Junia Flavia," the archdeacon said.

Flavia rose to her feet. "I didn't know that you knew me, sir."

The archdeacon smiled warmly. "I know all the affairs of His Holiness, including who his guests are. I am Rufus. We have come to restore the flow of the fountains that make this water living. Shall we return at another time?"

"I am pleased to make your acquaintance, Archdeacon Rufus," Flavia said with a respectful bow. "Please, come and attend to your work. It is past time for me to be going."

Rufus nodded and signaled for the workman to proceed. As Flavia stepped past the archdeacon on the way to the door, she noticed him catch sight of her face. The kindly elder reached to a cloth draped over his belt. "Your face is wet," he observed. "Would you like a towel?"

"No, thank you," Flavia replied. "All is as it should be."

<hr>

JULY 326

Pope Sylvester glanced around the reception hall at the Lateran Palace, making sure it was suitably appointed for him to meet with today's guests and conduct the day's business. The room had a long, strange history. For centuries, it served as the meeting place for the clients of the Laterani clan, until, through family connections, the mansion came into Empress Fausta's hands. Her evil brother Maxentius gave it to his Praetorian prefect, Pompeianus, a man as wicked as his master. During that time, the reception hall was bedecked with idols and other pagan finery.

But then Constantine took possession of the building when he defeated Maxentius in war. His first action was to destroy his enemy's adjacent cavalry camp; his second was to give the beautiful palace to Pope Miltiades. That holy bishop, of blessed memory, turned the reception room into a church meeting hall. However, now that the Church of the Savior stood next door, Sylvester had returned the hall to its original purpose of meeting guests. And today's first visitor would be an interesting one. Sylvester smiled as he realized he would be meeting with the best—and only!—undercover spy the Roman catholic church had ever had.

When all seemed ready for the day's business, Sylvester settled into his episcopal throne in the hall's exedra. Since to remain seated was an honor, while having to stand indicated inferior status, Sylvester had ordered chairs to be set around his throne to avoid the appearance of pride and image-consciousness. Thus, it would be clear to everyone that all brethren were equal before the Lord. And as Christ said, it was the lowly and meek who would inherit the earth.

A short while later, Archdeacon Rufus entered the room with Brandulf Vitus Rex, the former speculator who was now a deacon and papal legate. Like so many Germani, Rex was taller than the average Roman, with the wide shoulders and powerful build of his people. He was tastefully dressed in a tunic overlain by the silken dalmatic so popular in the east. Alongside him was his slender and beautiful wife, Junia Flavia, a woman with an equally dignified bearing and an impeccable Christian reputation.

When the archdeacon and the two guests were seated on the chairs around Sylvester, he greeted them warmly in the name of the Lord. "The church isn't used to having spies like the government does," he said to Rex after the Christian pleasantries were over. "Yet information is a neutral thing. It can be acquired for holy purposes as well as nefarious ones. Come now, Vitus. Tell me about your latest endeavors. It must bring back memories of your days as a speculator."

Rex chuckled and gave a little nod of agreement. "I've been interviewing more people and corroborating more stories over the past few weeks than I ever did in service to the legions. And I even performed an infiltration that my classmates in cadet school would have said was impossible."

"What was it?" Sylvester asked, his curiosity piqued.

"I managed to enter the Pantheon and listen in on a Manichaean liturgy."

"That doesn't seem so remarkable. The doors of the Pantheon are often open to the public."

Rex grinned in the brash way that made him so likable. "Who said anything about the doors? They wouldn't let me in. I couldn't use them."

Sylvester sat back in his chair, arching his eyebrows. "But . . . there's only one other opening in the Pantheon."

"That's right. A good speculator must adapt to whatever the field of operations provides. So I used the only opening I had available."

"You went in through the *eye*?"

"With a rope, yes."

"But that ceiling is ten stories high! And it's a straight drop to the floor!"

Rex shrugged. "I was a sailor for many years. I learned to tie a good knot."

Sylvester could only marvel and shake his head. "The church has few men like you, Brother Vitus. We are grateful for the services you can provide. Tell us, then, what you learned as you observed the doings of the Manichaeans. It is hard-won information indeed."

"You will not be pleased to hear the report I'm about to give, Your Holiness. The Manicheans have grown strong in this city—stronger even than we had suspected. Their numbers have grown, and not just by converting the pagans to their belief. Many people who now call themselves Manichaeans were once with us in the orthodox faith. This is by their design. Their leaders have sent out the common folk—they call them 'Hearers'—to attend our churches and persuade our people to go over to them."

"It is just as the apostle predicted," Archdeacon Rufus said sadly. "'Savage wolves will come in among you, not sparing the flock.' Unfortunately, the Roman flock is spread over a large pasture. The shepherds cannot be everywhere at once!"

"But the eye of the Good Shepherd sees all," Flavia reminded the gathered men.

Sylvester nodded at the fortifying word from his lone female guest. "Thank you for that word of truth, sister." He turned back to Rex. "What are the Manichaeans saying about the Nicene Creed? All our people consider it a great victory for the deity of Christ."

"The Manichaean leaders have been talking about it to their people as well. But what you and I consider a victory for truth, they view as an opportunity to expand. Though they don't hold to the creed's doctrine, they believe they can use it to steal some sheep from our flock."

Sylvester grimaced, and he noticed the same expression come to the archdeacon's face. Both of them felt the pastor's ever-present burden to protect the lambs that God had entrusted to their care. "What is their strategy, Vitus?" Sylvester pressed. "Understanding this is perhaps the greatest contribution your speculator skills can make to the church."

"I will tell you exactly what I observed from Quintus. He gave a demonstration with all his people watching. He placed two identical apples upon the altar. Then he cut one with a knife and ate the bite. After he had swallowed it, he said, 'Delicious! Now I shall try this other one to see if it's just as good.' But when he pressed it hard with his knife, it crumbled into dust."

"Crumbled? Like chalk?"

"Yes. The apple was made of plaster and painted red. It was from the theater, as when craftsmen make props to use in plays."

"And what was the point of Quintus's little lesson?"

"He held up a piece of the plaster apple and said something like this: 'Just as this apple looks real but is not, so was the body of Jesus Christ. He looked like a real man to the eyes of the apostles. But for a god to become a man is unworthy of a divine being. If Christ is one with God, he cannot be one with mankind. His body only seemed to be human. But in fact, it was an illusion.'"

"That is the heresy of the Docetists!" Flavia exclaimed. "It has plagued the church since the earliest days when Gnosticism was rampant."

"And now it has arisen again under a new name," Rufus agreed.

Rex nodded grimly. "The Manichaeans are a sect with many followers, all of whom have been ordered to sneak into the churches and spread this false doctrine."

As Sylvester contemplated the dire news, he felt a mixture of anger at the threat to his sheep and zeal to defend them from theological harm. Rising from his throne, he announced, "This danger warrants drastic measures. Vitus and Candida, I want you to meet me at the front steps of this palace in one hour. I will take you with me on an essential errand. In the meantime, prepare yourselves in prayer. We have some high-level business to conduct."

At the appointed time, Sylvester met the married couple at the palace entrance just as he had said. He had donned his most formal attire and wore fine leather shoes. All his other appointments for the day had been postponed.

The threesome headed east beside the city wall and soon came to the Sessorian Palace. The grand old mansion was home to two empresses, and it was about to house an emperor as well. A church messenger had been sent ahead to alert Empress Helena that the pope wished an audience with her about a pressing matter. Helena had received the message with approval and replied that she would make her throne room ready.

After entering the palace, Sylvester was shown to the throne room in a reversal of the way his day had started. Now he was the one bringing petitions that needed attention from a more powerful person. Though the inversion of roles was humbling, Sylvester reminded himself that humility was the hallmark of a pastor—just as it was the mark of the Savior who had humbled himself to become a man and die a criminal's death.

"Welcome, Holy Father," Helena said when Sylvester was escorted into the hall by two imperial bodyguards. Her tone seemed more friendly than formal. "And greetings to you also, Brother Rex and Sister Flavia. What urgent matter brings such reputable visitors before me today?"

"A grave concern, Your Majesty. It is the heresy of the Manichaeans. I have it on good authority from these eyewitnesses"—Sylvester gestured toward his two Christian spies—"that the sect is planning a major offensive maneuver against God's church."

"You use the language of war," Helena observed. "What kind of 'maneuver' is being devised?"

When Sylvester indicated that Rex should speak, he stepped forward with crisp military bearing and said, "They will turn the Nicene Creed against the catholics, Your Majesty. Because it so clearly affirms the deity of Christ, they have declared that our Lord cannot be a true man. They take an either-or view on this. If God, then not a man."

Helena gave a small shrug. "One might call this erroneous, or even blasphemous. Yet to be a Manichee is no crime—unless you wish me to start a persecution against them?"

"Never!" Sylvester cried. "Such a thing is far from the mind of any Christian. We do not deal out the violence and bloodshed that has been wreaked upon us."

"What then do you seek from me?"

"I am not sure," Sylvester admitted. "I came here today with an open mind. Does so pious an empress have any ideas about how to handle this situation?"

Helena tilted her chin and gazed at the ceiling as she considered the matter for a few moments. Finally, she said, "My son shall arrive soon in Rome. He could issue directives that do not persecute yet mandate true belief in Christ for all the citizenry."

Although Flavia had been silent so far, she spoke up now in a way that was both humble and firm. "Compelled belief is no belief at all, my lady. People must be persuaded by the inherent truth of an idea, not by laws and edicts from on high."

Helena nodded gently. "Well stated, Junia Flavia. Such is my conviction as well." The empress turned back to Sylvester. "How about some public debates, then? Let the people engage with the ideas on both sides and determine the truth for themselves."

"That approach has been tried," Sylvester replied. "In Alexandria, they did it with the Arians. Nothing was achieved except for each side to harden into even more vehement factions, like the supporters of the chariot teams."

"It is true," Rex agreed. "I was part of all that. It didn't work."

Helena raised her palms and shrugged. "Then are we defeated, my friends? Is prayer the only recourse we have left? Prayer is powerful, of course. But God wishes us to couple our prayers with resolute deeds upon a wise course of action. Our problem is that we can't seem to find an action to perform."

Sylvester did, in fact, feel that he had reached a dead end. He was about to bid Helena farewell for now and retire to consider the matter further when Rex did something strange. The tall barbarian knelt and touched the floor. "I remember what you once scattered here," he said to the empress on her throne. "You poured out the soil of Hierusalem so that this might be holy ground. I believe we should find our solution by considering that holy city."

"Go on," Helena invited. "Your words intrigue me."

Rex stood up so he could properly address the queen. "Hierusalem is the city of David. His psalms show us his deep love for God. David's spiritual zeal kept Israel's heart turned toward the Lord. A leader like that can carry a nation's faith on his shoulders. Today we need a new King David to lead the Romans to God through his godly example."

For a long time, Helena was silent as she contemplated Rex's words. Sylvester understood not to speak too quickly but to linger in the silence and let the empress process her thoughts. *Lord, give her wisdom*, he prayed. *Let the outcome of this meeting be from you!*

When Helena was finally ready to speak, a sadness seemed to descend upon her. "This idea will not work," she announced, "at least not for Rome."

Sylvester was surprised to hear the empress be so negative. "Why not?"

"Because my son will never make his permanent home in this city. Constantine hates Rome because he feels unwelcome here. The senators annoy him like gnats. The old bureaucracy feels to him like a valve that has rusted shut. Perhaps while he is here, his faith in Christ could serve as the public example you seek. But as soon as he leaves—which he certainly will—the Romans will lapse back into their old ways."

Sylvester felt a new pang of discouragement at these words. Although he had thought Rex's idea was brilliant, he now realized that Helena was right. Constantine was no solution. Even if he were pious enough to influence the populace toward God, he wouldn't stay around long enough to make substantive changes in Roman society.

"Your Majesty, may I clarify something?" Rex asked.

"Of course," the empress said. "What is it?"

"When I spoke of a new King David, I was well aware that your son wouldn't remain in Rome. His future is in Byzantium—or New Rome, as they call it now. Constantine isn't our King David. He represents someone else in my biblical comparison."

Helena leaned forward in her seat. "Who?"

"He is Jesse, my lady."

Now the throne room fell silent. Sylvester watched as a dawning smile came to Helena's face, which couldn't help but bring one to his own as well. Each person here knew the scriptures well enough to catch Rex's intended meaning. Jesse was King David's father.

"This is truly a noble idea!" the empress exclaimed.

Sylvester thought so too. "It is time for the city of Rome to have a permanent Christian caesar," he declared. "An orthodox and catholic leader who will guide his people in the ways of the Lord. Like King David of old, he shall lead the citizens to godly worship."

"All hail Caesar Crispus!" Helena cried.

Sylvester lifted his gaze to the heavens. "And all hail Caesar's Lord!"

<hr />

Though the queasiness in Empress Fausta's stomach was unpleasant, it was nothing compared to her dismay at what it probably meant. She stared listlessly at her morning meal of honeyed bread, trying not to think about the facts that burdened her mind. Last month, she missed her womanly flow, and now it had happened again. She was unusually tired. Her breasts were tender and swollen. She had felt nauseated every morning for the past week. Convincing herself it was from too much wine, she had abstained from strong drink the previous evening. Yet here was that same morning sickness, plaguing her again.

Fausta could take no more of the honey's sweet odor, so she shoved away the plate. But getting rid of the repugnant food didn't alleviate the nausea. She hurried to the chamber pot, retched twice, then vomited into it. After wiping her mouth, she finally accepted the truth.

I am with child.

A tiny bit of comfort came from acknowledging the dreadful fact. Though it was scary, at least the mental effort of denial was over. Perhaps the anticipation was worse than the actual consequences? But then Fausta's inner voice of warning kicked in. *Your husband is going to be furious! You've had no marital union that could make the child his. Fausta, admit it—you've got an imperial bastard on your hands. What are you going to do about it?*

There was no question that she had to do something drastic. A queen who conceived out of wedlock was—at minimum—an outcast. Fausta knew she would be kicked out of the palace and exiled to some remote place. Poverty and shame would be her lot for the rest of her life, assuming she wasn't killed by her enraged husband. Constantine had a terrible temper when he felt betrayed. His Christian faith might not be enough to stop his violent rampage.

A maid entered the room to empty the chamber pot, but Fausta waved her away from it. "Go find the bodyguard Pantera," she ordered. "Send him here through the servants' halls so no one will see him."

A short while later, Fausta's lover arrived at her room. He tried to greet her warmly, but she kept him at a distance. "I am carrying your child."

Pantera paused as he absorbed the news. "Did you not take the wild carrot elixir?" he finally asked.

"I missed it a few times!" Fausta snapped. "What do you want me to do? Am I Chronos, that I can roll back the wheel of time and do it over again?"

"Be at peace, my darling," Pantera soothed. "I have a remedy for you. I know a woman who handles things like this."

Pantera's comforting words actually did give Fausta some hope, for she desperately wanted a solution. "Who is it?"

"I will take you to her tonight. In the meantime, have a slave bring you the ragged tunic and cloak of a peasant, then meet me at the side door when full darkness has set in."

Fausta fretted and paced around her chambers all day. When dusk arrived, she stared out her window. The stubborn sun seemed reluctant to go down. Finally, when the sky was black, Fausta donned a long cloak over her plain woolen tunic, pulled the hood over her head, and exited through the kitchen into an alley beside the palace. Pantera was there with a torch. "Follow me," he said.

The furtive twosome walked to the Gardens of Pallas, a lush park with umbrella pines and manicured hedges. The gurgle of trickling water from a nymphaeum obscured the sounds of their footfalls. Eventually, they came to a city gate whose archway supported an aqueduct. After Pantera slipped the night watchman a coin, he opened a small door that led onto the Labicana Way.

Once she had exited the city, Fausta glanced apprehensively at her surroundings. As was common at most of Rome's gates, an opportunistic little community had sprung up here. Though it probably bustled with activity during the daytime, everything was quiet now. Empty stalls lined the road for vendors who hawked their cheap wares by day and retreated into their hovels at night. Litter bearers could also be hired during daylight hours, since mule-drawn carts were forbidden in the city. Hostlers provided stabling for the animals of newly arrived travelers, while ramshackle inns offered sleep or other pleasures in exchange for a few copper coins. It was a shabby environment. Fausta felt disgust for the filthy, money-grubbing denizens of this makeshift village.

"I'm going back to the palace," she told Pantera. "I can't stand this place."

"No! Stay with me, my darling. We're almost at our destination. I promise you, it'll be worth it. All your problems will soon be gone."

Fausta acquiesced, so Pantera led her to a dilapidated cottage at the edge of the village. Behind it was nothing but the empty darkness of the suburban landscape. Rays of yellow light escaped through the cracks in the house's crumbling mortar. After Pantera rapped on the door, a croaky voice said, "Enter!" He pushed open the door and ducked as he went inside. Fausta reluctantly followed him.

The one-room cottage was lit by a single oil lamp. Its walls were lined with shelves filled with terracotta jars of all sizes. There was no bed, only a pallet upon the floor. A workbench occupied the center of the room, its surface littered with mortars, pestles, and glass bottles. And behind the workbench was the most wrinkled woman Fausta had ever seen. Yet while her face was shriveled like a prune, her eyes were lively and bright, even bewitching.

"I am called Pharmakis," the old hag said. "I welcome all visitors into my home, whether human or divine."

"We are human," Fausta said firmly.

"Are you? Who really knows?" The cryptic statement drew a cackle from Pharmakis. Shaking away the thought, she reached to a vial and inspected it by the lamplight. "Pantera tells me you might wish to purchase this."

Fausta eyed the green bottle. "What is it?"

"An essence of bitter herbs known only to me. The shepherds of the mountains bring me what I need. Or sometimes I meet traders from afar. Every road leads to Rome, you know. But only one road leads away."

Fausta had no idea what that meant. Before she could even guess, the old woman said in a matter-of-fact voice, "You are pregnant. You wish to abort your child. This potion will surely do the deed. Yet all sorcery takes its toll. You must be prepared for that."

Abortion! It wasn't something Fausta had yet considered, at least not from a potion. Peasant women were known to drink strange brews, but the upper classes typically withdrew to some quiet retreat where a doctor would prescribe hot baths, bloodletting, and vigorous shaking for several days. If that didn't work, there were surgical options. But potions were fearful, magical things. Only witches dealt in such enchanted concoctions. Indeed, that was what Pharmakis's nickname meant: a sorceress. Fausta wasn't sure she was prepared for such a drastic approach.

"What effects will this potion have?" she asked the witch.

"A violent one, no doubt! There will be pain. There will be groaning, retching, and bleeding from the nethers. But it will last only a day . . . no more than two. And my result is guaranteed, with no permanent effects. The same can't be said for the doctors' silly methods. They often don't work. And they leave lasting damage to the body."

Horrified by these words, Fausta spun to face Pantera, who was standing quietly to the side. "You never should have brought me to this miserable house!" she complained. "Can you imagine such things happening to me in the palace? Everyone would hear it. The rumors would fly. I'd be judged guilty of adultery even without the baby. This is no solution at all!"

For the first time, Pantera's face turned fearful. "Think of me, my darling!" he pleaded. "If you are found out, I'll be crucified. I cannot face such agony! Persevere in this plan, I beg you!"

"You are just a commoner," Fausta said coldly. "Your agony means little in comparison to mine."

Staggered by these words, Pantera could make no reply. Only Pharmakis seemed undisturbed by the turbulent emotions swirling in the cottage. She sorted through the vials on her workbench until she found the one she wanted. It was made of red glass and had a cork stopper. "The dark world offers many kinds of magic," she said in her raspy voice. "I could offer you a different route to reach your desired end."

"We'll try anything!" Pantera cried. "What is it?"

"If you can't remove the child, your other option is to blame it upon a rapist. This potion will stupefy a man and dull his memory. All you have to do is drug some lecherous fool and bring him naked to your bed. Then cry for help and claim there was a violent encounter. No one will doubt your word against his, and he won't have the wits to deny it. Every husband understands that a ravished wife is guilty of no crime. His fury will be directed at the culprit instead of at you."

The devious idea instantly appealed to Fausta. It didn't require abortion by surgery or potions. At full term, she could go off and have the baby, then give it to a Christian family to raise—a practice for which they were famous. The only downside to the plan was that some innocent servant would have to be framed, then probably be sentenced to crucifixion. Yet that was a small price to pay in times of need. More slaves could always be found.

"This plan could work," Pantera said excitedly. "Slaves are notorious for being lusty. Pick someone to blame, buttercup, and I'll make it happen."

Fausta's crafty mind immediately settled on the perfect candidate for the crime. It would solve all her problems and make everything right in the world. Yet Fausta didn't trust Pharmakis to keep the secret. "I will not say his name in front of any witnesses," she announced.

"Whisper it to me, then."

Fausta stepped close to Pantera. He lowered his head so she could speak into his ear. When she gave him the name, a smirk immediately came to his face. His green eyes danced at the prospect of carrying out the plan and freeing himself of blame. "Your words are like the command of a goddess to me," he said. "I will start making the arrangements right away."

<hr />

Since Fausta was anxious and had no reason to delay, Pantera's plan was implemented the next day. Fausta told her lover she didn't want to know the details of how he administered the drug, only where she needed to be and when. "I will come get you when the hour has grown late," Pantera promised, then said no more.

By nightfall, Fausta had grown terribly nervous. A raging thunderstorm outside only added to her tension and unease. She steeled herself by considering the dire consequences that would befall her if the plan didn't succeed. It was after midnight when she finally heard three sharp knocks on the door—the prearranged signal from Pantera. *Time to do the deed, Fausta. Take courage!*

She left her bedroom wearing a cloak over her night shift. Silently, she followed Pantera to another part of the palace by way of slaves' passages that were deserted at this hour. They arrived at a bedroom door for which Pantera—since he was a royal bodyguard—had a key. He unlocked the door but did not open it.

Pantera took Fausta's cloak from her, which made her feel exposed in her thin linen shift. He ripped the fabric at her neckline, then tore the hem of the shift as well. Next he drew a knife from his belt. After slicing his palm, he smeared blood on the shift, as well as on Fausta's face and legs. With the costume now ready for the deadly charade, Pantera eased open the bedroom door. The darkness inside was forbidding.

"Go on," Pantera whispered. "The man is drugged and lies in a stupor upon the bed. Do this brave thing, my darling, and set us free." With a kiss upon Fausta's bloody cheek, he nudged her into the bedroom and shut the door behind her.

The click of the latch seemed loud in the stillness. Fausta waited until her eyes had adjusted to the dark. A formless shape lay on the bed, as inert and unmoving as a corpse. *Did Pantera give him too much potion? He might be dead! Get out now while you still can!*

Yet Fausta didn't leave. Her feet seemed anchored to the floor. By an act of will, she took a step forward, then another. She reached the bed. The man was quiet—yet he was breathing. Fausta moved aside the covers and slipped into bed with him.

With blood-smeared hands, Fausta removed her night shift. The silken bedcovers felt cold against her bare skin. She grasped the man's hand, half expecting him to awaken, but he only grunted and smacked his lips before quieting again. Fausta tied the neck string of her shift around his wrist, then bunched it up and curled his fingers around the garment.

For a long moment, she lay quietly beside the designated victim, gathering her strength before heading into the storm she was about to create. Finally, the tension became too much. She could delay no longer. It was time for hysterical theatrics like never before.

"Help!" she screamed as she burst from the bed. *"Save me!"*

Fausta ran to a wine cart and knocked it over with a crash, sending glass shards and red wine skittering across the floor. One jug didn't break, so she hurled it against the bedroom door and shattered it. Then she clawed at a tapestry until she managed to rip it from the wall. Its support rod clattered loudly as it struck the ground.

She heard running footsteps and distraught voices in the hallway outside. Shrieking like a maniac, Fausta burst from the bedroom, not caring that she wore only her undergarments in front of the palace servants. Chambermaids and page boys stared at her with wild eyes. But Pantera, dressed in the uniform of an imperial bodyguard, had arrived to take command. His drawn sword was in his hand.

"My lady, you are safe!" he exclaimed. "No one can hurt you now!"

"He already did!" Fausta wailed as she recoiled from the gaping doorway. "He ravished me in his bed! He defiled the empress of Rome!"

"Who was it?" Pantera demanded with fire in his eyes. "I will slay him now!"

Fausta's accusing finger shot toward the dark opening like an arrow. "Him!"

323

A muscular young man stood in the doorway, naked and confused. His hair was tousled. His eyes were dull. And in his balled fist he held a bloody night shift.

"It can't be!" cried a valet.

Fausta whirled to face the man who had spoken. "It . . . was . . . *him*," she snarled through gritted teeth. The valet cringed and shrank back.

Pantera set the point of his sword against the criminal's ribs. "You are under arrest," he announced. "One false move, and I run you through."

"Wh-what?" was all the young man could say.

Pantera gave his prisoner a poke with the tip of his sword. "Get moving!" he ordered, then motioned for the onlookers to step aside. The stunned crowd parted to let the two men through. Fausta watched the naked man shuffle down the hallway in confusion and shame.

"You'll pay for this crime with your life, Crispus!" she shouted after him. "Not even your God can save you now!"

—✺—

Constantine gazed appreciatively at the beautiful marble arch on the country road in front of him. Though it commemorated his victory in war, this arch was unlike the one next to the Flavian Amphitheater inside the capital city. That one was two-dimensional—like a gate through which someone passes from one side to the other. But this arch had four piers arranged in a square, which meant its central vault could be placed over a crossroads. One road came in from the east and exited to the west. And the arch's north-south axis was the Flaminian Way that ran from northern Italy straight into Rome.

"The area hasn't changed much over the years," Constantine observed to the bodyguards who accompanied him. He gestured to the landscape around him. "The countryside is just as I recall it. My commander's tent was right here. And the battle began"—Constantine pointed to a line of reddish cliffs far to the south—"right over there, at Red Rocks."

"I remember it, Your Highness. I was there that day," one of the bodyguards said.

Constantine's head swiveled to look at the man. "You fought for me that day?"

"Indeed, I did," the heavyset veteran replied. "I was eighteen and newly enrolled in the legions. We pushed hard toward the bridge. I took a spear point in the thigh—but not before killing three of Maxentius's men."

Constantine reached to his belt and unbuckled the sword on his hip. Though its hilt was inlaid with silver and its scabbard was encrusted with jewels, it was no merely ornamental weapon. The blade was forged from good steel that kept a fine edge.

Constantine handed the sword to the faithful soldier who had distinguished himself at the Milvian Bridge. "A brave deed deserves a worthy gift," he said. After the soldier bowed humbly and received the weapon, Constantine clapped him on the back. "Loyalty is an important virtue. Show it to me, and I will show it to you in return. Come now, gentlemen. Let us head back to the wagon train. The cook has probably got a stew bubbling over the fire."

The cook did have a roadside feast ready, and afterward, Constantine slept well in his tent. As a military emperor, he didn't feel the need to stay in the imperial inns at every stop. Since he had grown accustomed to camping while on army campaigns, he actually preferred his tent to the crowded government establishments. He arose the next morning in good spirits and set out before the sun had grown hot. By midday, his traveling party had reached the Milvian Bridge. Constantine called for a halt so he could step out of his carriage and walk across the arched span.

Although this was the scene of the battle's climax, the current bridge made of stone wasn't the one Constantine had crossed fourteen years ago when he fought his brother-in-law for control of Rome. Back then, Maxentius strategically cut this bridge, making it unusable by either army. Then he ordered a temporary bridge to be constructed alongside it, rigged with a trap that was supposed to plunge Constantine into the Tiberis.

But thanks be to God, the trap failed, and it was Maxentius who drowned that day. Once victory was assured and the opposing troops had begun to flee, the speculator Rex fished Maxentius's corpse from the river, then severed its head with a single slash of his sword. After another soldier mounted the head on a spear, everyone paraded into Rome.

As Constantine stared at the spot where Maxentius had straddled his warhorse, shouting threats and curses at the height of the battle, he muttered,

"You were a terrible general, Maxentius, and an even worse brother-in-law. You got just what you deserved." Though a gust of wind stirred the trees along the riverbank, the ghost of Maxentius made no reply.

When the wagon train finally drew near to Rome's walls, Constantine could hear the happy rumble of a cheering crowd rising from the city. The closer he approached, the louder it got. By the time he could clearly see the walls, he discerned that the ramparts were lined with well-wishers who were celebrating and waving banners. "Bring me a horse," he said to one of his bodyguards. "I'll ride into Rome through this gate like a victor once again."

The Flaminian Gate was wide open as Constantine passed through, riding erect in the saddle on the best-looking stallion the wagon train could provide. Boisterous crowds thronged the Broadway, waving, shouting acclamations, and casting flowers onto the emperor's path as his white stallion passed by. Constantine couldn't help but wonder if the people of Rome had turned out like this for Crispus when he arrived a few weeks ago. *I hope so*, he thought as he gazed at the enthusiastic citizens on either side of his horse. *Just as the people love the father, so they should love the son. What could be more Christian than that?*

The emperor's bodyguards, aided by the Urban Cohorts, pushed the crowds back and cleared the street all the way to the Capitoline Hill. Now that the cavalcade had arrived in the heart of Rome, the well-wishers who lined the thoroughfare were of a higher social class. Many of the men wore the toga, the traditional garment of white wool that had fallen out of favor everywhere in the empire but here. One of the aristocrats, a distinguished-looking fellow whom Constantine didn't know, shouted, "Will you go up to the temple, Your Highness?" With a sweep of his hand, he gestured to the Temple of Jupiter atop Rome's highest hill. "Crispus passed it by, and that offended many of us."

"Get used to the offense, Senator. The old has passed away. Behold—the new has come!" Constantine turned his horse away from the hill so that its arse was facing Jupiter. As if on cue, the stallion chose that moment to lift its tail and drop some moist, green nuggets onto the street.

"It's an omen!" cried one of the onlookers with religious awe on his face.

"The old gods are caca," Constantine agreed—and the senator's fierce scowl told him everything he needed to know about how the pagan aristocracy would receive him while he was here.

As he proceeded into the ancient Forum, Constantine paused in front of the Rostra. It was a speaker's platform that took its name from the prows of conquered ships that adorned its front. Dismounting for a brief impromptu speech, Constantine walked up the steps of the Rostra and faced the waiting crowd in the Forum. On his right was the Temple of Saturn, which these days functioned more as a bank than a place of religious devotion. On his left was the Senate House, the sacred seat of government since the time of the old Republic. And just behind him was the Navel of Rome—a round monument that served as the symbolic belly button of the imperial body. Every street and highway throughout the empire measured its distance from this spot. It wasn't too much to say that the whole world revolved around the place where Constantine now stood.

He kept his speech brief, making it more of a greeting and explanation of his visit than a formal oration. "Fourteen years ago, I entered this public square as a liberator," he declared to the adoring masses. "Now I do so again! This time, you aren't under the cruel hand of a human tyrant. Yet you are subjected to tyranny nonetheless! The old gods hold you in bondage. When I came to you before, I had only just met the true God of heaven. His symbol had appeared to me in the light of the sun—a cross that proclaimed, 'Conquer by this sign.' Now I know this God more fully, and I have come to bring him to you, my beloved people! For twenty years, I have reigned over the Roman Empire. In the next twenty—I tell you this boldly today—my realm shall be transformed into a Christian empire!"

"Never!" shouted a senator from the steps of the Senate House. He was immediately joined by several other jeering men in togas. "Rome belongs to Jupiter!" one of them accused, wagging his finger in a dogmatic way.

"Get back to the east with your weird cult!" yelled someone out in the Forum. When a rock went sailing past Constantine—its thrower impossible to discern in the crowd—Constantine knew it was time to go. All it would take was one rock hitting him for the rumor to spread across the empire that the people of Rome had rejected their augustus. The cheering crowds would be forgotten, and only that one act would stand out, emboldening any potential challengers. Constantine descended from the

Rostra, remounted his white stallion, and quickly exited the Forum on the Sacred Way.

The street passed beside the Flavian Amphitheater, then went through Constantine's second great arch, the one shaped like a gateway that commemorated his victory over Maxentius. Now Constantine's entourage took an eastward turn, bypassing the Palatine Hill and heading straight for the Sessorian Palace instead.

As he approached the imperial residence, Constantine began to imagine the warm reception he would receive there—a stark contrast to the rock-throwing incident in the Forum. His beloved family would be waiting for him at the palace. The plan was for them to be standing on the porch to receive him as the father of the family. Dignified Helena would be positioned in front of the main door, with Fausta on her right and Crispus on her left. Fausta's boys—Constantine Secundus, Constantius, and even little Constans—would be there too. Bishop Sylvester and his churchmen would also be present, and so would the Praetorian prefect, a Christian convert by the name of Junius Bassus.

But when Constantine arrived at the Sessorian, the key element of his plan was missing. As expected, there was a trumpet fanfare, soldiers in fine array, and many dignitaries from political and ecclesiastical circles. Yet the imperial family was absent. Instead, Bishop Sylvester alone welcomed Constantine at the front door. "A grave illness has befallen both of the empresses," he whispered by way of explanation, "or so it was told to me."

After some final greetings to the gathered assembly, Constantine entered the palace and was escorted to his private chambers. His wife was nowhere to be seen, nor his mother, nor any of his sons or daughters. The servants were evasive when Constantine inquired about his family. They would only refer to a "sickness" that had recently come to the Sessorian. *Is a plague starting in Rome?*

A wine cart was in the corner of the imperial bedroom, and Constantine wasn't the type of ruler who expected a slave to fetch his every drink. To demand such pampering on the battlefield wasn't a good look in front of the men, and his wartime habit of pouring his own drinks had stayed with him in civilian life. Constantine filled a goblet with a dark brown vintage that wasn't too fruity or sweet but tasted of good Italian soil. After downing it thirstily, he poured himself a second glass to savor, then stepped out to the balcony.

The Sessorian wasn't located on a hill, so the balcony gave no grand view of Rome. Instead, Constantine gazed upon a courtyard adorned with fountains but soon found himself feeling dizzy. He retired back inside to get out of the hot sun yet found that the shady interior of the palace didn't help. "Must be the rigors of travel," he told himself.

Outside the door, the sound of anguished weeping began to draw nearer. It was a feminine voice making the racket, a lone woman who somehow managed to wail like a crowd of mourners at a funeral. Then Fausta burst into the room with shrieks of distress. Her bodyguard accompanied her, a swarthy fellow with piercing green eyes. Fausta rushed to Constantine and fell into his arms in a cascade of tears.

"Wh-what's going on here?" he asked in a shaky voice. He wondered if he was supposed to be more tenderhearted in a moment like this, but he felt confused about the right way to respond.

"He violated me!" Fausta screamed. "He snatched me to his bed and ravished me!"

A volcanic explosion of rage welled up in Constantine. Anger was a simple emotion that his addled mind didn't have to comprehend because he could feel it in his bones. A twisted grimace came to his face, and he reached out with fingers like talons to choke the offending bodyguard who would surely perish this day.

"No, not him!" Fausta screamed as she moved to protect the bodyguard. "Pantera nobly helped me, and he has arrested the vile perpetrator."

Though Constantine lowered his arms, the rage still boiled within him. "Who, then?"

"Crispus raped me. He said it was time for me to be with a real man."

Hearing that the violator was his own son didn't quench Constantine's rage but stoked it even higher because of the colossal treachery involved. A rape by a stranger was bad enough—but a son against his stepmother? Such a vile thing was unheard of in Roman history, a deed as wicked as anything Constantine could imagine. So staggering was the news that he had to sit on a nearby divan. His head swam with turbulent emotions—fury, vengefulness, betrayal, shame, and jealousy. Beneath all these feelings was a foggy sense of disorientation.

"This deed cannot be allowed to stand!" Fausta insisted, her shrill voice bringing Constantine's attention back to his wife. "The death penalty is demanded!"

"N-no, I don't think . . ." Constantine allowed his words to trail off because he wasn't sure what to do here.

"Will you let yourself be shamed in front of everyone?" Fausta shot back. "When Lucretia was raped in the days of the kings, was not Tarquinius killed? Or if you want examples from our scriptures, what about Dinah? What about Tamar? God took vengeance on their attackers. He put them to death! Can you do any less?"

"But . . . he is my son . . ."

"Which makes the crime all the more worthy of capital punishment! King David was betrayed by Absalom—and what did God do? He caught the man's head in a tree until he could be killed with javelins. Don't you see how God's punishment for betrayal is always death?"

"I s-suppose," Constantine answered. He had never known Fausta to cite the scriptures so much. Apparently she had been reading deeply in the divine books.

The exertion of thinking made Constantine feel sleepy. He reclined on the divan and rested his head on a cushion. The two people in the room seemed to fade from his consciousness. "I will decide this matter tomorrow," he told the woman who was speaking with him.

"No!" she insisted. "The prosecutors have prepared the death warrant already. The penalty is well deserved for such a heinous crime." The woman turned to the green-eyed man and received a tablet from him. "The wax is soft in this document. It only awaits your signet, then Crispus will be executed immediately."

Since Constantine's eyelids felt heavy, he let them fall shut. Surely he could converse with these people while his eyes were closed. "Betrayal . . . death . . ." he mumbled.

"He shamed you, my darling," the female voice said.

"Curse him!" Constantine exclaimed, then added, "I'm tired. Leave me, all of you." He waved his hand toward where he thought the door might be.

Ending this arduous conversation came as a great relief to Constantine. All he wanted to do was drift toward sleep. Barely aware of the sensation, he felt a delicate hand grasp his left wrist, manipulating the ring on his finger. Something waxy brushed against his knuckles. There was a pressing movement—then the soft hand released his wrist and let his arm fall back to his side.

"He will regret it in the morning," a male voice said.

"I will take care of that," came the reply, then all was lost to darkness.

—◦◦◦—

For probably the twentieth time this night, Crispus rose from the cot in his cell and peered from one of the narrow windows. The locked room was situated at the top of a guard tower in Rome's outer wall. Crispus could see the Sessorian Palace inside the city and the abandoned Circus Varianus on the outside. Strangely, the city walls had been built right through the middle of the circus, bisecting its width and making it a relic where no chariots would ever race again. As Crispus looked down onto the former racetrack, he couldn't help but wish for a chariot to whisk him away. While he knew such a conveyance was unlikely to appear, he had every intention of finding some other means of escape.

Mighty God, deliver me from the lies of evildoers!

Crispus understood he had been given some kind of mind-dulling drug on the night that Fausta falsely accused him. He had spent the following day sleeping off its effects in the cell, so now his mind was clear again. And his body was strong too, because the guards had brought him food when he finally woke up around sunset. They had even brought him his own clothing instead of giving him rags to wear. Rejuvenated, he had paced around his cell through much of the night, imagining different means of escape. No solution had yet presented itself. But Crispus was confident that the Lord would show him the way. Sunrise was coming soon—and like the scriptures said, God's mercies were new every morning.

The mercy of God found a strange way to present itself when two rough soldiers came to Crispus's cell at first light. They wore armor and had swords belted on their hips. "Turn around," one of the men ordered gruffly. He carried a spear and seemed to be the leader. When Crispus complied with the command, his wrists were clamped into manacles behind his back.

The guards trundled Crispus downstairs and out to the racetrack—on the suburban side of the walls, not inside the city. Three horses were waiting there. "Mount up," the leader commanded. A mounting block was provided since Crispus couldn't use his hands. When he was situated on horseback, the other soldiers swung into the saddles of their horses, then the threesome headed out of the circus's crumbling gates and into the countryside. One man rode in front of Crispus and the other behind. Crispus noticed that the second man had two ominous items attached to his saddle: a shortbow and a shovel.

Eventually they came to a major highway that Crispus recognized as the Labicana Way. After an hour's ride, the lead soldier stopped at the sixth milestone and turned off the pavement onto a dirt track to the north. They traveled for about a mile into the deep woods. At last, they came to an abandoned villa that must have been very luxurious in its day. Not far away, Crispus could see the arches of the Aqua Marcia bringing clear mountain water into the city. The whole area was deserted and secluded.

"This will do," the leader said. "Dismount, Crispus, or we'll drag you out of the saddle."

The soldier's gruff tone and informal address told Crispus everything he needed to know. Normally, a legionary would be terrified to speak that way to an emperor. The fact that these men spoke so disrespectfully meant they didn't think Crispus would be around much longer. *It's now or never*, he realized.

The second soldier, a man with a spindly neck like an ostrich, unfastened Crispus's manacles and handed him the shovel. "Dig a hole," he ordered with a shove to the shoulder. "Go on. Don't stop until we say so." He snickered after he issued his command.

Crispus's eyes surveyed the ground and the surrounding area. After a moment, he turned back to his captors. "I can't dig here."

"You'll dig where we say, rapist!" the leader roared. To back up his point, he brandished his long cavalry lance.

"Then you'll be out here all day under the hot sun. See how the ground is hard baked? But if I step over here"—Crispus walked a few paces away—"the land can easily be dug. See this line of mounded earth? It is soft under the spade and will turn easily."

The two soldiers exchanged glances, then the leader shrugged. "Fine," he muttered. "Just get it done. Make it deep. And leave a big pile of earth beside it."

The ostrich-necked soldier brandished his bow and a fistful of arrows. "I'm a deadly shot, so don't try to run or you're going down."

Crispus began to excavate what he now knew was intended to be his grave. There was no other explanation for the day's events—the rough treatment, the secrecy, the remote location. Crispus would dig a hole, then be stabbed by a lance or shot with arrows. The soldiers would backfill the dirt over his corpse and no one would ever see him again. At least, that was the intent of these evil men. But God had provided a miraculous means of escape!

While the soldiers loafed under a shady tree, Crispus dug through the low, grassy ridge and into the soft soil beneath. Soon the hole was waist-deep. He kept going until it reached to his shoulders—and that was when his shovel struck what he was expecting: masonry.

With a rapid heartbeat not only from exertion, Crispus jabbed and stomped on the stonework until it gave way. A burst of cool air whooshed up from the hole. With a few more hard kicks, he enlarged the opening until it was big enough to climb into. He had discovered what he knew the line of mounded earth must indicate: a branch of the Aqua Marcia that ran to the old villa and once supplied it with water. Today, it was bone dry—a perfect escape tunnel provided by the hand of the Lord.

"What's taking so long?" shouted one of the men from beneath the tree. "You don't need to dig all the way to Hades. We'll send you there soon enough!"

"There are some heavy rocks to dislodge," Crispus called back. "Take your ease, men. I'll have them out in no time."

He bent to the hole in the aqueduct and slithered into it like a badger into his den. The walls were narrow and confining. But since aqueduct pipes needed frequent maintenance, they were always constructed large enough so the watermen could move inside them.

With his head ducked low, Crispus immediately began to shuffle in the direction of the abandoned villa. He had no intention of going toward the main line, for the absence of water in the conduit showed it had been bricked up, and there might not be an access hole anywhere along its length. Soon enough, however, he did come to a manhole in the opposite direction. Though it provided some light, its opening was barred with iron and clogged with debris, so Crispus kept going. He carried the shovel in case he might need to dig his way out.

The aqueduct spur terminated in a holding tank from which pipes exited to supply the villa. Just like the tunnel, the tank was completely dry. And to Crispus's great relief, nothing but a large clay tile covered the hatch that the house's workmen once used to access the reservoir. He pushed it aside with his shovel and clambered out of the tank.

There was no time to waste, so Crispus immediately began to run. He had gone only a few steps when he heard hoofbeats behind him. Whirling, he found the ostrich-necked soldier astride his mount and bearing down hard. His cavalry spatha was raised to deliver a death blow. Yet Crispus still had the shovel in his hands, so he stabbed it like a spear, knocking his assailant from the saddle before the sword could do its murderous work. The man landed on his back after tumbling over the horse's rump. Dazed, he lay still. Before the fellow could collect his wits, Crispus jammed the shovel's blade into his throat and drove it all the way into the soil. A fountain of blood jetted up, and the man's eyes glazed over in death.

A fierce battle cry and more hoofbeats made Crispus turn again. The lead soldier was galloping into the fray. From the way the rider held his lance, Crispus could tell he was a proficient cavalryman. No shovel strike from a man on foot was going to win that battle.

The dead man's horse wasn't far away, so Crispus ran to it and snatched a bow and arrow from its saddle. Nocking the arrow as he turned, he let it fly, then dove out of the way just as the spearman lunged. The blade of the lance whiffed past Crispus as he rolled across the grass. Scrambling to his feet, he prepared for further combat—but it wasn't needed. The arrow had flown true. The soldier was lying on the ground with the feathered shaft protruding from his chest.

Crispus knelt beside him. The pallor upon the man's face showed that death would come quickly. His fingertips held a slip of papyrus, half drawn from his belt pouch. It was a centurion's warrant of execution. "My . . . orders," the man gurgled as frothy blood bubbled on his lips. "I knew . . . it was wrong."

"I forgive you," Crispus assured him. "You were brave in battle." It was the last thing the man heard in this mortal life. With two fingers, Crispus closed the dead man's vacant eyes, then he sprinkled a little dirt on his chest. Every warrior, even one with evil orders, deserved to be buried in the precious soil of his homeland.

After hitching the three horses together, Crispus mounted the strongest one and headed across the country toward the north. His goal was to reach the Salarian Way, for that road led to Truentinum on the Adriatic Sea. Crispus knew he could find some of his loyal navy boys in that port. If he could get aboard a warship, he could find a safe place in the empire to sort out Fausta's false accusations.

The journey across the width of the Italian peninsula took only three days because Crispus rode fast and alternated his weight among the horses. He traveled by moonlight and slept in remote barns during the day. At one point, a widowed farmwife took him in and provisioned him with enough food to make it to the coast.

"What can they do to me if they find out?" she asked with a shrug. "I'm old. I don't fear death anymore."

"You aren't going to die anytime soon, madam," Crispus replied. "You have much to live for. You shall be handsomely rewarded once I am free again."

Unfortunately, when Crispus arrived at the seaside town of Truentinum, he found that freedom was farther away than he thought. The port wasn't the safe haven he had been hoping for. Though he was able to locate some of his former men in the navy, he also discovered that word of his escape had preceded him there. The army had used a carrier pigeon to send an alert over the Apennines. Now he was a wanted man, even in a town far from Rome.

Crispus's loyalists, however, hadn't been idle. They had arranged for a fast liburnian to set sail under cover of darkness. The goal was to reach Ravenna, a naval stronghold where the enlisted men adored their caesar. The bogus warrant of execution would hold little force among the soldiers and sailors who had fought under Crispus's command in the Hellespont.

The first day of the journey went without opposition, and the liburnian made good time. But on the second day out of Truentinum, three warships were spotted coming down from the north in battle formation. When the ships didn't turn aside but stayed on an intercept course, the crew knew what it meant. Apparently, word had reached Ravenna of Crispus's whereabouts and someone had authorized his arrest. "Head out to open sea!" Crispus ordered. "We can beat them to Pola. I have supporters there too."

Though the chase lasted all afternoon, by the end of the day Crispus realized he wasn't going to make it to Pola. Liburnians were quicker vessels at close range and more maneuverable in battle, but in a sustained course along a straight line, the greater sailcloth and manpower of a trireme couldn't be overcome. The coastline around Pola was in sight when the three warships caught up to the liburnian and surrounded it. After the enemy flagship pulled a little ahead, it turned inward with the intent to ram. There was nothing for Crispus to do but call for a halt and see what his captors would say.

The captain of the flagship was a highly decorated officer Crispus didn't know. From his appearance and demeanor, he seemed to be a good seaman. His tone wasn't threatening when he spoke, just efficient and brusque. "Are you Caesar Crispus?" he asked, though the answer was obvious. The captain was just making sure he had established the proper legalities.

"I am," Crispus replied.

The captain displayed a parchment whose writing was brief. An official wax seal was affixed upon it. "This is a copy of your death warrant," the captain said without any sign of emotion. "It demands your immediate execution. But as a mercy"—he held up a gourd flask—"I will allow you to drink a sleep potion first."

Crispus shook his head. "I shall do no such thing! There has been no trial. Nothing about this action is in accord with Roman law. The accusations against me are utterly false."

"What do I care? I am no lawyer. I'm just an admiral who does what he's told."

Crispus straightened to his full height, which was considerable. With command authority in his voice, he said, "Then here is what I tell you, Admiral! I am Flavius Julius Crispus, a caesar of the Roman Empire. I order you to stand down! You shall not enforce that false document. It has no legal validity whatsoever."

A steely look came to the admiral's eyes. After handing the death warrant to an associate, he drew his sword and stepped forward until he was nose-to-nose with Crispus.

"Kneel down," he ordered. "This is the last time I will offer you the sleep potion. Take it or leave it."

"I refuse your accursed potion," Crispus declared, "and I refuse to bow to you."

The admiral's motion was swift—the adept response of a man accustomed to many years of battle. He plunged his blade into Crispus's body just below the breastbone. Though there wasn't much pain, the blood loss from the liver would be massive. Crispus looked down at the sword's hilt in disbelief. His vision clouded, and the hilt grew indistinct. The world swam dizzily around him. As he collapsed at the admiral's feet and the earthly world receded, the last words he heard were chilling.

"You will surely bow," the admiral declared, "for Rome is forever Caesar's lord."

11

The disappearance of Caesar Crispus had set the Sessorian Palace abuzz with chatter, not to mention all the gossip sweeping the streets of Rome. Some people thought he was guilty of a terrible crime, ranging from the rape of his stepmother to an assassination attempt on Constantine. Others didn't believe a word of it, suspecting that something else must be afoot. Rex didn't know what to believe. But unlike the palace servants and street-corner gossips, he had the ability to find out some facts.

"Let's go inspect his cell," he told Flavia. "That's the first place to start."

The cell where Crispus had been detained, according to several of the palace bodyguards, was a room at the top of a nearby watchtower in Rome's walls. When Rex arrived there, he decided it was a strange structure to call a "watchtower," for it commanded no view except the inside of a now-defunct racetrack. The engineers of the Aurelian Walls often didn't bother to demolish whatever was in the way of their fortification. They just drew their line where they wanted it to go, and if a sturdy building stood in the way, it meant that much less wall had to be put up. In this case, they had built the wall right through the Circus Varianus, including the so-called watchtower that watched over nothing.

"It seems silly to put a tower in the middle of a chariot track," Flavia remarked.

338

"Nothing about this makes sense. But let's go up anyway and see what we can find."

Now that the caesar had disappeared, this remote part of the wall had gone back to its normal state of having few soldiers on the ramparts. Rex saw no one as he climbed the tower's spiral staircase with Flavia behind him. Upon reaching a sturdy door at the top, he tried the latch and found it locked. He turned to Flavia. "Can I have one of your—" he began, then grinned as she handed him exactly what he wanted.

"I know you by now," she said sweetly, "even before you speak."

After picking the lock with Flavia's hairpin, Rex gave it back to her and entered the cell. It was a drab place whose only furniture was a wooden frame with a straw mattress on it. The room had two windows, one on each side of the tower. Its roof was made of terra-cotta tiles that were undisturbed.

Flavia walked over to a chamber pot in the corner. After kneeling and opening it, she grimaced and turned away, quickly replacing the tight-fitting lid. "Recent use," she informed Rex with her nose scrunched up.

"Now we know for sure that someone was here. But we don't know who. The caca of a caesar stinks just like anyone else's."

As Flavia glanced around the room, her face went from the scowl at the bad odor to a look of sudden discovery. She crawled over to the cot and reached under it. A moment later she brought forth her prize. "This fibula isn't like anyone else's!" she exclaimed. "Only the rich could afford it!"

Rex caught the brooch when Flavia pitched it to him. Its basic structure was the same as any other clasp that would hold a cloak in place. But Flavia was right about its value. It was made from gold and decorated with the head of an eagle carved in ivory. "No commoner would own this," Rex agreed. "Crispus was surely here. Now we just have to figure out where he went."

"How?"

"Come take a look," Rex said when Flavia stood up. He pointed out the window and showed her the sandy surface of the circus's racetrack. Three lines of hoofprints came in from one side. They were joined in the middle by human tracks from the tower. Then the three mounted riders left the circus at its far end where it exited into the countryside.

Flavia glanced up at Rex. "Can you follow that trail?"

"Let's find out," he replied as he started for the door.

After descending from the tower and scanning the racetrack's surface, Rex found the print he needed. The impression was made by a hoof shod with iron, a practice not often seen in Italy's dry climate. Horseshoes were more common in the colder, wetter parts of the empire. Yet this horse was wearing them, making a distinctive print that could be followed by a trained eye as long as the earth was soft.

The tracks headed from the circus across the countryside in an easterly direction. Rex and Flavia were on foot, so the hike would take them longer than if they were riding. Yet they had no time constraints for this fact-finding mission, which was a direct request from the pope. Being on foot actually made it easier for Rex and Flavia to stay in contact with the hoofprints as they followed the trail.

Soon, however, they hit the Labicana Way. Tracking a horse was impossible on its hard surface—but that didn't mean the end of the quest. "Watch for any prints that turn off the road," Rex said to Flavia. "You look left. I'll look right."

The day grew hotter as the couple trudged under the hot sun. A few times they found tracks to one side or the other, but none were from an iron-shod horse. At midday, they stopped to rest under a shady tree and ate a lunch from Rex's pack. They had just resumed their walking when Flavia called out, "Tracks leaving the road!" She gestured to a thin trail that led off through the shrubbery beside a milestone that marked the sixth mile from the city.

When Rex bent down to examine the soil, it didn't take him long to find the prints of the horseshoes. "We're back on the trail," he announced, beckoning Flavia to follow him into the woods.

They went for about a mile into the forest, never losing the trail because there had been no rain since the night Crispus was arrested. The tracks ended at a strange discovery. A hole had been dug into the earth, at the bottom of which was a broken aqueduct conduit. Then two of the horses—including the one with the horseshoes—had moved toward a nearby villa that had fallen into ruin. From the length of the horses' strides, they appeared to have been galloping. Clearly, something strange had happened here.

"Stay close," Rex said, setting his hand on his dagger's hilt. "And stay alert."

Everything was quiet and still at the old villa. No voices could be heard, not even birdsong. Death seemed to haunt the place. "Look!" Flavia hissed, grasping Rex's arm and pointing across a grassy field. "Someone is lying on the ground."

The man didn't move as the pair approached, and Rex quickly discerned that the fellow was dead. A shovel had pierced his throat. Nearby was a second man, also dead, this one from an arrow. Although flies buzzed over both corpses, decomposition hadn't set in, so they couldn't have been here for more than a day. The men were dressed in military uniforms, but their weapons had been taken. Rex approached the soldier who had a higher-quality outfit and seemed to be the leader. A little dirt was sprinkled upon his chest. Kneeling beside the corpse, Rex drew a piece of papyrus from the dead man's fingers. The Latin script was an imperial death warrant—and the condemned convict was Caesar Crispus.

Rex stood up, tucking the warrant into his belt pouch. "They brought him out here to kill him secretly."

"But the horses are gone and these soldiers are unburied. That means Crispus must have escaped."

"Men like him often do," Rex said. "Let's head back into the city. There's nothing more we can do here today."

After the long trek back to the Sessorian, Rex and Flavia slipped a surreptitious message to Crispus's loyal valet to request a private meeting. The valet, a man named Scipio, agreed to meet them in the imperial bedchamber later that evening. He let them in the door when they arrived and quickly shut it behind them.

Through a series of questions, Rex determined that Caesar Crispus had been feeling ill the night that everything happened. He went to bed early to try and sleep it off. That was the last time Scipio saw him until the accusations came from Fausta in the middle of the night. "I know he didn't do it!" Scipio exclaimed. "He had a look in his eyes that I've never seen before—like he was unaware of his surroundings. And why would he attack Fausta? He could have any woman he wants. Nothing about this makes sense!"

"We agree," Flavia said. "Do you think there was a plot against him?"

"Yes! I think Fausta's bodyguard is involved—Pantera, they call him. He

341

always seems to be part of the action. Somehow, he's in the know, or in just the right spot."

Rex and Flavia exchanged glances. They had both noticed Pantera's familiarity with the empress during the trip from Nicomedia to Rome. "Where is he now?" Rex asked.

"The royal family is at a big meeting with some senators on the Palatine, so all the bodyguards are with them."

"Then I'm going to inspect Pantera's belongings while he's out," Rex said. "It might provide some evidence."

"His bed in the barracks is easy to find. It has a panther's claw carved into it."

"That's all I need to know. You've been very helpful, Scipio. Say a prayer for your master, because he's in deep trouble."

"I have been praying earnestly!" Scipio replied as he let Rex and Flavia out the door.

The guardsmen's lodgings were in a wing of the Sessorian Palace not far from the imperial bedchambers. The door to their barracks wasn't locked because nobody would dare to steal from this tight-knit brotherhood. Rex knew that if he were caught rifling through their things, it would create a lot of trouble—a situation he wanted to avoid.

"I'll keep a lookout in the hall," Flavia said. "If anyone starts coming, I'll warn you."

"I won't take long," Rex promised, then gave his wife a kiss on the cheek and darted into the barracks.

The bed with the panther's claw carving was one of twelve bunks in the room. Rex hurried over to it and opened the trunk at its foot. Nothing of interest was inside—just clothing, a sheathed sword, a cookpot, some jars of food. Then Rex spotted the glass bottle.

It was a little red vial with a cork stopper in it. After opening it, he gave it a sniff, then tasted a drop on his tongue. From the pungent, earthy taste, Rex immediately recognized the concoction's main ingredient. *Mushrooms!* Certain kinds of this fungus could induce terrible confusion in the mind. Some speculators used mushroom elixirs for espionage or interrogation. Though Rex didn't have that specialized training, he knew the basics. This potion, taken in a high enough dose, would create profound disorientation and memory loss. An imperial bodyguard had no good reason to have such a powerful substance in his footlocker. Could Pantera have administered this drug to Crispus without his knowledge?

Rex had just put the vial back in the trunk and closed its lid when he heard Flavia speak in the hallway. "Sir, can you help me?" she called to an unknown visitor. Rex drew his dagger and crept to the door. Instead of trying to step outside now—since a bodyguard had obviously shown up unexpectedly—he waited to see how things would play out.

"I seem to have taken a wrong turn," Flavia went on. "Can you escort me to Her Majesty's guest quarters?"

A male voice answered in words Rex couldn't quite hear, though the tone sounded agreeable. Soon everything was silent again. When Rex peeked into the hall, it was empty, so he slipped out and made his way back to the palace's guest rooms by a different route. Flavia was there waiting for him.

"Nice work," he told her. "We make a good team."

She smiled back at him. "We've been dodging soldiers since the first day we met." After pausing, she asked, "So, what did you find in there?"

"A potion that makes people confused and forgetful. I think Pantera probably gave it to Crispus. He's working with Fausta to get the caesar condemned and exiled."

"I knew it!" Flavia exclaimed. "We have to tell Constantine what's really happening!"

But Rex shook his head. "Not yet. All we've got so far is guesswork. We need real proof to back up an accusation like this. I'm going to ask Scipio to tell the palace servants to keep an eye on Pantera. We'll offer a reward for anything suspicious. The slaves see everything. If something happens out of the ordinary, we'll know about it right away."

Unfortunately, Pantera did nothing during the next few days except carry out his normal duties. One servant reported he was going to Fausta's chambers more often than usual, and Rex rewarded that information with some small copper coins. But the real money was reserved for the person who could report something big—and one week after the alert was put out, someone did.

Rex was awakened just after falling asleep by a knock on the door of the guest room he was sharing with Flavia. Groggily, he answered the door and found Scipio standing there. "Get dressed, quick!" the valet whispered. "Pantera is leading three of his comrades out of the palace. They're armed. And they're bringing torches. I'll stall them as long as I can. Meet me at the side door as soon as possible." And with those words, Scipio hurried away.

"What's happening?" Flavia whispered from the bed as Rex pulled his tunic over his head.

"Pantera is up to something. He and three other men are going out undercover. Bodyguards don't have any business sneaking out at night." Rex swung a cloak around his shoulders and fastened the pin. "I'll be back before dawn," he promised his wife—without telling her that he had also buckled on a sword.

The nocturnal foursome wasn't hard to follow because the soldiers wore hobnailed boots, which made a characteristic clacking sound on Rome's paved streets. Since Rex's shoes were of a civilian sort, he was able to follow the men without being noticed. They proceeded across the entire width of the city and finally came to the gate that led out to the Salarian Way. After pausing to pay the night watchman a few coins, the bodyguards exited through a little door that was opened for them within the huge gate. Rex waited a few moments, then did the same. The watchman took the money and opened the door again without comment. Clearly, this was how he augmented his meager government salary.

Pantera and his band lit their torches now that they were outside the city walls. Rex followed the bobbing lights on the road ahead until they turned aside and entered a necropolis. Soon, the lights stopped moving. The men assembled in a dense thicket that had grown up around the ancient tombs.

As Rex watched from behind a clump of shrubbery, four more men emerged from the underbrush and stepped into the circle of light from the torches. They, too, were soldiers—but they were standard legionaries, not members of the palace bodyguard. Their leader carried the vine staff of a centurion.

"We've brought you the prize," the centurion said, then gestured toward one of his subordinates behind him. The legionary brought forth a stone ossuary and set it on the ground among the men.

"I will inspect it," Pantera said, "lest you falsely try to claim the reward." While one of his assistants held a torch over him, Pantera knelt beside the ossuary and lifted the lid. Satisfied by what he found inside, he set the top back in place and stood up. Turning toward his own men, he said, "Pay him in full."

Pantera's three accompanying bodyguards withdrew leather sacks from beneath their capes—six in all. Rex could hear the jingle of coins in them. The centurion chuckled greedily as he received the payment. After he passed the sacks to his legionaries, who hid them beneath their cloaks, the two groups stepped back from each other. The ossuary remained on the ground between them.

"Do we take the prize with us?" asked one of the palace guardsmen.

"Too dangerous," Pantera said. "Too many eyes in the city. It is enough that I have seen it. My word will be sufficient for Her Majesty."

"But we can't leave it sitting on the ground!" the man protested.

"Of course not." Pantera gestured toward a nearby mausoleum with tangled ivy engulfing its entrance. "Put it in there. Clearly, no one is visiting that tomb anymore."

The three palace bodyguards worked the heavy stone out of its opening while the centurion departed along with his men and their money sacks. After the ossuary was stored inside the mausoleum, the big tombstone was shoved back into place. Then Pantera's group started back into the city—but Rex had no intention of staying with them.

When everything had been quiet for a long time, Rex moved out of his hiding place. Though the tombstone was heavy, he was able to use a thick branch as a lever and force it ajar. One of the soldiers had left behind a spent torch, which still smoldered enough for Rex to light a resinous twig from a nearby pine. With this miniature torch in his hand, he wriggled past the tombstone and slipped into the ancient mausoleum.

The air inside the enclosure was musty and dank. The ossuary had been set on a slab next to the crumbly skeleton of some long-forgotten Roman. Rex held his twig in his teeth to provide light while he worked. His heart was beating fast as he grasped the heavy stone lid in two hands and set it aside. Then he looked inside the ossuary.

The sight was terrible to behold. A sickening horror struck Rex, making him turn away his face. *My God! No! How can it be?*

Compelled to look again—to make sure the dreadful nightmare was, in fact, the truth—Rex forced his gaze back to the box. His second look was just as horrifying as the first. Tears of frustration came to his eyes, the helpless feeling of knowing that a grievous crime had been perpetrated and nothing could be done about it. Everything in Rome was about to change for the worse.

After putting the lid back on the box, Rex carried it to the mausoleum's narrow opening and pushed it through. Then he slipped through the crack and exited the tomb. Though the cool night air felt better than the mustiness inside, Rex wasn't refreshed. A gruesome task lay ahead of him, and there was nothing he could do to avoid it. Heavyhearted yet resolved to see it through, Rex picked up the ossuary and began the long walk back to the palace with the severed head of Caesar Crispus.

⚬⚬⚬

It was a dark day—and Empress Helena had the feeling it was about to get much darker.

Two churchmen were coming to see her at the Sessorian Palace, and the fact that they were coming together didn't bode well. *Perhaps it is for devising a strategy*, she tried to convince herself. *Or maybe they have good news about my grandson and they want to tell me in person?* Despite these hopeful thoughts, a terrible sense of foreboding had taken hold of Helena. She feared that the bishops Ossius and Sylvester were coming to give her pastoral care in a time of grief.

When the two bishops arrived, they were ushered straight to the residential part of the palace. Helena didn't have the heart right now for the pomp and circumstance of an imperial audience in the reception hall. Instead, she met Ossius and Sylvester in a small, enclosed garden where curious eyes wouldn't be a problem. Only one trusted handmaiden was there. Helena wasn't sure she could remain dignified if the news were bad, and she didn't want the servants gossiping about her emotional breakdown.

"I greet thee in the name of the Lord," Sylvester said stiffly. His face had a somber appearance that Helena took as a bad sign. Ossius stood behind him, holding a small treasure chest by its two handles. The sturdy wooden box was ironbound and had a secure latch on it. Helena couldn't fathom why the men would be bringing money today. *Maybe a bribe to free Crispus from imprisonment?*

After Ossius also offered a Christian greeting, Sylvester asked Helena to take a seat on a marble bench in the little garden. It was a pleasant spot, shaded by an ivy-covered trellis. A slight breeze stirred the leaves above. Sylvester sat down beside Helena on the bench, then surprised her by taking her hand in a comforting way.

"My lady," he said, "I am sorry to inform you that wicked men have slain your beloved grandson."

For a long moment, no one said a word. Helena felt like she might vomit. She clenched her hands into fists, squeezing Sylvester's fingers as if they were twigs she was trying to break. Yet he didn't flinch, nor even seem to feel it. A rapid series of thoughts tumbled through Helena's mind, each one claiming to be true until the next one replaced it. *These men are lying and plotting against me! They are mistaken and got wrong information! I'm dreaming and about to wake up! I'm losing my mind and this isn't real! I'm losing my hearing and I misunderstood! It's true, but God will raise him from the dead!*

Rapid breaths began to escape Helena's lips. Her chest heaved up and down. She panted as she tried to get enough air in the tiny garden whose walls seemed to be closing around her. *I must be . . . no, he can't be . . . no, they are . . . but this isn't . . .*

Helena released Sylvester's hand and leapt to her feet. "NO!" she screamed to the heavens with her head thrown back. "NO!" she cried again with her palms to the sky. "It can't be true! It can't be—"

Words failed to materialize in her throat, which felt as dry as a sandy desert. She staggered back onto the bench beside Sylvester, coughing and clasping her neck. The handmaiden stationed in the corner of the garden rushed forward and handed her a silver goblet. Helena sputtered as she put it to her lips, choked down some water, then hurled the goblet against the wall. Its clatter sounded indistinct and distant in Helena's fogged mind.

"I am very sorry," Sylvester said tenderly. "Crispus will rise again in the resurrection. This is not the end."

Now anger flooded Helena's heart. "I refuse to believe it. It's . . . it's not true. It cannot be. Everyone is mistaken."

Sylvester sighed and nodded. "Those who grieve often deny. Unfortunately, that luxury isn't afforded to you. An empress who denies a truth like this is in danger herself. That is why we have brought proof."

Ossius had been standing to the side of the garden while Sylvester took the lead. Now the Spanish bishop set his money chest on another bench in the garden. After glancing at Sylvester and receiving a nod, he looked at Helena and said, "The evildoers beheaded him, my lady. Crispus is surely gone from this life and awaits the trumpet of Jesus Christ." After patting the top of the wooden box, he added, "There can be no doubt, if you know what I mean."

A dawning horror seized Helena as she began to grasp the import of Ossius's words. *That chest contains no treasure! It contains . . .*

Once again, Helena began to pant for breath. Her chest felt tight, like someone was drawing a band around it. The handmaiden hurried to bring another goblet of water, but Helena waved it away. Instead, she met the servant's eyes. "Tell me what is in that chest."

But Sylvester intervened before the wide-eyed maid could respond. He stood up and whispered in the girl's ear, then turned back to Helena. "She will declare if she sees confirmation of what I just told you. There is no need to utter terrible things or describe sights that will never be forgotten by those who hear the words. Only a yes or a no is required here."

Ossius beckoned for the girl to come near. Tentatively, she approached. He opened the lid of the chest. "Young lady," he said, "do your eyes now witness proof of Caesar Crispus's departure from this earthly life? If so, take courage, then turn around and say 'yes' to your mistress with a clear testimony."

To her credit, the handmaiden rose to the challenge. After bowing to Helena, she said in a firm voice that did not waver, "Your Majesty, I testify to you, yes, your grandson is dead."

So be it, Helena said to herself.

Now, it is time to get even.

—◦◦◦—

The past few days had been the most hellish of Constantine's life. No one knew where Crispus was. Every new report seemed to contradict the last. Fausta, of course, kept wailing about Crispus's attack on her. Other accusations were running rampant as well, rumors of secret plots and palace intrigues. Some people spoke of insurrection . . . invasion armies . . . civil war on the horizon. Strident voices demanded swift justice for crimes real or imagined. There was even a widespread belief that legal documents had been sent out under the imperial seal. Death warrants. Edicts of execution. Whether those documents had been enforced—or even truly existed—who could say?

The death penalty against Crispus? Hot anger flared within Constantine as he contemplated the possibility that Fausta's accusations were actually true. *How dare he attack my wife! An outrage! Death is too good for a son who . . .*

Constantine's thoughts broke off as the jealous rage in his soul evaporated, replaced immediately by sorrow, by pity, by paternal longing. *Where are you, my beloved son?* Tears came to Constantine's eyes as he pictured Crispus in some remote dungeon—alone, falsely accused, wondering why his father had turned against him. *Crispus! I love you! Come back to me!*

And so it went—on and on. Constantine had been cycling through turbulent feelings like these for ten days. It was a fiery torment that seemed to have no end. None of his emotions were stable enough to linger for very long. Yet each one hurt like hell while it lasted.

A commotion outside the room caught Constantine's attention. Commotions were, of course, ever present these days. Someone was always screaming, or complaining, or warning, or accusing. This time, the wailing voice sounded like his mother. A bodyguard was trying to stop her from advancing. *Might as well give it up, fellow. You'd have better luck trying to stop the waves from crashing onto the beach. Nobody can stop my mother.* And with that, Helena burst into Constantine's private chambers like an arrow shot from a bow.

"Murder!" she screamed. "They've murdered your son!"

An icy chill coursed through Constantine—a powerful, shocking feeling that terrified and energized him at the same time. He had been holding on to the hope that Crispus was alive and innocent of all crimes. Now Helena seemed to have information that would prove otherwise. Constantine's mind refused to believe it.

"Just another rumor," he declared with a dismissive wave of his hand, as if saying so would make it true.

Helena, though, was undeterred. "It is no rumor! Your son is dead. He's *dead*, I tell you! Look here. I have proof!"

A container was in Helena's palm, a beautiful silver jewelry box. Constantine approached his mother. "What is it?"

"See for yourself." She opened the box and extended her hand. A curled lock of hair was inside, the russet color of . . .

"No," Constantine whispered as he backed away from what his eyes beheld. "It can't be his."

Though Helena's response was factual, her tone brimmed with barely controlled rage. "Your son is dead," she repeated. "This was clipped from his severed head, which is here in this palace."

God help me!

Constantine staggered backward as he realized Helena's assertions were true. At some point, he would surely feel grief, but now he was seized with a burning desire for revenge against the perpetrators of this terrible crime. "Who did this?" he demanded through gritted teeth.

"Fausta arranged it! She is with child—all the palace servants know this now. And the baby's father is her bodyguard, the man with green eyes like a panther. Together they have conspired against Crispus!"

Helena's use of her beloved grandson's name caused a fountain of tears to burst from her. She stumbled to a nearby divan and collapsed upon it. Constantine was trying to figure out what to do next when two new arrivals rushed into the room. It was Empress Fausta, accompanied by—of all people—the man called Pantera.

"Lies!" screamed Fausta. "All lies! Don't believe anything this woman tells you! Not a word she says is true!"

"It's all true!" Helena countered from her couch. "Be gone, murderer! You deserve death for your crimes! And take your lover with you!"

Constantine's head was spinning from all the accusations. He felt like a whirlwind had taken up residence in his soul. Normally he was in command of every situation. Now he couldn't distinguish truth from falsehood. There was no such thing as reality here, only a series of competing illusions. Never had he been so confused about what to do.

He turned toward Fausta with a fierce glare. "Is it true you are with child?"

"Yes . . . from the attack Crispus made on me."

"How could you know already?"

"Women know such things," Fausta said evasively.

"I think you're lying. I think—"

Pantera interrupted Constantine's hypothesis by stepping forward and kneeling in a humble way. In his hand was a tablet that he extended for examination. "Your Highness, I believe you know the truth in your heart. Look here at the evidence of your clear thinking about these matters."

Constantine snatched the tablet from Pantera. It took him only a moment to determine what it was: the death warrant for Caesar Crispus. And at the bottom, beneath the writing in the wax, was the impression from his own ring. He took a step back, stunned by what he was seeing. "I . . . I authorized this?"

"Yes, Your Highness," Pantera said in a strong, clear voice. "In your weariness from travel, you must have forgotten it. Yet you issued this command because you knew the truth. Crispus ravished Fausta, sir. That is a fact. I have seen the evidence with my own eyes. It is undeniable. It truly happened."

Fausta's expression turned tender. She approached Constantine and softly put a hand on his arm. "I am not guilty of sin, my darling. Another one is. And you have acted swiftly against his crimes."

"She's tricking you!" Helena shouted as she rose from the couch.

"ENOUGH!"

The room fell silent when the furious command exploded from Constantine's lips. Everyone seemed taken aback by his fierce demeanor. He glared at each person in the room, his eyes shifting from one to the next. In all the tumult, one thing had become clear to Constantine: this whole thing had to go away. *Erase it all,* he told himself. *Every bit of it. Grieve in private if you must. But publicly—you have to make this disappear forever!*

Constantine strode over to his mother, who shrank back from him as he approached. She had never done that before. Yet Constantine thought it was probably a good reaction this time. Fear was necessary now.

"Give me that," he demanded, holding out his hand.

"Give you what?"

"You know what I mean!" Constantine roared. His wide-eyed mother handed over the silver box with the lock of hair in it. Turning away from her, Constantine went to the balcony and hurled the repugnant thing out of his sight.

"But that is—" Helena started to say until Constantine rebuked her with a curse. Chastened by his harsh language, she held her tongue.

"I hereby damn the memory of Caesar Crispus," Constantine announced with steely determination in his voice. At these words, Helena began to whimper, while Fausta seemed triumphant. Damnation of memory was a terrible penalty, a sentence designed to destroy all recollection of a public figure. No longer would any monument bear Crispus's name, nor any document make mention of him. All the records of his life would be obliterated. No one would speak of him ever again. It would be as if this young man had never existed.

Although a giddy smile was plastered on Fausta's face, Constantine intended to make it disappear. He turned toward her, and the intensity of his step as he stalked over brought sudden apprehension to her posture. She withdrew toward Pantera, who was standing nearby. Fausta's instinctive response lent ferocity to Constantine's words. "You will kill it," he said, jabbing a finger toward her belly. "Within a week, it must be done. If not, it is off to a distant island for you, never to return." Constantine leaned close to Fausta and drilled her with his stare. "And I mean *never*."

The prospect of lifelong exile had clearly gotten Fausta's attention. She lowered her gaze and nodded obediently. "Yes, my lord. It shall be done as you command."

"One life in exchange for another," he added. "Then all shall be even again."

But Helena denounced this plan. "You would commit the sin of abortion?" she cried. "The innocent child pays the price while this adulterer gets away with her crime?"

Fausta whirled toward her mother-in-law like a cornered badger. "I am no criminal!"

"You're a killer!" Helena shot back.

"Be quiet, both of you!" Constantine bellowed. "I have spoken! Heed my commands, or I swear to God, you will all pay a terrible price!"

Both women knew Constantine meant what he said. Though they lapsed into sullen silence, the glare between them was like daggers flying across the room.

Now Constantine went to the door of his chamber and stepped into the hallway. When he returned a few moments later, three bodyguards trailed him with unsheathed swords in their hands. Pantera's eyes bugged out as Constantine darted to him and grabbed a wad of his tunic. He hurled the swarthy man into the bodyguards' grasp. The tips of their swords surrounded him, each poised to strike like a scorpion awaiting any movement from its prey.

"Shall we do it here?" one of the guardsmen asked.

"I would never let this man's filth stain my bedroom," Constantine said disdainfully. His accusing gaze was fixed on Fausta as he spoke. Unable to endure the intense look, she glanced away. Constantine turned back to the bodyguards surrounding Pantera. "Take him away."

"What should we do with him, Your Highness?"

"Hold him overnight. Then tomorrow, throw him to the lions in the amphitheater."

The fearsome punishment caused Fausta to let out a whimper, though she quickly choked it off. Constantine's head swiveled toward her. "My decree bothers you?"

She swallowed hard, then met Constantine's gaze. "No, my lord. This fellow means nothing to me. I care not what happens to him."

"Get him out of my sight," Constantine said coldly. The bodyguards began to drag the wailing Pantera out of the room. Yet just as they reached the door, Constantine stopped them. "One more thing!"

The lead guardsman turned around. "Yes, my lord?"

"I said 'throw him to the lions,' but I have changed my mind. Make sure it is panthers instead."

"As you wish," replied the bodyguard, then Pantera was no more.

With these matters resolved, there was nothing left to say. Helena and Fausta seemed anxious to depart, having experienced enough emotional trauma for one day. Neither of them wanted to wait around and see if things could get any worse. "Leave me, both of you," Constantine said. Helena rose from her couch and exited, followed soon after by Fausta. A welcome silence descended upon the room.

Standing in place because he was too exhausted to move, Constantine closed his eyes and breathed rhythmically for a long time. Never had he experienced such a terrible day, not even in war when the battle didn't go his way. All his energy seemed to be drained away. He felt empty, depleted, utterly spent.

When he had finally calmed himself—or at least grown blessedly numb—he stepped out to the balcony. It was a private spot, not open to anyone's view, and that was what he wanted. A screen of cypress trees surrounded the balcony, their boughs fragrant and soothing. Constantine inhaled their scent and let the afternoon sun warm his face. Yet as he moved his head, something flashed in the corner of his vision. Focusing on it, he discovered that a metallic object was snagged in the dense cypress foliage.

The silver box that Helena brought!

Tentatively, he approached the little container and removed it from the branches. The box was made of wood, overlaid with delicate silver filigree. Its clasp was still secured.

Dare I open it?

Constantine couldn't resist. Lifting the lid, he gazed at the single lock of hair. It was the reddish color he knew so well . . . the hue not only of Crispus but of his mother, the sweet and delicate Minervina whom Constantine had so dearly loved. The lock of hair seemed innocent as it lay there in the box, almost childlike. Yet a bit of darkened blood on the curl proved that this young man had come to a violent end.

At last, the grief began to hit. Crispus was gone, truly gone. Constantine would never see his son's handsome face again. Crispus had an easy laugh, a confident step, a bright future. Now he was gone . . . forever.

By my own order!

Although the grief was bad enough, when combined with shame, it was more than Constantine could bear. The bloodguilt of such a terrible deed was beyond repair. God would surely cast him aside. Constantine's Christian faith had lasted for a few years—but now what? In just one day, it had shriveled up and died. The righteous God of Christianity would look down on the earth and see nothing but a murderer and villain. Crispus's death wasn't like killing in war, which was allowable. This was filicide, compounded afterward by abortion. No one could forgive sins like that. Not even Jesus Christ.

But . . .
Perhaps there is another in the heavens who can?

⚊⚊⚉⚊⚊

All things considered, Fausta believed that recent events had worked out pretty well for her. Yes, she had lost Pantera. Her lover was devoured by panthers, just like Constantine had commanded. Fausta didn't watch it, of course, or attend the games that day. Yet everyone in the palace was talking about it, and some of them were eyewitnesses. They all agreed that Pantera didn't handle himself with courage. He squealed with fear, then lost control of his bowels as the cats approached. Though that was known to happen to the victims in the amphitheater, people generally assumed it wouldn't happen to soldiers or imperial bodyguards. Pantera's cowardice was widely viewed as a disgrace.

Fausta wasn't brokenhearted about the man's death, because she had never loved him. Her dalliances with Pantera were more about exciting experiences than actual affection. And the truth was, he had become a serious liability. The conception of a baby had changed everything for the worse. Fortunately, that problem was about to disappear from this earth just like Pantera.

It was early morning, before the day had yet grown warm, when Fausta arrived at the bathhouse that served the Sessorian Palace. The facility was deserted, not only because people didn't typically use the baths at such an early hour, but also because everyone—except the necessary servants—had been forbidden from entering the building. Today, the baths were reserved only for the empress's use.

"What a run-down place," Fausta said to herself as she disrobed in the changing room and wrapped a towel around her body. Though the Sessorian baths had once been magnificent, they were now showing their age. The place had the aura of an aristocratic dame whose beauty had faded but who must have been dazzling back in her heyday. Fausta's critical eye noticed the decay more than the former grandeur. "The whole building needs to be torn down," she muttered.

As she took a seat on a marble bench to slip her feet into some wooden clogs, a dizzy spell hit her. She steadied herself with both hands on the bench and waited for it to pass. Instead, it grew worse. For a long time, she sat with her eyes closed and her head spinning. Once, she felt the need to vomit, but eventually that feeling passed. Only after what must have been half an hour did Fausta feel able to stand again.

Here we go, she thought. *Just put up with it as long as you must. A day of enduring such trials is a small price to pay for a return to normalcy.*

Fausta wasn't worried about the dizzy spell because she knew exactly what had caused it. Last night, then again at dawn, a physician had administered drugs to start the abortion process. Now the extreme heat would finish the job. *All I have to do is wait*, Fausta reminded herself. *I'll deliver the fetus in the privacy of my bedchamber. The doctor will discard it, and no one will know it was from Pantera!*

Fausta's secret fear had been that the baby would have piercing green eyes like its father. Now that wouldn't matter. No one would ever see the tiny creature except a midwife and a doctor—and they weren't part of the palace staff, so they had no knowledge of Pantera. A feeling of exultation came to Fausta as she finally stood up and left the changing room. *I'm going to get away with it!*

She walked to the sauna, the only room in the bathhouse she planned to visit today. Normally, bathers would alternate from warm to hot to cool, then start the process over again. But today was all about extreme heat. The doctor had ordered Fausta to linger for as long as she could in the sauna, which was known for getting overheated at times. Even the caldarium—the hot pool room—wasn't hot enough for the purposes of abortion. The dry heat of the sauna most enervated the body and caused the necessary convulsions of the womb.

The furnace man was checking the sauna's temperature when Fausta arrived. He was an unkempt fellow with stubble on his jowls and hairy forearms. His only garments were a loincloth and cheap sandals made of rope. Though he should have bowed when an augusta approached, he seemed to have forgotten the proper demeanor of slaves.

But Fausta didn't have time for reprimands. "I want the heat turned up to the limits of human endurance," she told the slovenly worker. "When you think you've got it hot enough, throw on another log."

"As you wish," replied the furnace man with a curt nod of his head. He turned away and headed downstairs to tend the fire.

Fausta stepped out of her clogs and unwrapped the towel from around her body. As she was about to enter the sauna, she painfully stubbed her toe on a protruding pavestone. "Damned old place!" she shouted at the ceiling, then stepped into the sauna. As if to confirm her curse, she had a hard time shutting the warped door but was finally able to yank it into place. The sauna wouldn't get hot enough without a tight seal to keep the heat from escaping.

Stone risers around the little round room provided places for Fausta to sit. She spread her towel on the top tier near the ceiling, where the heat was the greatest. Though the air in the sauna was dry, a sheen of sweat soon glistened on her body. But Fausta didn't mind a good sweat; it was an excellent way to purge oneself of impurities. She was determined to stay in the heat longer than she ever had before. Today, the impurity she needed to purge from her body was of a more substantial sort.

Downstairs, the furnace man must have been doing his job well, for the heat was surely intense. Yet even when it began to grow arduous, Fausta didn't budge. Finally, unable to tolerate the heat any longer, she moved down to the bottom tier and spread her towel there. The temperature at that lower level was only slightly diminished.

Another dizzy spell came over Fausta, which she considered a sign of good things to come. She placed both palms on the travertine seat to keep from toppling over. Her mind felt slow and sluggish—whether from the extreme heat or the doctor's drugs, she didn't know. *Not . . . long . . . now*, she told herself. *Just . . . hang . . . on.*

When a painful spasm racked Fausta's abdomen, she felt relieved. The sharp pang in her womb meant the abortion process had begun. Soon, she could exit the sauna and go lie in her bed to let the events unfold. But before she left the heat, she wanted to make sure the process was truly underway and wouldn't falter. She forced herself to wait a little longer.

The second contraction was even more acute than the first. It seemed to engulf her whole body, its pain like the stab of a knife. Now Fausta knew the time to leave had come. Naked, weak, and sweating profusely, she rose from her seat and staggered to the door.

And it wouldn't open.

She pushed on the door and tried to jiggle it, but the wooden barrier refused to move. Though a wave of panic rushed upon Fausta, she ignored her fearful thoughts and focused on the one task before her. *Push . . . hard!*

She did—yet there was still no movement.

Fausta lowered her shoulder and gave the door a full-bodied shove. It didn't yield, not even a little. The door felt like it was more than just stuck—like it had been firmly barred on the other side. More panic arose, and this time, Fausta couldn't bat it away.

"Help!" she screamed, slapping the wood with her palm. "Open up! I need help!" But no one came. The only sound was the dull roar inside her head.

Fausta knelt down, then lay prone on the sauna's floor and put her nose and lips near the bottom of the door. Perhaps she could receive some cool air from underneath? Yet there was no refreshment, no relief from the life-draining heat. More feebly than before, she banged on the door with her palm and yelled again for help. Nothing changed. There were no sounds of response, no voices of salvation.

The torrid heat was unbearable. Fausta could feel that her body had become overheated from within. If she hadn't already been lying on the floor, she surely would have collapsed. To stand up now would be impossible.

Terrified at the prospect of her death, Fausta tried again to summon help. But no words formed in her mouth, only a feeble groan. Soon she would faint, and from that stupor she would never wake up. Yet was that so bad? The horror of her imminent demise was balanced by the instant relief it would bring. *Just . . . let . . . go . . .*

NO!

Gathering all her remaining strength, Fausta uttered one last plea. "Venus!" she cried to the ceiling, to the stars, to the heavens of the eternal goddess. "Save me!"

At last, a voice responded from the other side of the door. It was a female voice, firm and clear. Yet her words held out no hope. Instead, the message was one of condemnation. "There is no salvation," the speaker said, "for those who murder the innocent."

Was . . . that . . . Venus?

As the deep darkness closed around Fausta and the light of her consciousness dimmed, a final realization came to her flickering mind. The voice she had heard wasn't the goddess of love.

It was the voice of Helena Augusta.

━◦◦◦━

AUGUST 326

Sorrow pressed hard upon Constantine's heart. His burdens were heavy. His sins were manifold. His bloodguilt was enormous. The Christian God had surely abandoned him. *But*, he reasoned, *perhaps Jupiter has not?*

"Your conveyance awaits you, my lord," said the doorman at the Sessorian Palace. Hardly aware of what he was doing, Constantine stepped out into the hot sunshine and took a seat in his fancy litter. Then the eight beefy porters picked it up and began to move through the streets of Rome.

Constantine had recently learned some more facts about his son's death. The night of the alleged rape, Crispus was affected by some kind of mind-numbing potion. He wasn't guilty of any crime. Fausta had falsely accused him. Nonetheless, he was now dead. And so was Fausta. An accident had occurred at the baths during her abortion.

Is that really what it was—an accident? Helena had hinted that something else was being planned. "She should be executed for what she did," Helena had said.

"Yes, she should," Constantine had agreed. "But I can't do that publicly."

"May your will be done," was Helena's cryptic reply.

Did my words give tacit permission for capital punishment?

Nothing was clear to Constantine anymore—nothing except a few essential truths that shined like lighthouse beacons in a fog of uncertainty. One was that his wife had been guilty of death-deserving crimes. It could no longer be denied. She had committed adultery, murder, and high treason. No queen who did those things had ever been allowed to live.

Another truth was that three members of his family were now dead: his son, his wife, and an unknown infant. Their deaths had been brutal. Stabbing. Beheading. Overheating. Suffocation. Abortion. Terrible deaths involving great pain and suffering. Violence had come to the clan of Constantine.

The third truth was the clearest of all in Constantine's mind: this whole episode had to go away—far, far away. It had to disappear from the eyes of the public. More importantly, it had to disappear from Constantine's blackened soul. A washing like that would require a god who was less strict and demanding than the one found in the Christian scriptures. Fortunately, such a god existed. In fact, he lived nearby. His home was the Capitoline Hill.

The litter bearers arrived at the foot of the Capitoline and set down their burden in front of the Senate House. Today, Constantine didn't intend to ascend the holy hill. That would come in due time. Instead, he had summoned the High Priest of Jupiter to meet him privately inside the legislative building where the Senate normally gathered for debate. Imperial bodyguards and some policemen from the Urban Cohorts were stationed at the front entrance to keep the masses away. Even the senators had been temporarily excluded from their assembly hall. Constantine stepped out of the litter and hurried inside the Senate House, then the doors were shut behind him.

The High Priest of Jupiter was standing beside the Altar of Winged Victory. Two chairs were there, so Constantine sat down and the priest followed suit. Though the High Priest wasn't equal in power to an emperor, he was certainly Constantine's social peer—an aristocrat from an eight-hundred-year-old Roman family. The man's toga was beautifully tailored, and the cap on his head bore the olivewood spike that signaled his high religious status.

He greeted Constantine warmly and respectfully, then asked, "How might I help you, Your Majesty?"

Constantine had no intention of dragging this matter out, for it weighed too heavily on his mind. "I need cleansing from sin," he announced.

The High Priest considered his reply for a long moment. "Sin is a primitive concept," he finally said. "It was concocted by the Jews. And it is an obsession of the new cult that emerged from them, led by their crucified criminal. But our religion makes no place for that idea. The gods do not care about your moral life. They only want to be worshiped correctly with ritual and offering."

"I know the gods overlook our petty crimes. Yet they grow agitated when men shed blood unjustly. Consider the Furies. They avenge the wrong deeds of men. The gods certainly aren't oblivious to"—Constantine paused to choose his words carefully—"the immoral things an emperor may have done."

"Be that as it may," the High Priest said, "we do not have a means of atonement for sins. Sacrifices please the gods by their propriety and costliness, not as an expiation by blood."

Constantine leaned forward in his chair. "Then I wish to make a costly sacrifice to Father Jupiter, the Best and Greatest. It will be a pure, white ox, given to the god according to all the rules. Jupiter will look favorably on me, and the cosmos will be restored."

"If you say so," the High Priest answered agreeably. "A sacrifice at the Capitol by the Augustus at the climax of his Twentieth Year is a worthy and befitting deed. The people will see your true piety and rejoice in your repudiation of that strange cult of the Jew."

"Arrange it for three days hence," Constantine commanded. "It must be preceded by a public parade." After some specific details were discussed and various plans were made, he thanked the High Priest, then rose from his seat and ended the meeting.

On the appointed day for the public sacrifice, Constantine dressed in the full regalia of a Roman emperor. He wore a robe made of the finest wool, dyed to a deep purple and fringed with golden tassels. Gem-studded shoes bedecked his feet and a diadem of gold and pearls was on his brow. His inner voice whispered to him as he got dressed, *You traitor! You wore these same garments at Nicaea!* but he pushed that memory out of his mind. He didn't want to think about the Christian God anymore because his holy standards were too hard for mortals to bear. Constantine didn't have the strength for such high demands.

Just before leaving the palace to head to the parade's starting point, Constantine retrieved the silver box that held Crispus's lock of hair. He transferred the reddish curl into a slip of parchment, folded it, and tucked it into his belt pouch where it would be close at hand. After the sacrifice to Jupiter had been made, Constantine intended to burn the wisp of hair as well. In this way, he would relinquish all memory of his son forever. It would be a lavish and costly gift to Jupiter, which would surely avert the wrath of the gods.

The parade formally began at the Arch of Constantine, which served as a gateway into the heart of Rome. Arrayed in his regal attire, the emperor mounted a chariot drawn by eight noble stallions. Above his head, emblazoned upon the arch, was the relief sculpture that depicted his great triumph at the Milvian Bridge. The arch's inscription declared that the victory had been won "by the prompting of the Divinity." Though the senators who erected the arch used that phrase as a veiled reference to the Christian God, the terminology was vague enough to include Jupiter as well. And Jupiter was a god whose yoke was easy and whose burden was light.

With a snap of the reins, Constantine expertly guided the chariot beneath the arch, then took a left turn at the Flavian Amphitheater. Crowds lined both sides of the royal procession, kept back from the rolling chariot by the Urban Cohorts in full dress uniform. After also navigating through the Arch of Titus, Constantine headed toward the Forum on Sacred Street. To his right was the mighty basilica—the biggest in the empire—that Maxentius initiated but Constantine completed, installing his own colossal image in the hall's apse instead of his fallen enemy's. After passing the basilica and the Temple of the Divine Julius, where the famed general Julius Caesar was cremated after his assassination, the imperial chariot entered the Forum proper. Many senators thronged the way ahead, their gleaming white togas rippling like sea surf on this windy day.

Once the chariot had reached the Rostra, Constantine halted the stallions and handed the reins to a charioteer who was especially popular with the crowds. That man moved the vehicle away so Constantine could ascend on foot toward the mighty height of the Capitoline, the highest hill in Rome. The little lane that climbed its flank was called the Clivus. At the summit of the Clivus was the Capitol—the Temple of Jupiter. This deity was known as the father of the gods, the wielder of the thunderbolt, the eternal protector of Rome. Upon that ancient, rugged hill, the High Priest would meet with the emperor. There, the divine world would be conjoined with earthly, mortal life. A white ox would shed its blood, the people would marvel, and a beloved son would be relinquished forever and ever.

All the imperial splendor of the day came down to this one moment. Everything was just as it should be. Constantine stood at the foot of the Capitoline Hill while the aristocrats and commoners cheered him on. He was about to start up the slope when a lone man appeared on the Clivus ahead, declaring that none of this would be allowed to stand.

"Who shall go up to the mountain of the Lord? Who shall stand in his holy place?" the man cried in a voice endowed with power from on high. As he spoke, he raised his cross-shaped staff to the sky. A stunned silence descended on the watching crowd; and into that silence, the man projected his holy words. "He who is innocent in his hands and pure in his heart! He who has not lifted up his soul to vain idols, nor sworn deceitfully to his neighbor. This one shall receive a blessing from the Lord and mercy from God his Savior!" The speaker was Pope Sylvester, the fearless bishop of the Roman catholic church.

"Do not bar my way," Constantine said, though not in a tone of anger or warning. Something significant was happening here—something he could feel but not define. A whisper in his soul told him not to speak harshly.

"Why do you ascend to the house of demons?" Sylvester asked. "They do not have what you seek, my brother."

"And what do I seek?"

"Absolution from your sins! You seek divine forgiveness for the death of Caesar Crispus, whose execution order went out under your seal."

At the confirmation of this terrible charge—which many in Rome had suspected but no one had known for certain—an angry murmur rippled through the crowd. Some people even booed and hissed, for Crispus was much loved and his undeserved death struck everyone as tragic. Constantine cringed, not only because of the bystanders' accusing eyes, but even more because of the Accuser's diabolical assault upon his soul.

Yet Sylvester directed his gaze toward the disgruntled crowd. "Silence!" he barked, thrusting forth his palm. "Which of you is innocent of sins against the Almighty?" The sharp rebuke quieted the restless bystanders, and their murmuring ceased.

Now that the truth had been cast into the open, Constantine decided to take matters firmly in hand. "You are right that I seek absolution for my wrongdoing," he said to the bishop. "In the fog of confusion and deceit that enveloped my palace, I allowed a death warrant to go out beneath my seal. I did not try to recall it, for anger and vengeance had a hold on me. I believed things I shouldn't have entertained. I gave credence to crafty lies. Now my son is dead. And I am to blame." Though these facts were horrific, it felt good to speak the truth publicly.

Sylvester took a few steps down the incline of the Clivus, aided by his cross-shaped staff. Now he faced Constantine from only a few paces away. "So you admit it is for forgiveness that you are climbing this wicked hill behind me?"

"Should I not want the Best and Greatest to favor me?"

"Yes!" Sylvester roared with holy fire in his eyes. "But you will not find him in a temple made by human hands." He gestured toward the sky with his staff. "The one true God is enthroned in heaven. Only he can forgive sins—and he does it not by the blood of bulls and goats but by the blood of his own Son! Sinners are made holy through the sacrifice of Christ's body, once for all. The ancient prophet says, 'He was wounded for our sins, he was bruised for our iniquities. The chastisement of our peace was laid on him, and by his welts we are healed.'"

A hard gust of wind blew through the Forum, forcing Constantine to step back from the Clivus onto flat ground. Although part of him wanted to press forward, something inside him seemed to prevent it.

As he stood rooted in place, an idea crystallized in his mind, an insight prompted by Sylvester's words. It was a new realization about Jesus, whom Constantine had always understood as a conqueror who beat the Romans at their own game by coming back alive after they crucified him. While that was certainly true, Sylvester had just said something else about the cross: Jesus's death was a sacrifice for sin. The cross was where the Son of God took upon himself the sins of the world. Though Constantine had heard such language before, his mind had always skipped over it in favor of the victory motif. But now, with the burden of his own sins upon him . . . he finally understood.

A sharp, authoritative voice snapped Constantine's awareness back to his surroundings. "Rome worships the ancient gods!" the voice said. Constantine turned and saw the speaker was a toga-clad senator. "Go up the hill and do your duty. Show the people what the empire is all about!"

"Go on," added another senator, waving his hand toward the gleaming temple on the heights. "The High Priest awaits you up there. Do what a Roman should do!"

But Constantine backed away from the Clivus. "I cannot."

Jeers and boos erupted from many in the crowd, causing Constantine's bodyguards to surround him in a protective circle. The ridicule of the senators seemed most vociferous of all. Yet the sudden opposition only strengthened Constantine's resolve. He turned his back on the Capitoline Hill and began to proceed with firm steps out of the Forum.

"Rome follows Jupiter!" someone shouted.

"But your emperor follows Christ," Constantine replied.

As he walked back along Sacred Street and exited the Forum, the crowd grew more agitated. The way was narrow here, and the people pressed close despite the bodyguards' efforts to keep everyone at bay. Some people threw pieces of food, and even a few rocks came sailing at Constantine. One of them hit him in the ribs—a remarkable act of treason, even though it was just a glancing blow. Constantine was wondering how he was going to make it through the constriction ahead when someone joined him at his right hand.

"Get back, all of you, in the name of the Lord!" Sylvester shouted to the ruffians who blocked the way. He jabbed his staff toward them, and they shrank back—perhaps from religious awe, or perhaps even from the mighty hand of God.

"We should step inside the basilica," Sylvester advised. "The guards can bar the door until the people disperse. Then you can go home. More troops can be summoned to escort you back to your palace."

It was a wise idea, and since the basilica was close, Constantine darted up the steps and let the soldiers and policemen shut the door behind him and the bishop. Immediately, the clamor outside diminished to a low rumble in the background. The New Basilica was a stout edifice with massive walls and heavy masonry. Whatever was happening in the street wasn't going to make its way inside such an impregnable building.

Now that things had settled, Sylvester let out a deep sigh. "Let us calm ourselves for a moment," he said, then closed his eyes and stood quietly in the vast, empty hall. As Constantine examined the bishop's face, he decided there was nothing compelling about Sylvester's physical appearance. He was just an average-looking middle-aged man. Even so, Sylvester had a commanding spirituality that few could resist and none could ignore.

After both men had regained a sense of equilibrium, they began to walk toward the apse at the far end of the hall. The image there seemed to draw them—not an idol, but a colossal depiction of Constantine seated on a throne. The enormous statue dwarfed the two men, making them seem smaller and smaller the closer they approached. Originally, Maxentius had commissioned this sculpture of himself, but the head of Constantine was carved instead and placed on the preexisting torso. Now it was Constantine's marble eyes that gazed toward the heavens, while the real eyes of the flesh-and-blood Constantine gazed up at the giant work of art.

When the two men reached the statue's base, they stopped to contemplate its marvelous height. Though Constantine was a tall man, he came only partway up the shin of the seated figure before him. Yet it wasn't the sculpture's legs that arrested his attention, nor the hands, nor even the face. It was the item in the emperor's hand: a long wooden staff with a crossbeam about two-thirds of the way up. A plain flag hung from the transverse bar, its fabric dyed bright red.

Is it a Christian cross? Like everything else in this age of transition, the imagery was ambiguous and liminal. It could be an army standard. It could be a government banner. It could be a bishop's staff. It could be a symbol of Jesus Christ. Maybe it was all these at once.

Sylvester turned toward Constantine and gave him a gentle smile. "I am glad you didn't sacrifice to Jupiter," he said quietly. "Today you survived a great crisis in your faith."

"It would have been a wicked deed," Constantine acknowledged, then paused before adding, "but not the hardest task of the day."

And with those words, the dam broke. All the pent-up emotions in Constantine's soul came flooding out. He began to weep in the empty basilica—not loudly yet deeply, with shoulder-heaving sobs and an abundance of tears. They were tears of many emotions: grief for what had been lost, shame for what had been done, regret for what had not been done, and longing for what still might be. But most of all, they were tears of contrition—for Constantine now understood that he was a greater sinner than any other man.

"Join me, brother," Sylvester said as he knelt down, then stretched out on the floor. "Join me at the foot of the cross."

The two men lay prone before the wooden pole in the statue's hand. Each of them gripped its thick shaft where it rested on the marble floor. Meanwhile, something else was in Constantine's other hand. Before he assumed his humble position, he had removed the lock of Crispus's hair from the pouch at his belt.

Constantine's tears flowed freely, welling up from his broken heart, drenching his cheeks and the floor of the basilica built in his honor. "Crispus," he whispered, fingering the lock of hair. "I am sorry. Oh, my son! I am so . . . so . . . sorry." Terrible guilt took hold of Constantine, and his next words came out as a groan. "God in heaven! Forgive me! Jesus Christ, have mercy on me, a sinner!"

Although Sylvester made no spoken reply, Constantine felt his friend's hand come to rest upon his shoulder. It signaled presence in sorrow, brotherly companionship, and acceptance.

A sense of hope returned to Constantine as the two men lay side by side. The bishop had proclaimed truth today. The hill of Calvary, not the Capitoline Hill, was the only place of forgiveness, the sole means of removing the stain of sin. The cross was a reminder that the Heavenly Father had given up his Son so that a human father could see his son again. *In this sign*, God had promised the world, *you shall be forgiven!*

At last, Constantine rose from the floor to a kneeling position. Sylvester did the same. Constantine tucked the lock of hair back into his pouch, grateful he didn't have to burn it. The two men stared at the giant statue looming over them. Its placid gaze was transfixed not on them but on the distant heavenly heights.

"It is a remarkably good resemblance," Sylvester observed. "The sculptor was skilled."

"It looks just like me. Yet it tells a giant lie."

"What lie, my brother?"

"It declares to everyone who beholds it, 'Caesar is Lord!'"

"Is he not?"

"So I believed for many years," Constantine replied. "But now I know that Jesus alone is Lord."

ACT 3

HUMANITY

12

It was a beautiful late-summer day in Rome—breezy, not too warm, and sunny, yet with enough puffy clouds in the sky to take the edge off the sun's glare.

"This is a fitting day to dedicate the shrine where Peter is buried," Bishop Ossius declared.

"And where our baby is buried," Flavia said to Rex, though not loudly enough for anyone else to hear. The final resting place of their stillborn son next to the apostle's grave wasn't a subject she wanted to bring up publicly— yet it wasn't something she wanted to forget either.

Over the past few years, a massive construction project had been taking place at the Vatican Hill. This gentle slope wasn't one of the seven original hills of Rome but was located outside the city walls and across the Tiberis River. Long ago, the wicked emperor Nero killed Saint Peter in a circus on that hill, then the Roman Christians buried their beloved apostle in the adjacent cemetery. Over the centuries, the cemetery expanded and the local believers slowly forgot the precise location of Peter's grave—until a few years ago, when Flavia and Rex discovered it again. Yet the discovery wasn't without opposition from God's enemies. A fierce confrontation with an evil man had resulted in Flavia's first miscarriage.

"Nikasius," she whispered, recalling the name she and Rex had given their son. "Someday I shall see you again, little one."

Emperor Constantine had declared today to be a public holiday in honor of the shrine's dedication. The group of Christians proceeding out to the Vatican Hill along with Flavia and Rex comprised a substantial portion of the Roman church, both clergy and laity. In addition to Pope Sylvester, all the priests from Rome's neighborhood congregations had been invited. Countless monks, nuns, deacons, and deaconesses had likewise been asked to participate. They were joined on the road by a throng of common Christians who wanted to be part of the festivities. Although Constantine wasn't going to be at the shrine today, his mother would be representing the imperial family. And since Helena was always attended by Bishop Ossius, he would be at her side. Flavia's and Rex's invitations had come from him.

"I can see the platform from here," Rex said after he and Flavia crossed the Tiberis. "Can you see its shape past those trees?" He pointed toward the west, and Flavia followed the line with her eyes.

"It's much bigger than I imagined!" she exclaimed once she recognized the outline of the structure. "That church is going to be enormous!"

"Constantine doesn't do anything on a small scale."

"Neither does his mother," Flavia answered with a grin.

As the Christian procession drew near the site and the platform came into clearer view, Flavia could discern that it was not only large but also extremely solid. The construction crews had cut off a large portion of the Vatican Hill's summit. The excavated soil and rubble had been dumped into retaining walls raised to the height of the hill's new level. Once all the fill dirt was in place and the surface was compacted, the result was a large, flat area—the platform to which the travelers were journeying today. Although no church had yet been built on the platform, the hill was now crowned by a stable foundation from which the Basilica of Saint Peter would soon rise.

After leaving the main road, Flavia followed the rest of the pilgrims along a narrow pathway that ascended the hillside and gave access to the platform's top. Arriving upon it, she stamped her foot and found the surface to be just as solid as she had expected.

"I bet the new church will stand here for a thousand years," she marveled.

Rex nodded. "Maybe even longer."

As Flavia walked toward the platform's far end, she tried to imagine what was under her feet, now covered by a vast amount of fill dirt. This whole place was once a necropolis—a city of the dead. Three centuries' worth of graves, tombs, and mausoleums were once scattered along the Vatican Hill, with little alleys running between them to form a sort of "city."

Terrible events had happened in those alleys, events Flavia didn't like to recall. There had been a lightning strike, a vicious battle with an evil foe, and a fall from the heights of Nero's nearby circus. That fall had taken Nikasius's life. Flavia instinctively drew closer to Rex, and he clasped her hand. Though he didn't say anything, she knew that he, too, was remembering the epic battle and tragic outcome. Constantine's workmen had buried the surrounding land and its structures, but no one could bury the difficult memories Rex and Flavia shared.

The countryside pilgrims made their way to a little edifice at the far end of the platform. Today's dedication ceremony was not for the basilica—that would require many more years to erect—but for the shrine over Peter's grave, which the basilica would one day surround. The crowd of pilgrims encircled the newly built monument, pressing close to it in their holy fervor yet kept back from the structure itself by Helena's bodyguards. An awning had been set up for the empress, and she stood beneath it in royal dignity. On her right was Sylvester and on her left was Ossius. Rex and Flavia were allowed to draw close to the empress, though not under the awning itself.

"Look at those beautiful columns," Flavia said to Rex while they waited for the ceremony to begin. "It must be hard to sculpt stone into spirals like that. They look more like twisted tree trunks than pillars."

"It takes a skillful hand to do that," Rex agreed.

The four gently spiraled columns supported two bronze arches that crisscrossed at their zeniths. From their juncture dangled a beautiful gold lamp. Beneath the lamp was the grave monument itself. Marble cladding now encased the structure built by earlier Christians to mark Peter's grave. Although that former "trophy" could no longer be seen, everyone knew what was inside the marble and under the floor: the original burial place of the apostle, along with his relics in a special receptacle. *And my baby lies there too*, Flavia thought. She took comfort in knowing that when the day came for Christ to blow his final trumpet, Nikasius and Peter would rise together and join their Savior for eternity.

Once all the Christians had assembled at the shrine, it was time to begin the dedication ceremony. Although various participants had different roles to play—offering invocations, singing hymns, anointing the monument's four corners, and lighting the lamp for the first time—Pope Sylvester served as the overseer of the proceedings. He used King Solomon's dedication of the Jewish temple as his guide: not by sacrificing animals but by taking up Solomon's humble desire that this house of worship would become a focal point of prayer to the Living God.

To emphasize that desire, Sylvester asked Empress Helena to be the first to pray at the shrine. After she had knelt in front of it and prayed silently, she stood up and returned to her place beneath the awning. Then Sylvester began to offer some closing words of exhortation. His theme was the importance of believing in the real manhood of Christ.

"Just as the blessed apostle Peter was a real man, so, too, was our Lord," Sylvester declared. "Whenever Peter caught a fish, he broiled it and ate it along with the rest of the Twelve. Can anyone believe that the Savior rejected the food as the disciples sat around their campfire? Of course not! Jesus took a piece of that fish and ate it, just like the others. Though he was God, he was also a true man with flesh like ours. Do not listen to the Manichaeans, who declare that Jesus only 'seemed' to be human. No, my people! We must believe that the infant in the manger . . . the carpenter of Nazareth . . . the Lamb upon the cross—this very One was incarnate and enfleshed, having a body just like ours in every way."

From the cheers and hurrahs that arose, Flavia could see that the bishop's words were having a powerful effect. Sylvester didn't let up, but pressed his point. "Right here at this monument, we have proof of Peter's humanity," he went on. "His bones lie beneath our feet. But do such relics exist for our Lord?" The bishop's gestures and the expression on his face indicated he wanted an actual answer.

"No!" the people cried.

"And why not?"

"He is risen!" someone shouted.

"You are right!" Sylvester answered with a gratified smile. "No bones of our Savior shall ever be found. And yet, there are other proofs of his historical life and work. But since the Lord did not come to Rome like Peter and Paul, the reminders of his life must be sought elsewhere. That is why our pious emperor is sending his beloved representative"—Sylvester swept his hand toward Empress Helena—"on a mission to the holy land! There she will find and uncover the places where our Lord walked, fed the hungry, healed the sick, died on the cross, and burst from his tomb. For too long, those holy places have lain hidden. Now let them see the light of day once again!"

The cheer that Sylvester's words elicited seemed loud enough to be heard throughout the peninsula of Italy. Flavia had to cover her ears because the noise was so deafening. Only when Helena stepped from beneath her awning did the ovation subside so everyone could hear what she would say. Raising her hands to the heavens, she announced, "I accept the mission of Constantine! In obedience to my son, I shall lead a holy pilgrimage to Israel. My visit shall begin in Hierusalem, where, by God's grace, Christians will once again pray at the foot of the cross. For it is only at Calvary that true forgiveness can be found!"

True forgiveness . . .

At Calvary.

In Hierusalem!

Flavia stepped closer to Rex, then gently pulled his sleeve so he would bend down for her to speak in his ear. "We must go there too," she told him while the crowd celebrated around her.

"All the way to Hierusalem?"

"Yes," Flavia replied, "and straight to the foot of the cross."

<hr />

The warrior Geta had every reason to be bitter. His lot in life had been hard. And things didn't look like they'd be getting better anytime soon.

Geta limped his way through the streets of Aelia Capitolina—the true name of this backwater city, not the stupid "Hierusalem" the Christians liked to use. Their religion was the cause of many of Geta's problems. He hated all Christians and prayed that the gods of Rome—or his own Germanic gods—would smite anyone who worshiped the Jewish criminal who was crucified in this city.

Fifteen years ago, Geta's life had held so much promise. Things were vastly different in those days. He was an outstanding cadet in speculator school, able to run faster and fight harder than any of his peers. Then he got a commission into the Roman army as an elite operative and quickly caught the eye of his superiors. He was even the son of Emperor Licinius by his concubine Inga, a connection that would surely prove beneficial when the right time came. The future seemed unimaginably bright. *Now all that is gone!*

The last time Geta saw Licinius was upon the walls of Thessalonica at the failed escape attempt. Caesar Crispus, the pretty-boy prince with a charming smile, had arrested them both. Geta was demoted and sent to serve with the Tenth Legion on the fringe of the empire in Palaestina. As for Licinius— who could say where he was being held now? Probably in a dungeon much worse than the cell Geta had tried to rescue him from. Constantine was a cruel and vindictive overlord who took vengeance on his rivals.

The sun was hot on this late summer day, but Geta pressed toward his destination. Walking long distances was difficult due to his limp from a broken leg many years ago. A man had stamped on his shin in a fierce duel, and the injury had been crippling. Though Geta could still get around, he couldn't march with the troops or fight in combat. That meant only the most menial jobs in the army were available to him. Once he had been an invincible speculator. Now he was a cleaner of the latrines. That was Geta's downward trajectory in life. Every morning when he woke up, he had to swallow the bitter pill of the Fates . . . then do it again on the morrow.

The main street of Aelia, known as the Great Cardo, was bustling with midday activity. The grand avenue ran north and south, bisecting the city into halves. Colonnades on both of its sides allowed pedestrians to walk in the shade, giving shopkeepers the chance to snare them as they passed. Geta reached an intersection and turned right. After descending a steep slope, he crossed the Lower Cardo, which ran through the ravine called the Valley of the Cheesemakers. The effort of ascending the valley's other side brought sweat to Geta's brow. At last, he reached flat ground near the smaller of Aelia's two forums. Just beyond that was his destination: the temple of the healing god, Aesculapius Serapis.

The focal point of Aesculapius's worship was the healing waters gathered in twin pools. Even the magician Jesus, when he walked the streets of Aelia before his well-deserved execution by Pilate, had drawn upon these waters' power when he healed a paralytic. The Christians believed the claim of their scriptures that an angel would stir up the Pool of Bethesda and the first person into the water would be healed. Little did those fools know that their "Christ" was just a charlatan and their "angel of the Lord" was actually Aesculapius!

An attendant greeted Geta at the gateway into the temple complex. "You have a gift for the god?" he asked.

Geta withdrew a coin pouch from his knapsack and handed over a silver argenteus. "May I find favor before the mighty one," he said as he entered the holy precinct.

The worship of Aesculapius—who was associated at this shrine with Serapis, the Aegyptian god of healing—normally involved three aspects. First, there had to be a cleansing of the body and spirit. Then there was an overnight stay during which the god would visit the sleeper in a dream. Finally, there was a prescribed therapy given by the god—or maybe even a miraculous cure.

Geta went through the first step by bathing in the temple's pools and washing himself with ritual ablutions. He also cleansed himself with oil and a strigil, then spent the afternoon contemplating an idol in a small, quiet garden. It took him all afternoon to go through the process. By the end of the day, he was hungry, yet his body was relaxed. "Drink this," said one of the Aesculapian priests as Geta got ready for sleep. "It is a potion that opens you to dreams."

During the night, a dream did come to Geta—not a tranquil one but a terrible nightmare. He tossed and turned beneath his covers, sweating and afraid. Dangers seemed to close in, and a shadowy figure in black entered his room. Then a serpent appeared, entwined around a pole. "You need many treatments!" the snake said in a whispery voice as it loomed over the bed. "Come back and worship me every week with many gifts, and you shall be healed." Geta thought he heard the sound of someone exiting the bedroom, but he couldn't be certain because the dream world was mixed with the real in his mind. After the figure in black departed, the room fell silent again.

The next morning, a priest interpreted Geta's nighttime visitation from Aesculapius. "Clearly, your limp cannot be cured at once. That is why the snake told you to return often. Over time, there are massages and stretches that will reshape the joints of the leg. Perhaps even the bone can be re-formed. It will require many visits here."

"And many gifts to the god?"

"Of course. How else would he be prompted to notice your sufferings? He is a deity, after all. He does not experience the things of mortals, nor observe them unless you draw his eye to your plight."

"I shall do it," Geta vowed. "My limp vexes me. It is the cause of all my problems."

The Aesculapian priest smiled wisely at this. "Your healing is assured, my friend. Go now and receive your massage. Then I will see you again, one week hence. Bring the same silver coin—and if you also offered some sweet cakes to the god, that would probably be noticed by his all-seeing eye."

"Yes. I will bring silver and sweet cakes. Soon I shall be whole again."

"Not soon," the priest countered. "But eventually. Farewell."

After the massage, Geta did feel more limber and quicker of step. He walked back through the streets of Aelia Capitolina to the ruins of its citadel, where three towers from the original fortress were still standing, only one fully intact. When the defensive walls were destroyed long ago, these towers remained as a fortification for the city's garrison. The Tenth Legion had manned a camp here for many years, though few soldiers were left now that the bulk of the troops had been transferred to a distant seaport.

Geta's leg was starting to ache again as he made his way toward his barracks. When he reached the building, a messenger was waiting. "The new centurion has arrived from Caesarea," the man announced. "He demands your presence right away."

"What would he want with me?"

The messenger shrugged. "I do not know. I only know you had better go at once. He seems like a harsh commander."

Geta straightened his tunic and smoothed his rumpled hair with his fingers before heading to the camp headquarters. It was located inside the tower called Hippicus. Upon entering, Geta was immediately ushered into his commander's presence.

"You are Valerius Geta?" the centurion asked. He was oiling a sword blade while he talked, and as he moved the rag, the veins on his muscular forearms stood out like vines on a tree branch.

"Yes, sir."

"Valerius, eh? The family name of Licinius. Any relation to the former augustus?"

"His son, sir. Not by a legitimate union, but by a courtesan of high esteem."

"Would it surprise you to learn that your father has been executed?"

Wait . . . did he say . . . executed? My father is dead? Curse Constantine and his double-dealing ways!

Despite Geta's shock and anger at the announcement, he managed to control his response. Though the news was disturbing, he didn't let it show. And he certainly didn't doubt the centurion's words. Powerful warlords like Licinius usually didn't last long after they lost their battles against their rivals. Geta took another moment to collect himself, then said, "I had not heard that, sir."

"It happened last summer, with much secrecy. We are only now learning of it. Does it disappoint you?"

"Perhaps you can understand, sir, it saddens me. That is natural for a son. And yet"—Geta gathered his strength for a colossal lie—"my loyalty is not to Licinius but to the rightful augustus of our realm, Emperor Constantine."

"So you say, son of Licinius! The army does not agree." The muscular centurion sheathed the sword he was oiling, then walked around to his desk and bent over a ledger. After writing a brief note in it, he said, "Valerius Geta, you are being dishonorably discharged from the Tenth Legion Fretensis. Your crimes have become known to us, including the escape attempt at Thessalonica. Your pension is revoked, along with the allotment of land that would have been yours with an honorable discharge. And do not try to complain! Just be glad you weren't executed for your treason." The centurion pushed the ledger across the desk. "Sign here before you leave the premises. Or make an *X* if that's all you can do."

Stunned, Geta couldn't move. It was only when the centurion barked another sharp order that Geta finally shuffled to the desk, wrote his name next to the words *dishonorably discharged*, and set down the stylus with a shaky hand.

"You may leave now," the centurion said with a backhanded wave.

Geta's mind reeled. Hardly able to comprehend what had just happened, he turned to leave the centurion's office. He had just reached the door when his commander stopped him. "Wait! I have one more order before you go."

Geta turned around. "Yes, sir?" he said meekly, knowing that any hint of disrespect could result in a harsh whipping, or even death. He was just an expendable civilian now.

"Clean the latrines on your way out of camp. They're filthy. Leaving them in good shape is the least you can do for the army you have served so poorly."

Though Geta had many things he wanted to say in response, he knew that uttering any of them would get him killed on the spot. There was only one reply he could make. "Yes, sir," he said with a bow that looked humble—though inside, he was seething. "It has been my greatest honor to serve Rome."

"Rome doesn't need you anymore," the centurion said.

———

The ship Flavia was about to board was a trading vessel known for its speed more than the size of its hold. Called the *Gazelle*, it had established a place for itself in Mediterranean shipping by transporting goods that were highly valuable yet quickly perishable. It was said that the *Gazelle* could bring unsalted fish from Carthago to a table in Rome without any spoilage. On today's journey, however, the swift freighter wouldn't be transporting any fish. The cargo was of infinitely greater value. Empress Helena and her retinue were about to embark on their pilgrimage to the holy land of God.

"I can't believe I'm wearing a soldier's uniform again," Rex said to Flavia as he stood beside her on the dock at Portus. "I keep trying to leave my army career behind, but it keeps finding me anew."

"Because you're good at it," Flavia replied. "The imperial family needs you. They know what you can do."

"I can at least do better than the man I replaced. My work probably won't get me thrown to the panthers."

Flavia shook her head and shuddered, then let that fearsome subject drop away. Instead, she bent down and picked up her leather travel bag, which was fully packed and heavy. "Ready to board?" she asked as she started toward the gangplank—and was gratified to find that Rex didn't try to carry her pack for her as if she was incapable. By now, he knew when to be gallant and when to hold back.

They had just stowed their belongings below deck and returned topside when they were greeted by Pope Sylvester, who had come aboard to pray with the empress and wish everyone well. "Vitus and Candida!" he called. "Come over here. I wish to speak with you."

When they reached the bishop, he drew them close and spoke in a serious tone. "I want you to obtain some things for me in the holy land."

"What sorts of things?" Rex asked.

"*Real* things. Tangible objects that are connected with the scriptures or the Savior. He was an actual man who walked this earth. His feet went here and there to places that truly existed—and still exist three hundred years later. I need proof of this. Reminders for God's people that their Jesus didn't just 'seem' to be human, but he was a true man in every way."

"We will do it," Rex promised.

"And may the Lord lead us to many evidences," Flavia added.

Sylvester took each of them by the hand. "My prayers will go with you," he said with a gentle squeeze. "God speed you on your way, my children."

The *Gazelle* finally set sail about an hour later. Rex had declared it to be a beautifully built ship, with taut, well-trimmed sails and just the right lines for speed. When the vessel made it all the way to Neapolis on the first day, Rex told Flavia that this was surely going to be a swift and efficient trip.

And it was. At the end of two weeks, the travelers reached the island of Cyprus. In the port of Paphos, the captain decreed a one-day stopover to make some minor repairs and give his crew a rest. Rex and Flavia used the opportunity to go for a walk in the countryside, a welcome change from the feel of a ship rolling under their feet.

Flavia had gotten ahead of Rex a little ways when a movement near her feet caught her eye. She froze. Terror seized her as she spotted a huge viper, angry and coiled within striking distance of her exposed ankles. It was as thick as her forearm, with brown spots along its body and a triangular head that signaled its poisonous bite. The eyes of the snake were thin slits, watching her every move. A malevolent hissing warned her to stay back—but Flavia was afraid to retreat lest she prompt a deadly strike.

"R-Rex!" she cried in a shuddery voice. "Snake!"

"Stand still! Don't make a move. Then step back when I tell you." Rex circled the snake and approached from its side. He held a hiking stick, which he extended until he had caught the viper's attention. "Slowly step away," he ordered when the hissing creature had turned its head, and Flavia was able to do so without incident. Rex retreated as well. They decided to head back to the ship rather than risk another encounter with the deadly serpents in the area.

Two days later, after spending the night in the open sea, the *Gazelle* sailed into the spacious harbor of Caesarea, capital of Palaestina. It was a remarkable city, carved out of the seashore and endowed with magnificent buildings by the ancient Jewish king, Herod the Great. A lofty temple dedicated to Herod's patron, Caesar Augustus, met any traveler who entered the harbor. Today, however, the temple didn't bustle with emperor worship like it had in times past.

Helena's retinue was met at the docks by the city's scholarly bishop, Eusebius. Because of his short stature and round belly, his walk as he approached the empress on the pier reminded Flavia of a duck's waddle. Helena dipped her chin graciously to the little bishop, then everyone followed him toward Herod's former palace, where the imperial visitors would be staying. The palace was situated on a peninsula that jutted into the sea—still impressive even now, three and a half centuries after its construction.

During the week that the travelers stayed in Caesarea, Bishop Eusebius announced his intention to join the pilgrimage to Hierusalem. Technically, because Caesarea was the regional capital, its bishop had supervision over all other churches in Palaestina. But the bishop of Hierusalem's church, a man named Macarius, didn't like that arrangement. He had even gotten Emperor Constantine to grant him some independence while they were at Nicaea.

"You'll like Bishop Macarius," Rex assured Flavia. "He doesn't look at all like a churchman. He's rugged and has long hair. His arms are strong because he works with wood in his spare time."

"I've heard his doctrine is orthodox as well."

"He is a workman approved unto God in two ways," Rex quipped.

Though Flavia rolled her eyes, she also had to smile at the thought that her barbarian husband could make a biblical joke. For many years such a thing would have seemed impossible to her.

The overland journey to Hierusalem required an overnight stay at Lydda, where Saint Peter had healed a paralytic, according to the *Book of Acts*. The next day, as the imperial carriages ascended from the coastal lowlands into the Judean hills, Flavia began to grow increasingly excited. *Hierusalem . . . at last!* It was a lifelong dream of hers to enter the city of God and discover its mysteries. She was certain the Lord would speak to her from his holy habitation. *But what will he have to say?*

The road from Caesarea entered Hierusalem at a huge, monumental gate. Passing through it, Flavia found herself in a public square with a tall column at its center. On top of it was a golden statue of Emperor Hadrian. Though he had been an efficient emperor in many ways, he also had a bad reputation among Christians for what he did to Hierusalem. Around a hundred years after the time of Christ, Hadrian decided to refound the city in honor of the pagan gods. He called it Aelia after his own family name, then added the term *Capitolina* to signal its dedication to the divine triad of Jupiter, Juno, and Minerva, who were worshiped on Rome's Capitoline Hill. Hadrian erected many temples around the city. He even dared to build a shrine to Jupiter on the Temple Mount itself. All Jews were banished from the region, including many Jewish Christians. Fortunately, some Christians of Gentile birth had been able to keep the word of Christ alive in the city where he was crucified and resurrected.

A wealthy local businessman had vacated his home near the camp of the Tenth Legion so Empress Helena could stay there. Rex and Flavia were given lodging in a beautiful guesthouse next door, not far from the Hippicus tower in the citadel. Immediately, Flavia fell in love with the guesthouse. The graceful old building was made of white, rough-hewn stone, and its floors were strewn with eastern carpets. There were many cozy nooks and decorative arches. Bronze lampstands and potted palms in the corners gave the place a charming, exotic feel. Its Christian proprietor called it Glory House.

After all the travel, Empress Helena declared that she needed a few days of rest in her new home, so for the moment, Rex found himself without many duties as a guardsman. "How about we explore the city tomorrow?" he asked Flavia as they were getting ready for bed.

"I can't think of anything I'd like more."

"I can," Rex said with a mischievous grin, then blew out the lamp in their room.

The next morning was blue-skied and pleasantly cool now that it was early October. Flavia washed in the room's basin, then joined Rex for a light breakfast in the quaint courtyard at the front of Glory House. They were finishing up their meal when they noticed a boy of about twelve eyeing them from a nearby bench. His complexion was brown, and his eyes were lively and intelligent. Rex waved at him in a friendly way, and that was enough to prompt the boy to approach their table.

"I know you," the boy said. "I was at Nicaea for the council, and I observed all you did. I am grateful for it. You defended true doctrine—both of you."

Rex chuckled and pushed out a wooden bench with his foot. "Then it seems we should make your acquaintance, young sir! Come sit at our table." After Rex introduced himself and Flavia, they learned that the boy's name was Cyril. He was an assistant to Bishop Macarius and was studying for a future career in the church.

"I can show you around the city," Cyril offered. "I know everything about Hierusalem, especially as it relates to our faith." The boy smiled, then added, "And I know secret ways to get into hidden places."

"You're just my kind of lad," Rex said with a laugh as the threesome headed out to the city streets.

Cyril led Rex and Flavia to the Great Cardo that divided the city in half. "This street was the outer wall of the city in the time of Jesus," the boy told them. "The Lord did all of his work to the east of here. The western side was outside the walls."

From the Cardo, the tour wandered through the side streets of Hierusalem where many generations of Christians had lived and worshiped. Cyril pointed out all the important sites, including two ancient house churches where believers still met today. The larger of them was the church where Macarius now presided. It was the former home of Mary, the mother of John Mark. The second story of the house was the Upper Room—the site of the Last Supper and the place where the Holy Spirit first descended upon the church. A grapevine was growing there, so Rex broke off a branch as a memento of the place where the cup of the Lord came to represent his blood.

Next, Cyril headed into the countryside to the south of the city. The ravine known as the Valley of the Cheesemakers descended to meet the valley called Gehenna, where the Old Testament said babies were sacrificed to evil gods, making it a hellish location. Fortunately, Cyril took Rex and Flavia to a different place: an enclosed pool fed by the ancient Gihon spring. Now it was decorated with pagan nymphs frolicking in the nude.

"King David drank these waters," Cyril said, "and Jesus called it the Pool of Siloam. He made mud from his saliva, then told a man born blind to wash in this pool. It healed him."

Rex removed an army canteen from his satchel. "I will collect some of this water. Pope Sylvester will be delighted to have it."

From the low-lying Pool of Siloam, the three now began to climb an ancient pilgrimage route up to the Temple Mount. Flavia soon found herself out of breath and sweating now that the day had warmed. Once she drew near to the platform's surface, she grew excited to see what was on top. She knew the Jewish temple wouldn't be there; Emperor Titus had destroyed it sixty years before the time of Hadrian. Even so, this was Mount Moriah—the summit King David had purchased for God's temple. Solomon had carried out David's idea in glorious fashion. *Somewhere up here*, Flavia reminded herself as she topped the Mount, *is the very spot where God dwelled in the Holy of Holies!*

Unfortunately, just as Cyril had warned her before they began to climb, the place was a disappointment. Wicked Titus had completely destroyed the house of the Lord. Then Hadrian had made the blasphemy even worse by erecting the temple to Jupiter. As always, Jupiter sought the high places, for he was a minion of the ultimate climber—Satan, who raised himself up in pride before Almighty God. Flavia didn't even bother to ascend the temple steps to look around from its porch. She approached only as far as two statues of Hadrian and his successor, Antoninus Pius, then turned her back on the demonic place with a sense of sorrow and indignation.

"Is there nothing left from the time of the Lord?" Rex asked Cyril. "We know the Savior's feet walked here. He came as a boy to talk with the rabbis, and again as a teacher himself. But it seems like everything is now pagan."

"Follow me," Cyril said. "I will show you a special, forgotten place."

The youth led his two fellow explorers to a region of the Temple Mount obscured by debris that had accumulated over many decades of neglect. Vines and shrubs had engulfed whatever structures once stood here.

"From all the columns, it looks like some kind of colonnade," Rex observed.

Cyril nodded. "It was the Royal Portico, I believe."

The threesome came to an impenetrable wall of vegetation and ancient ruins. Yet when Cyril tugged on a certain vine, a gap opened in the leafy obstacle. "Go in," he encouraged with a gesture of his hand. Flavia was the first to dart through.

A staircase lay before her, crumbling and cluttered with rubble yet sturdy enough to climb. Flavia ascended it. Arriving at the top, a wide vista met her eyes. She stood at one of the four corners of the Temple Mount. The place was situated high above the surrounding city and gave an expansive view of the ravines and hills around Mount Moriah.

In the waist-high wall that guarded the sheer edge of the platform, there was a niche where a person could stand. It was almost like a little pulpit. Rex went to it and peered over the wall. When Flavia joined him, she saw that the drop to the pavement below was dizzying. This high place was a vantage point that overlooked all of Hierusalem.

"There's an inscription here," Rex said to Cyril, running his finger along letters carved into the niche. "It's in Hebrew. Can you read it?"

Cyril shook his head. "No, but I copied it and showed it to a rabbi. It says this is the 'place of trumpeting, to declare the Sabbath.' The rabbi told me this was where a shofar was blown at sunset to let the city know the Sabbath was beginning. But that's not all. There's something else special about this place."

Impressed by the boy's inquisitive nature and knowledge of the city, Flavia exclaimed, "Cyril, you amaze me! Perhaps someday you should be the bishop of Hierusalem."

"If the Lord wills it, I would serve," he replied modestly.

"So what else is special about this place?" Rex asked.

"Jesus himself stood here. The scriptures say the devil took him to the pinnacle of the Temple and tempted him to throw himself down and let angels catch him. This is the Temple's highest point—right here. Jesus refused to show his glory in a prideful way. He said, 'Do not put the Lord your God to the test.'"

Rex knelt down and removed a loose pavestone from the niche. Since the whole area was exposed to the weather and had fallen into decay, the stone's removal was an act of preservation more than desecration. "I will keep this safe," Rex said. "The Christians of Rome can view it and be strengthened to overcome their temptations to pride and self-glory."

"We've found some good relics today," Flavia remarked after Rex had tucked the stone into his satchel. "The grapevine of the Upper Room. The healing waters of Siloam. And now an actual stone where Christ stood and resisted Satan."

Rex patted his satchel and nodded. "It's a start, but we need to find more. What I'd really like to discover is something related to Christ's resurrection."

At these words, Cyril let out a little chuckle. An impish expression also came to the boy's face. "What is it?" Flavia asked him.

Though Cyril didn't want to answer at first, he was finally coaxed into saying, "I think you're about to find what you seek."

The intriguing words caught the attention of Rex and Flavia. When they pressed Cyril some more, they learned he had eavesdropped on a secret meeting last night between Bishop Macarius and Empress Helena. "I overheard them by accident," Cyril explained, then sheepishly admitted, "but I stayed around to listen."

Rex had to smile and shake his head at the boy's audacity. "Sounds like something I would have done. What did you hear?"

"Big news! Emperor Constantine has authorized the excavation of Christ's tomb. It's the main reason he sent his mother here."

Astonished, Flavia asked, "You know where the tomb is?"

"Not for sure. But we have strong traditions. One of our elders—he's close to a hundred years old—he says he knows the place. He insists his grandfather told him. Memories like that are common in the Hierusalem church. We pass down the lore of our sacred places. How could God's people ever forget such things?"

The idea of visiting Jesus's tomb fascinated Flavia. From the look on Rex's face, she could tell he was excited too. "Let's go there now!" he exclaimed.

"We can't," said Cyril.

"Why not?"

"It's underneath a huge amount of earth. Hadrian buried the tomb that the earliest believers said was the Lord's. He ordered a public square to be built over it. And right in the middle of the plaza, he put up a temple to the foulest goddess of them all—Aphrodite."

Rex and Flavia exchanged glances, then smiles came to both of their faces. "Are you remembering what I'm remembering?" she asked him.

"Yes! That day in Corinthus!"

Flavia took her husband by the hand. "We toppled Aphrodite's idol that day," she said. "Now it's time to dethrone her once and for all."

———

OCTOBER 326

The news acquired by Cyril in his accidental eavesdropping soon proved correct: Constantine had, indeed, ordered the demolition of the Temple of Aphrodite. Over the course of about a week, a team of workers was brought in from the vicinity of Hierusalem and throughout the province of Palaestina. Even the few remaining soldiers of the Tenth Legion were assigned to the demolition job—a task they knew well, since digging earthworks was part of every legionary's basic duties.

Rex was able to watch the proceedings as they developed because Empress Helena wanted to visit the site every day and observe what was being done. His only assignment was to remain close to her side and make sure she was safe. She often stood for so long under a purple awning at the edge of the temple precinct that Flavia finally arranged for a cushioned chair to be brought in. "How kind of you!" Helena said as she took her seat in the shade.

From this makeshift throne, the new queen of the Christian empire watched the gradual dethroning of the Queen of Heaven. Aphrodite was known elsewhere by other names: Venus among the Latins, Ishtar or Astarte among the timeless cultures of the east. She ruled from the sky and oversaw fertility, sexuality, and love. Her star was the first to appear in the night sky and the last to leave it at dawn. But while she was an ancient goddess, she wasn't invincible. Her time in Hierusalem had finally come to an end. Yet as it turned out, she wasn't going down without a fight.

Once the work crew was assembled and equipped, the dismantling of the temple commenced. From the very start, it was a difficult job, plagued by more delays and obstacles than anyone had expected. Even from his vantage point next to the empress, Rex could feel the tension among the workers. Many of them didn't want to be there, so a spirit of rivalry prevailed instead of cooperation. The crew was often afflicted by strife and arguments. Tools and personal possessions kept going missing. The frequency of work injuries—some of them serious—seemed to be higher than normal for such a job. Even the two supervising bishops, Macarius and Eusebius, were at odds with each other. The outcome of this project would have major implications for their respective churches, so both men were tense and found it hard to reconcile their differences.

Yet despite all the problems, the Temple of Aphrodite gradually came down. Once the roof tiles and ceiling beams were removed, the light of the sun shone upon the idol for the first time in almost two hundred years. "Go look at her, Rex," the empress said. "Report back to me what you see."

After Rex walked across the plaza and went inside the now-roofless temple, he returned to Helena's side. "She is seated on a throne in the form of a seashell," he reported. "Delfini are swimming on either side of her, and doves sit on her shoulders. She wears a crown of stars. Her body is naked, though her lower half is draped with a cloth."

"At least that's better than what they have out here," Flavia said, indicating a marble statue that stood on a nearby hillock. In that depiction of Aphrodite, the goddess was entirely nude and painted in lifelike fashion. The statue was perched on a stony outcrop that protruded from the temple platform. Although no one was currently excavating that part of the temple complex, Rex knew it was on Helena's agenda because the local Christians claimed the outcrop was the ancient hill of Calvary. Each item was supposed to proceed in due time, and demolishing the temple was the first order of business.

It took two more days to knock down the temple's walls, which left Aphrodite sitting alone and exposed in the plaza. Ropes were attached to the idol, then men with machines whose wheels were turned by oxen began trying to pull it down. Yet the ancient cement of Hadrian—or perhaps some demonic contrivance—resisted the laborers' efforts. Rex was watching the proceedings intently when one of the machines shattered under the immense strain, drawing a terrible bellow from the oxen. Shards of wood went flying into the air, and Rex winced when he realized that body parts were part of that carnage as well. Flavia also groaned and covered her eyes. Apparently the goddess of love was hell-bent on vengeance today.

The accident, combined with the arrival of the first autumn rains, made Helena stay away from the work site for a while. Only when the weather turned nice again did she go back. But Flavia no longer joined them, for she had taken ill with a fever that kept her bedridden. Fortunately, there were some imperial handmaidens who could look after her, so Rex wasn't worried about leaving his wife for part of the day. Yet since Flavia was normally so healthy, her sudden sickness seemed like a visitation from the evil spirits that had been stirred up in Hierusalem. Rex made sure to have an elder from a nearby church anoint Flavia with oil like the scriptures commanded.

When he returned with Helena to the seat under the awning, Rex found that the temple was completely gone and the flagstones of the plaza were being removed one by one. Husky men with iron bars pried them out, then two-man crews carried away the heavy pavers. Underneath the flagstones was a sandy muck filled with masonry rubble and chunks of broken statuary—infertile soil that could only serve as the substrate for the platform, not for agriculture.

Eventually, all the flagstones were removed and the crew began to excavate the fill dirt by digging it with shovels and dumping it into baskets. Gangs of workers passed the baskets from one to another until the last man emptied the basket onto a cart that would discard the debris outside the city. Soon a round crater was formed like those found in volcanic regions. It grew wider and deeper every day, even when rainstorms impeded the progress.

One of the most enthusiastic workers—if not the strongest of them—was little Cyril. With his quick energy, he wasn't hard to spot among all the more sluggish and plodding workmen at the site. Cyril worked long hours while wearing nothing but a loincloth. During the afternoon rest breaks, he would frequently lounge near the empress's awning and converse with Rex. Sometimes he would even chat with Helena, who quickly grew fond of him and commented on his sharp mind. She started sharing her flavored water and raisin cakes with Cyril during the breaks.

As the fill dirt was removed, the outlines of an ancient quarry began to emerge. The pick marks made by the stonecutters of long ago could still be seen on the quarry's walls. Hadrian's workers had backfilled the quarry pit to create a level platform for the temple. Bishop Eusebius, who was a scholarly historian, considered this a promising sign that the team was digging in the right place. "Quarries were often turned into cemeteries when they were used up because of all the holes hewn from the rock," he remarked. "After a few decades passed, they often became gardens too, because fresh soil accumulated on the bottom. Both of those facts fit with Christ's burial in the scriptures. I expect we shall find his tomb soon."

As if to prove the bishop right, a gaping hole opened up the next day in the muddy crater that had been carved out of the quarry pit. It looked like a portal into Hades, so the workers backed away from it with superstitious awe. Cyril, however, wasn't afraid. He approached the hole with a lamp and gazed into it. And then, without warning, the edge of the hole collapsed and the underworld swallowed him whole.

Rex didn't wait for any of the crewmen to initiate a rescue. Bolting from Helena's side as if shot from a sling, he descended into the crater and scrambled across its gooey bottom toward the hole. An overnight rainstorm had made the soil unstable, so Rex knew he was in significant danger. Any hollow space beneath the surface was liable to collapse, just as it had for Cyril. But Rex was determined not to let Aphrodite claim the life of the boy he had come to admire so much.

Stepping gingerly to the edge of the hole, Rex shouted into it. "Cyril! Can you hear me?" Since there was no answer, Rex snatched up a nearby spade and thrust its blunt end into the opening. "Grab on to the pole, and I'll pull you out!"

What happened next was so swift and violent that Rex could barely comprehend it. The whole earth seemed to give way in a cascade of mud and rubble. A landslide plunged Rex down into an abyss while spinning him like a child's doll and bombarding him with rocky blows. Light and dark flashed in every direction as Rex lost all sense of up and down. His nostrils and mouth became clogged with grit and sludge. After tumbling for what seemed like an hour but was probably just a snap of the fingers, the turbulence stopped as Rex slammed into something solid. Pain shot through his body at the impact. A dreadful darkness and silence engulfed him. Then all was still.

I can't breathe!

The constriction around Rex was like being encased in cement. A giant wave of panic rose up in him, stealing what little breath was left. Only a tiny bit of air remained in a small pocket in front of his face. Soon, suffocation would kill him—and he would already be buried in his tomb.

God! Save me!

Rex squirmed and wriggled, but the earth refused to release its cruel, unyielding grip. A strange laughter echoed through his mind, sounding otherworldly and surreal. The pressure on his chest grew heavier. The blackness was complete. Rex had descended into hell, and there was nothing he could do about it.

And that was when he felt his right arm move.

He pushed again, using all his strength. His hand seemed to break through the compacted soil into some kind of cavity or empty space beneath the earth. Rex found he could wiggle his fingers freely and even his wrist. By making circular motions with his arm, he was able to widen the hole until his whole arm was free. Soon he was able twist his body into the opening. Wriggling like a mole in its den, he broke free of the soil's grasp and tumbled into a sheltered cave. A mound of hard bedrock was all around him. It contained a saving refuge with enough air to breathe—at least for the moment.

Turning around in the mouth of the cave, Rex began to claw at the soil in search of Cyril. A faint moaning indicated the direction to dig, and soon the sounds grew louder. Rex sensed movement in the black earth, then felt a slender shoulder in his hand. He scooped away the dirt from around Cyril's head, creating a place for him to breathe. The boy sputtered and moaned but couldn't form coherent words. After clearing away more soil, Rex was able to draw Cyril by the armpits into the cavity beside him.

"Th-thank y-y-you," Cyril said after coughing and spitting out gobs of mud. The effort of speaking was enough for the moment, so he lay still next to Rex in their little refuge in the underworld.

Time passed. How long? Perhaps it was three hours. Perhaps it was three days. Perhaps it was three years. *Did it matter?* Time down here was meaningless, for there was no sight, no sound, no sign of life—only the ageless silence of the grave. And then a sunbeam touched Rex's eye, shining like a star in the darkness. Salvation was at hand.

"Dig faster!" shouted a voice. The sound of scraping drew nearer, along with vibrations and movements in the soil. Footsteps tramped here and there. Men grunted and yelled, their words muffled yet audible. A spadeful of dirt was hauled away, and with its removal, the pinpoint of light from above became a brilliant ray. At the same moment, a refreshing wind blew away the stale air of the cavity beneath the earth. "Here I am!" Rex yelled. When he clasped the hand that reached down to him, he was lifted out of the shadows and into the sunshine. At last, he was back in the land of the living.

After helping Cyril exit the cavity as well, Rex found he didn't have the strength to climb out of the earthen crater that had almost killed him. Instead, he and Cyril sat in silence near the cave that had been their salvation. Neither of them wanted to talk about their close brush with death.

Meanwhile, a buzz of activity swirled around them. As more dirt was cleared away by lines of men passing baskets, it became clear that the mound of bedrock into which Rex had crashed during the landslide was a protuberance that stuck up from the quarry's floor. The lump had been left behind when the quarry was abandoned. Within the lump was the cavity that had saved two lives today.

Cyril was eyeing the cave's entrance. His boyish energy must have returned, because he stood up and approached the mound of rock. The workmen had partially revealed something to the side of the entrance—something large and curved. Cyril brushed away more soil, then stepped back. "Rex, come see this! It's a tombstone!"

When Rex drew near, he could see that Cyril was right. The cavity was indeed a tomb, and the curved piece was its rolling gravestone. Rex knelt at the mouth of the opening and dug his fingers into the earth on the quarry's floor. Beneath the rubbly dirt, Rex discovered a rich, dark loam with lots of plant material in it. "This is garden soil," he said to Cyril.

They exchanged excited glances, for both of them knew what this meant. Cyril had just started to enter the cavity to explore its recesses when Rex caught his arm. "Not yet," he said, then pointed to the rim of the crater. "Her Majesty should authorize it before anyone goes in. She's coming down now."

All the excitement had brought Eusebius and Macarius to the work site.

The two bishops helped the empress descend partway into the crater. But even with their assistance, she had to stop short of the cavity because of the muddy, uneven ground. "Praise the Lord that you survived, Rex!" she called to him. "And praise the Lord for what he is showing us."

"What's inside that opening?" Macarius asked.

"I don't know," Rex replied. "We have only been a short way into its mouth."

Helena waved her hand to grant permission. "Go see. Then tell us what you find."

Rex entered the cavity again, followed closely by Cyril. Now that more soil had been cleared from the entrance, the light inside was sufficient to look around. The cavity had two sections, a vestibule and a room beyond. This architecture immediately confirmed it was a tomb, for most under-ground crypts were constructed like that. A few objects were strewn on the floor of the vestibule. Rex picked them up, then returned to the open air with them.

"I found a pig's skull in the outer room," he called back to the empress and the two bishops. "There is also a sacrificial knife."

"And a very old chamber pot!" Cyril added, holding it up to the sunlight.

The two churchmen grimaced at this discovery. "Clearly, a pagan attempt at desecration!" Eusebius cried. "Anything else?"

"I'll check the second room," Rex answered, then went back inside.

A sense of awe now descended on him as he realized where he was. This place was almost certainly the tomb of Jesus Christ. The garden soil . . . the rock-cut tomb . . . the rolling stone . . . the lack of other graves in the area . . . the intentional defilement of its sanctity . . . and most of all, the unbroken tradition within the Hierusalem church that claimed Hadrian had covered the Lord's tomb with the Aphrodite temple—all these factors testified together that this must be the right place. Only one thing remained to be confirmed.

Ducking his head, Rex went from the vestibule into the rear chamber. It was a simple space. The ceiling was low. There was a burial slab. It was on the right, just as Mark's gospel described. And there was nothing else. The tomb was empty.

Rex stepped back outside. The bishops waited expectantly beside the empress as they stood in the mud. Even the workmen had stopped their labors. They set down their baskets and leaned on their shovels, eager to hear what would be said.

"He is not here," Rex declared.

"He is risen!" the bishops cried in unison. At this shout, a great cheer erupted from the gathered crowd.

Helena Augusta raised her palms and lifted her gaze to the heavens. "Here we shall build the Church of the Resurrection," she declared, "and may the Lord reveal his mercies from this place."

<hr>

Geta couldn't believe what his eyes were seeing. After all he had been through—the mockery, the limping, the menial jobs, the rejection by the army—at last, the gods were favoring him. They were giving him a chance for sweet revenge.

Though Geta wasn't in the army anymore, he had joined the work crew that had descended upon Hierusalem. Over the past month, he had helped tear down the Temple of Aphrodite, clear the plaza's flagstones, and dig a crater into the dirt beneath the pavement. It had been difficult work, plagued by not only mishaps and delays but also frequent arguments among the laborers. Yet now Geta understood why the gods had brought him through those arduous times to this very day. Soon he would get revenge on his ancient enemy: Brandulf Rex, the man who crippled his leg so many years ago.

"Brothers, always!" they used to say to each other when they were comrades in war.

"To the death!" the other would reply.

That's right, Geta swore to himself, giving the warrior's oath a new meaning. *To the death sounds like a good fate for you!*

Of course, it wouldn't be easy. Rex looked just as strong today as when Geta first met him as a cadet at the speculator academy in the Alps. Rex's blond hair no longer hung below his shoulders, and his beard didn't dangle from his chin like it once did. His frame had obviously filled out, yet not in the manner of someone who had let himself go with age. If anything, Rex looked more muscular and powerful now than when he was in the army. His years at the oar had probably done that. Geta decided he would have to take Rex by surprise in any future attack. An equal fight wouldn't turn out well for Geta, just like it hadn't the first time they met in combat.

For a long while, Geta leaned on his shovel and watched the proceedings from the rim of the crater. Rex was down there at the bottom with the empress and her churchmen, celebrating their discovery of Christ's tomb. *What a pitiful deity!* The fact that this god's most eminent shrine was a tomb struck Geta as utterly ridiculous. *Why not a throne in a temple? Why not a mountaintop? Why not the heavens themselves?* The god Jesus was associated with no high place, no star, no impressive idol bedecked with gold and gems. *What kind of god would appear as a crucified man born in a stable?* The things the Christians believed and preached about their deity deserved no respect in the Roman Empire—which was why stupid Emperor Constantine was the perfect match for this absurd new religion.

"Hey, barbarian, get back to work!" barked the overseer supervising Geta's crew of diggers. The money was good, so Geta was glad for the job, especially since his army pension had been revoked. Even though the labor itself was drudgery, he couldn't complain about the pay. After finishing his shift, he set his shovel on a rack, took the copper coins allotted to him by the boss, and left the work site for the day.

But instead of heading back to his rented room in a widow's home, Geta made his way toward Aelia Capitolina's second forum. As always, the downhill trudge into the Valley of the Cheesemakers and the uphill climb on the other side made his leg ache, but he consoled himself with the hope that after a few months of visiting the Temple of Aesculapius, the expensive therapy he was receiving would finally begin to work. However, Aesculapius wasn't the god he wanted to visit today. In fact, it wasn't a god at all. Geta's destination was the shrine of a goddess. Her name was Nemesis.

The shrine was more like a grotto than a temple, just a recessed alcove in a wall. Greenery overhung the niche, well watered by the mist from a nearby fountain, so the place felt secluded and sacred. The idol depicted Nemesis with her wings spread wide. She held a whip in one hand and a measuring rod in the other. Beneath her feet, she trampled a prostrate and defeated man. These were her important symbols, for Nemesis was the goddess of revenge. She measured the wrongs of mankind, then punished those misdeeds with her whip until the malefactor was subdued. Now it was time for Nemesis to become aware of Brandulf Rex so she could exact her retribution from him.

"Sir, do you wish to rebalance the scales of justice?" asked a voice behind Geta.

He turned to see that a seller of curse tablets had spoken to him. "I do," Geta replied. "I seek aid from the divine world for an act of vengeance."

The man was glad to sell Geta the necessary items, and Geta was equally glad to part with a silver coin to purchase them. He received a thin sheet of lead, a stylus, and a nail. With the stylus, he wrote out his plea upon the soft leaden tablet:

> Lady Nemesis, I pray thee, bind Brandulf Rex in cords of affliction. See and behold the injury he has done to me, and avenge it with thy righteous hand. Make his mind dark and his body weak. Grant me the good luck to hurt him in the most terrible way. And when that day comes, and thou shalt give me that chance, grant me also the divine strength to take my revenge. Do it speedily, I pray thee, O Queen Augusta. I am Valerius Geta, wrongly injured, pious, deserving of justice.

Geta rolled the tablet into a tight cylinder so no one could ever read it and provide a countermeasure to its magic. Just to make certain of this, Geta picked up a rock and pounded the iron nail through the cylinder. Now it was sealed, and Rex was bound by the curse. There was only one thing left to do: offer the tablet to the goddess.

In front of the idol was a deep, green pool whose surface was covered with a mucky scum. Its depths could be seen by no eyes except those of Nemesis herself. Geta pitched the rolled-up curse into the pool. Immediately, it disappeared. Now the deed was complete.

"Grant me your favor against my enemy," Geta whispered to the goddess.

"Gladly," she replied upon the wind.

13

The discovery of Christ's tomb in Hierusalem prompted Empress Helena to announce she would be taking a victory tour across Palaestina. The news was satisfying to the people of the land because they had come to love their queen for her piety and generosity of spirit. One of the purposes of the tour was to spread charity among the peasants of the countryside, not just to Christians but even to pagans and Jews in a show of imperial goodwill.

Another purpose was to investigate holy sites for building new churches and shrines. "God knew just the bodyguard I would need," Helena told Rex as they were preparing to leave the mansion where she was staying. "Not only a capable protector but a field scout who can explore curious places." Rex had to admit, he did seem like the right man for the job. When he said as much to the empress, she simply replied, "God foresees all."

The royal procession began its great journey by walking along the city's main west-to-east road called the Decumanus. Hierusalem had two public forums and this street linked them, so it was an important civic avenue. But for the local Christians, these two forums and the road joining them had a more spiritual significance. The western forum and its former Temple of Aphrodite marked the place of the Savior's crucifixion, while the eastern forum had been built over the ruins of the Antonia Fortress, where the trials of Jesus had taken place. That meant the Decumanus was the very

398

street Jesus had walked with the crossbeam upon his shoulders from his trial to his death.

"This is a way of great suffering and sorrow!" Helena proclaimed to the crowds that lined either side of the street. "Yet it led to the forgiveness of sins!" When Helena made the sign of the cross over herself, many of the adoring onlookers did likewise.

As the royal procession passed the Bethesda Pool, a beggar with a paralyzed leg stumbled into the street and fell at Helena's feet. "Lady, have mercy!" he cried. "The angel no longer stirs the waters. I shall never be healed!"

Helena beckoned for her handmaiden to give her a money pouch. Reaching into the purse, Helena produced a silver coin. "May God have mercy on—"

Before she could finish her blessing, the beggar snatched the purse and scampered on two perfectly fine legs toward a door that an accomplice had thrown open in a streetfront wall. No doubt it would be slammed shut and barred once the thief darted through. Pursuit would then be impossible.

But Rex was too fast. He caught the speedy little fellow by the collar just as he was about to escape through the door. Yanking the thief by his garment, Rex retrieved the coin purse, then dragged the criminal to Helena.

"Your purse, my lady," Rex said with a bow as he gave her back the money. Then he pulled aside another guardsman. "Take this man back to the camp and tell the centurion what happened. Justice will be swift, I'm sure."

Helena, however, had different plans. "If God's justice is all we ever receive," she said to the onlookers, "who among us could stand? His mercy is needed as well." For a long moment, she was silent as she considered that thought. The hushed crowd waited to see what would happen. Helena picked up the silver coin that had fallen to the street when the thief grabbed the bag. After handing it to the wide-eyed fellow, she added a second coin, then said, "Go in peace, my son, and sin no more."

The outcome drew a great cheer from the crowd. "Queen Helena the Gracious!" someone shouted, and others immediately followed suit. While the acclamations were ringing in the air, the weasely thief took the coins and escaped the public eye through his accomplice's doorway.

"God's mercy be upon you, Queen Helena!" shouted a young woman with a pregnant belly.

"I need it," Helena murmured, then resumed her procession through the streets.

The royal entourage left Hierusalem through the Sheep Gate and descended into the Kidron Valley. Most of the city dwellers didn't follow them out from the walls, though a few of the more enthusiastic well-wishers continued, and Rex constantly had to keep them back from the empress. She proceeded along the valley's length until they came to a garden full of olive trees and flowerpots of white autumn crocuses. A timeworn building stood next to the garden, its multiple windows and outdoor dining area testifying that it was some kind of inn. From its front door, an old man emerged, hobbling on an olivewood cane that was as gnarly as he was.

"Welcome to the Garden of Gethsemane," the man said in a surprisingly strong voice for someone of his age. "I am the keeper of this hostel for the Lord's pilgrims who come here. And are we not all pilgrims of one form or another?"

"Indeed, we are," Helena agreed. "What is your name, brother?"

"Sopater, I am called, Your Majesty. I am the fifth in my line to bear that name. All of us have been caretakers of this hostel. Believers in the Lord have been coming here for centuries to pray where the Savior prayed."

Helena approached the old man and took his hand in hers, then humbly kissed his knuckles. "Sopater, I shall reside with you tonight in this holy place. Please do not call me by any imperial titles. Refer to me only as 'sister.'"

"I will . . . sister," the innkeeper said, making a visible effort to speak so casually to the empress. "Come now and take some rest while I prepare cool drinks. Then, when the sun has gone lower in its course, let us ascend the mountain."

After an afternoon nap, the empress emerged from her room wearing a plain tunic of everyday cloth and a wrap of undyed wool. She was adorned with no finery or jewels. Only a carved wooden cross dangled from a thong around her neck. "I am ready to go up."

Sopater led her to a trail behind the inn, and they began to climb. Rex followed them with a sword on his belt. The rocky trail ascended the flank of the Mount of Olives via numerous switchbacks. Everyone kept up a good pace, even Sopater, who proved himself energetic and spry despite his cane. The sun's rays felt pleasantly warm to Rex as the day gave way to the cool November evening.

Eventually the three hikers reached a rocky ledge near the summit. Its vista offered a beautiful view of Hierusalem spread out before them. The late-day sunshine seemed to bathe the holy city in liquid gold. All of its buildings glowed with heavenly flame, while the surrounding hills looked like burnished bronze. Surely there was no other city like this on earth.

Sopater, however, didn't pause to consider the view. He walked over to a clump of bushes. With the aid of his cane, he pulled aside some branches, revealing an opening in the rock face. "Look here," he said to Helena.

"What is it?"

"This entrance opens to a cave where people can stand. There is a ring for campfires and a crevice above it for smoke. Our family has always believed that the Savior gave his discourse about the end of the world from here. The *Gospel of Matthew* says the disciples asked him privately about these things. We think this was the very place."

"Perhaps Jesus spent the night in there too?" Rex suggested.

"It is likely. The Zealots used to do that on Mount Arbel. Whenever I show pilgrims this spot, I always quote this saying from *Luke*: 'He was teaching during the day in the Temple, and in the evening he went out, lodging on the mountain called Olivet.'" Sopater gestured toward the Temple Mount on the other side of the valley. "That is where the Temple used to be. A place like this must have been where our Lord sought shelter for the night. Like any man, he would have sought protection from the weather. And he would need a fire for cooking and warmth."

Rex stooped and looked into the entrance. Sopater was right—the cave inside was spacious and its floor was flat and dry. It would have made an excellent shelter. "May I take a blackened rock from the ring?" Rex asked his guide.

Sopater shrugged. "There are many, and we have no use for them. Take what you wish."

Rex opened his satchel and entered the cave. After he had collected a fire-charred stone, he emerged to find Helena standing off to the side of the ledge, praying with her eyes upon Hierusalem and her palms raised to heaven. The two men let her pray for as long as she wished. When she finished, she turned back to them. Immediately, though, her gaze moved beyond them as she pointed to a bare, stony outcrop above the cave. "Is that the highest point of the mountain?"

Sopater nodded. "Yes, Your M—yes, my sister. We hold it to be the place of the Lord's ascension."

"Rex, climb up there and bring me a rock from which the feet of Jesus went back to heaven," Helena said. "And keep one for your collection too. We have just found the site of my second church in the holy land. We shall call it the Olivet Church."

After Rex had clambered up and returned with the holy relics, the three-some proceeded back down the trail to the hostel. It was dark by the time they arrived. One of the queen's handmaidens had a meal of lentil stew bubbling over a brazier, augmented by plain bread and water. Rex was glad to see Flavia assisting the handmaiden. Recovered, at last, from her sick-ness, Flavia had been able to join the journey. Everything was tranquil and quiet in the courtyard of the inn. The pilgrims shared a simple meal out of a common cookpot, then retired to their rooms for the night.

Rex and Flavia, however, weren't sleepy. They left the courtyard and decided to stroll for a while in the Garden of Gethsemane. The ancient olive trees loomed overhead, forming a kind of tunnel through which they could walk. They came to a firepit with a couple of log benches beside it, worn smooth by many years of sitting. A fire striker was beside the ring of stones, so Rex threw a spark onto some dry tinder and soon had a cheerful blaze going. Meanwhile, Flavia went over to a vat brimming with olives since the harvest was now in full swing. She returned with the newly cured olives and sat beside Rex on the log. For a long time, they enjoyed the quiet evening together, munching on their snack and listening to the cooing of doves.

"How old do you think these trees are?" Flavia finally asked.

"The heartwood is gone. It takes a long time for that to happen. These trees might have been here for a thousand years. Maybe more. It's not impossible that King Solomon could have planted them thirteen hundred years ago."

"There was an olive tree in Sicilia that the Phoenicians left records about.

It was seventeen hundred years old." Flavia smiled mischievously at Rex, then stood up. After popping an olive into her mouth, she plucked the pit from her lips and walked to a nearby place that was open to the sky. She made a hole in the soil with her finger, dropped in the seed, spat into the hole with unladylike accuracy, and covered it again with dirt. Returning to her seat beside Rex, she said, "Who knows? Maybe some pilgrim will see that tree seventeen hundred years from now."

Rex had to grin at his wife's playful action. "A woman like you deserves a legacy like that."

The humorous remark made Flavia laugh in an affectionate way. Rex put his arm around her shoulders and drew her close. They remained quiet for a while, contemplating the flames that danced among the olivewood sticks. Eventually, once the air had started to turn chilly, they returned to their room in the hostel. A charcoal brazier had given the room a pleasant warmth, and the bedcovers were scented with lavender. Soon they were both asleep.

But late that night, Rex's dreams took an ominous turn. A horrible figure appeared to him, indistinct yet obviously monstrous. The evil creature chased Rex through a forest with a chalice of poison in its hand. Branches reached out and snagged Rex's garments, entangling him so that he couldn't move. The demon clutched Rex's throat and tried to force him to drink the deadly draught. Rex resisted, turning his head this way and that, but it was futile. The monster was too strong. It forced open Rex's mouth and sent poison cascading over his face . . . down his throat . . . into the depths of his soul.

"No!" he cried, sitting up in bed. Slick sweat was upon his body, and the chamber felt smoky and hot. A dark presence seemed to threaten him even though he was awake.

"Rex, what is it?" Flavia asked from beside him.

"Nightmare. I'm going out for some air."

He threw a cloak around his shoulders and left the room. Stepping into the garden, he found a quiet place in a shaft of moonlight. He knelt beside a large boulder, its solidity providing comfort as he sought to calm his emotions. Rex's forehead was still wet with sweat, and when he wiped it, he half expected to see blood like the Lord himself. Yet the moisture was clear and nothing seemed amiss. A terrible poison hadn't taken control of his body. Even so, he couldn't shake the feeling that his death was imminent.

A stick snapped behind him. Rex leapt to his feet, whirling to confront his enemy with a racing heart. But it was no enemy who approached. It was Flavia, faithful and true. She came to Rex's side and drew him to his former kneeling position beside the boulder. "I will keep watch with you," she said, "for as long as it takes."

Side by side, the couple prayed in silence. Rex found that his wife's presence helped his equilibrium to return. Though it didn't happen right away, Rex eventually found that his sense of foreboding had lifted. The dark spirits that clawed at his soul no longer prowled so close but had retreated into the olive trees around him.

A long time had passed—an hour? maybe two?—when Flavia finally broke the silence. "Look there."

Rex raised his eyes to find his wife pointing toward the east. He gazed in that direction and saw that the sky had brightened. The sunrise was on its way. Only one pinpoint of light remained in the blue-black sky above the growing dawn.

"Venus still lurks in the dark," Rex said.

"No," Flavia replied, shaking her head. "She has fled, for the Bright Morning Star has come."

———❦———

After the overnight stay at the Mount of Olives, Empress Helena took the next month to make a circuit through the desert to the south of Hierusalem. As Flavia traveled with the entourage, she kept a diary so she wouldn't forget all the places she was seeing. At each site mentioned in scripture, Rex collected another memento or relic, which Flavia carefully noted in her diary. It wasn't long before he'd accumulated an impressive collection. Rex kept everything in a wooden lockbox, wrapping each item in a soft cloth to protect it from damage.

The imperial procession headed deep into the Palaestinian wilderness, descending through barren ravines to the salty sea devoid of all life. The two local bishops, Eusebius of Caesarea and Macarius of Hierusalem, served as guides. Each of them had a different kind of knowledge. Eusebius was the more historical and scholarly of the two, while Macarius was more aware of popular Christian traditions. It was Macarius who noted that the road they were traveling was the same one mentioned by Jesus in the parable of the Good Samaritan. But upon reaching Iericho—formerly a great city, now just a minor village—Eusebius was able to explain exactly where the walls had fallen down when Iosue and the Israelites attacked it. Macarius added that the local believers still venerated the memory of Rahab, the courageous prostitute who helped Iosue, and of Zacchaeus, who repented of his dishonest tax collection when he was called by Jesus.

From Iericho, the empress traveled down to Mamre, where the Jewish patriarch Abraham was visited by two angels and an appearance of Christ. Rex collected an acorn from the Oak of Mamre, under which Abraham had pitched his tent and entertained his guests. The travelers went next to Petra, an ancient Arabian trading center with incredible buildings carved into the canyon walls. Flavia found the place captivating and exotic during the three days she was there.

After reaching the southern port city of Aila, where the seaside was sparkling and lovely, the entourage traveled farther down the coast on a ship, then ventured far into the desert. An arduous journey by camel train brought them to an encampment at the base of Mons Sinai. Although ascending the rugged mountain was impossible for the empress, Rex and some of the other bodyguards decided to head up to the summit, led by one of the monks who lived at the foot of the mountain.

"I'm not missing that," Flavia told Rex as the men were about to leave. She had donned a pair of sturdy boots and held a staff in her hand. A large skin of water was slung over her shoulder on a strap. She also had a waterproof cloak with a hood since the weather could be stormy this time of year, especially in the high mountains.

"I never imagined for a moment that we could leave you behind," Rex answered with a grin. "In fact, I thought you'd probably lead the way."

Although Flavia didn't actually lead the way, she hiked so vigorously and kept up so well with the men that they gave her the honor of stepping first upon the summit where Moses received the Torah. Flavia felt a sense of awe as she imagined God's presence on this lofty place. The view of the horizon in all directions made her feel small and insignificant before the greatness of the Lord. "El Shaddai, I worship you," she said—and when a distant thundercloud rumbled in response, the eyes of everyone on the mountaintop widened with holy fear. They quickly descended from the summit where God had once been manifest in smoke and fire.

From Mons Sinai, the queen's retinue headed up to the Mediterranean coast, passing through the substantial cities of Gaza and Ascalon. Helena visited with the local bishops there and also with the important politicians who ran those cities. It was late in December by the time the travelers finally left Ascalon and began to ascend from the coastal plain into the hill country again. Their destination was Bethlehem, which prompted a vigorous discussion about the Nativity as everyone rode toward that little town.

"The precise date of Christ's birth is a matter of dispute in the church," said the scholarly Eusebius. He was wearing a broad-brimmed hat as he rode on a mule, but even so, his forehead was sweaty. After mopping his face, he added, "The Latins hold to one date, but here in the east, we hold to another."

Empress Helena was riding a white mule with an especially smooth gait. "I have always heard it was the eighth before the Kalends of January. That is only two days from now—the twenty-fifth day in December."

"Yes, my sister," Eusebius agreed, using the term of address Helena had adopted on her pilgrimage. "That is indeed the date observed by Rome and the church in the west. But here in the east, we calculate it as twelve days afterward—the Day of Manifestation, the sixth in January."

Flavia found herself intrigued by this topic, for she had never heard it addressed before, at least not by experts. Since she was riding behind Rex's horse as he protected the queen's right flank, she was able to overhear the conversation. Although she wanted to ask questions, she decided to remain quiet and see where the discussion went.

"It seems the Christian church should have remembered such an important day," Helena remarked. "How strange that there should be two days competing for the honor."

"The earliest believers didn't observe birthdays," Macarius explained. "That practice is associated with good luck and astrology, which have no part in our faith. So we have received no ancient traditions about this. Yet because the Gospels so clearly describe the Lord's birth, it was natural to start wondering when it happened. Eastern theologians determined it to be the sixth day in January. But the west uses the December date."

Helena frowned at these words. "Our whole empire should have one date for everyone. I will speak to my son about this. Perhaps we Christians can unify our practices."

"Do not use the December date," Macarius advised. "It comes from the pagan worship of the Unconquered Sun."

"No, it doesn't," Rex said firmly.

The interjection from the queen's bodyguard seemed to catch everyone by surprise. All eyes now swung toward Rex. "You think not?" asked Eusebius in a less-than-friendly tone. "Perhaps you can illumine us, then, my brother."

Although Rex was no bishop, nor even a high-level churchman, he didn't seem intimidated by the skeptical response or the stares. Even so, Flavia felt a little defensive on his behalf. She wanted to remind everyone that her husband wasn't just a soldier on guard duty. He was a deacon of the Alexandrian church and a teacher of theology. He even wore the ring of a papal legate.

But Flavia quickly discovered she didn't have to worry about Rex. He had a ready answer to the query, and his voice was confident as he gave it. "No one in Rome thinks Jesus was a sun god, at least no one who is educated in such matters. It is true that the twenty-fifth day of December is dedicated to the sun. The emperor Aurelian decreed it. But long before that, the Christians started keeping it as the day of Christ's birth for an entirely different reason than sun worship."

"And what reason is that?" asked Eusebius, who seemed surprised by Rex's assertion.

"Because our theologians believe the Christ child was conceived in the Virgin's womb on the same date he was crucified. That was in the springtime. The Jewish Passover that year has been computed as the eighth day before the Kalends of April—the twenty-fifth of March. So if that was also the day of conception, and you count forward nine months from the conception, you come to the twenty-fifth day in December. That is why the western Christians observe it as the Savior's birthday, not because of the sun god."

"It is a trustworthy belief!" Helena declared. "I shall tell it to Constantine. All the people will celebrate the December date for the Nativity. We shall be unified across the realm."

"As you wish, my lady," Macarius said graciously.

Something happened then that no one else noticed, not even Rex, whose eyes were scanning the roadside ahead. Only Flavia observed it from her position behind her husband. The two bishops, Macarius and Eusebius, exchanged a glance that signaled their disagreement with what Helena had just decreed. It wasn't a conspiratorial glance, at least not in the sense that they meant to do her harm. Yet each of them seemed to say to each other, "We do not approve of this. But let's stay silent for now." Flavia felt sure that what she had seen was more than mere intuition. However, since she didn't know what to make of it, she filed it away for later consideration.

Dusk had come to the sky by the time the travelers finally reached the outskirts of Bethlehem. "Do you think there will be room for us at the inn?" Rex asked Flavia, making a joke that surely every Christian had made for centuries when arriving in this town. She smiled back at Rex and replied that guest rooms were always available to empresses, even if not for peasant girls with seemingly illegitimate babies.

The next morning, Helena arose early to visit the stable that the locals asserted was the location of Jesus's birth. Just as at Hierusalem, so here the evil emperor Hadrian had tried to obliterate the place by turning it into a pagan shrine. Trees had been planted to convert the site into a sacred grove for the god Adonis, the lover of Aphrodite and a heavenly embodiment of Hadrian's handsome boyfriend, Antinous. In recent years, however, the place had fallen into disuse by the pagans. Now the Christians were trying to reclaim it.

"Look here," Bishop Macarius said as he pulled aside some shrubbery and debris near a cave in the side of the hill. He was a physically fit man who had no trouble removing the tangled foliage that would have made chubby Eusebius start huffing and puffing. Macarius gestured to a rectangle of ruined masonry that surrounded the mouth of the cave and abutted the hillside. "Do you see the outline?"

"It's a house," Rex said as he examined what Macarius was trying to reveal. "Israelite homes always had a yard enclosed by walls."

Macarius's face lit up at Rex's confirmation of his point. "That's right! And they kept their animals within the walls for safety and warmth. Here, the cave would have served as the stable for the residence, no question."

"What is inside it?" Helena asked.

"Come see, my sister," Macarius replied.

The empress went to the cave's opening and peered inside, though she didn't stoop low enough to enter. The others each took turns looking into the stable. When Flavia's turn came, she saw that the snug little space would have served well as a place to house a donkey or a few sheep and goats. A wooden feeding trough filled with fresh hay was in the middle of the room. Some oil lamps and a small brazier for incense had been set on the floor.

"The local Christians maintain this place for spiritual devotion," Macarius said. "Many pilgrims come here for the festival in January."

"Soon to be December," Helena corrected.

Macarius dipped his chin politely. "As you wish, Your Majesty." And again, Flavia saw him exchange a quick glance with Eusebius.

Since there wasn't much else to see at the cave of Christ's birth, the empress left with her advisers to draw up plans for the Church of the Nativity. That evening, after everyone had retired to their rooms in Bethlehem's brand-new hostel for pilgrims, Rex opened his box of relics and spread them on the bed. He had thirty or forty items in the collection, each with a plausible connection to a biblical site, and some even with a connection to Jesus himself. Rex's newest acquisition was wrapped in a piece of sackcloth: a few strands of hay and a splinter of wood from the feeding trough in the stable that had once sheltered Iosef and the Virgin.

"Surely that isn't the same trough Jesus was laid in," Flavia remarked. "Why would anyone still have the original? Who would have kept it for all those years?"

"It's a lookalike," Rex agreed. "It's only there as a reminder. The original is long gone. And that hay was freshly cut."

"So why bring all these relics back to Rome if they're not real?"

"Define real," Rex countered.

Flavia had to take some time to consider her husband's inquiry. Though she believed in the quest for relics just as much as Rex did, thinking about his question helped to clarify the reasons behind her beliefs. Finally, she offered her answer: "I think 'real' means anything that actually happened in history."

"Like Jesus coming to earth? God in the flesh?"

"Yes, exactly. That actually happened, so it's real."

"But it happened three hundred years ago. How do you know it was real?"

"The scriptures say so."

"What scriptures? Show me."

A little exasperated, Flavia went to her traveling bag and withdrew the *Gospel of Luke.* Turning the pages of the codex, she found the passage she wanted and read it aloud: "And she brought forth her firstborn son, and swaddled him, and laid him in a trough because there was no place for them in the lodging."

Rex gently took hold of Flavia's index finger and traced its tip along the smooth page of her book. "Do you feel that?"

"Of course."

"Although truth is always truth," Rex said, "how do you *receive* the truth? Ideas come to you by physical means—words on a page, for example. A book . . . a voice . . . a sight that you witness. Your mind was created to gain truth through your body. Touching. Seeing. Hearing. Even tasting."

"Almost everything I know comes through my senses," Flavia admitted.

"That's true for everyone. We are embodied people." Rex handed Flavia the rough splinter of wood he had taken from the feeding trough, then once again traced her fingertip along its length. "This fragment confirms what you already know. Does it matter that it isn't the actual wood? Not really. It's still tied to this place, so it has the power to remind you of your beliefs. Objects can convey messages about what happened in history. They strengthen our faith."

Flavia stared at the splinter in her palm. "I guess that's what faith is—to live in the present and hope in the future because we are confident in the past."

A big grin came to Rex's face. "That's right! And it's hard to have faith. We can all use a little reminder of our story from time to time."

After a little more silent contemplation, Rex rose from the edge of the bed and held open the piece of sackcloth. Flavia placed the wooden splinter into the cloth next to the strands of hay. Rex folded it, put it in his lockbox, and stowed the relics under the bed.

"Tomorrow is the twenty-fifth of December," Flavia said. "The day when God sent his Son into the world, only a few steps from here."

Instead of answering, Rex scooped Flavia into an embrace. She responded by encircling his body with her arms and resting her head on his chest. For a long while they stood like that, tranquil and content on this silent, holy night.

"What a mystery the Incarnation is," Flavia finally whispered as her husband held her close.

"Glory to God in the highest," Rex replied.

—◦◦◦—

MARCH 327

The Apostle Felix stood at an upstairs window in the House of Mani and gazed across the street at decrepit old Santa Sabina. Felix found it hard to believe he was once the priest of that church, back when Lady Sabina Sophronia and her daughter, Junia Flavia, were its leading patrons. That seemed like a different world to Felix, an era long gone and happily forgotten. Back then, the catholics were the strongest Christians in Rome. But now the true Manichaean church was on the rise and the catholic congregations were dwindling. "Good riddance, you blind fools," Felix said, then turned away from the window and went downstairs to await the arrival of his guest.

He didn't have long to wait, for the Apostle Quintus was a well-organized and punctual man. Those were the exact traits that made him so valuable when he served Pope Sylvester as an archdeacon in the papal residence. Now, however, Quintus had seen the light. He had become a follower of the truly divine prophet: not Jesus Christ, but Mani of Persia, who had revealed the Heavenly Way more clearly than the physical and earthbound doctrines of the catholics. That deluded form of Christianity emphasized the disgusting idea that God had taken on flesh as a man. "Good riddance," Felix muttered again, though not loud enough for Quintus to hear as he entered the house.

"Let us go to the rear garden," Felix said after he had exchanged greetings with his guest. He led Quintus to a courtyard whose walls dribbled with piped-in water that trickled through bright, green moss. The water made a pleasant, natural sound as it landed in a pool that ran around the base of the walls. In the middle of the room, which was open to the sky, was a flagstone area with two chairs in it. The garden was like a moist grotto a spiritual seeker might find in the faraway east. Here in Rome, it was a

411

suitable place for Manichaeans to meet, for it symbolized Light, Life, and Paradise—three things that could be found only by separating oneself from anything belonging to the human body.

"Tell me about your conventicle in the Pantheon," Felix said when the men were seated. "I hear it is thriving and growing beyond all expectations."

"That is true," Quintus acknowledged. "And conversely, the catholic churches are shrinking. Few pagans are joining us, but many former catholics are coming over. They can see that our way is more intellectual and enlightened."

"And our banquets are more lavish too!"

Felix's quip didn't bring a smile to Quintus's face. Instead, he said sternly, "I've been meaning to talk to you about that. You ought not be serving meat and strong drink to the Hearers. That is not the teaching of our religion."

"Nothing forbids those things for the Hearers," Felix countered. "Only the Elect. And even if it is a sin for the common folk, we can easily forgive them afterward. But we can't give up those banquets, Apostle Quintus. It keeps the people coming through our doors."

"That is another thing! We shouldn't be calling ourselves 'apostles.' That title is reserved only for those sent out by Mani."

Felix waved his hand dismissively. "There are some who follow our Seven Books strictly and others who give them a looser interpretation. I am one of those, my brother, because it gets the results we want."

Though Quintus frowned at this remark, he let the subject drop. Felix went on to give a report of his own conventicle on the Aventine Hill. It was growing rapidly, adding more people each week at the expense of Santa Sabina across the street. Some Sun Days, fewer than ten people showed up at that false church.

"One time," Felix exulted, "no one came at all! Father Vincentius presided over a Eucharist in an empty church. Ha! I was sure to let him know that the House of Mani was overflowing the same day. The Hibernian's face grew as red as his hair!"

"A great victory for us," Quintus said as he fiddled with a loose thread on his sleeve.

"Not yet, my brother. Victory is close, but not yet in hand. There is one more secret deed we must accomplish. Then total victory will be ours."

The cryptic remark made Quintus raise his eyes to meet Felix's gaze. "What secret deed?"

Instead of revealing his plans right away, Felix probed for a little more information from his guest. "What was the name of our man inside the Lateran Palace? That slave with the purple stain on his face?"

"Primus, he is called. He sides with us, or anyone who rewards him with money or sweets."

"Yes, that's him—Primus. I have dealt with him before. He's a spiritual mercenary. Grovels before whoever offers him a trinket. That makes him useful, of course."

Since Quintus made no reply, Felix kept probing for more information. "Is the Lateran Basilica secure?"

"Secure? You mean like against thieves?"

"Or anyone who would wish to enter."

"I suppose it is secure at night. By day, many people visit it."

"We must gain control of it," Felix declared.

The shocking statement brought a look of surprise to Quintus's face. "It is the foremost catholic church! What would that gain us?"

"You said it yourself! It's the foremost church in this city. It's visible to everyone as a center of religious power. The same goes for the shrine of Peter out on the Vatican, though I tried my hardest to stop that."

"I remember the affair with the relics," Quintus said quietly. "Your snaky friend was killed."

Felix put his fist to his chest. "The spark of the Aegyptian Asp lives on right here." After a moment of sober reflection, Felix returned to his main point. "We must take over the Lateran Basilica and the palace. That is the head of the body—the source that feeds the rest. If the Manichaeans controlled that church, we would control the shape of Christianity throughout the city. Picture it, Quintus! We could bend everyone to Manichaeism and destroy those crude myths about saving crucifixion. The faith of Mani would shine forth in Rome. And as Rome goes, so goes the whole world."

"Your plans are expansive," Quintus admitted. "But you have one problem. The bishop would never let it happen. Sylvester is too strong for you."

"That is why he must be removed."

At those words, Quintus immediately recoiled. His former look of surprise now turned to suspicion, maybe even disgust. "What do you mean, 're-moved'?"

"I mean, judged by the hand of God. That is what the Father of Greatness does. Wherever there is a servant of darkness, he shines down his burn-ing light until it's gone. He obliterates the wicked by the brilliance of his cleansing fire. And he uses people like us to accomplish such holy deeds."

"So that is your secret plan? To obliterate Sylvester by fire?"

"An inner fire," Felix said. "A burning from within. A consuming pain that eliminates and destroys him."

The narrowing of Quintus's eyes revealed that anger had finally come to him. "Speak plainly! What do you intend?"

Before answering, Felix offered a prayer in his heart. *O Light Above, help this man understand that your purifying and cleansing ways must sometimes be painful!* The quick prayer gave Felix the courage he needed to state his full intent. Quintus's cooperation was essential for the plan to succeed, since only the former archdeacon had the necessary contacts inside the Lateran Palace.

"I intend to poison the false bishop Sylvester," Felix announced. "When he is gone, his church will be ours. Then, one by one, the catholic congrega-tions of Rome will die out as Mani becomes all in all."

Quintus leapt to his feet and stared down at Felix in his chair. "I toler-ated your feasts of meat and wine," he said, his eyes blazing with righteous indignation. "I even tolerated your twisting of our scriptures and doctrines. But this I will not tolerate! Manichaeism is nonviolent! And Sylvester was—" Quintus broke off for a moment, then corrected his wording as he finished his thought. "Sylvester *is* my friend, and I will do him no harm."

Now Felix stood up too. Though he was a tall man, Quintus was even taller, so Felix didn't try to engage him in a staredown. Instead, he simply said, "Your courage fails you, brother. It seems you aren't able to do what is required to cleanse the earth of darkness."

"Poisoning the bishop of Rome is no part of Manichaeism," Quintus declared, then turned abruptly and marched out of the room.

Perhaps not, Felix thought as he watched the man leave. *But it should be.*

✦

MAY 327

Flavia stepped from the dock and into the fishing boat with a helping hand from Rex since the morning was breezy and the Sea of Galilee was choppy today. Though the faint light of dawn was visible in the eastern sky, the orb of the sun hadn't yet risen above the mountains. That mattered little, of course, to the fishermen who owned the boat. They could sail by the full light of the sun, or by the moon, or by no light at all. Catching fish at night was how they made their living. Today, however, they had a much easier way to earn income: simply transport Empress Helena and her attendants up to Capernaum.

The past four months of Flavia's life had been the most peaceful she had ever experienced. After spending the Nativity season at Bethlehem, the empress had decided to take up residence beside the Sea of Galilee until the coolness of winter gave way to the pleasant warmth of spring. The town of Tiberias had been her official base, yet she also spent time in a villa on the sea's opposite shore. Wherever she went, Rex and a few other bodyguards accompanied her. Flavia had found the Galilean pace of life to be slow and relaxed, a welcome change from constant travel and the bustle of big cities. Flavia's spring had been spent walking along the waterfront with Rex, writing in her diary, and visiting quaint villages nearby. Life was indeed sweet. Her only regret was that her mother, who was back in Rome, hadn't been able to experience the tranquility as well.

Since today was the Sabbath, the queen's retinue was planning to attend the ancient church in Capernaum. Unlike the area around Hierusalem, where the Jews were evicted by Hadrian long ago, the Christians of Galilee still came from a Jewish background. That meant they met on the seventh day of the week instead of the first. The pastor of the church—or the "rabbi," as his followers still called him—was named Isaac ben Yehudah. Jewish Christianity fascinated Empress Helena, so she visited the church in Capernaum often to experience its unique flavor.

"Did you remember to bring the letter?" Rex asked Flavia as he took a seat next to her in the boat's stern.

"Right here," she replied, patting the satchel at her side. Though mail couldn't be sent from the villa where the empress was staying, Capernaum had a postal station connected with the tax office, so letters could be dispatched from there. Last night, Flavia wrote to her friend Athanasius in Alexandria. She and Rex had decided not to go back and live in that city, so they were bequeathing all their possessions to the local church.

"I'm sure the bishop will understand," Rex said as he gestured toward Flavia's satchel. "Our things will provide a lot of charity for the poor. I wonder what they'll do with the apartment?"

"Maybe some monastic brothers will live in it," Flavia suggested. "It's near the Serapeum, so some scholars of the church could live there and make use of the library."

Rex nodded. "Good idea."

"Does it make you sad to send the letter?"

"To give away all our possessions? Not really. We didn't have much. Nothing that can't be replaced."

"But it's also the end of a season for us. A phase of our lives that's over."

Rex slipped his arm around Flavia's shoulder as they sat side by side. "We did have some good years in Aegyptus."

"And some hardships," Flavia added, then felt her husband draw her a little closer. They lapsed into silence as they sifted their thoughts. Now their future was wide open. All they could do was let the wind and the waves take them where they would.

After about two hours of northward sailing on the Sea of Galilee, the boat drew near to Capernaum. The empress was met at the dock by Rabbi Isaac. Though he spoke Greek with her, his language was interspersed with Aramaic words. "Shalom to you in the name of Yeshua HaMashiach," he said with a deep bow. Helena greeted him warmly, referring to him by his Aramaic name, "Yitzhak." Then everyone proceeded to the House of Peter.

The residential compound where Peter once lived was constructed of black basalt stones like every other house in the area. There wasn't much to it. A few nondescript buildings faced a courtyard, adjoined by a second residence that had belonged to his brother, Andrew. Soon after Peter's martyrdom in Rome, the local Christians had turned the main room of his house into a church. The walls were covered in plaster to give it greater beauty, and oil lamps now made the place bright and cheerful. A large stone jar in the corner contained wine, while a table next to it held cakes of unleavened bread. Also on the table were some wooden cups and a silver ladle.

Rabbi Isaac's sermon focused on the passage from the *Gospel of Matthew* in which Jesus healed Peter's mother-in-law and cast out many demons. "It happened in this very room," Isaac declared. "Our Lord touched the mother of Shimon Kepha's wife upon the hand, and the fever left her, and she rose up and served him. But I ask you: *Why* did she serve him?"

"Because he was a rabbi," said one of the elders from the bench reserved for them. "And rabbis deserve honor."

When Isaac shook his head, another man offered his answer. "Because she was a woman, and it is a woman's place to cook for men."

"Our wives do cook for us," Isaac admitted, "but that was not why she did it."

"What then?" asked the first elder impatiently. "Do not make sport with us, Yitzhak!"

Despite the rebuke, Isaac still didn't answer right away. Instead, he re-read his chosen passage from the *Gospel of Matthew*—first in Greek, then in Aramaic. After both readings were complete, Isaac raised his eyes to the small crowd in the church and said, "Mar Yeshua healed the woman by touching her hand. Therefore it is with her hand that she served him. For whatever is touched by Yeshua becomes devoted to the service of the Holy One, blessed be he."

The rabbi's explanation caused murmurs of approval to erupt from the congregation. Everyone could see the wisdom of the interpretation. Yet the person who marveled most was Empress Helena. She rose to her feet and exclaimed, "I, too, have been touched by Yeshua! And here is my service. On this very site we shall build the fourth church of the holy land. After the Resurrection, the Olivet, and the Nativity, there shall be, right here, the Church of the House of Peter."

"Surround this place with walls," Isaac advised, "yet madam, please do not tear down what is already here."

"It shall be done as you say," Helena agreed.

After the service was complete, including a Eucharist whose liturgical rhythms were still very close to a seder, the people of Capernaum were treated to a great banquet at imperial expense. There was abundant food and drink, and much laughter, and even some dancing. Only when the sun was low in the sky did the fishing boat finally take the royal entourage back to the villa on the sea's eastern shore. Sunset was close when Flavia stepped onto the dock where she had started the long day. Her heart felt full to overflowing, satisfied by the fellowship in Yeshua and the abiding presence of Ruach HaKodesh.

"Would you like to watch the sun go down over the sea?" Rex asked her as everyone made their way from the waterfront back to the villa. When Flavia agreed, he said, "I'll meet you at the beach. Let me get some blankets since the night has turned chilly."

Flavia separated from the group and went to an out-of-the-way spot where the Sea of Galilee met the sandy shoreline. Far across the water, the twinkling lights of Tiberias were visible as shop owners and householders started to light their evening lamps. Above the town, the sky was ablaze with an orange glow.

The sun had just touched the distant hillside when Rex arrived with a heavy woolen blanket and a pillow. He sat down on the beach beside Flavia and they snuggled into the blanket, content to remain quiet for a while in this lonely and lovely place. The rays of the setting sun played across the ruffled water and seemed to reach all the way to the waves lapping at their feet, like a glowing path inviting them onto the shimmering lake.

"I wonder what it was like for Peter to walk across that sea," Flavia mused. "It must have been scary out there in the deep water with waves and storms all around."

"Do you think you would have sunk like him?"

"Only if I forgot where to put my eyes."

Rex nodded thoughtfully. "It's easy to do."

Too easy, Flavia thought. *Lord, help my unbelief!*

After the sun had gone down behind Tiberias, the stars began to appear in the darkening sky. Soon the entire swath of the Milky Way was visible across the firmament. It was a moonless night, so the stars appeared especially brilliant. None of them seemed like malevolent demons tonight, but like diamonds scattered onto a black cloth by the generous hand of God.

Their delicate beauty made Flavia feel romantic. She nestled closer to

Rex inside the warm confines of their blanket. "I love you so much," she whispered.

His reply touched the deepest recesses of Flavia's heart. "You are mine forever," he said. "You and no other."

The married couple's kiss soon became something more. As desire rose in them, they reclined on the beach, unseen by human eyes yet visible to the approving gaze of God. He had declared their love to be good, so they rejoiced to enact the union of two into one. On this dark and starry night, the husband and wife expressed their affection in the intimate way God had designed. Flavia gave herself to Rex and he to her, until, at last, they were spent and stillness came to them again.

The warmth of Rex's body within the blanket's cocoon lulled Flavia into a deep sleep. For a long time, she lay still, at peace in her slumber. It was late in the night when something strange awakened her. At first, she couldn't perceive what it was. Then she heard faint shouts . . . saw a flickering light . . . smelled the aroma of smoke.

"Rex, wake up!" she cried, shaking him. "Something's burning!"

Immediately, Rex was awake and on his feet, a trait ingrained in all special forces operatives. "It's the villa," he said as he studied the eerie orange glow. "Don't stay here or you could get trapped if those trees catch the flame. Run down shore and you'll be safe."

After Rex broke into a run toward the house, Flavia paused and considered what to do. Though she knew she would be safe if she moved away, she didn't want to abandon the empress in her moment of need. So instead of escaping the conflagration, Flavia followed Rex to see if there was anything she could do. Even one extra person on a bucket brigade could make a difference. Flavia found she didn't have the heart to flee from danger at such an urgent time.

It didn't take long to realize the fire was a big one. The whole villa was ablaze. Flames leapt from nearly every window and danced above the roof, sending a column of black smoke into the sky. The intense heat was shattering the roof tiles in staccato explosions. Though a few people were running here and there, no one had started any kind of effort to put out the fire. Apparently the villa would be lost.

The acrid haze that surrounded the house made Flavia's eyes water, but she pressed ahead to see if anyone was injured and could be dragged away from harm. A kitchen maid staggered from a doorway and Flavia caught her just before she fell to the ground. Supporting the girl in her arms, Flavia helped her to the beach where the air was better, then returned to see what else she could do.

The smoke column was thicker now, rising up and spreading out like the wings of a bat. For a moment, two swirling sparks looked like the baleful eyes of a demon as it loomed over the house, dancing and writhing in wicked glee. "You have no power!" Flavia cried, shaking her fist at the apparition. Her shout caused her to inhale a lungful of ashy smoke. She fell to her knees, coughing against the cinders that had invaded her body to burn her from within.

A frightened wailing made Flavia look up at the highest window in the villa. It was a grand window on the top floor that offered a vista of the lawn sloping down to the sea. A desperate figure was there, enveloped in billowing darkness. Although the flames had not yet reached that spot, their red tongues licked from the windows on either side, hungry to consume whatever was in their path. It wouldn't be long before the fire reached the center window as well.

"Help me!" cried the terrified person in the window. Though the voice was hoarse and muffled, Flavia immediately realized who it was. *Empress Helena!*

Before Flavia could make a move toward the window, she saw Rex come dashing around the corner. The firelight revealed that his face was smudged with soot and his garments were singed. Yet Rex wasn't overcome by the hellish flames. He was ready to do battle with them all night. Stationing himself beneath the window, he yelled up to the empress, "Climb down, Your Majesty! You've got to get out of there!"

"It's . . . too . . . far!" she cried between hacking coughs.

"You must!"

Helena's only response was to swoon, overcome by the smoke and perhaps also by fear. Rex didn't hesitate. As soon as he saw the empress slump to the floor and disappear, he sprinted to the waterfront and returned with something bulky in his arms. "You men, help me!" he shouted to a pair of servants wandering around in the confusion. By the time Rex reached the base of the window again, he had recruited two more helpers. "Spread this out!" he ordered the foursome. "Pull it taut!"

Through the gloom, Flavia discerned that the men held a fishing net. Terror seized her as she realized what Rex was planning to do. "Almighty God, protect him," she prayed as she watched Rex begin to scale the exterior of the house toward Helena's window far above.

Like a spider on a wall, Rex made his way upward, using decorative ornaments, the lower window frames, and even the rough stonework as footholds and handholds. Once, his foot slipped, and Flavia gasped as he dangled from two hands. Yet Rex managed to find purchase again and keep going. Finally, he reached the top windowsill and disappeared into the smoke being belched out of the house.

For a long time, there was no movement, no sign of life. The center window was no longer dark, for the flames had reached that room and an evil glow backlit the billowing smoke. Sparks and embers shot from the window as if ejected from a volcano. A crafty voice started whispering fearful words in Flavia's ear. *The s-s-smoke overcame him. His body is burning! His flesh is melting! He is in agony! You'll never s-s-see him again . . . not in thi-s-s-s world or the next!*

"No! Christ is Victor!" Flavia cried—and at the same moment, Rex burst from the darkness with Helena Augusta in his arms.

"Hold that net, men!" Rex called down to his helpers. "Here we come!"

There was no time for him to clamber out of the window or sit on its sill before jumping. Nor did Rex try to lower Helena down. Instead, he just leapt into the air while cradling the empress against himself.

The freefall seemed to happen in slow motion. As Flavia watched, Rex pivoted midair so that his body would hit first and cushion the fall. He landed in the middle of the net, which was now held fast by eight or nine men who had joined the rescue effort. The net bowed in the middle and bounced the jumpers twice. Then, as they came to rest in its center, a great cheer went up from the men. "The queen is saved!" shouted the soot-blackened servants.

Though she was coughing from the smoke she had inhaled, Helena was not physically injured. She extricated herself from the net, supported by Rex's arm around her waist. "Th-thank you," she murmured as everyone backed away from the house. It was a total loss. The place could not be saved. Yet it seemed that most of its residents had escaped.

At a safe distance from the blaze, near the refreshing breezes of the waterfront, Rex and Flavia caught their breath and regrouped. Twice, Rex's tunic had caught on fire, but he had swatted out the flames before they could burn his skin. Even so, his normally thick beard had been singed down to stubble on one of his cheeks. His eyebrow on that side was also gone.

"I yanked open our bedroom door and the flames leapt out," he explained.

"You went inside? Rex, we have nothing that's worth risking your life for!"

"Yes we do—the relics!" His face fell as he spoke. "They're gone. All of them. The box was nothing but charcoal. Everything was consumed."

Flavia put her hand on his wrist, then met his eyes with a tender gaze. "I'm sorry, my beloved. That is a great loss."

"I will get more!" Rex vowed.

"The Lord our God will provide," Flavia said.

—◦◦◦—

The burning of the villa signaled to Empress Helena that it was time to return to Hierusalem. But before departing, she went around the Sea of Galilee to her base in Tiberias, where the good Jewish doctors were able to nurse her back to full health. They paid particular attention to her lungs, which had inhaled copious amounts of smoke and fumes. Helena was in her late seventies, so any ailment took longer to heal. Yet soon enough, the healthy air on the western side of the sea did its rejuvenating work. On the tenth day before the Kalends of June, Helena's retinue set out for the Holy City. Once again, Rex found himself on the road next to the empress, protecting her right flank like a dutiful guardsman.

The rescue at the villa, however, had altered the long-standing dynamic between them. Helena had known Rex for many years in his professional capacity. Their first interaction was in faraway Gaul, seventeen years ago, when the empress asked the teenaged Rex to convey a message to Constantine in the middle of an important meeting. But now, after the fire, Helena seemed to treat Rex like her own grandson. She doted on him—not quite as much as she had Caesar Crispus, yet with a similar dynamic. It was a mixture of gratitude, affection, and esteem, probably with some grief and loss mixed in. Rex had rescued Helena once already when he swept her from an enemy encampment on horseback, which had earned her respect. Now the rescue from the hellfire at the villa seemed to have made an even deeper impression on the queen. Rex decided to maintain his normal professional demeanor with her while also trying to minister, as much as possible, to a Christian ruler whose burdens were heavy.

When Helena arrived in Hierusalem, she took up residence in the same mansion as before, so Rex and Flavia found themselves back in the charming Glory House next door. The morning after their arrival, everyone went to the construction site at the tomb of Christ. When Rex saw it, he could hardly believe how much had changed. The plaza that had housed the Temple of Aphrodite was completely gone. Likewise, the crater that had been dug underneath it had also disappeared. The area had been so thoroughly excavated that it was now just an open rectangle with no sign of the fill dirt Hadrian's workers had brought in. Even the former quarry, which had become a garden in Jesus's day, had been chipped away by the hewing of many pickaxes. Now the whole area was just an empty expanse awaiting future construction. It was entirely flat except for one lonely protuberance in the middle: the mound of rock containing the tomb that had held the Savior's body for three days but couldn't keep him in.

And yet, as Rex scanned the work site, his eyes shifted to a second mound about a stone's throw from the empty tomb. This rocky mound, too, hadn't been removed. The workers clearly could have done so, which meant the little hill was intended to be preserved just like the rock that contained the holy tomb. *What is it?*

Bishops Macarius and Eusebius were busy explaining the construction plans to Helena. Rex caught the attention of little Cyril, the boy who served Macarius, and waved him over. "What's that second hill over there?"

"Golgotha," Cyril answered. "Or *Calvary* as they call it in your tongue. The Place of the Skull."

"Yes, of course," Rex said, shaking his head with some embarrassment that he hadn't identified the hillock. The site was so transformed that he was a bit disoriented. Yet now Rex recognized the place. The local authorities used to crucify criminals on that hill, back in the days when this area was outside Hierusalem's walls. It was a chunk of unquarried stone near a gate that led from the city to the garden. Crosses had stood there for many years, until Hadrian built his temple platform and put a lascivious idol of Aphrodite right on the place of crucifixion. With all the landmarks gone, it wasn't easy to recognize what was what, but Cyril's reminder made everything fall into place.

Bishop Macarius called Cyril back to his side. "I want to show Her Majesty the size of the church we're planning," he told the boy. "You know where the corner markers are. Go run the outline so the empress can imagine it."

Cyril dutifully obeyed, smiling and waving from each marker before running the line to the next one. Soon he had traced the full rectangle of the intended basilica and returned to his original spot.

"Aha!" Helena exclaimed. "I see it now. It's big!"

"Yes, Your Majesty," Macarius agreed. "It will be just as your son commanded, so the new church might be worthy of such a holy place." He turned back to the work site and called out, "Cyril! Show the queen the courtyard too!"

Cyril nodded, then ran the four corners of a planned courtyard that would surround the Lord's tomb. An encasing structure would be built around the rock-cut tomb to protect it from the elements, but otherwise it would be open to the sky. One wall of the courtyard would be the façade of the new church, while the other three would enclose the area within a colonnade, forming a quiet and sheltered place for worshiping the Risen Christ.

"And will Golgotha be inside the courtyard too?" Helena asked. "I have in mind to search the earth around it for fragments of our Lord's cross."

"It will also be enclosed," Macarius said, "and we can consider such excavations another day."

As the bishop of Hierusalem spoke these words, he glanced at Eusebius for the briefest of moments. Just then, Rex felt Flavia poke him. "Did you see that?" she whispered as she leaned close. "It's what I've been telling you! Those two are at odds with Helena for some reason." Rex nodded and turned his attention back to the empress, resolving to keep an eye on this matter and see where it would lead.

About a week later, Rex and Flavia were eating a midday meal at Glory

House when Cyril showed up, dirt-smudged and out of breath. "You have to come see this!"

Rex smiled at the boy's enthusiasm. "What is it?"

"A secret tunnel! Deep under the foundations of Hadrian. Come quick! The workers just discovered it."

"Have you told Macarius?"

"Not yet."

"Keep it a secret," Rex advised, then rose from the table and followed Cyril with Flavia at his side.

A short walk down the Great Cardo brought the threesome to the construction site. Laborers were scurrying everywhere, yet the place to which Cyril led them was an out-of-the-way spot near an old retaining wall from the Hadrianic construction. The wall was made of huge stone blocks that used to support the temple platform but would now form a foundation for the Church of the Resurrection. All the wall's blocks abutted one another. However, at the place Cyril indicated, the removal of some debris had revealed an opening between two of the blocks. When Rex drew closer to examine it, he felt cool air blowing out, and he could see from the darkness stretching away that the opening didn't end at a shallow niche. It was essentially a doorway into the underworld.

He turned back to Cyril. "We need lights."

The boy scampered away and quickly returned with three lamps the workers used during the evening shift. Since they were already lit, Rex led the way into the hole with Flavia and Cyril trailing him.

Although the passage was narrow, it was straight—clearly the work of human hands and not a natural cavity. "Someone built this on purpose," Flavia said from behind, noticing the same thing. Rex grew more excited to discover where the tunnel would lead.

The three explorers encountered no twists or bends as they went deeper into the heart of the earth. Fortunately, the air remained cool and fresh. A slight breeze in Rex's face told him that somewhere, cracks or crevices connected to the surface, providing adequate circulation. Though he had to stoop to make his way forward, he kept going until he finally came to a tiny room with a ceiling high enough for him to stand erect. It was a dead end. There was nowhere else to go.

Flavia held up her lamp and inspected her surroundings. "What is this place?"

Rex ran his hand along the walls, which were a jumble of rough blocks and smooth ashlars, all held together with mortar. "These stones aren't like the ones outside. I think they were reused from earlier constructions to create this secret room."

"But who puts a room in the middle of a temple foundation?" Flavia asked.

For a long moment, no one said anything. It was Cyril who finally voiced the idea that had begun to gather in Rex's mind too. "Christians! Believers who wanted to get as close as possible to what they knew was under Aphrodite's temple!"

"That makes sense," Rex said. "But it's hard to say for sure."

Flavia walked over to the corner of the room, investigating something that had caught her eye. Squatting down, she brushed some dust from the wall and examined it with her lamp, then looked over her shoulder with a triumphant expression. "Rex! Come see this!"

After kneeling next to her, Rex realized that Flavia had discovered a work of art. In black ink, someone had drawn a ship. Its mast was lowered and its sail furled, indicating it had reached its destination. And beneath the ship was an amazing inscription: "DOMINE IVIMUS."

"What does it say?" Cyril asked, peering over Rex's shoulder. He couldn't read the inscription because it was in Latin.

"Lord, we have come," Rex said. "And the use of Latin means these people sailed from far away to get here. This room must have been a pilgrimage destination for them."

"Non est hic," Flavia said solemnly, "surrexit enim, sicut dixit. Venite, videte locum ubi positus erat Dominus."

The Latin words nearly drove Cyril crazy with curiosity. "Ah! What are you saying, Flavia? Explain the mystery to me!"

Flavia switched back to Greek and said, "Those were the words of the angel at the empty tomb. 'He is not here, for he has risen, just as he said. Come, see the place where the Lord was laid.' It's from Matthew's gospel." Tracing her finger along the inscription beneath the ship, she added, "These people obeyed the command. They came here and saw the place—as close as they could get. Then they wrote, 'Lord, we have come' to record their obedience."

"This is a very ancient shrine," Rex said. "A holy place for earlier Christians. We should tell Helena right away. Let's go back to the daylight."

The three explorers left the underground chapel and retraced their steps through the narrow passage. One spot in particular was difficult to navigate due to the uneven ground, so each of them reached out and touched the same place on the wall. "Look how many hands have touched this stone," Cyril observed by the light of his lamp as he brought up the rear. "It's worn smooth."

Suddenly Flavia gasped. Rex immediately turned to see what was the matter. His wife had stopped walking, and her face held a stunned expression. Her mouth was open, and her eyes were wide. "What is it?" Rex asked.

"The oblong stone back in the chapel! It was set into the wall—did you notice it?"

"I saw lots of stones. I didn't notice a particular one."

"There was a rectangular one about the height of our eyes. And Rex, its whole surface was polished like this. Not just by stonecutters. I mean polished by many hands touching it."

"So?"

"So the pilgrims must have known it was holy. They revered it."

Rex was intrigued now. "What do you think it could be?"

"Maybe it was the slab that the Lord's body was laid on?" Cyril suggested.

"Let's have a look," Flavia said.

Back in the chapel, the three explorers stood before the polished stone. Now that they examined it more closely, another thing about the stone became obvious: it wasn't mortared into place like all the others in the wall. It was set horizontally into a recess, wedged tight enough to be unobtrusive, yet able to be removed by anyone who would.

"Let's take it out," Rex said. "Maybe there's something written on the back of it. You two get ready to grab that end. I'll pull out this one. We'll set it on the floor right here."

After Rex got his fingers behind the stone, a hard yank brought his end out of the wall. Carefully, Flavia and Cyril gripped their side, then they all laid the heavy stone on the floor with the polished side down. There was no writing on the back. And it didn't look to Rex like a grave slab. It was just a standard piece of marble that—

"Look what's in the hole!" Cyril cried.

Rex and Flavia immediately stood up and followed Cyril's gaze. The light of the boy's lamp illuminated something deep inside the recess that the stone had been covering.

A rugged beam made of wood.

Rex felt a chill run through his body. The hairs on his forearms stood on end as he realized what this timber was. He had seen many of them over the years, so there could be no doubt about its purpose. In the beam's center was a hole that identified it as a *patibulum*—the crosspiece used for a crucifixion. It would be placed on the upright *stipes*, which had a peg on top to fit into the hole, creating a sturdy T-shaped structure.

"Look at this," Flavia whispered in holy awe. Tentatively, she raised her finger and brought it close to one end of the crossbeam. "A nail hole, reddened by blood."

"And another at the other end," Cyril added. "There can be no doubt."

Reaching into the recess, Rex carefully lifted out the crossbeam. It was heavy—a burden that would quickly exhaust anyone trying to carry it upon his shoulders. Rex cradled it in his arms without letting it touch the ground. "We have to show this to the augusta right away. What we have here is the relic of all relics." He glanced at Flavia, remembering her words to him after the fire. "God has indeed provided," he said, and Flavia nodded back.

Because the underground passageway was narrow, Rex and Flavia carried the crossbeam together, each holding one end. Cyril led the way, walking backward while holding the lamps low so the walkers could see their footing. In this way, they soon approached the exit. The rectangle of light seemed to overwhelm Rex's eyes after his sojourn in the heart of the earth.

As Rex was stepping out of the tunnel, a pebble rolled beneath his foot. To steady himself, he thrust his other foot forward. In that moment, as his foot came down hard, he was assaulted by a thunderbolt of pain. "Argh!" he cried as white-hot fire shot up his leg from his heel. He collapsed to the ground, dropping the crossbeam with a clatter. Dizziness swamped him because the pain was so intense. A wave of nausea washed over him and threatened to make him vomit. Snatching his ankle, he bent his foot around and inspected his sole. A nail was there, having pierced his shoe and thrust itself into his heel. "Aaaahhh!" he cried again as he pulled out the nail and cast it aside. Blood welled up from the hole and dribbled onto the sand. Though the pain subsided a little, it still felt like a hot iron was being pressed into his flesh.

"What do you think you're doing?" demanded an authoritative voice.

Through eyes squinted against the pain and the glare of the sun, Rex looked up to see Bishop Eusebius. Behind him was the taller Macarius. The looks on their faces were stern and disapproving.

"We'll take that," Macarius said, motioning to some workers to confiscate the crossbeam.

Eusebius jabbed his finger at Rex. "Don't speak a word about this to anyone, on pain of excommunication." He looked over at Flavia, then added, "You too, little miss!"

"And you, Cyril!" Macarius said.

Flavia knelt down by Rex, her eyes wide with concern. "Should we summon a doctor?"

Rex shook his head, then managed to stand up with Flavia's help. He kept his weight off his injured foot and supported himself by leaning on his wife. Glancing around, he discerned that the workers had taken away the crossbeam. He turned his gaze toward the stern-faced Macarius and Eusebius. "What are you two up to?"

"The will of the Lord," Eusebius shot back. "So don't you get in the way."

Though Rex wanted to respond with a sharp reply, a squeeze of his hand from Flavia reminded him to be quiet instead. He checked his words and closed his mouth. Flavia, too, was silent. Their lack of a response seemed to perplex the two bishops. Finally, Eusebius gave an awkward wave of his hand. "Let's be going," he said, and Macarius nodded his agreement. The two men departed and soon were gone from sight.

The pain in Rex's heel had dulled to a throbbing ache. He knew he could make it back to the guesthouse by hobbling on the ball of his foot and leaning on Flavia. His real frustration wasn't the loss of his mobility but the bishops' confiscation of the crossbeam. "What a time to step on a nail!" he complained.

"I don't believe it was just a nail," Flavia said, drawing a little closer to Rex. "I think it was also the poisonous fang of a snake."

—∾—

JUNE 327

It was dawn on the Day of the Sun—the Day of Resurrection, the Lord's Day. Helena Augusta believed it was only right to dedicate the shrine of the empty tomb at such a time as this.

The mound of rock in the middle of the construction site had been enclosed in a protective cladding that people were calling the Aedicule, or "little shrine." Now, instead of bare rock, visitors to the holy place saw a round chapel with a conical roof. A porch in front of the entrance, supported by four columns, covered the anteroom that had preceded Christ's burial chamber. As of yet, no one had gone into the inner sanctum to pray, for that was the purpose of today's ceremony.

Although Bishop Macarius of Hierusalem was presiding over the dedication today—as was only right, since this was his home city—Helena had asked to be intimately involved in everything that was being done. A symbolic and deeply meaningful ritual had been planned for the day. All the preparations had been shown to Helena and rehearsed. Now the moment to begin had arrived.

As the summer sun was rising over the city's skyline to the east, the bishop went to the porch of the Aedicule with a powerful implement in his hands. It was a large burning glass, the mysterious lens that could make fire from the rays of the sun. The lens had been set into a wooden stand, which Macarius positioned at the entrance to the Aedicule. This caused a pinpoint of light to be focused on the interior wall of the Lord's tomb.

Macarius entered the burial chamber, and Helena followed him. On the holy slab to the right, where the body of Christ had lain, some special implements had been placed. Using a pair of tweezers, Macarius picked up a dark and very dry piece of charred cloth. Although the sun's rays weren't as strong now as they would be later in the day, the pinpoint of light on the wall was sufficient to bring forth a tendril of smoke from the charcloth, then an ember. Immediately, Macarius set it in a nest of tinder and blew on it until he had a flame. He set the burning tinder in a clay bowl. From this he lit a torch whose head contained the ores of Magnesia. The large torch blazed to life and illuminated the tomb in a brilliant white light.

Outside the Aedicule, a choir of monastic brothers responded to the light from within by chanting a Christian hymn. Their sonorous voices combined to make a hauntingly beautiful and timeless sound. Helena closed her eyes and listened as the monks sang:

> O Joyful Light of the holy glory of the immortal Father!
> O heavenly, holy, blessed Jesus Christ!
> Having come to the rising of the sun,
> having seen the light of dawn,
> we praise the Father, Son, and Holy Spirit—one God!
> Worthy are you at all times to be hymned with reverent
>   voices,
> O Son of God, O Giver of Life,
> for which the world glorifies you!

No sooner had the monks finished their song than Macarius emerged from the tomb with the torch. By the strength of its blazing fire, he lit an oil lamp on a bronze stand outside the Aedicule. "Today I light the eternal flame of the Ever-Risen Christ!" the bishop declared. "All hail the Lord Jesus, the Light of the World!"

In response, the crowd of monks, nuns, churchmen, and commoners recited the words of God's throne room in heaven, crying, "Worthy are you, our Lord and God, to receive glory and honor and power! For you created all things, and because of your will they existed and were created!"

Now it was time for private prayers inside the Aedicule. One by one, the appointed worshipers knelt on the floor of the burial chamber while resting their arms upon the holy slab, lifting up holy hands to the Lord. Although Helena could have been the first to pray in the shrine, that honor was given instead to the elderly bishop Paphnutius, the confessor who had been blinded in one eye and maimed in one leg during the persecutions. After his prayers were complete, it was Helena's turn to go in.

The interior of the tomb had been left in its original state without any attempt to smooth the rough-cut walls or install decorative marble over the slab. The only adornments were some lamps that hung from the ceiling and three painted pictures of Jesus: one of him being cradled in the lap of Mary, one of him being baptized in the Iordanes River, and one of his glorious face with radiant sunbeams behind his head. A golden censer also sat on the holy slab, perfuming the place with its fragrance and picturing the prayers rising to heaven.

Helena knelt down awkwardly, since her almost eighty years of life had taken their toll on her body. Yet she managed to assume the humble posture of prayer, leaning forward with her elbows resting on the slab. At first, her prayers felt obligatory and rote. But soon the power and majesty of the Lord began to dawn upon her in this sacred and dynamic place. She felt herself growing smaller as God grew greater. Though she was an augusta of the Roman Empire, the Lord Jesus Christ was the King of Glory and Ruler of All.

A heavy weight settled onto Helena's shoulders, a burden she couldn't throw off or escape. It was a spiritual burden, so it couldn't be removed by human hands. Deeply embedded memories started flitting through her mind: a door too hot to touch . . . a log wedged against an upturned stone to bar the door . . . a pitiful cry for help . . . fingernails clawing at the base of the door . . . desperate gasps for breath. The remembered images and sounds were hard for Helena to bear. And yet, beneath these terrible memories was also the indulgent satisfaction of a bodily lust, a delight more intense than sex, riches, or power. Only one kind of gratification could be more satisfying than these. *Vengeance.*

"Vengeance is mine," declared the painted face of Jesus on the icon. Though his lips did not move, the voice was real to Helena nonetheless. The gaze of Christ was stern, passionless, convicting. "It is mine to repay. Not yours. *Mine.*"

"Ohhhhh," Helena groaned, overwhelmed by the burden of her guilt. It seemed to press down on her like a physical weight. Still kneeling, she laid her torso on the holy slab, facedown upon the stone, and splayed out her arms with palms upward in desperate supplication. "I am a murderer!" she cried. "Forgive me, Father, for I have sinned! I took vengeance on the killer of my grandson!"

Outside the Aedicule, the monastic choir resumed its singing. Tears flowed from Helena's eyes as the monks' rhythmic, resonant words reached inside the empty tomb and touched her soul. "Kyrie-e-e-e, elei-i-i-son!" the brothers intoned in long, sonorous chants. "Chri-i-i-i-ste, elei-i-i-son!"

"Lord, have mercy on me!" Helena repeated, adding her own desire to the reverberant voices of the monks. "Christ, have mercy on me, a sinner!"

With that cry, the burden lifted from the empress's shoulders. She stood up again, buoyed by a lightness not of this world. Now the dawn's light shone directly into the chamber, its golden beams illuminating the rock-cut tomb. Helena could feel its warmth on her face—a gentle touch, a welcome embrace. It enlivened her, not by its own innate power but by the splendor of the Sun of Righteousness, who inhabited the heavenly rays.

As Helena strode boldly from the Aedicule, Bishop Macarius hailed her with upraised hands and the words of holy scripture. "Wake up, O sleeper!" he shouted triumphantly. "Rise up from the dead, and Christ will shine on you!"

"Amen!" cried all the people gathered around the Aedicule. As Helena's gaze went from face to face, she greeted each person with her eyes. They were Christians of every sort, ranging across the whole spectrum of humanity. From honored bishops to peasant believers, from rich ladies to humble monks, from strong soldiers to crippled beggars, from brown-skinned easterners to dark Africans and pale Germani . . . all these people made up the church of Jesus Christ. Each one was called by God, forgiven of trespasses, and united with the Risen Lord.

And then, as Helena gazed on the jubilant faces gathered around the Aedicule, her eyes fell on one person whose expression was serious and concerned. She knew this man. He wasn't someone from Hierusalem, but a friend and confidante from far away. He was Vincentius, the red-haired priest from the Aventine Hill—and his somber presence here, in this joyful moment, could only mean one thing.

Something big had happened back in Rome.

14

With the help of two T-shaped crutches under his arms, Rex hobbled into a private room at the Christian guesthouse where he and Flavia were staying. He fell heavily into a seat and set the crutches aside. "I hate these things," he muttered.

Flavia felt sorry for Rex because she knew nothing bothered her husband more than being limited. Rex was a man of action who grew frustrated whenever he was hemmed in. However, the nail wound in Rex's foot had grown infected, making it painful for him to put any weight on it. It was going to take some time for the poultices beneath his bandages to do their work and for God's healing touch to restore Rex's snake-bitten heel.

"I know it's a struggle," Flavia said supportively, though without any pity in her voice. "But you're strong. You'll get through it eventually."

"I guess so," Rex replied.

Flavia plumped the cushions on the other two chairs in the room, then poured water from a jug into four cups on a tray. Empress Helena was due here shortly. Because of Vincentius's arrival from Rome, a secret meeting was arranged after the dedication ceremony at the Aedicule. Vincentius had some urgent news to report, a dire announcement from the pope that the queen needed to hear for herself. Instead of discussing the matter in the mansion next door—where the servants might not be trustworthy—Helena had agreed to come to the private room at Glory House so no unauthorized ears would be listening. There she could speak freely with the two papal legates.

The empress was wearing a plain tunic and a veil over her face when she arrived. Vincentius came in behind her. After they had taken their seats in the private room, Flavia closed the door and returned to Rex's side.

Helena folded back her veil. "Tell me your business," she said matter-of-factly. "I am ready to listen, then to do whatever I can to address your concerns."

Vincentius wasted no time getting to his point. "The Manichaeans have staged a coup against Pope Sylvester," he announced with visible anger on his face. "They've put the Lateran Church and palace under a blockade. The bishop has barred himself inside and refuses to come out. But there's no food getting in, so when it runs out, there will be a confrontation. Maybe a violent one. This is basically siege warfare against God's church. We need help, Your Highness."

For a long moment, Empress Helena was silent as she considered her reply. Then she asked, "What about the Praetorian prefect—Junius Bassus? Has he not intervened? He could send in the Urban Cohorts to break the siege."

"Bassus is a believer like us, so he would be willing to help. But his power has become more bureaucratic than military these days. And his rival, the urban prefect, sides with the Manichaeans. He has forbidden all military intervention. So it's a stalemate, Your Majesty, until you declare your will in this matter. Sylvester has sent me for your decision."

Once again, Helena paused before giving an answer. When she finally spoke, Rex was impressed with her wisdom. "I side with the pope," the queen said. "However, this problem cannot be resolved by a direct command from me. It has to be determined by the people themselves or it will not last. Matters of faith have to emerge from the free choice of the human spirit, not from government mandate. And certainly not from policemen and punishments."

"Then you will do nothing?" demanded hot-headed Vincentius, speaking more vehemently than he should to the augusta.

Helena's reply, however, was mild. "I did not say I would do nothing, Father Vincentius. I only said I would not compel belief at the point of a sword." She turned to Rex. "You're a papal legate too. That ring on your finger proves you have Sylvester's trust. What do you think ought to be done here, Rex?"

Rex collected his thoughts for a moment, then said, "I think you are right that faith shouldn't be forced on people. Violence doesn't stamp out religion. It only makes martyrs for the rest to admire. The people of Rome need to be convinced of the truth for themselves."

"And how do we convince them, my son?"

"There might be a way," Rex suggested.

Flavia glanced at Rex's face, knowing he would seek her advice with his eyes about what to say next. He did, and she nodded at him, encouraging him to proceed. She wanted him to speak about what he knew, even though he had been warned not to.

Rex shifted his gaze back to Helena. "We have made a great discovery, Your Majesty. It is a relic that should be brought to Rome on your authority. Let it be installed in the Sessorian Palace on public display. Everyone can come see it and be strengthened to accept the true faith. Though no one will be forced to believe by imperial power, they will know where you stand. You will be declaring those words of Iosue, 'As for me and my house, we will serve the Lord, for he is holy.'"

"And what is this great discovery?"

"We have found what we believe to be the cross of Jesus Christ."

At this announcement, Vincentius leapt from his seat, and even Helena sat up straight in her chair with her eyes wide. "Can it be true?" she marveled.

"We think so, based on solid evidence. It is the crossbeam only, not the trunk. I am writing a full report of the discovery, which I will submit to you with all the facts."

"And where is the crossbeam now?"

When Flavia saw Rex hesitate, she intervened with a diplomatic answer she hoped would be acceptable to everyone. "Bishop Macarius has possession of the holy relic. A message from you to him is all it will take to have it shipped to Rome."

"I shall do it," the empress said. "And I deputize you men, as papal legates, to make sure the shipment is made."

"God be praised!" Vincentius exclaimed. Then he smiled sheepishly and admitted, "This is much better than what I had in mind. Thank you, Your Majesty."

The meeting adjourned, and the empress returned to her lodging. Rex submitted his report the next day, and the courier reported that Helena had followed through on her promise by writing a directive to Bishop Macarius. But that evening, little Cyril arrived at the guesthouse around dusk with a concerned look on his face. He approached Flavia in the common room. "Eusebius is coming to visit my master," he told her in a hushed tone. "Tonight, after dark. And there's a traveling carriage being packed and hitched to mules. Something strange is going on—and I think it has to do with the crossbeam."

"Are you able to listen in?" she asked.

A sly grin came to the boy's face as he nodded. "There's a storeroom beneath the rooftop where they always meet. It's a terrace with a nice view of the city. But under the place where they sit, I can hear everything through the floor."

"Do it," Flavia said.

"Come with me, Flavia. I want you to hear it too. Then we can make better plans."

Though Cyril's suggestion caught Flavia by surprise, she instantly knew he was right. The high stakes here required the kind of stealth and craftiness Rex usually asserted as a spy. But since he was laid up with an injury, that responsibility now fell to her. "I'll get my wrap," she told her clever little friend, "then you lead the way."

Since Bishop Macarius lived nearby, the two spies soon reached his house. The doorway to the storeroom was used only by the household servants. Cyril knew where they hid the key, so he retrieved it and opened the door. When Flavia slipped inside, she found a small room full of spare garments, dried foodstuffs, and other charitable goods for the poor. A single lamp on a stand provided just enough light for her to pick her way through the gloom.

"Stand over here," Cyril whispered, beckoning Flavia to his side. He pointed above his head at the wooden beams that supported a floor of reeds covered with mud plaster. Putting his mouth next to Flavia's ear, he said, "They'll sit above us, under an awning."

It wasn't long before voices and footsteps overhead proved Cyril right.

Once the men were settled, Flavia found that she could indeed make out their words. Eusebius's squeakier tone contrasted with Macarius's robust manner of speaking. No one else was part of their conversation.

"We cannot disobey the augusta's direct order," Macarius said. "It would be disastrous for us to resist her openly."

"But that crossbeam must never make it to Rome," Eusebius countered. "If Sylvester gets ahold of it, his church will always be above ours. The Romans will rise above the Greek church forever. They already have the bones of Saint Peter. Give them the cross too and every pilgrim in the world will go there instead of here."

So that's it—ecclesiastical politics! Rome versus Palaestina. West versus east. These two conniving bishops want to fortify their own churches at Sylvester's expense!

"Do you think it's actually the true cross?" Macarius asked.

"As a historian, I have to admit, the evidence is strong. The drawing of the ship provides good corroboration."

"I agree. No one must ever find out about this relic."

"I'm certainly not going to mention the crossbeam in my books! Too many people would accept it. We need to eliminate any movable relic that other churches can obtain. Let the world come to us, not Rome."

Let the world come to both! Flavia thought. She and Cyril exchanged disgusted glances. They both knew how much Sylvester could use support right now. Yet these two eastern bishops were playing politics instead of helping a brother in need. Their actions weren't worthy of their pastoral office.

"I thought about sending a substitute beam," Macarius said. "But what good would that do? The people of Rome would just venerate that one instead. And if the augusta ever found out . . ." Though Macarius didn't finish his statement, the ominous nature of his warning was clear. Such an action would be considered high treason.

"So are we stuck, then? Does Sylvester's church rise above ours forever?"

"I have hired a man," Macarius said.

There was silence for a long moment. Then Eusebius asked, "What kind of man?"

"A crafty man. Strong and capable. Experienced in stealthy ways. He's unknown to anyone in high places. And he's going to take care of this problem for us."

"Where did you find this man?"

"Disgruntled local worker. That's all you need to know."

"What is his mission, then?"

"To tie the crossbeam to an anchor and throw it overboard on the first windy day. We'll say it was 'lost at sea' during a tempest. Happens all the time. Cargo gets misplaced . . . moved around . . . jettisoned by frightened sailors. No one will ever know what happened."

"That's a dangerous plan, Macarius! It could get us into serious trouble. Not just with the augusta. Maybe the augustus too."

"I know. I have considered that. But I believe Christ would want me to do this for the sake of Hierusalem."

No he wouldn't! Flavia wanted to yell through the floor. *He would want you to help a brother who's under attack from heretics!*

The mention of Christ caused the two men to forget their scheming for the moment and turn their attention to an ongoing theological argument between them. Macarius accused Eusebius of still harboring Arian ideas even though he had signed the Nicene Creed. For his part, Eusebius didn't totally deny it. They spent a good half hour debating back and forth about the eternality and consubstantiality of the Son and the Father. Eventually, though, they set aside their differences and came back to the subject of the crossbeam.

"The relic is going to be shipped out of Caesarea's harbor," Macarius said. "You have to go there and make arrangements. My man is expecting you to meet him at the dock and pay him a deposit as he boards. We'll also need a spy among the crew to make sure the job gets done. Only when that wood is deep in the ocean will my man get his full reward."

"Very well. I can leave tomorrow morning. It will be good to finally be home."

"No," Macarius countered, "you have to leave right now. That's why I called you here tonight."

After a long pause, Eusebius said, "What?"

"You have to leave right now. I've got a carriage with lanterns waiting for you downstairs. It's light and fast. The coachmen are smugglers who are used to driving in the dark."

"I can't leave tonight!" Eusebius screeched. "I'm not packed. I'm not ready."

"There will be food and blankets in the carriage. You can sleep your way to Caesarea. It'll take you all night, but you'll arrive by sunrise."

"I can't!"

"You have to, brother. Be brave."

"What's the big rush?" wailed the distraught Eusebius. "Why now?"

"Because my man has already taken the crossbeam to the port," Macarius replied, "and he's leaving on the first ship tomorrow for Rome. Soon that relic will be at the bottom of the sea. Your job is to make sure it happens."

Making a nighttime ride from Hierusalem to Caesarea had been the last thing Rex expected to do when he woke up this morning. But Flavia's news that the crossbeam was on its way to oblivion had changed Rex's plans. He had quickly thrown a few things in a saddlebag, then hobbled to the legionary camp headquarters to obtain a swift postal pony. "On the direct authority of the augusta," he had told the hostler, and the man didn't argue. He knew Rex was the captain of the queen's bodyguard, and he had no desire to hinder a royal command.

Flavia had insisted on riding along as well. Since plenty of ponies were available because no one else was out at night, Rex had agreed. His wife was an experienced equestrian, sitting comfortably in the saddle and accustomed to long-distance travel. The two riders made the seventy-mile journey by moonlight, exchanging their mounts five times at way stations along the route. They saw no one on the road except when passing through an occasional village. Military rations of waybread and posca, eaten in the saddle, helped keep up their strength. Even so, the ride was tiring, and Rex looked forward to its end.

Just before dawn, the lanterns of Caesarea's eastern gatehouse finally came into view. A wide thoroughfare led directly from the gate to the Temple of Caesar Augustus that overlooked the harbor. Normally, Rex would have gone there by foot, but with his injury it was faster to travel in a litter carried by four stout slaves. Flavia climbed into a litter of her own. After crossing the width of the city—not a long distance since the urban area extended up and down the coast more than inland—the porters arrived at the temple. As soon as they set down the litter, Rex exited from it, put his crutches under his arms, and started toward the waterfront with Flavia at his side.

"Look!" she cried, pointing across the harbor. "A ship is leaving already!"

Rex saw it too—a large freighter with a gooshecked sternpost that honored the sea goddess Isis. Its shape was sleek rather than tubby. Even as Rex watched, the ship glided past Caesarea's lighthouse into the open sea. The waves beyond the harbor were rough today. The smoke from the lighthouse swirled erratically in the breeze, and ragged clouds that hinted at rain scudded across the sky.

A man's voice made Rex turn his head. The speaker was Bishop Eusebius, his face haggard and tired yet triumphant. "What you seek is gone," he informed Rex. "Do not keep chasing after lowly things."

"Sir, the cross of our Lord is no lowly thing."

"Bah! Our empire needs a heavenly cross, not an earthly one. Salvation is found in the spiritual Word who dwells above."

"But the Word became flesh and dwelled among us," Rex replied. "Never forget that, my brother."

When Eusebius tsked and rolled his eyes, Rex turned away from him and spoke privately to Flavia. "We have to stop that ship. Only the navy can do it now."

"Let's go see the harbormaster," she agreed.

Though the naval headquarters for Caesarea's harbor wasn't far away, it still took Rex an annoyingly long time to make his way there. He was sweaty by the time he arrived. Even at this early hour, the office was staffed and operational because maritime traffic was already moving in and out of the port. Rex entered the front office and approached a clerk behind a desk.

"What's your business?" asked the clerk. His expression was skeptical as he scanned Rex's disheveled appearance.

Rex stood up straight—though on one foot—instead of leaning on his crutches. "I am here on a mission from Empress Helena Augusta. Her Majesty's most earnest wishes are at stake. I must see the harbormaster immediately."

Despite Rex's impressive statement, the clerk still looked doubtful. None-theless, he stood up from his desk. "Come with me," he said, beckoning with his hand. "The harbormaster hasn't arrived yet. I'll let you speak with his optio." The clerk led Rex into the next room, though he made Flavia wait in the front office.

The optio was a man named Andronicus. As it turned out, he was a fellow Christian who was willing to help. He confirmed that the ship that had left at sunrise, the *Grey Goose*, was headed to Rome with a cargo of cedar timbers and purple cloth. But when Rex explained that he wanted a warship sent out to overtake the *Grey Goose* and conduct an inspection, Andronicus balked. "We don't do that sort of thing," he said with a shake of his head. "That freighter is safely underway and has done nothing wrong. I cannot authorize such an action."

Rex could feel his frustration begin to boil over. One of the most precious objects on earth was about to be lost forever, and this military bureaucrat was going to stand by and let it happen. "You have to get me out there," Rex insisted. "Her Majesty demands it!"

But Andronicus wouldn't budge. "Can you prove you're here on her be-half? You could be anyone off the street. I'm sorry, sir, but no valid orders have come down to me through the chain of command."

"I am the chain of command!" Rex snapped. "The augusta orders you to send out a warship immediately!"

"I can't, sir. It's just not something we do."

"Today it is," said a new voice in the room.

When Rex turned around, his mouth fell open as he discovered who had made the welcome statement. It was Cato, a navy commander whom Rex had known long ago at Thessalonica. On his uniform he wore the insignia that identified him as the harbormaster. And behind him was his wife, Marcia, accompanied by Flavia with a huge grin on her face.

"Cato!" Rex exclaimed. "What are you doing here?"

Cato took the hand of his plump yet stately wife and stroked it affec-tionately. "My little turtledove wanted to come to the land of Jesus, so I requested a transfer to Palaestina. Why not? Shouldn't my sweet buttercup be happy?"

"Of course I should, darling," Marcia cooed. "The scriptures teach it! And today you can make me happy by doing whatever Flavia asks. I owe this woman a great debt. She bore witness to the gospel when I was in darkness. God used her to save my soul!"

"Whatever you say, honeybee," the doting husband said. Then he turned to Andronicus and barked, "Get the *Valiant* out of the harbor immediately! I want a full crew on the oars and a tight sail to the wind. We can be on the *Grey Goose*'s tail within an hour."

"Yes, sir," the optio replied with a fist to his chest and a dip of his chin. He hurried from the room to carry out his commander's order.

Dark clouds were on the horizon and whitecaps were on the swells when the *Valiant* left the port with Rex and Flavia aboard. Cato was right—within an hour, they had caught sight of the *Grey Goose* in the sea-lane ahead. Though the harbormaster hadn't come out with the ship, he had appointed one of his most skillful crews to do the job Rex had requested.

The warship pulled alongside the freighter and ordered it to stop, then a boarding plank was stretched from one vessel to the other. No soldier from the *Valiant* was allowed to board the commercial ship because this was just an inspection, not a military seizure. But Rex was fine with that. He didn't need anything more than a chance to examine the hold. The crossbeam was like nothing else, so it would be recognizable.

Rex crossed over to the *Grey Goose*—not an easy task in the rough seas while limping on the ball of his injured foot—then turned and helped Flavia across as well. When the merchant captain greeted his unwanted guests rather gruffly, Rex promised him that his ship would soon be underway again. "You have something onboard of great importance to the augusta," Rex told the captain. "I'll take it and be gone as quickly as possible."

"Just get it over with," the captain muttered.

The ship's crew seemed a little bewildered by the unexpected naval intervention. Some of them were as annoyed as their captain. They grumbled, yet complied, when Rex instructed them to open the hatch to the hold. Peering down, he could see huge cedar logs below. He was about to descend when Flavia grabbed his sleeve. "What is that man doing?"

Rex turned and followed her pointing finger to a lone figure on the aft deck, partially obscured by the gooseneck decoration that capped the stern-post. He was a tall, muscular fellow whose blond hair signaled Germanic ancestry. His back was to the rest of the ship as he lugged a heavy stone anchor to an opening in the railing that surrounded the aft deck.

"Stop right there!" Rex shouted as he hobbled closer to see what the man was up to. "Imperial navy orders!"

But Rex's sharp command only made the man move faster. Lugging the rectangular block of stone in two hands, he reached the opening just as Rex climbed a short staircase onto the deck. Since the deck extended far out from the stern, the place where the man stood offered a straight drop into the sea. "Halt!" Rex barked again. And this time, the man obeyed.

As the stranger turned around, three shocking realizations struck Rex in quick succession. The first was that the man holding the anchor was Geta—Rex's long-lost comrade from cadet school whose betrayal had turned best friends into mortal enemies. Second, when Geta's glance darted to the side of the deck, Rex noticed that the crossbeam of Christ was there, resting against the railing. And third, Rex realized that the sacred relic was in grave danger. Geta had fastened it by a rope to the anchor he held in his arms.

"This time, you lose," Geta snarled, then heaved his burden into the sea.

The anchor's plunge into the abyss sent the rope slithering across the deck like a swift snake. "No!" Flavia screamed as the rope went taut and started to drag the crossbeam toward the opening.

Rex responded instinctively. Ignoring the pain in his foot, he dove across the planking and grabbed hold of the rope. The heavy weight at the end of it spun him around and would have yanked him overboard except Rex managed to brace his feet against the railing on either side of the opening. A hot spike of agony shot up his leg from his wounded heel, making him groan from the pain as well as the strain on his arms. Yet the crossbeam was still on the deck. It lay just behind Rex, not far from the opening. Only his endurance right now would save it from destruction.

Hand over hand, Rex began to haul up the rope to bring the anchor back onboard. The ship rolled and tossed in the waves, and a stiff wind whipped at his face. With a loud crack, the flimsy railing began to break loose from the planking where Rex's foot was braced against it.

"You can go in too!" Geta screamed, shoving Rex from behind and trying to push him overboard. When that didn't work, he began to pummel Rex, who could only hunch his shoulders and take the beating. Letting go of the rope now would send the crossbeam hurtling into the depths forever.

Geta's fist caught Rex on the side of the head, stunning him for a moment. Half the line he had just hauled up slipped through his hands and plummeted back into the sea. Rex realized he couldn't win this fight—not against two opponents. Either Geta or the weight of the anchor could be battled, but not both at the same time. Despair came with that realization—and that was when Flavia cried, "Rex, it's free!"

He looked over his shoulder to see his wife standing triumphantly beneath the gooseneck symbol of Isis with the end of the rope in her hand. Flavia's face shone in a fleeting ray of the sun, and her hair billowed behind her like a victorious war banner. *She untied the knot!*

Rex glanced at the crossbeam and confirmed that the anchor line was no longer attached to it. With great relief, he released his hold on the rope and let it snake away. Its tail flew from Flavia's hand and disappeared from sight like Leviathan returning to his watery lair.

Still seated at the railing's opening, Rex turned his attention back to the deck. He found himself greeted by Geta's furious stare. The look on his face was a combination of frustration, shock, disappointment, and fury. His mission had been thwarted just when success was at hand. Though his glance went to the crossbeam, Rex shook his head and said, "Not a chance." Both men knew Geta couldn't throw the heavy timber overboard while Rex was there to prevent it.

The captain of the *Grey Goose* stood at the head of the stairs with a club in his hand. "You three, come here to me at once!" he snapped. His face was stern, and he had ten strong sailors down on the main deck to back up his command.

Instead of obeying, Geta picked up another anchor and cradled it against his chest. It was a much smaller one, the kind made of wood and iron, to be used with a ship's rowboat. "You took everything from me," he growled at Rex through gritted teeth.

"No. Your decisions were your own."

Geta's eyes narrowed to slits. "Now *this* is my decision," he hissed.

Before Rex could scramble to his feet, Geta snatched Flavia by the wrist. He dragged her to the railing and tumbled overboard with her body

445

entwined against his. Flavia shrieked as they fell off the deck. Then they disappeared from sight.

But Rex was already in motion. He launched himself over the rail and inhaled a deep breath before hitting the water. Down into the murky depths he swam, following the trajectory he thought Flavia had taken. Though the water was cloudy, he caught a flash of movement deep below—fearfully deep. Kicking his legs, he pushed ahead, his eyes fixed on the flash of white that he hoped was Flavia's gown.

When Rex reached the spot, he found his wife struggling to ascend. She had freed herself from Geta yet was making no upward progress. Swimming deeper, Rex found Geta clutching her ankle. His death wish was dragging him to the bottom of the sea, and his devilish plan was to take Flavia with him.

With violent force, Rex pried Geta's claws from Flavia's foot. Released from her captor's grip, she finally began to make her way upward. But the surface was far, and she had been under for a long time. Rex twisted in the water and also began to ascend. He clasped Flavia's wrist and began drawing her to the world above with powerful kicks.

Yet before he could reach the life-giving air, he felt Flavia's efforts weaken. *No! Stay with me, beloved!* Spurred by his fear of a terrible loss, Rex rose higher and higher. He surged through the water as if propelled by a powerful force. Yet Flavia was limp now. His own lungs were in agony, and his breath was almost spent. *God in heaven! Save us!*

Rex burst from the abyss like a captive escaping from his cell. With a mighty tug of his arm, he pulled Flavia alongside him, drawing her from death's grip into the bright sunlight and blessed air of salvation. He gasped and gulped and inhaled, but more importantly, so did Flavia. She treaded water beside him, panting with her head thrown back and her face to the sky.

"We're alive!" Rex yelled, exulting in the joy of defying the ocean's depths. "Thank you, God! We're alive!" Though Flavia wasn't yet able to speak, Rex could see from her exhilarated nods that she, too, was grateful to be alive.

Glancing around to get his bearings, Rex saw that the rough seas had separated the two ships. The *Grey Goose* was the nearer of the two, easily distinguishable from the *Valiant* by its different construction and lack of oars. "We can make it," Rex said as he began to swim toward it.

"Right . . . beside . . . you," Flavia replied.

Though the two exhausted swimmers were buffeted by the salty waves, they managed to make progress toward the merchant ship. As they approached it, they could see the crew cheering them from the rails. "Only . . . a little more!" Rex said between breaths.

Flavia increased her efforts. "I'll . . . beat . . . you," she answered with a determined grin.

Rex was admiring his wife's plucky spirit when a viselike grip encircled his throat. "Now you die!" Geta snarled in his ear, renewing the battle in the sea just when salvation had seemed near. The former speculator choked Rex with deadly force, and no amount of resistance or thrashing was able to break his grip.

"Cease and desist!" shouted an authoritative voice from above. It was the *Valiant*'s captain, who had maneuvered his warship close to the combatants in the sea. Although several archers stood next to him with drawn bows, there was little they could do. Any arrow they might let loose was as likely to pierce one man as the other in the heaving surf.

Rex clawed at the fingers that pressed against his throat, though he resisted with less vigor than before. The constriction of his windpipe was taking its terrible toll. Already breathless and fatigued when he was attacked, Rex was weakening. His mind had grown foggy, and his will to live was starting to fade. *No!* he told himself. *Keep fighting!*

At that moment, Rex felt his entire body get lifted by a rising swell. Flavia's voice spoke to him, not from afar but at his side. "Take this!" she shouted as she put a thick rope into his hands. The powerful wave carried them both higher, seeming to raise them even above the ships on either side. It billowed upward like a mighty mountain. Geta, too, was lifted by its power. And then, as the wave crested and began to curl down again, the rushing of so much water threatened to plunge its three riders into the depths of the sea.

"Hang on!" Flavia urged, and Rex did. He clenched the rope—which the men of the *Grey Goose* had thrown to her—as the wave tried to drag him away. Rex's entire body was extended, and his arms were stretched above his head. Flavia was beside him in the same position. Their lifeline was taut as it ran back to the merchant ship, the only thing keeping them from being swept along with the wave's churning momentum.

But Geta, who had no life-saving rope, was torn away from Rex by the awesome power of the sea. The mighty breaker gripped Geta in its bubbling fist and hurled him toward the *Valiant* at breakneck speed. He smashed into the hull like a catapult stone striking a fortress wall. His body went limp. Then the watery abyss swallowed Geta once again.

With the wave's force spent, the lifeline went slack upon the ocean's surface. The sailors aboard the *Grey Goose* reeled in Rex and Flavia until they were near the hull. A rope ladder was dropped down the side, and they clambered aboard. Nothing had ever felt as good to Rex as the solid decking beneath his feet.

Yet even in his exhausted state, he couldn't rest until he knew the crossbeam was safe. He returned to the aft deck, not even limping because the arousal of his body for combat had deadened all his awareness of pain. Ascending the steps, Rex was gratified to see the beam lying almost exactly where he had left it. Apparently, no one aboard knew what this precious relic was, so they had ignored it during the fierce battle in the sea.

"Rex! Come quick!" Flavia cried as she peered over the rail. He joined her and saw Geta in the water, his head barely above the ocean's surface. Only by a desperate churning of his legs was he able to stay afloat. Strangely, his arms hung limp and useless at his sides. Geta's impact against the *Valiant*'s hull must have paralyzed his upper limbs. In these rough seas, it was only a matter of time before he went down for good.

A wave washed over Geta's head, making him vanish for a moment before popping up again. No longer was his face angry or hateful, just sad and afraid. He locked his gaze with Rex in a way that aroused deep memories. This man was once Rex's comrade in war, his friend in need, his trusted ally in the battles of life. All that was gone now, lost in a swirl of betrayal, bitterness, and blame. A once-vibrant friendship was about to disappear when the next wave took the wounded warrior to his death.

"Brothers, always!" Geta shouted up to Rex, staring at him with big, fearful eyes.

"From death to life!" came the reply—but not from Rex's lips.

He turned to see something whose spiritual power staggered him. Rex's jaw dropped and he could utter no words, only marvel at the mighty deed he was witnessing. Flavia had hoisted the crossbeam to her shoulders like the Savior himself. Though she was burdened by the beam's weight, her steps were strong as she strode to the ship's rail. And then, while Rex watched in awe, Flavia hurled the trophy of grace into the turbulent sea.

〰

July 327

Sylvester gazed from an upstairs window of the Lateran Palace at a scene he never thought he would see in his lifetime. An unruly mob of people who called themselves Christians—but who actually blended Jesus's teachings with the heretical doctrines of Mani—had surrounded the bishop's residence and were besieging it like foot soldiers attacking a castle. The agitated Manichaeans had been joined by a large band of ruffians, forming a crowd big enough to create a total blockade around not only the palace but the adjacent basilica as well. So far, neither the Senate nor the urban prefect nor the Praetorian prefect had put a stop to it. The politicians were all testing the winds to see what the empire's new religious policy would be. Everyone was in waiting mode, hoping for an imperial solution from afar.

My solution comes from afar, Sylvester reminded himself, *from the heights of heaven!*

As he had done often over the past seven weeks, the bishop again said a prayer for God's speedy deliverance in a time of hardship and distress. Sylvester closed his petition by reciting the Lord's Prayer out loud. The phrase "Give us this day our daily bread" had taken on new meaning during the deprivation caused by the blockade.

Ever since Felix had surrounded the papal residence, the Christians trapped inside had been living off the stores intended for charitable distribution. Those supplies had been depleted during the seven-week siege, so now everyone was down to one meal a day—a thin gruel made from wheat that was normally baked into bread for the poor. Yet even that food was running out, and the water in the cistern was dangerously low as well. Sylvester knew the status quo couldn't last much longer. Things would come to a head soon. *Lord, have mercy on your people!*

In contrast to the situation inside the palace and church, the besiegers seemed to have no shortage of food. They had essentially set up camp in the streets, and Felix had supplied them with braziers for cooking their meals. Even now, as Sylvester watched from the window, some men were grilling pork sausages over hot coals. The delicious smell made Sylvester's mouth water and his stomach rumble.

"What do you see down there?" a woman asked.

Sylvester turned to find Sabina Sophronia approaching him in the hallway. As usual, she was accompanied by Bishop Ossius, her constant companion. "The Manichaeans like to cook their food near our windows," Sylvester replied. "It is yet another way of putting pressure on us without an outright attack."

Sophronia set her hand upon her stomach. "When I'm this hungry, I'd call it an attack. It might not draw blood, but it's just as hostile as stones and arrows. We can't go on much longer like this."

"We are used to fasting, but even the most arduous fast must eventually end," the Spanish bishop added. His handsome face looked gaunt and hollow. Sylvester had heard that Ossius had been giving portions of his gruel to Sophronia.

A pair of benches was nearby in the hallway, so Sylvester gestured for his friends to sit down, then he took a seat across from them. "I suspect Vincentius will be back soon with an answer from Empress Helena. Her son has given her total authority over Rome. Surely she will support our cause."

"Even if she does, will the people go along with it?" Ossius asked. "Felix has captured the Hall of the Church in Trans Tiberim. That was our first church in the city! They've also gained control of Saint Peter's shrine at the Vatican. And Quintus controls the Pantheon. Those are important monuments. The people are starting to say that God favors the Manichaeans instead of us."

Sylvester sucked in his breath at the dire news. "You know for sure they say this, my brother?"

"Yes. Our friends on the outside throw potsherds to us with writing on them. We received this information last night."

"Well, the Manichaeans may have taken hold of those buildings," Sylvester said, "but I do not think they can enter the cathedral. Our defenses are secure."

But Ossius grimaced and shook his head. "Even the most fortified citadel can be breached with enough time or determination."

"Should we further strengthen our doors?"

"Our best defense is your presence among us," Sophronia replied. "You have great respect in this city. You have proven yourself to be a man of God. The people of Rome know this—and Felix knows how they feel. He has refrained from a direct attack because he fears it would turn public opinion against him."

"I must show myself, then," Sylvester mused, rubbing his stubbly chin, which in normal times would have been smooth-shaven. "Perhaps I should make an address from the balcony, even if just briefly. Everyone could see that we remain resolute, entrusting ourselves to God."

Sophronia nodded vigorously at this suggestion. "Yes, Your Holiness! Speak God's word of rebuke against this madness. I do not think the masses want to follow the Manichaeans. It's just that there's spiritual confusion in the air. The unclean spirits are at work. You should invoke Christ's power against them."

"I will do it," Sylvester vowed. "On the morrow, I will go out and offer a reminder of our Lord's victory over evil. Let us pray that it will be well-received."

Without embarrassment, Ossius took Sophronia's hand in his. "We will surely join you in this prayer, my brother. You can count on the two of us to stand with you."

"That is much strength indeed," Sylvester answered with heartfelt gratitude.

After the time of prayer with his friends, Sylvester made his daily pastoral rounds through the palace, lifting the spirits of his little lambs who were trapped inside. Everyone was steadfast yet also tense as they played the stressful waiting game that seemed to have no end. Sylvester decided to cross over to the basilica through a connecting walkway—another area the besiegers had not yet dared to invade—to check on the clergy who were holding the church for the catholics.

The priest and three monks inside possessed good morale and adequate food. They had pushed some heavy cabinets against the basilica's doors and barred them with bronze lampstands. Fortunately, the clerestory windows were too high for any invaders to reach, and the aisle windows, though lower, had a lattice in them that wouldn't be easy to penetrate. For now, at least, the church was secure against trespassing just like the palace. Yet like Bishop Ossius had said, even the most well-defended fortress could be breached if the invaders were determined enough.

As dusk fell, Sylvester joined the thirty or so people in the palace for the evening meal. Once again, it was plain water to drink and gruel to eat—but to everyone's surprise, a Christian outside had managed to dash through the blockade and toss a packet of dried mushrooms and salted sardines onto a balcony. The palace servant named Primus, who was serving in the kitchen as the cook, had cut up the treat into savory bits and sprinkled it into the gruel, adding flavor and nourishment that everyone appreciated.

"The Israelites in the wilderness received quail from heaven. How much more of a miracle is fish?" Sylvester quipped as Primus handed him his bowl. The pope's attempt at humor did get a few chuckles, though the lightened mood didn't last for long.

After the meal, a hymn was sung and vespers were said. The young men discussed who would take turns patrolling the hallways to watch for intruders, then everyone retired to bed. Sylvester undressed in his bedroom and blew out his lamp. A moonbeam from the window made a pale square upon the floor. Too tired to bother with closing the shutters, Sylvester just pulled the blanket over his head and rolled the other way. It wasn't long before he fell into a deep slumber.

He had been asleep for what seemed like several hours when a sharp, stabbing pain awakened him. At first, he thought he had been knifed, but the room was empty and dark. Sweat broke out on Sylvester's forehead, and he struggled not to vomit as waves of nausea made him gag and retch.

When the second pang hit, Sylvester knew he was in trouble. Its pain was much worse than the first—so bad he thought he might pass out. He moaned at the agony, which felt as if his entire digestive tract had been dissolved by acid. Dizziness made the room spin out of control. Rising from the bed, he stumbled toward the chamber pot, knowing he would need it for one reason or another. Yet before he could get there, a weakness in his legs made him collapse to the floor. He couldn't rise, nor even lift his hands. Terrified, Sylvester realized that this affliction might be more than an illness, but an attack that would claim his life.

"Lord!" he gasped. "Keep . . . my flock!"

The words had just left Sylvester's lips when the third pang hit. This time, the pain was beyond human endurance. He cried out as his body convulsed in deep torment. The wracking pain made his limbs tremble uncontrollably. And then, as darkness descended like a veil over his eyes, Sylvester released his grip on the world and gazed upon it no more.

<hr/>

After traveling up Italy's unremarkable coast for several days, Flavia found the protruding arms of Portus's harbor to be a welcome sight. It meant she had finally reached Rome—a city that, no matter where else she traveled in the empire, would always feel like home.

"Trim those sails! And keep a steady hand on the tiller!" shouted one of the proficient sailors who had helped to make the run from Caesarea to Rome in the excellent time of only three weeks. Like all the crew, he was a tanned and wiry man who had been sailing for many years.

When the harbormaster, Cato, had finally realized what Rex and Flavia were attempting to do, he ordered the *Valiant* to be recalled into the port and dispatched his swiftest messenger vessel instead. It was a ship built for speed, with sleek lines, virtually no cargo, and a top-notch crew. Since he was an important official at Caesarea, Cato had been one of the first people to welcome Empress Helena to Palaestina. He understood exactly what she was up to, and he wanted to do everything in his power to help her transport the sacred crossbeam to Rome.

The sacred crossbeam . . . such a powerful image of Christ's saving work!

Flavia wasn't sure whether that ancient timber—now wrapped in protective padding and securely stowed in the hold—was the actual patibulum on which the Lord had been crucified. Certainly it could be. The supporting evidence for it was solid. Or maybe it was just wishful thinking. That could be the case as well. Yet like Rex had said earlier when they discussed the matter, even a mistaken relic could serve as a powerful memorial of Christ's historical act. The crossbeam would remind everyone that the crucifixion was no myth. The Savior had won eternal life upon the literal hill of Calvary.

The possibility that the crossbeam was the authentic patibulum of Christ made Flavia's action on Geta's behalf all the more shocking. But when she hurled the precious relic into the sea, her only thought had been to save him from drowning. The floating timber had indeed been his life preserver. Despite his paralyzed arms, the defeated warrior had managed to heave his body over the beam and entwine it with his legs, which kept him alive until he could be rescued.

Astonished by Flavia's risky act, Rex had later asked her, "How did you know it wouldn't sink?"

"I didn't," she had replied. "But I knew that he who hung upon it had also walked on water. I figured he could do a miracle again to save a dying man." Rex had nodded at those words, then kissed Flavia's forehead in a gesture of love and respect.

Despite Geta's rescue from certain death, his emotions had remained troubled. In fact, his mind seemed to have gone blank. His only request was to be taken to Rome; he would say no more than that. Since Geta's violent lust for revenge had been drained away by his ordeal—and his paralysis made him no threat—Rex and Flavia had agreed that he could travel with them in the swift ship. Geta had spent the whole journey in the empty hold, lying in a hammock and gazing absently out of a tiny opening in the hull. Though Rex brought him food and tried to reach out to him, Geta seemed lost in his own little world. He often mumbled incoherently. Rex finally decided to give his old friend the space he so obviously desired.

As the messenger ship now rounded Portus's lighthouse and slipped into the harbor, Rex came forward from the rear deck and approached Flavia in the prow. His stride toward her was normal, for his foot had finished healing during the three-week journey.

"I'll never forget the wonders of Palaestina," he said as he joined her at the railing, "but it feels right for us to be here in Italy."

"I think so too. But I'll feel even better once I know the bishop is safe and the Roman Christians are back under his care."

"It won't be long. They won't abandon their first love. All they need is a good reminder—and we're bringing them the best reminder they could ever have."

Once the ship was moored at the dock, Rex and Flavia disembarked with two strong sailors carrying the crossbeam behind them. It was wrapped in soft sheepskins, then an outer covering of sturdy leather, all fastened by thongs. No one paid it much mind, for a package like that could be almost anything.

A river barge brought Rex, Flavia, and the precious relic up the Tiberis to the Emporium in Rome. There they transferred into a litter with curtains to block them from view. Because of the extra weight of the timber resting between the two passengers, Rex paid a bonus to have the litter carried by a ten-man team.

As the litter was borne along, Flavia reclined on its cushions and listened to the familiar hubbub of the city outside. But once they began to descend the flank of the Caelian Hill, more aggressive sounds began to meet her ears. Instead of the good-natured din of a bustling city, Flavia heard raucous shouts and angry taunting—and the racket only grew louder as they approached their destination.

When they arrived at the Lateran Palace, the tension in the air was palpable. Peeking out past the curtains, Flavia found the people encircling the palace and basilica to be a rougher lot than she had expected. The ruffians and thugs seemed to outnumber the more austere and aloof Manichaeans. Although Father Vincentius had described how Felix set up a blockade around the cathedral, he hadn't portrayed the besiegers as a criminal element. Evidently the situation had deteriorated in the weeks since Vincentius departed from Rome. Now the Lateran neighborhood felt like a volcano that was rumbling and smoking, ready to explode with deadly fire at any moment.

"Set us down over there," Rex instructed the porters. They carried the litter to the narrow lane he had indicated, a relatively quiet place since the shops that lined it were all shuttered. Rex removed the crossbeam from the litter and sent the porters on their way. "We need to find a place to store this until we can figure out how to get inside the palace," he said to Flavia.

Jiggling the shutters of the closed shops, Flavia found one of them to be loose. The establishment was a skewered-meat restaurant with a street-front serving window. When Flavia tugged hard on the shutter, a gap opened above the counter. "I think we could squeeze the beam in there."

"Perfect. No one will be inside that restaurant anytime soon—not with this band of troublemakers around."

Once they slipped the crossbeam through the opening and hid it from view on the countertop, Flavia let the shutters close, and the restaurant assumed its nondescript, closed-down appearance again. With Rex at her side, she returned to the main street, and together they milled around in the crowd. Though they pretended to wander aimlessly, they were actually listening for the people's mood.

Quickly, they discovered the reason for the crowd's agitation. Something violent had happened to Pope Sylvester overnight. Some said it was sickness; others claimed an assassination attempt. There was even gossip suggesting he had died. Though no one knew exactly what had happened to the bishop, the general consensus was that God had judged him—which meant now was the time to take action.

"We should break down the doors!" many of the besiegers said. "The cathedral is ours! The catholics deserve it no more!" Even the more peaceful Manichaeans were advocating aggression and violence, egged on by the riffraff interspersed among them.

When Flavia heard one rough-looking character use the term "Pope Felix," she pulled Rex close and spoke urgently in his ear. "These people are ready to attack. It's like the buildup before an insurrection. They could go at any moment. We have to warn our friends!"

"I'm sure they can sense it too," Rex answered with a grimace, then assured Flavia he agreed that getting inside the building was the top priority.

After doing a complete circuit around the palace and basilica, Flavia found herself discouraged. The besiegers were concentrated near all the access points into the papal complex, making entry impossible. She sighed and shook her head in frustration—and that was when she noticed a familiar look in Rex's eyes. She could almost see the wheels of his mind turning. Apparently her husband, the unstoppable speculator, was on the move again.

"What are you thinking?" she asked him with an arch of her eyebrows.

A satisfied smile turned up the corners of Rex's mouth. "I'm thinking I've found a way in. Follow me."

He took her around to the rear of the palace, where there was an enclosed garden with high walls around it. Flavia could see no entrances here—no doors, no windows, not even a tree or other high point by which to climb over the wall. Again, she gave Rex a quizzical look. "Have you sprouted wings, my love?"

Rex pointed to a row of locked-up shops that abutted the palace's rear wall. "We can go through one of those. I'm sure I can pick the lock."

"But those shops don't access the palace. No house would allow a doorway into it from a row of rentals like that."

"True. But we won't be using a door." Smiling mischievously, Rex pointed to a shop whose sign indicated it was a restaurant specializing in soups and stews. "See that chimney? I know where it is in the palace because I once stayed in a guest room next to it. There's a big fireplace that faces the garden. But since that's a soup restaurant, it has to be using the chimney too. There must be separate fireboxes going up into the same flue. How else could they heat a cauldron in that restaurant? So we should be able to get from one side to the other, as long as we don't mind getting soot on ourselves."

"Let's get filthy, then," Flavia said with a grin. "Whatever it takes to get inside."

"We'll go as soon as it's dark. First, let's get something to eat while we still can."

After a quick meal, Flavia returned with Rex to the place where they had hidden the crossbeam. It was, of course, exactly where they had left it. They moved it to a narrow alley across from the soup restaurant, remaining in the shadows while they waited for the sun to go down. To reach the restaurant, they would have to cross a wide street that would make them visible to any watchers. A group of men were huddled over a grill fire a short distance away, but fortunately, they seemed more interested in their cooking than what any pedestrians around them might be up to.

When full darkness had set in, Rex made his move. Striding briskly into the open, he crossed to the soup restaurant's door and knelt in the shadows. A piece of metal wire twisted off a cheap brooch he'd purchased at a nearby store served as his lock pick. Flavia started to grow nervous as Rex fiddled with the lock. She looked over at the men by the brazier, but they were otherwise occupied. When she glanced back at Rex, she saw that he was already recrossing the street toward her.

"I got it," he said. "The door is ajar. We can take the beam right in. Let's keep a smooth pace, slow and steady. No jerky movements to catch the eye. As soon as a cloud covers the moon, we go."

Rex took one end of the crossbeam in his hands, and Flavia held the other. Her heart was beating fast as she waited for the right opportunity. The moment the sky darkened, Rex moved, and Flavia followed him from her hiding place and into the open street. She was halfway across when a voice from the brazier barked, "Hey, you! Stop right there!"

She froze, her heart lurching in her chest. Slowly, she turned her head . . . and found that the watchman's attention had been drawn by some other fellow on the far side of the brazier. The watchers were all manhandling him and sending him away. Rex resumed moving, and Flavia followed him straight into the restaurant. Her heartbeat still hadn't slowed when he closed the door behind them and latched it shut.

"Th-that was close," she said.

"It scared me too," Rex admitted.

They set down the crossbeam and examined the fireplace by the faint moonlight that filtered through the shutters. A copper cookpot hung on an arm over a half-burnt log, but Rex swung it out of the way. Squatting, he looked up into the chimney. A smile came to his lips, then he stood up inside the flue. "The two fireboxes join at about my eye level," he said. "I'll lower it just a bit." A scraping sound, followed by a shower of crumbled mortar, indicated that Rex was loosening some bricks. One by one, he handed them out to Flavia, about thirty in all. "That should be low enough. Can you drag those two crates over here?"

Flavia brought them near, one about half the size of the other. Together they formed a stair step that allowed Rex to get higher into the flue. After some wriggling and grunting, his legs disappeared. The next thing Flavia heard was, "I'm in. Let's transfer the beam."

After she had stood the crossbeam on its end—still protected by its padding and outer wrap—Rex was able to lift it up into the chimney, then draw it down to his side. Now Flavia clambered into the firebox and stepped onto the crates. Upon entering the dark and narrow flue, which reeked of smoky, sulfurous dust, Flavia found that her joke about getting filthy wasn't as clever as she had thought at the time. The space was cramped, grimy, and smelly.

But since there was no way to go but forward, she didn't hesitate. Flavia resolved not to mind the filth but to squeeze right up into the chimney and slither over to the other side.

Even with the lowered opening Rex had created, it wasn't easy. The tight confines made moving difficult. In the end, she went over headfirst with her feet sticking straight up the flue. Yet Rex was there to support her weight as he gently let her down. Flavia rolled out of the wide stone hearth and into the moonlit garden at the rear of the Lateran Palace. Compared to the hellish chimney, the place seemed more beautiful than Eden.

A gardener's shed in the corner of the courtyard served as a safe place to store the crossbeam for the moment. After hiding it there, Rex and Flavia entered the palace itself and hailed a household maid. Though she was startled to see the two visitors at night and feared they were attackers, Flavia assured her they meant no harm.

"Where can I find 'Charis'?" she asked, using the alias Sophronia had adopted to obscure her identity.

"The lady is upstairs taking care of His Holiness," answered the girl. "God save him—he's so near death."

Flavia and Rex exchanged worried glances, then hurried to Sylvester's bedroom. The door was ajar, and light was visible from inside the room. Peeking in, Flavia saw her mother seated at the pope's bedside. Two other people were there as well: Bishop Ossius and a man Flavia recognized as Diogenes, the palace doctor and surgeon.

Sophronia's face was filled with surprise and joy when Flavia knocked and was admitted into the bedroom. "My sweet girl!" she cried, rising from her chair. Sophronia didn't even mind getting covered in soot as she hugged Flavia after her long sojourn in Palaestina.

Rex explained to everyone that they had just snuck into the palace through an unused fireplace. Although that prompted some initial specu-lation about the possibility of smuggling in food, Rex shook his head. "Food isn't your problem anymore," he told everyone. "An attack is imminent."

"Yes, because they believe the pope is about to die," Ossius said bitterly. "And unless God intervenes, he very well might. Then Felix will sweep in, and the people will acclaim him as their bishop. God forbid that such heresy should ever be voiced in his holy church!"

Flavia glanced over at Sylvester, who was jaundiced and looked more unconscious than asleep as he lay motionless on the bed. Truly, his situation seemed dire. "It is a malady of the liver," explained Diogenes. "He also has a great turbulence of the bowels, and—"

The doctor's medical diagnosis was interrupted by the clamor of a scuffle in the streets. Flavia was instantly on the alert. *Has the attack begun?*

Rex ran to the window and stepped out to the balcony. Rough voices were crying, "Stop him!" and "Grab that man!"

"Throw it to me, quick!" Rex yelled to someone below.

The clatter of rocks hitting the palace sounded like vicious hailstones hurled by angry gods. Several of them even smashed against the double doors of the balcony. Yet Rex didn't come inside to avoid the barrage. He remained in place for a few moments longer, then finally darted back into the safety of the bedroom. Something strange was in his hand.

Rex revealed his prize to the others in the room. It was a wad of tattered rags bound with twine. After untying the knots, Rex folded back the cloths to reveal a piece of pottery with writing on it, the kind of note the Greeks called an *ostrakon*.

"Another message from our friends!" Ossius exclaimed. "Read it aloud, Rex!"

Rex's eyes widened as he scanned the writing. "It is from Archdeacon Quintus," he announced, drawing gasps of surprise from his listeners. Flavia knew Quintus had gone over to the Manichaeans. Why was he now sending a message to the besieged residents of the palace?

When Rex started reading, an awed silence descended on the little group gathered at Sylvester's bedside. Flavia could hardly believe what she was hearing. It was so marvelous that it could only be miraculous. Archdeacon Quintus had reached his breaking point. He could no longer abide the evil things being done by the Manichaeans. Now he was repenting of his heresy, and he wished to come back to the catholic faith.

Yet there was more—and when Flavia heard what Quintus had written next, she had to reach over and grasp her mother's hand. "Praise God!" Sophronia cried as Rex read the words aloud.

"'I have learned the terrible news of what Felix has done,'" Rex quoted as his eyes scanned the ostrakon. "'He has poisoned my friend, my brother

Sylvester, the rightful bishop of Rome. So I write to you with great urgency. The poison that Felix sent was deadly mushrooms. The slave Primus substituted it in the bishop's dish. But there is an antidote—the extract called sillybum from the seed of the milk thistle.'"

Rex raised his eyes from the potsherd in his hand. "Quintus goes on to give details about its dosage and use. Do we have this substance in the palace?"

The doctor bent down to his satchel of bottles and surgical tools, then stood up again with a vial in his hand. "Of course," he answered. "It is a common medicine for indigestion. I never would have guessed it could help so serious a malady as our brother has."

"That is the way of the Lord," Ossius declared. "He takes up the common things of this world and makes them sublime. Let us prepare this substance right away, my friends! And then let us discover what our mighty God is about to do."

⚬⚬⚬

The attack on the Lateran Church of the Savior began at dawn.

Rex was asleep beside Flavia in the room next door to her mother's. Last night, after leaving Sylvester's bedroom, they retrieved the crossbeam for safekeeping, then washed themselves of the chimney's grime and went straight to bed. Sleep had come quickly to them both. But now the blaring of a trumpet jolted Rex out of his dreams and back into the world of struggle and strife.

Flavia heard it too. She sat up in her bed next to Rex and listened with him for a moment. Along with the trumpet's call to action, there was much angry shouting in the streets. And then came an enormous crash—the reverberating, metallic sound of bronze smashing against bronze.

"They're ramming the front doors," Flavia said with a shake of her head. "So it begins."

Rex threw aside the covers and went to the window. He could see the adjacent basilica from his vantage point, though not its front door. Violent marauders were wreaking havoc in the streets, hurling stones at the basilica and attacking the citizenry with sticks or their fists.

Surprisingly, however, the number of attackers and defenders seemed evenly matched. The Manichaeans and their associated band of ruffians were being opposed by a substantial number of stalwart Romans. Apparently, many locals supported the catholics and didn't want to see the foremost church in the city captured in an illegal attack.

"I've got to get out there," Rex said, turning away from the window and picking up a clean tunic. It was made of plain wool, undyed, like the monastic brothers wore.

"I know. And I'm coming with you." As Flavia reached for her own garment, one of the pale linen dresses worn by the nuns, Rex knew better than to protest. His wife had faced many dangers at his side, and she wasn't about to stop now. Nor did he want her to. Her bravery was one of the many reasons he loved her so much.

After Rex had donned his tunic and shoes, he returned to the window. The situation had deteriorated and the fighting had become even more intense. Instead of just men with clubs and rocks, archers had joined the fray. They were shooting arrows at the basilica's defenders. Rex saw corpses in the streets with shafts protruding from their bodies.

"The Manichaeans have started using bows," he said as he took his sword belt from a peg on the wall. He was buckling it on when Flavia softly placed her hand on his.

"This battle is the Lord's," she said, "and it must be fought in a different way."

Rex met Flavia's gaze, and in that moment, a profound understanding passed between them. Flavia's expression communicated more to Rex than words ever could. Never had he gone into battle without a sword—but never had there been a battle quite like this one. *Our fight is not against flesh and blood*, Flavia reminded him with her eyes, *but against the cosmic powers of darkness, against the spiritual forces of evil in the heavens.*

"I would be defenseless without a weapon."

"I didn't say you shouldn't have a weapon," she replied, "just a different one."

Flavia's glance shifted to the oblong bundle beneath her bed. Rex drew it out and cut the cords that bound it. Though its outer covering was blackened with soot, the wool inside was as white as snow. Flavia joined Rex as they knelt beside the sacred crossbeam and gazed at its old, rugged wood.

Tentatively, she reached out her hand and touched its surface. "The middle is worn smooth here."

"From many backs rubbing against it," Rex said solemnly. "Agonized people pushing up against the nails of their feet. Pulling up against the nails of their hands. Just to get one more breath before sagging in exhaustion. Then suffocating, and doing it again. Sometimes for several days."

"Ahhh," Flavia murmured. "The Lord's suffering is so terrible to imagine."

"Which is why it is the height of love."

Flavia's finger went to one of the nail holes, stained a deep crimson by ancient blood. "Is this really the true cross, Rex? Could it have been preserved for three hundred years?"

"I've seen buildings whose timbers were laid down in the time of the Republic. That was what? Six hundred years ago? There are shipwrecks from a thousand years ago. Wood can last for many centuries. So, yes, this could be the actual wood of the cross."

"But *is* it?"

Rex nodded thoughtfully. "I think it is when you believe it is. Faith is what matters to God. And he helps our weak faith. He gives us things to touch with our hands so we can believe with our hearts."

Flavia raised her eyes from the cross to look at Rex's face. "I believe God is going to do something great today."

"Then let's discover it together," he replied, "like we have since the first day we met."

Rex's mind flashed back to the perilous day when he first saw Flavia being mistreated by her accusers. Their enemies had been human that day, and also bestial. Today their opponents would be spiritual, and thus far more powerful. *But who is the King of glory?* Rex asked himself. *The LORD strong and mighty. The LORD mighty in battle!*

He rose to his feet with one end of the crossbeam in his hands. Flavia picked up the other end, and they took it out to the hallway. Instead of carrying it lengthwise, they walked side by side, a husband and wife equally yoked and ready for war.

They went downstairs and reached the front atrium of the palace. As they prepared to head out to the turbulent streets, a woman's voice spoke to them from behind. Looking over their shoulders at the same moment,

Rex and Flavia found Sophronia dressed in her finest gown and bearing a torch. "I will make a way for you," she said simply.

"And I will assist," Ossius said, entering the atrium from a different wing of the palace. He wore the robes of the clergy and carried an olivewood staff. Rex wasn't surprised that both of them knew to arrive at this moment. Things were happening now—spiritual things that could be discerned only by spiritual people. The absence of Sophronia and Ossius at such a time as this would have been more surprising than their presence.

Two strong deacons pulled aside the furniture that had been shoved against the door as a barricade. Though Rex could hear shouting outside, so far, the main impetus of the attack had been directed against the basilica instead of the residence. He knew no one outside was expecting a sortie from the palace, so a quick exit from its front door would take the besiegers by surprise. One of the deacons put his hand on the latch, then glanced at Rex, awaiting his signal.

"Ready?" Rex asked his friends.

"For all my life," Flavia said, then the deacon opened the door to hell.

The maelstrom in the streets hit Rex in the face like a boxer's fist. The battle was far more violent and chaotic than he had expected. Evidently the palace's thick walls had muffled the sound well, for now that he was out in the fray, the clamor was overwhelming. Blood ran in the gutters. Deadly missiles hurtled back and forth. Injured men lay everywhere on the ground, moaning, writhing, or clutching at arrow shafts that had pierced them. Rex had been in combat before, so he knew warfare when he saw it. This was every bit the real thing. The pall of death was in the air. The laughter of dark spirits cackled in the background—ungraspable in the tumult yet undeniably there. Today, as always in the days of war, the devourers of human souls would satisfy their infernal cravings.

A Manichaean holding a garden rake ran close with malice in his stride. Droplets of blood speckled his face—whether his own or someone else's was impossible to say. His eyes were wild as he shouted, "For Mani!" even though Mani was a pacifist. He swung the rake in a wide arc, but Ossius blocked it with his staff. The two sticks locked against each other as the adversaries pushed hard and vied for supremacy. Only when Sophronia waved her torch in the Manichaean's face did he relent and back away. "Be gone!" Ossius commanded him in an authoritative voice. The crazed man dashed off to see who else he might accost.

Rex and Flavia continued their side-by-side walk toward the basilica's front door. Though the fighting swirled around them, the attackers who came near were either driven off by Ossius and Sophronia or they withdrew from the strangeness of the procession in the street. At one point, Rex heard an arrow whizz past his head. Just after that, a rock hit his chest and bounced away. Another one glanced off Flavia's arm, making her wince. Yet they kept going, undeterred, until they arrived at the basilica's front steps.

A gang of men—not practicing Manichaeans but hardened fellows who looked like hired mercenaries—had rigged up a battering ram from a roof rafter and a bronze cauldron. Its repeated clanging was the background beat of the evil symphony being played today by devilish hands. One of the basilica's front doors had been battered into submission and was hanging loose on its hinges. Only the furniture piled up behind it prevented anyone from entering.

But Rex could see that was about to change. The mercenaries gave another hard smash to the furniture, sending it flying backward in a shower of splinters and dust. A gap opened up, wide enough for the invaders to get in. Yet even as the besiegers swarmed inside the church, they were followed by many locals determined to defend the basilica from foreign occupation. The fighting in the streets had just entered the holy precincts of God.

Stepping past shards of wood and chunks of marble, Rex and Flavia threaded their way through the debris and entered the basilica. It wasn't dark inside, for the high clerestory windows streamed in light from the east. Though men were fighting in pockets here and there, dodging and thrusting among the columns of the aisles, a pathway was clear up the center of the nave.

With Sophronia going ahead and Ossius bringing up the rear, Rex and Flavia carried the crossbeam toward the apse. Arriving beneath a half dome painted blue and speckled with golden stars, they laid the timber on the altar of the Lateran Basilica. The four friends gathered behind the altar. The ornate bible of the scriptures lay upon it—the very book the foursome had struggled so hard to bring to God's people in Rome.

Placing one hand on the Word of God and another on the beam, Rex proclaimed in a loud voice, "Brothers and sisters, today I declare to you a great wonder!"

And someone shot him with an arrow.

The impact against Rex's shoulder felt like being stabbed with a hot iron. His left arm flew backward, and he felt blood spatter his cheek. The burning pain coursed up his neck and down his chest. Glancing to his shoulder, he saw no shaft there, only a reddening stain on his tunic. The arrowhead had nicked the muscle at the top of his shoulder above his collarbone. Though it was a flesh wound that hurt, and it might affect any fighting he would have to do today, the injury wouldn't be fatal.

Rex was gathering himself for another shout when something far more extraordinary caught the crowd's attention. Above the din of combat arose a strange and mystical sound. It was singing—the sonorous chant of monks reciting a psalm in unison.

Adtollite portas principes vestras, they sang, *et elevamini portae aeternales. Et introibit Rex gloriae!* "Lift up your gates, O princes, and be elevated, O eternal gates. And the King of glory shall come in!"

The chanting monks entered the basilica in single file. Although some of the fighting slowed as the combatants pulled back to consider this strange development, it was only when two figures entered behind the monks that the strife ceased altogether. For a moment, the pair was backlit against the jagged gap of the doorway, so Rex couldn't see who they were. But when they stepped into the basilica's light, everyone gasped at once. It was Bishop Sylvester of Rome, leaning on the arm of Archdeacon Quintus.

The two churchmen proceeded slowly up the center of the nave. Sylvester was clad in the tunic and rope belt of a peasant, and his feet were bare in humble simplicity. The archdeacon walked at his side and helped the bishop when he struggled. As the pope drew near to the altar, Rex could see that his complexion was still yellowed from the poison's effect on his liver. Even so, he was here, walking in the basilica—a drastic change from last night when he looked like a man about to die.

When Sylvester reached the apse, Quintus helped him stand behind the altar. Rex stepped out of his way and gave the bishop his rightful place. As the monks finished their chant, a holy silence descended on the church. Every ear—of both friend and foe—was listening for what Sylvester would say.

"The Lord be with you!" he cried.

"And with your spirit!" came the instinctive response from all the catholics in the hall.

"Lift up your hearts!"

"We lift them up to the Lord."

"Let us give thanks to the Lord."

"It is right and just," agreed the people of God.

And with that, Sylvester launched into a Eucharistic liturgy no one could have imagined would be celebrated today in the Lateran Basilica. The ancient words comforted the hearts of the faithful, intrigued the hearts of the curious, and repelled the hearts of the unrepentant. Some of the Manichaeans began to slink away, throwing down their rocks and sticks in disgust. Even the hired mercenaries, who had no interest in spiritual matters, began to leave as it became obvious that the tide had turned against them.

The brief liturgy soon reached its climax: the moment when Christ's saving work upon the cross was proclaimed by the breaking of bread. Sylvester held up a loaf for all to see and said, "When he was handed over to willing suffering—in order to undo death, shatter the chains of the devil, stomp down on hell, illumine the righteous, and display his resurrection—he took bread and gave thanks, saying, 'Take, eat, this is my body which is broken for you. Do this in remembrance of me!'"

The instant Sylvester tore the unleavened loaf, a great tumult arose in the basilica. The few remaining besiegers, knowing they had been defeated, fled out the door. But those who held the true faith came surging forward, rejoicing to find their salvation in the crucified and risen Christ. A throng of worshipers crowded around the altar, praising God in the highest. Their joyous faces were turned up toward the sunshine that flooded the church. Sylvester and Quintus distributed fragments of bread to the people, then did the same with a chalice of wine.

When the liturgy was complete, Sylvester beckoned for Rex and Flavia to come near to him. Though the bishop's purposes hadn't wavered all morning, Rex could see that his strength was flagging and he needed to get back to bed. Sylvester's voice had a tired, breathy quality when he spoke. "Brother Vitus and Sister Candida, this is a marvel you have brought to us from Palaestina. Announce it to the people, please, then lead us back to the residence."

Rex and Flavia picked up the two ends of the crossbeam and brought it around to the front of the altar. The people gaped at it, knowing it must be something great. But when Rex proclaimed, "Christians of Rome, behold this gift from Hierusalem! We believe our mighty God has revealed the true cross of the Lord Jesus!" the awe in the people's hearts could not be contained. They fell back from the holy relic, their eyes wide. Many of them made exclamations of wonder or praise, while others signed themselves with the cross. Such a thing had never before been witnessed by anyone in Rome.

With Ossius and Sophronia once more clearing the way, Rex and Flavia began to walk down the nave toward the door. Behind them was Pope Sylvester, staggering a little as he leaned on Quintus yet determined to see his task through to the end. The delighted onlookers stood on either side. They were a great host whose numbers had swollen now that the fighting outside had ceased. All the faithful had rushed into the basilica to rejoice in the victory.

As Rex neared the door, one last commotion broke out in the street. There were shouts of "Halt!" and "Grab that man!" The clatter of hobnailed boots against the pavement told Rex that the Urban Cohorts had finally gotten involved. Then a shadow darkened the door of God's church as someone evil darted inside.

Felix!

The look on his face was like that of a rabid animal that raves before it dies. Felix's hair, normally coiffed to perfection, was all askew. His garments were blood-smeared and torn. But the most terrible thing of all was what he held in his hand: an archer's bow and arrow.

Felix didn't hesitate when he entered the basilica. Spotting Sylvester, he took a step to the right to give himself a direct line of sight without the procession standing in the way. Then he nocked the arrow in his bow, drew back the string to his chin, and aimed his deadly dart at the bishop.

"Use the beam!" Flavia cried, shifting her feet.

Rex followed her lead and swung the crossbeam around so it would stand in the arrow's flight path. A look of fierce determination was on Felix's face. His eyes narrowed as he focused his aim. Then, sneering in triumph, he released the arrow with an evil flourish of his hand.

A shout of dread went up in the hall as the swift missile was loosed. At the same moment, the Urban Cohorts burst into the basilica like enraged hornets looking for an enemy to sting. They tackled Felix and pinned him to the ground. Though no one stabbed him, they held him fast. "You'll die for that deed!" shouted a centurion.

Rex's eyes met Flavia's above the crossbeam. Their gaze shifted down to its length—and what they discovered wasn't what they expected. No arrowhead had impaled the wood. The timber was just as it was before. Then a wail erupted from behind them where Sylvester had been standing.

After setting the beam on the floor, Rex turned around and rushed over to the bishop. He was still upright, though leaning feebly on Quintus. There was no blood upon him. *The arrow missed!*

Only then did Rex notice what was at Sylvester's feet. A man was lying on the floor. His eyes were closed. His limp arms were splayed out like the Savior himself. And from his ribs protruded an arrow shaft. It had gone in deep—too far to be survived.

Geta.

"This man leapt in front of the arrow," Sylvester said. "He gave his life for me."

Rex knelt beside his old friend, his comrade from the days of their youth. Already, Geta's face was pale. The frothy blood on his lips was a sign every soldier recognized: a fatal piercing of the lung. Rex cupped his friend's bearded face in his palm. "Geta, can you hear me?"

The warrior's eyes fluttered open. At first, his stare was glazed over, but then recognition came to him. "R-R-Rex . . ."

"Yes, it's me! I'm here with you."

The light was fading fast from Geta's eyes. He coughed up more blood, bright red and bubbly. "B-b-b . . ." he gasped, struggling to form his words.

"You can do it," Rex encouraged.

"B-brothers . . ." Geta managed to say, then paused, collecting his strength before trying again. "In Christ," he finished.

Hot tears flooded Rex's eyes. Those words were a promise of eternal life that he had not expected to hear. Rex let out an anguished groan as deep emotions wrenched his soul. "Then I'll see you again!" he cried. "We shall ride together as servants of the King!"

A mental image came to Rex then, a perception so vivid and clear that it seemed like a heavenly vision. He could see Geta riding on horseback in all his warrior's strength. His posture was erect in the saddle, his head held high, his body thick and powerful. A lance was in one hand and a shield in the other. Down his back trailed a long, blond braid—a sign of Geta's Germanic heritage that he shared with Rex. In the distance, a trumpet sounded, and Geta turned his handsome face to answer its call. Then, in a wash of tears, the vision dissolved.

Rex looked down and discovered that Geta had passed. With a gentle hand, he closed his comrade's eyes. Flavia knelt beside Rex, taking his other hand in hers.

"Jesus is Lord," Rex declared, and began to weep.

15

Although the mausoleum on the Ostian Way was a dark place, it wasn't gloomy or fearful to Flavia. She viewed her family's burial vault as a place not of defeat but of victory in Christ. Most of her ancestors who had been interred here were Christians—some still sleeping in the sealed niches while their bodies decayed, others having been transferred to ossuaries after the process was complete. Yet no one here had been cremated. Christians didn't intentionally destroy the body Jesus was going to raise up on the Last Day. Bodily resurrection was the joyful expectation for all believers in the Risen Lord. Christian burial testified to this confident hope of eternal life.

Flavia stood beside her mother—both women veiled in black—in the quietness of the mausoleum. The building's outer door was open, providing enough light to see the inscriptions on the graves. Flavia traced her fingers along the letters of the marble slab that, only hours before, had been put in place to seal the most recent burial. "Valerius Geta, may you live in ☧," the epitaph read. It was followed by the date of Geta's burial, the Ides of July, then a depiction of a flying dove with an olive branch in its beak.

"It is right to bury Geta here," Flavia murmured. "His family was lost to him. But when he found Christ, he gained a new one for eternity."

Sophronia nodded and made the sign of the cross over herself. "Thanks be to God."

The two women exited the mausoleum but left its door ajar, knowing the

471

gravediggers would attend to it. A mule cart with a driver awaited them not far away, since the distance from the Lateran Palace to the necropolis outside the walls was too great to come on foot. Yet before the women reached their cart, they paused at the burial place of Saint Paul. It was a simple grave from the time of Nero, marked by only a plain stone. A later generation of Christians had adorned it with a small trophy to make it stand out.

"Bishop Sylvester has his eye on this spot," Sophronia said. "Now that the monument of Peter on the Vatican is getting a basilica over it, this grave is next on his list. A church will rise here as well."

"That is only fitting. Peter and Paul were the two great apostles who came to Rome. We should remember their burial places and celebrate their—*oh!*"

A spasm of nausea struck Flavia, making her stomach lurch. "What's the matter?" her mother asked with a look of concern. But Flavia couldn't answer. Turning away, she rushed to a nearby clump of shrubbery and darted into the thicket. After retching three times, her breakfast came up. Only then did the nauseous feeling subside.

Sophronia followed Flavia into the bushes and put her hand on her daughter's shoulder. "Are you sick, my love?"

Flavia shook her head, then smiled in a way that seemed to catch her mother by surprise. She had been waiting for the right moment to tell Sophronia about her recent bouts of nausea. Now the time had come. "It has been happening every morning for about two weeks," Flavia announced. She grinned even wider as she saw the dawning understanding come to Sophronia's face. "And I haven't been in the way of women this month."

"You're pregnant!" Sophronia exclaimed, throwing her arms around Flavia with unbridled enthusiasm and rocking her back and forth. "It is the great handiwork of God!" She hugged Flavia joyously for a long time, then finally separated and looked into her face. "Do you know when it happened?"

Flavia nodded. "Beside the Sea of Galilee. Under the stars."

"Ah! That is beautiful! Just this morning, I read the psalm that says, 'He numbers the multitudes of the stars, he calls them all by names.'" Sophronia arched her eyebrows in a playfully inquisitive way. "God's role is to name the stars, but to us he gives the job of naming our children. Have you considered it yet?"

Again, Flavia nodded. "It if it is a girl, we thought to call her 'Galilea' after the place of her conception."

"That is both lovely and well-suited. What if it is a boy?"

"Rex and I were thinking that 'Pistis' would be a good name for a boy."

"How come?"

Gesturing over her shoulder toward the family mausoleum, Flavia said, "Remember our servant Pistis? He was a man of godly character—a man who lived up to the meaning of his name. He kept his 'faith' in God despite adversity. Rex and I would want our son to be a man of faith like that."

"The Sea of Galilee was a place for testing faith," Sophronia observed. "Saint Peter was tested on its waters. He stepped out of the boat and walked upon the waves. And when he started to sink, the Lord caught him by the hand. Do you recall what he said then?"

As Jesus's words came to Flavia's mind, powerful emotions also rose within her—a sense of humility before her own shortcomings, combined with gratitude for God's grace. "I recall," she said quietly. "'O you of little faith, why did you doubt?' And I admit, I doubted too." Touching her abdomen, she added, "I doubted I would ever see this day again. Yet here it is."

"We all doubt sometimes, my love. The question is not whether we will doubt but whether we stay there or move back to the solid rock of faith. I think you found your footing again, even before God answered your prayers the way you wanted."

"He has surely answered my prayers. And for that, I am grateful."

Flavia's words brought a feeling of worship to her heart. She lifted her face to the sky and raised her palms toward the heavens. Then, borrowing the words of the disciples in the boat, she made them her own and said, "Truly . . . *truly*, my Lord . . . you are the Son of God."

—◦◦◦—

NOVEMBER 327

Athanasius removed his sandals so he could walk on the beach without getting them sandy. The place was just outside the walls of Alexandria, a short distance from the Moon Gate. The city's bishop, Alexander, was sitting on a sedan chair near the sea. A recent illness had robbed him of the

473

ability to walk. The old man stared at the rolling waves while several other Aegyptian churchmen stood around him.

When Athanasius reached the group, he came around the chair and knelt before Alexander in the sand. "You summoned me, Papa?" he asked, using the common term of address for the bishop of Alexandria—though the Romans used its Latin form for their "pope" as well.

"Yes, my son," Alexander said in a hoarse voice. He motioned for the other churchmen to step away and give him some privacy, then turned his attention back to Athanasius. "Do you remember what happened here the first time I saw you?"

"Of course, Papa. It remains vivid in my mind to this day."

"Tell me the story."

"It was summertime. I was playing on the beach with some other boys. After swimming in the sea, we decided to play 'church.' Of course, I was the bishop. The other boys were still naked from our swimming, so they were the catechumens to be baptized. With a seashell, I poured water over their heads and pretended to baptize them."

"In what name, my son?"

"The Father, the Son, and the Holy Spirit—just as the Savior commands us in the *Gospel of Matthew*."

Alexander chuckled at the memory, smiling and shaking his head as he enjoyed the fond recollection. "And what happened next?" he asked, then immediately answered his question before Athanasius could respond. "I called you into my residence and inquired about what you had done. You had recited the liturgy of the church in exactly the right words! Those boys were pious believers, each one of them. There was no reason to think they hadn't been rightly baptized by you, their little bishop with a stout heart. So I declared it a valid baptism."

A coughing fit came upon Alexander, but he shook it away as quickly as he could. Smiling warmly, he leaned close and said, "It is time, Athanasius, for your childhood faith to be tested. I want you to become the next bishop of this city."

The announcement caught Athanasius by surprise, and his heartbeat quickened. "But you are—" he began, then was interrupted by a wave of Alexander's hand.

"I am dying, my son," the bishop said. "Soon I shall see the Good Shepherd and his heavenly flock. You must lead his earthly flock in my place."

Athanasius felt a heavy load descend upon him—not only the weight of grief for the imminent loss of his mentor but also the responsibility of pastoral ministry. To be charged with the care of eternal souls was always a difficult burden to bear. "Perhaps you will recover," he suggested. "It could happen! You might be the bishop for many more years."

"I will not recover. An old man knows when his time has come. My life is ending. Your life as a pastor is about to begin."

"But I am not yet thirty years of age!" Athanasius exclaimed. He knew it was a silly protest, for it was only a matter of months until he would reach the required age for a bishop according to church law. Yet somehow, Athanasius hoped that if he could invalidate the ordination on a technicality, he could keep his beloved bishop alive for just a while longer.

"You have proven yourself faithful over many years," Alexander said. "It will be enough."

Turning stiffly in his chair, he signaled for the other churchmen to come close again. In addition to several bishops from around the Nilus delta, some desert monks were there as well. Among them was the revered brother Anthony, one of the first men ever to retreat to the wilderness as a hermit. He was a gnarled and wizened fellow, bent out of shape by his hard life and frequent combat with demons. Yet his soul was as straight as an arrow—an arrow that was always pointed toward God.

When the churchmen had reassembled around Alexander's chair, he announced in a loud voice, "Behold! It is to Athanasius that I give my episcopal ring." He took it off his finger and handed it to his successor. "This man stands for true doctrine. He holds to the full and undiminished deity of our Lord! Rightly has God appointed him for this hour, and for the arduous task that lies ahead."

"A wise choice," Anthony said. The elderly monk's words carried so much weight that all the other churchmen murmured and nodded their agreement.

Another coughing fit came upon Alexander, this one lasting for a longer time. His personal valet poured him a cup of water from a canteen, which helped Alexander collect himself. Once he was composed again, he said,

"Do not imagine that the heresy of Arius is completely vanquished. It is not! Despite our victory at Nicaea, some bishops still believe Christ is a mere creature, a being of lesser glory. They cannot wait to start spewing those lies again. I fear that Constantine's sons may side with them once they come into imperial power."

"Especially now that Caesar Crispus has passed into the bosom of the Lord," said Anthony. His remark elicited grave nods from the churchmen.

"Athanasius, rise to your feet," Alexander commanded. After he had complied, the bishop asked him, "Do you accept this great responsibility, my son?"

"I do, Papa—fearfully, yet with steadfast faith as well."

"Then hand me that ring."

Athanasius gave it back to Alexander, then held out his left hand. The bishop placed the ring on Athanasius's third finger. Its gemstone was red like the blood of Christ, and its gold circle was the sign of a glorious King. "I will shepherd the flock of God to the best of my abilities," Athanasius promised, "even if I have to stand against the whole world."

"I have always known it," Alexander said, closing his eyes as if with great weariness. His face was pale and his cheeks were gaunt. "Now I can die in peace. Lord, come quickly."

"It is time to take the holy father back to his residence," the valet announced, and everyone could see it was so.

The Aegyptian bishops left the beach together in a hired boat that would take them to the city's harbor, from where they could each make their way home. Meanwhile, the monks carried the bishop in his sedan chair back inside the city through the Moon Gate.

Athanasius returned to his home on the lower slopes of the Serapeum's hill. The apartment was previously owned by that orthodox and godly couple, Brandulf Vitus Rex and Junia Flavia Candida. Though it had once been tastefully decorated, now the place looked more like a scriptorium than a home. Books, scrolls, pens, inkpots, and scraps of papyrus were scattered everywhere. Yet Athanasius thought that Rex and Flavia wouldn't mind. They valued books as vessels of sacred theology.

Athanasius went to the cabinet where the holy scriptures were kept. In Rome, the church had recently made a beautiful edition of all the canonical writings under a single cover. Although such a great bible had not yet been achieved in Alexandria, many Christians were talking it over. It would no doubt happen soon, once everyone was in agreement about which books should be included in the tome. But the Alexandrian church wasn't quite there yet. Until then, the books of the canon were kept as separate volumes.

However, there was no debate about the canonicity of the book Athanasius removed from the cabinet. It was the *Gospel of John*, the most theological of the four. He laid the codex on a reading bench, untied its thong, and opened its stiff leather cover. After signing himself with the cross, he took off his ring and laid it upon the sacred page, then read aloud the gospel's opening lines: Ἐν ἀρχῇ ἦν ὁ λόγος, καὶ ὁ λόγος ἦν πρὸς τὸν θεόν, καὶ θεὸς ἦν ὁ λόγος.

Having recited the inspired words, Athanasius meditated on their truth. In the beginning was the Logos. He was with God, and he *was* God. Not a lesser being. Not diminished in his glory. Certainly not a time-bound creature! The Logos—Jesus Christ, the incarnate Word—was fully divine in every way.

Athanasius picked up the episcopal ring and put it back on his finger. "Strengthen me, Lord!" he cried with great depth of feeling. "When you take our brother Alexander into your bosom, according to your purpose and will, then make me—O Lord, by your grace!—make me a worthy successor in your holy church."

FEBRUARY 328

"You look more handsome now than the day I met you," Flavia told Rex as she straightened the brooch on his cloak and brushed away a bit of lint from his shoulder. Rex found himself pleased by the compliment. Although he was by no means an old man at age thirty-four, it was always nice to hear that your wife still found you handsome.

Rex was dressed today in full imperial regalia, with a plumed helmet and plenty of polished brass. He even had a gold-tipped spear. However, despite all the finery, the day was a sad one. Empress Helena had died of old age not long ago while on her pilgrimage in the east. Her body had been embalmed and brought to the capital for burial, just as she had requested. Rome was her beloved city, so she wanted to rest here until the day of resurrection. Rex had been asked to serve in Helena's honor guard. Ironically, it was the same ceremonial role he had occupied when he first met her in faraway Germania.

Glancing out the window, Rex was a little disheartened to see that a winter rain was falling and the day was blustery and cold. "Are you sure you can make it?" he asked his very pregnant wife. Of course, he already knew how she would answer. Flavia wasn't about to miss the empress's funeral. Rex just wanted to hear her confident assurance that she was up for the long walk into the suburbs.

"I have a thick cloak," Flavia said with a shrug. "It's made of good wool. It has a hood. My shoes are warm." And that was that.

The funeral procession began at the front steps of the Lateran Palace. The imperial guardsmen in their splendid uniforms accompanied the royal casket, which was beautifully carved from expensive wood. It rested upon a horse-drawn cart draped with boughs of winter holly. Pope Sylvester—now fully recovered from the mushroom poison—led the procession through the streets, accompanied by dignified musicians with flutes instead of pagan wailing.

When the procession neared the Gardens of Pallas in the southeastern corner of Rome, Rex scanned the crowd traveling beside the empress's casket, looking for his wife. Since Flavia had been staying near Rex as everyone walked along, he was quickly able to spot her. Though he couldn't make any visible motions toward her because of his ceremonial duties, he caught her eye and indicated the gardens with a slight tip of his head. Flavia's smile and nod told him she remembered their visit to that wooded park on the first day they met. They had been fleeing from pursuers in the streets of Rome and took refuge in a dense thicket near a fountain. *Geta was with us that day*, Rex recalled. *We were such close friends! He was gallant. He helped me escape with Flavia.* Sighing, Rex shook away the memory and returned his mind to the present—though not before whispering, "See you soon, brother," as the walkers left the garden behind.

After exiting Rome through the gate that led onto the Labicana Way, the funeral procession traveled for an hour until it reached a suburban villa at the third milestone. The place was called "Two Laurels" because of the two trees that commemorated a pair of martyrs buried there. Previously, the cemetery had belonged to Rex's old army unit, the Imperial Horse Guard. Now there was a large Christian hall covering many graves in the floor. And attached to that hall was one of the most magnificent buildings Rex had ever seen: the brand-new Mausoleum of Helena.

The horse-drawn cart carrying the empress's casket stopped outside the mausoleum. It was a round building with a dome on top whose only architectural rival in Rome was the famous Pantheon. The building's height was imposing, and its façade was beautifully decorated. But as impressive as it looked from the outside, when Rex entered it along with the other guardsmen carrying the casket, an amazing scene met his eyes.

The interior was lavishly adorned with beautiful marbles in colorful geometric patterns. Arched recesses encircled the rotunda, each with lampstands and Christian paintings in them. A bronze chandelier dangled from the ceiling, its candles adding their light to the illumination from the lamps and the high windows. The high dome above was painted midnight blue, and it gleamed with hundreds of golden stars. Directly across from the entrance was a huge sarcophagus made of the finest purple marble—soon to be the final resting place of Empress Helena Augusta.

With great formality and elaborate ceremony, the shrouded body in the casket was transferred into the sarcophagus and the lid was lowered. The porphyry marble—a type of stone used only by emperors—had been carved with depictions of galloping cavalrymen defeating enemies and taking captives. After a trumpet fanfare was played to signal that this was a moment of victory, everyone adjourned into the adjacent basilica. Rex proceeded there with the rest of the attendees so that Pope Sylvester could deliver the funeral eulogy.

The pope's speech centered on the theme of Christ's glory. Although Empress Helena was a revered and honored person, Sylvester emphasized that her glory was nothing compared to the grandeur of Christ. Even Emperor Constantine, who was far away in his new capital of "Constantinople" building a bright future, had no glory at all when compared to Jesus's infinite splendor. Sylvester kept returning to the text in *Isaiah* that said, "I am the Lord God. That is my name. I will not give my glory to another, nor my praises to graven images."

As the pope spoke to the gathered crowd in the funeral hall, Rex scanned the onlookers until he finally met Flavia's gaze. Although once again he could not use any gestures, he gave her a look of wide-eyed wonder and rolled his eyes to indicate their surroundings. She nodded and also glanced around to show that she understood. They were both witnessing a significant moment, something they never could have imagined even a few years ago.

The people standing in this hall were some of the leading citizens of Rome. Many of the richest and most powerful senators were here along with their wives. And beyond the aristocrats, a broad segment of Roman society was represented—soldiers, government officials, churchmen, and a large crowd of commoners, both men and women. Their listening ears received not the traditional words of prideful conquest but pastoral exhortations to Christian humility and worship. The gathered people of the imperial capital were hearing the leader of the Roman catholic church exalt the name of Christ. Not one pagan priest was present in the building. No sign of the gods could be found. No idols loomed over the people. Instead, this grand imperial occasion was a Christian meeting in every way.

"No longer shall human worship be given to graven images!" Sylvester thundered from his speaker's stand. "Those days are dead and gone. A new age is being birthed as we speak!"

As Rex gazed at his wife, he saw her hand unconsciously drop to her pregnant belly. The juxtaposition of her action and the pope's words brought sudden understanding to Rex's mind. *Societies have lives,* he realized. *They are born. They expand. They grow mighty. They wane. And then they die, to be replaced by whatever is next.* With clarity of insight, Rex perceived that he was living through one of these old-to-new transitions. The Roman Empire of Jupiter was coming to an end. Centuries of paganism would soon fade away. Now the Christian Empire of Jesus was rising to take its place.

"What's next, Lord?" Rex whispered to the ceiling. "Will we be faithful?"

It was Pope Sylvester who offered the hopeful reply Rex wanted to hear. *"Non nobis, Domine, non nobis, sed nomini tuo da gloriam!"*

"Let it be so," Rex whispered as he prayed for his society's future. "Not to us, O Lord. Not to us, but to your name let glory be given."

<hr />

"It looks good," Flavia declared. "After all its journeys, it has finally found a permanent home."

Rex chuckled as he stood at Flavia's side. "Not long ago, I thought it was about to find a home at the bottom of the sea."

"Would that have been so terrible?" Flavia shot back with an arch of her eyebrows.

"It would have been God's will, I suppose. But apparently the Lord had something else in mind."

The crossbeam of the Savior rested on a marble column in the former meeting hall of the Sessorian Palace. Empress Helena's last will and testament had bequeathed the whole building to the catholic church. Now the hall was going to be reconstructed into a special chapel for the display of the Holy Cross.

Sophronia and Ossius were looking at the new installation along with Rex and Flavia. It was Sophronia who voiced what Flavia also hoped would be the result of the crossbeam's residence in Rome. "Everyone can come here and view it," Sophronia said. "People who can't travel to Palaestina can make a pilgrimage and see this relic instead. Standing in this church will be like standing on a little piece of Hierusalem in Italy."

"The crossbeam is proof of Christ's humanity," Ossius added. "It shows he was no cosmic symbol of good and evil. He was a man who died with nails in his hands and love in his heart."

"But is it the real wood?" Flavia asked.

Ossius shrugged. "We cannot know for sure. What we do know is that our Lord's crucifixion was real. Here before us stands a tangible reminder of that."

Death and life, Flavia mused as she gazed at the crossbeam. *Death on a piece of timber . . . life and light bursting from a rock-cut tomb . . . bread and wine as a mysterious remembrance . . . the Risen Lord united with his people!*

As she considered these profound things, she felt Rex take her hand. "Thank you," he whispered.

She glanced sideways at him, unsure of what he meant. "For what?"

"For speaking the gospel to me all those years ago. For pointing me to the cross. For leading me to salvation when I was in darkness."

Rex had never expressed such a thing before, at least not in so direct a way. Flavia found her heart powerfully moved by his words. When she first met him, he was a pagan barbarian with a violent streak. Now he was a mature Christian husband and soon-to-be father—with just enough barbarian left in him to keep things interesting.

"Oh, Rex," she said, squeezing his hand. "I'm glad God made you his own. And I'm glad I could be part of that journey."

"I think our journey has only just begun," he replied.

The foursome left the chapel and exited the palace. It was a short walk from the Sessorian to the Lateran Palace where everyone was staying. Yet when they arrived there, Flavia sensed something strange in her mother's demeanor. She had a hesitant spirit, and she kept looking to Ossius for confirmation that she should speak. Finally, Flavia asked directly, "Mother, is everything alright?"

Sophronia collected herself as she turned to face Flavia. "Beloved, I am moving to Hispania."

For a long moment, Flavia was absolutely silent. The news was so surprising that everyone stood still except for Rex, who came to Flavia's side because he knew she would need support. At last, Flavia gathered her thoughts enough to say, "With Bishop Ossius, I assume?"

The handsome bishop took Sophronia's hand in his. "Yes, Flavia. I am moving back to my home at Corduba, and I have invited your mother to come with me. We will not cohabit—that is not proper for Christians to do. Yet we will live in close proximity, and we'll share our lives in celibate friendship."

"Th-this is what you wish, Mother?"

"Yes, my love. More than anything."

"Why not just marry?" Rex demanded in a voice not altogether free of exasperation. "You're clearly in love. Marriage is a gift from God. Just be together as man and wife!"

Sophronia and Ossius both shook their heads with equal vehemence. "That is not our interpretation of scripture's guidance," Sophronia said. "We must live according to the Word of God as we understand it."

Ossius's tone was gentle yet firm as he tried to explain. "To do what you're suggesting would be to violate our consciences before God. We believe in celibate clergy." The bishop put his hand on Rex's shoulder. "Do not pity us, my brother. Marriage is good, yes. There is no question about that. But so is celibacy for those who are called to it. Not everyone believes marital consummation is the height of all human experiences. Could it be that something deeper is to be found in this other way of life? Something that takes us close to God by a different path? We believe this. And we are committed to it. Trust me when I say that I know this to be true, even if you, as a young man, find it hard to believe."

A bright smile came to Sophronia's face. She seemed relieved to have finally expressed what had been burdening her. "We are happy like this," she told Flavia earnestly. "Ossius promises me that Hispania is beautiful! I can think of no better purpose for my life than to spend it with him, helping him in his work as a bishop. Given the beliefs of the Spanish church, and the things Ossius has stood for, a marriage would mean the end of his ministry. But our holy friendship will be a beautiful testimony to something else. We are"—she glanced affectionately at the bishop—"we are excited about what lies ahead."

Though Flavia found herself delighted by her mother's happiness, one troublesome thing remained. Flavia's hand instinctively went to her belly. "But what about . . ."

Sophronia immediately understood. "I shall visit often. Do you know how far Corduba is from the coast?" When Flavia shook her head, Sophronia said, "Only two days! And ships sail from Hispania constantly. The Romans need their garum, you know. Your baby will have a doting grandmother, of that you can be certain."

"And even a grandfather of sorts, if you should allow it," Ossius said with genuine affection.

With those hopeful words, a sense of relief came to Flavia. Rex put his arm around her shoulders, adding his comforting presence to Sophronia's and Ossius's assurances. Though these developments were unexpected, now that they had been explained, they didn't seem too hard to bear. Flavia could see that only in this way would her mother be at peace. Sophronia's life would take this necessary path. It was a gift from God, a mark of his faithfulness.

Lord, why are you so good to us? Flavia wondered.

Because my banner over you is love, was God's gently whispered reply.

The best view overlooking the city of Rome was to be found atop the Aventine Hill. Rex and Flavia sat side by side on the steps of the Temple of Ceres, enjoying the cool evening and the interplay of light and shadow as the sun went down. Behind them, the former temple to the goddess of grain was now shuttered and locked. The people would no longer seek their daily bread from a goddess but from the Bread of Life himself.

Rex stretched out his hand and pointed to the city's amphitheater, its stone arches bronzed by sunset's dusky light. "Remember when that wild cow almost trampled you?" The words sounded unreal to Rex as he recalled the event. It seemed like something out of a legend—yet both of them knew it had actually happened.

"A fierce lion saved me that day," Flavia said.

"As I recall, it was a lioness."

"No," she countered, encircling his arm with hers and tipping her head onto his shoulder, "it was a mighty lion with a golden mane."

Rex smiled at his wife's analogy. He knew he was no lion, just a regular man doing the best he could in a hostile world. At times he accomplished great things. Other times he failed miserably. But either way, Rex was glad to know that Flavia viewed him like that. "Thank you," he said quietly. "Your support means everything to me. I'll need it in the days ahead."

Flavia glanced sideways at him with a mischievous smile. "You certainly will, Father Vitus."

"Hey! Can we not use my baptismal name? It just doesn't sound like me."

"Alright," Flavia agreed. "We'll go with Father Rex. That has a good ring to it. You're going to be a great priest. I'm confident of that."

Rex again felt grateful for his wife's support in uncertain times. Only two days ago, Pope Sylvester had named him as the pastor of the Church of Saint Sabina—the former house church in Flavia's home. Long ago, Felix was its pastor, but that evildoer had been banished to the mines for attempted murder. Father Vincentius was the church's next priest, and he led the congregation well. Yet the pope now needed Vincentius for other duties.

"I can think of no one better than you for this appointment," Sylvester had said to Rex. "You're theologically instructed. You've been a teacher and a deacon. Your life experience is broader than anyone I know. But most of all, you know what it means to receive divine grace."

"I do," Rex had agreed. "It reaches all the way down to the lowest point. Then it digs even lower and finds the people like me."

"And that, my son, is why you are ready to be a pastor."

Rex's mind returned to the present as he gazed upon Rome. The distant horizon reminded him of open possibilities, of remote places unknown to him but well known to the God who sees all. "I'll do my best," he told Flavia. "And I'm glad you're doing it with me."

"We were meant to do this together, Rex. Just like we were meant to share all those adventures across the earth. We faced so many perils—things I don't even want to recall! We left one child buried on the Vatican. Another in Alexandria. The Lord tested us at every turn. But now, it seems, he has brought us to a place of peace. We have a new house on this hill. We have a ministry to share. Our future is bright."

"I keep thinking of the scripture that says, 'The old things have passed away. Behold, the new has come.' That's how I feel. Like the turning of an age is upon us. I'm ready for it."

"Me too," Flavia said and then she gasped in a way that made Rex's heart leap.

"What is it?" he cried in sudden fear. A look of pain was on Flavia's face, and her hand clutched the folds of her gown at her waist.

"My water just broke." After wincing for a long moment, she breathed a sigh of relief. "The contraction has passed. But there will be more. Let's get home and call the midwife. It's time."

Rex helped Flavia to her feet and supported her as she descended the temple's steps. Their new house, located adjacent to the church, wasn't far away. Even so, Rex felt anxious to get his wife there as quickly as possible.

"I can't believe we're having a baby!" he exclaimed as they walked side by side toward their home.

"Actually," Flavia said with the gentle laugh Rex knew so well, "I think it's going to be twins."

Bryan Litfin is the author of several works of nonfiction about the ancient church, including *Wisdom from the Ancients*, *Early Christian Martyr Stories*, *After Acts*, and *Getting to Know the Church Fathers*. A former professor of theology at the Moody Bible Institute, Litfin earned his PhD in religious studies from the University of Virginia and his ThM in historical theology from Dallas Theological Seminary. He is currently the Head of Strategy and Advancement at Clapham School, a classical Christian school in Wheaton, Illinois. He and his wife have two adult children and live in Wheaton, Illinois. Learn more at bryanlitfin.com.

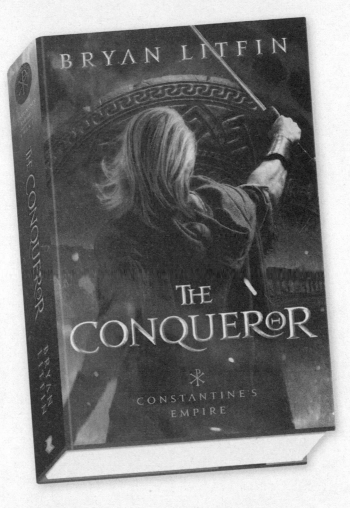

Rex and Flavia Embark on a
QUEST TO HELP FURTHER THE ANCIENT CHURCH

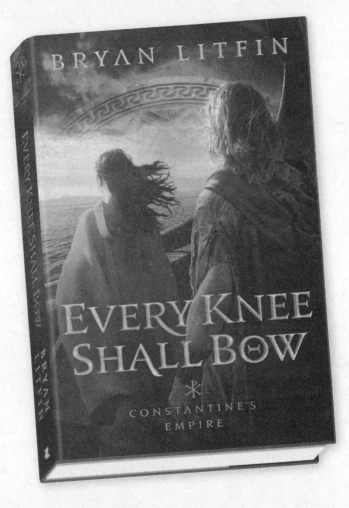

The year is AD 316. Imperial persecution has officially ended. For the first time in history, the Roman emperor supports the church. But the fledgling faith's future still hangs in the balance.

MEET BRYAN

Follow along at

BRYANLITFIN.COM

to stay up to date on exclusive news,
upcoming releases, and more!

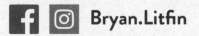 Bryan.Litfin